CITY
SLEUTHS
AND
TOUGH
GUYS

Books by David Willis McCullough

People, Books & Book People

Brooklyn . . . And How It Got That Way

Great Detectives: A Century of the
Best Mysteries from England
and America (editor)

American Childhoods:
An Anthology (editor)

CITY SLEUTHS AND TOUGH GUYS

Edited by
David Willis
McCullough

Houghton Mifflin Company

Boston 1989

Copyright © 1989 by Houghton Mifflin Company
All rights reserved

No part of this work may be reproduced or transmitted in any form
or by any means, electronic or mechanical, including photocopying
and recording, or by any information storage or retrieval system
without the prior written permission of the copyright owner unless
such copying is expressly permitted by federal copyright law. With
the exception of nonprofit transcription in Braille, Houghton Mifflin
is not authorized to grant permission for further uses of copyrighted
selections reprinted in this book without the permission of their
owners. Permission must be obtained from the individual copyright
owners as identified herein. Address requests for permission to make
copies of Houghton Mifflin material to Permissions, Houghton Mifflin
Company, 2 Park Street, Boston, Massachusetts 02108.

Library of Congress Cataloging-in-Publication Data

City sleuths and tough guys / edited by David Willis McCullough.
p.   cm.
Bibliography: p.
ISBN 0-395-51318-9
1. Detective and mystery stories.   I. McCullough, David W.
PN6120.95.D45C58   1989 89-1960
808.83'872 — dc19   CIP

Printed in the United States of America

Q 10 9 8 7 6 5 4 3 2 1

For Norma and Jim Marshall,
veterans of the Brooklyn crime scene

CONTENTS

INTRODUCTION
DAVID WILLIS McCULLOUGH

When Charlotte Brontë mentioned sleuths, as she did in at least one
of her novels, she was writing about dogs, bloodhounds that the Scots
used to pursue wild game and occasionally, with perhaps more glee,
wilder human fugitives. That's also the meaning of the word as used
by the stranger in Marie Belloc Lowndes's short story "The Lodger"
when he moves into the Buntings' spare room. We, of course, with
the advantage of hindsight and perhaps because we have seen the
Alfred Hitchcock film, know that he is Jack the Ripper. To the Buntings, he is simply a much-needed paying guest. "My name is Sleuth,"
he says. "S-l-e-u-t-h. Think of a hound, Mrs. Bunting, and you'll never
forget my name."

That grand old warhorse, *The Oxford English Dictionary*, suggests
that using *sleuth* to mean "detective" is an Americanism, something
along the line of calling a lift an elevator or a public school a private
school. But it is an Americanism that has stuck, with one slight change.
The word has become a literary one. No one, except perhaps as a
joke, would ever call a real detective a sleuth, which only underlines
how fanciful the fictional detective is, no matter how hard-boiled he
or she seems to be.

In Bill Pronzini and Marcia Muller's mammoth *1001 Nights,* an
encyclopedic guide to everything they believe worth reading in the
mystery and detective fiction line, the editors use a classification system
that accurately reflects mystery fans' love for defining, redefining, and
narrowing the categories of their passion. The list includes Action
and Adventure, Amateur Detective, Comedy (far too few, I'm afraid),
Classic Sleuth, Espionage, Historical, Private Eye, Police Procedural,

Psychological Suspense, Romantic Suspense, Thriller, and Whodunit. No Psychological Suspense fan would be caught dead reading something in the Romantic Suspense field — or vice versa — but probably neither would be averse to establishing new genres, such as Psychological Romantic Suspense or Romantic Psychological Suspense, which of course would be very different from each other. Would a Private Eye fan dip into a Police Procedural? Well, maybe. Would a Dashiell Hammett fan, even trapped overnight in a fogged-in airport, turn to Agatha Christie?

Which brings us to our basic division: hard-boiled versus soft, city versus country. The poet W. H. Auden, an enthusiastic mystery reader with a knack — or a weakness — for spotting religious allegory, wrote fondly of crime novels set in "Eden-like" English country houses, traditional whodunits in which there are inevitably a titled eccentric, a doddering vicar, and a curious relative just back from Australia. In them he found echoes of Adam's fall and the sure and certain hope of redemption. Meanwhile, far from Eden (in Los Angeles, to be exact), Raymond Chandler, who had become bored stiff with literary English mannerisms and Americans who affected them, wrote of getting murder back into the hands of people who are good at it. By that he meant Americans, city people, people who know how to find a taxi on a rainy night or a good drink after hours.

There is all sorts of snobbery at work here, both straight-on and reverse. Chandler's essay "The Simple Art of Murder" has become holy writ for the hard-boiled school. The faithful can recite passages ("Down these mean streets a man must go who is not himself mean, who is neither tarnished nor afraid") the way early Christians could recite the Nicene Creed. Chandler, writing in 1944, called for stories with realistic settings, realistic characters, and a hero-detective who is "the best man in his world and a good enough man for any world . . . a relatively poor man, or he would not be a detective at all . . . a common man or he could not go among common people . . . a lonely man and his pride is that you will treat him as a proud man or be very sorry you ever saw him."

Writing a little more than forty years earlier, G. K. Chesterton — whose detective, Father Brown, bears little resemblance to Chandler's Philip Marlow — also saw the detective as a lonely, noble figure: "No one can have failed to notice that in these [popular mystery] stories the hero or the investigator crosses London with something of the loneliness and liberty of a prince in a tale of elfland, that in the course of that incalculable journey the causal omnibus assumes the primal colours of a fairy ship. The lights of the city begin to glow like innumerable goblin eyes, since they are the guardians of some secret, however crude, which the writer knows and the reader does not."

Chesterton wrote those words in 1902, in an essay called "A Defense of Detective Stories," which may be the first example of a major writer seriously examining what was considered a form of entertainment best suited to the lower classes, a judgment Chesterton, in fact, clearly shared. He compares the mystery story ("however crude") with the *Iliad,* describes the detective in terms that Chandler or John D. MacDonald or Elmore Leonard could probably accept. But he adds one more point, a key point. He recognizes the curious way detective fiction celebrates — however perversely — the city. He writes that "it is the earliest and only form of popular literature in which is expressed some sense of the poetry of modern life" — by which he means city life. Chesterton then compares what he calls the "conscious" poetry of the city with the "unconscious" poetry of the countryside:

> The crest of the flower or the pattern of the lichen may or may not be significant symbols. But there is no stone in the street and no brick in the wall that is not actually a deliberate symbol — a message from some man, as much as if it were a telegram or a post-card. The narrowest street possesses, in every crook and twist of its intention, the soul of the man who built it, perhaps long in his grave. Every brick has as human a hieroglyph as if it were a graven brick of Babylon; every slate of the roof is as educational a document as if it were a slate covered with addition and subtraction sums. Anything which tends, even under the fantastic form of the minutiae of Sherlock Holmes, to assert this romance of detail in civilization, to emphasize this unfathomably human character in flints and tiles, is a good thing.

One man's notion of a "good thing" might, to another, sound suspiciously like patronizing "good works," especially when Chesterton goes on to say, "It is good that the average man should fall into the habit of looking imaginatively at ten men in the street, even if it is only on the chance that the eleventh be a notorious thief." But it is only a matter of time, and distance, before one writer's consciously poetic cityscape may become another's exercise in brutal realism. Whatever his motive, Chesterton understood the basic fact: the detective story is an urban art form.

In the popular imagination the city is made for crime. From the dawn of civilization, it's the place mothers have warned their restless children about. Auden calls the idyllic settings of British country house mysteries "the Great Good Place" where crime is unimaginable, and cities "the Great Wrong Place" where crime is all too expected. The myth of the dangerous city gave birth to the suburbs. The city became a place to escape from, and the daydreams of all too many city people are taken up with country houses and long, peaceful weekends far from the threat of the stranger's corpse on the front stoop or the drug addict breaking in from the fire escape. Or, for that matter, a place far from the utterly ordinary reality of dirty streets and noisy traffic.

In the popular imagination the city is harsh reality, while the country is a place of enchantment and peace. Norman Rockwell worked in rural Stockbridge, not Brooklyn. Saints and utopian theorists may have written of the City of God and the New Jerusalem or other urban paradises, but in the nineteenth century, when men actually tried to build their backwoods utopias (to use Arthur Bestor's phrase), they put their Oneidas and New Harmonys and Sabbathday Lakes as far as they could from the temptations — and the everyday realities — of the city.

Fans of the country house mystery are in the game for the puzzle, perhaps for the play of manners. Eyes are diverted away from the well-dressed body on the library floor, but they need not be. There is rarely a sign of blood. The fine Aubusson rug on which the poor victim sprawls is never stained or ruined. Fans of the city novel are in it for the grit, the danger, the sense that — however theatrical the situation may seem — they are in touch with what passes for reality. Yet the crime story also offers a perhaps unrealistic hope for order that is often missing in "real" city life. The detective, by his very nature, finds patterns and logic in what seems to be chaos. The traditional detective story, by *its* very nature, ends with a solution and a sense of justice being done. The defining quality of the city dweller is probably a well-honed sense of skepticism — a sucker may be born every minute, but he's born out of town — and what better quality is there for a detective? Or for a reader about detectives?

The crime story was born in the city and grew up there. Summer vacations in country houses and vicarages came later. Paris was the detective's first home. A rogue named François Eugène Vidocq first dabbled in crime and served time in prison, then worked as an informer for Napoleon, a position he somehow parlayed into becoming the first chief of the Sûreté, the national police force. Many of the agents he hired were old friends from his former life, and the "crimes" they solved may well have been engineered by Vidocq himself. In 1832 he opened his own private detective agency, but first he published his memoirs, four volumes of fanciful crime-busting adventure full of disguises and elaborate sleuthing. Vidocq's *Mémoires* — perhaps his most successful con job is that they continue to be classified in the libraries of the world as nonfiction — became the model of the modern detective story.

When Edgar Allan Poe, whom Americans like to think of as the father of the detective story, wrote his mysteries featuring the "ratiocinist" C. Auguste Dupin (Poe never used the word *detective*), he set his tales in Paris, even rewriting a sensational New York City killing so it would have a Parisian setting. E. T. A. Hoffmann, who the Germans like to think invented the detective story, also used Paris as his crime scene; his "Das Fräulein von Scuderi," set in the Paris of Louis XIV, was published in 1818 and predated Vidocq.

The British candidate for inventor of the detective novel, William Godwin, wrote even earlier (*Things as They Are; or, The Adventures of Caleb Williams* was published in 1794). Although the murder his detective avenges did not take place in a city, the philosophy underlying the book — that the justice system and the established rule of law is totally corrupt — is one that would appeal to the hard-boiled crime writers of the 1930s. Godwin's daughter Mary was the author of *Frankenstein,* and giving him the inventor's title has the tidy effect of keeping the makers of literary prototypes in one family.

As the nineteenth century progressed, Paris was replaced by London as the favorite crime capital, largely due to the popularity of Arthur Conan Doyle's Sherlock Holmes and his imitators. In time, thanks largely to Dashiell Hammett and his followers, the shift would move farther west to New York, Los Angeles, and San Francisco, and later to other outposts as scattered as Stockholm, Amsterdam, and Tokyo.

In fact, the particular city is probably unimportant in crime fiction. Individual landmarks may pop up to tell us we are in Vienna with Harry Lime or Malmö with Martin Beck or Santa Barbara with Lew Archer, but in the reader's mind the back alleys, the rain-slick streets, and the neon glare all come down to the universal crime city of the mind. In *Gorky Park,* Martin Cruz Smith made Moscow, a city he had visited only briefly as a tourist and which most of his readers knew not at all, seem stunningly real, largely by making it as drab and as matter-of-fact as Raymond Chandler's Los Angeles or Elmore Leonard's Detroit. The secret is in the humdrum details of any city: it becomes mysterious and threatening by removing the exotic and the picturesque, the stuff of Sunday travel supplements, and leaving the bare bones of fear, the instinct to walk clear of the shadows.

The modern city novel is the one honed by Dashiell Hammett and dozens of now forgotten pulp magazine hacks, polished by Raymond Chandler, brought to studied perfection by Ross Macdonald, and currently being remade by a new generation. Robin W. Winks, a Yale professor who is a professional historian of the British Empire and an amateur historian of the mystery novel, pretty much covers the territory when he defines it this way:

> The Western moves to the city; behind the façade of toughness is some-one sentimental enough to care about both truth and people, though truth comes first; dialogue is used to reveal character, and character to motivate plot; the reader is steadily pushed to the limit of what he will find too tough, in language, situation, visual image; a quiet competence stands revealed behind a shabby exterior. Forty bucks a day buys the expertise but not the person.

There is also the *sound* of a city story, partly dialogue, partly a deadpan narrative style that doesn't quite mask a hidden romanticism. Here are a few spare — and utterly typical — paragraphs from a short story by Paul Cain, a pulp writer of the 1930s and 1940s whose name never became a household word. Druse, the detective, has just knocked on Mrs. Hanan's door.

> Druse bowed slightly, said: "How do you do."
> She smiled, and her eyes were heavy, nearly closed. "Swell — and you?"
> He came slowly into the room, put his hat on the table, asked: "May we sit down?"
> "Sure." She jerked her head towards a chair, stayed where she was.
> Druse said, "You're drunk."
> "Right."
> He smiled, sighed gently. "A commendable condition. I regret exceedingly that my stomach does not permit it." He glanced casually about the room. In the comparative darkness of a corner, near a heavily draped window, there was a man lying on his back on the floor. His arms were stretched out and back, and his legs were bent under him in a curious broken way, and there was blood on his face.
> Druse raised his thick white eyebrows, spoke without looking at Mrs. Hanan: "Is *he* drunk, too?"
> She laughed shortly. "Uh-huh — in a different way." She nodded towards a golf-stick on the floor near the man. "He had a little too much niblick."

The flat, secretly florid style is the key to the success of these stories. Ellery Queen, writing about Dashiell Hammett, points out that Hammett's plots were sometimes outrageously romantic and asks, what makes critics and readers think he is a hard-boiled realist? "The secret is Hammett's method. Hammett tells his modern fables in *terms* of realism. . . . The stories are flamboyant extravaganzas but the characters in those stories are authentic human beings who talk, think, and act like real people. Their speech is tough, earthy, two-syllabled; their desires, their moods, their frustrations, are cut open, laid bare, probed with frank, hard fingers." Ross Macdonald, talking about his own style, says he patterned the "talking voice" of his detective, Lew Archer, on the understated one used by James M. Cain* in *The Postman Always Rings Twice*: "You can say almost anything about anything with a tone like that." Hammett stated the formula more succinctly in *The Maltese Falcon*: "The cheaper the crook, the gaudier the patter."

The Maltese Falcon was published in 1930, the best of the Raymond Chandler novels a decade or so later. That means the form has had a half century to flourish or atrophy. The city crime story itself has gone off in several directions. The detective may be a private citizen who solves crimes during idle moments (which means the author must be ingenious in finding excuses for encountering murder), or a private eye with clients continually arriving at the office door, or a police officer with a busy caseload. There is even the Ed McBain trick of having the detective be not just one person but an entire police precinct. Detectives have been popping up in new venues — Albany, St. Paul, Pittsburgh, you name it. There has been a flowering of gay and lesbian detectives since Joseph Hansen broke the ice. Women detectives, thanks to writers such as Sara Paretsky and Sue Grafton, no longer are expected to act — or look — like Miss Marple.

Clichés have developed: the narrator with a voice like Howard Duff's, the distant wail of a saxophone, the whiskey bottle in the bottom desk drawer, the loveless melancholy of the alcoholic detective both on and off the wagon (many of the pioneer detective writers were themselves alcoholics — Hammett, Chandler, Cornell Woolrich, Paul Cain, Jim Thompson — which may have had something to do with this).

And with time there has been a reaction against Chandler's philosophizing in "The Simple Art of Murder." Roger Simon, creator of the Los Angeles detective Moses Wine, threw down the gauntlet at the Fourth International Crime Writers Congress in 1988 by saying

---

*In a 1975 interview, Cain (then eighty-three years old) told me that his writing style was curiously influenced by the testimony of Roxy Stinson during the congressional hearing following the Teapot Dome scandal of the Harding administration. Roxy was the divorced wife of one of the principals, and she knew all the secrets. "Her testimony ran for days in the *New York Times*," Cain said, "and it was a literary sensation. She spoke in nothing but clichés, but she made them work." He continued, "I hadn't begun *Postman* at that time, and [Roxy] taught me respect for the cliché. I'd say she influenced me plenty."

that he was tired of hearing about those "mean streets," that Philip Marlowe was passé, that he could never get a girl today and probably never could. Ross Macdonald has criticized Chandler's sense of good and evil as "conventional to the point of occasional old-maidishness." The British crime writer Robert Barnard has satirized him for putting a "fuzzy glow around the private eye, as in a not-too-good Victorian painting of Christ or King Arthur."

But the contemporary fictional detective, even if she is a woman who drinks Perrier and jogs every morning along Lake Michigan, owes more to those sullen, hard-drinking old boys of the 1930s than to real-life private eyes who probably spend most of their time tracking down hidden property in divorce cases. It is a tradition that maintains itself simply by the weight of its existence. The new detectives even admit to reading about the old-timers. Carolyn Wheat's investigative Brooklyn lawyer Cassandra Jameson can refer to predecessors as familiar as Perry Mason and as obscure as Evan Tanner. Loren D. Estleman's Detroit private eye Amos Walker can muse that nothing in the world of crime makes sense and that it "rarely does outside Nero Wolfe."

Back in 1929, Dorothy L. Sayers, who did not write city crime novels, even though her beloved Lord Peter Wimsey maintained digs in London, published a twelve-hundred-page anthology called *Omnibus of Crime*. In its preface she warned that the reading public would soon catch on to the mystery writer's limited bag of tricks and that the detective novel might be on the way to extinction. (The "crime thriller," on the other hand, being, she believed, a more debased art form, would continue to exist as long as crime exists.) Several decades later, in 1962, mystery fiction still seemed as healthy as ever when an East German critic named Ernst Kaemmel came up with a new dire warning. He declared that the existence of detective fiction was impossible in a socialist state because its very being is a product of the evils of capitalism. With capitalism's certain collapse, he predicted, the detective novel would "likewise disappear one day."

While we await that unlikely day, and while homegrown mystery writers begin to be published even in Moscow, the following stories set in cities in the United States, Britain, Japan, France, Hong Kong, Malaysia, and the Netherlands may help while away the hours. Most of the stories are from the point of view of the sleuths, but from time to time one of the bad guys is also heard from.

CITY
SLEUTHS
AND
TOUGH
GUYS

RAYMOND
CHANDLER

AN ESSAY

THE SIMPLE ART OF MURDER

There is a vague hint of the poseur about Raymond Chandler (1888–1959), like one of those suspiciously well-dressed barflies who make a point of letting their fellow customers know that they were made for better things than drinking boilermakers at four in the afternoon. At some point, the reader suspects, Chandler decided that if he couldn't be as authentically tough a writer as Hammett he could damn well be a lot more poetic. The critic and mystery writer Julian Symons has said that we read Chandler "first of all for the writing." That's a judgment Chandler would have written approving letters about (he was a marvelous correspondent, as Frank MacShane's edition of Selected Letters of Raymond Chandler *makes clear).*

He was born in Chicago, educated in England, worked as a journalist in London, spent World War I first in the Canadian army and then in the Royal Air Force. After the war he returned to America. He wrote, several decades later, to a British publisher: "I arrived in California with a beautiful wardrobe, a public school accent, no practical gifts for earning a living, and a contempt for the natives which, I am sorry to say, has to some measure persisted to this day." After failing at just about everything he tried, including the oil business, he began writing for pulp magazines and published his first novel, The Big Sleep, *when he was fifty-one. Its hero is private eye Philip Marlowe; six other Marlowe novels would follow.*

"The Simple Art of Murder," his often quoted statement of what detective fiction should be, was first published in The Atlantic Monthly *in 1944.*

FICTION IN ANY FORM has always intended to be realistic. Old-fashioned novels which now seem stilted and artificial to the point of burlesque did not appear that way to the people who first read them. Writers like Fielding and Smollett could seem realistic in the modern sense because they dealt largely with uninhibited characters, many of whom were about two jumps ahead of the police, but Jane Austen's chronicles of highly inhibited people against a background of rural gentility seem real enough psychologically. There is plenty of that kind of social and emotional hypocrisy around today. Add to it a liberal dose of intellectual pretentiousness and you get the tone of the book page in your daily paper and the earnest and fatuous atmosphere breathed by discussion groups in little clubs. These are the people who make best sellers, which are promotional jobs based on a sort of indirect snob appeal, carefully escorted by the trained seals of the critical fraternity, and lovingly tended and watered by certain much too powerful pressure groups whose business is selling books, although they would like you to think they are fostering culture. Just get a little behind in your payments and you will find out how idealistic they are.

The detective story for a variety of reasons can seldom be promoted. It is usually about murder and hence lacks the element of uplift. Murder, which is a frustration of the individual and hence a frustration of the race, may have, and in fact has, a good deal of sociological implication. But it has been going on too long for it to be news. If the mystery novel is at all realistic (which it very seldom is) it is written in a certain spirit of detachment; otherwise nobody but a psychopath would want to write it or read it. The murder novel has also a depressing way of minding its own business, solving its own problems and answering its own questions. There is nothing left to discuss, except whether it was well enough written to be good fiction, and the people who make up the half-million sales wouldn't know that anyway. The detection of quality in writing is difficult enough even for those who make a career of the job, without paying too much attention to the matter of advance sales.

The detective story (perhaps I had better call it that, since the English formula still dominates the trade) has to find its public by a slow process of distillation. That it does do this, and holds on thereafter with such tenacity, is a fact; the reasons for it are a study for more patient minds than mine. Nor is it any part of my thesis to maintain that it is a vital and significant form of art. There are no vital and significant forms of art; there is only art, and precious little of that. The growth of populations has in no way increased the amount; it has merely increased the adeptness with which substitutes can be produced and packaged.

Yet the detective story, even in its most conventional form, is difficult to write well. Good specimens of the art are much rarer than good serious novels. Second-rate items outlast most of the high-velocity fiction, and a great many that should never have been born simply refuse to die at all. They are as durable as the statues in public parks and just about as dull.

This fact is annoying to people of what is called discernment. They do not like it that penetrating and important works of fiction of a few years back stand on their special shelf in the library marked "Best-sellers of Yesteryear" or something, and nobody goes near them but an occasional shortsighted customer who bends down, peers briefly, and hurries away; while at the same time old ladies jostle each other at the mystery shelf to grab off some item of the same vintage with such a title as *The Triple Petunia Murder Case* or *Inspector Pinchbottle to the Rescue*. They do not like it at all that "really important books" (and some of them are too, in a way) get the frosty mitt at the reprint counter while *Death Wears Yellow Garters* is put out in editions of fifty or one hundred thousand copies on the newsstands of the country, and is obviously not there just to say goodbye.

To tell the truth, I do not like it very much myself. In my less stilted moments I too write detective stories, and all this immortality makes just a little too much competition. Even Einstein couldn't get very far if three hundred treatises of the higher physics were published every year, and several thousand others in some form or other were hanging around in excellent condition, and being read too.

Hemingway says somewhere that the good writer competes only with the dead. The good detective story writer (there must after all be a few) competes not only with all the unburied dead but with all the hosts of the living as well. And on almost equal terms; for it is one of the qualities of this kind of writing that the thing that makes people read it never goes out of style. The hero's tie may be a little out of the mode and the good gray inspector may arrive in a dogcart instead of a streamlined sedan with siren screaming, but what he does when he gets there is the same old futzing around with timetables and bits of charred paper and who trampled the jolly old flowering arbutus under the library window.

I have, however, a less sordid interest in the matter. It seems to me that production of detective stories on so large a scale, and by writers whose immediate reward is small and whose meed of critical praise is almost nil, would not be possible at all if the job took any talent. In that sense the raised eyebrow of the critic and the shoddy merchandising of the publisher are perfectly logical. The average detective story is probably no worse than the average novel, but you never see the average novel. It doesn't get published. The average — or only slightly above average — detective story does. Not only is it published but it is sold in small quantities to rental libraries and it is read. There are even a few optimists who buy it at the full retail price of two dollars, because it looks so fresh and new and there is a picture of a corpse on the cover.

And the strange thing is that this average, more than middling dull, pooped-out piece of utterly unreal and mechanical fiction is really not very different from what are called the masterpieces of the art. It drags on a little more slowly, the dialogue is a shade grayer, the cardboard out of which the characters are cut is a shade thinner, and the cheating is a little more obvious. But it is the same kind of book. Whereas the good novel is not at all the same kind of book as the bad novel. It is about entirely different things. But the good detective story and the bad detective story are about exactly the same things, and they are about them in very much the same way. There are reasons for this too, and reasons for the reasons; there always are.

I suppose the principal dilemma of the traditional or classic or straight deductive or logic and deduction novel of detection is that for any approach to perfection it demands a combination of qualities not found in the same mind. The coolheaded constructionist does not also come across with lively characters, sharp dialogue, a sense of pace, and an acute use of observed detail. The grim logician has as much atmosphere as a drawing board. The scientific sleuth has a nice new shiny laboratory, but I'm sorry I can't remember the face. The fellow who can write you a vivid and colorful prose simply will not be bothered with the coolie labor of breaking down unbreakable alibis.

The master of rare knowledge is living psychologically in the age of the hoop skirt. If you know all you should know about ceramics and Egyptian needlework, you don't know anything at all about the police. If you know that platinum won't melt under about 3000° F. by itself, but will melt at the glance of a pair of deep blue eyes if you put it near a bar of lead, then you don't know how men make love in the twentieth century. And if you know enough about the elegant *flânerie* of the pre-war French Riviera to lay your story in that locale, you don't know that a couple of capsules of barbital small enough to be swallowed will not only not kill a man — they will not even put him to sleep if he fights against them.

Every detective story writer makes mistakes, of course, and none will ever know as much as he should. Conan Doyle made mistakes which completely invalidated some of his stories, but he was a pioneer, and Sherlock Holmes after all is mostly an attitude and a few dozen lines of unforgettable dialogue. It is the ladies and gentlemen of what Mr. Howard Haycraft (in his book *Murder for Pleasure*) calls the Golden Age of detective fiction that really get me down. This age is not remote. For Mr. Haycraft's purpose it starts after the First World War and lasts up to about 1930. For all practical purposes it is still here. Two thirds or three quarters of all the detective stories published still adhere to the formula the giants of this era created, perfected, polished, and sold to the world as problems in logic and deduction.

These are stern words, but be not alarmed. They are only words. Let us glance at one of the glories of the literature, an acknowledged masterpiece of the art of fooling the reader without cheating him. It is called *The Red House Mystery,* was written by A. A. Milne, and has been named by Alexander Woollcott (rather a fast man with a superlative) "one of the three best mystery stories of all time." Words of that size are not spoken lightly. The book was published in 1922 but is timeless, and might as easily have been published in July 1939, or, with a few slight changes, last week. It ran thirteen editions and seems to have been in print, in the original format, for about sixteen years. That happens to few books of any kind. It is an agreeable book, light, amusing in the *Punch* style, written with a deceptive smoothness that is not so easy as it looks.

It concerns Mark Ablett's impersonation of his brother Robert, as a hoax on his friends. Mark is the owner of the Red House, a typical laburnum-and-lodge-gate English country house. He has a secretary who encourages him and abets him in this impersonation, and who is going to murder him if he pulls it off. Nobody around the Red House has ever seen Robert, fifteen years absent in Australia and known by repute as a no-good. A letter is talked about (but never shown) announcing Robert's arrival, and Mark hints it will not be a pleasant occasion. One afternoon, then, the supposed Robert arrives, identifies himself to a couple of servants, is shown into the study. Mark goes in after him (according to testimony at the inquest). Robert is then found dead on the floor with a bullet hole in his face, and of course Mark has vanished into thin air. Arrive the police, who suspect Mark must be the murderer, remove the débris, and proceed with the investigation — and in due course, with the inquest.

Milne is aware of one very difficult hurdle and tries as well as he can to get over it. Since the secretary is going to murder Mark, once Mark has established himself as Robert, the impersonation has to continue and fool the police. Since, also, everybody around the Red

House knows Mark intimately, disguise is necessary. This is achieved by shaving off Mark's beard, roughening his hands ("not the hands of a manicured gentleman" — testimony), and the use of a gruff voice and rough manner.

But this is not enough. The cops are going to have the body and the clothes on it and whatever is in the pockets. Therefore none of this must suggest Mark. Milne therefore works like a switch engine to put over the motivation that Mark is such a thoroughly conceited performer that he dresses the part down to the socks and underwear (from all of which the secretary has removed the maker's labels), like a ham blacking himself all over to play Othello. If the reader will buy this (and the sales record shows he must have), Milne figures he is solid. Yet, however light in texture the story may be, it is offered as a problem of logic and deduction.

If it is not that, it is nothing at all. There is nothing else for it to be. If the situation is false, you cannot even accept it as a light novel, for there is no story for the light novel to be about. If the problem does not contain the elements of truth and plausibility, it is no problem; if the logic is an illusion, there is nothing to deduce. If the impersonation is impossible once the reader is told the conditions it must fulfill, then the whole thing is a fraud. Not a deliberate fraud, because Milne would not have written the story if he had known what he was up against. He is up against a number of deadly things, none of which he even considers. Nor, apparently, does the casual reader, who wants to like the story — hence takes it at its face value. But the reader is not called upon to know the facts of life when the author does not. The author is the expert in the case.

Here is what this author ignores:

1. The coroner holds formal jury inquest on a body for which no legal competent identification is offered. A coroner, usually in a big city, will sometimes hold inquest on a body that *cannot* be identified, if the record of such an inquest has or may have a value (fire, disaster, evidence of murder). No such reason exists here, and there is no one to identify the body. Witnesses said the man said he was Robert Ablett. This is mere presumption, and has weight only if nothing conflicts with it. Identification is a condition precedent to an inquest. It is a matter of law. Even in death a man has a right to his own identity. The coroner will, wherever humanly possible, enforce that right. To neglect it would be a violation of his office.

2. Since Mark Ablett, missing and suspected of the murder, cannot defend himself, all evidence of his movements before and after the murder is vital (as also whether he has money to run away on); yet

all such evidence is given by the man closest to the murder and is without corroboration. It is automatically suspect until proved true.

3. The police find by direct investigation that Robert Ablett was not well thought of in his native village. Somebody there must have known him. No such person was brought to the inquest. (The story couldn't stand it.)

4. The police know there is an element of threat in Robert's supposed visit, and that it is connected with the murder must be obvious to them. Yet they make no attempt to check Robert in Australia, or find out what character he had there, or what associates, or even if he actually came to England, and with whom. (If they had, they would have found out he had been dead three years.)

5. The police surgeon examines a body with a recently shaved beard (exposing unweathered skin) and artificially roughened hands, but it is the body of a wealthy, soft-living man, long resident in a cool climate. Robert was a rough individual and had lived fifteen years in Australia. That is the surgeon's information. It is impossible he would have noticed nothing to conflict with it.

6. The clothes are nameless, empty, and have had the labels removed. Yet the man wearing them asserted an identity. The presumption that he was not what he said he was is overpowering. Nothing whatever is done about his peculiar circumstance. It is never even mentioned as being peculiar.

7. A man is missing, a well-known local man, and a body in the morgue closely resembles him. It is impossible that the police should not at once eliminate the chance that the missing man *is* the dead man. Nothing would be easier than to prove it. Not even to think of it is incredible. It makes idiots of the police, so that a brash amateur may startle the world with a fake solution.

The detective in the case is an insouciant amateur named Anthony Gillingham, a nice lad with a cheery eye, a nice little flat in town, and that airy manner. He is not making any money on the assignment, but is always available when the local gendarmerie loses its notebook. The English police endure him with their customary stoicism, but I shudder to think what the boys down at the Homicide Bureau in my city would do to him.

There are even less plausible examples of the art than this. In *Trent's Last Case* (often called "the perfect detective story") you have to accept the premise that a giant of international finance, whose lightest frown makes Wall Street quiver like a chihuahua, will plot his own death so as to hang his secretary, and that the secretary when pinched will maintain an aristocratic silence — the old Etonian in him, maybe. I have known relatively few international financiers, but I rather think the author of this novel has (if possible) known fewer.

There is another one, by Freeman Wills Crofts (the soundest builder of them all when he doesn't get too fancy), wherein a murderer, by the aid of make-up, split-second timing, and some very sweet evasive action, impersonates the man he has just killed and thereby gets him alive and distant from the place of the crime. There is one by Dorothy Sayers in which a man is murdered alone at night in his house by a mechanically released weight which works because he always turns the radio on at just such a moment, always stands in just such a position in front of it, and always bends over just so far. A couple of inches either way and the customers would get a rain check. This is what is vulgarly known as having God sit in your lap; a murderer who needs that much help from Providence must be in the wrong business.

And there is a scheme of Agatha Christie's featuring M. Hercule Poirot, that ingenious Belgian who talks in a literal translation of school-boy French. By duly messing around with his "little gray cells" M. Poirot decides that since nobody on a certain through sleeper could have done the murder alone, everybody did it together, breaking the process down into a series of simple operations like assembling an egg beater. This is the type that is guaranteed to knock the keenest mind for a loop. Only a halfwit could guess it.

There are much better plots by these same writers and by others of their school. There may be one somewhere that would really stand up under close scrutiny. It would be fun to read it, even if I did have to go back to page 47 and refresh my memory about exactly what time the second gardener potted the prize-winning tea-rose begonia. There is nothing new about these stories and nothing old. The ones I mentioned are all English because the authorities, such as they are, seem to feel that the English writers had an edge in this dreary routine and that the Americans, even the creator of Philo Vance, only make the Junior Varsity.

This, the classic detective story, has learned nothing and forgotten nothing. It is the story you will find almost any week in the big shiny magazines, handsomely illustrated, and paying due deference to virginal love and the right kind of luxury goods. Perhaps the tempo has become a trifle faster and the dialogue a little more glib. There are more frozen daiquiris and stingers and fewer glasses of crusty old port, more clothes by *Vogue* and décors by *House Beautiful,* more chic, but not more truth. We spend more time in Miami hotels and Cape Cod summer colonies and go not so often down by the old gray sundial in the Elizabethan garden.

But fundamentally it is the same careful grouping of suspects, the same utterly incomprehensible trick of how somebody stabbed Mrs. Pottington Postlethwaite III with the solid platinum poniard just as she flatted on the top note of the "Bell Song" from *Lakmé* in the presence of fifteen ill-assorted guests; the same ingénue in fur-trimmed pajamas screaming in the night to make the company pop in and out of doors and ball up the timetable; the same moody silence next day as they sit around sipping Singapore slings and sneering at each other, while the flatfeet crawl to and fro under the Persian rugs, with their derby hats on.

Personally I like the English style better. It is not quite so brittle and the people as a rule just wear clothes and drink drinks. There is more sense of background, as if Cheesecake Manor really existed all around and not just in the part the camera sees; there are more long walks over the downs and the characters don't all try to behave as if they had just been tested by MGM. The English may not always be the best writers in the world, but they are incomparably the best dull writers.

There is a very simple statement to be made about all these stories: they do not really come off intellectually as problems, and they do not come off artistically as fiction. They are too contrived, and too little aware of what goes on in the world. They try to be honest, but honesty is an art. The poor writer is dishonest without knowing it, and the fairly good one can be dishonest because he doesn't know what to be honest about. He thinks a complicated murder scheme which baffled the lazy reader, who won't be bothered itemizing the details, will also baffle the police, whose business is with details.

The boys with their feet on the desks know that the easiest murder case in the world to break is the one somebody tried to get very cute with; the one that really bothers them is the murder somebody thought of only two minutes before he pulled it off. But if the writers of this fiction wrote about the kind of murders that happen, they would also have to write about the authentic flavor of life as it is lived. And since they cannot do that, they pretend that what they do is what should be done. Which is begging the question — and the best of them know it.

In her introduction to the first *Omnibus of Crime,* Dorothy Sayers wrote: "It [the detective story] does not, and by hypothesis never can, attain the loftiest level of literary achievement." And she suggested somewhere else that this is because it is a "literature of escape" and not "a literature of expression." I do not know what the loftiest level of literary achievement is: neither did Aeschylus or Shakespeare; neither does Miss Sayers. Other things being equal, which they never are, a more powerful theme will provoke a more powerful performance. Yet some very dull books have been written about God, and some very fine ones about how to make a living and stay fairly honest. It is always a matter of who writes the stuff, and what he has in him to write it with.

As for "literature of expression" and "literature of escape" — this is critics' jargon, a use of abstract words as if they had absolute meanings. Everything written with vitality expresses that vitality: there are no dull subjects, only dull minds. All men who read escape from something else into what lies behind the printed page; the quality of the dream may be argued, but its release has become a functional necessity. All men must escape at times from the deadly rhythm of their private thoughts. It is part of the process of life among thinking beings. It is one of the things that distinguish them from the three-toed sloth; he apparently — one can never be quite sure — is perfectly content hanging upside down on a branch, not even reading Walter Lippmann. I hold no particular brief for the detective story as the ideal escape. I merely say that *all* reading for pleasure is escape, whether it be Greek, mathematics, astronomy, Benedetto Croce, or The Diary of the Forgotten Man. To say otherwise is to be an intellectual snob, and a juvenile at the art of living.

I do not think such considerations moved Miss Dorothy Sayers to her essay in critical futility.

I think what was really gnawing at Miss Sayers' mind was the slow realization that her kind of detective story was an arid formula which could not even satisfy its own implications. It was second-grade literature because it was not about the things that could make first-grade literature. If it started out to be about real people (and she could write about them — her minor characters show that), they must very soon do unreal things in order to form the artificial pattern required by the plot. When they did unreal things, they ceased to be real themselves. They became puppets and cardboard lovers and papier-mâché villains and detectives of exquisite and impossible gentility.

The only kind of writer who could be happy with these properties was the one who did not know what reality was. Dorothy Sayers' own stories show that she was annoyed by this triteness; the weakest element in them is the part that makes them detective stories, the strongest the part which could be removed without touching the "problem of logic and deduction." Yet she could not or would not give her characters their heads and let them make their own mystery. It took a much simpler and more direct mind than hers to do that.

*

In *The Long Week End,* which is a drastically competent account of English life and manners in the decades following the First World War, Robert Graves and Alan Hodge gave some attention to the detective story. They were just as traditionally English as the ornaments of the Golden Age, and they wrote of the time in which these writers were almost as well known as any writers in the world. Their books in one form or another sold into the millions, and in a dozen languages. These were the people who fixed the form and established the rules and founded the famous Detection Club, which is a Parnassus of English writers of mystery. Its roster includes practically every important writer of detective fiction since Conan Doyle.

But Graves and Hodge decided that during this whole period only one first-class writer had written detective stories at all. An American, Dashiell Hammett. Traditional or not, Graves and Hodge were not fuddy-duddy connoisseurs of the second-rate; they could see what went on in the world and that the detective story of their time didn't; and they were aware that writers who have the vision and the ability to produce real fiction do not produce unreal fiction.

How original a writer Hammett really was it isn't easy to decide now, even if it mattered. He was one of a group — the only one who achieved critical recognition — who wrote or tried to write realistic mystery fiction. All literary movements are like this; some one individual is picked out to represent the whole movement; he is usually the culmination of the movement. Hammett was the ace performer, but there is nothing in his work that is not implicit in the early novels and short stories of Hemingway.

Yet, for all I know, Hemingway may have learned something from Hammett as well as from writers like Dreiser, Ring Lardner, Carl Sandburg, Sherwood Anderson, and himself. A rather revolutionary debunking of both the language and the material of fiction had been going on for some time. It probably started in poetry; almost everything does. You can take it clear back to Walt Whitman, if you like. But Hammett applied it to the detective story, and this, because of its heavy crust of English gentility and American pseudogentility, was pretty hard to get moving.

I doubt that Hammett had any deliberate artistic aims whatever; he was trying to make a living by writing something he had firsthand information about. He made some of it up; all writers do; but it had a basis in fact; it was made up out of real things. The only reality the English detection writers knew was the conversational accent of Surbiton and Bognor Regis. If they wrote about dukes and Venetian vases, they knew no more about them out of their own experience than the well-heeled Hollywood character knows about the French

Modernists that hang in his Bel-Air château or the semi-antique Chippendale-cum-cobbler's bench that he uses for a coffee table. Hammett took murder out of the Venetian vase and dropped it into the alley; it doesn't have to stay there forever, but it looked like a good idea to get as far as possible from Emily Post's idea of how a well-bred debutante gnaws a chicken wing.

Hammett wrote at first (and almost to the end) for people with a sharp, aggressive attitude to life. They were not afraid of the seamy side of things; they lived there. Violence did not dismay them; it was right down their street. Hammett gave murder back to the kind of people that commit it for reasons, not just to provide a corpse; and with the means at hand, not hand-wrought dueling pistols, curare, and tropical fish. He put these people down on paper as they were, and he made them talk and think in the language they customarily used for these purposes.

He had style, but his audience didn't know it, because it was in a language not supposed to be capable of such refinements. They thought they were getting a good meaty melodrama written in the kind of lingo they imagined they spoke themselves. It was, in a sense, but it was much more. All language begins with speech, and the speech of common men at that, but when it develops to the point of becoming a literary medium it only looks like speech. Hammett's style at its worst was as formalized as a page of *Marius the Epicurean;* at its best it could say almost anything. I believe this style, which does not belong to Hammett or to anybody, but is the American language (and not even exclusively that anymore), can say things he did not know how to say, or feel the need of saying. In his hands it had no overtones, left no echo, evoked no image beyond a distant hill.

Hammett is said to have lacked heart; yet the story he himself thought the most of is the record of a man's devotion to a friend. He was spare, frugal, hard-boiled, but he did over and over again what only the best writers can ever do at all. He wrote scenes that seemed never to have been written before.

With all this he did not wreck the formal detective story. Nobody can; production demands a form that can be produced. Realism takes too much talent, too much knowledge, too much awareness. Hammett may have loosened it up a little here, and sharpened it a little there. Certainly all but the stupidest and most meretricious writers are more conscious of their artificiality than they used to be. And he demonstrated that the detective story can be important writing. *The Maltese Falcon* may or may not be a work of genius, but an art which is capable of it is not "by hypothesis" incapable of anything. Once a detective story can be as good as this, only the pedants will deny that it *could* be even better.

Hammett did something else; he made the detective story fun to write, not an exhausting concatenation of insignificant clues. Without him there might not have been a regional mystery as clever as Percival Wilde's *Inquest,* or an ironic study as able as Raymond Postgate's *Verdict of Twelve,* or a savage piece of intellectual double-talk like Kenneth Fearing's *The Dagger of the Mind,* or a tragi-comic idealization of the murderer as in Donald Henderson's *Mr. Bowling Buys a Newspaper,* or even a gay Hollywoodian gambol like Richard Sale's *Lazarus No. 7.*

The realistic style is easy to abuse: from haste, from lack of awareness, from inability to bridge the chasm that lies between what a writer would like to be able to say and what he actually knows how to say. It is easy to fake; brutality is not strength, flipness is not wit, edge-of-the-chair writing can be as boring as flat writing; dalliance with promiscuous blondes can be very dull stuff when described by goaty young men with no other purpose in mind than to describe dalliance with promiscuous blondes. There has been so much of this sort of thing that if a character in a detective story says "Yeah," the author is automatically a Hammett imitator.

And there are still a number of people around who say that Hammett did not write detective stories at all — merely hard-boiled chronicles of mean streets with a perfunctory mystery element dropped in like the olive in a martini. These are the flustered old ladies — of both sexes (or no sex) and almost all ages — who like their murders scented with magnolia blossoms and do not care to be reminded that murder is an act of infinite cruelty, even if the perpetrators sometimes look like playboys or college professors or nice motherly women with softly graying hair.

There are also a few badly scared champions of the formal or classic mystery who think that no story is a detective story which does not pose a formal and exact problem and arrange the clues around it with neat labels on them. Such would point out, for example, that in reading *The Maltese Falcon* no one concerns himself with who killed Spade's partner, Archer (which is the only formal problem of the story), because the reader is kept thinking about something else. Yet in *The Glass Key* the reader is constantly reminded that the question is who killed Taylor Henry, and exactly the same effect is obtained — an effect of movement, intrigue, cross-purposes, and the gradual elucidation of character, which is all the detective story has any right to be about anyway. The rest is spillikins in the parlor.

*

But all this (and Hammett too) is for me not quite enough. The realist in murder writes of a world in which gangsters can rule nations and almost rule cities, in which hotels and apartment houses and celebrated restaurants are owned by men who made their money out of brothels, in which a screen star can be the finger man for a mob, and the nice man down the hall is a boss of the numbers racket; a world where a judge with a cellar full of bootleg liquor can send a man to jail for having a pint in his pocket, where the mayor of your town may have condoned murder as an instrument of money-making, where no man can walk down a dark street in safety because law and order are things we talk about but refrain from practicing; a world where you may witness a holdup in broad daylight and see who did it, but you will fade quickly back into the crowd rather than tell anyone, because the holdup men may have friends with long guns, or the police may not like your testimony, and in any case the shyster for the defense will be allowed to abuse and vilify you in open court, before a jury of selected morons, without any but the most perfunctory interference from a political judge.

It is not a fragrant world, but it is the world you live in, and certain writers with tough minds and a cool spirit of detachment can make very interesting and even amusing patterns out of it. It is not funny that a man should be killed, but it is sometimes funny that he should be killed for so little, and that his death should be the coin of what we call civilization. All this still is not quite enough.

In everything that can be called art there is a quality of redemption. It may be pure tragedy, if it is high tragedy, and it may be pity and irony, and it may be the raucous laughter of the strong man. But down these mean streets a man must go who is not himself mean, who is neither tarnished nor afraid. The detective in this kind of story must be such a man. He is the hero; he is everything. He must be a complete man and a common man and yet an unusual man. He must be, to use a rather weathered phrase, a man of honor — by instinct, by inevitability, without thought of it, and certainly without saying it. He must be the best man in his world and a good enough man for any world. I do not care much about his private life; he is neither a eunuch nor a satyr; I think he might seduce a duchess and I am quite sure he would not spoil a virgin; if he is a man of honor in one thing, he is that in all things.

He is a relatively poor man, or he would not be a detective at all. He is a common man or he could not go among common people. He has a sense of character, or he would not know his job. He will take no man's money dishonestly and no man's insolence without a due and dispassionate revenge. He is a lonely man and his pride is that you will treat him as a proud man or be very sorry you ever saw him. He talks as the man of his age talks — that is, with rude wit, a lively sense of the grotesque, a disgust for sham, and a contempt for pettiness.

The story is this man's adventure in search of a hidden truth, and it would be no adventure if it did not happen to a man fit for adventure. He has a range of awareness that startles you, but it belongs to him by right, because it belongs to the world he lives in. If there were enough like him, the world would be a very safe place to live in, without becoming too dull to be worth living in.

FRANÇOIS EUGÈNE
VIDOCQ

THE CLUE
OF THE
YELLOW
CURTAINS

*François Eugène Vidocq (1775–1857) was a criminal, a prison inmate, a
police informer, first chief of the French Police de Sûreté, and founder of the
first private detective agency. He was also the titular author (the books were
actually ghost-written) of a collection of sometimes dubious memoirs that began
appearing in 1828 and established the form modern detective fiction would
follow. Vidocq presents himself as a master of disguises, as an acute observer
of the telltale clue, and as a somewhat scientific detective who maintained
detailed files on criminals and criminal activity. He was also fond of grand
generalizations, such as noting that most criminals are bowlegged.*

*Vidocq's story — which often sounds too good to be true — appealed to
writers. His friend Balzac used him in several novels under the name Vautrin,
and other novelists — including Hugo, Dumas, Bulwer-Lytton, and Dickens — seem to have borrowed from him. Julian Symons, the British mystery
writer and historian of the crime novel, even suspects that the Deerslayer's
fascination with the variation in Indians' footprints in the novels of James
Fenimore Cooper owes much to Vidocq. But Vidocq's most important American
student was probably Edgar Allan Poe.*

This translation of a section of the Mémoires *is by Edwin Gile Rich.*

AFTER THEY HAD SERVED several sentences, two escaped convicts,
Goreau and Florentin, alias Châtelain, were held at Bicêtre as incor-
rigible thieves. Wearied of their sojourn in the cells where they might
as well have been buried alive, they sent a letter to M. Henry [a police
official] in which they offered to furnish information which would
make it possible to take several of their comrades who were daily

committing robberies in Paris. One named Fossard, a man sentenced to life imprisonment who had escaped from prison several times, was the one they designated as the most adroit, at the same time representing him as the most dangerous. "He was," they wrote, "unrivaled in boldness, and he should be approached only after precautions had been taken, in view of the fact that he was always armed to the teeth, and was resolved to blow out the brains of the police agent who was daring enough to try to arrest him."

The chiefs of the administration asked nothing better than to deliver the capital of such a scoundrel. Their first thought was to use me to discover him, but the informers had observed to M. Henry that I was too well known to Fossard and his concubine not to fail in such a delicate operation in case I was entrusted with it. So it was decided to have recourse to the regular police. The information necessary to direct their search was put at their disposal, but, whether they were unlucky or did not care to meet Fossard, "armed to the teeth," he continued his exploits. The numerous complaints to which his activity gave rise announced that, in spite of their apparent zeal, these gentlemen, according to their custom, were making much noise but doing little work.

The result was that one day the Prefect, who wanted more work and less noise, summoned them and reproached them, probably rather severely, to judge from the discontent which they were unable to repress on this occasion. They were just coming from this blowing-up when I happened to meet one of them named M. Yvrier. I bowed to him; he came toward me, almost swollen to bursting with rage. When he was near me, he said: "Oh, there you are, monsieur the doer of great things. You're the cause of our being reprimanded on account of one called Fossard, escaped convict, who, it is pretended, is in Paris. To hear Monsieur the Prefect one would think that the only one in the administration capable of anything is you. If Vidocq, he told us, had been sent in pursuit, there's no doubt that he would have been arrested long ago. Come along, M. Vidocq, make a slight attempt to find him; you who are so adroit, prove that you have as much shrewdness as they say you have."

M. Yvrier was an old man, and I had need to respect his age, not to retort with temper to his impertinent attack. Although I felt piqued at the tone of bitterness which he took in talking to me, I was not at all angry and contented myself by answering that for the moment I had hardly the leisure to busy myself with Fossard; that I was saving his capture for the first of January to offer him as a New Year's gift, as I had offered the famous Delzève the previous year.

"Go your way," answered M. Yvrier, irritated by this persiflage, "the result will show us what you are — a presumptuous man, a trouble-maker." He left me muttering in his teeth some other qualifications I did not understand.

After this scene, I went to M. Henry's office and told him about it. "Oh, so they're mad," he said, laughing. "So much the better."

Then he gave me the following information:

"Fossard lives in Paris in a street which leads from the market to the boulevard, that is to say, starting with the rue Comtesse d'Artois to rue Poissonnière, passing through rue Montorgueil and Petit Carreau. It is not known on what floor he lives, but the windows of his apartment may be recognized by yellow silk curtains and others of embroidered muslin. There is living in the same house a small dwarf, a seamstress, a friend of the girl who lives with Fossard."

As one can see, this information was not so precise as to enable one to go straight to the end. A dwarf and yellow curtains, with other curtains of embroidered muslin, were certainly not easy to find in a space as large as that which I had to explore. Without a doubt such a combination of circumstances would present itself more than once. How many dwarfs, old and young, could be counted in Paris, and who could number the yellow curtains? To sum up, the data were rather vague; however, the problem must be solved. I would try and see whether my lucky genius, as a result of my investigations, would not lead me to put my finger on the exact spot.

I did not know where to start. However, as I foresaw that in my rounds I should meet principally women of the people, that is to say, the gossips, I soon fixed on the sort of disguise suitable to assume. It was obvious that I needed to appear as a very respectable gentleman. Consequently, by means of some artificial wrinkles, a queue, white crêpe, and a large gold-headed cane, a three-cornered hat, buckles, appropriate trousers and coat, I changed myself into one of those good sixty-year-old citizens whom all the old maids consider well preserved. I had the complete appearance and dress of one of those rich men whose ruddy and winsome faces indicate ease and the fancy of making the happiness of some unfortunate woman past middle age. I was certain that all the dwarfs would desire me, and then I had the appearance of such an honest man that it was impossible that they should scruple to receive me.

Disguised in this way, I started to go up and down the streets, nose in the air, noting all the curtains of the color which had been described to me. I was so occupied with this census that I neither heard nor saw anything around me. If I had been a little less wealthy in appearance, I should have been taken for a metaphysician or perhaps a poet.

Twenty times I just missed being crushed under cabs; from all sides I heard cries of "Look out! Look out!" and turned to find myself under a wheel or embracing a horse. Sometimes, too, while I was wiping off the foam that covered my sleeve, a cut of the whip reached my face; or, when the driver was less brutal, there were pretty thoughts of this nature, "Get out, old dummy!" One even went so far, I remember, as to call me "old cocked hat"!

This review of yellow curtains was not the affair of a day. I wrote more than a hundred and fifty in my notes. And I could not tell but what the curtains behind which Fossard hid had been sent to the cleaner and replaced by white, green, or red. No matter, if luck was against me, it could also be favorable. So I took courage, and although it was very painful for a sexagenarian to climb and descend a hundred and fifty staircases, that is to say, about seven hundred and fifty flights of stairs, as I felt my legs strong and my breath deep, I undertook the task, sustained by a hope of the same kind as led the Argonauts to voyage in search of the Golden Fleece. I was searching for my dwarf. In my ascents on how many landings did I play the sentinel for entire hours in the persuasion that my lucky star would show her to me! The heroic Don Quixote was never more ardent in the pursuit of his Dulcinea. I knocked at the doors of all the dressmakers; I examined them all one after the other; but there were no dwarfs. They were all ravishing.

I passed several days in this way without meeting the shadow of my aim. It was a devilish trade; I was worn out every evening, and I had to begin again every morning. Still, if I had dared to ask questions, perhaps some charitable soul would have set me on the way, but I was afraid of giving the game away. In the end, worn out by this maneuver, I tried another means.

I had noticed that dwarfs are generally chatterers and curious; nearly always it is they who make the talk of the quarter, and when they do not, they record it for use as slander; nothing happens that they do not know. Starting with these data, I concluded that under the pretext of getting provisions the unknown who had already caused me so many steps would, no more than any of the rest, neglect to gossip with the milkman, the baker, and fruiterer, mercer, or grocer. In consequence I decided to place myself within reach of the largest possible number of these media of talk. And as there is no dwarf who in her desire for a husband does not make a parade of all her merits as a housekeeper, I was persuaded that as mine would get up early, to see her I had to arrive early on the scene of my observations. I was there at daybreak.

I employed my first session in orienting myself. The question was to what dairy my dwarf would give the preference. Undoubtedly to the one which was nearest, where there was the most talk, and which was most frequented. That at the corner of the rue Thévenot appeared to combine these conditions. Around it were small jars for everyone, and in the middle of a crowded circle, the merchant never stopped serving or talking. The customers formed a queue, but that did not disturb me. The important thing was that I had recognized a meeting-place, and I promised myself that I would not let it out of my sight.

I was there at my second session, impatiently on the lookout for a female dwarf, but only young girls came. With their graceful figures and slender forms there was not one who was not as straight as an "I." I was in despair. . . . At last my star appeared on the horizon; it was the model, the Venus of dwarfs. It seemed to me that I saw one of those fairies of the Middle Ages, in whom a deformity was one charm the more. This super-natural being approached the milk-seller and talked to her for some time, as I had expected. Then she took the cream, at least that was what she had asked for, and went into the grocer's; then she stopped a moment with the tripe dealer, who gave her some lights, probably for her cat. Then, her purchases finished, she went into the side entrance of a house, the ground floor of which was occupied by a cooper. My gaze at once turned to the windows, but I did not see the yellow curtains for which I had sighed. However, remembering the thought which had already come to mind, that curtains, no matter what the shade, have not the immovability of a dwarf, I decided not to withdraw until I had had an interview with the little prodigy whose appearance had pleased me so much. I imagined that in spite of my disappointment about one of the major circumstances which were to be my guides, the interview would furnish me some light.

I decided to go upstairs. When I reached the mezzanine floor, I asked on what floor a small, slightly deformed woman lived.

"Do you want to talk to the dressmaker?" was the reply, laughing in my face.

"Yes, it's the dressmaker, a person with one shoulder slightly prominent."

They laughed again, and pointed to the third-floor front. Although the neighbors were very obliging, I was on the point of taking offense at their jeering hilarity. They were really impolite; but my tolerance was so great that I willingly forgave them for finding the situation comic. Besides, was I not a good man? So I kept to my role. They had pointed out the door; I knocked, and it was opened. There was my dwarf. After the usual excuses on the importunity of my visit, I asked her to grant me a short audience, adding that I had to talk of an affair of personal interest to me.

"Mademoiselle," I said, with a sort of solemnity, after she had made me seat myself opposite her, "you do not know the reason which has brought me to you, but, when you learn, perhaps my course will arouse your interest."

The dwarf imagined that I was going to make a declaration. The color mounted to her face, and her gaze became animated, although she forced herself to lower her eyes. I went on:

"Without doubt you will be astonished that at my age one can be as much in love as at twenty."

"Oh, monsieur, you are still robust," said my amiable dwarf.

"I am very well," I answered, "but that isn't the question. You know that in Paris it is not rare for a man and a woman to live together without being married."

"What do you take me for, monsieur, to make me such a proposition?" cried the dwarf, without waiting for me to finish. Her mistake made me smile.

"I did not come to make you a proposition," I replied. "I only want you to be so kind as to give me certain information about a young lady who, I have been told, lives in this house with a man who passes as her husband."

"I don't know her," the dwarf answered dryly.

Then I gave her a rough description of Fossard and his mistress Tonneau.

"Oh, I know him," she said. "A man about your figure, nearly as stout as you are, about thirty or thirty-five, a fine gallant; the lady, an attractive brunette, beautiful eyes, fine teeth, superb eyelashes, a slight growth of hair on her upper lip, a turned-up nose, and with all that an appearance of kindness and modesty. They lived here, but they moved a little while ago."

I begged her to give me their new address, and on her reply that she did not know it, I pleaded with her tearfully to help me to find an unfortunate creature whom I still loved in spite of her perfidy. The dressmaker was touched by my tears; I saw that she was moved, and I became more and more pathetic.

"Oh, her infidelity will kill me! Take pity on a poor husband, I conjure you; do not hide their retreat; I will owe you more than life itself!"

Dwarfs are sympathetic; in addition, a husband is in their eyes so precious a treasure that they cannot understand how a wife can be unfaithful, so my dressmaker was horrified, sympathized with me most sincerely, and protested that she wanted to be useful to me.

"Unfortunately," she added, "their moving was done by commissionaires who are strangers in the quarter. I am completely ignorant where they have gone or what has become of them, but if you would see the owner . . ."

The good faith of this woman was obvious. I went to see the owner. All he could tell me was that they had paid the rent, and had no references.

Aside from the certainty that I had discovered Fossard's former lodgings, I was hardly further along than before. Nevertheless, I did not want to abandon the game without exhausting all means of inquiry. Ordinarily the commissionaires of one quarter know those of another; so I questioned those in the rue du Petit Carreau, to whom I represented myself as a deceived husband, and one of them pointed out to me one of his colleagues who had helped in moving my rival's furniture.

I saw the individual indicated and told him my pretended history. He listened to me, but he was a knave and intended to play me up. I pretended not to see it, and to recompense him for having promised to take me next day to the place where Fossard had moved, I gave him two five-franc pieces. They were spent the same day on the girls.

The first interview took place two days after Christmas. We were to see each other again on the twenty-eighth. There was no time to lose if I was to be ready on the first of January. I was prompt at the rendezvous; the commissionaire, whom I had had followed by my agents, was careful not to be missing. Again some five-franc pieces passed from my purse to his. I also paid for his lunch. Finally, he decided to start, and we arrived near a pretty house, situated at the corner of the rue Duphot and rue Saint-Honoré. "Here it is," he said. "We'll find out in the wine-cellar downstairs whether they're still here." He wanted me to regale him for the last time. I was not deaf; I went in and we emptied a bottle of Beaune together.

I withdrew in the certainty that at last I had found the refuge of my pretended wife and her seducer. I no longer needed my guide, so I dismissed him, expressing my full gratitude. But to assure myself that he did not take money from both sides, I recommended my agents to watch him closely and, above all, to prevent his coming back to the wine merchant's. To be frank, I had him locked up, a just reprisal. "My friend," I said to him, "I have given the police a five-hundred-franc note to recompense the one who leads me to find my wife. It belongs to you, and I'm going to give you a note so that you can get it." In fact I gave him a note which he took to M. Henry. "Take the gentleman to the cash-box," the latter ordered. The cash-box was the dépôt, where my commissionaire had time to recover from his joy.

It had not been demonstrated that Fossard's home had been pointed out to me. However, I reported to the authorities what had happened, and I was immediately provided with an order to effect the arrest. Then the rich man changed suddenly into a coalman, and in this guise, under which neither my mother nor the employees of the Prefecture who saw me most frequently would have made me out, I busied myself in studying the ground on which I had to operate.

Fossard's friends — that is to say, his denouncers — had advised that the agents charged with the arrest should be warned that he always had on him a dagger and pistols; and that a double-barreled gun was hidden in a cambric handkerchief which he held constantly in his hand. This advice made precautions necessary; besides, from Fossard's known character they were convinced that he would not hesitate at murder to escape a condemnation worse than death. I wanted to operate so that I should not be a victim, and it seemed that a way considerably to diminish the danger was to have an understanding in advance with the wine merchant who was Fossard's landlord.

This wine merchant was a good man, but the police have such a bad reputation that it is not always easy to induce honest folk to lend their assistance. I decided to assure myself of his cooperation by binding him to me in his own interests. I had already had some sessions with him in both my disguises, and I had had the leisure to become acquainted with the locality and to get in touch with the personnel of the shop. I went back in my ordinary clothes, and told the good man that I wanted to speak to him in private. He entered a room with me, and I spoke to him nearly as follows:

"I am ordered to warn you on the part of the police that you are to be robbed. The thief who has prepared this coup and will perhaps execute it himself lodges in your house. The woman who lives with him sometimes comes in and places herself near your wife in the bar. While she has been talking to her, she has managed to procure the impression of the key which opens the door through which they can enter. All has been foreseen; the spring on the alarm bell will be cut with scissors, while the door will be ajar. Once inside, they will rapidly go up to your chamber. If they have the slightest fear of your waking up, as you are engaged with a most consummate rascal, I don't need to explain the rest."

"They'll do us in!" said the terrified wine merchant, and he at once called his wife to give her the news.

"Well, my dear, we must distrust everyone! So that Madame Hazard wants to cut our throats? They'll come to butcher us this very night?"

"No, no, sleep in peace," I answered. "It's not for tonight. The receipts aren't good enough; they'll wait. But if you're discreet, and will consent to help me, we'll put everything in good order."

Madame Hazard was the girl Tonneau; she had taken this name, the only one under which Fossard was known in the house. I engaged the wine merchant and his wife, who were terrified by my confidence, to receive their tenants, whose projects I had revealed, with the same kindliness as usual. It need not be asked whether they were disposed to serve me. It was arranged between us that I should hide in a small room at the foot of the staircase so that I could watch Fossard pass in and out, and, in addition, arrange for an occasion to seize him.

The twenty-ninth of December I was at my post early. It was excessively cold; my watch was long, and the more uncomfortable in that we were without a fire; motionless, and my eye riveted to a hole made in the shutters, I was hardly at my ease. At last, toward three o'clock, a man went out. I followed; it was Fossard. Until then I had had some doubts. Certain of his identity, I wanted to execute my writ immediately, but the agent with me pretended that he had seen the terrible pistol. I hastened my step to verify the fact. I passed Fossard, and retracing my steps I regretted to see that the agent was not mistaken. To attempt the arrest was to expose myself, and perhaps uselessly. I then decided to postpone the party, and recalling that a fortnight previously I had flattered myself that I would hand over Fossard only on the first of January, I was almost pleased by the delay. Until then I must not relax my vigilance.

At eleven o'clock the thirty-first of December, when all my batteries were mounted, Fossard came back; he suspected nothing and went up the stairs humming. Twenty minutes after, the disappearance of his light indicated that he was in bed. The propitious moment had come. The commissioner and the gendarmes whom I had warned were waiting at the nearest post, and I summoned them. They entered without making a noise, and we at once began to deliberate on the means of taking Fossard without running the risk of being killed or wounded. They were persuaded that at the least surprise this brigand would defend himself with determination.

My first thought was not to act before daylight. I was informed that Fossard's companion came down very early to get milk; we could then seize the woman, take her key, and suddenly enter her lover's room. But what would happen if, contrary to custom, he came down first? This thought led me to think of another expedient.

The wine merchant's wife, to whom, as I had learned, Madame Hazard was kindly disposed, had one of her nephews with her. He was a boy of ten, rather intelligent for his age, and most precocious in his desire for money in that he was a Norman. I promised him a reward on condition that, in the pretense that his aunt was ill, he would ask Madame Hazard to give him some cologne. I practiced the little man in assuming the piteous tones fitting to such a circumstance, and when I was satisfied with him, I distributed the roles. The dénouement was near. I made everyone take off his shoes and I took off my own so that we should not be heard in going upstairs. The little man was in his shirt; he rang; there was no answer; he rang again. "Who is it?" someone asked. "It's me, Madame Hazard; Louis; my aunt's ill and begs you to give her a little cologne; she's dying. I have a light."

The door opened; but hardly had the girl Tonneau presented herself than two strong gendarmes seized her and placed a towel over her mouth to prevent her crying out. At the same instant, more rapid than the lion which leaps upon its prey, I sprang on Fossard. Stunned by the event, already bound and tied in his bed, he was my prisoner before he had time to make a single gesture or proffer a single word. His astonishment was so great that it was nearly an hour before he could utter a word. When a light was brought and he saw my blackened face and my clothes of a coalman, he showed such an increase of terror that I thought he believed the Devil had him. When he came to himself, he thought of his arms, his pistols and dagger, which were on a table; his gaze turned in that direction; he gave a start, but that was all. Deprived of his power to do injury, he was docile and content to fret.

A search was made in the domicile of this brigand reputed to be so fearful, and a quantity of diamonds and jewels and the sum of eight to ten thousand francs were discovered. While the search was going on, Fossard had recovered his spirits and confided to me that he still had hidden ten thousand-franc notes. "Take them," he said, "we'll share them, or rather you'll keep what you want." In fact, I took the notes as he desired.

We got into a cab and were soon at M. Henry's office, where the objects found at Fossard's were deposited. They were again inventoried; when the last article was reached, "There's nothing left to us but to close the procès-verbal," said the commissioner who had accompanied me for the sake of the regularity of the expedition. "One moment," I cried, "here are ten thousand francs which the prisoner handed to me." And I exhibited the sum, to the great regret of Fossard, who gave me one of those looks which mean, "That's a trick I'll never forgive."

EDGAR ALLAN POE

THE MYSTERY OF MARIE ROGÊT

In 1841, when he introduced C. Auguste Dupin in "The Murders in the Rue Morgue," Edgar Allan Poe (1809–1849) had been an unsuccessful poet, an unread novelist, and a journeyman critic and magazine editor. He had already published, in a magazine he edited, "The Fall of the House of Usher," but all his best-known work was ahead of him. With the creation of Dupin, he experienced his first hint of fame. He had just created the American detective story. After publishing two more stories — "The Mystery of Marie Rogêt" and "The Purloined Letter" — he wrote to a friendly critic: "These tales of ratiocination owe most of their popularity to being something in a new key. I do not mean to say they are not ingenious — but people think them more ingenious than they are — on account of their method and air of method." In other words, Poe saw the stories as conjuring tricks.

In "Marie Rogêt," Poe transported a real New York crime — the disappearance and death of Mary Rogers, a Wall Street area tobacco shop clerk, that era's version of a Playboy bunny — to Paris, changed the names of the people involved, broadened the Seine until it resembled the Hudson, and tried to solve a crime — using real newspaper accounts — that had baffled the police.

The result is probably the least well known of the Dupin stories. But watching Poe at work on his conjuring act is first-rate entertainment. John Walsh has written a fascinating account of the Rogers case, Poe the Detective, *which suggests that Poe may not have been as honest with his clues as he claims.*

The footnotes are Poe's own.

THERE ARE FEW PERSONS, even among the calmest thinkers, who

have not occasionally been startled into a vague yet thrilling half-credence in the supernatural, by *coincidences* of so seemingly marvellous a character that, as *mere* coincidences, the intellect has been unable to receive them. Such sentiments — for the half-credences of which I speak have never the full force of *thought* — are seldom thoroughly stifled unless by reference to the doctrine of chance, or, as it is technically termed, the Calculus of Probabilities. Now this Calculus is, in its essence, purely mathematical; and thus we have the anomaly of the most rigidly exact in science applied to the shadow and spirituality of the most intangible in speculation.

The extraordinary details which I am now called upon to make public, will be found to form, as regards sequence of time, the primary branch of a series of scarcely intelligible *coincidences,* whose secondary or concluding branch will be recognized by all readers in the late murder of MARY CECILIA ROGERS, at New York.*

When, in an article entitled "The Murders in the Rue Morgue," I endeavored, about a year ago, to depict some very remarkable features in the mental character of my friend, the Chevalier C. Auguste Dupin, it did not occur to me that I should ever resume the subject. This depicting of character constituted my design; and this design was fulfilled in the train of circumstances brought to instance Dupin's idiosyncrasy. I might have adduced other examples, but I should have proven no more. Late events, however, in their surprising development, have startled me into some farther details, which will carry with them the air of extorted confession. Hearing what I have lately heard,

---

*On the original publication of "Marie Rogêt," the foot-notes now appended were considered unnecessary; but the lapse of several years since the tragedy upon which the tale is based, renders it expedient to give them, and also to say a few words in explanation of the general design. A young girl, *Mary Cecilia Rogers*, was murdered in the vicinity of New York; and, although her death occasioned an intense and long-enduring excitement, the mystery attending it had remained unsolved at the period when the present paper was written and published (November, 1842). Herein, under pretence of relating the fate of a Parisian *grisette*, the author has followed, in minute detail, the essential, while merely paralleling the inessential facts of the real murder of Mary Rogers. Thus all argument founded upon the fiction is applicable to the truth: and the investigation of the truth was the object.

The "Mystery of Marie Rogêt" was composed at a distance from the scene of the atrocity, and with no other means of investigation than the newspapers afforded. Thus much escaped the writer of which he could have availed himself had he been on the spot, and visited the localities. It may not be improper to record, nevertheless, that the confessions of *two* persons, (one of them the Madame Deluc of the narrative) made, at different periods, long subsequent to the publication, confirmed, in full, not only the general conclusion, but absolutely *all* the chief hypothetical details by which that conclusion was attained.

it would be indeed strange should I remain silent in regard to what I both heard and saw so long ago.

Upon the winding up of the tragedy involved in the deaths of Madame L'Espanaye and her daughter, the Chevalier dismissed the affair at once from his attention, and relapsed into his old habits of moody reverie. Prone, at all times, to abstraction, I readily fell in with his humor; and, continuing to occupy our chambers in the Faubourg Saint Germain, we gave the Future to the winds, and slumbered tranquilly in the Present, weaving the dull world around us into dreams.

But these dreams were not altogether uninterrupted. It may readily be supposed that the part played by my friend, in the drama at the Rue Morgue, had not failed of its impression upon the fancies of the Parisian police. With its emissaries, the name of Dupin had grown into a household word. The simple character of those inductions by which he had disentangled the mystery never having been explained even to the Prefect, or to any other individual than myself, of course it is not surprising that the affair was regarded as little less than miraculous, or that the Chevalier's analytical abilities acquired for him the credit of intuition. His frankness would have led him to disabuse every inquirer of such prejudice; but his indolent humor forbade all farther agitation of a topic whose interest to himself had long ceased. It thus happened that he found himself the cynosure of the political eyes; and the cases were not few in which attempt was made to engage his services at the Prefecture. One of the most remarkable instances was that of the murder of a young girl named Marie Rogêt.

This event occurred about two years after the atrocity in the Rue Morgue. Marie, whose Christian and family name will at once arrest attention from their resemblance to those of the unfortunate "cigar-girl," was the only daughter of the widow Estelle Rogêt. The father had died during the child's infancy, and from the period of his death, until within eighteen months before the assassination which forms the subject of our narrative, the mother and daughter had dwelt together in the Rue Pavée Saint Andrée;* Madame there keeping a *pension*, assisted by Marie. Affairs went on thus until the latter had attained her twenty-second year, when her great beauty attracted the notice of a perfumer, who occupied one of the shops in the basement of the Palais Royal, and whose custom lay chiefly among the desperate adventurers infesting that neighborhood. Monsieur Le Blanc† was not unaware of the advantages to be derived from the attendance of

*Nassau Street.
†Anderson.

the fair Marie in his perfumery; and his liberal proposals were accepted eagerly by the girl, although with somewhat more of hesitation by Madame.

The anticipations of the shopkeeper were realized, and his rooms soon became notorious through the charms of the sprightly *grisette*. She had been in his employ about a year, when her admirers were thrown into confusion by her sudden disappearance from the shop. Monsieur Le Blanc was unable to account for her absence, and Madame Rogêt was distracted with anxiety and terror. The public papers immediately took up the theme, and the police were upon the point of making serious investigations, when, one fine morning, after the lapse of a week, Marie, in good health, but with a somewhat saddened air, made her re-appearance at her usual counter in the perfumery. All inquiry, except that of a private character, was of course immediately hushed. Monsieur Le Blanc professed total ignorance, as before. Marie, with Madame, replied to all questions, that the last week had been spent at the house of a relation in the country. Thus the affair died away, and was generally forgotten; for the girl, ostensibly to relieve herself from the impertinence of curiosity, soon bade a final adieu to the perfumer, and sought the shelter of her mother's residence in the Rue Pavée Saint Andrée.

It was about three years after this return home, that her friends were alarmed by her sudden disappearance for the second time. Three days elapsed, and nothing was heard of her. On the fourth her corpse was found floating in the Seine,* near the shore which is opposite the Quartier of the Rue Saint Andrée, and at a point not very far distant from the secluded neighborhood of the Barrière du Roule.†

The atrocity of this murder, (for it was at once evident that murder had been committed,) the youth and beauty of the victim, and, above all, her previous notoriety, conspired to produce intense excitement in the minds of the sensitive Parisians. I can call to mind no similar occurrence producing so general and so intense an effect. For several weeks, in the discussion of this one absorbing theme, even the momentous political topics of the day were forgotten. The Prefect made unusual exertions; and the powers of the whole Parisian police were, of course, tasked to the utmost extent.

Upon the first discovery of the corpse, it was not supposed that the murderer would be able to elude, for more than a very brief period,

*The Hudson.
†Weehawken.

the inquisition which was immediately set on foot. It was not until the expiration of a week that it was deemed necessary to offer a reward; and even then this reward was limited to a thousand francs. In the mean time the investigation proceeded with vigor, if not always with judgment, and numerous individuals were examined to no purpose; while, owing to the continual absence of all clue to the mystery, the popular excitement greatly increased. At the end of the tenth day it was thought advisable to double the sum originally proposed; and, at length, the second week having elapsed without leading to any discoveries, and the prejudice which always exists in Paris against the Police having given vent to itself in several serious *émeutes,* the Prefect took it upon himself to offer the sum of twenty thousand francs "for the conviction of the assassin," or, if more than one should prove to have been implicated, "for the conviction of any one of the assassins." In the proclamation setting forth this reward, a full pardon was promised to any accomplice who should come forward in evidence against his fellow; and to the whole was appended, wherever it appeared, the private placard of a committee of citizens, offering ten thousand francs, in addition to the amount proposed by the Prefecture. The entire reward thus stood at no less than thirty thousand francs, which will be regarded as an extraordinary sum when we consider the humble condition of the girl, and the great frequency, in large cities, of such atrocities as the one described.

No one doubted now that the mystery of this murder would be immediately brought to light. But although, in one or two instances, arrests were made which promised elucidation, yet nothing was elicited which could implicate the parties suspected; and they were discharged forthwith. Strange as it may appear, the third week from the discovery of the body had passed, and passed without any light being thrown upon the subject, before even a rumor of the events which had so agitated the public mind, reached the ears of Dupin and myself. Engaged in researches which had absorbed our whole attention, it had been nearly a month since either of us had gone abroad, or received a visiter, or more than glanced at the leading political articles in one of the daily papers. The first intelligence of the murder was brought us by G——, in person. He called upon us early in the afternoon of the thirteenth of July, 18 —, and remained with us until late in the night. He had been piqued by the failure of all his endeavors to ferret out the assassins. His reputation — so he said with a peculiarly Parisian air — was at stake. Even his honor was concerned. The eyes of the public were upon him; and there was really no sacrifice which he would not be willing to make for the development of the mystery. He concluded a somewhat droll speech with a compliment upon what he was pleased to term the *tact* of Dupin, and made him a direct, and certainly a liberal proposition, the precise nature of which I do not feel myself at liberty to disclose, but which has no bearing upon the proper subject of my narrative.

The compliment my friend rebutted as best he could, but the proposition he accepted at once, although its advantages were altogether provisional. This point being settled, the Prefect broke forth at once into explanations of his own views, interspersing them with long comments upon the evidence; of which latter we were not yet in possession. He discoursed much, and beyond doubt, learnedly; while I hazarded an occasional suggestion as the night wore drowsily away. Dupin, sitting steadily in his accustomed arm-chair, was the embodiment of respectful attention. He wore spectacles, during the whole interview; and an occasional glance beneath their green glasses, sufficed to convince me that he slept not the less soundly, because silently, throughout the seven or eight leaden-footed hours which immediately preceded the departure of the Prefect.

In the morning, I procured, at the Prefecture, a full report of all the evidence elicited, and, at the various newspaper offices, a copy of every paper in which, from first to last, had been published any decisive information in regard to this sad affair. Freed from all that was positively disproved, this mass of information stood thus:

Marie Rogêt left the residence of her mother, in the Rue Pavée St. Andrée, about nine o'clock in the morning of Sunday, June the twenty-second, 18 — . In going out, she gave notice to a Monsieur Jacques St. Eustache,* and to him only, of her intention to spend the day with an aunt who resided in the Rue des Drômes. The Rue des Drômes is a short and narrow but populous thoroughfare, not far from the banks of the river, and at a distance of some two miles, in the most direct course possible, from the *pension* of Madame Rogêt. St. Eustache was the accepted suitor of Marie, and lodged, as well as took his meals, at the *pension*. He was to have gone for his betrothed at dusk, and to have escorted her home. In the afternoon, however, it came on to rain heavily; and, supposing that she would remain all night at her aunt's, (as she had done under similar circumstances before,) he did not think it necessary to keep his promise. As night drew on, Madame Rogêt (who was an infirm old lady, seventy years of age,) was heard to express a fear "that she should never see Marie again;" but this observation attracted little attention at the time.

*Payne.

On Monday, it was ascertained that the girl had not been to the Rue des Drômes; and when the day elapsed without tidings of her, a tardy search was instituted at several points in the city, and its environs. It was not, however, until the fourth day from the period of her disappearance that any thing satisfactory was ascertained respecting her. On this day, (Wednesday, the twenty-fifth of June,) a Monsieur Beauvais,* who, with a friend, had been making inquiries for Marie near the Barrière du Roule, on the shore of the Seine which is opposite the Rue Pavée St. Andrée, was informed that a corpse had just been towed ashore by some fishermen, who had found it floating in the river. Upon seeing the body, Beauvais, after some hesitation, identified it as that of the perfumery-girl. His friend recognized it more promptly.

The face was suffused with dark blood, some of which issued from the mouth. No foam was seen, as in the case of the merely drowned. There was no discoloration in the cellular tissue. About the throat were bruises and impressions of fingers. The arms were bent over on the chest and were rigid. The right hand was clenched; the left partially open. On the left wrist were two circular excoriations, apparently the effect of ropes, or of a rope in more than one volution. A part of the right wrist, also, was much chafed, as well as the back throughout its extent, but more especially at the shoulder-blades. In bringing the body to the shore the fishermen had attached to it a rope; but none of the excoriations had been effected by this. The flesh of the neck was much swollen. There were no cuts apparent, or bruises which appeared the effect of blows. A piece of lace was found tied so tightly around the neck as to be hidden from sight; it was completely buried in the flesh, and was fastened by a knot which lay just under the left ear. This alone would have sufficed to produce death. The medical testimony spoke confidently of the virtuous character of the deceased. She had been subjected, it said, to brutal violence. The corpse was in such condition when found, that there could have been no difficulty in its recognition by friends.

The dress was much torn and otherwise disordered. In the outer garment, a slip, about a foot wide, had been torn upward from the bottom hem to the waist, but not torn off. It was wound three times around the waist, and secured by a sort of hitch in the back. The dress immediately beneath the frock was of fine muslin; and from this a slip eighteen inches wide had been torn entirely out — torn very evenly and with great care. It was found around her neck, fitting

---

*Crommelin.

loosely, and secured with a hard knot. Over this muslin slip and the slip of lace, the strings of a bonnet were attached; the bonnet being appended. The knot by which the strings of the bonnet were fastened, was not a lady's, but a slip or sailor's knot.

After the recognition of the corpse, it was not, as usual, taken to the Morgue, (this formality being superfluous,) but hastily interred not far from the spot at which it was brought ashore. Through the exertions of Beauvais, the matter was industriously hushed up, as far as possible; and several days had elapsed before any public emotion resulted. A weekly paper,* however, at length took up the theme; the corpse was disinterred, and a re-examination instituted; but nothing was elicited beyond what has been already noted. The clothes, however, were now submitted to the mother and friends of the deceased, and fully identified as those worn by the girl upon leaving home.

Meantime, the excitement increased hourly. Several individuals were arrested and discharged. St. Eustache fell especially under suspicion; and he failed, at first, to give an intelligible account of his whereabouts during the Sunday on which Marie left home. Subsequently, however, he submitted to Monsieur G——, affidavits, accounting satisfactorily for every hour of the day in question. As time passed and no discovery ensued, a thousand contradictory rumors were circulated, and journalists busied themselves in *suggestions*. Among these, the one which attracted the most notice, was the idea that Marie Rogêt still lived — that the corpse found in the Seine was that of some other unfortunate. It will be proper that I submit to the reader some passages which embody the suggestion alluded to. These passages are *literal* translations from L'Etoile,† a paper conducted, in general, with much ability.

Mademoiselle Rogêt left her mother's house on Sunday morning, June the twenty-second, 18 — , with the ostensible purpose of going to see her aunt, or some other connexion, in the Rue des Drômes. From that hour, nobody is proved to have seen her. There is no trace or tidings of her at all. * * * * There has no person, whatever, come forward, so far, who saw her at all, on that day, after she left her mother's door. * * * * Now, though we have no evidence that Marie Rogêt was in the land of the living after nine o'clock on Sunday, June the twenty-second, we have proof that, up to that hour, she was alive. On Wednesday noon, at twelve, a female body was discovered afloat on the shore of the Barrière du Roule. This was, even if we presume that Marie Rogêt was thrown into the river within three hours after she left her mother's

*The "N. Y. Mercury."
†The "N. Y. Brother Jonathan," edited by H. Hastings Weld, Esq.

house, only three days from the time she left her home — three days to an hour. But it is folly to suppose that the murder, if murder was committed on her body, could have been consummated soon enough to have enabled her murderers to throw the body into the river before midnight. Those who are guilty of such horrid crimes, choose darkness rather than light. * * * * Thus we see that if the body found in the river *was* that of Marie Rogêt, it could only have been in the water two and a half days, or three at the outside. All experience has shown that drowned bodies, or bodies thrown into the water immediately after death by violence, require from six to ten days for sufficient decomposition to take place to bring them to the top of the water. Even where a cannon is fired over a corpse, and it rises before at least five or six days' immersion, it sinks again, if left alone. Now, we ask what was there in this case to cause a departure from the ordinary course of nature? * * * * If the body had been kept in its mangled state on shore until Tuesday night, some trace would be found on shore of the murderers. It is a doubtful point, also, whether the body would be so soon afloat, even were it thrown in after having been dead two days. And, furthermore, it is exceedingly improbable that any villains who had committed such a murder as is here supposed, would have thrown the body in without weight to sink it, when such a precaution could have so easily been taken.

The editor here proceeds to argue that the body must have been in the water "not three days merely, but, at least, five times three days," because it was so far decomposed that Beauvais had great difficulty in recognizing it. This latter point, however, was fully disproved. I continue the translation:

What, then, are the facts on which M. Beauvais says that he has no doubt the body was that of Marie Rogêt? He ripped up the gown sleeve, and says he found marks which satisfied him of the identity. The public generally supposed those marks to have consisted of some description of scars. He rubbed the arm and found *hair* upon it — something as indefinite, we think, as can readily be imagined — as little conclusive as finding an arm in the sleeve. M. Beauvais did not return that night, but sent word to Madame Rogêt, at seven o'clock, on Wednesday evening, that an investigation was still in progress respecting her daughter. If we allow that Madame Rogêt, from her age and grief, could not go over, (which is allowing a great deal,) there certainly must have been some one who would have thought it worth while to go over and attend the investigation, if they thought the body was that of Marie. Nobody went over. There was nothing said or heard about the matter in the Rue Pavée St. Andrée, that reached even the occupants of the same building. M. St. Eustache, the lover and intended husband of Marie, who boarded in her mother's house, deposes that he did not hear of the discovery of the body of his intended until the next morning, when M. Beauvais came into his chamber and told him of it. For an item of news like this, it strikes us it was very coolly received.

In this way the journal endeavored to create the impression of an apathy on the part of the relatives of Marie, inconsistent with the supposition that these relatives believed the corpse to be hers. Its insinuations amount to this: — that Marie, with the connivance of her friends, had absented herself from the city for reasons involving a charge against her chastity; and that these friends, upon the discovery of a corpse in the Seine, somewhat resembling that of the girl, had availed themselves of the opportunity to impress the public with the belief of her death. But L'Etoile was again over-hasty. It was distinctly proved that no apathy, such as was imagined, existed; that the old lady was exceedingly feeble, and so agitated as to be unable to attend to any duty; that St. Eustache, so far from receiving the news coolly, was distracted with grief, and bore himself so frantically, that M. Beauvais prevailed upon a friend and relative to take charge of him, and prevent his attending the examination at the disinterment. Moreover, although it was stated by L'Etoile, that the corpse was reinterred at the public expense — that an advantageous offer of private sepulture was absolutely declined by the family — and that no member of the family attended the ceremonial: — although, I say, all this was asserted by L'Etoile in furtherance of the impression it designed to convey — yet *all* this was satisfactorily disproved. In a subsequent number of the paper, an attempt was made to throw suspicion upon Beauvais himself. The editor says:

> Now, then, a change comes over the matter. We are told that, on one occasion, while a Madame B—— was at Madame Rogêt's house, M. Beauvais, who was going out, told her that a *gendarme* was expected there, and that she, Madame B., must not say anything to the *gendarme* until he returned, but let the matter be for him. * * * * In the present posture of affairs, M. Beauvais appears to have the whole matter locked up in his head. A single step cannot be taken without M. Beauvais; for, go which way you will, you run against him. * * * * * For some reason, he determined that nobody shall have any thing to do with the proceedings but himself, and he has elbowed the male relatives out of the way, according to their representations, in a very singular manner. He seems to have been very much averse to permitting the relatives to see the body.

By the following fact, some color was given to the suspicion thus thrown upon Beauvais. A visiter at his office, a few days prior to the girl's disappearance, and during the absence of its occupant, had observed *a rose* in the key-hole of the door, and the name *"Marie"* inscribed upon a slate which hung near at hand.

The general impression, so far as we were enabled to glean it from the newspapers, seemed to be, that Marie had been the victim of *a gang* of desperadoes — that by these she had been borne across the river, maltreated and murdered. Le Commerciel,* however, a print of extensive influence, was earnest in combating this popular idea. I quote a passage or two from its columns:

> We are persuaded that pursuit has hitherto been on a false scent, so far as it has been directed to the Barrière du Roule. It is impossible that a person so well known to thousands as this young woman was, should have passed three blocks without some one having seen her; and any one who saw her would have remembered it, for she interested all who knew her. It was when the streets were full of people, when she went out. * * * It is impossible that she could have gone to the Barrière du Roule, or to the Rue des Drômes, without being recognized by a dozen persons; yet no one has come forward who saw her outside of her mother's door, and there is no evidence, except the testimony concerning her *expressed intentions*, that she did go out at all. Her gown was torn, bound round her, and tied; and by that the body was carried as a bundle. If the murder had been committed at the Barrière du Roule, there would have been no necessity for any such arrangement. The fact that the body was found floating near the Barrière, is no proof as to where it was thrown into the water. * * * * * A piece of one of the unfortunate girl's petticoats, two feet long and one foot wide, was torn out and tied under her chin around the back of her head, probably to prevent screams. This was done by fellows who had no pocket-handkerchief.

A day or two before the Prefect called upon us, however, some important information reached the police, which seemed to overthrow, at least, the chief portion of Le Commerciel's argument. Two small boys, sons of a Madame Deluc, while roaming among the woods near the Barrière du Roule, chanced to penetrate a close thicket, within which were three or four large stones, forming a kind of seat, with a back and footstool. On the upper stone lay a white petticoat; on the second a silk scarf. A parasol, gloves, and a pocket-handkerchief were also here found. The handkerchief bore the name "Marie Rogêt." Fragments of dress were discovered on the brambles around. The earth was trampled, the bushes were broken, and there was every evidence of a struggle. Between the thicket and the river, the fences

---

*N.Y. "Journal of Commerce."

were found taken down, and the ground bore evidence of some heavy burthen having been dragged along it.

A weekly paper, Le Soleil,* had the following comments upon this discovery — comments which merely echoed the sentiment of the whole Parisian press:

> The things had all evidently been there at least three or four weeks; they were all mildewed down hard with the action of the rain, and stuck together from mildew. The grass had grown around and over some of them. The silk on the parasol was strong, but the threads of it were run together within. The upper part, where it had been doubled and folded, was all mildewed and rotten, and tore on its being opened. * * * * The pieces of her frock torn out by the bushes were about three inches wide and six inches long. One part was the hem of the frock, and it had been mended; the other piece was part of the skirt, not the hem. They looked like strips torn off, and were on the thorn bush, about a foot from the ground. * * * * * There can be no doubt, therefore, that the spot of this appalling outrage has been discovered.

Consequent upon this discovery, new evidence appeared. Madame Deluc testified that she keeps a roadside inn not far from the bank of the river, opposite the Barrière du Roule. The neighborhood is secluded — particularly so. It is the usual Sunday resort of blackguards from the city, who cross the river in boats. About three o'clock, in the afternoon of the Sunday in question, a young girl arrived at the inn, accompanied by a young man of dark complexion. The two remained here for some time. On their departure, they took the road to some thick woods in the vicinity. Madame Deluc's attention was called to the dress worn by the girl, on account of its resemblance to one worn by a deceased relative. A scarf was particularly noticed. Soon after the departure of the couple, a gang of miscreants made their appearance, behaved boisterously, ate and drank without making payment, followed in the route of the young man and girl, returned to the inn about dusk, and re-crossed the river as if in great haste.

It as soon after dark, upon this same evening, that Madame Deluc, as well as her eldest son, heard the screams of a female in the vicinity of the inn. The screams were violent but brief. Madame D. recognized not only the scarf which was found in the thicket, but the dress which was discovered upon the corpse. An omnibus-driver, Valence,† now also testified that he saw Marie Rogêt cross a ferry on the Seine, on

*Phil. "Sat. Evening Post," edited by C. J. Peterson, Esq.
†Adam.

the Sunday in question, in company with a young man of dark complexion. He, Valence, knew Marie, and could not be mistaken in her identity. The articles found in the thicket were fully identified by the relatives of Marie.

The items of evidence and information thus collected by myself, from the newspapers, at the suggestion of Dupin, embraced only one more point — but this was a point of seemingly vast consequence. It appears that, immediately after the discovery of the clothes as above described, the lifeless, or nearly lifeless body of St. Eustache, Marie's betrothed, was found in the vicinity of what all now supposed the scene of the outrage. A phial labelled "laudanum," and emptied, was found near him. His breath gave evidence of the poison. He died without speaking. Upon his person was found a letter, briefly stating his love for Marie, with his design of self-destruction.

"I need scarcely tell you," said Dupin, as he finished the perusal of my notes, "that this is a far more intricate case than that of the Rue Morgue; from which it differs in one important respect. This is an *ordinary*, although an atrocious instance of crime. There is nothing peculiarly *outré* about it. You will observe that, for this reason, the mystery has been considered easy, when, for this reason, it should have been considered difficult, of solution. Thus, at first, it was thought unnecessary to offer a reward. The myrmidons of G——— were able at once to comprehend how and why such an atrocity *might have been* committed. They could picture to their imaginations a mode — many modes — and a motive — many motives; and because it was not impossible that either of these numerous modes and motives *could* have been the actual one, they have taken it for granted that one of them *must*. But the ease with which these variable fancies were entertained, and the very plausibility which each assumed, should have been understood as indicative rather of the difficulties than of the facilities which must attend elucidation. I have before observed that it is by prominences above the plane of the ordinary, that reason feels her way, if at all, in her search for the true, and that the proper question in cases such as this, is not so much 'what has occurred?' as 'what has occurred that has never occurred before?' In the investigations at the house of Madame L'Espanaye,* the agents of G——— were discouraged and confounded by that very *unusualness* which, to a properly regulated intellect, would have afforded the surest omen of success; while this same intellect might have been plunged in despair at the ordinary character of all that met the eye in the case of

*See "Murders in the Rue Morgue."

the perfumery-girl, and yet told of nothing but easy triumph to the functionaries of the Prefecture.

"In the case of Madame L'Espanaye and her daughter, there was, even at the beginning of our investigation, no doubt that murder had been committed. The idea of suicide was excluded at once. Here, too, we are freed, at the commencement, from all supposition of self-murder. The body found at the Barrière du Roule, was found under such circumstances as to leave us no room for embarrassment upon this important point. But it has been suggested that the corpse discovered, is not that of the Marie Rogêt for the conviction of whose assassin, or assassins, the reward is offered, and respecting whom, solely, our agreement has been arranged with the Prefect. We both know this gentleman well. It will not do to trust him too far. If, dating our inquiries from the body found, and thence tracing a murderer, we yet discover this body to be that of some other individual than Marie; or, if starting from the living Marie, we find her, yet find her unassassinated — in either case we lose our labor; since it is Monsieur G—— with whom we have to deal. For our own purpose, therefore, if not for the purpose of justice, it is indispensable that our first step should be the determination of the identity of the corpse with the Marie Rogêt who is missing.

"With the public the arguments of L'Etoile have had weight; and that the journal itself is convinced of their importance would appear from the manner in which it commences one of its essays upon the subject — 'Several of the morning papers of the day,' it says, 'speak of the *conclusive* article in Monday's Etoile.' To me, this article appears conclusive of little beyond the zeal of its inditer. We should bear in mind that, in general, it is the object of our newspapers rather to create a sensation — to make a point — than to further the cause of truth. The latter end is only pursued when it seems coincident with the former. The print which merely falls in with ordinary opinion (however well founded this opinion may be) earns for itself no credit with the mob. The mass of the people regard as profound only him who suggests *pungent contradictions* of the general idea. In ratiocination, not less than in literature, it is the *epigram* which is the most immediately and the most universally appreciated. In both, it is of the lowest order of merit.

"What I mean to say is, that it is the mingled epigram and melodrame of the idea, that Marie Rogêt still lives, rather than any true plausibility in this idea, which have suggested it to L'Etoile, and secured it a favorable reception with the public. Let us examine the heads of this journal's argument; endeavoring to avoid the incoherence with which it is originally set forth.

"The first aim of the writer is to show, from the brevity of the interval between Marie's disappearance and the finding of the floating corpse, that this corpse cannot be that of Marie. The reduction of this interval to its smallest possible dimension, becomes thus, at once, an object with the reasoner. In the rash pursuit of this object, he rushes into mere assumption at the outset. 'It is folly to suppose,' he says, 'that the murder, if murder was committed on her body, could have been consummated soon enough to have enabled her murderers to throw the body into the river before midnight.' We demand at once, and very naturally, *why*? Why is it folly to suppose that the murder was committed *within five minutes* after the girl's quitting her mother's house? Why is it folly to suppose that the murder was committed at any given period of the day? There have been assassinations at all hours. But, had the murder taken place at any moment between nine o'clock in the morning of Sunday, and a quarter before midnight, there would still have been time enough 'to throw the body into the river before midnight.' This assumption, then, amounts precisely to this — that the murder was not committed on Sunday at all — and, if we allow L'Etoile to assume this, we may permit it any liberties whatever. The paragraph beginning 'It is folly to suppose that the murder, etc.,' however it appears as printed in L'Etoile, may be imagined to have existed actually *thus* in the brain of its inditer — 'It is folly to suppose that the murder, if murder was committed on the body, could have been committed soon enough to have enabled her murderers to throw the body into the river before midnight; it is folly, we say, to suppose all this, and to suppose at the same time, (as we are resolved to suppose,) that the body was *not* thrown in until *after* midnight'— a sentence sufficiently inconsequential in itself, but not so utterly preposterous as the one printed.

"Were it my purpose," continued Dupin, "merely to *make out a case* against this passage of L'Etoile's argument, I might safely leave it where it is. It is not, however, with L'Etoile that we have to do, but with the truth. The sentence in question has but one meaning, as it stands; and this meaning I have fairly stated: but it is material that we go behind the mere words, for an idea which these words have obviously intended, and failed to convey. It was the design of the journalist to say that, at whatever period of the day or night of Sunday this murder was committed, it was improbable that the assassins would have ventured to bear the corpse to the river before midnight. And herein lies, really, the assumption of which I complain. It is assumed that the murder was committed at such a position, and under such circumstances, that *the bearing it* to the river became necessary. Now, the assassination might have taken place upon the river's brink, or on the river itself; and, thus, the throwing the corpse in the water might have been resorted to, at any period of the day or night, as the most obvious and most immediate mode of disposal. You will understand that I suggest nothing here as probable, or as coincident with my own opinion. My design, so far, has no reference to the *facts* of the case. I wish merely to caution you against the whole tone of L'Etoile's *suggestion,* by calling your attention to its *ex parte* character at the outset.

"Having prescribed thus a limit to suit its own preconceived notions; having assumed that, if this were the body of Marie, it could have been in the water but a very brief time; the journal goes on to say:

> All experience has shown that drowned bodies, or bodies thrown into the water immediately after death by violence, require from six to ten days for sufficient decomposition to take place to bring them to the top of the water. Even when a cannon is fired over a corpse, and it rises before at least five or six days' immersion, it sinks again if let alone.

"These assertions have been tacitly received by every paper in Paris, with the exception of Le Moniteur.* This latter print endeavors to combat that portion of the paragraph which has reference to 'drowned bodies' only, by citing some five or six instances in which the bodies of individuals known to be drowned were found floating after the lapse of less time than is insisted upon by L'Etoile. But there is something excessively unphilosophical in the attempt on the part of Le Moniteur, to rebut the general assertion of L'Etoile, by a citation of particular instances militating against that assertion. Had it been possible to adduce fifty instead of five examples of bodies found floating at the end of two or three days, these fifty examples could still have been properly regarded only as exceptions to L'Etoile's rule, until such time as the rule itself should be confuted. Admitting the rule, (and this Le Moniteur does not deny, insisting merely upon its exceptions,) the argument of L'Etoile is suffered to remain in full force; for this argument does not pretend to involve more than a question of the *probability* of the body having risen to the surface in less than three days; and this probability will be in favor of L'Etoile's position until the instances so childishly adduced shall be sufficient in number to establish an antagonistical rule.

"You will see at once that all argument upon this head should be urged, if at all, against the rule itself; and for this end we must examine the *rationale* of the rule. Now the human body, in general, is neither

*The "N. Y. Commercial Advertiser," edited by Col. Stone.

much lighter nor much heavier than the water of the Seine; that is to say, the specific gravity of the human body, in its natural condition, is about equal to the bulk of fresh water which it displaces. The bodies of fat and fleshy persons, with small bones, and of women generally, are lighter than those of the lean and large-boned, and of men; and the specific gravity of the water of a river is somewhat influenced by the presence of the tide from sea. But, leaving this tide out of question, it may be said that *very* few human bodies will sink at all, even in fresh water, *of their own accord.* Almost any one, falling into a river, will be enabled to float, if he suffer the specific gravity of the water fairly to be adduced in comparison with his own — that is to say, if he suffer his whole person to be immersed, with as little exception as possible. The proper position for one who cannot swim, is the upright position of the walker on land, with the head thrown fully back, and immersed; the mouth and nostrils alone remaining above the surface. Thus circumstanced, we shall find that we float without difficulty and without exertion. It is evident, however, that the gravities of the body, and of the bulk of water displaced, are very nicely balanced, and that a trifle will cause either to preponderate. An arm, for instance, uplifted from the water, and thus deprived of its support, is an additional weight sufficient to immerse the whole head, while the accidental aid of the smallest piece of timber will enable us to elevate the head so as to look about. Now, in the struggles of one unused to swimming, the arms are invariably thrown upwards, while an attempt is made to keep the head in its usual perpendicular position. The result is the immersion of the mouth and nostrils, and the inception, during efforts to breathe while beneath the surface, of water into the lungs. Much is also received into the stomach, and the whole body becomes heavier by the difference between the weight of the air originally distending these cavities, and that of the fluid which now fills them. This difference is sufficient to cause the body to sink, as a general rule; but is insufficient in the cases of individuals with small bones and an abnormal quantity of flaccid or fatty matter. Such individuals float even after drowning.

"The corpse, being supposed at the bottom of the river, will there remain until, by some means, its specific gravity again becomes less than that of the bulk of water which it displaces. This effect is brought about by decomposition, or otherwise. The result of decomposition is the generation of gas, distending the cellular tissues and all the cavities, and giving the *puffed* appearance which is so horrible. When this distension has so far progressed that the bulk of the corpse is materially increased without a corresponding increase of *mass* or weight, its specific gravity becomes less than that of the water displaced, and it forthwith makes its appearance at the surface. But decomposition is modified by innumerable circumstances — is hastened or retarded by innumerable agencies; for example, by the heat or cold of the season, by the mineral impregnation or purity of the water, by its depth or shallowness, by its currency or stagnation, by the temperament of the body, by its infection or freedom from disease before death. Thus it is evident that we can assign no period, with any thing like accuracy, at which the corpse shall rise through decomposition. Under certain conditions this result would be brought about within an hour; under others, it might not take place at all. There are chemical infusions by which the animal frame can be preserved *forever* from corruption; the Bi-chloride of Mercury is one. But, apart from decomposition, there may be, and very usually is, a generation of gas within the stomach, from the acetous fermentation of vegetable matter (or within other cavities from other causes) sufficient to induce a distension which will bring the body to the surface. The effect produced by the firing of a cannon is that of simple vibration. This may either loosen the corpse from the soft mud or ooze in which it is imbedded, thus permitting it to rise when other agencies have already prepared it for so doing; or it may overcome the tenacity of some putrescent portions of the cellular tissue; allowing the cavities to distend under the influence of the gas.

"Having thus before us the whole philosophy of this subject, we can easily test by it the assertions of L'Etoile. 'All experience shows,' says this paper, 'that drowned bodies, or bodies thrown into the water immediately after death by violence, require from six to ten days for sufficient decomposition to take place to bring them to the top of the water. Even when a cannon is fired over a corpse, and it rises before at least five or six days' immersion, it sinks again if let alone.'

"The whole of this paragraph must now appear a tissue of inconsequence and incoherence. All experience does *not* show that 'drowned bodies' *require* from six to ten days for sufficient decomposition to take place to bring them to the surface. Both science and experience show that the period of their rising is, and necessarily must be, indeterminate. If, moreover, a body has risen to the surface through firing of cannon, it will *not* 'sink again if let alone,' until decomposition has so far progressed as to permit the escape of the generated gas. But I wish to call your attention to the distinction which is made between 'drowned bodies,' and 'bodies thrown into the water immediately after death by violence.' Although the writer admits the distinction, he yet includes them all in the same category. I have shown how it is that the body of a drowning man becomes specifically heavier than its bulk of water, and that he would not sink at all, except for the struggles by which he elevates his arms above the surface, and his gasps for breath while beneath the surface — gasps which supply by water the place of the original air in the lungs. But these struggles and these gasps would not occur in the body 'thrown into the water immediately after death by violence.' Thus, in the latter instance, *the body, as a general rule, would not sink at all* — a fact of which L'Etoile is evidently ignorant. When decomposition had proceeded to a very great extent — when the flesh had in a great measure left the bones — then, indeed, but not *till* then, should we lose sight of the corpse.

"And now what are we to make of the argument, that the body found could not be that of Marie Rogêt, because, three days only having elapsed, this body was found floating? If drowned, being a woman, she might never have sunk; or having sunk, might have reappeared in twenty-four hours, or less. But no one supposes her to have been drowned; and, dying before being thrown into the river, she might have been found floating at any period afterwards whatever.

" 'But,' says L'Etoile, 'if the body had been kept in its mangled state on shore until Tuesday night, some trace would be found on shore of the murderers.' Here it is at first difficult to perceive the intention of the reasoner. He means to anticipate what he imagines would be an objection to his theory — viz: that the body was kept on shore two days, suffering rapid decomposition — *more* rapid than if immersed in water. He supposes that, had this been the case, it *might* have appeared at the surface on the Wednesday, and thinks that *only* under such circumstances it could so have appeared. He is accordingly in haste to show that it *was not* kept on shore; for, if so, 'some trace would be found on shore of the murderers.' I presume you smile at the *sequitur*. You cannot be made to see how the mere *duration* of the corpse on the shore could operate to *multiply traces* of the assassins. Nor can I.

" 'And furthermore it is exceedingly improbable,' continues our journal, 'that any villains who had committed such a murder as is here supposed, would have thrown the body in without weight to sink it, when such a precaution could have so easily been taken.' Observe, here, the laughable confusion of thought! No one — not even L'Etoile — disputes the murder committed *on the body found*. The marks of violence are too obvious. It is our reasoner's object merely to show that this body is not Marie's. He wishes to prove that *Marie* is not assassinated — not that the corpse was not. Yet his observation proves only the latter point. Here is a corpse without weight attached. Murderers, casting it in, would not have failed to attach a weight. Therefore it was not thrown in by murderers. This is all which is proved, if any thing is. The question of identity is not even approached, and L'Etoile has been at great pains merely to gainsay now what it has admitted only a moment before. 'We are perfectly convinced,' it says, 'that the body found was that of a murdered female.'

"Nor is this the sole instance, even in this division of his subject, where our reasoner unwittingly reasons against himself. His evident object, I have already said, is to reduce, as much as possible, the interval between Marie's disappearance and the finding of the corpse. Yet we find him *urging* the point that no person saw the girl from the moment of her leaving her mother's house. 'We have no evidence,' he says, 'that Marie Rogêt was in the land of the living after nine o'clock on Sunday, June the twenty-second.' As his argument is obviously an *ex parte* one, he should, at least, have left this matter out of sight; for had any one been known to see Marie, say on Monday, or on Tuesday, the interval in question would have been much reduced, and, by his own ratiocination, the probability much diminished of the corpse being that of the *grisette*. It is, nevertheless, amusing to observe that L'Etoile insists upon its point in the full belief of its furthering its general argument.

"Reperuse now that portion of this argument which has reference to the identification of the corpse by Beauvais. In regard to the *hair* upon the arm, L'Etoile has been obviously disingenuous. M. Beauvais, not being an idiot, could never have urged, in identification of the corpse, simply *hair upon its arm*. No arm is *without* hair. The *generality* of the expression of L'Etoile is a mere perversion of the witness' phraseology. He must have spoken of some *peculiarity* in this hair. It must have been a peculiarity of color, of quantity, of length, or of situation.

" 'Her foot,' says the journal, 'was small — so are thousands of feet. Her garter is no proof whatever — nor is her shoe — for shoes and garters are sold in packages. The same may be said of the flowers in her hat. One thing upon which M. Beauvais strongly insists is, that the clasp on the garter found, had been set back to take it in. This amounts to nothing; for most women find it proper to take a pair of garters home and fit them to the size of the limbs they are to encircle, rather than to try them in the store where they purchase.' Here it is difficult to suppose the reasoner in earnest. Had M. Beauvais, in his search for the body of Marie, discovered a corpse corresponding in general size and appearance to the missing girl, he would have been warranted (without reference to the question of habilment at all) in forming an opinion that his search had been successful. If, in addition to the point of general size and contour, he had found upon the arm a peculiar hairy appearance which he had observed upon the living Marie, his opinion might have been justly strengthened; and the increase of positiveness might well have been in the ratio of the peculiarity, or unusualness, of the hairy mark. If, the feet of Marie being small, those of the corpse were also small, the increase of probability that the body was that of Marie would not be an increase in a ratio merely arithmetical, but in one highly geometrical, or accumulative. Add to all this shoes such as she had been known to wear upon the day of her disappearance, and, although these shoes may be 'sold in packages,' you so far augment the probability as to verge upon the certain. What, of itself, would be no evidence of identity, becomes through its corroborative position, proof most sure. Give us, then, flowers in the hat corresponding to those worn by the missing girl, and we seek for nothing farther. If only *one* flower, we seek for nothing farther — what then if two or three, or more? Each successive one is multiple evidence — proof not *added* to proof, but *multiplied* by hundreds or thousands. Let us now discover, upon the deceased, garters such as the living used, and it is almost folly to proceed. But these garters are found to be tightened, by the setting back of a clasp, in just such a manner as her own had been tightened by Marie, shortly previous to her leaving home. It is now madness or hypocrisy to doubt. What L'Etoile says in respect to this abbreviation of the garter's being an usual occurrence, shows nothing beyond its own pertinacity in error. The elastic nature of the clasp-garter is self-demonstration of the *unusualness* of the abbreviation. What is made to adjust itself, must of necessity require foreign adjustment but rarely. It must have been by an accident, in its strictest sense, that these garters of Marie needed the tightening described. They alone would have amply established her identity. But it is not that the corpse was found to have the garters of the missing girl, or found to have her shoes, or her bonnet, or the flowers of her bonnet, or her feet, or a peculiar mark upon the arm, or her general size and appearance — it is that the corpse had each, and *all collectively*. Could it be proved that the editor of L'Etoile *really* entertained a doubt, under the circumstances, there would be no need, in his case, of a commission *de lunatico inquirendo*. He has thought it sagacious to echo the small talk of the lawyers, who, for the most part, content themselves with echoing the rectangular precepts of the courts. I would here observe that very much of what is rejected as evidence by a court, is the best of evidence to the intellect. For the court, guiding itself by the general principles of evidence — the recognized and *booked* principles — is averse from swerving at particular instances. And this steadfast adherence to principle, with rigorous disregard of the conflicting exception, is a sure mode of attaining the *maximum* of attainable truth, in any long sequence of time. The practice, *in mass,* is therefore philosophical; but it is not the less certain that it engenders vast individual error.*

"In respect to the insinuations levelled at Beauvais, you will be willing to dismiss them in a breath. You have already fathomed the true character of this good gentleman. He is a *busy-body,* with much of romance and little of wit. Any one so constituted will readily so conduct himself, upon occasion of *real* excitement, as to render himself liable to suspicion on the part of the over-acute, or the ill-disposed. M. Beauvais (as it appears from your notes) had some personal interviews with the editor of L'Etoile, and offended him by venturing an opinion that the corpse, notwithstanding the theory of the editor, was, in sober fact that of Marie. 'He persists,' says the paper, 'in asserting the corpse to be that of Marie, but cannot give a circumstance, in addition to those which we have commented upon, to make others believe.' Now, without readverting to the fact that stronger evidence 'to make others believe,' could *never* have been adduced, it may be remarked that a man may very well be understood to believe, in a case of this kind, without the ability to advance a single reason for the belief of a second party. Nothing is more vague than impressions of individual identity. Each man recognizes his neighbor, yet there are few instances in which any one is prepared to *give a reason* for his recognition. The editor of L'Etoile had no right to be offended at M. Beauvais' unreasoning belief.

"The suspicious circumstances which invest him, will be found to tally much better with my hypothesis of *romantic busy-bodyism,* than with the reasoner's suggestion of guilt. Once adopting the more charitable interpretation, we shall find no difficulty in comprehending the rose in the key-hole; the 'Marie' upon the slate; the 'elbowing the male relatives out of the way;' the 'aversion to permitting them to see the body;' the caution given to Madame B —— , that she must hold no conversation with the *gendarme* until his return (Beauvais'); and, lastly, his apparent determination 'that nobody should have anything to do

*"A theory based on the qualities of an object, will prevent its being unfolded according to its objects; and he who arranges topics in reference to their causes, will cease to value them according to their results. Thus the jurisprudence of every nation will show that, when law becomes a science and a system, it ceases to be justice. The errors into which a blind devotion to *principles* of classification has led the common law, will be seen by observing how often the legislature has been obliged to come forward to restore the equity its scheme had lost." — *Landor.*

with the proceedings except himself.' It seems to me unquestionable that Beauvais was a suitor of Marie's; that she coquetted with him; and that he was ambitious of being thought to enjoy her fullest intimacy and confidence. I shall say nothing more upon this point; and, as the evidence fully rebuts the assertion of L'Etoile, touching the matter of *apathy* on the part of the mother and other relatives — an apathy inconsistent with the supposition of their believing the corpse to be that of the perfumery-girl — we shall now proceed as if the question of *identity* were settled to our perfect satisfaction."

"And what," I here demanded, "do you think of the opinions of Le Commerciel?"

"That, in spirit, they are far more worthy of attention than any which have been promulgated upon the subject. The deductions from the premises are philosophical and acute; but the premises, in two instances, at least, are founded in imperfect observation. Le Commerciel wishes to intimate that Marie was seized by some gang of low ruffians not far from her mother's door. 'It is impossible,' it urges, 'that a person so well known to thousands as this young woman was, should have passed three blocks without some one having seen her.' This is the idea of a man long resident in Paris — a public man — and one whose walks to and fro in the city, have been mostly limited to the vicinity of the public offices. He is aware that *he* seldom passes so far as a dozen blocks from his own *bureau,* without being recognized and accosted. And, knowing the extent of his personal acquaintance with others, and of others with him, he compares his notoriety with that of the perfumery-girl, finds no great difference between them, and reaches at once the conclusion that she, in her walks, would be equally liable to recognition with himself in his. This could only be the case were her walks of the same unvarying, methodical character, and within the same *species* of limited region as are his own. He passes to and fro, at regular intervals, within a confined periphery, abounding in individuals who are led to observation of his person through interest in the kindred nature of his occupation with their own. But the walks of Marie may, in general, be supposed discursive. In this particular instance, it will be understood as most probable, that she proceeded upon a route of more than average diversity from her accustomed ones. The parallel which we imagine to have existed in the mind of Le Commerciel would only be sustained in the event of the two individuals' traversing the whole city. In this case, granting the personal acquaintances to be equal, the chances would be also equal that an equal number of personal recounters would be made. For my own part, I should hold it not only as possible, but as very far more than probable, that Marie might have proceeded, at any given period, by any one of the many routes between her own residence and that of her aunt, without meeting a single individual whom she knew, or by whom she was known. In viewing this question in its full and proper light, we must hold steadily in mind the great disproportion between the personal acquaintances of even the most noted individual in Paris, and the entire population of Paris itself.

"But whatever force there may still appear to be in the suggestion of Le Commerciel, will be much diminished when we take into consideration *the hour* at which the girl went abroad. 'It was when the streets were full of people,' says Le Commerciel, 'that she went out.' But not so. It was at nine o'clock in the morning. Now at nine o'clock of every morning in the week, *with the exception of Sunday,* the streets of the city are, it is true, thronged with people. At nine on Sunday, the populace are chiefly within doors *preparing for church.* No observing person can have failed to notice the peculiarly deserted air of the town, from about eight until ten on the morning of every Sabbath. Between ten and eleven the streets are thronged, but not at so early a period as that designated.

"There is another point at which there seems a deficiency of *observation* on the part of Le Commerciel. 'A piece,' it says, 'of one of the unfortunate girl's petticoats, two feet long, and one foot wide, was torn out and tied under her chin, and around the back of her head, probably to prevent screams. This was done by fellows who had no pocket-handkerchiefs.' Whether this idea is, or is not well founded, we will endeavor to see hereafter; but by 'fellows who have no pocket-handkerchiefs,' the editor intends the lowest class of ruffians. These, however, are the very description of people who will always be found to have handkerchiefs even when destitute of shirts. You must have had occasion to observe how absolutely indispensable, of late years, to the thorough blackguard, has become the pocket-handkerchief."

"And what are we to think," I asked, "of the article in Le Soleil?"

"That it is a pity its inditer was not born a parrot — in which case he would have been the most illustrious parrot of his race. He has merely repeated the individual items of the already published opinion; collecting them, with a laudable industry, from this paper and from that. 'The things had all *evidently* been there,' he says, 'at least, three or four weeks, and there can be *no doubt* that the spot of this appalling outrage has been discovered.' The facts here re-stated by Le Soleil, are very far indeed from removing my own doubts upon this subject, and we will examine them more particularly hereafter in connexion with another division of the theme.

"At present we must occupy ourselves with other investigations. You cannot fail to have remarked the extreme laxity of the examination of the corpse. To be sure, the question of identity was readily determined, or should have been; but there were other points to be ascertained. Had the body been in any respect *despoiled*? Had the deceased any articles of jewelry about her person upon leaving home? if so, had she any when found? These are important questions utterly untouched by the evidence; and there are others of equal moment, which have met with no attention. We must endeavor to satisfy ourselves by personal inquiry. The case of St. Eustache must be re-examined. I have no suspicion of this person; but let us proceed methodically. We will ascertain beyond a doubt the validity of the *affidavits* in regard to his whereabouts on the Sunday. Affidavits of this character are readily made matter of mystification. Should there be nothing wrong here, however, we will dismiss St. Eustache from our investigations. His suicide, however corroborative of suspicion, were there found to be deceit in the affidavits, is, without such deceit, in no respect an unaccountable circumstance, or one which need cause us to deflect from the line of ordinary analysis.

"In that which I now propose, we will discard the interior points of this tragedy, and concentrate our attention upon its outskirts. Not the least usual error, in investigations such as this, is the limiting of inquiry to the immediate, with total disregard of the collateral or circumstantial events. It is the mal-practice of the courts to confine evidence and discussion to the bounds of apparent relevancy. Yet experience has shown, and a true philosophy will always show, that a vast, perhaps the larger portion of truth, arises from the seemingly irrelevant. It is through the spirit of this principle, if not precisely through its letter, that modern science has resolved to *calculate upon the unforeseen*. But perhaps you do not comprehend me. The history of human knowledge has so uninterruptedly shown that to collateral, or incidental, or accidental events we are indebted for the most numerous and most valuable discoveries, that it has at length become necessary, in any prospective view of improvement, to make not only large, but the largest allowances for inventions that shall arise by chance, and quite out of the range of ordinary expectation. It is no longer philosophical to base, upon what has been, a vision of what is to be. *Accident* is admitted as a portion of the substructure. We make chance a matter of absolute calculation. We subject the unlooked for and unimagined, to the mathematical *formulae* of the schools.

"I repeat that it is no more than fact, that the *larger* portion of all truth has sprung from the collateral; and it is but in accordance with the spirit of the principle involved in this fact, that I would divert inquiry, in the present case, from the trodden and hitherto unfruitful ground of the event itself, to the cotemporary circumstances which surround it. While you ascertain the validity of the affidavits, I will examine the newspapers more generally than you have as yet done. So far, we have only reconnoitred the field of investigation; but it will be strange indeed if a comprehensive survey, such as I propose, of the public prints, will not afford us some minute points which shall establish a *direction* for inquiry."

In pursuance of Dupin's suggestion, I made scrupulous examination of the affair of the affidavits. The result was a firm conviction of their validity, and of the consequent innocence of St. Eustache. In the mean time my friend occupied himself, with what seemed to me a minuteness altogether objectless, in a scrutiny of the various newspaper files. At the end of a week he placed before me the following extracts:

About three years and a half ago, a disturbance very similar to the present, was caused by the disappearance of this same Marie Rogêt, from the *parfumerie* of Monsieur Le Blanc, in the Palais Royal. At the end of a week, however, she re-appeared at her customary *comptoir,* as well as ever, with the exception of a slight paleness not altogether usual. It was given out by Monsieur Le Blanc and her mother, that she had merely been on a visit to some friend in the country; and the affair was speedily hushed up. We presume that the present absence is a freak of the same nature, and that, at the expiration of a week, or perhaps of a month, we shall have her among us again. — *Evening Paper — Monday, June 23.**

An evening journal of yesterday, refers to a former mysterious disappearance of Mademoiselle Rogêt. It is well known that, during the week of her absence from Le Blanc's *parfumerie,* she was in the company of a young naval officer, much noted for his debaucheries. A quarrel, it is supposed, providentially led to her return home. We have the name of the Lothario in question, who is, at present, stationed in Paris, but, for obvious reasons, forbear to make it public. — *Le Mercurie — Tuesday Morning, June 24.*†

An outrage of the most atrocious character was perpetrated near this city the day before yesterday. A gentleman, with his wife and daughter, engaged, about dusk, the services of six young men, who were idly

*"N. Y. Express."
†"N. Y. Herald."

rowing a boat to and fro near the banks of the Seine, to convey him across the river. Upon reaching the opposite shore, the three passengers stepped out, and had proceeded so far as to be beyond the view of the boat, when the daughter discovered that she had left in it her parasol. She returned for it, was seized by the gang, carried out into the stream, gagged, brutally treated, and finally taken to the shore at a point not far from that at which she had originally entered the boat with her parents. The villains have escaped for the time, but the police are upon their trail, and some of them will soon be taken. — *Morning Paper* — *June 25.**

We have received one or two communications, the object of which is to fasten the crime of the late atrocity upon Mennais;† but as this gentleman has been fully exonerated by a legal inquiry, and as the arguments of our several correspondents appear to be more zealous than profound, we do not think it advisable to make them public. — *Morning Paper* — *June 28.‡*

We have received several forcibly written communications, apparently from various sources, and which go far to render it a matter of certainty that the unfortunate Marie Rogêt has become a victim of one of the numerous bands of blackguards which infest the vicinity of the city upon Sunday. Our own opinion is decidedly in favor of this supposition. We shall endeavor to make room for some of these arguments hereafter. — *Evening Paper* — *Tuesday, June 31.§*

On Monday, one of the bargemen connected with the revenue service, saw an empty boat floating down the Seine. Sails were lying in the bottom of the boat. The bargeman towed it under the barge office. The next morning it was taken from thence, without the knowledge of any of the officers. The rudder is now at the barge office. — *Le Diligence* — *Thursday, June 26.***

Upon reading these various extracts, they not only seemed to me irrelevant, but I could perceive no mode in which any one of them could be brought to bear upon the matter in hand. I waited for some explanation from Dupin.

"It is not my present design," he said, "to *dwell* upon the first and second of these extracts. I have copied them chiefly to show you the extreme remissness of the police, who, as far as I can understand

---

*"N. Y. Courier and Inquirer."
†Mennais was one of the parties originally suspected and arrested, but discharged through total lack of evidence.
‡"N. Y. Courier and Inquirer."
§"N. Y. Evening Post."
**"N. Y. Standard."

from the Prefect, have not troubled themselves, in any respect, with an examination of the naval officer alluded to. Yet it is mere folly to say that between the first and second disappearance of Marie, there is no *supposable* connection. Let us admit the first elopement to have resulted in a quarrel between the lovers, and the return home of the betrayed. We are now prepared to view a second *elopement* (if we *know* that an elopement has again taken place) as indicating a renewal of the betrayer's advances, rather than as the result of new proposals by a second individual — we are prepared to regard it as a 'making up' of the old *amour,* rather than as the commencement of a new one. The chances are ten to one, that he who had once eloped with Marie, would again propose an elopement, rather than that she to whom proposals of elopement had been made by one individual, should have them made to her by another. And here let me call your attention to the fact, that the time elapsing between the first ascertained, and the second supposed elopement, is a few months more than the general period of the cruises of our men-of-war. Had the lover been interrupted in his first villainy by the necessity of departure to sea, and had he seized the first moment of his return to renew the base designs not yet altogether accomplished — or not yet altogether accomplished *by him*? Of all these things we know nothing.

"You will say, however, that, in the second instance, there was *no* elopement as imagined. Certainly not — but are we prepared to say that there was not the frustrated design? Beyond St. Eustache, and perhaps Beauvais, we find no recognized, no open, no honorable suitors of Marie. Of none other is there any thing said. Who, then, is the secret lover, of whom the relatives (*at least most of them*) know nothing, but whom Marie meets upon the morning of Sunday, and who is so deeply in her confidence, that she hesitates not to remain with him until the shades of the evening descend, amid the solitary groves of the Barrière du Roule? Who is that secret lover, I ask, of whom, at least, *most* of the relatives know nothing? And what means the singular prophecy of Madame Rogêt on the morning of Marie's departure? — 'I fear that I shall never see Marie again.'

"But if we cannot imagine Madame Rogêt privy to the design of elopement, may we not at least suppose this design entertained by the girl? Upon quitting home, she gave it to be understood that she was about to visit her aunt in the Rue des Drômes, and St. Eustache was requested to call for her at dark. Now, at first glance, this fact strongly militates against my suggestion; — but let us reflect. That she *did* meet some companion, and proceed with him across the river, reaching the Barrière du Roule at so late an hour as three o'clock in the afternoon, is known. But in consenting so to accompany this individual, (*for whatever purpose — to her mother known or unknown,*) she must have thought of her expressed intention when leaving home, and of the surprise and suspicion aroused in the bosom of her affianced suitor, St. Eustache, when, calling for her, at the hour appointed, in the Rue des Drômes, he should find that she had not been there, and when, moreover, upon returning to the *pension* with this alarming intelligence, he should become aware of her continued absence from home. She must have thought of these things, I say. She must have foreseen the chagrin of St. Eustache, the suspicion of all. She could not have thought of returning to brave this suspicion; but the suspicion becomes a point of trivial importance to her, if we suppose her *not* intending to return.

"We may imagine her thinking thus — 'I am to meet a certain person for the purpose of elopement, or for certain other purposes known only to myself. It is necessary that there be no chance of interruption — there must be sufficient time given us to elude pursuit — I will give it to be understood that I shall visit and spend the day with my aunt at the Rue des Drômes — I will tell St. Eustache not to call for me until dark — in this way, my absence from home for the longest possible period, without causing suspicion or anxiety, will be accounted for, and I shall gain more time than in any other manner. If I bid St. Eustache call for me at dark, he will be sure not to call before; but, if I wholly neglect to bid him call, my time for escape will be diminished, since it will be expected that I return the earlier, and my absence will the sooner excite anxiety. Now, if it were my design to return *at all* — if I had in contemplation merely a stroll with the individual in question — it would not be my policy to bid St. Eustache call; for, calling, he will be *sure* to ascertain that I have played him false — a fact of which I might keep him for ever in ignorance, by leaving home without notifying him of my intention, by returning before dark, and by then stating that I had been to visit my aunt in the Rue des Drômes. But, as it is my design *never* to return — or not for some weeks — or not until certain concealments are effected — the gaining of time is the only point about which I need give myself any concern.'

"You have observed, in your notes, that the most general opinion in relation to this sad affair is, and was from the first, that the girl had been the victim of *a gang* of blackguards. Now, the popular opinion, under certain conditions, is not to be disregarded. When arising of itself — when manifesting itself in a strictly spontaneous manner — we should look upon it as analogous with that *intuition* which is the idiosyncrasy of the individual man of genius. In ninety-nine cases from the hundred I would abide by its decision. But it is important that we find no palpable traces of *suggestion.* The opinion must be rigorously *the public's own;* and the distinction is often exceedingly difficult to perceive and to maintain. In the present instance, it appears to me that this 'public opinion,' in respect to *a gang,* has been super-induced by the collateral event which is detailed in the third of my extracts. All Paris is excited by the discovered corpse of Marie, a girl young, beautiful and notorious. This corpse is found, bearing marks of violence, and floating in the river. But it is now made known that, at the very period, or about the very period, in which it is supposed that the girl was assassinated, an outrage similar in nature to that endured by the deceased, although less in extent, was perpetrated, by a gang of young ruffians, upon the person of a second young female. Is it wonderful that the one known atrocity should influence the popular judgment in regard to the other unknown? This judgment awaited direction, and the known outrage seemed so opportunely to afford it! Marie, too, was found in the river; and upon this very river was this known outrage committed. The connexion of the two events had about it so much of the palpable, that the true wonder would have been a *failure* of the populace to appreciate and to seize it. But, in fact, the one atrocity, known to be so committed, is, if any thing, evidence that the other, committed at a time nearly coincident, was *not* so committed. It would have been a miracle indeed, if, while a gang of ruffians were perpetrating, at a given locality, a most unheard-of wrong, there should have been another similar gang, in a similar locality, in the same city, under the same circumstances, with the same means and appliances, engaged in a wrong of precisely the same aspect, at precisely the same period of time! Yet in what, if not in this marvellous train of coincidence, does the accidentally *suggested* opinion of the populace call upon us to believe?

"Before proceeding farther, let us consider the supposed scene of the assassination, in the thicket at the Barrière du Roule. This thicket, although dense, was in the close vicinity of a public road. Within were three or four large stones, forming a kind of seat with a back and footstool. On the upper stone was discovered a white petticoat; on the second, a silk scarf. A parasol, gloves, and a pocket-handkerchief, were also here found. The handkerchief bore the name, 'Marie Rogêt.' Fragments of dress were seen on the branches around. The earth was trampled, the bushes were broken, and there was every evidence of a violent struggle.

"Notwithstanding the acclamation with which the discovery of this thicket was received by the press, and the unanimity with which it was supposed to indicate the precise scene of the outrage, it must be admitted that there was some very good reason for doubt. That it *was* the scene, I may or I may not believe — but there was excellent reason for doubt. Had the *true* scene been, as Le Commerciel suggested, in the neighborhood of the Rue Pavée St. Andrée, the perpetrators of the crime, supposing them still resident in Paris, would naturally have been stricken with terror at the public attention thus acutely directed into the proper channel; and, in certain classes of minds, there would have arisen, at once, a sense of the necessity of some exertion to redivert this attention. And thus, the thicket of the Barrière du Roule having been already suspected, the idea of placing the articles where they were found, might have been naturally entertained. There is no real evidence, although Le Soleil so supposes, that the articles discovered had been more than a very few days in the thicket; while there is much circumstantial proof that they could not have remained there, without attracting attention, during the twenty days elapsing between the fatal Sunday and the afternoon upon which they were found by the boys. 'They were all *mildewed* down hard,' says Le Soleil, adopting the opinions of its predecessors, 'with the action of the rain, and stuck together from *mildew*. The grass had grown around and over some of them. The silk of the parasol was strong, but the threads of it were run together within. The upper part, where it had been doubled and folded, was all *mildewed* and rotten, and tore on being opened.' In respect to the grass having 'grown around and over some of them,' it is obvious that the fact could only have been ascertained from the words, and thus from the recollections, of two small boys; for these boys removed the articles and took them home before they had been seen by a third party. But grass will grow, especially in warm and damp weather, (such as was that of the period of the murder,) as much as two or three inches in a single day. A parasol lying upon a newly turfed ground, might, in a week, be entirely concealed from sight by the upspringing grass. And touching that *mildew* upon which the editor of Le Soleil so pertinaciously insists, that he employs the word no less than three times in the brief paragraph just quoted, is he really unaware of the nature of this *mildew*? Is he to be told that it is one of the many classes of *fungus*, of which the most ordinary feature is its upspringing and decadence within twenty-four hours?

"Thus we see, at a glance, that what has been most triumphantly adduced in support of the idea that the articles had been 'for at least three or four weeks' in the thicket, is most absurdly null as regards any evidence of that fact. On the other hand, it is exceedingly difficult to believe that these articles could have remained in the thicket specified, for a longer period than a single week — for a longer period than from one Sunday to the next. Those who know any thing of the vicinity of Paris, know the extreme difficulty of finding *seclusion,* unless at a great distance from its suburbs. Such a thing as an unexplored, or even an unfrequently visited recess, amid its woods or groves, is not for a moment to be imagined. Let any one who, being at heart a lover of nature, is yet chained by duty to the dust and heat of this great metropolis — let any such one attempt, even during the week-days, to slake his thirst for solitude amid the scenes of natural loveliness which immediately surround us. At every second step, he will find the growing charm dispelled by the voice and personal intrusion of some ruffian or party of carousing blackguards. He will seek privacy amid the densest foliage, all in vain. Here are the very nooks where the unwashed most abound — here are the temples most desecrate. With sickness of the heart the wanderer will flee back to the polluted Paris as to a less odious because less incongruous sink of pollution. But if the vicinity of the city is so beset during the working days of the week, how much more so on the Sabbath! It is now especially that, released from the claims of labor, or deprived of the customary opportunities of crime, the town blackguard seeks the precincts of the town, not through love of the rural, which in his heart he despises, but by way of escape from the restraints and conventionalities of society. He desires less the fresh air and the green trees, than the utter *license* of the country. Here, at the road-side inn, or beneath the foliage of the woods, he indulges, unchecked by any eye except those of his boon companions, in all the mad excess of a counterfeit hilarity — the joint offspring of liberty and of rum. I say nothing more than what must be obvious to every dispassionate observer, when I repeat that the circumstance of the articles in question having remained undiscovered, for a longer period than from one Sunday to another, in *any* thicket in the immediate neighborhood of Paris, is to be looked upon as little less than miraculous.

"But there are not wanting other grounds for the suspicion that the articles were placed in the thicket with the view of diverting attention from the real scene of the outrage. And, first, let me direct your notice to the *date* of the discovery of the articles. Collate this with the date of the fifth extract made by myself from the newspapers. You will find that the discovery followed, almost immediately, the urgent communications sent to the evening paper. These communications, although various, and apparently from various sources, tended all to the same point — viz., the directing of attention to *a gang* as the perpetrators of the outrage, and to the neighborhood of the Barrière du Roule as its scene. Now here, of course, the suspicion is not that, in consequence of these communications, or of the public attention by them directed, the articles were found by the boys; but the suspicion might and may well have been, that the articles were not *before* found by the boys, for the reason that the articles had not before been in the thicket; having been deposited there only at so late a period as at the date, or shortly prior to the date of the communications, by the guilty authors of these communications themselves.

"This thicket was a singular — an exceedingly singular one. It was unusually dense. Within its naturally walled enclosure were three extraordinary stones, *forming a seat with a back and footstool.* And this thicket, so full of a natural art, was in the immediate vicinity, *within a few rods,* of the dwelling of Madame Deluc, whose boys were in the habit of closely examining the shrubberies about them in search of the bark of the sassafras. Would it be a rash wager — a wager of one thousand to one — that *a day* never passed over the heads of these boys without finding at least one of them ensconced in the umbrageous hall, and enthroned upon its natural throne? Those who would hesitate at such a wager, have either never been boys themselves, or have forgotten the boyish nature. I repeat — it is exceedingly hard to comprehend how the articles could have remained in this thicket undiscovered, for a longer period than one or two days; and that thus there is good ground for suspicion, in spite of the dogmatic ignorance of Le Soleil, that they were, at a comparatively late date, deposited where found.

"But there are still other and stronger reasons for believing them so deposited, than any which I have as yet urged. And, now, let me beg your notice to the highly artificial arrangement of the articles. On the *upper* stone lay a white petticoat; on the *second* a silk scarf; scattered around, were a parasol, gloves, and a pocket-handkerchief bearing the name, 'Marie Rogêt.' Here is just such an arrangement as would *naturally* be made by a not-over-acute person wishing to dispose the articles *naturally.* But it is by no means a *really* natural arrangement. I should rather have looked to see the things *all* lying on the ground and trampled under foot. In the narrow limits of that bower, it would have been scarcely possible that the petticoat and scarf should have retained a position upon the stones, when subjected to the brushing to and fro of many struggling persons. 'There was evidence,' it is said, 'of a struggle; and the earth was trampled, the bushes were broken,' — but the petticoat and the scarf are found deposited as if upon shelves.

'The pieces of the frock torn out by the bushes were about three inches wide and six inches long. One part was the hem of the frock and it had been mended. They *looked like strips torn off.*' Here, inadvertently, Le Soleil has employed an exceedingly suspicious phrase. The pieces, as described, do indeed 'look like strips torn off;' but purposely and by hand. It is one of the rarest of accidents that a piece is 'torn off,' from any garment such as is now in question, by the agency *of a thorn.* From the very nature of such fabrics, a thorn or nail becoming entangled in them, tears them rectangularly — divides them into two longitudinal rents, at right angles with each other, and meeting at an apex where the thorn enters — but it is scarcely possible to conceive the piece 'torn off.' I never so knew it, nor did you. To tear a piece *off* from such a fabric, two distinct forces, in different directions, will be, in almost every case, required. If there be two edges to the fabric — if, for example, it be a pocket-handkerchief, and it is desired to tear from it a slip, then, and then only, will the one force serve the purpose. But in the present case the question is of a dress, presenting but one edge. To tear a piece from the interior, where no edge is presented, could only be effected by a miracle through the agency of thorns, and no *one* thorn could accomplish it. But, even where an edge is presented, two thorns will be necessary, operating, the one in two distinct directions, and the other in one. And this in the supposition that the edge is unhemmed. If hemmed, the matter is nearly out of the question. We thus see the numerous and great obstacles in the way of pieces being 'torn off' through the simple agency of 'thorns;' yet we are required to believe not only that one piece but that many have been so torn. 'And one part,' too, *'was the hem of the frock!'* Another piece was *'part of the skirt, not the hem,'* — that is to say, was torn completely out, through the agency of thorns, from the unedged interior of the dress! These, I say, are things which one may well be pardoned for disbelieving; yet, taken collectedly, they form, perhaps, less of reasonable ground for suspicion, than the one startling circumstance of the articles' having been left in this thicket at all, by any *murderers* who had enough precaution to think of removing the corpse. You will not have apprehended me rightly, however, if you suppose it my design to *deny* this thicket as the scene of the outrage. There might have been a wrong *here,* or, more possibly, an accident at Madame Deluc's. But, in fact, this is a point of minor importance. We are not engaged in an attempt to discover the scene, but to produce the perpetrators of the murder. What I have adduced, notwithstanding the minuteness with which I have adduced it, has been with the view, first, to show the folly of the positive and headlong assertions of Le Soleil, but secondly and chiefly, to bring you, by the most natural route, to a further contemplation of the doubt whether this assassination has, or has not been, the work of *a gang*.

"We will resume this question by mere allusion to the revolting details of the surgeon examined at the inquest. It is only necessary to say that his published *inferences,* in regard to the number of the ruffians, have been properly ridiculed as unjust and totally baseless, by all the reputable anatomists of Paris. Not that the matter *might not* have been as inferred, but that there was no ground for the inference: — was there not much for another?

"Let us reflect now upon 'the traces of a struggle;' and let me ask what these traces have been supposed to demonstrate. A gang. But do they not rather demonstrate the absence of a gang? What *struggle* could have taken place — what struggle so violent and so enduring as to have left its 'traces' in all directions — between a weak and defenceless girl and the *gang* of ruffians imagined? The silent grasp of a few rough arms and all would have been over. The victim must have been absolutely passive at their will. You will here bear in mind that the arguments urged against the thicket as the scene, are applicable, in chief part, only against it as the scene of an outrage committed by *more than a single individual.* If we imagine but *one* violator, we can conceive, and thus only conceive, the struggle of so violent and so obstinate a nature as to have left the 'traces' apparent.

"And again. I have already mentioned the suspicion to be excited by the fact that the articles in question were suffered to remain *at all* in the thicket where discovered. It seems almost impossible that these evidences of guilt should have been accidentally left where found. There was sufficient presence of mind (it is supposed) to remove the corpse; and yet a more positive evidence than the corpse itself (whose features might have been quickly obliterated by decay,) is allowed to lie conspicuously in the scene of the outrage — I allude to the handkerchief with the *name* of the deceased. If this was accident, it was not the accident *of a gang.* We can imagine it only the accident of an individual. Let us see. An individual has committed the murder. He is alone with the ghost of the departed. He is appalled by what lies motionless before him. The fury of his passion is over, and there is abundant room in his heart for the natural awe of the deed. His is none of that confidence which the presence of numbers inevitably inspires. He is *alone* with the dead. He trembles and is bewildered. Yet there is a necessity for disposing of the corpse. He bears it to the river, but leaves behind him the other evidences of guilt; for it is difficult, if not impossible to carry all the burthen at once, and it will be easy to return for what is left. But in his toilsome journey to the water his fears redouble within him. The sounds of life encompass his path. A dozen times he hears or fancies the step of an observer. Even the very lights from the city bewilder him. Yet, in time, and by long and frequent pauses of deep agony, he reaches the river's brink, and disposes of his ghastly charge — perhaps through the medium of a boat. But *now* what treasure does the world hold — what threat of vengeance could it hold out — which would have power to urge the return of that lonely murderer over that toilsome and perilous path, to the thicket and its blood-chilling recollections? He returns *not*, let the consequences be what they may. He *could* not return if he would. His sole thought is immediate escape. He turns his back *forever* upon those dreadful shrubberies, and flees as from the wrath to come.

"But how with a gang? Their number would have inspired them with confidence; if, indeed, confidence is ever wanting in the breast of the arrant blackguard; and of arrant blackguards alone are the supposed *gangs* ever constituted. Their number, I say, would have prevented the bewildering and unreasoning terror which I have imagined to paralyze the single man. Could we suppose an oversight in one, or two, or three, this oversight would have been remedied by a fourth. They would have left nothing behind them; for their number would have enabled them to carry *all* at once. There would have been no need of *return*.

"Consider now the circumstance that, in the outer garment of the corpse when found, 'a slip, about a foot wide, had been torn upward from the bottom hem to the waist, wound three times round the waist, and secured by a sort of hitch in the back.' This was done with the obvious design of affording *a handle* by which to carry the body. But would any *number* of men have dreamed of resorting to such an expedient? To three or four, the limbs of the corpse would have afforded not only a sufficient, but the best possible hold. The device is that of a single individual; and this brings us to the fact that 'between the thicket and the river, the rails of the fences were found taken down, and the ground bore evident traces of some heavy burden having been dragged along it!' But would a *number* of men have put themselves to the superfluous trouble of taking down a fence, for the purpose of dragging through it a corpse which they might have *lifted over* any fence in an instant? Would a *number* of men have so *dragged* a corpse at all as to have left evident *traces* of the dragging?

"And here we must refer to an observation of Le Commerciel; an observation upon which I have already, in some measure, commented.

'A piece,' says this journal, 'of one of the unfortunate girl's petticoats was torn out and tied under her chin, and around the back of her head, probably to prevent screams. This was done by fellows who had no pocket-handkerchiefs.'

"I have before suggested that a genuine blackguard is never *without* a pocket-handkerchief. But it is not to this fact that I now especially advert. That it was not through want of a handkerchief for the purpose imagined by Le Commerciel, that this bandage was employed, is rendered apparent by the handkerchief left in the thicket; and that the object was not 'to prevent screams' appears, also, from the bandage having been employed in preference to what would so much better have answered the purpose. But the language of the evidence speaks of the strip in question as 'found around the neck, fitting loosely, and secured with a hard knot.' These words are sufficiently vague, but differ materially from those of Le Commerciel. The slip was eighteen inches wide, and therefore, although of muslin, would form a strong band when folded or rumpled longitudinally. And thus rumpled it was discovered. My inference is this. The solitary murderer, having borne the corpse, for some distance, (whether from the thicket or elsewhere) by means of the bandage *hitched* around its middle, found the weight, in this mode of procedure, too much for his strength. He resolved to drag the burthen — the evidence goes to show that it *was* dragged. With this object in view, it became necessary to attach something like a rope to one of the extremities. It would be best attached about the neck, where the head would prevent its slipping off. And, now, the murderer bethought him, unquestionably, of the bandage about the loins. He would have used this, but for its volution about the corpse, the *hitch* which embarrassed it, and the reflection that it had not been 'torn off' from the garment. It was easier to tear a new slip from the petticoat. He tore it, made it fast about the neck, and so *dragged* his victim to the brink of the river. That this 'bandage,' only attainable with trouble and delay, and but imperfectly answering its purpose — that this bandage was employed *at all*, demonstrates that the necessity for its employment sprang from circumstances arising at a period when the handkerchief was no longer attainable — that is to say, arising, as we have imagined, after quitting the thicket, (if the thicket it was), and on the road between the thicket and the river.

"But the evidence, you will say, of Madame Deluc, (!) points especially to the presence of *a gang*, in the vicinity of the thicket, at or about the epoch of the murder. This I grant. I doubt if there were not a *dozen* gangs, such as described by Madame Deluc, in and about the vicinity of the Barrière du Roule at *or about* the period of this tragedy. But the gang which has drawn upon itself the pointed animadversion, although the somewhat tardy and very suspicious evidence of Madame Deluc, is the *only* gang which is represented by that honest and scrupulous old lady as having eaten her cakes and swallowed her brandy, without putting themselves to the trouble of making her payment. *Et hinc illae irae?*

"But what *is* the precise evidence of Madame Deluc? 'A gang of miscreants made their appearance, behaved boisterously, ate and drank without making payment, followed in the route of the young man and girl, returned to the inn *about dusk,* and recrossed the river as if in great haste.'

"Now this 'great haste' very possibly seemed *greater* haste in the eyes of Madame Deluc, since she dwelt lingeringly and lamentingly upon her violated cakes and ale — cakes and ale for which she might still have entertained a faint hope of compensation. Why, otherwise, since it was *about dusk,* should she make a point of the *haste?* It is no cause for wonder, surely, that even a gang of blackguards should make *haste* to get home, when a wide river is to be crossed in small boats, when storm impends, and when night *approaches.*

"I say *approaches;* for the night had *not yet arrived.* It was only *about dusk* that the indecent haste of these 'miscreants' offended the sober eyes of Madame Deluc. But we are told that it was upon this very evening that Madame Deluc, as well as her eldest son, 'heard the screams of a female in the vicinity of the inn.' And in what words does Madame Deluc designate the period of the evening at which these screams were heard? 'It was *soon after dark,*' she says. But 'soon *after* dark,' is, at least, *dark;* and '*about dusk*' is as certainly daylight. Thus it is abundantly clear that the gang quitted the Barrière du Roule *prior* to the screams overheard (?) by Madame Deluc. And although, in all the many reports of the evidence, the relative expressions in question are distinctly and invariably employed just as I have employed them in this conversation with yourself, no notice whatever of the gross discrepancy has, as yet, been taken by any of the public journals, or by any of the Myrmidons of police.

"I shall add but one to the arguments against *a gang;* but this *one* has, to my own understanding at least, a weight altogether irresistible. Under the circumstances of large reward offered, and full pardon to any King's evidence, it is not to be imagined, for a moment, that some member of *a gang* of low ruffians, or of any body of men, would not long ago have betrayed his accomplices. Each one of a gang so placed, is not so much greedy of reward, or anxious for escape, as *fearful of betrayal.* He betrays eagerly and early that *he may not himself be betrayed.* That the secret has not been divulged, is the very best of proof that it is, in fact, a secret. The horrors of this dark deed are known only to *one,* or two, living human beings, and to God.

"Let us sum up now the meagre yet certain fruits of our long analysis. We have attained the idea either of a fatal accident under the roof of Madame Deluc, or of a murder perpetrated, in the thicket at the Barrière du Roule, by a lover, or at least by an intimate and secret associate of the deceased. This associate is of swarthy complexion. This complexion, the 'hitch' in the bandage, and the 'sailor's knot,' with which the bonnet-ribbon is tied, point to a seaman. His companionship with the deceased, a gay, but not an abject young girl, designates him as above the grade of the common sailor. Here the well written and urgent communications to the journals are much in the way of corroboration. The circumstance of the first elopement, as mentioned by Le Mercurie, tends to blend the idea of this seaman with that of the 'naval officer' who is first known to have led the unfortunate into crime.

"And here, most fitly, comes the consideration of the continued absence of him of the dark complexion. Let me pause to observe that the complexion of this man is dark and swarthy; it was no common swarthiness which constituted the *sole* point of remembrance, both as regards Valence and Madame Deluc. But why is this man absent? Was he murdered by the gang? If so, why are there only *traces* of the assassinated *girl*? The scene of the two outrages will naturally be supposed identical. And where is his corpse? The assassins would most probably have disposed of both in the same way. But it may be said that this man lives, and is deterred from making himself known, through dread of being charged with the murder. This consideration might be supposed to operate upon him now — at this late period — since it has been given in evidence that he was seen with Marie — but it would have had no force at the period of the deed. The first impulse of an innocent man would have been to announce the outrage, and to aid in identifying the ruffians. This, *policy* would have suggested. He had been seen with the girl. He had crossed the river with her in an open ferry-boat. The denouncing of the assassins would have appeared, even to an idiot, the surest and sole means of relieving himself from suspicion. We cannot suppose him, on the night of the fatal Sunday, both innocent himself and incognizant of an outrage committed. Yet only under such circumstances is it possible to imagine that he would have failed, if alive, in the denouncement of the assassins.

"And what means are ours, of attaining the truth? We shall find these means multiplying and gathering distinctness as we proceed. Let us sift to the bottom this affair of the first elopement. Let us know the full history of 'the officer,' with his present circumstances, and his whereabouts at the precise period of the murder. Let us carefully compare with each other the various communications sent to the evening paper, in which the object was to inculpate *a gang*. This done, let us compare these communications, both as regards style and MS., with those sent to the morning paper, at a previous period, and insisting so vehemently upon the guilt of Mennais. And, all this done, let us again compare these various communications with the known MSS. of the officer. Let us endeavor to ascertain, by repeated questionings of Madame Deluc and her boys, as well as of the omnibus-driver, Valence, something more of the personal appearance and bearing of the 'man of dark complexion.' Queries, skilfully directed, will not fail to elicit, from some of these parties, information on this particular point (or upon others) — information which the parties themselves may not even be aware of possessing. And let us now trace *the boat* picked up by the bargeman on the morning of Monday the twenty-third of June, and which was removed from the barge-office, without the cognizance of the officer in attendance, and *without the rudder*, at some period prior to the discovery of the corpse. With a proper caution and perseverance we shall infallibly trace this boat; for not only can the bargeman who picked it up identify it, but the *rudder is at hand*. The rudder *of a sail-boat* would not have been abandoned, without inquiry, by one altogether at ease in heart. And here let me pause to insinuate a question. There was no *advertisement* of the picking up of this boat. It was silently taken to the barge-office, and as silently removed. But its owner or employer — how *happened* he, at so early a period as Tuesday morning, to be informed, without the agency of advertisement, of the locality of the boat taken up on Monday, unless we imagine some connexion with the *navy* — some personal permanent connexion leading to cognizance of its minute interests — its petty local news?

"In speaking of the lonely assassin dragging his burden to the shore, I have already suggested the probability of his availing himself *of a boat*. Now we are to understand that Marie Rogêt *was* precipitated from a boat. This would naturally have been the case. The corpse could not have been trusted to the shallow waters of the shore. The peculiar marks on the back and shoulders of the victim tell of the bottom ribs of a boat. That the body was found without weight is also corroborative of the idea. If thrown from the shore a weight would have been attached. We can only account for its absence by supposing the murderer to have neglected the precaution of supplying himself with it before pushing off. In the act of consigning the corpse to the water, he would unquestionably have noticed his oversight; but then no remedy would have been at hand. Any risk would have been preferred to a return to that accursed shore. Having rid himself of his ghastly charge, the murderer would have hastened to the city. There, at some obscure wharf, he would have leaped on land. But the boat — would he have secured it? He would have been in too great haste for such things as securing a boat. Moreover, in fastening it to the wharf, he would have felt as if securing evidence against himself. His natural thought would have been to cast from him, as far as possible, all that had held connection with his crime. He would not only have fled from the wharf, but he would not have permitted *the boat* to remain. Assuredly he would have cast it adrift. Let us pursue our fancies. — In the morning, the wretch is stricken with unutterable horror at finding that the boat has been picked up and detained at a locality which he is in the daily habit of frequenting — at a locality, perhaps, which his duty compels him to frequent. The next night, *without daring to ask for the rudder,* he removes it. Now *where* is that rudderless boat? Let it be one of our first purposes to discover. With the first glimpse we obtain of it, the dawn of our success shall begin. This boat shall guide us, with a rapidity which will surprise even ourselves, to him who employed it in the midnight of the fatal Sabbath. Corroboration will rise upon corroboration, and the murderer will be traced."

[For reasons which we shall not specify, but which to many readers will appear obvious, we have taken the liberty of here omitting, from the MSS. placed in our hands, such portion as details the *following up* of the apparently slight clew obtained by Dupin. We feel it advisable only to state, in brief, that the result desired was brought to pass; and that the Prefect fulfilled punctually, although with reluctance, the terms of his compact with the Chevalier. Mr. Poe's article concludes with the following words. — *Eds.**]

It will be understood that I speak of coincidences *and no more.* What I have said above upon this topic must suffice. In my own heart there dwells no faith in praeter-nature. That Nature and its God are two, no man who thinks, will deny. That the latter, creating the former, can, at will, control or modify it, is also unquestionable. I say "at will;" for the question is of will, and not, as the insanity of logic has assumed,

*Of the Magazine in which the article was originally published.

of power. It is not that the Deity *cannot* modify his laws, but that we insult him in imagining a possible necessity for modification. In their origin these laws were fashioned to embrace *all* contingencies which *could* lie in the Future. With God all is *Now*.

I repeat, then, that I speak of these things only as coincidences. And farther: in what I relate it will be seen that between the fate of the unhappy Mary Cecilia Rogers, so far as that fate is known, and the fate of one Marie Rogêt up to a certain epoch in her history, there has existed a parallel in the contemplation of whose wonderful exactitude the reason becomes embarrassed. I say all this will be seen. But let it not for a moment be supposed that, in proceeding with the sad narrative of Marie from the epoch just mentioned, and in tracing to its *dénouement* the mystery which enshrouded her, it is my covert design to hint at an extension of the parallel, or even to suggest that the measures adopted in Paris for the discovery of the assassin of a *grisette*, or measures founded in any similar ratiocination, would produce any similar result.

For, in respect to the latter branch of the supposition, it should be considered that the most trifling variation in the facts of the two cases might give rise to the most important miscalculations, by diverting thoroughly the two courses of events; very much as, in arithmetic, an error which, in its own individuality, may be inappreciable, produces, at length, by dint of multiplication at all points of the process, a result enormously at variance with truth. And, in regard to the former branch, we must not fail to hold in view that the very Calculus of Probabilities to which I have referred, forbids all idea of the extension of the parallel: — forbids it with a positiveness strong and decided just in proportion as this parallel has already been long-drawn and exact. This is one of those anomalous propositions which, seemingly appealing to thought altogether apart from the mathematical, is yet one which only the mathematician can fully entertain. Nothing, for example, is more difficult than to convince the merely general reader that the fact of sixes having been thrown twice in succession by a player at dice, is sufficient cause for betting the largest odds that sixes will not be thrown in the third attempt. A suggestion to this effect is usually rejected by the intellect at once. It does not appear that the two throws which have been completed, and which lie now absolutely in the Past, can have influence upon the throw which exists only in the Future. The chance for throwing sixes seems to be precisely as it was at any ordinary time — that is to say, subject only to the influence of the various other throws which may be made by the dice. And this is a reflection which appears so exceedingly obvious that attempts to controvert it are received more frequently with a derisive smile than with anything like respectful attention. The error here involved — a gross error redolent of mischief — I cannot pretend to expose within the limits assigned me at present; and with the philosophical it needs no exposure. It may be sufficient here to say that it forms one of an infinite series of mistakes which arise in the path of Reason through her propensity for seeking truth *in detail*.

MARIE BELLOC LOWNDES

THE LODGER

In 1911, twenty-three years after the unsolved Jack the Ripper murders shocked Victorian London, Marie Belloc Lowndes (1868–1947) published "The Lodger," a short story that came to embody the way most people remember the crimes.

Mrs. Lowndes, sister of the writer Hilaire Belloc, later expanded her story into a novel that has been filmed at least four times, the most famous being Alfred Hitchcock's 1926 version. Her other novels, most of which have historical settings and feature plots with strong overtones of sexual and psychological terror, include The Chink in the Armour *and* Letty Lynton. *Commenting on her technique as a writer of mysteries, Mrs. Lowndes once said, "What has always seemed to me of paramount interest . . . is contained not in the word 'Who?' but in the word 'Why?' "*

"THERE HE IS at last, and I'm glad of it, Ellen. 'Tain't a night you would wish a dog to be out in."

Mr. Bunting's voice was full of unmistakable relief. He was close to the fire, sitting back in a deep leather armchair — a clean-shaven, dapper man, still in outward appearance what he had been so long and now no longer was — a self-respecting butler.

"You needn't feel so nervous about him; Mr. Sleuth can look out for himself, all right." Mrs. Bunting spoke in a dry, rather tart tone. She was less emotional, better balanced, than was her husband. On her the marks of past servitude were less apparent, but they were there all the same — especially in her neat black stuff dress and scrupulously clean, plain collar and cuffs. Mrs. Bunting, as a single woman, had been for long years what is known as a useful maid.

"I can't think why he wants to go out in such weather. He did it in last week's fog, too," Bunting went on complainingly.

"Well, it's none of your business — now, is it?"

"No, that's true enough. Still, 'twould be a very bad thing for us if anything happened to him. This lodger's the first bit of luck we've had for a very long time."

Mrs. Bunting made no answer to this remark. It was too obviously true to be worth answering. Also she was listening — following in imagination her lodger's quick, singularly quiet — "stealthy," she called it to herself — progress through the dark, fog-filled hall and up the staircase.

"It isn't safe for decent folk to be out in such weather — not unless they have something to do that won't wait till tomorrow." Bunting had at last turned round. He was now looking straight into his wife's narrow, colorless face; he was an obstinate man, and liked to prove himself right. "I read you out the accidents in *Lloyd's* yesterday — shocking, they were, and all brought about by the fog! And then, that 'orrid monster at his work again —"

"Monster?" repeated Mrs. Bunting absently. She was trying to hear the lodger's footsteps overhead; but her husband went on as if there had been no interruption.

"It wouldn't be very pleasant to run up against such a party as that in the fog, eh?"

"What stuff you do talk!" she said sharply, and then she got up suddenly. Her husband's remark had disturbed her. She hated to think of such things as the terrible series of murders that were just then horrifying and exciting the nether world of London. Though she enjoyed pathos and sentiment — Mrs. Bunting would listen with mild amusement to the details of a breach-of-promise action — she shrank from stories of either immorality or physical violence.

Mrs. Bunting got up from the straight-backed chair on which she had been sitting. It would soon be time for supper.

She moved about the sitting room, flecking off an imperceptible touch of dust here, straightening a piece of furniture there.

Bunting looked around once or twice. He would have liked to ask Ellen to leave off fidgeting, but he was mild and fond of peace, so he refrained. However, she soon gave over what irritated him of her own accord.

But even then Mrs. Bunting did not at once go down to the cold kitchen, where everything was in readiness for her simple cooking. Instead, she opened the door leading into the bedroom behind, and there, closing the door quietly, stepped back into the darkness and stood motionless, listening.

At first she heard nothing, but gradually there came the sound of someone moving about in the room just overhead; try as she might, however, it was impossible for her to guess what her lodger was doing. At last she heard him open the door leading out on the landing. That meant that he would spend the rest of the evening in the rather cheerless room above the drawing-room floor — oddly enough, he liked sitting there best, though the only warmth obtainable was from a gas stove fed by a shilling-in-the-slot arrangement.

It was indeed true that Mr. Sleuth had brought the Buntings luck, for at the time he had taken their rooms it had been touch and go with them.

After having each separately led the sheltered, impersonal, and, above all, the financially easy existence that is the compensation life offers to those men and women who deliberately take upon themselves the yoke of domestic service, these two, butler and useful maid, had suddenly, in middle age, determined to join their fortunes and savings.

Bunting was a widower; he had one pretty daughter, a girl of seventeen, who now lived, as had been the case ever since the death of her mother, with a prosperous aunt. His second wife had been reared in the Foundling Hospital, but she had gradually worked her way up into the higher ranks of the servant class and as useful maid she had saved quite a tidy sum of money.

Unluckily, misfortune had dogged Mr. and Mrs. Bunting from the very first. The seaside place where they had begun by taking a lodging house became the scene of an epidemic. Then had followed a business experiment which had proved disastrous. But before going back into service, either together or separately, they had made up their minds to make one last effort, and, with the little money that remained to them, they had taken over the lease of a small house in the Marylebone Road.

Bunting, whose appearance was very good, had retained a connection with old employers and their friends, so he occasionally got a good job as waiter. During this last month his jobs had perceptibly increased in number and in profit; Mrs. Bunting was not superstitious, but it seemed that in this matter, as in everything else, Mr. Sleuth, their new lodger, had brought them luck.

As she stood there, still listening intently in the darkness of the bedroom, she told herself, not for the first time, what Mr. Sleuth's departure would mean to her and Bunting. It would almost certainly mean ruin.

Luckily, the lodger seemed entirely pleased both with the rooms and with his landlady. There was really no reason why he should ever leave such nice lodgings. Mrs. Bunting shook off her vague sense of apprehension and unease. She turned round, took a step forward, and, feeling for the handle of the door giving into the passage, she opened it, and went down with light, firm steps into the kitchen.

She lit the gas and put a frying pan on the stove, and then once more her mind reverted, as if in spite of herself, to her lodger, and there came back to Mrs. Bunting, very vividly, the memory of all that had happened the day Mr. Sleuth had taken her rooms.

The date of this excellent lodger's coming had been the twenty-ninth of December, and the time late afternoon. She and Bunting had been sitting, gloomily enough, over their small banked-up fire. They had dined in the middle of the day — he on a couple of sausages, she on a little cold ham. They were utterly out of heart, each trying to pluck up courage to tell the other that it was no use trying anymore. The two had also had a little tiff on that dreary afternoon. A newspaper seller had come yelling down the Marylebone Road, shouting out, " 'Orrible murder in Whitechapel!" and just because Bunting had an old uncle living in the East End he had gone and bought a paper, and at a time, too, when every penny, nay, every halfpenny, had its full value! Mrs. Bunting remembered the circumstances because that murder in Whitechapel had been the first of these terrible crimes — there had been four since — which she would never allow Bunting to discuss in her presence, and yet which had of late begun to interest curiously, uncomfortably, even her refined mind.

But, to return to the lodger. It was then, on that dreary afternoon, that suddenly there had come to the front door a tremulous, uncertain double knock.

Bunting ought to have got up, but he had gone on reading the paper and so Mrs. Bunting, with the woman's greater courage, had gone out into the passage, turned up the gas, and opened the door to see who it could be. She remembered, as if it were yesterday instead of nigh on a month ago, Mr. Sleuth's peculiar appearance. Tall, dark, lanky, an old-fashioned top hat concealing his high bald forehead, he had stood there, an odd figure of a man, blinking at her.

"I believe — is it not a fact that you let lodgings?" he had asked in a hesitating, whistling voice, a voice that she had known in a moment to be that of an educated man — of a gentleman. As he had stepped into the hall, she had noticed that in his right hand he held a narrow bag — a quite new bag of strong brown leather.

Everything had been settled in less than a quarter of an hour. Mr. Sleuth had at once "taken" to the drawing-room floor, and then, as

Mrs. Bunting eagerly lit the gas in the front room above, he had looked around him and said, rubbing his hands with a nervous movement, "Capital — capital! This is just what I've been looking for!"

The sink had specially pleased him — the sink and the gas stove. "This is quite first-rate!" he had exclaimed, "for I make all sorts of experiments. I am, you must understand, Mrs. — er — Bunting, a man of science." Then he had sat down — suddenly. "I'm very tired," he had said in a low tone, "very tired indeed! I have been walking about all day."

From the very first the lodger's manner had been odd, sometimes distant and abrupt, and then, for no reason at all that she could see, confidential and plaintively confiding. But Mrs. Bunting was aware that eccentricity has always been a perquisite, as it were the special luxury, of the well born and well educated. Scholars and such-like are never quite like other people.

And then, this particular gentleman had proved himself so eminently satisfactory as to the one thing that really matters to those who let lodgings. "My name is Sleuth," he said, "S-l-e-u-t-h. Think of a hound, Mrs. Bunting, and you'll never forget my name. I could give you references," he had added, giving her, as she now remembered, a funny sidewise look, "but I prefer to dispense with them. How much did you say? Twenty-three shillings a week, with attendance? Yes, that will suit me perfectly; and I'll begin by paying my first month's rent in advance. Now, four times twenty-three shillings is" — he looked at Mrs. Bunting, and for the first time he smiled, a queer, wry smile — "ninety-two shillings."

He had taken a handful of sovereigns out of his pocket and put them down on the table. "Look here," he had said, "there's five pounds; and you can keep the change, for I shall want you to do a little shopping for me tomorrow."

After he had been in the house about an hour, the bell had rung, and the new lodger had asked Mrs. Bunting if she could oblige him with a loan of a Bible. She brought up to him her best Bible, the one that had been given to her as a wedding present by a lady with whose mother she had lived for several years. This Bible and one other book, of which the odd name was Cruden's Concordance, formed Mr. Sleuth's only reading: he spent hours each day poring over the Old Testament and over the volume which Mrs. Bunting had at last decided to be a queer kind of index to the Book.

However, to return to the lodger's first arrival. He had had no luggage with him, barring the small brown bag, but very soon parcels had begun to arrive addressed to Mr. Sleuth, and it was then that

Mrs. Bunting first became curious. These parcels were full of clothes; but it was quite clear to the landlady's feminine eye that none of these clothes had been made for Mr. Sleuth. They were, in fact, second-hand clothes, bought at good secondhand places, each marked, when marked at all, with a different name. And the really extraordinary thing was that occasionally a complete suit disappeared — became, as it were, obliterated from the lodger's wardrobe.

As for the bag he had brought with him, Mrs. Bunting had never caught sight of it again. And this also was certainly very strange.

Mrs. Bunting thought a great deal about that bag. She often wondered what had been in it; not a nightshirt and comb and brush, as she had at first supposed, for Mr. Sleuth had asked her to go out and buy him a brush and comb and toothbrush the morning after his arrival. That fact was specifically impressed on her memory, for at the little shop, a barber's, where she had purchased the brush and comb, the foreigner who had served her had insisted on telling her some of the horrible details of the murder that had taken place the day before in Whitechapel, and it had upset her very much.

As to where the bag was now, it was probably locked up in the lower part of a chiffonier in the front sitting room. Mr. Sleuth evidently always carried the key of the little cupboard on his person, for Mrs. Bunting, though she looked well for it, had never been able to find it.

And yet never was there a more confiding or trusting gentleman. The first four days that he had been with them he had allowed his money — the considerable sum of one hundred and eighty-four pounds in gold — to lie about wrapped up in pieces of paper on his dressing table. This was a very foolish, indeed a wrong thing to do, as she had allowed herself respectfully to point out to him; but as only answer he had laughed, a loud, discordant shout of laughter.

Mr. Sleuth had many other odd ways; but Mrs. Bunting, a true woman in spite of her prim manner and love of order, had an infinite patience with masculine vagaries.

On the first morning of Mr. Sleuth's stay in the Buntings' house, while Mrs. Bunting was out buying things for him, the new lodger had turned most of the pictures and photographs hanging in his sitting room with their faces to the wall! But this queer action on Mr. Sleuth's part had not surprised Mrs. Bunting as much as it might have done; it recalled an incident of her long-past youth — something that had happened a matter of twenty years ago, at a time when Mrs. Bunting, then the still youthful Ellen Cottrell, had been maid to an old lady. The old lady had a favorite nephew, a bright, jolly young gentleman who had been learning to paint animals in Paris; and it was he who had had the impudence, early one summer morning, to turn to the wall six beautiful engravings of paintings done by the famous Mr. Landseer! The old lady thought the world of those pictures, but her nephew, as only excuse for the extraordinary thing he had done, had observed that "they put his eye out."

Mr. Sleuth's excuse had been much the same, for, when Mrs. Bunting had come to his sitting room and found all her pictures, or at any rate all those of her pictures that happened to be portraits of ladies, with their faces to the wall, he had offered as only explanation, "Those women's eyes follow me about."

Mrs. Bunting had gradually become aware that Mr. Sleuth had a fear and dislike of women. When she was "doing" the staircase and landing, she often heard him reading bits of the Bible aloud to himself, and in the majority of instances the texts he chose contained uncomplimentary reference to her own sex. Only today she had stopped and listened while he uttered threateningly the awful words, "A strange woman is a narrow pit. She also lieth in wait as for a prey, and increaseth the transgressors among men." There had been a pause, and then had come, in a high singsong, "Her house is the way to hell, going down to the chambers of death." It had made Mrs. Bunting feel quite queer.

The lodger's daily habits were also peculiar. He stayed in bed all the morning and sometimes part of the afternoon, and he never went out before the streetlamps were alight. Then there was his dislike of an open fire; he generally sat in the top front room, and while there he always used the large gas stove, not only for his experiments, which he carried on at night, but also in the daytime, for warmth.

But there! Where was the use of worrying about the lodger's funny ways? Of course Mr. Sleuth was eccentric; if he hadn't been "just a leetle 'touched' upstairs" — as Bunting had once described it — he wouldn't be their lodger now; he would be living in a quite different sort of way with some of his relations, or with a friend of his own class.

Mrs. Bunting, while these thoughts galloped disconnectedly through her brain, went on with her cooking, doing everything with a certain delicate and cleanly precision.

While in the middle of making the toast on which was to be poured some melted cheese, she suddenly heard a noise, or rather a series of noises. Shuffling, hesitating steps were creaking down the house above. She looked up and listened. Surely Mr. Sleuth was not going out again into the cold, foggy night? But no; for the sounds did not continue down the passage leading to the front door.

The heavy steps were coming slowly down the kitchen stairs. Nearer and nearer came the thudding sounds, and Mrs. Bunting's heart began to beat as if in response. She put out the gas stove, unheedful of the fact that the cheese would stiffen and spoil in the cold air; and then she turned and faced the door. There was a fumbling at the handle, and a moment later the door opened and revealed, as she had known it would, her lodger.

Mr. Sleuth was clad in a plaid dressing gown, and in his hand was a candle. When he saw the lit-up kitchen, and the woman standing in it, he looked inexplicably taken aback, almost aghast.

"Yes, sir? What can I do for you, sir? I hope you didn't ring, sir?" Mrs. Bunting did not come forward to meet her lodger; instead, she held her ground in front of the stove. Mr. Sleuth had no business to come down like this into her kitchen.

"No, I — I didn't ring," he stammered. "I didn't know you were down here, Mrs. Bunting. Please excuse my costume. The truth is, my gas stove has gone wrong, or, rather, that shilling-in-the-slot arrangement has done so. I came down to see if *you* had a gas stove. I am going to ask leave to use it tonight for an experiment I want to make."

Mrs. Bunting felt troubled — oddly, unnaturally troubled. Why couldn't the lodger's experiment wait till tomorrow? "Oh, certainly, sir; but you will find it very cold down here." She looked round her dubiously.

"It seems most pleasantly warm," he observed, "warm and cozy after my cold room upstairs."

"Won't you let me make you a fire?" Mrs. Bunting's housewifely instincts were roused. "Do let me make you a fire in your bedroom, sir; I'm sure you ought to have one there these cold nights."

"By no means — I mean, I would prefer not. I do not like an open fire, Mrs. Bunting." He frowned, and still stood, a strange-looking figure, just inside the kitchen door.

"Do you want to use this stove now, sir? Is there anything I can do to help you?"

"No, not now — thank you all the same, Mrs. Bunting. I shall come down later, altogether later — probably after you and your husband have gone to bed. But I should be much obliged if you would see that the gas people come tomorrow and put my stove in order."

"Perhaps Bunting could put it right for you, sir. I'll ask him to go up."

"No, no — I don't want anything of that sort done tonight. Besides, he couldn't put it right. The cause of the trouble is quite simple. The machine is choked up with shillings: a foolish plan, so I have always felt it to be."

Mr. Sleuth spoke very pettishly, with far more heat than he was wont to speak; but Mrs. Bunting sympathized with him. She had always suspected those slot-machines to be as dishonest as if they were human. It was dreadful, the way they swallowed up the shillings!

As if he were divining her thoughts, Mr. Sleuth, walking forward, stared up at the kitchen slot-machine. "Is it nearly full?" he asked abruptly. "I expect my experiment will take some time, Mrs. Bunting."

"Oh, no, sir; there's plenty of room for shillings there still. We don't use our stove as much as you do yours, sir. I'm never in the kitchen a minute longer than I can help this cold weather."

And then, with him preceding her, Mrs. Bunting and her lodger made a slow progress to the ground floor. There Mr. Sleuth courteously bade his landlady good night and proceeded upstairs to his own apartments.

Mrs. Bunting again went down into her kitchen, again she lit the stove, and again she cooked the toasted cheese. But she felt unnerved, afraid of she knew not what. The place seemed to her alive with alien presences, and once she caught herself listening, which was absurd, for of course she could not hope to hear what her lodger was doing two, if not three, flights upstairs. She had never been able to discover what Mr. Sleuth's experiments really were; all she knew was that they required a very high degree of heat.

The Buntings went to bed early that night. But Mrs. Bunting intended to stay awake. She wanted to know at what hour of the night her lodger would come down into the kitchen, and, above all, she was anxious as to how long he would stay there. But she had had a long day, and presently she fell asleep.

The church clock hard by struck two in the morning, and suddenly Mrs. Bunting awoke. She felt sharply annoyed with herself. How could she have dropped off like that? Mr. Sleuth must have been down and up again hours ago.

Then, gradually, she became aware of a faint acrid odor; elusive, almost intangible, it yet seemed to encompass her and the snoring man by her side almost as a vapor might have done.

Mrs. Bunting sat up in bed and sniffed; and then, in spite of the cold, she quietly crept out of the nice, warm bedclothes and crawled along to the bottom of the bed. There Mr. Sleuth's landlady did a very curious thing; she leaned over the brass rail and put her face close to the hinge of the door. Yes, it was from there that this strange, horrible odor was coming; the smell must be very strong in the passage. Mrs. Bunting thought she knew now what became of those suits of clothes of Mr. Sleuth's that disappeared.

As she crept back, shivering, under the bedclothes, she longed to give her sleeping husband a good shake, and in fancy she heard herself saying: "Bunting, get up! There is something strange going on downstairs that we ought to know about."

But Mr. Sleuth's landlady, as she lay by her husband's side, listening with painful intentness, knew very well that she would do nothing of the sort. The lodger had a right to destroy his clothes by burning if the fancy took him. What if he did make a certain amount of mess, a certain amount of smell, in her nice kitchen? Was he not — was he not such a good lodger! If they did anything to upset him, where could they ever hope to get another like him?

Three o'clock struck before Mrs. Bunting heard slow, heavy steps creaking up her kitchen stairs. But Mr. Sleuth did not go straight up to his own quarters, as she expected him to do. Instead, he went to the front door and, opening it, put it on the chain. At the end of ten minutes or so he closed the front door, and by that time Mrs. Bunting had divined why the lodger had behaved in this strange fashion — it must have been to get the strong acrid smell of burning wool out of the passage. But Mrs. Bunting felt as if she herself would never get rid of the horrible odor. She felt herself to be all smell.

At last the unhappy woman fell into a deep, troubled sleep; and then she dreamed a most terrible and unnatural dream; hoarse voices seemed to be shouting in her ear, " 'Orrible murder off the Edgeware Road!" Then three words, indistinctly uttered, followed by "— at his work again! Awful details!"

Even in her dream Mrs. Bunting felt angered and impatient; she knew so well why she was being disturbed by this horrid nightmare. It was because of Bunting — Bunting, who insisted on talking to her of those frightful murders, in which only morbid, vulgar-minded people took any interest. Why, even now, in her dream, she could hear her husband speaking to her about it.

"Ellen" — so she heard Bunting say in her ear — "Ellen, my dear, I am just going to get up to get a paper. It's after seven o'clock."

Mrs. Bunting sat up in bed. The shouting, nay, worse, the sound of tramping, hurrying feet smote on her ears. It had been no nightmare, then, but something infinitely worse — reality. Why couldn't Bunting have lain quietly in bed awhile longer, and let his poor wife go on dreaming? The most awful dream would have been easier to bear than this awakening.

She heard her husband go to the front door, and, as he bought the paper, exchange a few excited words with the newspaper boy. Then he came back and began silently moving about the room.

"Well!" she cried. "Why don't you tell me about it?"

"I thought you'd rather not hear."

"Of course I like to know what happens close to our own front door!" she snapped out.

And then he read out a piece of the newspaper — only a few lines, after all — telling in brief, unemotional language that the body of a woman, apparently done to death in a peculiarly atrocious fashion some hours before, had been found in a passage leading to a disused warehouse off the Marylebone Road.

"It serves that sort of hussy right!" was Mrs. Bunting's only comment.

When Mrs. Bunting went down into the kitchen, everything there looked just as she had left it, and there was no trace of the acrid smell she had expected to find there. Instead, the cavernous whitewashed room was full of fog, and she noticed that, though the shutters were bolted and barred as she had left them, the windows behind them had been widely opened to the air. She, of course, had left them shut.

She stooped and flung open the oven door of her gas-stove. Yes, it was as she had expected; a fierce heat had been generated there since she had last used the oven, and a mass of black, gluey soot had fallen through to the stone floor below.

Mrs. Bunting took the ham and eggs that she had bought the previous day for her own and Bunting's breakfast, and broiled them over the gas ring in their sitting room. Her husband watched her in surprised silence. She had never done such a thing before.

"I couldn't stay down there," she said, "it was so cold and foggy. I thought I'd make breakfast up here, just for today."

"Yes," he said kindly, "that's quite right, Ellen. I think you've done quite right, my dear."

But when it came to the point, his wife could not eat any of the nice breakfast she had got ready; she only had another cup of tea.

"Are you ill?" Bunting asked solicitously.

"No," she said shortly, "of course I'm not ill. Don't be silly! The thought of that horrible thing happening so close by has upset me. Just hark to them, now!"

Through their closed windows penetrated the sound of scurrying feet and loud, ribald laughter. A crowd, nay, a mob, hastened to and from the scene of the murder.

Mrs. Bunting made her husband lock the front gate. "I don't want any of those ghouls in here!" she exclaimed angrily. And then, "What a lot of idle people there must be in the world," she said.

The coming and going went on all day. Mrs. Bunting stayed indoors; Bunting went out. After all, the ex-butler was human — it was
natural that he should feel thrilled and excited. All their neighbors
were the same. His wife wasn't reasonable about such things. She
quarreled with him when he didn't tell her anything, and yet he was
sure she would have been angry with him if he had said very much
about it.

The lodger's bell rang about two o'clock, and Mrs. Bunting prepared the simple luncheon that was also his breakfast. As she rested
the tray a minute on the drawing-room floor landing, she heard Mr.
Sleuth's high, quavering voice reading aloud the words:

"She saith to him, Stolen waters are sweet, and bread eaten in secret
is pleasant. But he knoweth not that the dead are there; and that her
guests are in the depths of hell."

The landlady turned the handle of the door and walked in with
the tray. Mr. Sleuth was sitting close by the window, and Mrs. Bunting's Bible lay open before him. As she came in he hastily closed the
Bible and looked down at the crowd walking along the Marylebone
Road.

"There seem a great many people out today," he observed, without
looking round.

"Yes, sir, there do." Mrs. Bunting said nothing more, and offered
no other explanation; and the lodger, as he at last turned to his landlady, smiled pleasantly. He had acquired a great liking and respect for
this well-behaved, taciturn woman; she was the first person for whom
he had felt any such feeling for many years past.

He took a half sovereign out of his waistcoat pocket; Mrs. Bunting
noticed that it was not the same waistcoat Mr. Sleuth had been wearing
the day before. "Will you please accept this half sovereign for the use
of your kitchen last night?" he said. "I made as little mess as I could,
but I was carrying on a rather elaborate experiment."

She held out her hand, hesitated, and then took the coin.

As she walked down the stairs, the winter sun, a yellow ball hanging
in the smoky sky, glinted in on Mrs. Bunting, and lent blood-red
gleams, or so it seemed to her, to the piece of gold she was holding
in her hand.

It was a very cold night — so cold, so windy, so snow-laden the
atmosphere, that everyone who could do so stayed indoors. Bunting,
however, was on his way home from what had proved a very pleasant
job; he had been acting as waiter at a young lady's birthday party,
and a remarkable piece of luck had come his way. The young lady
had come into a fortune that day, and she had had the gracious, the

surprising thought of presenting each of the hired waiters with a sovereign.

This birthday treat had put him in mind of another birthday. His daughter Daisy would be eighteen the following Saturday. Why shouldn't he send her a postal order for half a sovereign, so that she might come up and spend her birthday in London?

Having Daisy for three or four days would cheer up Ellen. Mr. Bunting, slackening his footsteps, began to think with puzzled concern of how queer his wife had seemed lately. She had become so nervous, so "jumpy," that he didn't know what to make of her sometimes. She had never been a really good-tempered woman — your capable, self-respecting woman seldom is — but she had never been like what she was now. Of late she sometimes got quite hysterical; he had let fall a sharp word to her the other day, and she had sat down on a chair, thrown her black apron over her face, and burst out sobbing violently.

During the last ten days Ellen had taken to talking in her sleep. "No, no, no!" she had cried out, only the night before. "It isn't true! I won't have it said! It's a lie!" And there had been a wail of horrible fear and revolt in her unusually quiet, mincing voice. Yes, it would certainly be a good thing for her to have Daisy's company for a bit. Whew! It *was* cold; and Bunting had stupidly forgotten his gloves. He put his hands in his pockets to keep them warm.

Suddenly he became aware that Mr. Sleuth, the lodger who seemed to have "turned their luck," as it were, was walking along on the opposite side of the solitary street.

Mr. Sleuth's tall, thin figure was rather bowed, his head bent toward the ground. His right arm was thrust into his long Inverness cape; the other occasionally sawed the air, doubtless in order to help him keep warm. He was walking rather quickly. It was clear that he had not yet become aware of the proximity of his landlord.

Bunting felt pleased to see his lodger; it increased his feeling of general satisfaction. Strange, was it not, that that odd, peculiar-looking figure should have made all the difference to his (Bunting's) and Mrs. Bunting's happiness and comfort in life?

Naturally, Bunting saw far less of the lodger than did Mrs. Bunting. Their gentleman had made it very clear that he did not like either the husband or wife to come up to his rooms without being definitely asked to do so, and Bunting had been up there only once since Mr. Sleuth's arrival five weeks before. This seemed to be a good opportunity for a little genial conversation.

Bunting, still an active man for his years, crossed the road and, stepping briskly forward, tried to overtake Mr. Sleuth; but the more he hurried, the more the other hastened, and that without even turning to see whose steps he heard echoing behind him on the now freezing pavement.

Mr. Sleuth's own footsteps were quite inaudible — an odd circumstance, when you came to think of it, as Bunting did think of it later, lying awake by Ellen's side in the pitch-darkness. What it meant was, of course, that the lodger had rubber soles on his shoes.

The two men, the pursued and the pursuer, at last turned into the Marylebone Road. They were now within a hundred yards of home, and so, plucking up courage, Bunting called out, his voice echoing freshly on the still air:

"Mr. Sleuth, sir! Mr. Sleuth!"

The lodger stopped and turned round. He had been walking so quickly, and he was in so poor a physical condition, that the sweat was pouring down his face.

"Ah! So it's you, Mr. Bunting? I heard footsteps behind me, and I hurried on. I wish I'd known that it was only you; there are so many queer characters about at night in London."

"Not on a night like this, sir. Only honest folk who have business out of doors would be out such a night as this. It *is* cold, sir!" And then into Bunting's slow and honest mind there suddenly crept the query as to what Mr. Sleuth's own business out could be on this cold, bitter night.

"Cold?" the lodger repeated. "I can't say that I find it cold, Mr. Bunting. When the snow falls the air always becomes milder."

"Yes, sir, but tonight there's such a sharp east wind. Why, it freezes the very marrow in one's bones!"

Bunting noticed that Mr. Sleuth kept his distance in a rather strange way: he walked at the edge of the pavement, leaving the rest of it, on the wall side, to his landlord.

"I lost my way," he said abruptly. "I've been over Primrose Hill to see a friend of mine, and then, coming back, I lost my way."

Bunting could well believe that, for when he had first noticed Mr. Sleuth he was coming from the east, and not, as he should have done if walking home from Primrose Hill, from the north.

They had now reached the little gate that gave onto the shabby, paved court in front of the house. Mr. Sleuth was walking up the flagged path, when, with a "By your leave, sir," the ex-butler, stepping aside, slipped in front of his lodger, in order to open the front door for him.

As he passed by Mr. Sleuth the back of Bunting's bare left hand brushed lightly against the long Inverness cape the other man was wearing, and, to his surprise, the stretch of cloth against which his hand lay for a moment was not only damp, damp from the flakes of snow that had settled upon it, but wet — wet and gluey. Bunting thrust his left hand into his pocket; it was with the other that he placed the key in the lock of the door.

The two men passed into the hall together. The house seemed blackly dark in comparison with the lighted-up road outside; and then, quite suddenly, there came over Bunting a feeling of mortal terror, an instinctive knowledge that some terrible and immediate danger was near him. A voice — the voice of his first wife, the long-dead girl to whom his mind so seldom reverted nowadays — uttered in his ear the words, "Take care!"

"I'm afraid, Mr. Bunting, that you must have felt something dirty, foul, on my coat? It's too long a story to tell you now, but I brushed up against a dead animal — a dead rabbit lying across a bench on Primrose Hill."

Mr. Sleuth spoke in a very quiet voice, almost in a whisper.

"No, sir, no, I didn't notice nothing. I scarcely touched you, sir." It seemed as if a power outside himself compelled Bunting to utter these lying words. "And now, sir, I'll be saying good night to you," he added.

He waited until the lodger had gone upstairs, and then he turned into his own sitting room. There he sat down, for he felt very queer. He did not draw his left hand out of his pocket till he heard the other man moving about in the room above. Then he lit the gas and held up his left hand; he put it close to his face. It was flecked, streaked with blood.

He took off his boots, and then, very quietly, he went into the room where his wife lay asleep. Stealthily he walked across to the toilet table and dipped his hand into the water jug.

The next morning Mr. Sleuth's landlord awoke with a start; he felt curiously heavy about the limbs and tired about the eyes.

Drawing his watch from under his pillow, he saw that it was nearly nine o'clock. He and Ellen had overslept. Without waking her, he got out of bed and pulled up the blind. It was snowing heavily, and, as is the way when it snows, even in London, it was strangely, curiously still.

After he had dressed he went out into the passage. A newspaper and a letter were lying on the mat. Fancy having slept through the postman's knock! He picked them both up and went into the sitting room; then he carefully shut the door behind him and, tossing the letter aside, spread the newspaper wide open on the table and bent over it.

As Bunting at last looked up and straightened himself, a look of inexpressible relief shone upon his stolid face. The item of news he had felt certain would be there, printed in big type on the middle sheet, was not there.

He folded the paper and laid it on a chair, and then eagerly took up his letter.

Dear Father [it ran]: I hope this finds you as well as it leaves me. Mrs. Puddle's youngest child has got scarlet fever, and aunt thinks I had better come away at once, just to stay with you for a few days. Please tell Ellen I won't give her no trouble.

> Your loving daughter,
> Daisy

Bunting felt amazingly lighthearted, and, as he walked into the next room, he smiled broadly.

"Ellen," he cried out, "here's news! Daisy's coming today. There's scarlet fever in their house, and Martha thinks she had better come away for a few days. She'll be here for her birthday!"

Mrs. Bunting listened in silence; she did not even open her eyes. "I can't have the girl here just now," she said shortly. "I've got just as much as I can manage to do."

But Bunting felt pugnacious, and so cheerful as to be almost light-headed. Deep down in his heart he looked back to last night with a feeling of shame and self-rebuke. Whatever had made such horrible thoughts and suspicions come into his head?

"Of course Daisy will come here," he said shortly. "If it comes to that, she'll be able to help you with the work, and she'll brisk us both up a bit."

Rather to his surprise, Mrs. Bunting said nothing in answer to this, and he changed the subject abruptly. "The lodger and me came in together last night," he observed. "He's certainly a funny kind of gentleman. It wasn't the sort of night one would choose to go for a walk over Primrose Hill, and yet that was what he had been doing — so he said."

It stopped snowing about ten o'clock, and the morning wore itself away.

Just as twelve was striking, a four-wheeler drew up to the gate. It was Daisy — pink-cheeked, excited, laughing-eyed Daisy, a sight to gladden any father's heart. "Aunt said I was to have a cab if the weather was bad," she said.

There was a bit of a wrangle over the fare. King's Cross, as all the world knows, is nothing like two miles from the Marylebone Road, but the man clamored for one-and-sixpence, and hinted darkly that he had done the young lady a favor in bringing her at all.

While he and Bunting were having words, Daisy, leaving them to it, walked up the path to the door where her stepmother was awaiting her.

Suddenly there fell loud shouts on the still air. They sounded strangely eerie, breaking sharply across the muffled, snowy air.

"What's that?" said Bunting, with a look of startled fear. "Why, whatever's that?"

The cabman lowered his voice: "Them are crying out that 'orrible affair at King's Cross. He's done for two of 'em this time! That's what I meant when I said I might have got a better fare. I wouldn't say anything before Missy there, but folk 'ave been coming from all over London — like a fire; plenty of toffs, too. But there — there's nothing to see now!"

"What! Another woman murdered last night?" Bunting felt and looked convulsed with horror.

The cabman stared at him, surprised. "Two of 'em, I tell yer — within a few yards of one another. He 'ave got a nerve —"

"Have they caught him?" asked Bunting perfunctorily.

"Lord, no! They'll never catch 'im! It must 'ave happened hours and hours ago — they was both stone-cold. One each end of an archway. That's why they didn't see 'em before."

The hoarse cries were coming nearer and nearer — two news vendors trying to outshout each other.

" 'Orrible discovery near King's Cross!" they yelled exultantly. And as Bunting, with his daughter's bag in his hand, hurried up the path and passed through his front door, the words pursued him like a dreadful threat.

Angrily he shut out the hoarse, insistent cries. No, he had no wish to buy a paper. That kind of crime wasn't fit reading for a young girl, such a girl as was his Daisy, brought up as carefully as if she had been a young lady by her strict Methody aunt.

As he stood in his little hall, trying to feel "all right" again, he could hear Daisy's voice — high, voluble, excited — giving her stepmother a long account of the scarlet fever case to which she owed her presence in London. But as Bunting pushed open the door of the sitting room, there came a note of sharp alarm in his daughter's voice, and he heard her say: "Why, Ellen! Whatever is the matter? You do look bad!" and his wife's muffled answer: "Open the window — do."

Rushing across the room, Bunting pushed up the sash. The newspaper sellers were now just outside the house. "Horrible discovery near King's Cross — a clue to the murderer!' they yelled. And then, helplessly, Mrs. Bunting began to laugh. She laughed and laughed and laughed, rocking herself to and fro as if in an ecstasy of mirth.

"Why, father, whatever's the matter with her?" Daisy looked quite scared.

"She's in 'sterics — that's what it is," he said shortly. "I'll just get the water jug. Wait a minute."

Bunting felt very put out, and yet glad, too, for this queer seizure of Ellen's almost made him forget the sick terror with which he had been possessed a moment before. That he and his wife should be obsessed by the same fear, the same terror, never crossed his simple, slow-working mind.

The lodger's bell rang. That, or the threat of the water jug, had a magical effect on Mrs. Bunting. She rose to her feet, still trembling, but composed.

As Mrs. Bunting went upstairs she felt her legs trembling under her, and put out a shaking hand to clutch at the banister for support. She waited a few minutes on the landing, and then knocked at the door of her lodger's parlor.

But Mr. Sleuth's voice answered her from the bedroom. "I'm not well," he called out querulously; "I think I caught a chill going out to see a friend last night. I'd be obliged if you'll bring me up a cup of tea and put it outside my door, Mrs. Bunting."

"Very well, sir."

Mrs. Bunting went downstairs and made her lodger a cup of tea over the gas ring, Bunting watching her the while in heavy silence.

During their midday dinner the husband and wife had a little discussion as to where Daisy should sleep. It had already been settled that a bed should be made up for her in the sitting room, but Bunting saw reason to change this plan. As the two women were clearing away the dishes, he looked up and said shortly: "I think 'twould be better if Daisy were to sleep with you, Ellen, and I were to sleep in the sitting room."

Ellen acquiesced quietly.

Daisy was a good-natured girl; she liked London, and wanted to make herself useful to her stepmother. "I'll wash up; don't you bother to come downstairs," she said.

Bunting began to walk up and down the room. His wife gave him a furtive glance; she wondered what he was thinking about.

"Didn't you get a paper?" she said at last.

"There's the paper," he said crossly, "the paper we always do take in, the *Telegraph*." His look challenged her to a further question.

"I thought they were shouting something in the street — I mean just before I was took bad."

But he made no answer; instead, he went to the top of the staircase and called out sharply: "Daisy! Daisy, child, are you there?"

"Yes, Father," she answered from below.

"Better come upstairs out of that cold kitchen."

He came back into the sitting room again.

"Ellen, is the lodger in? I haven't heard him moving about. I don't want Daisy to be mixed up with him."

"Mr. Sleuth is not well today," his wife answered. "He is remaining in bed a bit. Daisy needn't have anything to do with him. She'll have her work cut out looking after things down here. That's where I want her to help me."

"Agreed," he said.

When it grew dark, Bunting went out and bought an evening paper. He read it out of doors in the biting cold, standing beneath a street-lamp. He wanted to see what was the clue to the murderer.

The clue proved to be a very slender one — merely the imprint in the snowy slush of a half-worn rubber sole; and it was, of course, by no means certain that the sole belonged to the boot or shoe of the murderer of the two doomed women who had met so swift and awful a death in the arch near King's Cross station. The paper's special investigator pointed out that there were thousands of such soles being worn in London. Bunting found comfort in that obvious fact. He felt grateful to the special investigator for having stated it so clearly.

As he approached his house, he heard curious sounds coming from the inner side of the low wall that shut off the courtyard from the pavement. Under ordinary circumstances Bunting would have gone at once to drive whoever was there out into the roadway. Now he stayed outside, sick with suspense and anxiety. Was it possible that their place was being watched — already?

But it was only Mr. Sleuth. To Bunting's astonishment, the lodger suddenly stepped forward from behind the wall onto the flagged path. He was carrying a brown-paper parcel, and as he walked along the new boots he was wearing creaked and the tap-tap of wooden heels rang out on the stones.

Bunting, still hidden outside the gate, suddenly understood what his lodger had been doing the other side of the wall. Mr. Sleuth had been out to buy himself a pair of boots and had gone inside the gate to put them on, placing his old footgear in the paper in which the new boots had been wrapped.

Bunting waited until Mr. Sleuth had let himself into the house; then he also walked up the flagged pathway, and put his latchkey in the door.

In the next three days each of Bunting's waking hours held its meed of aching fear and suspense. From his point of view, almost any alternative would be preferable to that which to most people would have seemed the only one open to him. He told himself that it would be ruin for him and for his Ellen to be mixed up publicly in such a terrible affair. It would track them to their dying day.

Bunting was also always debating within himself as to whether he should tell Ellen of his frightful suspicion. He could not believe that what had become so plain to himself could long be concealed from all the world, and yet he did not credit his wife with the same intelligence. He did not even notice that, although she waited on Mr. Sleuth as assiduously as ever, Mrs. Bunting never mentioned the lodger.

Mr. Sleuth, meanwhile, kept upstairs; he had given up going out altogether. He still felt, so he assured his landlady, far from well.

Daisy was another complication, the more so that the girl, whom her father longed to send away and whom he would hardly let out of his sight, showed herself inconveniently inquisitive concerning the lodger.

"Whatever does he do with himself all day?" she asked her step-mother.

"Well, just now he's reading the Bible," Mrs. Bunting had answered very shortly and dryly.

"Well, I never! That's a funny thing for a gentleman to do!" Such had been Daisy's pert remark, and her stepmother had snubbed her well for it.

Daisy's eighteenth birthday dawned uneventfully. Her father gave her what he had always promised she should have on her eighteenth birthday — a watch. It was a pretty little silver watch, which Bunting had bought secondhand on the last day he had been happy; it seemed a long time ago now.

Mrs. Bunting thought a silver watch a very extravagant present, but she had always had the good sense not to interfere between her husband and his child. Besides, her mind was now full of other things. She was beginning to fear that Bunting suspected something, and she was filled with watchful anxiety and unease. What if he were to do anything silly — mix them up with the police, for instance? It certainly would be ruination to them both. But there — one never knew, with men! Her husband, however, kept his own counsel absolutely.

Daisy's birthday was on Saturday. In the middle of the morning Ellen and Daisy went down into the kitchen. Bunting didn't like the feeling that there was only one flight of stairs between Mr. Sleuth and himself, so he quietly slipped out of the house and went to buy himself an ounce of tobacco.

In the last four days Bunting had avoided his usual haunts. But today the unfortunate man had a curious longing for human companionship — companionship, that is, other than that of Ellen and Daisy. This feeling led him into a small, populous thoroughfare hard by the Edgeware Road. There were more people there than usual, for the housewives of the neighborhood were doing their marketing for Sunday.

Bunting passed the time of day with the tobacconist, and the two fell into desultory talk. To the ex-butler's surprise, the man said nothing at all to him on the subject of which all the neighborhood must still be talking.

And then, quite suddenly, while still standing by the counter, and before he had paid for the packet of tobacco he held in his hand, Bunting, through the open door, saw, with horrified surprise, that his wife was standing outside a greengrocer's shop just opposite. Muttering a word of apology, he rushed out of the shop and across the road.

"Ellen!" he gasped hoarsely. "You've never gone and left my little girl alone in the house?"

Mrs. Bunting's face went chalky white. "I thought you were indoors," she said. "You *were* indoors. Whatever made you come out for, without first making sure I was there?"

Bunting made no answer; but, as they stared at each other in exasperated silence, *each knew that the other knew.*

They turned and scurried down the street.

"Don't run," he said suddenly. "We shall get there just as quickly if we walk fast. People are noticing you, Ellen. Don't run."

He spoke breathlessly, but it was breathlessness induced by fear and excitement, not by the quick pace at which they were walking.

At last they reached their own gate. Bunting pushed past in front of his wife. After all, Daisy was his child — Ellen couldn't know how he was feeling. He made the path almost in one leap, and fumbled for a moment with his latchkey. The door opened.

"Daisy!" he called out in a wailing voice. "Daisy, my dear, where are you?"

"Here I am, Father; what is it?"

"She's all right!" Bunting turned his gray face to his wife. "She's all right, Ellen!" Then he waited a moment, leaning against the wall of the passage. "It did give me a turn," he said. And then, warningly, "Don't frighten the girl, Ellen."

Daisy was standing before the fire in the sitting room, admiring herself in the glass. "Oh, Father," she said, without turning round, "I've seen the lodger! He's quite a nice gentleman — though, to be sure, he does look a cure! He came down to ask Ellen for something, and we had quite a nice little chat. I told him it was my birthday, and he asked me to go to Madame Tussaud's with him this afternoon." She laughed a little self-consciously. "Of course I could see he was 'centric, and then at first he spoke so funnily. 'And who be you?' he says, threatening-like. And I says to him, 'I'm Mr. Bunting's daughter, sir.' 'Then you're a very fortunate girl' — that's what he said, Ellen — 'to 'ave such a nice stepmother as you've got. That's why,' he says, 'you look such a good, innocent girl.' And then he quoted a bit of the prayer book at me. 'Keep innocency,' he says, wagging his head at me. Lor'! It made me feel as if I was with Aunt again."

"I won't have you going out with the lodger — that's flat." He was wiping his forehead with one hand, while with the other he mechanically squeezed the little packet of tobacco, for which, as he now remembered, he had forgotten to pay.

Daisy pouted. "Oh, Father, I think you might let me have a treat on my birthday! I told him Saturday wasn't a very good day — at least, so I'd heard — for Madame Tussaud's. Then he said we could go early, while the fine folk are still having their dinners. He wants you to come, too." She turned to her stepmother, then giggled happily. "The lodger has a wonderful fancy for you, Ellen; if I was Father, I'd feel quite jealous!"

Her last words were cut across by a loud knock on the door. Bunting and his wife looked at each other apprehensively.

Both felt a curious thrill of relief when they saw that it was only Mr. Sleuth — Mr. Sleuth dressed to go out: the tall hat he had worn when he first came to them was in his hand, and he was wearing a heavy overcoat.

"I saw you had come in" — he addressed Mrs. Bunting in his high, whistling, hesitating voice — "and so I've come down to ask if you and Miss Bunting will come to Madame Tussaud's now. I have never seen these famous waxworks, though I've heard of the place all my life."

As Bunting forced himself to look fixedly at his lodger, a sudden doubt, bringing with it a sense of immeasurable relief, came to him. Surely it was inconceivable that this gentle, mild-mannered gentleman could be the monster of cruelty and cunning that Bunting had but a moment ago believed him to be!

"You're very kind, sir, I'm sure." He tried to catch his wife's eye, but Mrs. Bunting was looking away, staring into vacancy. She still, of course, wore the bonnet and cloak in which she had just been out to do her marketing. Daisy was already putting on her hat and coat.

Madame Tussaud's had hitherto held pleasant memories for Mrs. Bunting. In the days when she and Bunting were courting they often spent part of their "afternoon out" there. The butler had an acquaintance, a man named Hopkins, who was one of the waxworks' staff, and this man had sometimes given him passes for "self and lady." But this was the first time Mrs. Bunting had been inside the place since she had come to live almost next door, as it were, to the big building.

The ill-sorted trio walked up the great staircase and into the first gallery; and there Mr. Sleuth suddenly stopped short. The presence of those curious, still figures, suggesting death in life, seemed to surprise and affright him.

Daisy took quick advantage of the lodger's hesitation and unease.

"Oh, Ellen," she cried, "do let us begin by going into the Chamber of Horrors! I've never been in there. Aunt made Father promise he wouldn't take me, the only time I've ever been here. But now that I'm eighteen I can do just as I like; besides, Aunt will never know!"

Mr. Sleuth looked down at her.

"Yes," he said, "let us go into the Chamber of Horrors; that's a good idea, Miss Bunting."

They turned into the great room in which the Napoleonic relics are kept, and which leads into the curious, vaultlike chamber where waxen effigies of dead criminals stand grouped in wooden docks. Mrs. Bunting was at once disturbed and relieved to see her husband's old acquaintance, Mr. Hopkins, in charge of the turnstile admitting the public to the Chamber of Horrors.

"Well, you *are* a stranger," the man observed genially. "I do believe this is the very first time I've seen you in here, Mrs. Bunting, since you married!"

"Yes," she said, "that is so. And this is my husband's daughter, Daisy. I expect you've heard of her, Mr. Hopkins. And this" — she hesitated a moment — "is our lodger, Mr. Sleuth."

But Mr. Sleuth frowned and shuffled away. Daisy, leaving her stepmother's side, joined him.

Mrs. Bunting put down three sixpences.

"Wait a minute," said Hopkins. "You can't go into the Chamber of Horrors just yet. But you won't have to wait more than four or five minutes, Mrs. Bunting. It's this way, you see; our boss is in there, showing a party round." He lowered his voice. "It's Sir John Burney — I suppose you know who Sir John Burney is?"

"No," she answered indifferently, "I don't know that I ever heard of him." She felt slightly — oh, very slightly — uneasy about Daisy.

She would like her stepdaughter to keep well within sight and sound. Mr. Sleuth was taking the girl to the other end of the room.

"Well, I hope you never *will* know him — not in any personal sense, Mrs. Bunting." The man chuckled. "He's the Head Commissioner of Police — that's what Sir John Burney is. One of the gentlemen he's showing round our place is the Paris Prefect of Police, whose job is on all fours, so to speak, with Sir John's. The Frenchy has brought his daughter with him, and there are several other ladies. Ladies always like 'orrors, Mrs. Bunting; that's our experience here. 'Oh, take me to the Chamber of 'Orrors!' — that's what they say the minute they gets into the building."

A group of people, all talking and laughing together, were advancing from within toward the turnstile.

Mrs. Bunting stared at them nervously. She wondered which of them was the gentleman with whom Mr. Hopkins had hoped she would never be brought into personal contact. She quickly picked him out. He was a tall, powerful, nice-looking gentleman with a commanding manner. Just now he was smiling down into the face of a young lady. "Monsieur Barberoux is quite right," he was saying, "the English law is too kind to the criminal, especially to the murderer. If we conducted our trials in the French fashion, the place we have just left would be very much fuller than it is today! A man of whose guilt we are absolutely assured is oftener than not acquitted, and then the public taunt us with 'another undiscovered crime'!"

"D'you mean, Sir John, that murderers sometimes escape scot-free? Take the man who has been committing all those awful murders this last month. Of course, I don't know much about it, for father won't let me read about it, but I can't help being interested!" Her girlish voice rang out, and Mrs. Bunting heard every word distinctly.

The party gathered round, listening eagerly to hear what the Head Commissioner would say next.

"Yes." He spoke very deliberately. "I think we may say — now, don't give me away to a newspaper fellow, Miss Rose — that we do know perfectly well who the murderer in question is —"

Several of those standing nearby uttered expressions of surprise and incredulity.

"Then why don't you catch him?" cried the girl indignantly.

"I didn't say we know *where* he is; I only said we know *who* he is; or, rather, perhaps I ought to say that we have a very strong suspicion of his identity."

Sir John's French colleague looked up quickly. "The Hamburg and Liverpool man?" he said interrogatively.

The other nodded. "Yes. I suppose you've had the case turned up?"

Then, speaking very quickly, as if he wished to dismiss the subject from his own mind and from that of his auditors, he went on:

"Two murders of the kind were committed eight years ago — one in Hamburg, the other just afterward in Liverpool, and there were certain peculiarities connected with the crimes which made it clear they were committed by the same hand. The perpetrator was caught, fortunately for us red-handed, just as he was leaving the house of his victim, for in Liverpool the murder was committed in a house. I myself saw the unhappy man — I say unhappy, for there is no doubt at all that he was mad" — he hesitated, and added in a lower tone — "suffering from an acute form of religious mania. I myself saw him, at some length. But now comes the really interesting point. Just a month ago this criminal lunatic, as we must regard him, made his escape from the asylum where he was confined. He arranged the whole thing with extraordinary cunning and intelligence, and we should probably have caught him long ago were it not that he managed, when on his way out of the place, to annex a considerable sum of money in gold with which the wages of the staff were about to be paid."

The Frenchman again spoke. "Why have you not circulated a description?" he asked.

"We did that at once" — Sir John Burney smiled a little grimly — "but only among our own people. We dare not circulate the man's description among the general public. You see, we may be mistaken, after all."

"That is not very probable!" The Frenchman smiled a satirical little smile.

A moment later the party were walking in Indian file through the turnstile, Sir John Burney leading the way.

Mrs. Bunting looked straight before her. Even had she wished to do so, she had neither time nor power to warn her lodger of his danger.

Daisy and her companion were now coming down the room, bearing straight for the Head Commissioner of Police. In another moment Mr. Sleuth and Sir John Burney would be face to face.

Suddenly Mr. Sleuth swerved to one side. A terrible change came over his pale, narrow face; it became discomposed, livid with rage and terror.

But, to Mrs. Bunting's relief — yes, to her inexpressible relief — Sir John Burney and his friends swept on. They passed by Mr. Sleuth unconcernedly, unaware, or so it seemed to her, that there was anyone else in the room but themselves.

"Hurry up, Mrs. Bunting," said the turnstile keeper. "You and your friends will have the place all to yourselves." From an official he had become a man, and it was the man in Mr. Hopkins that gallantly addressed pretty Daisy Bunting. "It seems strange that a young lady like you should want to go in and see all those 'orrible frights," he said jestingly.

"Mrs. Bunting, may I trouble you to come over here for a moment?" The words were hissed rather than spoken by Mr. Sleuth's lips.

His landlady took a doubtful step forward.

"A last word with you, Mrs. Bunting." The lodger's face was still distorted with fear and passion. "Do you think to escape the consequences of your hideous treachery? I trusted you, Mrs. Bunting, and you betrayed me! But I am protected by a higher power, for I still have work to do. Your end will be bitter as wormwood and sharp as a two-edged sword. Your feet shall go down to death, and your steps take hold on hell." Even while Mr. Sleuth was uttering these strange, dreadful words, he was looking around, his eyes glancing this way and that, seeking a way of escape.

At last his eyes became fixed on a small placard placed about a curtain. "Emergency Exit" was written there. Leaving his landlady's side, he walked over to the turnstile. He fumbled in his pocket for a moment, and then touched the man on the arm. "I feel ill," he said, speaking very rapidly, "very ill indeed! It's the atmosphere of this place. I want you to let me out by the quickest way. It would be a pity for me to faint here — especially with ladies about." His left hand shot out and placed what he had been fumbling for in his pocket on the other's bare palm. "I see there's an emergency exit over there. Would it be possible for me to get out that way?"

"Well, yes, sir. I think so." The man hesitated; he felt a slight, a very slight, feeling of misgiving. He looked at Daisy, flushed and smiling, happy and unconcerned, and then at Mrs. Bunting. She was very pale, but surely her lodger's sudden seizure was enough to make her feel worried. Hopkins felt the half sovereign pleasantly tickling his palm. The Prefect of Police had given him only half a crown — mean, shabby foreigner!

"Yes, I can let you out that way," he said at last, "and perhaps when you're standing out in the air on the iron balcony you'll feel better. But then, you know sir, you'll have to come round to the front if you want to come in again, for those emergency doors only open outward."

"Yes, yes," said Mr. Sleuth hurriedly, "I quite understand! If I feel better I'll come in by the front way, and pay another shilling — that's only fair."

"You needn't do that if you'll just explain what happened here."

The man went and pulled the curtain aside, and put his shoulder against the door. It burst open, and the light for a moment blinded Mr. Sleuth. He passed his hand over his eyes.

"Thank you," he said, "thank you. I shall get all right here."

Five days later Bunting identified the body of a man found drowned in the Regent's Canal as that of his late lodger; and the morning following, a gardener working in the Regent's Park found a newspaper in which were wrapped, together with a half-worn pair of rubber-soled shoes, two surgical knives. This fact was not chronicled in any newspaper; but a very pretty and picturesque paragraph went the round of the press, about the same time, concerning a small box filled with sovereigns which had been forwarded anonymously to the Governor of the Foundling Hospital.

Mr. and Mrs. Bunting are now in the service of an old lady, by whom they are feared as well as respected, and whom they make very comfortable.

MARCEL ALLAIN
AND
PIERRE SOUVESTRE

PRINCESS
SONIA'S
BATH

The film director Louis Malle calls Fantomâs "one of the greatest characters
of French popular literature." Fantomâs was a crook, of course, a dashing,
mysterious master of a thousand disguises who put the lie to the silly notion
that crime doesn't pay. He is what Professor Moriarty might have become if
that "Napoleon of crime" had had a Paris tailor and no Sherlock Holmes to
bother with. Fantomâs first appeared as the eponymous hero of a novel of
comic-strip complexity in 1911. Before the series ran its course, there were
thirty-one sequels. The poet Apollinaire called Fantomâs *"one of the richest*
works that exists." It inspired James Joyce to make up a word: enfantomastic.
　　The authors — Marcel Allain (1885–1969) and Pierre Souvestre (1874–
1914) — were both law students who turned to journalism and began their
collaboration when they worked on the trade magazine Poids Lourds *("Heavy*
Trucks"). The poet John Ashbery calls them "inspired hacks."
　　"Princess Sonia's Bath" is a chapter from the first Fantomâs adventure.

FOUR MONTHS had passed since Etienne Rambert had been acquitted
at the Cahors courthouse, and the world was beginning to forget the
Beaulieu tragedy as it had already almost forgotten the mysterious
murder of Lord Beltham. Juve alone did not allow his daily occupations to put the two cases out of his mind. True, he had ceased to
make any direct inquiries and gave no outward signs that he still had
any interest in those cases; but the detective knew very well that in
both of them he was contending with no ordinary murderer and he
was content to remain in the shadows, waiting and watching, seemingly
inactive, waiting for some slip to betray the person or persons who

had perpetrated two of the most puzzling murders that he had ever had to deal with.

It was the end of June, and Paris was beginning to empty out. But the spring had been late and cold that year, and although July was only a couple of days away, society lingered on in the capital; luxuriously appointed carriages still swept along the Champs Elysées as the audiences poured out of theaters and concert halls, and fashionably attired people still thronged the broad pavements and gathered before the brilliantly lighted cafés on the Rond-Point; even at that late hour the Champs Elysées was as animated as it was during the busiest hours of the day.

At the Royal Palace Hotel the entire staff still hurried about the vast entrance halls and the palatial public rooms on the ground floor; for it was the hour when the guests were returning from their evening's amusements, and the spacious vestibules of the immense hotel were crowded with men in evening dress, young fellows in dinner jackets, and women in low-cut gowns.

A young and fashionable woman got out of a perfectly appointed victoria, and M. Louis, the manager of the staff, came forward and bowed deeply, as he did only to clients of the very highest distinction. The lady responded with a gracious smile, and the manager called a servant: "The elevator for Madame la Princesse Sonia Danidoff," and the next moment this beautiful vision, who had created a sensation merely by passing through the hall, had disappeared within the elevator and was borne up to her apartments.

Princess Sonia was one of the most important clients that the Royal Palace Hotel possessed. She belonged to one of the greatest families in the world, being, by her marriage to Prince Danidoff, cousin to the emperor of Russia and, so, connected to many people of royal blood. Still barely thirty years of age, she was not pretty but remarkably lovely, with wonderful blue eyes that formed a strange and bewitching contrast to the heavy masses of black hair that framed her face. A woman of immense wealth and sophistication, the princess spent six months of the year in Paris, where she was a well-known and much liked figure in the most exclusive circles; she was clever and cultivated, a first-rate musician, and her reputation was impeccable, although only very seldom was she accompanied by her husband, whose duties as grand chamberlain to the czar kept him almost continuously in Russia. When in Paris she occupied a suite of four rooms on the third floor of the Royal Palace Hotel, a suite identical in its layout and luxuriousness with that reserved for sovereigns who came there incognito.

The princess passed through her drawing room, a vast, round room with a superb view over the Arc de Triomphe, and went into her bedroom where she switched on the electric light.

"Nadine," she called, in her grave, melodious voice, and a young girl, almost a child, sprang from a low divan hidden in a corner. "Nadine, take off my cloak and unfasten my hair. Then you can leave; it is late, and I am tired."

The little maid obeyed, helped her mistress to put on a silk dressing gown, and loosened the masses of her hair. The princess passed a hand across her brow, as if to brush away a headache.

"Before you go, get a bath ready for me; I think that would relax me."

Ten minutes later Nadine crept back like a shadow and found the princess standing dreamily on the balcony, inhaling deep breaths of the pure night air. The child kissed the tips of her mistress's fingers. "Your bath is ready," she said, and then withdrew.

A few more minutes passed, and Princess Sonia, half undressed, was just going into her dressing room when suddenly she turned and went back to the middle of the bedroom which she had been on the point of leaving.

"Nadine," she called, "are you still there?" No answer came. "I must have been dreaming," the princess murmured, "but I thought I heard someone moving about."

Sonia Danidoff was not unusually nervous, but like most people who live mostly alone and in large hotels, she was in the habit of being careful, and wished to make sure that no uninvited person had gotten into her rooms. She made a rapid survey of her bedroom, glanced into the brilliantly lighted drawing room, and then moved to her bed and saw that the electric bell board, which enabled her to summon any of her own or the hotel's servants, was in perfect order. Then, satisfied, she went into her dressing room, quickly slipped off the rest of her clothes, and plunged into the perfumed water of her bath.

She thrilled with pleasure as her limbs, so tired after a long evening, relaxed in the warm water. On a table close to the bath she had placed a volume of old Muscovite folk tales, and she was glancing through these by the shaded light from a lamp above her when a fresh sound made her start. She sat up quickly in the water and looked around her. There was nothing there. Then a little shiver shook her and she sank down again in the warm bath with a laugh at her own nervousness. And she was just beginning to read once more when suddenly a strange voice, with an unmistakable ring of malice in it, sounded in her ear. Someone was looking over her shoulder and reading aloud the words she had just begun!

Before Sonia Danidoff had time to utter a cry or make a movement, a strong hand was over her lips, and another gripped her wrist, preventing her from reaching the button of the electric bell that was fixed among the taps. The princess almost fainted. She was expecting some horrible shock, expecting to feel some weapon that would take her life, when the pressure on her mouth and the grip on her wrist gradually relaxed; and at the same moment the mysterious individual who had taken her by surprise moved around the bathtub and stood in front of her.

He was a man of about forty years of age, and extremely well dressed. A perfectly cut dinner jacket proved that the strange visitor was no lowly dweller of the Paris slums, no thug such as the princess had read terrifying descriptions of in luridly illustrated newspapers. The hands that had held her motionless, and which now restored to her liberty of movement, were white and well manicured and adorned with a few plain rings. The man's face was a distinguished one, and he wore a very fine black beard; slight baldness added to the height of a naturally large forehead. But what struck the princess most, although she had no heart to observe the man very carefully, was the abnormal size of his head and the number of wrinkles that ran right across his temples, following the line of the eyebrows.

In silence and with trembling lips Sonia Danidoff made an instinctive effort again to reach the electric bell, but with a quick movement the man caught her shoulder and prevented her from doing so. There was a cryptic smile on the stranger's lips, and with a furious blush Sonia Danidoff dived back again into the milky water in the bath.

The man stood in perfect silence, and at length the princess mastered her terror and spoke to him.

"Who are you? What do you want? Go at once or I will call for help."

"Above all things, do not call out, or you are a dead woman!" said the stranger harshly. Then he gave a little ironical shrug of his shoulders. "As for ringing — that would not be easy; you would have to leave the water to do so! And, besides, I would object."

"If it is money or jewelry you want," said the princess between clenched teeth, "take them! But please go!"

The princess had laid several rings and bracelets on the table by her side, and the man glanced at them now, but without paying much attention to what the princess said.

"Those trinkets are not bad," he said, "but your signet ring is much finer," and he calmly took the princess's hand in his and examined the ring that she had kept on her third finger. "Don't be frightened," he added as he felt her hand trembling. "Let us chat, if you don't mind! There is nothing especially tempting about jewels apart from their personality," he said after a little pause, "apart, I mean, from the person who habitually wears them. But the bracelet on a wrist, or the necklace round a neck, or the ring upon a finger is another matter!"

Princess Sonia was as pale as death and utterly at a loss to understand what this extraordinary visitor was driving at. She held up her ring finger and made a frightened little apology.

"I cannot take this ring off; it fits too tightly."

The man laughed grimly.

"That does not matter in the least, Princess. Anyone who wanted to get a ring like that could do it quite simply." He felt absent-mindedly in his waistcoat pocket and produced a miniature razor, which he opened. He flashed the blade before the terrified eyes of the princess. "With a sharp blade like this a skillful man could cut off the finger that carried such a splendid jewel in a couple of seconds," and then, seeing that the princess, in fresh panic, was on the very point of screaming, quick as a flash he laid the palm of his hand over her lips, while still speaking in gentle tones to her. "Please do not be so terrified; I suppose you take me for some common hotel thief, but, Princess, can you really believe that I am anything of the kind?"

The man's tone was so earnest, and there was so deferential a look in his eyes, that the princess recovered some of her courage.

"But I do not know who you are," she said half-questioningly.

"So much the better," the man replied; "there is still time to make one another's acquaintance. I know who you are, and that is the main thing. You do not know me, Princess? Well, I assure you that on many occasions I have mingled with the blessed company of your adorers!"

The princess's anger rose steadily with her courage.

"Sir," she said, "I do not know if you are joking or if you are talking seriously, but your behavior is extraordinary, hateful, disgusting —"

"It is merely original, Princess, and it pleases me to reflect that if I had wanted to be presented to you in the ordinary way, in one of the many drawing rooms we both frequent, you would certainly have taken much less notice of me than you have taken tonight; from the persistence of your gaze I can see that from this day onward not a single feature of my face will be unfamiliar to you, and I am convinced that, whatever happens, you will remember it for a very long time."

Princess Sonia tried to force a smile. She had recovered her self-possession and was wondering what kind of man she had to deal with. If she was still not quite persuaded that this was not a vulgar thief, and if she had little faith in his professions of admiration for herself, she was considerably alarmed by the idea that she was alone with a lunatic. The man seemed to read her thoughts for he, too, smiled a little.

"I am glad to see, Princess, that you have a little more self-confidence now; we shall be able to arrange things much more easily. You are certainly much calmer, much less uneasy now. Oh, yes, you are!" he added, checking her protest. "Why, it is quite five minutes since you last tried to ring for help. We are getting on. Besides, I somehow can't picture the Princess Sonia Danidoff, wife of the grand chamberlain and cousin of His Majesty the emperor of all the Russias, allowing herself to be surprised alone with a man whom she did not know. If she were to ring, and someone came, how would the princess account for the gentleman to whom she had accorded an audience in the most delightful but certainly the most private of all her apartments?"

"But tell me," pleaded the poor woman, "how did you get in here?"

"That is not the question," the stranger replied. "The problem actually before us is, how am I to get out? For, of course, Princess, I shall not be so indelicate as to prolong my visit unduly. I hope only that you will permit me to repeat it on some other evening soon." He turned his head, and plunging his hand into the bath in the most natural manner possible, took out the thermometer which was floating on the perfumed water. "Thirty degrees centigrade, Princess! Your bath is getting cold; you must get out!"

In her blank astonishment Princess Sonia did not know whether to laugh or cry. Was she alone with a monster who, after having played with her as a cat plays with a mouse, would suddenly turn on her and kill her? Or was this merely some harmless lunatic? Whatever the case might be, the man's last words had made her aware that her bath really was getting cold. A shiver shook her whole frame, and yet —

"Oh, go, please go!" she implored him.

He shook his head, an ironical smile in his eyes.

"For pity's sake," she entreated him again, "have mercy on a helpless woman!"

The man appeared to be considering.

"It is very embarrassing," he murmured, "and yet we must decide on something soon, for I am most anxious you should not take a chill. Oh, it is very simple, Princess; of course you know the arrangement of everything here so well that you could find your dressing gown at once, by merely feeling your way? We will put out the light, and then you will be able to get out of the bath in the dark without the least fear." He was on the very point of turning off the switch of the lamp when he stopped abruptly and came back to the bath. "I was forgetting that exasperating bell," he said. "A movement is so very easily made; suppose you were to ring inadvertently, and regret it afterward?" Putting his idea into action, the man made a quick cut with his razor and severed the two electric wires several feet above the ground. "That is perfect," he said. "By the way, I don't know where these other two wires go that run along the wall, but it is best to be on the safe side. Suppose there were another bell." He lifted his razor once more and was trying to sever the electric wires when the steel blade cut the insulator and an alarming flash of light resulted. The man leaped into the air and dropped his razor. "Good Lord!" he growled. "I suppose that will make you happy, Madame; I have burned my hand most horribly! These must be wires for the light! But no matter; I have still got one good hand, and that will be enough for me to secure the darkness that you desire. And anyhow, you can press the button of your bell as much as you like; it won't ring. So I am sure of a few more minutes in your company.

Sudden darkness fell upon the room. Sonia Danidoff hesitated for a moment and then half rose in the bath. All her pride as a great lady was in revolt. If she must defend her honor and her life, she was ready to do so, and desperation would give her strength; but in any event she would be better out of the water and on her feet, prepared. The darkness was complete, both in the bathroom and in the adjacent bedroom, and the silence was absolute. Standing up in the bath, Sonia Danidoff swept her arms around in a circle to feel for any obstacle. Her touch met nothing. She drew out one foot, and then the other, sprang toward the chair on which she had left her dressing gown, slipped into it with feverish haste, slid her feet into her slippers, stood motionless for just a second, and then, with sudden decisiveness, moved to the switch by the door and turned on the light.

The man had gone from the bathroom, but taking two steps toward her bedroom Sonia Danidoff saw him smiling at her from the far end of that room.

"Sir," she said, "this — pleasant visit — has lasted long enough. You must go. You must!"

"Must?" the stranger echoed. "That is a word that is not often said to me. But you are forgiven for not knowing that, Princess. I forgot for the moment that I have not been formally introduced to you. But what is on your mind now?"

Between them was a little writing desk, on the top of which was lying the tiny inlaid revolver that Sonia Danidoff always carried when she went out at night. If she could get to it, it would be a potent argument to induce this stranger to obey her. The princess also knew that in the drawer of that desk which she could actually see half open, she had placed, only a few minutes before going in to her bath, a pocketbook filled with bank notes for 120,000 francs, money she had withdrawn from the strongbox of the hotel that very morning in order to meet some bills next day. She looked at the drawer and wondered if the pocketbook were still there, or if this mysterious admirer of hers was only a vulgar hotel thief after all. The man had followed her eyes to the revolver.

"That is an unusual knickknack to find in a lady's room, Princess," and he sprang in front of her as she was taking a step toward the desk, and grabbed the revolver. "Do not be alarmed," he added, noticing her little gesture of terror. "I would not do you an injury for anything in the world. I shall be delighted to give this back to you in a minute, but first let me render it harmless." He deftly slipped the six cartridges out of the barrel and then handed the now useless weapon to the princess with a gallant little bow. "Do not laugh at my extreme caution; accidents happen so easily!"

It was in vain that the princess tried to get near her writing desk to ascertain if the drawer had been tampered with; the man stayed between her and it all the time, still smiling, still polite, but watching every movement she made. Suddenly he took his watch from his pocket.

"Two o'clock! Already! Princess, you will be annoyed with me for having imposed upon your hospitality to such an extent. I must go!" He appeared not to notice the sigh of relief that broke from her but went on in a melodramatic tone. "I shall take my departure, not through the window like a lover, nor up the chimney like a thief, nor yet through a secret door behind the tapestry like a bandit in romantic tales, but like a gentleman who has come to pay his tribute of homage and respect to the most enchanting woman in the world — through the door!" He made a movement as if to go, and came back. "And what are you thinking of doing now, Princess? Perhaps you will be angry with me? Possibly some unpleasant discovery, made after my departure, will inspire your animosity against me? You might even ring as soon as my back is turned and alarm the staff, merely to embarrass me in my exit and without paying any attention to the possible subsequent scandal. That is a complex arrangement of bells and telephones beside your bed! It would be a pity to spoil such a pretty thing, and besides, I hate doing unnecessary damage!" The princess's eyes turned once more to the drawer; it was practically certain that her money was not there now! But the man again interrupted her thoughts. "What can I be thinking of? Just imagine my not having presented myself to you even yet! But as a matter of fact I do not want to tell you my name out loud; it is a romantic one, utterly inappropriate to the typically modern environment in which we now stand. Ah, if we were only on the steep side of some mountain with the moon like a great lamp above us, or by the shore of some wild ocean, there would be some glamour in proclaiming my identity in the silence of the night, or in the midst of lightning and thunder as a hurricane swept the seas! But here — in a third-floor suite of the Royal Palace Hotel, surrounded by telephones and electric lights, and standing by a window overlooking the Champs Elysées — it would be positively anachronistic!" He took a card out of his pocket and drew near the little writing desk. "Allow me, Princess, to slip my card into this drawer, left open on purpose, it would seem," and while the princess uttered a little cry she could not repress, he did just that. "And now, Princess," he went on, compelling her to retreat before him as he moved to the door of the anteroom opening on to the corridor, "you are too well bred, I am sure, not to wish to conduct your visitor to the door of your suite." His tone altered abruptly, and in a deep imperious voice that made the princess quake he ordered her: "And now, not a word, not a cry, not a movement until I am outside, or I will kill you!"

Clenching her fists and summoning all her strength to prevent herself from swooning, Sonia Danidoff led the man to the anteroom door. Slowly she unlocked the door and held it open, and the man stepped quietly out. The next second he was gone!

Leaping back into her bedroom Sonia Danidoff set off every bell ringing; with great presence of mind she telephoned down to the hall porter: "Don't let anybody go out! I have been robbed!" and she pressed hard on the special button that set the great alarm bell clanging. Footsteps and voices resounded in the corridor; the princess knew that help was coming and ran to open her door. The night watchman and the manager of the third floor came running up and bellboys appeared at the end of the corridor.

"Stop him! Stop him!" the princess shouted. "He has only just gone out; a man in a dinner jacket with a black beard!"

A lad came hurrying out of the elevator.

"Where are you going? What is the matter?" inquired the hall porter, whose office was at the far end of the hall, next to the courtyard of the hotel, the door into which he had just closed.

"I don't know," he answered. "There is a thief in the hotel! They are calling from the other side."

"It's not in your area, then? By the way, what floor are you on?"

"The second."

"All right," said the hall porter, "it's the third floor that they are calling from. Go up and see what is wrong."

The lad turned on his heel, and disregarding the sign forbidding staff to use the guest elevator, hurried back into it and upstairs again. He was a solidly built fellow, with a smooth face and red hair. On the third floor he stopped immediately opposite Sonia Danidoff's suite. The princess was standing at her door, taking no notice of the watchman Muller's efforts to calm her, and mechanically twisting between her fingers the blank visiting card that her strange visitor had left in place of her pocketbook and the 120,000 francs. There was no name whatever on the card.

"Well," said Muller to the redheaded lad, "where do you come from?"

"I'm the new man on the second floor," the fellow answered. "The hall porter sent me up to find out what was going on."

"Going on!" said Muller. "Somebody has robbed the princess. Here, send someone for the police at once."

"I'll run, sir," and as the elevator, instead of being sent down, had carelessly been sent up to the top floor, the young fellow ran down the staircase at full speed.

Through the telephone, Muller was just ordering the hall porter to send for the police when the second-floor servant rushed up and caught him by the arm, dragging him away from it.

"Open the door, for the Lord's sake! I'm off to the police station," and the hall porter made haste to facilitate his departure.

Through the top floor echoed more cries of astonishment. The servants had been alarmed by the uproar and, surprised to see the elevator stop and nobody get out of it, they opened the door and found a heap of clothing, a false beard, and a wig. Two housemaids and a valet gazed in amazement at these extraordinary things and never thought of informing the manager, M. Louis. Meantime, however, that gentleman had hurried through the mazelike service passages of the hotel and had just reached the third floor when he was stopped by the Baronne Van den Rosen, one of the hotel's oldest clients.

"M. Louis!" she exclaimed, bursting into sobs. "I have just been robbed of my diamond necklace. I left it in a jewel case on my table before going down to dinner. When I heard the noise just now, I got up and looked through my jewel case, and the necklace is not there."

M. Louis was too dazed to reply. Muller ran up to him.

"Princess Sonia Danidoff's pocketbook has been stolen," he announced, "but I have had the hotel doors locked and we shall be sure to catch the thief."

The princess came up to explain matters, but at that moment the servants came down from upstairs, bringing with them the articles of disguise that they had found in the elevator. They laid these on the ground without a word, and M. Louis was staring at them when Muller had a sudden inspiration.

"M. Louis, what is the new man on the second floor like?"

Just at that instant a servant appeared at the end of the corridor, a middle-aged man with white whiskers and a bald head.

"There he is, coming toward us," M. Louis replied. "His name is Arnold."

"Good God!" cried Muller. "And the redheaded fellow?" M. Louis shook his head, not understanding, and Muller tore himself away and rushed down to the hall porter. "Has he gone out? Has anyone gone out?"

"No one," said the porter, "except, of course, the servant from the second floor, whom you sent for the police."

"The redheaded fellow?" Muller inquired.

"Yes, that's the one."

Princess Sonia Danidoff lay back in an armchair, receiving the anxious attentions of Nadine, her Circassian maid. M. Louis was holding salts to her nose. The princess still held the card left by the mysterious stranger who had just robbed her so cleverly of 120,000 francs. As she slowly came to, the princess, fascinated, gazed at the card, and this time her haggard eyes grew wide with astonishment. For upon the card, which until now had appeared immaculately white, letters were gradually becoming visible, and the princess read:

"Fan — tô — mas!"

EDGAR WALLACE

THE INVESTORS

Trivia experts may remember Edgar Wallace (1875–1932) as the British novelist who wrote the film script for King Kong, *but in his day he was called the King of the Thrillers. Someone — probably a press agent or a graduate student — figured that one out of every four books read in England in the 1920s and 1930s was written by Wallace. Most of them — with such heroes as Derrick Yale ("the amazing psychometrical detective"), Surefoot Smith, the Black (a masked American spy who runs around in a black outfit), the Ringer, the Twister, the Squealer, and Four Square Jane — are best forgotten.*

But his truly memorable creation is Mr. J. G. Reeder, who with his unvarying commuter schedule and tightly rolled umbrella seems a caricature of the mild-mannered bachelor London clerk. In fact, he is all that, but he is also a detective with the mind of a master criminal. And he is armed, which is unusual for a British detective in 1925. There's a knife in that umbrella handle and a pistol in a hidden pocket. Best of all, Mr. Reeder — or is it Mr. Wallace? — has a sly sense of humor.

THERE ARE SEVEN million people in Greater London and each one of those seven millions is in theory and practice equal under the law and commonly precious to the community. So that, if one is wilfully wronged, another must be punished; and if one dies of premeditated violence, his slayer must hang by the neck until he be dead.

It is rather difficult for the sharpest law-eyes to keep tag of seven million people, at least one million of whom never keep still and are generally unattached to any particular domicile. It is equally difficult to place an odd twenty thousand or so who have domiciles but no human association. These include tramps, aged maiden ladies in affluent circumstances, peripatetic members of the criminal classes, and other friendless individuals.

Sometimes uneasy inquiries come through to headquarters. Mainly they are most timid and deferential. Mr. X. has not seen his neighbour, Mr. Y., for a week. No, he doesn't know Mr. Y. Nobody does. A little old man who had no friends and spent his fine days pottering in a garden overlooked by his more gregarious neighbour. And now Mr. Y. potters no more. His milk has not been taken in; his blinds are drawn. Come a sergeant of police and a constable who break a window and climb through, and Mr. Y. is dead somewhere — dead of starvation or a fit of suicide. Should this be the case, all is plain sailing. But suppose the house empty and Mr. Y. disappeared. Here the situation becomes difficult and delicate.

Miss Elver went away to Switzerland. She was a middle-aged spinster who had the appearance of being comfortably circumstanced. She went away, locked up her house, and never came back. Switzerland looked for her; the myrmidons of Mussolini, that hatefully efficient man, searched North Italy from Domodossola to Montecatini. And the search did not yield a thin-faced maiden lady with a slight squint.

And then Mr. Charles Boyson Middlekirk, an eccentric and over-powering old man who quarrelled with his neighbours about their noisy children, he too went away. He told nobody where he was going. He lived alone with his three cats and was not on speaking terms with anybody else. He did not return to his grimy house.

He too was well off and reputedly a miser. So was Mrs. Athbell Marting, a dour widow who lived with her drudge of a niece. This lady was in the habit of disappearing without any preliminary announcement of her intention. The niece was allowed to order from the local tradesmen just sufficient food to keep body and soul together, and when Mrs. Marting returned (as she invariably did) the bills were settled with a great deal of grumbling on the part of the payer, and that was that. It was believed that Mrs. Marting went to Boulogne or to Paris or even to Brussels. But one day she went out and never came back. Six months later her niece advertised for her, choosing the cheapest papers — having an eye to the day of reckoning.

"Queer sort of thing," said the Public Prosecutor, who had before him the dossiers of four people (three women and a man) who had so vanished in three months.

He frowned, pressed a bell, and Mr. Reeder came in. Mr. Reeder took the chair that was indicated, looked owlishly over his glasses, and shook his head as though he understood the reason for his summons and denied his understanding in advance.

"What do you make of these disappearances?" asked his chief.

"You cannot make any positive of a negative," said Mr. Reeder carefully. "London is a large place full of strange, mad people who live such — um — commonplace lives that the wonder is that more of them do not disappear in order to do something different from what they are accustomed to doing."

"Have you seen these particulars?"

Mr. Reeder nodded.

"I have copies of them," he said. "Mr. Salter very kindly —"

The Public Prosecutor rubbed his head in perplexity.

"I see nothing in these cases — nothing in common, I mean. Four is a fairly low average for a big city —"

"Twenty-seven in twelve months," interrupted his detective apologetically.

"Twenty-seven — are you sure?" The great official was astounded.

Mr. Reeder nodded again.

"They were all people with a little money; all were drawing a fairly large income, which was paid to them in bank-notes on the first of every month — nineteen of them were, at any rate. I have yet to verify eight — and they were all most reticent as to where their revenues came from. None of them had any personal friends or relatives who were on terms of friendship, except Mrs. Marting. Beyond these points of resemblance there was nothing to connect one with the other."

The Prosecutor looked at him sharply, but Mr. Reeder was never sarcastic. Not obviously so, at any rate.

"There is another point which I omitted to mention," he went on. "After their disappearance no further money came for them. It came for Mrs. Marting when she was away on her jaunts, but it ceased when she went away on her final journey."

"But twenty-seven — are you sure?"

Mr. Reeder reeled off the list, giving name, address, and date of disappearance.

"What do you think has happened to them?"

Mr. Reeder considered for a moment, staring glumly at the carpet.

"I should imagine that they were murdered," he said, almost cheerfully, and the Prosecutor half rose from his chair.

"You are in your gayest mood this morning, Mr. Reeder," he said sardonically. "Why on earth should they be murdered?"

Mr. Reeder did not explain. The interview took place in the late afternoon, and he was anxious to be gone, for he had a tacit appointment to meet a young lady of exceeding charm who at five minutes after five would be waiting on the corner of Westminster Bridge and Thames Embankment for the Lee car.

The sentimental qualities of Mr. Reeder were entirely unknown. There are those who say that his sorrow over those whom fate and ill-fortune brought into his punitive hands was the veriest hypocrisy. There were others who believed that he was genuinely pained to see a fellow-creature sent behind bars through his efforts and evidence.

His housekeeper, who thought he was a woman-hater, told her friends in confidence that he was a complete stranger to the tender emotions which enlighten and glorify humanity. In the ten years which she had sacrificed to his service he had displayed neither emotion nor tenderness except to inquire whether her sciatica was better or to express a wish that she should take a holiday by the sea. She was a woman beyond middle age, but there is no period of life wherein a woman gives up hoping for the best. Though the most perfect of servants in all respects, she secretly despised him, called him, to her intimates, a frump, and suspected him of living apart from an ill-treated wife. This lady was a widow (as she had told him when he first engaged her) and she had seen better — far better — days.

Her visible attitude toward Mr. Reeder was one of respect and awe. She excused the queer character of his callers and his low acquaintances. She forgave him his square-toed shoes and high, flat-crowned hat, and even admired the ready-made Ascot cravat he wore and which was fastened behind the collar with a little buckle, the prongs of which invariably punctured his fingers when he fastened it. But there is a limit to all hero-worship, and when she discovered that Mr. Reeder was in the habit of waiting to escort a young lady to town every day, and frequently found it convenient to escort her home, the limit was reached.

Mrs. Hambleton told her friends — and they agreed — that there was no fool like an old fool, and that marriages between the old and the young invariably end in the divorce court (December *v.* May and July). She used to leave copies of a favourite Sunday newspaper on his table, where he could not fail to see the flaring headlines:

OLD MAN'S WEDDING ROMANCE
WIFE'S PERFIDY BRINGS GREY HAIR IN SORROW
TO THE LAW COURTS.

Whether Mr. Reeder perused these human documents she did not know. He never referred to the tragedies of ill-assorted unions, and went on meeting Miss Belman every morning at nine o'clock and at five-five in the afternoons whenever his business permitted.

He so rarely discussed his own business or introduced the subject that was exercising his mind that it was remarkable he should make even an oblique reference to his work. Possibly he would not have done so if Miss Margaret Belman had not introduced (unwillingly) a leader of conversation which traced indirectly to the disappearances.

They had been talking of holidays: Margaret was going to Cromer for a fortnight.

"I shall leave on the second. My monthly dividends (doesn't that sound grand?) are due on the first —"

"Eh?"

Reeder slued round. Dividends in most companies are paid at half-yearly intervals.

"Dividends, Miss Margaret?"

She flushed a little at his surprise and then laughed.

"You didn't realise that I was a woman of property?" she bantered him. "I receive ten pounds a month — my father left me a little house property when he died. I sold the cottages two years ago for a thousand pounds and found a wonderful investment."

Mr. Reeder made a rapid calculation.

"You are drawing something like 12½ per cent," he said. "That is indeed a wonderful investment. What is the name of the company?"

She hesitated.

"I'm afraid I can't tell you that. You see — well, it's rather secret. It is to do with a South American syndicate that supplies arms to — what do you call them — insurgents! I know it is rather dreadful to make money that way — I mean out of arms and things, but it pays terribly well and I can't afford to miss the opportunity."

Reeder frowned.

"But why is it such a terrible secret?" he asked. "Quite a number of respectable people make money out of armament concerns."

Again she showed reluctance to explain her meaning.

"We are pledged — the shareholders, I mean — not to divulge our connection with the company," she said. "That is one of the agreements I had to sign. And the money comes regularly. I have had nearly £300 of my thousand back in dividends already."

"Humph!" said Mr. Reeder, wise enough not to press his question. There was another day tomorrow.

But the opportunity to which he looked forward on the following morning was denied to him. Somebody played a grim "joke" on him — the kind of joke to which he was accustomed, for there were men who had good reason to hate him, and never a year passed but one or the other sought to repay him for his unkindly attentions.

"Your name is Reeder, ain't it?"

Mr. Reeder, tightly grasping his umbrella with both hands, looked over his spectacles at the shabby man who stood at the bottom of the steps. He was on the point of leaving his house in the Brockley Road for his office in Whitehall, and since he was a methodical man and worked to a time table, he resented in his mild way this interruption which had already cost him fifteen seconds of valuable time.

"You're the fellow who shopped Ike Walker, ain't you?"

Mr. Reeder had indeed "shopped" many men. He was by profession a shopper, which, translated from the argot, means a man who procures the arrest of an evildoer. Ike Walker he knew very well indeed. He was a clever, a too clever, forger of bills of exchange, and was at that precise moment almost permanently employed as orderly in the convict prison at Dartmoor, and might account himself fortunate if he held this easy job for the rest of his twelve years' sentence.

His interrogator was a little hard-faced man wearing a suit that had evidently been originally intended for somebody of greater girth and more commanding height. His trousers were turned up noticeably; his waistcoat was full of folds and tucks which only an amateur tailor would have dared, and only one superior to the criticism of his fellows would have worn. His hard, bright eyes were fixed on Mr. Reeder, but there was no menace in them so far as the detective could read.

"Yes, I was instrumental in arresting Ike Walker," said Mr. Reeder, almost gently.

The man put his hand in his pocket and brought out a crumpled packet enclosed in green oiled silk. Mr. Reeder unfolded the covering and found a soiled and crumpled envelope.

"That's from Ike," said the man. "He sent it out of stir by a gent who was discharged yesterday."

Mr. Reeder was not shocked by his revelation. He knew that prison rules were made to be broken, and that worse things have happened in the best regulated jails than this item of a smuggled letter. He opened the envelope, keeping his eyes on the man's face, took out the crumpled sheet and read the five or six lines of writing.

Dear Reeder:
   Here is a bit of a riddle for you.
   What other people have got, you can have. I haven't got it, but it is coming to you. It's red-hot when you get it, but you're cold when it goes away.

                                        Your loving friend,
                                        Ike Walker
(doing a twelve year stretch because you went on the witness stand and told a lot of lies).

Mr. Reeder looked up and their eyes met.
"Your friend is a little mad, one thinks?" he asked politely.

"He ain't a friend of mine. A gent asked me to bring it," said the messenger.

"On the contrary," said Mr. Reeder pleasantly, "he gave it to you in Dartmoor Prison yesterday. Your name is Mills; you have eight convictions for burglary, and will have your ninth before the year is out. You were released two days ago — I saw you reporting at Scotland Yard."

The man was for the moment alarmed and in two minds to bolt. Mr. Reeder glanced along Brockley Road, saw a slim figure that was standing at the corner cross to a waiting tramcar, and, seeing his opportunity vanish, readjusted his time table.

"Come inside, Mr. Mills."

"I don't want to come inside," said Mr. Mills, now thoroughly agitated. "He asked me to give this to you and I've give it. There's nothing else —"

Mr. Reeder crooked his finger.

"Come, birdie!" he said, with great amiability. "And please don't annoy me! I am quite capable of sending you back to your friend Mr. Walker. I am really a most unpleasant man if I am upset."

The messenger followed meekly, wiped his boots with great vigour on the mat, and tiptoed up the carpeted stairs to the big study where Mr. Reeder did most of his thinking.

"Sit down, Mills."

With his own hands Mr. Reeder placed a chair for his uncomfortable visitor, and then, pulling another up to his big writing table, he spread the letter before him, adjusted his glasses, read, his lips moving, and then leaned back in his chair.

"I give it up," he said. "Read me this riddle."

"I don't know what's in the letter —" began the man.

"Read me this riddle."

As he handed the letter across the table, the man betrayed himself, for he rose and pushed back his chair with a startled, horrified expression that told Mr. Reeder quite a lot. He laid the letter down on his desk, took a large tumbler from the sideboard, inverted it, and covered the scrawled paper. Then:

"Wait," he said, "and don't move till I come back."

And there was an unaccustomed venom in his tone that made the visitor shudder.

Reeder passed out of the room to the bathroom, pulled up his sleeves with a quick jerk of his arm and, turning the faucet, let hot water run over his hands before he reached for a small bottle on a shelf, poured a liberal portion into the water and let his hands soak.

This done, for three minutes he scrubbed his fingers with a nail-brush, dried them, and, removing his coat and waistcoat carefully, hung them over the edge of the bath. He went back to his uncomfortable guest in his shirt-sleeves.

"Our friend Walker is employed in the hospital," he stated rather than asked. "What have you had there — scarlet fever or something worse?"

He glanced down at the letter under the glass.

"Scarlet fever, of course," he said, "and the letter has been systematically infected. Walker is almost clever."

The wood of a fire was laid in the grate. He carried the letter and the blotting-paper to the hearth, lit the kindling and thrust paper and letter into the flames.

"Almost clever," he said musingly. "Of course, he is one of the orderlies in the hospital. It was scarlet fever, I think you said?"

The gaping man nodded.

"Of a virulent type, of course. How very fascinating!"

He thrust his hands in his pockets and looked down benevolently at the wretched emissary of the vengeful Walker.

"You may go now, Mills," he said gently. "I rather think that you are infected. That ridiculous piece of oiled silk is quite inadequate — which means 'quite useless' — as a protection against wandering germs. You will have scarlet fever in three days, and will probably be dead at the end of the week. I will send you a wreath."

He opened the door, pointed to the stairway, and the man slunk out.

Mr. Reeder watched him through the window, saw him cross the street and disappear round the corner into the Lewisham High Road, and then, going up to his bedroom, he put on a newer frock-coat and waistcoat, drew on his hands a pair of fabric gloves and went forth to his labours.

He did not expect to meet Mr. Mills again, never dreaming that the gentleman from Dartmoor was planning a "bust" which would bring them again into contact. For Mr. Reeder the incident was closed.

That day news of another disappearance had come through from police headquarters, and Mr. Reeder was waiting at ten mintues before five at the rendezvous for the girl who, he instinctively knew, could give him a thread of the clue. He was determined that this time his inquiries should bear fruit; but it was not until they had reached the end of Brockley Road, and he was walking slowly up toward the girl's boarding-house, that she gave him a hint.

"Why are you so persistent, Mr. Reeder?" she asked, a little impatiently. "Do you wish to invest money? Because, if you do, I'm sorry I can't help you. That is another agreement we made, that we would not introduce new shareholders."

Mr. Reeder stopped, took off his hat, and rubbed the back of his head (his housekeeper, watching him from an upper window, was perfectly certain he was proposing and had been rejected).

"I am going to tell you something, Miss Belman, and I hope — er — that I shall not alarm you."

And very briefly he told the story of the disappearances and the queer coincidence which marked every case — the receipt of a dividend on the first of every month. As he proceeded, the colour left the girl's face.

"You are serious, of course?" she said, serious enough herself. "You wouldn't tell me that unless — The company is the Mexico City Investment Syndicate. They have offices in Portugal Street."

"How did you come to hear of them?" asked Mr. Reeder.

"I had a letter from their manager, Mr. De Silvo. He told me that a friend had mentioned my name, and gave full particulars of the investment."

"Have you that letter?"

She shook her head.

"No; I was particularly asked to bring it with me when I went to see them. Although, in point of fact, I never did see them," smiled the girl. "I wrote to their lawyers — will you wait? I have their letter."

Mr. Reeder waited at the gate while the girl went into the house and returned presently with a small portfolio, from which she took a quarto sheet. It was headed with the name of a legal firm, Bracher & Bracher, and was the usual formal type of letter one expects from a lawyer.

Dear Madam:

Re Mexico City Investment Syndicate: We act as lawyers to this syndicate, and so far as we know it is a reputable concern. We feel that it is only due to us that we should say that we do not advise investments in any concern which offers such large profits, for usually there is a corresponding risk. We know, however, that this syndicate has paid 12½ per cent and sometimes as much as 20 per cent, and we have had no complaints about them. We cannot, of course, as lawyers, guarantee the financial soundness of any of our clients, and can only repeat that, in so far as we have been able to ascertain, the syndicate conducts a genuine business and enjoys a very sound financial backing.

Yours faithfully,
Bracher & Bracher

"You say you never saw De Silvo?"

She shook her head.

"No; I saw Mr. Bracher, but when I went to the office of the syndicate, which is in the same building, I found only a clerk in attendance. Mr. De Silvo had been called out of town. I had to leave the letter because the lower portion was an application for shares in the syndicate. The capital could be withdrawn at three days' notice, and I must say that this last clause decided me; and when I had a letter from Mr. De Silvo accepting my investment, I sent him the money."

Mr. Reeder nodded.

"And you've received your dividends regularly ever since?" he said.

"Every month," said the girl triumphantly. "And really I think you're wrong in connecting the company with these disappearances."

Mr. Reeder did not reply. That afternoon he made it his business to call at 179 Portugal Street. It was a two-story building of an old-fashioned type. A wide flagged hall led into the building; a set of old-fashioned stairs ran up to the "top floor," which was occupied by a China merchant; and from the hall led three doors. That on the left bore the legend "Bracher & Bracher, Solicitors," and immediately facing was the office of the Mexican syndicate. At the far end of the passage was a door which exhibited the name "John Baston," but as to Mr. Baston's business there was no indication.

Mr. Reeder knocked gently at the door of the syndicate and a voice bade him come in. A young man, wearing glasses, was sitting at a typewriting table, a pair of dictaphone receivers in his ears, and he was typing rapidly.

"No, sir, Mr. De Silvo is not in. He only comes in about twice a week," said the clerk. "Will you give me your name?"

"It is not important," said Reeder gently, and went out, closing the door behind him.

He was more fortunate in his call upon Bracher & Bracher, for Mr. Joseph Bracher was in his office: a tall, florid gentleman who wore a large rose in his buttonhole. The firm of Bracher & Bracher was evidently a prosperous one, for there were half a dozen clerks in the outer office, and Mr. Bracher's private sanctum, with its big partner desk, was a model of shabby comfort.

"Sit down, Mr. Reeder," said the lawyer, glancing at the card.

In a few words Mr. Reeder stated his business, and Mr. Bracher smiled.

"It is fortunate you came to-day," he said. "If it were to-morrow we should not be able to give you any information. The truth is, we have had to ask Mr. De Silvo to find other lawyers. No, no, there is nothing wrong, except that they constantly refer their clients to us, and we feel that we are becoming in the nature of sponsors for their clients, and that, of course, is very undesirable."

"Have you a record of the people who have written to you from time to time asking your advice?"

Mr. Bracher shook his head.

"It is a curious thing to confess, but we haven't," he said; "and that is one of the reasons why we have decided to give up this client. Three weeks ago, the letter-book in which we kept copies of all letters sent to people who applied for a reference most unaccountably disappeared. It was put in the safe overnight, and in the morning, although there was no sign of tampering with the lock, it had vanished. The circumstances were so mysterious, and my brother and I were so deeply concerned, that we applied to the syndicate to give us a list of their clients, and that request was never complied with."

Mr. Reeder sought inspiration in the ceiling.

"Who is John Baston?" he asked, and the lawyer laughed.

"There again I am ignorant. I believe he is a very wealthy financier, but, so far as I know, he only comes to his office for three months in the year, and I have never seen him."

Mr. Reeder offered him his flabby hand and walked back along Portugal Street, his chin on his breast, his hands behind him dragging his umbrella, so that he bore a ludicrous resemblance to some strange tailed animal.

That night he waited again for the girl, but she did not appear, and although he remained at the rendezvous until half-past five he did not see her. This was not very unusual, for sometimes she had to work late, and he went home without any feeling of apprehension. He finished his own frugal dinner and then walked across to the boarding-house. Miss Belman had not arrived, the landlady told him, and he returned to his study and telephoned first to the office where she was employed and then to the private address of her employer.

"She left at half-past four," was the surprising news. "Somebody telephoned to her and she asked me if she might go early."

"Oh!" said Mr. Reeder blankly.

He did not go to bed that night, but sat up in a small room at Scotland Yard, reading the brief reports which came in from the various divisions. And with the morning came the sickening realisation that Margaret Belman's name must be added to those who had disappeared in such extraordinary circumstances.

He dozed in the big Windsor chair. At eight o'clock he returned to his own house and shaved and bathed, and when the Public Prosecutor arrived at his office he found Mr. Reeder waiting for him in the corridor. It was a changed Mr. Reeder, and the change was not due entirely to lack of sleep. His voice was sharper; he had lost some of that atmosphere of apology which usually enveloped him.

In a few words he told of Margaret Belman's disappearance.

"Do you connect De Silvo with this?" asked his chief.

"Yes, I think I do," said the other quietly, and then: "There is only one hope, and it is a very slender one — a very slender one indeed!"

He did not tell the Public Prosecutor in what that hope consisted, but walked down to the offices of the Mexico City Investment Syndicate.

Mr. De Silvo was not in. He would have been very much surprised if he had been. He crossed the hallway to see the lawyer, and this time he found Mr. Ernest Bracher present with his brother.

When Reeder spoke to the point, it was very much to the point.

"I am leaving a police officer in Portugal Street to arrest De Silvo the moment he puts in an appearance. I feel that you, as his lawyers, should know this," he said.

"But why on earth —?" began Mr. Joseph Bracher, in a tone of astonishment.

"I don't know what charge I shall bring against him, but it will certainly be a very serious one," said Reeder. "For the moment I have not confided to Scotland Yard the basis for my suspicions, but your client has got to tell a very plausible story and produce indisputable proof of his innocence to have any hope of escape."

"I am quite in the dark," said the lawyer, mystified. "What has he been doing? Is his syndicate a fraud?"

"I know nothing more fraudulent," said the other shortly. "Tomorrow I intend to obtain the necessary authority to search his papers and to search the room and papers of Mr. John Baston. I have an idea that I shall find something in that room of considerable interest to me."

It was eight o'clock that night before he left Scotland Yard, and he was turning toward the familiar corner, when he saw a car come from Westminster Bridge toward Scotland Yard. Somebody leaned out of the window and signalled him, and the car turned. It was a two-seater coupé, and the driver was Mr. Joseph Bracher.

"We've found De Silvo," he said breathlessly as he brought the car to a standstill at the curb and jumped out.

He was very agitated and his face was pale. Mr. Reeder could have sworn that his teeth were chattering.

"There's something wrong — very badly wrong," he went on. "My brother has been trying to get the truth from him — my God! If he has done these terrible things I shall never forgive myself."

"Where is he?" asked Mr. Reeder.

"He came just before dinner to our house at Dulwich. My brother and I are bachelors and we live there alone now, and he has been to dinner before. My brother questioned him and he made certain admissions which are almost incredible. The man must be mad."

"What did he say?"

"I can't tell you. Ernest is detaining him until you come."

Mr. Reeder stepped into the car and in a few minutes they were flying across Westminster Bridge toward Camberwell. Lane House, an old-fashioned Georgian residence, lay at the end of a countrified road which was, he found, a cul de sac. The house stood in grounds of considerable size, he noted as they passed up the drive and stopped before the porch. Mr. Bracher alighted and opened the door, and Reeder passed into a cosily furnished hall. One door was ajar.

"Is that Mr. Reeder?" He recognised the voice of Ernest Bracher, and walked into the room.

The younger Mr. Bracher was standing with his back to the empty fireplace; there was nobody else in the room.

"De Silvo's gone upstairs to lie down," explained the lawyer. "This is a dreadful business, Mr. Reeder."

He held out his hand and Reeder crossed the room to take it. As he put his foot on the square Persian rug before the fireplace, he realised his danger and tried to spring back, but his balance was lost. He felt himself falling through the cavity which the carpet hid, lashed out, and caught for a moment the edge of the trap, but as the lawyer came round and raised his foot to stomp upon the clutching fingers, Reeder released his hold and dropped.

The shock of the fall took away his breath, and for a second he sprawled, half lying, half sitting, on the floor of the cellar into which he had fallen. Looking up, he saw the older of the two leaning over. The square aperture was diminishing in size. There was evidently a sliding panel which covered the hole in normal times.

"We'll deal with you later, Reeder," said Joseph Bracher with a smile. "We've had quite a lot of clever people here —"

Something cracked in the cellar. The bullet seared the lawyer's cheek, smashed a glass chandelier to fragments, and he stepped back with a yell of fear. In another second the trap was closed and Reeder was alone in a small brick-lined cellar. Not entirely alone, for the automatic pistol he held in his hand was a very pleasant companion in that moment of crisis.

From his hip pocket he took a flat electric hand-lamp, switched on the current, and surveyed his prison. The walls and floor were damp; that was the first thing he noticed. In one corner was a small flight of brick steps leading to a locked steel door, and then:

"Mr. Reeder."

He spun around and turned his lamp upon the speaker. It was Margaret Belman, who had risen from a heap of sacks where she had been sleeping.

"I'm afraid I've got you into very bad trouble," she said, and he marvelled at her calm.

"How long have you been here?"

"Since last night," she answered. "Mr. Bracher telephoned me to see him, and he picked me up in his car. They kept me in the other room until tonight, but an hour ago they brought me here."

"Which is the other room?"

She pointed to the steel door. She offered no further details of her capture, and it was not a moment to discuss their misfortune. Reeder went up the steps and tried the door; it was fastened from the other side and opened inward, he discovered. There was no sign of a key-hole. He asked her where the door led, and she told him that it was to an underground kitchen and coal-cellar. She had hoped to escape, because only a barred window stood between her and freedom in the "little room" where she was kept.

"But the window was very thick," she said, "and of course I could do nothing with the bars."

Reeder made another inspection of the cellar, then sent the light of his lamp up at the ceiling. He saw nothing there except a steel pully fastened to a beam that crossed the entire width of the cellar.

"Now what on earth is he going to do?' he asked thoughtfully, and as though his enemies had heard the question and were determined to leave him in no doubt as to their plans, there came the sound of gurgling water, and in a second he was ankle-deep.

He put the light on to the place whence the water was coming. There were three circular holes in the wall, from each of which was gushing a solid stream.

"What is it?" she asked in a terrified whisper.

"Get on to the steps and stay there," he ordered peremptorily, and made investigation to see if it was possible to staunch the flow. He saw at a glance that this was impossible. And now the mystery of the disappearances was a mystery no longer.

The water came up with incredible rapidity, first to his knees, then to his thighs, and he joined her on the steps.

There was no possible escape for them. He guessed the water would come up only so far as would make it impossible for them to reach the beam across the roof or the pulley, the dreadful purpose of which he could guess. The dead must be got out of this charnel house in some way or other. Strong swimmer as he was, he knew that in the hours ahead it would be impossible to keep afloat.

He slipped off his coat and vest and unbuttoned his collar.

"You had better take off your skirt," he said in a matter-of-fact tone. "Can you swim?"

"Yes," she answered in a low voice.

He did not ask her the real question which was in his mind: for how long could she swim?

There was a long silence; the water crept higher; and then:

"Are you very much afraid?" he asked, and took her hand in his.

"No, I don't think I am," she said. "It is wonderful having you with me — why are they doing this?"

He said nothing, but carried the soft hand to his lips and kissed it.

The water was now reaching the top step. Reeder stood with his back to the iron door, waiting. And then he felt something touch the door from the other side. There was a faint click, as though a bolt had been slipped back. He put her gently aside and held his palms to the door. There was no doubt now: somebody was fumbling on the other side. He went down a step and presently he felt the door yield and come toward him, and there was a momentary gleam of light. In another second he had wrenched the door open and sprung through.

"Hands up!"

Whoever it was had dropped his lamp, and now Mr. Reeder focussed the light of his own torch and nearly dropped.

For the man in the passage was Mills, the ex-convict who had brought the tainted letter from Dartmoor!

"All right, guv'nor, it's a cop," growled the man.

And then the whole explanation flashed upon the detective. In an instant he had gripped the girl by the hand and dragged her through the narrow passage, into which the water was now steadily overrunning.

"Which way did you get in, Mills?" he demanded authoritatively.

"Through the window."

"Show me — quick!"

The convict led the way to what was evidently the window through which the girl had looked with such longing. The bars had been removed; the window sash itself lifted from its rusty hinges; and in another second the three were standing on the grass, with the stars twinkling above them.

"Mills," said Mr. Reeder, and his voice shook, "you came here to 'bust' this house."

"That's right," growled Mills. "I tell you it's a cop. I'm not going to give you any trouble."

"Skip!" hissed Mr. Reeder. "And skip quick! Now, young lady, we'll go for a little walk."

A few seconds later a patrolling constable was smitten dumb by the apparition of a middle-aged man in shirt and trousers, and a lady who was inadequately attired in a silk petticoat.

"The Mexican company was Bracher & Bracher," explained Reeder to his chief. "There was no John Baston. His room was a passage-way by which the Brachers could get from one room to the other. The clerk in the Mexican syndicate's office was, of course, blind; I spotted that the moment I saw him. There are any number of blind typists employed in the City of London. A blind clerk was necessary if the identity of De Silvo with the Brachers was to be kept a secret.

"Bracher & Bracher had been going badly for years. It will probably be found that they have made away with clients' money; and they hit upon this scheme of inducing foolish investors to put money into their syndicate on the promise of large dividends. Their victims were well chosen, and Joseph — who was the brains of the organisation — conducted the most rigorous investigation to make sure that these unfortunate people had no intimate friends. If they had any suspicion about an applicant, Brachers would write a letter deprecating the idea of an investment and suggesting that the too-shrewd dupe should find another and a safer method than the Mexican syndicate afforded.

"After they had paid one or two years' dividends the wretched investor was lured to the house at Dulwich and there scientifically killed. You will probably find an unofficial cemetery in their grounds. So far as I can make out, they have stolen more than a hundred and twenty thousand pounds in the past two years by this method."

"It is incredible," said the Prosecutor, "incredible!"

Mr. Reeder shrugged.

"Is there anything more incredible than the Burke and Hare murders? There are Burkes and Hares in every branch of society and in every period of history."

"Why did they delay their execution of Miss Belman?"

Mr. Reeder coughed.

"They wanted to make a clean sweep, but did not wish to kill her until they had me in their hands. I rather suspect" — he coughed again — "that they thought I had an especial interest in the young lady."

"And have you?" asked the Public Prosecutor.

Mr. Reeder did not reply.

DASHIELL
HAMMETT

THE
TENTH
CLEW

*Samuel Dashiell Hammett (1894–1961) is the detective writer all the others
would like to have been. He actually worked as a private eye (eight years as
a Pinkerton agent), and later he paid the bills working as a San Francisco
ad man while turning out crime stories for pulp magazines. His first four
novels (*Red Harvest, The Dain Curse, The Maltese Falcon, *and* The
Glass Key) *all ran first as serials in* Black Mask. The Maltese Falcon,
*which introduced Sam Spade of the Spade and Archer Detective Agency, was
published in hardcover in 1930, and became a landmark in American literature. The earlier novels — as well as a number of short stories, including
"The Tenth Clew" — featured the Continental Op, a nameless, all-business
detective who worked for a nationwide agency very like Pinkerton's.*

*In 1923, just as he was beginning his writing career, Hammett published
a list of twenty-nine numbered observations called "From the Memoirs of a
Private Detective" in H. L. Mencken's* Smart Set *magazine. Number 25
covered city crime versus country crime: "Going from the larger cities out into
the remote rural communities, one finds a steadily decreasing percentage of
crimes that have to do with money and a proportionate increase in the frequency
of sex as a criminal motive."*

*Number 27 touches on the Continental Op's problem in the following story.
The chief difference between a fictional crime and a real one is that "in the
former there is usually a paucity of clues and in the latter altogether too many."*

"MR. LEOPOLD GANTVOORT is not at home," the servant who opened
the door said, "but his son, Mr. Charles, is — if you wish to see him."

"No, I had an appointment with Mr. Leopold Gantvoort for nine or a little after. It's just nine now. No doubt he'll be back soon. I'll wait."

"Very well, sir."

He stepped aside for me to enter the house, took my overcoat and hat, guided me to a room on the second floor — Gantvoort's library — and left me. I picked up a magazine from the stack on the table, pulled an ash tray over beside me, and made myself comfortable.

An hour passed. I stopped reading and began to grow impatient. Another hour passed — and I was fidgeting.

A clock somewhere below had begun to strike eleven when a young man of twenty-five or -six, tall and slender, with remarkably white skin and very dark hair and eyes, came into the room.

"My father hasn't returned yet," he said. "It's too bad that you should have been kept waiting all this time. Isn't there anything I could do for you? I am Charles Gantvoort."

"No, thank you." I got up from my chair, accepting the courteous dismissal. "I'll get in touch with him tomorrow."

"I'm sorry," he murmured, and we moved toward the door together.

As we reached the hall an extension telephone in one corner of the room we were leaving buzzed softly, and I halted in the doorway while Charles Gantvoort went over to answer it.

His back was toward me as he spoke into the instrument.

"Yes. Yes, yes!" — sharply — "*What?* Yes" — very weakly — "Yes."

He turned slowly around and faced me with a face that was gray and tortured, with wide shocked eyes and gaping mouth — the telephone still in his hand.

"Father," he gasped, "is dead — killed!"

"Where? How?"

"I don't know. That was the police. They want me to come down at once."

He straightened his shoulders with an effort, pulling himself together, put down the telephone, and his face fell into less strained lines.

"You will pardon my —"

"Mr. Gantvoort," I interrupted his apology, "I am connected with the Continental Detective Agency. Your father called up this afternoon and asked that a detective be sent to see him tonight. He said his life had been threatened. He hadn't definitely engaged us, however, so unless you —"

"Certainly! You are employed! If the police haven't already caught the murderer I want you to do everything possible to catch him."

"All right! Let's get down to headquarters."

Neither of us spoke during the ride to the Hall of Justice. Gantvoort bent over the wheel of his car, sending it through the streets at a terrific speed. There were several questions that needed answers, but all his attention was required for his driving if he was to maintain the pace at which he was driving without piling us into something. So I didn't disturb him, but hung on and kept quiet.

Half a dozen police detectives were waiting for us when we reached the detective bureau. O'Gar — a bullet-headed detective sergeant who dresses like the village constable in a movie, wide-brimmed black hat and all, but who isn't to be put out of the reckoning on that account — was in charge of the investigation. He and I had worked on two or three jobs together before, and hit it off excellently.

He led us into one of the small offices below the assembly room. Spread out on the flat top of a desk there were a dozen or more objects.

"I want you to look these things over carefully," the detective-sergeant told Gantvoort, "and pick out the ones that belonged to your father."

"But where is he?"

"Do this first," O'Gar insisted, "and then you can see him."

I looked at the things on the table while Charles Gantvoort made his selections. An empty jewel case; a memorandum book; three letters in slit envelopes that were addressed to the dead man; some other papers; a bunch of keys; a fountain pen; two white linen handkerchiefs; two pistol cartridges; a gold watch, with a gold knife and a gold pencil attached to it by a gold-and-platinum chain; two black leather wallets, one of them very new and the other worn; some money, both paper and silver; and a small portable typewriter, bent and twisted, and matted with hair and blood. Some of the other things were smeared with blood and some were clean.

Gantvoort picked out the watch and its attachments, the keys, the fountain pen, the memorandum book, the handkerchiefs, the letters and other papers, and the older wallet.

"These were Father's," he told us. "I've never seen any of the others before. I don't know, of course, how much money he had with him tonight, so I can't say how much of this is his."

"You're sure none of the rest of this stuff was his?" O'Gar asked.

"I don't think so, but I'm not sure. Whipple could tell you." He turned to me. "He's the man who let you in tonight. He looked after Father, and he'd know positively whether any of these other things belonged to him or not."

One of the police detectives went to the telephone to tell Whipple to come down immediately.

I resumed the questioning.

"Is anything that your father usually carried with him missing? Anything of value?"

"Not that I know of. All the things that he might have been expected to have with him seem to be here."

"At what time tonight did he leave the house?"

"Before seven-thirty. Possibly as early as seven."

"Know where he was going?"

"He didn't tell me, but I supposed he was going to call on Miss Dexter."

The faces of the police detectives brightened, and their eyes grew sharp. I suppose mine did, too. There are many, many murders with never a woman in them anywhere; but seldom a very conspicuous killing.

"Who's this Miss Dexter?" O'Gar took up the inquiry.

"She's, well —" Charles Gantvoort hesitated. "Well, Father was on very friendly terms with her and her brother. He usually called on them — on her several evenings a week. In fact, I suspected that he intended marrying her."

"Who and what is she?"

"Father became acquainted with them six or seven months ago. I've met them several times, but don't know them very well. Miss Dexter — Creda is her given name — is about twenty-three years old, I should judge, and her brother Madden is four or five years older. He is in New York now, or on his way there, to transact some business for Father."

"Did your father tell you he was going to marry her?" O'Gar hammered away at the woman angle.

"No; but it was pretty obvious that he was very much — ah — infatuated. We had some words over it a few days ago — last week. Not a quarrel, you understand, but words. From the way he talked I feared that he meant to marry her."

"What do you mean 'feared'?" O'Gar snapped at that word.

Charles Gantvoort's pale face flushed a little, and he cleared his throat embarrassedly.

"I don't want to put the Dexters in a bad light to you. I don't think — I'm sure they had nothing to do with Father's — with this. But I didn't care especially for them — didn't like them. I thought they were — well — fortune hunters, perhaps. Father wasn't fabulously wealthy, but he had considerable means. And, while he wasn't feeble, still he was past fifty-seven, old enough for me to feel that Creda Dexter was more interested in his money than in him."

"How about your father's will?"

"The last one of which I have any knowledge — drawn up two or three years ago — left everything to my wife and me, jointly. Father's attorney, Mr. Murray Abernathy, could tell you if there was a later will, but I hardly think there was."

"Your father had retired from business, hadn't he?"

"Yes; he turned his import and export business over to me about a year ago. He had quite a few investments scattered around, but he wasn't actively engaged in the management of any concern."

O'Gar tilted his village constable hat back and scratched his bullet head reflectively for a moment. Then he looked at me.

"Anything else you want to ask?"

"Yes. Mr. Gantvoort, do you know or did you ever hear your father or anyone else speak of an Emil Bonfils?"

"No."

"Did your father ever tell you that he had received a threatening letter? Or that he had been shot at on the street?"

"No."

"Was your father in Paris in 1902?"

"Very likely. He used to go abroad every year up until the time of his retirement from business."

O'Gar and I took Gantvoort around to the morgue to see his father, then. The dead man wasn't pleasant to look at, even to O'Gar and me, who hadn't known him except by sight. I remembered him as a small wiry man, always smartly tailored, and with a brisk springiness that was far younger than his years.

He lay now with the top of his head beaten into a red and pulpy mess.

We left Gantvoort at the morgue and set out afoot for the Hall of Justice.

"What's this deep stuff you're pulling about Emil Bonfils and Paris in 1902?" the detective-sergeant asked as soon as we were out in the street.

"This: the dead man phoned the Agency this afternoon and said he had received a threatening letter from an Emil Bonfils with whom he had had trouble in Paris in 1902. He also said that Bonfils had shot at him the previous evening, in the street. He wanted somebody to come around and see him about it tonight. And he said that under no circumstances were the police to be let in on it — that he'd rather have Bonfils get him than have the trouble made public. That's all he would say over the phone; and that's how I happened to be on hand when Charles Gantvoort was notified of his father's death."

O'Gar stopped in the middle of the sidewalk and whistled softly.

"That's something!" he exclaimed. "Wait till we get back to head-quarters — I'll show you something."

Whipple was waiting in the assembly room when we arrived at headquarters. His face at first glance was as smooth and mask-like as when he had admitted me to the house on Russian Hill earlier in the evening. But beneath his perfect servant's manner he was twitching and trembling.

We took him into the little office where we had questioned Charles Gantvoort.

Whipple verified all that the dead man's son had told us. He was positive that neither the typewriter, the jewel case, the two cartridges, or the newer wallet had belonged to Gantvoort.

We couldn't get him to put his opinion of the Dexters in words, but that he disapproved of them was easily seen. Miss Dexter, he said, had called up on the telephone three times this night, at about eight o'clock, at nine, and at nine-thirty. She had asked for Mr. Leopold Gantvoort each time, but she had left no message. Whipple was of the opinion that she was expecting Gantvoort, and he had not arrived.

He knew nothing, he said, of Emil Bonfils or of any threatening letters. Gantvoort had been out the previous night from eight until midnight. Whipple had not seen him closely enough when he came home to say whether he seemed excited or not. Gantvoort usually carried about a hundred dollars in his pockets.

"Is there anything that you know of that Gantvoort had on his person tonight which isn't among these things on the desk?" O'Gar asked.

"No, sir. Everything seems to be here — watch and chain, money, memorandum book, wallet, keys, handkerchiefs, fountain pen — everything that I know of."

"Did Charles Gantvoort go out tonight?"

"No, sir. He and Mrs. Gantvoort were at home all evening."

"Positive?"

Whipple thought a moment.

"Yes, sir, I'm fairly certain. But I know Mrs. Gantvoort wasn't out. To tell the truth, I didn't see Mr. Charles from about eight o'clock until he came downstairs with this gentleman" — pointing to me — "at eleven. But I'm fairly certain he was home all evening. I think Mrs. Gantvoort said he was."

Then O'Gar put another question — one that puzzled me at the time.

"What kind of collar buttons did Mr. Gantvoort wear?"

"You mean Mr. Leopold?"

"Yes."

"Plain gold ones, made all in one piece. They had a London jeweler's mark on them."

"Would you know them if you saw them?"

"Yes, sir."

We let Whipple go home then.

"Don't you think," I suggested when O'Gar and I were alone with this desk-load of evidence that didn't mean anything at all to me yet, "it's time you were loosening up and telling me what's what?"

"I guess so — listen! A man named Lagerquist, a grocer, was driving through Golden Gate Park tonight, and passed a machine standing on a dark road, with its lights out. He thought there was something funny about the way the man in it was sitting at the wheel, so he told the first patrolman he met about it.

"The patrolman investigated and found Gantvoort sitting at the wheel — dead — with his head smashed in and this dingus" — putting one hand on the bloody typewriter — "on the seat beside him. That was at a quarter of ten. The doc says Gantvoort was killed — his skull crushed — with this typewriter.

"The dead man's pockets, we found, had all been turned inside out; and all this stuff on the desk, except this new wallet, was scattered about in the car — some of it on the floor and some on the seats. This money was there too — nearly a hundred dollars of it. Among the papers was this."

He handed me a sheet of white paper upon which the following had been typewritten:

L. F. G. —
  I want what is mine. 6,000 miles and 21 years are not enough to hide
you from the victim of your treachery. I mean to have what you stole.
                                                            E. B.

"L. F. G. could be Leopold F. Gantvoort," I said. "And E. B. could be Emil Bonfils. Twenty-one years is the time from 1902 to 1923, and 6,000 miles is, roughly, the distance between Paris and San Francisco."

I laid the letter down and picked up the jewel case. It was a black imitation leather one, lined with white satin, and unmarked in any way.

Then I examined the cartridges. There were two of them, S. W. .45-caliber, and deep crosses had been cut in their soft noses — an old trick that makes the bullet spread out like a saucer when it hits.

"These in the car, too?"

"Yep — and this."

From a vest pocket O'Gar produced a short tuft of blond hair — hairs between an inch and two inches in length. They had been cut off, not pulled out by the roots.

"Any more?"

There seemed to be an endless stream of things.

He picked up the new wallet from the desk — the one that both Whipple and Charles Gantvoort had said did not belong to the dead man — and slid it over to me.

"That was found in the road, three or four feet from the car."

It was of a cheap quality, and had neither manufacturer's name nor owner's initials on it. In it were two ten-dollar bills, three small newspaper clippings, and a typewritten list of six names and addresses, headed by Gantvoort's.

The three clippings were apparently from the Personal columns of three different newspapers — the type wasn't the same — and they read:

GEORGE — Everything is fixed. Don't wait too long.   D. D. D.

R. H. T. — They do not answer.   FLO

CAPPY — Twelve on the dot and look sharp.   BINGO

The names and addresses on the typewritten list, under Gantvoort's, were:

Quincy Heathcote, 1223 S. Jason Street, Denver; B. D. Thornton, 96 Hughes Circle, Dallas; Luther G. Randall, 615 Columbia Street, Portsmouth; J. H. Boyd Willis, 5444 Harvard Street, Boston; Hannah Hindmarsh, 218 E. 79th Street, Cleveland.

"What else?" I asked when I had studied these.

The detective-sergeant's supply hadn't been exhausted yet.

"The dead man's collar buttons — both front and back — had been taken out, though his collar and tie were still in place. And his left shoe was gone. We hunted high and low all around, but didn't find either shoe or collar buttons."

"Is that all?"

I was prepared for anything now.

"What the hell do you want?" he growled. "Ain't that enough?"

"How about fingerprints?"

"Nothing stirring! All we found belonged to the dead man."

"How about the machine he was found in?"

"A coupe belonging to a Dr. Wallace Girargo. He phoned in at six this evening that it had been stolen from near the corner of McAllister and Polk streets. We're checking up on him — but I think he's all right."

The things that Whipple and Charles Gantvoort had identified as belonging to the dead man told us nothing. We went over them carefully, but to no advantage. The memorandum book contained many entries, but they all seemed totally foreign to the murder. The letters were quite as irrelevant.

The serial number of the typewriter with which the murder had been committed had been removed, we found — apparently filed out of the frame.

"Well, what do you think?" O'Gar asked when we had given up our examination of our clews and sat back burning tobacco.

"I think we want to find Monsieur Emil Bonfils."

"It wouldn't hurt to do that," he grunted. "I guess our best bet is to get in touch with these five people on the list with Gantvoort's name. Suppose that's a murder list? That this Bonfils is out to get all of them?"

"Maybe. We'll get hold of them anyway. Maybe we'll find that some of them have already been killed. But whether they have been killed or are to be killed or not, it's a cinch they have some connection with this affair. I'll get off a batch of telegrams to the Agency's branches, having the names on the list taken care of. I'll try to have the three clippings traced, too."

O'Gar looked at his watch and yawned.

"It's after four. What say we knock off and get some sleep? I'll leave word for the department's expert to compare the typewriter with that letter signed E. B. and with that list to see if they were written on it. I guess they were, but we'll make sure. I'll have the park searched all around where we found Gantvoort as soon as it gets light enough to see, and maybe the missing shoe and the collar buttons will be found. And I'll have a couple of the boys out calling on all the typewriter shops in the city to see if they can get a line on this one."

I stopped at the nearest telegraph office and got off a wad of messages. Then I went home to dream of nothing even remotely connected with crime or the detecting business.

At eleven o'clock that same morning, when, brisk and fresh with five hours' sleep under my belt, I arrived at the police detective bureau, I found O'Gar slumped down at his desk, staring dazedly at a black shoe, half a dozen collar buttons, a rusty flat key, and a rumpled newspaper — all lined up before him.

"What's all this? Souvenir of your wedding?"

"Might as well be." His voice was heavy with disgust. "Listen to this: one of the porters of the Seamen's National Bank found a package in the vestibule when he started cleaning up this morning. It was this shoe — Gantvoort's missing one — wrapped in this sheet of a five-day-old *Philadelphia Record,* and with these collar buttons and this old key in it. The heel of the shoe, you'll notice, has been pried off, and is still missing. Whipple identifies it all right, as well as two of the collar buttons, but he never saw the key before. These other four collar buttons are new, and common gold-rolled ones. The key don't look like it had had much use for a long time. What do you make of all that?"

I couldn't make anything out of it.

"How did the porter happen to turn the stuff in?"

"Oh, the whole story was in the morning papers — all about the missing shoe and collar buttons and all."

"What did you learn about the typewriter?" I asked.

"The letter and the list were written with it, right enough; but we haven't been able to find where it came from yet. We checked up the doc who owns the coupe, and he's in the clear. We accounted for all his time last night. Lagerquist, the grocer who found Gantvoort, seems to be all right, too. What did you do?"

"Haven't had any answers to the wires I sent last night. I dropped in at the Agency on my way down this morning, and got four operatives out covering the hotels and looking up all the people named Bonfils they can find — there are two or three families by that name listed in the directory. Also I sent our New York branch a wire to have the steamship records searched to see if an Emil Bonfils had arrived recently; and I put a cable through to our Paris correspondent to see what he could dig up over there."

"I guess we ought to see Gantvoort's lawyer — Abernathy — and that Dexter woman before we do anything else," the detective-sergeant said.

"I guess so," I agreed. "Let's tackle the lawyer first. He's the most important one, the way things now stand."

Murray Abernathy, attorney-at-law, was a long, stringy, slow-spoken old gentleman who still clung to starched-bosom shirts. He was too full of what he thought were professional ethics to give us as much help as we had expected; but by letting him talk — letting him ramble along in his own way — we did get a little information from him. What we got amounted to this:

The dead man and Creda Dexter had intended being married the coming Wednesday. His son and her brother were both opposed to the marriage, it seemed, so Gantvoort and the woman had planned to be married secretly in Oakland, and catch a boat for the Orient that same afternoon; figuring that by the time their lengthy honeymoon was over they could return to a son and brother who had become resigned to the marriage.

A new will had been drawn up, leaving half of Gantvoort's estate to his new wife and half to his son and daughter-in-law. But the new will had not been signed yet, and Creda Dexter knew it had not been signed. She knew — and this was one of the few points upon which Abernathy would make a positive statement — that under the old will, still in force, everything went to Charles Gantvoort and his wife.

The Gantvoort estate, we estimated from Abernathy's roundabout statements and allusions, amounted to about a million and a half in cash value. The attorney had never heard of Emil Bonfils, he said, and had never heard of any threats or attempts at murder directed toward the dead man. He knew nothing — or would tell us nothing — that threw any light upon the nature of the thing that the threatening letter had accused the dead man of stealing.

From Abernathy's office we went to Creda Dexter's apartment, in a new and expensively elegant building only a few minutes' walk from the Gantvoort residence.

Creda Dexter was a small woman in her early twenties. The first thing you noticed about her were her eyes. They were large and deep and the color of amber, and their pupils were never at rest. Continuously they changed size, expanded and contracted — slowly at times, suddenly at others — ranging incessantly from the size of pinheads to an extent that threatened to blot out the amber irises.

With the eyes for a guide, you discovered that she was pronouncedly feline throughout. Her every movement was the slow, smooth, sure one of a cat; and the contours of her rather pretty face, the shape of her mouth, her small nose, the set of her eyes, the swelling of her brows, were all cat-like. And the effect was heightened by the way she wore her hair, which was thick and tawny.

"Mr. Gantvoort and I," she told us after the preliminary explanations had been disposed of, "were to have been married the day after tomorrow. His son and daughter-in-law were both opposed to the marriage, as was my brother Madden. They all seemed to think that the difference between our ages was too great. So to avoid any unpleasantness, we had planned to be married quietly and then go abroad for a year or more, feeling sure that they would all have forgotten their grievances by the time we returned.

"That was why Mr. Gantvoort persuaded Madden to go to New York. He had some business there — something to do with the disposal of his interest in a steel mill — so he used it as an excuse to get Madden out of the way until we were off on our wedding trip. Madden lived here with me, and it would have been nearly impossible for me to have made any preparations for the trip without him seeing them."

"Was Mr. Gantvoort here last night?" I asked her.

"No, I expected him — we were going out. He usually walked over — it's only a few blocks. When eight o'clock came and he hadn't arrived, I telephoned his house, and Whipple told me that he had left nearly an hour before. I called up again, twice, after that. Then, this morning, I called up again before I had seen the papers, and I was told that he —"

She broke off with a catch in her voice — the only sign of sorrow she displayed throughout the interview. The impression of her we had received from Charles Gantvoort and Whipple had prepared us for a more or less elaborate display of grief on her part. But she disappointed us. There was nothing crude about her work — she didn't even turn on the tears for us.

"Was Mr. Gantvoort here night before last?"

"Yes. He came over at a little after eight and stayed until nearly twelve. We didn't go out."

"Did he walk over and back?"

"Yes, so far as I know."

"Did he ever say anything to you about his life being threatened?"

"No."

She shook her head decisively.

"Do you know Emil Bonfils?"

"No."

"Ever hear Mr. Gantvoort speak of him?"

"No."

"At what hotel is your brother staying in New York?"

The restless black pupils spread out abruptly, as if they were about to overflow into the white areas of her eyes. That was the first clear indication of fear I had seen. But, outside of those telltale pupils, her composure was undisturbed.

"I don't know."

"When did he leave San Francisco?"

"Thursday — four days ago."

O'Gar and I walked six or seven blocks in thoughtful silence after we left Creda Dexter's apartment, and then he spoke.

"A sleek kitten — that dame! Rub her the right way, and she'll purr pretty. Rub her the wrong way — and look out for the claws!"

"What did that flash of her eyes when I asked about her brother tell you?" I asked.

"Something — but I don't know what! It wouldn't hurt to look him up and see if he's really in New York. If he is there today it's a cinch he wasn't here last night — even the mail planes take twenty-six or twenty-eight hours for the trip."

"We'll do that," I agreed. "It looks like this Creda Dexter wasn't any too sure that her brother wasn't in on the killing. And there's nothing to show that Bonfils didn't have help. I can't figure Creda being in on the murder, though. She knew the new will hadn't been signed. There'd be no sense in her working herself out of that three-quarters of a million berries."

We sent a lengthy telegram to the Continental's New York branch, and then dropped in at the Agency to see if any replies had come to the wires I had got off the night before.

They had.

None of the people whose names appeared on the typewritten list with Gantvoort's had been found; not the least trace had been found of any of them. Two of the addresses given were altogether wrong. There were no houses with those numbers on those streets — and there never had been.

What was left of the afternoon, O'Gar and I spent going over the street between Gantvoort's house on Russian Hill and the building in which the Dexters lived. We questioned everyone we could find — man, woman, and child — who lived, worked, or played along any of the three routes the dead man could have taken.

We found nobody who had heard the shot that had been fired by Bonfils on the night before the murder. We found nobody who had seen anything suspicious on the night of the murder. Nobody who remembered having seen him picked up in a coupe.

Then we called at Gantvoort's house and questioned Charles Gantvoort again, his wife, and all the servants — and we learned nothing. So far as they knew, nothing belonging to the dead man was missing — nothing small enough to be concealed in the heel of a shoe.

The shoes he had worn the night he was killed were one of three pairs made in New York for him two months before. He could have removed the heel of the left one, hollowed it out sufficiently to hide a small object in it, and then nailed it on again; though Whipple insisted that he would have noticed the effects of any tampering with the shoe unless it had been done by an expert repairman.

This field exhausted, we returned to the Agency. A telegram had just come from the New York branch, saying that none of the steamship companies' records showed the arrival of an Emil Bonfils from either England, France, or Germany within the past six months.

The operatives who had been searching the city for Bonfils had all come in empty-handed. They had found and investigated eleven person named Bonfils in San Francisco, Oakland, Berkeley, and Alameda. Their investigations had definitely cleared all eleven. None of these Bonfilses knew an Emil Bonfils. Combing the hotels had yielded nothing.

O'Gar and I went to dinner together — a quiet, grouchy sort of meal during which we didn't speak six words apiece — and then came back to the Agency to find that another wire had come in from New York.

> Madden Dexter arrived McAlpin Hotel this morning with Power of Attorney to sell Gantvoort interest in B. F. and F. Iron Corporation. Denies knowledge of Emil Bonfils or of murder. Expects to finish business and leave for San Francisco tomorrow.

I let the sheet of paper upon which I had decoded the telegram slide out of my fingers, and we sat listlessly facing each other across my desk looking vacantly each at the other, listening to the clatter of charwomen's buckets in the corridor.

"It's a funny one," O'Gar said softly to himself at last.

I nodded. It was.

"We got nine clews," he spoke again presently, "and none of them have got us a damned thing.

"Number one: the dead man called up you people and told you that he had been threatened and shot at by an Emil Bonfils that he'd had a run-in with in Paris a long time ago.

"Number two: the typewriter he was killed with and that the letter and list were written on. We're still trying to trace it, but with no breaks so far. What the hell kind of a weapon was that, anyway? It looks like this fellow Bonfils got hot and hit Gantvoort with the first thing he put his hand on. But what was the typewriter doing in a stolen car? And why were the numbers filed off it?"

I shook my head to signify that I couldn't guess the answer, and O'Gar went on enumerating our clews.

"Number three: the threatening letter, fitting in with what Gantvoort had said over the phone that afternoon.

"Number four: those two bullets with the crosses in their snoots.

"Number five: the jewel case.

"Number six: that bunch of yellow hair.

"Number seven: the fact that the dead man's shoe and collar buttons were carried away.

"Number eight: the wallet, with two ten-dollar bills, three clippings, and the list in it, found in the road.

"Number nine: finding the shoe next day, wrapped up in a five-day-old Philadelphia paper, and with the missing collar buttons, four more, and a rusty key in it.

"That's the list. If they mean anything at all, they mean that Emil Bonfils — whoever he is — was flimflammed out of something by Gantvoort in Paris in 1902, and that Bonfils came to get it back. He picked Gantvoort up last night in a stolen car, bringing his typewriter with him — for God knows what reason! Gantvoort put up an argument, so Bonfils bashed in his noodle with the typewriter, and then went through his pockets, apparently not taking anything. He decided that what he was looking for was in Gantvoort's left shoe, so he took the shoe away with him. And then — but there's no sense to the collar button trick, or the phony list, or —"

"Yes there is!" I cut in, sitting up, wide awake now. "That's our tenth clew — the one we're going to follow from now on. That list was, except for Gantvoort's name and address, a fake. Our people would have found at least one of the five people whose names were on it if it had been on the level. But they didn't find the least trace of any of them. And two of the addresses were of street numbers that didn't exist!

"That list was faked up, put in the wallet with the clippings and twenty dollars — to make the play stronger — and planted in the road near the car to throw us off-track. And if that's so, then it's a hundred to one that the rest of the things were cooked up too.

"From now on I'm considering all those nine lovely clews as nine bum steers. And I'm going just exactly contrary to them. I'm looking for a man whose name isn't Emil Bonfils, and whose initials aren't either E or B; who isn't French, and who wasn't in Paris in 1902. A man who hasn't light hair, doesn't carry a .45-caliber pistol, and has no interest in Personal advertisements in newspapers. A man who didn't kill Gantvoort to recover anything that could have been hidden in a shoe or on a collar button. That's the sort of a guy I'm hunting for now!"

The detective-sergeant screwed up his little green eyes reflectively and scratched his head.

"Maybe that ain't so foolish!" he said. "You might be right at that. Suppose you are — what then? That Dexter kitten didn't do it — it cost her three-quarters of a million. Her brother didn't do it — he's in New York. And, besides, you don't croak a guy just because you think he's too old to marry your sister. Charles Gantvoort? He and his wife are the only ones who make any money out of the old man dying before the new will was signed. We have only their word for it that Charles was home that night. The servants didn't see him between eight and eleven. You were there, and you didn't see him until eleven. But me and you both believe him when he says he *was* home all that evening. And neither of us think he bumped the old man off — though of course he might. Who then?"

"This Creda Dexter," I suggested, "was marrying Gantvoort for his money, wasn't she? You don't think she was in love with him, do you?"

"No. I figure, from what I saw of her, that she was in love with the million and a half."

"All right," I went on. "Now she isn't exactly homely — not by a long shot. Do you reckon Gantvoort was the only man who ever fell for her?"

"I got you! I got you!" O'Gar exclaimed. "You mean there might have been some young fellow in the running who didn't have any million and a half behind him, and who didn't take kindly to being nosed out by a man who did. Maybe — maybe."

"Well, suppose we bury all this stuff we've been working on and try out that angle."

"Suits me," he said, "Starting in the morning, then, we spend our time hunting for Gantvoort's rival for the paw of this Dexter kitten."

Right or wrong, that's what we did. We stowed all those lovely clews away in a drawer, locked the drawer, and forgot them. Then we set out to find Creda Dexter's masculine acquaintances and sift them for the murderer.

But it wasn't as simple as it sounded.

All our digging into her past failed to bring to light one man who could be considered a suitor. She and her brother had been in San Francisco three years. We traced them back the length of that period, from apartment to apartment. We questioned everyone we could find who even knew her by sight. And nobody could tell us of a single man who had shown an interest in her besides Gantvoort. Nobody, apparently, had ever seen her with any man except Gantvoort or her brother.

All of which, while not getting us ahead, at least convinced us that we were on the right trail. There must have been, we argued, at least one man in her life in those three years besides Gantvoort. She wasn't — unless we were very much mistaken — the sort of woman who would discourage masculine attention; and she was certainly endowed by nature to attract it. And if there was another man, then the very fact that he had been kept so thoroughly under cover strengthened the probability of him having been mixed up in Gantvoort's death.

We were unsuccessful in learning where the Dexters had lived before they came to San Francisco, but we weren't so very interested in their earlier life. Of course it was possible that some oldtime lover had come upon the scene again recently; but in that case it should have been easier to find the recent connection than the old one.

There was no doubt, our explorations showed, that Gantvoort's son had been correct in thinking the Dexters were fortune hunters. All their activities pointed to that, although there seemed to be nothing downright criminal in their pasts.

I went up against Creda Dexter again, spending an entire afternoon in her apartment, banging away with question after question, all directed toward her former love affairs. Who had she thrown over for Gantvoort and his million and a half? And the answer was always *nobody* — an answer that I didn't choose to believe.

We had Creda Dexter shadowed night and day — and it carried us ahead not an inch. Perhaps she suspected that she was being watched. Anyway, she seldom left her apartment, and then on only the most innocent of errands. We had her apartment watched whether she was in it or not. Nobody visited it. We tapped her telephone — and all our listening-in netted us nothing. We had her mail covered — and she didn't receive a single letter, not even an advertisement.

Meanwhile, we had learned where the three clippings found in the wallet had come from — from the Personal columns of a New York, a Chicago, and a Portland newspaper. The one in the Portland paper had appeared two days before the murder, the Chicago one four days before, and the New York one five days before. All three of those papers would have been on the San Francisco newsstands the day of the murder — ready to be purchased and cut out by anyone who was looking for material to confuse detectives with.

The Agency's Paris correspondent had found no less than six Emil Bonfilses — all bloomers so far as our job was concerned — and had a line on three more.

But O'Gar and I weren't worrying over Emil Bonfils any more — that angle was dead and buried. We were plugging away at our new task — the finding of Gantvoort's rival.

Thus the days passed, and thus the matter stood when Madden Dexter was due to arrive home from New York.

Our New York branch had kept an eye on him until he left that city, and had advised us of his departure, so I knew what train he was coming on. I wanted to put a few questions to him before his sister saw him. He could tell me what I wanted to know, and he might be willing to if I could get to him before his sister had an opportunity to shut him up.

If I had known him by sight I could have picked him up when he left his train at Oakland, but I didn't know him; and I didn't want to carry Charles Gantvoort or anyone else along with me to pick him out for me.

So I went up to Sacramento that morning, and boarded his train there. I put my card in an envelope and gave it to a messenger boy in the station. Then I followed the boy through the train, while he called out:

"Mr. Dexter! Mr. Dexter!"

In the last car — the observation-club car — a slender, dark-haired man in well-made tweeds turned from watching the station platform through a window and held out his hand to the boy.

I studied him while he nervously tore open the envelope and read my card. His chin trembled slightly just now, emphasizing the weakness of a face that couldn't have been strong at its best. Between twenty-five and thirty, I placed him; with his hair parted in the middle and slicked down; large, too-expressive brown eyes; small well-shaped nose; neat brown mustache; very red, soft lips — that type.

I dropped into the vacant chair beside him when he looked up from the card.

"You are Mr. Dexter?"

"Yes," he said. "I suppose it's about Mr. Gantvoort's death that you want to see me?"

"Uh-huh. I wanted to ask you a few questions, and since I happened to be in Sacramento, I thought that by riding back on the train with you I could ask them without taking up too much of your time."

"If there's anything I can tell you," he assured me, "I'll be only too glad to do it. But I told the New York detectives all I knew, and they didn't seem to find it of much value."

"Well, the situation has changed some since you left New York." I watched his face closely as I spoke. "What we thought of no value then may be just what we want now."

I paused while he moistened his lips and avoided my eyes. He may not know anything, I thought, but he's certainly jumpy. I let him wait a few minutes while I pretended deep thoughtfulness. If I played him right, I was confident I could turn him inside out. He didn't seem to be made of very tough material.

We were sitting with our heads close together, so that the four or five other passengers in the car wouldn't overhear our talk; and that position was in my favor. One of the things that every detective knows is that it's often easy to get information — even a confession — out of a feeble nature simply by putting your face close to his and talking in a loud tone. I couldn't talk loud here, but the closeness of our faces was by itself an advantage.

"Of the men with whom your sister was acquainted," I came out with it at last, "who, outside of Mr. Gantvoort, was the most attentive?"

He swallowed audibly, looked out of the window, fleetingly at me, and then out of the window again.

"Really, I couldn't say."

"All right. Let's get at it this way. Suppose we check off one by one all the men who were interested in her and in whom she was interested."

He continued to stare out of the window.

"Who's first?" I pressed him.

His gaze flickered around to meet mine for a second, with a sort of timid desperation in his eyes.

"I know it sounds foolish, but I, her brother, couldn't give you the name of even one man in whom Creda was interested before she met Gantvoort. She never, so far as I know, had the slightest feeling for any man before she met him. Of course it is possible that there may have been someone that I didn't know anything about, but —"

It did sound foolish, right enough! The Creda Dexter I had talked to — a sleek kitten as O'Gar had put it — didn't impress me as being at all likely to go very long without having at least one man in tow. This pretty little guy in front of me was lying. There couldn't be any other explanation.

I went at him tooth and nail. But when we reached Oakland early that night he was still sticking to his original statement — that Gantvoort was the only one of his sister's suitors that he knew anything about. And I knew that I had blundered, had underrated Madden Dexter, had played my hand wrong in trying to shake him down too quickly — in driving too directly at the point I was interested in. He was either a lot stronger than I had figured him, or his interest in concealing Gantvoort's murderer was much greater than I had thought it would be.

But I had this much: if Dexter was lying — and there couldn't be much doubt of that — then Gantvoort *had* had a rival, and Madden Dexter believed or knew that this rival had killed Gantvoort.

When he left the train at Oakland I knew I was licked, that he wasn't going to tell me what I wanted to know — not this night, anyway. But I clung to him, stuck at his side when we boarded the ferry for San

Francisco, in spite of the obviousness of his desire to get away from me. There's always a chance of something unexpected happening; so I continued to ply him with questions as our boat left the slip.

Presently a man came toward where we were sitting — a big burly man in a light overcoat, carrying a black bag.

"Hello, Madden!" he greeted my companion, striding over to him with outstretched hand. "Just got in and was trying to remember your phone number," he said, setting down his bag, as they shook hands warmly.

Madden Dexter turned to me.

"I want you to meet Mr. Smith," he told me, and then gave my name to the big man, adding, "he's with the Continental Detective Agency here."

That tag — clearly a warning for Smith's benefit — brought me to my feet, all watchfulness. But the ferry was crowded — a hundred persons were within sight of us, all around us. I relaxed, smiled pleasantly, and shook hands with Smith. Whoever Smith was, and whatever connection he might have with the murder — and if he hadn't any, why should Dexter have been in such a hurry to tip him off to my identity?— he couldn't do anything here. The crowd around us was all to my advantage.

That was my second mistake of the day.

Smith's left hand had gone into his overcoat pocket — or rather, through one of those vertical slits that certain styles of overcoats have so that inside pockets may be reached without unbuttoning the overcoat. His hand had gone through that slit, and his coat had fallen away far enough for me to see a snub-nosed automatic in his hand — shielded from everyone's sight but mine — pointing at my waist-line.

"Shall we go on deck?" Smith asked — and it was an order.

I hesitated. I didn't like to leave all these people who were so blindly standing and sitting around us. But Smith's face wasn't the face of a cautious man. He had the look of one who might easily disregard the presence of a hundred witnesses.

I turned around and walked through the crowd. His right hand lay familiarly on my shoulder as he walked behind me; his left hand held his gun, under the overcoat, against my spine.

The deck was deserted. A heavy fog, wet as rain — the fog of San Francisco Bay's winter nights — lay over boat and water, and had driven everyone else inside. It hung about us, thick and impenetrable; I couldn't see so far as the end of the boat, in spite of the lights glowing overhead.

I stopped.

Smith prodded me in the back.

"Farther away, where we can talk," he rumbled in my ear.

I went on until I reached the rail.

The entire back of my head burned with sudden fire . . . tiny points of light glittered in the blackness before me . . . grew larger . . . came rushing toward me. . . .

Semi-consciousness! I found myself mechanically keeping afloat somehow and trying to get out of my overcoat. The back of my head throbbed devilishly. My eyes burned. I felt heavy and logged, as if I had swallowed gallons of water.

The fog hung low and thick on the water — there was nothing else to be seen anywhere. By the time I had freed myself of the encumbering overcoat my head had cleared somewhat, but with returning consciousness came increased pain.

A light glimmered mistily off to my left, and then vanished. From out of the misty blanket, from every direction, in a dozen different keys, from near and far, fog-horns sounded. I stopped swimming and floated on my back, trying to determine my whereabouts.

After a while I picked out the moaning, evenly spaced blasts of the Alcatraz siren. But they told me nothing. They came to me out of the fog without direction — seemed to beat down upon me from straight above.

I was somewhere in San Francisco Bay, and that was all I knew, though I suspected the current was sweeping me out toward the Golden Gate.

A little while passed, and I knew that I had left the path of the Oakland ferries — no boat had passed close to me for some time. I was glad to be out of that track. In this fog a boat was a lot more likely to run me down than to pick me up.

The water was chilling me, so I turned over and began swimming, just vigorously enough to keep my blood circulating while I saved my strength until I had a definite goal to try for.

A horn began to repeat its roaring note nearer and nearer, and presently the lights of the boat upon which it was fixed came into sight. One of the Sausalito ferries, I thought.

It came quite close to me, and I halloed until I was breathless and my throat was raw. But the boat's siren, crying its warning, drowned my shouts.

The boat went on and the fog closed in behind it.

The current was stronger now, and my attempts to attract the attention of the Sausalito ferry had left me weaker. I floated, letting the water sweep me where it would, resting.

Another light appeared ahead of me suddenly — hung there for an instant — disappeared.

I began to yell, and worked my arms and legs madly, trying to drive myself through the water to where it had been.

I never saw it again.

Weariness settled upon me, and a sense of futility. The water was no longer cold. I was warm with a comfortable, soothing numbness. My head stopped throbbing; there was no feeling at all in it now. No lights, now, but the sound of fog-horns . . . fog-horns . . . fog-horns ahead of me, behind me, to either side; annoying me, irritating me.

But for the moaning horns I would have ceased all effort. They had become the only disagreeable detail of my situation — the water was pleasant, fatigue was pleasant. But the horns tormented me. I cursed them petulantly and decided to swim until I could no longer hear them, and then, in the quiet of the friendly fog, go to sleep. . . .

Now and then I would doze, to be goaded into wakefulness by the wailing voice of a siren.

"Those damned horns! Those damned horns!" I complained aloud, again and again.

One of them, I found presently, was bearing down upon me from behind, growing louder and stronger. I turned and waited. Lights, dim and steaming, came into view.

With exaggerated caution to avoid making the least splash, I swam off to one side. When this nuisance was past I could go to sleep. I sniggered softly to myself as the lights drew abreast, feeling a foolish triumph in my cleverness in eluding the boat. Those damned horns. . . .

Life — the hunger for life — all at once surged back into my being.

I screamed at the passing boat, and with every iota of my being struggled toward it. Between strokes I tilted up my head and screamed. . . .

When I returned to consciousness for the second time that evening, I was lying on my back on a baggage truck, which was moving. Men and women were crowding around, walking beside the truck, staring at me with curious eyes. I sat up.

"Where are we?" I asked.

A little red-faced man in uniform answered my question.

"Just landing in Sausalito. Lay still. We'll take you over to the hospital."

I looked around.

"How long before this boat goes back to San Francisco?"

"Leaves right away."

I slid off the truck and started back aboard the boat.

"I'm going with it," I said.

Half an hour later, shivering and shaking in my wet clothes, keeping my mouth clamped tight so that my teeth wouldn't sound like a dice-game, I climbed into a taxi at the Ferry Building and went to my flat.

There, I swallowed half a pint of whisky, rubbed myself with a coarse towel until my skin was sore, and, except for an enormous weariness and a worse headache, I felt almost human again.

I reached O'Gar by phone, asked him to come up to my flat right away, and then called up Charles Gantvoort.

"Have you seen Madden Dexter yet?" I asked him.

"No, but I talked to him over the phone. He called me up as soon as he got in. I asked him to meet me in Mr. Abernathy's office in the morning, so we could go over that business he transacted for Father."

"Can you call him up now and tell him that you have been called out of town — will have to leave early in the morning — and that you'd like to run over to his apartment and see him tonight?"

"Why yes, if you wish."

"Good! Do that. I'll call for you in a little while and go over to see him with you."

"What is —"

"I'll tell you about it when I see you," I cut him off.

O'Gar arrived as I was finishing dressing.

"So he told you something?" he asked, knowing of my plan to meet Dexter on the train and question him.

"Yes," I said with sour sarcasm, "but I came near forgetting what it was. I grilled him all the way from Sacramento to Oakland, and couldn't get a whisper out of him. On the ferry coming over he introduces me to a man he calls Mr. Smith, and he tells Mr. Smith that I'm a gum-shoe. This, mind you, all happens in the middle of a crowded ferry! Mr. Smith puts a gun in my belly, marches me out on deck, raps me across the back of the head, and dumps me into the bay."

"You have a lot of fun, don't you?" O'Gar grinned, and then wrinkled his forehead. "Looks like Smith would be the man we want then — the buddy who turned the Gantvoort trick. But what the hell did he want to give himself away by chucking you overboard for?"

"Too hard for me," I confessed, while trying to find which of my hats and caps would sit least heavily upon my bruised head. "Dexter knew I was hunting for one of his sister's former lovers, of course. And he must have thought I knew a whole lot more than I do, or he wouldn't have made that raw play — tipping my mitt to Smith right in front of me.

"It may be that after Dexter lost his head and made that break on the ferry, Smith figured that I'd be on to him soon, if not right away; and so he'd take a desperate chance on putting me out of the way. But we'll know all about it in a little while," I said, as we went down to the waiting taxi and set out for Gantvoort's.

"You ain't counting on Smith being in sight, are you?" the detective-sergeant asked.

"No. He'll be holed up somewhere until he sees how things are going. But Madden Dexter will have to be out in the open to protect himself. He has an alibi, so he's in the clear so far as the actual killing is concerned. And with me supposed to be dead, the more he stays in the open, the safer he is. But it's a cinch that he knows what this is all about, though he wasn't necessarily involved in it. As near as I could see, he didn't go out on deck with Smith and me tonight. Anyway he'll be home. And this time he's going to talk — he's going to tell his little story!"

Charles Gantvoort was standing on his front steps when we reached his house. He climbed into our taxi and we headed for the Dexters' apartment. We didn't have time to answer any of the questions that Gantvoort was firing at us with every turning of the wheels.

"He's home and expecting you?" I asked him.

"Yes."

Then we left the taxi and went into the apartment building.

"Mr. Gantvoort to see Mr. Dexter," he told the Philippine boy at the switchboard.

The boy spoke into the phone.

"Go right up," he told us.

At the Dexters' door I stepped past Gantvoort and pressed the button.

Creda Dexter opened the door. Her amber eyes widened and her smile faded as I stepped past her into the apartment.

I walked swiftly down the little hallway and turned into the first room through whose open door a light showed.

And came face to face with Smith!

We were both surprised, but his astonishment was a lot more profound than mine. Neither of us had expected to see the other; but I had known he was still alive, while he had every reason for thinking me at the bottom of the bay.

I took advantage of his greater bewilderment to the extent of two steps toward him before he went into action.

One of his hands swept down.

I threw my right fist at his face — threw it with every ounce of my 180 pounds behind it, reinforced by the memory of every second I had spent in the water, and every throb of my battered head.

His hand, already darting down for his pistol, came back up too late to fend off my punch.

Something clicked in my hand as it smashed into his face, and my hand went numb.

But he went down — and lay where he fell.

I jumped across his body to a door on the opposite side of the room, pulling my gun loose with my left hand.

"Dexter's somewhere around!" I called over my shoulder to O'Gar, who with Gantvoort and Creda was coming through the door by which I had entered. "Keep your eyes open!"

I dashed through the four other rooms of the apartment, pulling closet doors open, looking everywhere — and I found nobody.

Then I returned to where Creda Dexter was trying to revive Smith, with the assistance of O'Gar and Gantvoort.

The detective-sergeant looked over his shoulder at me.

"Who do you think this joker is?" he asked.

"My friend Mr. Smith."

"Gantvoort says he's Madden Dexter."

I looked at Charles Gantvoort, who nodded his head.

"This is Madden Dexter," he said.

We worked upon Dexter for nearly ten minutes before he opened his eyes.

As soon as he sat up we began to shoot questions and accusations at him, hoping to get a confession out of him before he recovered from his shakiness — but he wasn't that shaky.

All we could get out of him was:

"Take me in if you want to. If I've got anything to say I'll say it to my lawyer, and to nobody else."

Creda Dexter, who had stepped back after her brother came to, and was standing a little way off, watching us, suddenly came forward and caught me by the arm.

"What have you got on him?" she demanded, imperatively.

"I wouldn't want to say," I countered, "but I don't mind telling you this much. We're going to give him a chance in a nice modern court-room to prove that he didn't kill Leopold Gantvoort."

"He was in New York!"

"He was not! He had a friend who went to New York as Madden Dexter and looked after Gantvoort's business under that name. But if this is the real Madden Dexter then the closest he got to New York was when he met his friend on the ferry to get from him the papers connected with the B. F. & F. Iron Corporation transaction, and learned that I had stumbled upon the truth about his alibi — even if I didn't know it myself at the time."

She jerked around to face her brother.

"Is that on the level?" she asked him.

He sneered at her, and went on feeling with the fingers of one hand the spot on his jaw where my fist had landed.

"I'll say all I've got to say to my lawyer," he repeated.

"You will?" she shot back at him. "Well, I'll say what I've got to say right now!"

She flung around to face me again.

"Madden is not my brother at all! My name is Ives. Madden and I met in St. Louis about four years ago, drifted around together for a year or so, and then came to Frisco. He was a con man — still is. He made Mr. Gantvoort's acquaintance six or seven months ago, and was getting him all ribbed up to unload a fake invention on him. He brought him here a couple of times, and introduced me to him as his sister. We usually posed as brother and sister.

"Then, after Mr. Gantvoort had been here a couple times, Madden decided to change his game. He thought Mr. Gantvoort liked me, and that we could get more money out of him by working a fancy sort of badger-game on him. I was to lead the old man on until I had him wrapped around my finger — until we had him tied up so tight he couldn't get away — had something on him — something good and strong. Then we were going to shake him down for plenty of money.

"Everything went along fine for a while. He fell for me — fell hard. And finally he asked me to marry him. We had never figured on that. Blackmail was our game. But when he asked me to marry him I tried to call Madden off. I admit the old man's money had something to do with it — it influenced me — but I had come to like him a little for himself. He was mighty fine in lots of ways — nicer than anybody I had ever known.

"So I told Madden all about it, and suggested that we drop the other plan, and that I marry Gantvoort. I promised to see that Madden was kept supplied with money — I knew I could get whatever I wanted from Mr. Gantvoort. And I was on the level with Madden. I liked Mr. Gantvoort, but Madden had found him and brought him around to me; and so I wasn't going to run out on Madden. I was willing to do all I could for him.

"But Madden wouldn't hear of it. He'd have got more money in the long run by doing as I suggested — but he wanted his little handful right away. And to make him more unreasonable he got one of his jealous streaks. He beat me one night!

"That settled it. I made up my mind to ditch him. I told Mr. Gantvoort that my brother was bitterly opposed to our marrying, and he could see that Madden was carrying a grudge. So he arranged to send Madden East on that steel business, to get him out of the way until we were off on our wedding trip. And we thought Madden was completely deceived — but I should have known that he would see through our scheme. We planned to be gone about a year, and by that time I thought Madden would have forgotten me — or I'd be fixed to handle him if he tried to make any trouble.

"As soon as I heard that Mr. Gantvoort had been killed I had a hunch that Madden had done it. But then it seemed like a certainty that he was in New York the next day, and I thought I had done him an injustice. And I was glad he was out of it. But now —"

She whirled around to her erstwhile confederate.

"Now I hope you swing, you big sap!"

She spun around to me again. No sleek kitten, this, but a furious, spitting cat, with claws and teeth bared.

"What kind of looking fellow was the one who went to New York for him?"

I described the man I had talked to on the train.

"Evan Felter," she said, after a moment of thought. "He used to work with Madden. You'll probably find him hiding in Los Angeles. Put the screws on him and he'll spill all he knows — he's a weak sister! The chances are he didn't know what Madden's game was until it was all over."

"How do you like that?" she spat at Madden Dexter. "How do you like that for a starter? You messed up my little party, did you? Well, I'm going to spend every minute of my time from now until they pop you off helping them pop you!"

And she did, too — with her assistance it was no trick at all to gather up the rest of the evidence we needed to hang him. And I don't believe her enjoyment of her three-quarters of a million dollars is spoiled a bit by any qualms over what she did to Madden. She's a very respectable woman *now*, and glad to be free of the con man.

ROY VICKERS

THE
RUBBER
TRUMPET

Roy Vickers (1889–1965) wrote a number of crime stories and novels, but his creation in 1935 of Scotland Yard's fictional Department of Dead Ends was a stroke of genius. This is the dusty back attic where still mystifying clues from unsolved crimes are tucked away. The clues themselves are unremarkable — tortoiseshell toilet articles, a book of love poems, a doll, a yellow dress, a rubber trumpet — and they simply gather dust, in that uncomputerized age, until something in some more recent crime triggers the memory of someone in the department. The reader knows the details of the crime; the excitement comes in waiting for the event, or clue, that arouses memory.

"The Rubber Trumpet" was the first Department of Dead Ends story. Years after it was published in England, it came to the attention of Ellery Queen, much like a forgotten item on the department shelf. Ellery Queen encouraged Vickers to write more, and the series was reborn.

1

IF YOU WERE to enquire at Scotland Yard for the Department of Dead Ends you might be told, in all sincerity, that there is no such thing, because it is not called by that name nowadays. All the same, if it has no longer a room to itself, you may rest assured that its spirit hovers over the index files of which we are all so justly proud.

The Department came into existence in the spacious days of King Edward VII, and it took everything that the other departments rejected. For instance, it noted and filed all those clues that had the exasperating effect of proving a palpably guilty man innocent. Its shelves were crowded with exhibits that might have been in the Black Museum — but were not. Its photographs were a perpetual irritation to all rising young detectives, who felt that they ought to have found the means of putting them in the Rogues' Gallery.

To the Department, too, were taken all those members of the public who insist on helping the police with obviously irrelevant information and preposterous theories. The one passport to the Department was a written statement by the senior officer in charge of the case that the information offered was absurd.

Judged by the standards of reason and common sense, its files were mines of misinformation. It proceeded largely by guesswork. On one occasion it hanged a murderer by accidentally punning on his name.

It was the function of the Department to connect persons and things that had no logical connection. In short, it stood for the antithesis of scientific detection. It played always for a lucky fluke — to offset the lucky fluke by which the criminal so often eludes the police. Often it muddled one crime with another and arrived at the correct answer by wrong reasoning.

As in the case of George Muncey and the rubber trumpet.

And note, please, that the rubber trumpet had nothing logically to do with George Muncey, nor the woman he murdered, nor the circumstances in which he murdered her.

2

Until the age of twenty-six George Muncey lived with his widowed mother in Chichester, the family income being derived from a chemist's shop, efficiently controlled by Mrs. Muncey with the aid of a manager and two assistants, of whom latterly George was one. Of his early youth we know only that he won a scholarship at a day-school, tenable for three years, which was cancelled at the end of a year, though not, apparently, for misconduct. He failed several times to obtain his pharmaceutical certificate, with the result that he was eventually put in charge of the fancy soaps, the hot-water bottles, and the photographic accessories.

For this work he received two pounds per week. Every Saturday he handed the whole of it to his mother, who returned him fifteen shillings for pocket money. She had no need of the balance and only took it in order to nourish his self-respect. He did not notice that she bought his clothes and met all his other expenses.

George had no friends and very little of what an ordinary young man would regard as pleasure. He spent nearly all his spare time with his mother, to whom he was devoted. She was an amiable but very domineering woman and she does not seem to have noticed that her son's affection had in it a quality of childishness — that he liked her to form his opinions for him and curtail his liberties.

After his mother's death he did not resume his duties at the shop. For some eight months he mooned about Chichester. Then, the business having been sold and probate granted, he found himself in possession of some eight hundred pounds, with another two thousand pounds due to him in three months. He did not, apparently, understand this part of the transaction — for he made no application for the two thousand, and as the solicitors could not find him until his name came into the papers, the two thousand remained intact for his defence.

That he was a normal but rather backward young man is proved by the fact that the walls of his bedroom were liberally decorated with photographs of the actresses of the moment and pictures of anonymous beauties cut from the more sporting weeklies. Somewhat naïvely he bestowed this picture gallery as a parting gift on the elderly cook.

He drew the whole of the eight hundred pounds in notes and gold, said good-bye to his home and went up to London. He stumbled on cheap and respectable lodgings in Pimlico. Then, in a gauche, small-town way, he set out to see life.

It was the year when *The Merry Widow* was setting all London a-whistling. Probably on some chance recommendation, he drifted to Daly's Theatre, where he bought himself a seat in the dress-circle.

It was the beginning of the London season and we may assume that he would have felt extremely self-conscious sitting in the circle in his ready-made lounge suit, had there not happened to be a woman also in morning dress next to him.

The woman was a Miss Hilda Callermere. She was forty-three and if she escaped positive ugliness she was certainly without any kind of physical attractiveness, though she was neat in her person and reasonably well-dressed, in an old-fashioned way.

Eventually to the Department of Dead Ends came the whole story of his strange courtship.

There is a curious quality in the manner in which these two slightly unusual human beings approached one another. They did not speak until after the show, when they were wedged together in the corridor. Their voices seem to come to us out of a fog of social shyness and vulgar gentility. And it was she who took the initiative.

"If you'll excuse me speaking to you without an introduction, we seem to be rather out of it, you and I, what with one thing and another."

His reply strikes us now as somewhat unusual.

"Yes, rather!" he said. "Are you coming here again?"

"Yes, rather! I sometimes come twice a week."

During the next fortnight they both went three times to *The Merry Widow,* but on the first two of these occasions they missed each other. On the third occasion, which was a Saturday night, Miss Callermere invited George Muncey to walk with her on the following morning in Battersea Park.

Here shyness dropped from them. They slipped quite suddenly onto an easy footing of friendship. George Muncey accepted her invitation to lunch. She took him to a comfortably furnished eight-roomed house — her own — in which she lived with an aunt whom she supported. For, in addition to the house, Miss Callermere owned an income of six hundred pounds derived from gilt-edged investments.

But these considerations weighed hardly at all with George Muncey — for he had not yet spent fifty pounds of his eight hundred, and at this stage he had certainly no thought of marriage with Miss Callermere.

3

Neither of them had any occupation, so they could meet whenever they chose. Miss Callermere undertook to show George London. Her father had been a cheery, beery jerry-builder with sporting interests, and she had reacted from him into a parched severity of mind. She marched George round the Tower of London, the British Museum, and the like, reading aloud extracts from a guide-book. They went neither to the theatres nor to the music-halls, for Miss Callermere thought these frivolous and empty-headed — with the exception of *The Merry Widow,* which she believed to be opera, and therefore cultural. And the extraordinary thing was the George Muncey liked it all.

There can be no doubt that this smug little spinster, some sixteen years older than himself, touched a chord of sympathy in his nature. But she was wholly unable to cater for that part of him that had plastered photographs of public beauties on the walls of his bedroom.

She never went to *The Merry Widow* again, but once or twice he would sneak off to Daly's by himself. *The Merry Widow,* in fact, provided him with a dream-life. We may infer that in his imagination he identified himself with Mr. Joseph Coyne, who nightly, in the character of Prince Dannilo, would disdain the beautiful Sonia only to have her rush the more surely to his arms in the finale. Rather a dangerous fantasy for a backward young man from the provinces who was beginning to lose his shyness!

There was, indeed, very little shyness about him when, one evening after seeing Miss Callermere home, he was startled by the sight of a young parlourmaid, who had been sent out to post a letter, some fifty yards from Miss Callermere's house. If she bore little or no likeness to Miss Lily Elsie in the role of Sonia, she certainly looked quite lovely in her white cap and the streamers that were then worn. And she was smiling and friendly and natural.

She was, of course, Ethel Fairbrass. She lingered with George Muncey for over five minutes. And then comes another of those strange little dialogues.

"Funny a girl like you being a slavey! When's your evening off?"

"Six o'clock to-morrow. But what's it got to do with you?"

"I'll meet you at the corner of this road. Promise you I will."

"Takes two to make a promise. My name's Ethel Fairbrass, if you want to know. What's yours?"

"Dannilo."

"Coo! Fancy calling you that! Dannilo What?"

George had not foreseen the necessity for inventing a surname and discovered that it is quite difficult. He couldn't very well say "Smith" or "Robinson," so he said:

"Prince."

George, it will be observed, was not an imaginative man. When she met him the following night he could think of nowhere to take her but to *The Merry Widow*. He was even foolish enough to let her have a programme, but she did not read the names of the characters. When the curtain went up she was too entranced with Miss Lily Elsie, whom (like every pretty girl at the time) she thought she resembled, to take any notice of Mr. Joseph Coyne and his character name. If she had tumbled to the witless transposition of the names she might have become suspicious of him. In which case George Muncey might have lived to a ripe old age.

But she didn't.

4

Altogether, Ethel Fairbrass provided an extremely satisfactory substitute for the dream-woman of George's fantasy. Life was beginning
to sweeten. In the daylight hours he would enjoy his friendship with
Miss Callermere, the pleasure of which was in no way touched by his
infatuation for the pretty parlourmaid.

In early September Ethel became entitled to her holiday. She spent
the whole fortnight with George at Southend. And George wrote daily
to Miss Callermere, telling her that he was filling the place of a chemist-
friend of his mother's, while the latter took his holiday. He actually
contrived to have the letters addressed to the care of a local chemist.
The letters were addressed "George Muncey" while at the hotel the
couple were registered as "Mr. and Mrs. D. Prince."

Now the fictional Prince Dannilo was notoriously an open-handed
and free-living fellow — and Dannilo Prince proceeded to follow in
his footsteps. Ethel Fairbrass undoubtedly had the time of her life.
They occupied a suite. ("Coo! A bathroom all to our own two selves,
and use it whenever we like!")

He hired a car for her, with chauffeur — which cost ten pounds a
day at that time. He gave her champagne whenever he could induce
her to drink it and bought her some quite expensive presents.

It is a little surprising that at the end of a fortnight of this kind of
thing she went back to her occupation. But she did. There was nothing
of the mercenary about Ethel.

On his return to London, George was very glad to see Miss Callermere. They resumed their interminable walks and he went almost
daily to her house for lunch or dinner. A valuable arrangement, this,
for the little diversion at Southend had made a sizeable hole in his
eight hundred pounds.

It was a bit of a nuisance to have to leave early in order to snatch
a few minutes with Ethel. After Southend, the few snatched minutes
had somehow lost their charm. There were, too, Ethel's half-days and
her Sundays, the latter involving him in a great many troublesome
lies to Miss Callermere.

In the middle of October he started sneaking off to *The Merry Widow*
again. Which was a bad sign. For it meant that he was turning back
again from reality to his dream-life. The Reality, in the meantime,
had lost her high spirits and was inclined to weep unreasonably and
to nag more than a little.

At the beginning of November Ethel presented him with certain very valid arguments in favour of fixing the date of their wedding, a matter which had hitherto been kept vaguely in the background.

George was by now heartily sick of her and contemplated leaving her in the lurch. Strangely enough, it was her final threat to tell Miss Callermere that turned the scale and decided George to make the best of a bad job and marry her.

5

As Dannilo Prince he married her one foggy morning at the registrar's office in Henrietta Street. Mr. and Mrs. Fairbrass came up from Banbury for the wedding. They were not very nice about it, although from the social point of view the marriage might be regarded as a step up for Ethel.

"Where are you going for your honeymoon?" asked Mrs. Fairbrass. "That is — if you're going to *have* a honeymoon."

"Southend," said the unimaginative George, and to Southend he took her for the second time. There was no need for a suite now, so they went to a small family-and-commercial hotel. Here George was unreasonably jealous of the commercial travellers, who were merely being polite to a rather forlorn bride. In wretched weather he insisted on taking her for walks, with the result that he himself caught a very bad cold. Eucalyptus and hot toddy became the dominant note in a town which was associated in the girl's mind with champagne and bath salts. But they had to stick it for the full fortnight, because George had told Miss Callermere that he was again acting as substitute for the chemist-friend of his mother's in Southend.

According to the files of the Department, they left Southend by the three-fifteen on the thirtieth of November. George had taken first-class returns. The three-fifteen was a popular non-stop, but on this occasion there were hardly a score of persons travelling to London. One of the first-class carriages was occupied by a man alone with a young baby wrapped in a red shawl. Ethel wanted to get into this compartment, perhaps having a sneaking hope that the man would require her assistance in dealing with the baby. But George did not intend to concern himself with babies one moment before he would be compelled to do so, and they went into another compartment.

Ethel, however, seems to have looked forward to her impending career with a certain pleasure. Before leaving Southend she had paid a visit to one of those shops that cater for summer visitors and miraculously remain open through the winter. She had a bulky parcel, which she opened in the rather pathetic belief that it would amuse George.

The parcel contained a large child's bucket, a disproportionately small wooden spade, a sailing-boat to the scale of the spade, a length of Southend rock and a rubber trumpet, of which the stem was wrapped with red and blue wool. It was a baby's trumpet and of rubber so that it should not hurt the baby's gums. In the mouthpiece, shielded by the rubber, was a little metal contraption that made the noise.

Ethel put the trumpet to her mouth and blew through the metal contraption.

Perhaps, in fancy, she heard her baby doing it. Perhaps, after a honeymoon of neglect and misery, she was making a desperate snatch at the spirit of gaiety, hoping he would attend to her and perhaps indulge in a little horseplay. But for the actual facts we have to depend on George's version.

"I said 'Don't make that noise, Ethel — I'm trying to read' or something like that. And she said 'I feel like a bit of music to cheer me up' and she went on blowing the trumpet. So I caught hold of it and threw it out of the window. I didn't hurt her and she didn't seem to mind much. And we didn't have another quarrel over it and I went on reading my paper until we got to London."

At Fenchurch Street they claimed their luggage and left the station. Possibly Ethel abandoned the parcel containing the other toys, for they were never heard of again.

When the train was being cleaned, a dead baby was found under the seat of a first-class compartment, wrapped in a red shawl. It was subsequently ascertained that the baby had not been directly murdered but had died more or less naturally in convulsions.

But before this was known, Scotland Yard searched for the man who had been seen to enter the train with the baby, as if for a murderer. A platelayer found the rubber trumpet on the line and forwarded it. Detectives combed the shops of Southend and found that only one rubber trumpet had been sold — to a young woman whom the shopkeeper did not know. The trail ended here.

The rubber trumpet went to the Department of Dead Ends.

6

Of the eight hundred pounds there was a little over a hundred and fifty left by the time they returned from the official honeymoon at Southend. He took her to furnished rooms in Ladbroke Grove and a few days later to a tenement in the same district, which he furnished at a cost of thirty pounds.

She seems to have asked him no awkward questions about money. Every morning after breakfast he would leave the tenement, presumably in order to go to work. Actually he would loaf about the West End until it was time to meet Miss Callermere. He liked especially going to the house in Battersea for lunch on Sundays. And here, of course, the previous process reversed itself and it was Ethel who had to be told the troublesome lies that were so difficult to invent.

"You seem so different lately, George," said Miss Callermere one Sunday after lunch. "I believe you're living with a ballet girl."

George was not quite sure what a ballet girl was, but it sounded rather magnificently wicked. As he was anxious not to involve himself in further inventions, he said:

"She's not a ballet girl. She used to be a parlourmaid."

"I really only want to know one thing about her," said Miss Callermere. "And that is, whether you are fond of her?"

"No, I'm not!" said George with complete truthfulness.

"It's a pity to have that kind of thing in your life — you are dedicated to science. For your own sake, George, why not get rid of her?"

Why not? George wondered why he had not thought of it before. He had only to move, to stop calling himself by the ridiculous name of Dannilo Prince, and the thing was as good as done. He would go back at once and pack.

When he got back to the tenement, Ethel gave him an unexpectedly warm reception.

"You told me you were going to the S.D.P. Sunday Brotherhood, you did! And you never went near them, because you met that there Miss Callermere in Battersea Park, because I followed you and saw you. And then you went back to her house, which is Number Fifteen, Laurel Road, which I didn't know before. And what you can see in a dried-up old maid like that beats me. It's time she knew that she's rolling her silly sheep's eyes at another woman's husband. And I'm going to tell her before I'm a day older."

She was whipping on hat and coat and George lurched forward to stop her. His foot caught on a gas-ring, useless now that he had installed a gas-range — a piece of lumber that Ethel ought to have removed weeks ago. But she used it as a stand for the iron.

George picked up the gas-ring. If she were to go to Miss Callermere and make a brawl, he himself would probably never be able to go there again. He pushed her quickly on to the bed, then swung the gas-ring — swung it several times.

He put all the towels, every soft absorbent thing he could find, under the bed. Then he washed himself, packed a suitcase, and left the tenement.

He took the suitcase to his old lodgings, announced that he had come back there to live, and then presented himself at the house in Battersea in time for supper.

"I've done what you told me," he said to Miss Callermere. "Paid her off. Shan't hear from her any more."

The Monday morning papers carried the news of the murder, for the police had been called on Sunday evening by the tenants of the flat below. The hunt was started for Dannilo Prince.

By Tuesday the dead girl's parents had been interviewed and her life-story appeared on Wednesday morning.

> My daughter was married to Prince at the Henrietta Street registrar's office on November 16th, 1907. He took her straight away for a honeymoon at Southend, where they stayed a fortnight.

There was a small crowd at the bottom of Laurel Road to gape at the house where she had so recently worked as a parlourmaid. Fifty yards from Number Fifteen! But if Miss Callermere noticed the crowd she is not recorded as having made any comment upon it to anyone.

In a few days, Scotland Yard knew that they would never find Dannilo Prince. In fact, it had all been as simple as George had anticipated. He had just moved — and that was the end of his unlucky marriage. The addition of the murder had not complicated things, because he had left no clue behind him.

Now, as there was nothing whatever to connect George Muncey with Dannilo Prince, George's chances of arrest were limited to the chance of an accidental meeting between himself and someone who had known him as Prince. There was a hotel proprietor, a waiter, and a chambermaid at Southend, and an estate agent at Ladbroke Grove. And, of course, Ethel's father and mother. Of these persons only the estate agent lived in London.

A barrister, who was also a statistician, entertained himself by working out the averages. He came to the conclusion that George Muncey's chance of being caught was equal to his chance of winning the first prize in the Calcutta Sweep *twenty-three times in succession.*

But the barrister did not calculate the chances of the illogical guesswork of the Department of Dead Ends hitting the bull's-eye by mistake.

7

While the hue and cry for Dannilo Prince passed over his head, George Muncey dedicated himself to science with such energy that in a fortnight he had obtained a post with a chemist in Walham. Here he presided over a counter devoted to fancy soaps, hot-water bottles, photographic aparatus, and the like — for which he received two pounds a week and a minute commission that added zest to his work.

At Easter he married Miss Callermere in church. That lady had mobilised all her late father's associates and, to their inward amusement, arrayed herself in white satin and veil for the ceremony. As it would have been unreasonable to ask George's employers for a holiday after so short a term of service, the newly married couple dispensed with a honeymoon. The aunt entered a home for indigent gentlewomen with an allowance of a hundred a year from her niece. George once again found himself in a spacious, well-run house.

During their brief married life, this oddly assorted couple seem to have been perfectly happy. The late Mr. Callermere's friends were allowed to slip back into oblivion, because they showed a tendency to giggle whenever George absent-mindedly addressed his wife as "Miss Callermere."

His earnings of two pounds a week may have seemed insignificant beside his wife's unearned income. But in fact it was the basis of their married happiness. Every Saturday he handed her the whole of his wages. She would retain twenty-five shillings, because they both considered it essential to his self-respect that he should pay the cost of his food. She handed him back fifteen shillings for pocket-money. She read the papers and formed his opinions for him. She seemed to allow him little of what most men would regard as pleasure, but George had no complaint on this score.

Spring passed into summer and nearly everybody had forgotten the murder of Ethel Prince in a tenement in Ladbroke Grove. It is probably true to say that, in any real sense of the word, George Muncey had forgotten it too. He had read very little and did not know that murderers were popularly supposed to be haunted by their crime and to start guiltily at every chance mention of it.

He received no reaction whatever when his employer said to him one morning:

"There's this job-line of rubber trumpets. I took half a gross. We'll mark them at one-and-a-penny. Put one on your counter with the rubber teats and try them on women with babies."

George took one of the rubber trumpets from the cardboard case containing the half gross. It had red and blue wool wound about the stem. He put it next the rubber teats and forgot about it.

8

Wilkins, the other assistant, held his pharmaceutical certificate, but he was not stand-offish on that account. One day, to beguile the boredom of the slack hour after lunch, he picked up the rubber trumpet and blew it.

Instantly George was sitting in the train with Ethel, telling her not to make that noise. When Wilkins put the trumpet down, George found himself noticing the trumpet and thought the red and blue wool very hideous. He picked it up — Ethel's had felt just like that when he had thrown it out of the window.

Now it cannot for one moment be held that George felt anything in the nature of remorse. The truth was that the rubber trumpet, by reminding him so vividly of Ethel, had stirred up dormant forces in his nature. Ethel had been very comely and jolly and playful when one was in the mood for it — as one often was, in spite of everything.

The trumpet, in short, produced little more than a sense of bewilderment. Why could not things have gone on as they began? It was only as a wife that Ethel was utterly intolerable, because she had no sense of order and did not really look after a chap. Now that he was married to Miss Callermere, if only Ethel had been available on, say, Wednesday evenings and alternate Sundays, life would have been full at once of colour and comfort. . . . He tried to sell the trumpet to a lady with a little girl and a probable baby at home, but without success.

On the next day he went as far as admitting to himself that the trumpet had got on his nerves. Between a quarter to one and a quarter past, when Wilkins was out to lunch, he picked up the trumpet and blew it. And just before closing-time he blew it again, when Wilkins was there.

George was not subtle enough to humbug himself. The trumpet stirred longings that were better suppressed. So the next day he wrote out a bill for one-and-a-penny, put one-and-a-penny of his pocket money into the cash register and stuffed the trumpet into his coat pocket. Before supper that night he put it in the hot-water furnace.

"There's a terrible smell in the house. What did you put in the furnace, George?"

"Nothing."

"Tell me the truth, dear."

"A rubber trumpet stuck on my counter. Fair got on my nerves, it did. I paid the one-and-a-penny and I burnt it."

"That was very silly, wasn't it? It'll make you short in your pocket money. And in the circumstances I don't feel inclined to make it up for you."

That would be all right, George assured her, and inwardly throught how lucky he was to have such a wife. She could keep a fellow steady and pull him up when he went one over the odds.

Three days later his employer looked through the stock.

"I see that rubber trumpet has gone. Put up another. It may be a good line."

And so the whole business began over again. George, it will be observed, for all his unimaginativeness, was a spiritually economical man. His happy contentment with his wife would, he knew, be jeopardised if he allowed himself to be reminded of that other disorderly, fascinating side of life that had been presided over by Ethel.

There were six dozen of the rubber trumpets, minus the one burnt at home, and his employer would expect one-and-a-penny for each of them. Thirteen shillings a dozen. But the dozens themselves were thirteen, which complicated the calculation, but in the end he got the sum right. He made sure of this by doing it backwards and "proving" it. He still had twenty-three pounds left out of the eight hundred.

Mrs. Muncey had a rather nice crocodile dressing-case which she had bought for herself and quite falsely described as "gift of the bride-groom to the bride."

On the next day Geroge borrowed the crocodile dressing-case on the plea that he wished to bring some goods from the shop home for Christmas. He brought it into the shop on the plea that it contained his dinner jacket and that he intended to change at the house of a friend without going home that night. As he was known to have married "an heiress," neither Wilkins nor his employer was particularly surprised that he should possess a dinner jacket and a crocodile dressing-case in which to carry it about.

At a quarter to one, when he was again alone in the shop, he crammed half a gross (less one) of rubber trumpets into the crocodile dressing-case. When his employer came back from lunch he said:

"I've got rid of all those rubber trumpets, Mr. Arrowsmith. An old boy came in, said he was to do with an orphanage, and I talked him into buying the lot."

Mr. Arrowsmith was greatly astonished.

"Bought the lot, did you say? Didn't he ask for a discount?"

"No, Mr. Arrowsmith. I think he was a bit loopy myself."

Mr. Arrowsmith looked very hard at George and then at the cash register. Six thirteens, less one, at one-and-a-penny — four pounds, three and fivepence. It was certainly a very funny thing. But then, the freak customer appears from time to time and at the end of the day Mr. Arrowsmith had got over his surprise.

Journeying from Walham to Battersea, one goes on the Underground to Victoria Station, and continues the journey on the main line: From the fact that George Muncey that evening took the crocodile case to Victoria Station, it has been argued that he intended to take the rubber trumpets home and perhaps bury them in the garden or deal with them in some other way. But this ignores the fact that he told his wife he intended to bring home some goods for Christmas.

The point is of minor importance, because the dressing-case never reached home with him that night. At the top of the steps leading from the Underground it was snatched from him.

George's first sensation, on realising that he had been robbed, was one of relief. The rubber trumpets, he had already found, could not be burnt; they would certainly have been a very great nuisance to him. The case, he knew, cost fifteen guineas, and there was still enough left of the twenty-three pounds to buy a new one on the following day.

9

At closing-time the next day, while George and Wilkins were tidying up, Mr. Arrowsmith was reading the evening paper.

"Here, Muncey! Listen to this. 'Jake Mendel, thirty-seven, of no fixed abode, was charged before Mr. Ramsden this morning with the theft of a crocodile dressing-case from the precincts of Victoria Station. Mr. Ramsden asked the police what was inside the bag. "A number of toy trumpets, your worship, made of rubber. There were seventy-seven of 'em all told." Mr. Ramsden: "Seventy-seven rubber trumpets! Well, *now* there really is no reason why the police should not have their own band." (Laughter).' " Mr. Arrowsmith laughed too and then: "Muncey, that looks like your lunatic."

"Yes, Mr. Arrowsmith," said George indifferently, then went contentedly home to receive his wife's expostulations about a new crocodile dressing-case which had been delivered during the afternoon. It was not quite the same to look at, because the original one had been made to order. But it had been bought at the same shop and the manager had obliged George by charging the same price for it.

In the meantime, the police were relying on the newspaper paragraph to produce the owner of the crocodile case. When he failed to materialise on the following morning they looked at the name of the manufacturer and took the case round to him.

The manufacturer informed them that he had made that case the previous spring to the order of a Miss Callermere — that the lady had since married and that, only the previous day, her husband, Mr. Muncey, had ordered an exactly similar one but had accepted a substitute from stock.

"Ring up George Muncey and ask him to come up and identify the case — and take away these india-rubber trumpets!" ordered the Superintendent.

Mrs. Muncey answered the telephone and from her they obtained George's business address.

"A chemist's assistant!" said the Superintendent. "Seems to me rather rum. Those trumpets may be his employer's stock. And he may have been pinching 'em. Don't ring him up — go down. And find out if the employer has anything to say about the stock. See him before you see Muncey."

At Walham the Sergeant was taken into the dispensary, where he promptly enquired whether Mr. Arrowsmith had missed seventy-seven rubber trumpets from his stock.

"I haven't missed them — but I sold them the day before yesterday — seventy-seven, that's right! Or rather, my assistant, George Muncey, did. Here, Muncey!" And as George appeared:

"You sold the rest of the stock of those rubber trumpets to a gentleman who said he was connected with an orphanage — the day before yesterday it was — didn't you?"

"Yes, Mr. Arrowsmith," said George.

"Bought the lot without asking for a discount," said Mr. Arrowsmith proudly. "Four pounds, three shillings and fivepence. I could tell you of another case that happened years ago when a man came into this very shop and —"

The Sergeant felt his head whirling a little. The assistant had sold seventy-seven rubber trumpets to an eccentric gentleman. The goods had been duly paid for and taken away — and the goods were subsequently found in the assistant's wife's dressing-case.

"Did you happen to have a crocodile dressing-case stolen from you at Victoria Station the day before yesterday, Mr. Muncey?" asked the Sergeant.

George was in a quandary. If he admitted that the crocodile case was his wife's — he would admit to Mr. Arrowsmith that he had been lying when he had said that he had cleverly sold the whole of the seventy-seven rubber trumpets without even having to give away a discount. So:

"No," said George.

"Ah, I thought not! There's a mistake somewhere. I expect it's that manufacturer put us wrong. Sorry to have troubled you, gentlemen! Good morning!"

"Wait a minute," said Mr. Arrowsmith. "You *did* have a crocodile dressing-case here that day, Muncey, with your evening clothes in it. And you *do* go home by Victoria. But what is that about the trumpets, Sergeant? They couldn't have been in Mr. Muncey's case if he sold them over the counter."

"I don't know what they've got hold of, Mr. Arrowsmith, and that's a fact," said George. "I think I'm wanted in the shop."

George was troubled, so he got leave to go home early. He told his wife how he had lied to the police, and confessed to her about the trumpets. Soon she had made him tell her the real reason for his dislike of the trumpets. The result was that when the police brought her the original crocodile case she flatly denied that it was hers.

In law, there was no means by which the ownership of the case could be foisted upon the Munceys against their will. Pending the trial of Jake Mendel, the bag-snatcher, the crocodile case, with its seventy-seven rubber trumpets, was deposited with the Department of Dead Ends.

A few feet above it on a shelf stood the identical trumpet which George Muncey had thrown out of the window on the three-fifteen, non-stop Southend to Fenchurch Street, some seven months ago.

The Department took one of the trumpets from the bag and set it beside the trumpet on the shelf. There was no logical connection between them whatever. The Department simply guessed that there might be a connection.

They tried to connect Walham with Southend and drew blank. They traced the history of the seventy-seven Walham trumpets and found it simple enough until the moment when George Muncey put them in the crocodile case.

They went back to the Southend trumpet and read in their files that it had not been bought by the man with the baby but by a young woman.

Then they tried a cross-reference to young women and Southend. They found that dead end, the Ethel Fairbrass murder. They found:

"My daughter was married to Prince at the Henrietta Street registrar's office on November the sixteenth, 1907. He took her straight away for a honeymoon at Southend where they stayed a fortnight."

Fourteen days from November the sixteenth meant November the thirtieth, the day the rubber trumpet was found on the line.

One rubber trumpet is dropped on the railway line by (possibly) a young woman. The young woman is subsequently murdered (but not with a rubber trumpet). A young man behaves in an eccentric way with seventy-seven rubber trumpets more than six months later.

The connection was wholly illogical. But the Department specialised in illogical connections. It communicated its wild guess — in the form of a guarded Minute — to Detective-Inspector Rason.

Rason went down to Banbury and brought the old Fairbrass couple to Walham.

He gave them five shillings and sent them into Arrowsmith's to buy a hot-water bottle.

YOH SANO

NO PROOF

*The first Western-style mystery story by a Japanese writer published in Japan
was "The Two Sen Copper Coin." The year was 1923, and the author called
himself Edogawa Rampo, a name intended to sound a good deal like Edgar
Allan Poe. These classic tales came to be called* pazurras *(puzzlers). Later,
after World War II, came the Japanese version of the hard-boiled school, called*
haada-boirudo.

*Yoh Sano — the pseudonym of Ichiro Maruyama (b. 1928), a former news-
paperman who now lives in Kawasaki — is the prolific author of nearly a
hundred crime novels.*

The following story seems neither pazurra *nor* haada-boirudo *but more
the product of a culture that could produce* Rashomon, *with its four versions
of one incident, a rape.*

Chapter One: Noncriminal Owing to Impossibility

IN LEGAL TERMINOLOGY, an act is defined as noncriminal owing to
impossibility when, by the very nature of the act, the end is impossible
of achievement. The perpetrator of such an act is not liable to punishment under the law.

Police Inquest. In attendance:

Inquest chairman — Police Superintendent A.

Inquest vice-chairman — Police Superintendent B.

Criminal investigator — Police Superintendent C.

Chief of the Criminal Investigation Office — Police Inspector D.

Chief of the Inquest panel — Assistant Police Inspector E.

Members of the Inquest panel — Police Officers F, G, H, I, and J.

1

Police Inspector D: "When this case was first made public, the newspapers referred to it as the Mask Murder. As this suggests, it's a rather special crime — that is, a special case of unnatural death. It includes several problems that are difficult to interpret and deal with. We've called you together for this meeting so we can explain what's known about the case so far, and so you can hear directly the opinions of the people who were in charge of the investigation. First, Assistant Police Inspector E, could you outline the facts?"

Assistant Police Inspector E: "The incident occurred at about twelve twenty-five on the afternoon of Monday, January 6th, of this year. It happened on the roof of the home offices of the Chua Business Machines Company.

"Since it was the first day after the New Year's holiday, work was over at noon. Nine members of the business office staff went to the roof to have a group photograph taken. Keiji Nogami, twenty-three, was to take the picture. He was using a Nippon camera of the thirty-five-millimeter type.

"Nogami selected the place and set up the tripod. The people lined up, three squatting in front and five standing in back.

"Nogami looked into the viewfinder to focus the lens.

"I should explain that Nogami was using a black cloth to cover his head while he focused. This isn't required with a thirty-five-millimeter camera, but Nogami did it for a special reason. While under the black hood, he was putting on a monkey mask.

"Here's the mask. As you can see, it fits the head and is skillfully made to resemble a real monkey."

Police Inspector D: "Officer E, could you put the mask on so we can get an idea of the effect?"

Assistant Police Inspector E: "Sure."

Chairman A: "Terrific. It's the way people look in that movie about the world of monkeys."

Police Superintendent C: "You mean *Planet of the Apes.* Yes. I bet this mask's a copy of the makeup used in that film."

Assistant Police Inspector E: "Wait'll I take it off. There. Anyway, pretending it took time to focus the camera, Nogami put on this mask under the black cloth. Then he said something like, 'Say Cheese!' and poked his head out. He was wearing the mask. It gave the others a start. The shutter clicked. In other words, he was trying to take a photograph of the business department in a state of shock."

Vice-chairman B: "Does he always joke around like that?"

Assistant Police Inspector E: "No. I'll explain it later. But, as you can figure, he got a picture of surprised faces. Later, he voluntarily supplied the film to us. We had it printed. You have the picture there. As you can see, it's very interesting, because it shows facial expressions when something unexpected happens.

"Look at the man on the right in the front row. His eyes are open wider than the others'. He seems to be gasping. And the hand that's been on his knee is raised ever so slightly. The shutter was open for only one-five-hundredth of a second. The hand is arrested. But I was told that, later, it rose to the level of his eyes, where it seemed to move about, as if clutching for something.

"All the others immediately realized they were the victims of Nogami's joke and relaxed. Then they heard a horrible scream. They saw assistant department chief Junsuke Iwatsu, age fifty-three, fall forward. . . .

"This caused quite a commotion. The whole group gathered around Iwatsu and called to him. But Iwatsu was already stretched out straight and was no longer screaming.

"One of the group went downstairs and phoned for an ambulance, which quickly arrived on the scene. Oxygen and heart massage were administered. A neighborhood doctor rushed over and gave camphor injection. But Iwatsu didn't survive. He died.

"The coroner diagnosed the cause of death as acute cardiac insufficiency. Under ordinary conditions, Iwatsu's heart wasn't strong. The sudden shock of seeing the monkey mask must have caused his cardiac muscles to contract violently. This led to what is called cardioplegia, or paralysis of the heart."

2

Police Inspector D: "Thanks. Those are the facts of the case, then, roughly. Although the papers called it the Mask Murder, the word 'murder' is inappropriate, since there is no causal relation between the mask and the death of Junsuke Iwatsu."

Chairman A: "No relation! But he died from looking at the mask —"

Police Inspector D: "Sure, in that sense the mask's the cause and Iwatsu's death the result. In one sense there's a causal relation. But this doesn't constitute causal relation in the legal sense. Legally, a causal relation is recognized only when phenomenon A can be expected to produce result B."

Vice-chairman B: "Didn't Nogami know Iwatsu had a weak heart?"

Assistant Police Inspector E: "He said he knew. Iwatsu was obese. He weighed 78 kilograms and was only 163 centimeters tall. When he climbed steps he panted and suffered from shortness of breath. Other members of the business department noticed this. Iwatsu himself often said he ought to reduce, that his weight was bad on his heart. Nogami must've heard about it."

Vice-chairman B: "Nogami says he had no idea the surprise would be great enough to kill someone. I'm not defending him, but his idea seems to be common sense."

Police Superintendent C: "Yes. Even though a man's heart is weak, there's no reason to think a monkey mask'll kill him. If we interpret this as failure to warn a heart patient adequately and call it negligence resulting in fatality, it'd be foolish to hold a trial. The public prosecutor probably wouldn't issue an indictment. You'd have to make warnings to a heart patient who was confined to bed, but Iwatsu was healthy enough to go to work every day."

Chairman A: "I just remembered something — in a murder mystery about killing a heart patient with a snake. . . ."

Police Inspector D: "I read it, too. *Why Was the Horoscope Open?* by Seicho Matsumoto. But the circumstances are different. In that case, a heart patient tired himself taking part in a hunger strike for three days. When he came home, he wanted to look up something and opened the encyclopedia. Inside he found the skin of a snake, and this shocked him so much he died. Of course, intent to kill was proved against the murderer when it was found out he had deliberately weakened the victim by convincing him to take part in the three-day hunger strike."

Police Superintendent C: "But in court, how could you get a conviction in a case like that, unless the defendant confessed?"

Vice-chairman B: "What do you mean?"

Police Superintendent C: "Can a person die from the shock of seeing a snake skin? Good God. The defense would naturally insist it's impossible. It would be up to the judge. Everything depends on the way the judge sees the matter. If I were the defense attorney, even if the defendant admitted intent to kill, I'd plead noncriminal owing to impossibility."

Chairman A: "Noncriminal owing to impossibility? But the man's dead!"

Police Superintendent C: "Isn't that just piling up circumstances that have produced an effect? Surprise is basically not a murder method."

Police Inspector D: "Let's get back to the point. First there was thought of interpreting the case as negligence resulting in fatality. This proved impossible. Then we thought of accidental death. But, a new fact turned up. Officer E requested he be allowed to reinvestigate the whole thing. It seemes Nogami had a motive for killing Iwatsu, or at least that he stood to profit by Iwatsu's death."

Vice-chairman B: "You mean there's a possiblity of suspecting murder?"

Assistant Police Inspector E: "A possibility, yes. Nogami owed Iwatsu nearly one hundred thousand yen. I should like to ask Officer F, who investigated the facts, to report what he learned."

3

Police Officer F: "Actually, I got started on this in a very odd way. One morning on the train, about three days after the death, I happened to overhear two white-collar workers discussing the case. From the way they talked, I got the notion they must be employees of Chua Business Machines. One of them said that, now Iwatsu was dead, he'd have to go to another bookmaker. This led me to suspect that Iwatsu must've been a horse-race bookie for the people of Chua. I told my superiors about the idea. Then Officer H and I made the rounds of the Chua office asking questions. We questioned Iwatsu's family, too, and found that my impression of the conversation I heard on the train was right.

"It wasn't that Iwatsu really liked horse races. He had heard that bookies made money. After a little research, he decided to try his hand at it, moonlighting a little.

"In May of last year, he borrowed two hundred thousand yen from a home-loan company to use as starting capital. By the end of June, he'd paid back the loan. This means that in about a month, he was already breaking even or better."

Vice-chairman B: "Didn't anybody at the company complain?"

Police Officer F: "The office closes at noon on Saturday. He started taking bets after twelve. This didn't infringe on office work. On Sundays, he took bets over the phone in his home.

"He kept a record of all customers in the kind of notebook college students use, and carried it with him everywhere, in his briefcase. It was in the case the day he died. But the case was private effects and was turned over to the family. They had the notebook when I questioned them."

Vice-chairman B: "What made Iwatsu become a bookie? He have a girlfriend?"

Police Officer F: "Iwatsu had three children, a son and two daughters.

The oldest girl's married. The son, who's twenty-one, is a student in the humanities at a large university. He'd like to study abroad. Iwatsu figured he'd make enough money to help him.

"At first the son didn't want to show us the notebook. Claimed it didn't exist. We told him we'd come back with a search warrant. So he gave in. I think he was going to use it to try and collect from the people who owed his father money."

Police Superintendent C: "How much did he have out?"

Police Officer F: "Most people paid him back with their end-of-year bonuses. The total wasn't much; about three hundred thousand yen. There'd been a race five days before he died. He hadn't closed his records on that yet. He started on a pretty small scale, but by this time, a good bit of money was moving through his hands, for a bookie. Of the three hundred thousand he had out, Nogami owed ninety-three thousand."

Chairman A: "He must've been one of the big debtors."

Police Officer F: "He was second. Another person owed Iwatsu ninety-six thousand. With his bonus, Nogami brought his debt down to fifty thousand, but he had lost on a bet of forty-three thousand on the race the first week after New Year's."

Chairman A: "Who's the other big debtor?"

Police Officer F: "A Mr. Onuki, chief of the sales department. He's had debts of nearly a hundred thousand before. But he's always paid off when he won. Besides, his salary's big enough that a debt like this wouldn't cause him much worry. On the day of Iwatsu's death, as soon as work was over, he took a number of people from the sales department to a nearby mahjong parlor. He can't have had anything to do with the case."

Police Superintendent C: "But, even for Nogami, I doubt a hundred thousand's enough motive for murder."

Police Inspector D: "Of course, with the current inflation, one hundred thousand isn't much money. But if your creditor were to die without you doing the actual killing and without your being criminally liable, it might be tempting. A hundred thousand might be sufficient motive."

Police Superintendent C: "Hm. Not for murder. But a motive for action. Kind of, 'Let's give it a try.' If the guy dies, I'm ahead. In that sense, I suppose Nogami had a motive."

Vice-chairman B: "You take a pretty negative attitude, don't you?"

Police Superintendent C: "Not negative. It's a tricky legal point. We've got to be exact in our thinking."

Assistant Police Inspector E: "Well, I think we clearly established that

Nogami had what you've called a 'motive for action.' Next we questioned the other employees in the office to find out what kind of opinions they have about Nogami. We learned some strange things I'd like to ask Officer G to explain."

Police Officer G: "Superintendent B asked whether Nogami was in the habit of surprising people this way. Actually, that's an important point. From talking with his fellow workers, we found that what he did on the roof that day was most unusual for him."

Police Superintendent C: "How many people did you hear this from?"

Police Officer G: "All who were having their picture taken that day. They agreed it was unthinkable that Nogami would do such a thing.

"The department chief said Nogami's capable and serious about his work. But he's too negative. The chief was amazed that Nogami did anything like that. He never jokes in the office."

Vice-chairman B: "If that's how he is, I suppose they were plenty surprised by the monkey mask."

Police Officer G: "I'll say. Because of Nogami's personality, suddenly seeing a monkey face come out from under the black cloth must have added to the shock.

"But this made us wonder why he should act like that — on this day, I mean. Did he have some special plan? So, we questioned Nogami directly.

"He said he knows he has a negative personality and that he wants to improve it gradually. In the world of business, there's all kinds of competition. The most important thing is to win the recognition of your superiors. Nogami thought that instead of being retiring and conservative, he'd make a bigger impression if he did something wild occasionally. He made a New Year's resolution to try to change his personality. His first step was to startle his superiors and his coworkers with that monkey mask. At any rate, this is the way Nogami explained it to us."

Chairman A: "At first glance, it looks plausible. But, you think about it, it sounds cooked-up. He probably realized he'd be asked this kind of question and had good excuses ready."

Police Officer G: "Yes. I admit we had the same impression. But when we asked him further, he told us he'd written about it in his diary. He felt that to change his personality, he'd have to act the clown sometimes. He'd have to try to sell himself by being noisy and noticeable. His diary entry for New Year's day mentioned these things."

Police Superintendent C: "What's all that mean? He must've had a reason for wanting to change his personality."

Chairman A: "Wait a minute. This diary entry might be part of the plot. Nogami's ordinarily a quiet man. Suddenly he pulls this monkey-mask thing. He must've realized there would be people who'd think the whole thing odd. So he writes this business about personality change in his diary, ahead of time."

Police Officer G: "It's possible to view it like that. But it turns out someone else urged him to change his personality. A girl in the office named Mitsuko Sakaguchi."

Vice-chairman B: "She his girlfriend?"

Police Officer G: "Well, Nogami likes her. They see a good bit of each other. They went to a movie together on Saturday, January 4th. And the story is that Miss Sakaguchi suggested Nogami buy the monkey mask."

Police Superintendent C: "Sakaguchi suggested? Let's hear more about that."

Police Officer G: "After the movie, the two of them were strolling around and passed the famous Tamagawa toy shop. Mitsuko Sakaguchi spotted the monkey mask in the show window and said if he bought it, carried it secretly to the office, and suddenly put it on, he could give everybody a good surprise. Nogami went for the idea and decided to buy two masks, one for himself and one for her."

Assistant Police Inspector E: "He bought two?"

Police Officer G: "Yes. Miss Sakaguchi said she wanted to wear one. Nogami said he'd give it to her as a New Year's present, and bought two."

Police Superintendent C: "How old is she?"

Police Officer G: "Twenty-four. She's the girl at the far right in the back row."

Chairman A: "Ah, pretty good-looking. Certainly the sexiest of the three girls in the picture."

Vice-chairman B: "Yeah. The other two girls have their faces screwed up with surprise. Sakaguchi looks only mildly surprised. . . ."

Police Superintendent C: "Maybe Sakaguchi knew beforehand that Nogami was going to put the mask on. How about that?"

Police Officer G: "She says he didn't tell her. But when he put his head under the hood, she suspected he'd put it on. That's why she looks less surprised than anyone else in the picture."

Police Superintendent C: "Hm. . . . It's going to be hard to pin suspicion on Nogami. After all, he bought the mask at Sakaguchi's suggestion. It was Sakaguchi who said it would be fun to put the mask on in the office. He doesn't seem to have made preparations for the act himself."

4

Police Inspector D: "We already mentioned the murder mystery by Seicho Matsumoto. In that story, the victim was deadly afraid of snakes. This was why the shock he experienced on finding the snake skin in the encyclopedia killed him. Ordinary people wouldn't die of such a shock. After thinking about this, we began to wonder if anything similar pertained to Iwatsu."

Vice-chairman B: "I see. You tried to find out whether Iwatsu had any special dislike of monkeys?"

Police Inspector D: "Police Officers I and J investigated this. I'd like them to report."

Police Officer I: "At the chief's instruction, we called on Iwatsu's widow and asked if he had any special dislike for monkeys. At first she wouldn't give us a straight answer. She seemed to wonder why we asked. But we were reasonably sure she was hiding something. After we persisted, she finally told us.

"Iwatsu hated monkeys. Perhaps it'd be better to say he was terrified by them. For instance, he wouldn't stay in the room if *Planet of the Apes* was on TV. He didn't even like to flick past the channel showing it."

Police Superintendent C: "But why did Mrs. Iwatsu try to hide his fear of monkeys? When she heard he died of shock at seeing a monkey mask, you'd think she'd tell the police at once. It seems Officer F might've heard something about this fear in his questioning at the office. But he had to press her to tell him. It doesn't add up."

Police Officer I: "I see what you mean. But in his own lifetime, Iwatsu kept his fear of monkeys a secret from everyone. And his widow tried to hide it from us because she didn't want it to get out."

Police Superintendent C: "What's the need, hiding something like that?"

Police Officer I: "It's a strange story. He had a special reason. His wife was the only person who knew about it. He never even told his three children."

Vice-chairman B: "What was it? Why'd he keep it a secret?"

Police Officer I: "At the end of the war, Iwatsu was a college student. One day, a young man who did side work at the same place said he'd managed to get some monkey meat and would give some to Iwatsu. Iwatsu was happy to accept and went to his friend's place. In those days it was ordinarily impossible to get meat. Even monkey was considered a real treat."

Chairman A: "How did this friend come by the monkey meat?"

Police Officer I: "He was a student at a veterinary school and said he'd been given a monkey used for experiments. They made sukiyaki out of the meat. When they finished eating, the friend asked Iwatsu if he really thought it was monkey meat. Iwatsu asked him what he meant. The friend just grinned and said, 'Well, there's a maternity hospital next door.' "

Chairman A: "What? You mean it was the flesh of a child?"

Police Officer I: "When he heard this, Iwatsu thought so too. He suddenly vomited. He threw up everything he'd eaten right there."

Vice-chairman B: "A lot of funny things happened in those days. Maybe some maternity hospitals sold babies that had died of sickness."

Police Officer I: "There's no way of knowing. When the friend saw the effect his remark had on Iwatsu, he said he'd only been joking, that the meat was really monkey. But Iwatsu went on vomiting. The friend tried to convince him, but after a while Iwatsu left without saying a word. This happened thirty years ago, but it bred deep fear of monkeys in Iwatsu. His wife said she didn't find out about it till years after they were married. He made her promise never to tell. His children didn't know and there was no reason for anyone at the office to know."

Police Superintendent C: It's weird. I can hardly believe it."

Vice-chairman B: "No. You're too young to remember what it was like right after the war. Those of us who are older know such things happened then."

Police Superintendent C: "What I mean is, if such a thing happened, the chain of causes and effects is hard to accept. Why should this breed such deep fear of monkeys in the man that, thirty years later, he'd be killed seeing a monkey mask?"

Police Inspector D: "But the widow's story is true. Officer J found the friend and confirmed the facts. Officer J, tell us about it."

5

Police Officer J: "Mrs. Iwatsu said the veterinary student friend had a name with Funa-something in it. We checked and examined the register of veterinarians and discovered that a Doctor Funazaka who lives and works in Saitama Prefecture is about the right age. We went to Saitama for a talk. He told us that two years after the end of the war, he played a joke of this kind on one of his friends."

Chairman A: "A joke?"

Police Officer J: "The meat they had in the sukiyaki was actually horse meat. Pretending it was monkey is the kind of joke you could expect of a college student. Funazaka expected Iwatsu to be squeamish about the monkey meat. But he'd eaten it completely naturally. Funazaka thought he'd push it a little farther, suggesting it was human flesh. He laughed when he told us. But when he saw how violently Iwatsu reacted, he decided against telling the truth — that it was horse — and to go on insisting it was monkey."

Vice-chairman B: "In other words, Iwatsu was deceived for thirty years?"

Police Officer J: "Funazaka never saw Iwatsu after that and said he didn't know the incident made Iwatsu terrified of monkeys."

Police Superintendent C: "Does anyone at Chua Business Machines have any connection with Funazaka?"

Assistant Police Inspector E: "Far's we know, no. No one in the office, including Nogami and Mitsuko Sakaguchi, had any notion Iwatsu was afraid of monkeys."

Police Superintendent C: "Then there's no hope of establishing any legal causal relation between Nogami's monkey mask and Iwatsu's death. The only interpretation is that thoughtless mischief brought on a tragic effect."

Chairman A: "Why don't we just send a report to the prosecutor? What he does after that's up to him."

Police Superintendent C: "What can we say he's suspected of? Both murder and negligence resulting in fatality are out. If he'd put the mask on in the dead of night and frightened women, we might try for menacing. But this happened at noon. . . . Nobody could've thought Iwatsu would die. Even if we say Nogami had a motive . . ."

Chapter Two: Criminal Negligence

IN LEGAL TERMS, this means a failure to use a reasonable amount of care when such failure results in foreseeable injury or damage to another.

At a restaurant in the vicinity of Minato Police Station.

People in attendance at dinner meeting:

Police Inspector D.

Assistant Police Inspector E.

Police Officers F, G, H, I, and J.

Police Officer F: "I'm not convinced about the results of last week's inquest. Nogami had a motive and knew Iwatsu's heart was weak.

Maybe he felt he'd be none the worse if he failed, and that he should go ahead and try frightening Iwatsu with the mask. We could at least send the papers to the prosecutor. You agree?"

Police Inspector D: "But like Superintendent C said, what can we accuse him of?"

Police Officer G: "Yeah. But we could've hauled him in on a charge of violating the gambling laws. If we'd grilled him a little, he might've admitted intent to kill. Then we could've reported him on suspicion of murder."

Police Inspector D: "Still, there's something in what Superintendent C Says. Suppose he did admit intent to kill, then what?"

Assistant Police Inspector E: "You mean, noncriminal owing to impossibility? I'm not sure about that. In this case, I think we have what the murder mysteries call 'within the realm of criminal possibility.' Maybe the mask trick wouldn't work. But there was the possibility of succeeding. . . . Can't we interpret it that way?"

Police Officer F: "I agree. I did some study on this noncriminal-owing-to-impossibility thing. I found that legal precedent recognizes this only when the crime's absolutely impossible. In this case, Iwatsu's already dead. Superintendent C talks like he was the defense attorney."

Police Inspector D: "Still, how would it be if we sent the thing in before we were certain and the public prosecutor's boys came down on us? Even if we took it to trial, Nogami'd be almost certain to get off. If you think of it in terms of a man's human rights, you'll see we couldn't send in a report or indict when we're reasonably certain nothing can come of it."

Police Officer H: "Aside from all the tough legal points, I think there's something fishy about this Nogami. Until this year, he never kept a diary. Then suddenly he starts writing about how he's going to change his whole personality. I think it's a trick. . . ."

Police Inspector D: "We brought that up at the inquest. It's nothing but circumstantial evidence."

Police Officer H: "That's not what I mean. I mean, maybe this trick wasn't meant to have any connection with Iwatsu's death."

Assistant Police Inspector E: "I don't get you. What's it supposed to be connected with?"

Police Officer H: "Okay. Iwatsu died when they were having that photograph made. But Nogami didn't expect it to happen. This wasn't part of his plan."

Police Inspector D: "I think I see. You mean he was really planning something else?"

Police Officer H: "In the building where Nogami lives, there's a woman, Masako Hatakeyama. She's thirty-two. She's been married, but she's separated from her husband. Lives alone in an apartment and sells insurance for a living. The building superintendent's convinced there's something between Nogami and this Hatakeyama. Other people in the building suspect the same thing, so it's pretty nearly certain."

Police Officer I: "She good looking?"

Police Officer H: "No, you couldn't call her that. But she's got a sexy body. Nogami's a bachelor. If she'd let him, I'm sure he'd be happy to take her on."

Police Inspector D: "So?"

Police Officer H: "Their building's only two stories high, but there's a clothes-drying deck on the roof. When I visited the building, Mrs. Hatakeyama was hanging out clothes. As I glanced up, I thought, 'She'd better watch out.' "

Police Officer F: "Why? Could you see up her skirt?"

Police Officer H: "No, and anyway, she had on jeans. I mean the railing around the deck's so low. Only about forty centimeters. When I talked with the super, he admitted it and said that in one place the rail's broken. He always warns the tenants to be careful up there."

Assistant Police Inspector E: "Okay, I understand about the railing. But what's it go to do with Nogami?"

Police Officer H: "All right. She's up there on the deck, hanging out clothes. Nogami puts on the monkey mask and sneaks up there, too. When he sees his chance, he taps her on the shoulder."

Police Inspector D: "Yeah. That could give her a shock. She might forget about the low rail and fall off."

Police Officer H: "And what about Nogami? Would this be another case of noncriminal owing to impossibility?"

Police Inspector D: "Not this time. If the woman died, it'd clearly be negligence resulting in fatality. A person ought to know what could be the outcome of surprising somebody in a place like that. Reasonable caution is necessary. It would be a clear case of negligence. Any judge would recognize it."

Police Officer H: "Right. What's the maximum penalty for negligence resulting in fatality? Fifty thousand yen!"

Police Inspector D: "Right. But . . . wait. I get it. He could kill Hatakeyama, and make it look like negligence."

Police Officer H: "That's what I mean. The police would certainly take Nogami's personality into consideration. Nogami'd make it look like negligence, but it'd be possible to interpret the act as murder with deliberate intent to kill. No. If Nogami's a person who doesn't ordinarily joke like that, it would look suspicious. Naturally, it would look like he'd bought the monkey mask as part of the plan to kill."

Assistant Police Inspector E: "Yeah. But if he'd already pulled the mask trick on others, it'd seem to be only one of a series of pranks."

Police Officer F: "And the photography session would be perfect evidence. All the others would testify in his favor. What's more, there's the picture with the shocked look on everybody's face."

Police Officer H: "Then he writes in his diary that he's going to change his personality. With circumstantial evidence like that, the police would decide his joking had gone too far and Hatakeyama's death was the result. Penalty: fifty thousand yen."

Police Officer J: "Hold it. Has Nogami got a motive for murdering Hatakeyama?"

Police Officer H: "A case of man and woman. Hatakeyama's older than he is. She might not want to let him go. There are lots of cases of killings like that. Anyway, that's how it looks to me. I'm not saying we've found out for certain there's been talk of a break between them. But Nogami's fallen for Mitsuko Sakaguchi at the office. Hatakeyama could've been raising hell about that."

Police Officer G: "But would seeing a monkey mask make her fall off the roof? Of course, if she had some special fear of monkeys. Like Iwatsu, I mean . . ."

Police Inspector D: "That mask's very well made. Anybody'd be shocked if he found it suddenly in front of his face. She could fall. Even if nothing happened, the two of them could just laugh it off. . . ."

Police Officer H: "There's another point. Why'd he have to use the mask at all?"

Police Inspector D: "What d'you mean?"

Police Officer H: "As long's no one was around, he could just push her off. Then, when the police questioned him, he could say he'd frightened her when he was joking around with the mask."

Assistant Police Inspector E: "Right. He could simply have murdered her, then faked negligence."

Police Officer H: "Well, there's no proof for any of this. Its just a notion I got when I spotted that dangerous drying deck. I just thought something like this could've been what Nogami had in mind."

Police Inspector D: "In other words, you mean Iwatsu's death may've been a complete surprise to him?"

Assistant Police Inspector E: "But our hands are tied."

Chapter Three: Self-Defense

SELF-DEFENSE is legally defined as the right to defend oneself with whatever force is reasonably necessary against actual or threatened violence.

Inquest.

Attended by the same people as in Chapter One.

Assistant Police Inspector E: "We've heard a partial report. Now I'd like to outline the facts of the case in a more orderly fashion.

"At six forty-five in the evening, yesterday, an urgent phone call was received at police headquarters. The woman on the phone said, 'I've killed a man.' A headquarters patrol car rushed to the scene, Apartment 215, on the second floor of the Eiko Apartment Building, in Shibuya, Minato ward. Mitsuko Sakaguchi lived there — twenty-four, employed in a commercial firm. On the kitchen floor, next to the sink, lay a man. Mitsuko Sakaguchi was sitting next to him. She was only half conscious. The man had been stabbed in the left side of the chest with a sharp butcher knife and was already dead from loss of blood. The woman was arrested at once.

"For a while after she arrived at headquarters, Mitsuko Sakaguchi, the suspect, was unable to speak because of shock. When she calmed down, we went ahead with questioning. About two meters from the corpse was a large butcher knife. From the blood stains on it, we assumed it was the weapon. Immediately next to the corpse lay a blood-covered rubber monkey mask.

"The condition of the scene of the crime has been recorded in the color photo you have before you. In the lower left corner, you can make out the mask. It's the same kind of mask used in the New Year's photography session."

Vice-chairman B: "It looks like the same mask."

Assistant Police Inspector E: "If you remember, Mitsuko Sakaguchi was with Keiji Nogami when he bought two masks January 4th. She received a mask from him."

Vice-chairman B: "What happened to Nogami's mask?"

Assistant Police Inspector E: "He allowed us to keep it for a while. It was returned to him when the death of Iwatsu was declared accidental.

"To get back, then. When she calmed down, Mitsuko Sakaguchi confessed. The victim was Keiji Nogami. Of course, we didn't need Sakaguchi's confession to find this out. The officers who investigated the scene of the crime knew immediately."

Chairman A: "I think we said Sakaguchi and Nogami were on pretty close terms?"

Police Inspector D: "Yeah. Sakaguchi's supposed to have suggested Nogami try to change his personality. . . ."

Chairman A: "Does it have anything to do with a tangle in their love affair?"

Assistant Police Inspector E: "No. According to her confession, his death was completely accidental. At any rate, she had absolutely no intention of killing him.

"To explain: She invited Nogami to her apartment that evening for supper. They'd gone shopping together after work and arrived at the apartment about five forty-five. Mitsuko Sakaguchi went to the kitchen to prepare dinner. Keiji Nogami was in the next room watching TV. She was preparing a special fish soup that required a large fish head for broth. She was about to cut the fish head with the butcher knife.

"Just then she felt a tapping on her shoulder. Looking around, she saw a monkey standing there. Of course, it was Nogami up to his tricks. But without turning all the way around, she thrust the knife she was holding forward. It penetrated Nogami's chest on the left side. This concluded her statement."

Police Inspector D: "I might add, she said she was thinking about something entirely different when the monkey face suddenly appeared in front of her. She screamed as she thrust the knife into him."

Police Superintendent C: "In court, the defense is sure to claim self-defense. At that moment, she thought she was up against actual or threatened violence and acted to protect herself."

Chairman A: "But actually there was nothing to defend herself from."

Police Superintendent C: "It could be considered self-defense if she thought she was in danger. It would be mistaken self-defense."

Police Inspector D: "Still — you think she had to defend herself with a butcher knife?"

Police Superintendent C: "You mean excessive self-defense? But she said she was holding the knife at the time. If she'd drawn the knife out and then stabbed him again, it'd be excessive defense. But in this case . . ."

Assistant Police Inspector E: "Something doesn't sit right with me. Did she really think she was threatened with violence? I mean, look at that photograph. She shows less surprise than anyone else. She already had one experience with the monkey mask. Now it surprises her so much she stabs a man without thinking. I can't swallow that."

Vice-chairman B: "Yeah. But that time, she suspected he'd put the mask on. This time, she was thinking about something, when suddenly, right before her — the mask. The mask's really well done. I wonder if we ought to register an administrative warning about the way that thing's made?"

Police Superintendent C: "There'd be all kinds of hitches. Might violate freedom of expression or something like that. . . ."

Police Officer H: "Excuse me, but may I say something?"

Police Inspector D: "Sure."

Police Officer H: "Listening to what you said, I get the impression that if an indictment's made, the trial will be a hassle over whether this was or was not self-defense. I think it's possible to take a different viewpoint. I can explain. . . ."

Police Superintendent C: "Different viewpoint?"

Police Officer H: "I mean, all this was planned by Mitsuko Sakaguchi."

Police Inspector D: "Planned? How?"

Police Officer H: "On January 4th, Mitsuko Sakaguchi convinced Nogami to buy two masks, one for her. Then on January 6th, the other incident occurred. But I'd like to call your attention to one point. In this case, an adult man who puts on a monkey mask and taps a woman on the shoulder is killed. None of us doubts Nogami actually did this."

Vice-chairman B: "What d'you mean 'doubts'?"

Police Officer H: "Well, when we hear Nogami put on the mask, we're all psychologically prepared to think, 'Oh, him again.' "

Police Superintendent C: "True."

Police Officer H: "Let's pretend Iwatsu hadn't died when he did. In such a case, we'd have to ask ourselves whether Nogami was the kind of man to play jokes like that. We'd have asked around and would discover he played the same monkey-mask trick at New Year's. Then we'd have thought, 'Ha, he likes to go around surprising people.' We'd have believed her testimony."

Police Inspector D: "One stage is missing from your story, but the outcome's the same, all right."

Police Officer H: "But is it, really? She didn't plan on Iwatsu's death when she worked this out. But, after it happened, she still felt it'd work as she planned. I think this is where she made her mistake.

"Since Iwatsu's death, Nogami must have felt queasy about the damned mask. After all, a person died because he played a trick with it. And as a result he was investigated by the police. Is it likely he'd put the mask on to surprise Mitsuko Sakaguchi when he happened to be visiting her? Doesn't seem right, to me. He was probably nervous about the mask, anyway. I think he would've noticed she was holding a butcher knife. These are the reasons I can't believe what she says."

Chairman A: "All right. What then? You've been talking about a plan. Let's have more."

Police Officer H: "Well, I heard something. At first, I didn't pay much attention. Later, I got to thinking, and started worrying about it."

Assistant Police Inspector E: "What?"

Police Officer H: "Next door to Mitsuko Sakaguchi is a small boy, a sixth-grade pupil. She likes him very much and lets him come to her apartment to play checkers on Sundays. Last Sunday he came. He spotted that monkey mask and asked her to give it to him. She refused. She said she'd borrowed it from someone."

Assistant Police Inspector E: "What's funny about that?"

Police Officer H: "It could be just an excuse for turning the boy down. What worries me is why she refused him at all. She lives alone. If her family was with her, she might play with the mask to amuse them. But what did she intend doing with it? Why did she get Nogami to buy it? She never took it to the office with her. She didn't use it to play with the little boy next door. But when he asked for it, she refused. In other words, she was keeping something for which she had no use."

Police Superintendent C: "Yeah. Kind of unnatural."

Police Officer H: "She just might've had some purpose in getting Nogami to buy it and then keeping it without using it."

Assistant Police Inspector E: "Was that purpose a plan to kill Nogami?"

Police Officer H: "As I said earlier, Nogami must've felt a kind of aversion to that mask. I just believe he never did put it on.

"For instance, let's say while she was working in the kitchen, she called Nogami. When he comes close, she stabs him in the chest with the butcher knife. Then she drops the mask beside the body. Later she says to the police that she stabbed him in sudden surprise when seeing the mask."

Police Superintendent C: "A trumped-up self-defense. And to make it work, she had to have that mask."

Police Officer H: "Yeah. That explains getting Nogami to buy it, refusing to give it to the neighbor's boy, and keeping it with her in the apartment."

Police Inspector D: "But did she have a motive for killing Nogami?"

Police Officer H: "I don't know yet. She may've wanted to get away from him. He stuck with her, wouldn't let her go. . . ."

Police Superintendent C: "Then it becomes murder?"

Police Officer H: "In this case, there'd be no punishment if it was self-defense."

Police Inspector D: "We've got to have a winning card. To make her confess, we've got to have some conclusive fact."

Police Officer F: "There were no onions —"

Vice-chairman B: "Onions?"

Police Officer F: "Yes. You've got to have onions to make the kind of fish soup she was supposed to be making. I figured she was going to buy them later. But maybe she had no intention of making that fish soup at all."

Police Superintendent C: "Pretty good, now. You mean the whole fish-soup thing was just a trick? She'd have to work with something like a big fish head to need a sharp, heavy butcher knife. That what you're driving at?"

Police Officer F: "Yes. She must've thought a while before figuring out some dish that'd call for a sharp-pointed, heavy knife like she needed to make a fatal wound."

Police Inspector D: "Great. All right, Officer E. Grill Sakaguchi and question around to find out about her relations with Nogami. What d'you think, Superintendent C?"

Police Superintendent C: "Good idea. Looks like we better follow this up."

Vice-chairman B: "I still think we ought to say something to somebody about the way that monkey mask's made."

Police Superintendent C: "But that's a different matter."

WILLIAM CAMPBELL
GAULT

DEAD-END FOR DELIA

William Campbell Gault (b. 1910) has had a long and productive career,
stretching from a short story published by a pulp magazine in 1940 to a 1986
novel, The Chicano War, *that featured his best-known detective, a retired*
professional football player called Brock the Rock Callahan.

Ross Macdonald dedicated his novel The Blue Hammer *to Gault, a Santa*
Barbara neighbor, this way: "To Bill Gault, who knows that writing well is
the best revenge."

Nine of Gault's stories were published in Black Mask, *including "Dead-*
End for Delia" in 1950.

THE ONLY LIGHT in the alley came from the high, open windows of
the faded dancehall bordering its east length. From these same windows the clean melody of a tenor sax cut through the murky air of
the alley. There was nothing else around that was clean.

The warehouse running the west border of the alley was of grimy
red brick, the alley itself littered with paper and trash, cans, and
bottles. It was a dead-end alley, no longer used.

The beat officer was at its mouth, keeping the small crowd back,
and now the police ambulance came from the west, its siren dying in
a slow wail.

The beat officer said, "Better swing out and back in. Sergeant Kelley
with you?"

"No. Why?" The driver was frowning.

"It's his wife," the beat officer said. "She really got worked over."
"Dead?"

"Just died, two minutes ago. How she lived that long is a wonder."

The driver shook his head, and swung out to back into the mouth of the alley.

From the west again, a red light swung back and forth, and the scream of a high-speed siren pierced the night. The prowl car was making time. It cut over to the wrong side of the street and skidded for fifteen feet before stopping at the curb.

The man opposite the driver had the door open before the car came to rest, and he was approaching the beat patrolman while the driver killed the motor.

"Barnes? I'm Kelley. My wife —?"

"Dead, Sergeant. Two minutes ago."

Sergeant Kelley was a tall man with a thin, lined face and dark brown eyes. He stood there a moment, saying nothing, thinking of Delia, only half-hearing the trumpet that was now taking a ride at Dreamland, the Home of Name Bands.

Delia, who was only twenty-three to his thirty-seven, Delia who loved to dance, Delia of the fair hair and sharp tongue — was now dead. And that was her dirge, that trumpet taking a ride.

He shook his head and felt the trembling start in his hands. He took a step toward the other end of the alley, and the patrolman put a hand on his arm.

"Sergeant, I wouldn't. It's nothing to see. Unless you're a Homicide man, it's nothing you'd — Sergeant, don't."

Sergeant Kelley shook off the hand and continued down the alley.

Dick Callender of Homicide was talking to the M.E. He turned at the sound of Kelley's footsteps.

Dick said, "It's nothing to see, Pat."

Pat Kelley didn't answer him. There was enough light from the dancehall for him to see the bloody face of his wife and the matted hair above it. He hadn't seen her for four months.

Then he looked at Callender. "She say anything, Dick?"

"Just — *Tell Pat I'm sorry. Tell Pat Lois will know.* Make sense to you; the second sentence, I mean?"

"None," Pat lied. The band was playing a waltz, now.

Callender said, "We'll give it a lot of time. Homicide will shoot the works on this one."

Pat looked at him and used his title, now. "I want a transfer, Lieutenant. To Homicide." His voice was very quiet. "You can fix it."

A piece of dirty newspaper fluttered by, stirred by the night breeze. The white-coated men were laying the stretcher alongside the body.

Callender said, "We've got a lot of good men in Homicide, Pat." He didn't say, *And we want our suspects brought in alive.*

But Pat could guess he was thinking it. He said, "She left me, four months ago. I'm not going to go crazy on it, but I'd like the transfer."

"We'll see, Pat." The lieutenant put a hand on his shoulder. "Come on. I'll ride back to headquarters with you."

They went in the lieutenant's wagon. About halfway there, Pat said, "It could have been one of those — pick-up deals, some mug out of nowhere who'll go back to where he came from." Shame burned in him, but he had to get the words out.

Callender didn't look at him. "I've got Adams and Prokowski checking the dancehall. They're hard workers, good men."

Pat said nothing.

Callender went on, quietly. "There must be some angle you've got on it. Your wife must have thought you knew this — this Lois, or she wouldn't have mentioned it. She didn't have enough words left to waste any of them on some trivial matter."

"My wife knew a lot of people I didn't," Pat said. "My statement will include everything I know, Lieutenant. Have her sent to the Boone Mortuary on Seventh Street, will you? I'll talk to her mother tonight."

"She — was living with her mother, Pat?"

"No. I don't know where she's been living these past four months. But it wasn't with her mother. I wish to God it had been, now."

They made the rest of the trip in silence.

It was a little before midnight when Sergeant Pat Kelley, of the pawn shop and hotel detail, climbed the worn stairs of the four-story building on Vine. The place was quiet; these were working people and they got to bed early.

Mrs. Revolt lived on the third floor, in two rooms overlooking the littered back yard and the parking lot beyond. Pat knocked and waited.

There was the sound of a turning key, and then Mrs. Revolt opened the door. Her lined, weary face was composed, but her eyes quickened in sudden alarm at the sight of Pat.

"Pat, what is it?"

"I'd better come in," he said. "It's Delia, Mrs. Revolt. Something's happened . . ."

She pulled her wrapper tightly around her, as though to stiffen her body against his words. "Come in, come in. But what —? Pat, she's not — it's not —"

He came into the dimly lighted room with the rumpled studio couch, the gate-leg table with the brass lamp, the worn wicker chairs, the faded, dull brown rug. In this room, Delia Revolt had grown from an infant to the beauty of the block. In this room, Papa Revolt had died, and Pat had courted the Revolt miracle.

"Sit down, Mrs. Revolt," Pat said now.

She sat down in the wicker rocker. "She's dead, I know. She's dead. My Delia, oh Lord, she's dead." She rocked, then, back and forth, her eyes closed, her lips moving, no decipherable words coming out.

Pat sat on the wicker lounge. "She was found in an — she was found near the Dreamland dancehall. She's dead. There'll be detectives coming to see you; other detectives, Mrs. Revolt."

Her eyes opened, and she stopped rocking. "Murdered — Delia? It wasn't an accident? Murdered — Delia?"

He nodded. Her eyes closed again, and a strangled sound came from her tight throat, and she toppled sideways in the chair.

Pat got to her before she hit the floor. He put her on the studio couch, and was waiting with a glass of water when her eyes opened again.

Her voice was a whisper. "How did it happen?"

"She was hit with something blunt, concussion. Nobody knows anything else. But there's something I wanted you to know."

Fear in her eyes, now. She said nothing.

"Before she died, Delia mentioned a name. It was Lois. I told the officer in charge the name meant nothing to me. I told him I didn't know any Lois."

The frightened eyes moved around Pat's face. "Why did you say that?"

"Because they're going after this one. She's a cop's wife and they won't be pulling any punches. This man in charge, Callender, can be awful rough. I'd rather talk to Lois, myself."

"But why should they bother Lois?"

"Delia mentioned the name, before she died. They're not going to overlook anything and they're not going to be polite."

"All right, Pat. I had a feeling, when you knocked, something had happened. I've had a feeling about Delia, for years. You can go now; I'll be all right. I'll want to be alone."

She was under control, now, this woman who'd met many a tragedy, who'd just met her biggest one. The fortitude born of the countless minor tragedies was carrying her through this one.

Pat went from there to Sycamore. He was off duty, and driving his own car. On Sycamore, near Seventh, he parked in front of an old, red brick apartment building.

In the small lobby, he pressed the button next to the card which read: *Miss Lois Weldon.*

Her voice sounded metallic through the wall speaker. "Who's there?"

"It's Pat, Lois. Something has happened."

He was at the door when it buzzed.

She was waiting in her lighted doorway when he got off the self-service elevator on the fourth floor. She was wearing a maroon flannel robe piped in white, and no make-up. Her dark, soft hair was piled high on her head.

Her voice was quiet. "What's happened?"

"Delia's been murdered."

She flinched and put one hand on the door frame for support. "Pat, when — how —?"

"Tonight. In the alley next to the Dreamland ballroom. Slugged to death. She didn't die right away. She mentioned your name before she died."

"My name? Come in, Pat." Her voice was shaky.

There wasn't much that could be done about the apartment's arrangement, but color and taste had done their best with its appearance. Pat sat on a love seat, near the pseudo-fireplace.

Lois stood. "Now, what did she say?"

Pat frowned. "She said, 'Tell Pat I'm sorry. Tell Pat Lois will know.' She told that to Lieutenant Callender of Homicide, before she died. He asked me who Lois was, and I told him I didn't know."

"Why?"

"I was trying to protect you. It might have been dumb. But they're going to be rough in this case."

She sat down in a chair close by, staring at him. "I saw Delia two days ago, Thursday afternoon. She told me then that she was sorry she'd left you. Could it have been that, Pat?"

"It could have been. Yes, that's probably what she meant. What else did she tell you?"

"N-nothing. She was very vague. She'd — been drinking, Pat."

"Drinking? That's a new one for her. Was she working?"

"I didn't get that impression. She didn't tell me where she was living, either. Do you know?"

Pat shook his head, staring at the floor. The three of them had grown up in the same block on Vine, though they weren't of an age. Delia had been twenty-three, and Lois was — let's see, she was thirty and the fairly well paid secretary to a vice president of a text publishing firm. When Pat was twenty-two and freshly in uniform, he'd been Lois's hero, who'd been fifteen. At thirty-three, in another kind of uniform, U.S. Army, he'd been Delia's hero, and she'd been nineteen.

At the moment, he was an old man, and nobody's hero.

Lois said, "I guess you need a drink." She rose. "Don't try to think tonight, Pat. It won't be any good."

"I was without her for four months," he said, mostly to himself. "I got through that. I don't know about this. I don't seem to have any feelings at all. It's like I'm dead."

Her back was to him. "I know. That's the way I felt four years ago." She poured a stiff jolt of rye in the bottom of a tumbler.

"Four years ago?" He was only half listening.

"When you married her." She had no expression on her face as she walked over to him. Her hand was steady, holding out the drink.

He looked up to meet her gaze. "Lois, what are you —?"

"I just wanted you to know," she said, "and now. I'm glad you didn't tell that officer you knew me. That's a gesture I can hang on to. It will warm me, this winter."

"Lois —" he protested.

"Drink your drink," she said quietly. "Bottoms up."

He stared at her, and at the glass. He lifted it high and drained it. He could feel its warmth, and then he started to tremble.

"You're one of those black Irishmen," Lois said softly, "who can go all to hell over something like this. And wind up in the gutter. Or examine yourself a little better and decide she was a girl headed for doom from the day of her birth and all you really loved was her beauty."

"Stop talking, Lois. You're all worked up. I'd kill anybody else who talked like that, but I know you loved her, too."

"Who didn't love her? She was the most beautiful thing alive. But she was a kid, and she'd never be anything else. Even now you can see that, can't you?"

Pat stared at his empty glass, and rose.

"Thanks for the drink," he said, and walked to the door. There he paused, faced her. "It was probably a silly gesture, covering you. There'll be a million people who can tell them who Lois is. I'm sorry I got you up."

"Pat," she said, but he was through the door.

He caught a glimpse of her as he stepped into the elevator. She was like a statue, both hands on the door frame, watching him wordlessly. . . .

The Chief called him in, next morning. He was a big man and a blunt one. He said, "Callender tells me you want a transfer to Homicide for the time being."

Pat nodded, "Yes, sir."

"How is it you didn't tell Callender about this Lois Weldon last night? A half dozen people have told him about her since."

"I wasn't thinking last night, sir."

The Chief nodded. "You're too close to it, Sergeant. For anybody else, that would be withholding evidence. I'm overlooking it. But I'm denying your request for a temporary transfer to Homicide."

Pat stared at him, saying nothing.

The Chief stared back at him. "You'll want a few days leave."

"Maybe more." He omitted the "sir."

The Chief frowned and looked at his desk top. His eyes came up, again. "I don't like to hammer at you at a time like this. But why *more?* Were you planning to work on this outside of the department?"

Pat nodded.

"If I gave you a direct order not to that would be insubordination, Sergeant."

Pat said nothing.

The Chief said, "Those are my orders."

Pat took out his wallet and unpinned the badge. He laid it on the Chief's desk. "This isn't easy, sir, after fifteen years." He stood up, momentarily realizing what a damn fool speech that had been.

"You're being dramatic," the Chief said evenly. "The thing that makes a good officer is impartiality. Last night you tried to cover a friend. In your present mood, you might go gunning on a half-baked lead and do a lot of damage. This department isn't run that way. But it's your decision, Sergeant." He picked up the badge.

Pat started for the door, and the Chief's voice stopped him. "It would be smart to stay out of Lieutenant Callender's way."

Pat went out without answering. He stood there, in the main hall of Headquarters, feeling like a stranger for the first time in fifteen years. It was then he remembered Lois saying, *You're one of those black Irishmen who can go all to hell. . . .*

He wasn't that complicated, whether she knew it or not. His wife had been killed and it was a personal business with him. His job for fifteen years had been to protect the soft from violence and fraud and chicanery, and this time it was closer to home. Only a fool would expect him to continue checking pawn shops; he hadn't thought the Chief was a fool. But then, it wasn't the Chief's wife.

Detective Prokowski came along the hall and stopped at the sight of Pat.

Pat asked, "What did you find out at Dreamland last night, Steve?"

Prokowski licked his lower lip, frowning.

"Orders, Steve?" Pat asked quietly. "From the lieutenant?"

Prokowski didn't answer that. "Did your transfer go through?"

"No. I've left the force. Don't you want to talk about Dreamland? I won't remind you how long we've known each other."

"Keep your voice down," Prokowski said. "I'll see you at Irv's, at one-thirty."

"Sure. Thanks, Steve."

Irv's wasn't a cops' hangout. Prokowski was a Middle Westerner, originally, and a perfectionist regarding the proper temperature of draught beer. Irv had it at the proper temperature.

It was a hot day, for fall, and the beer was cool enough to sweat the glass without being cold enough to chill the stomach. Pat drank a couple of glasses, waiting for Steve.

Steve came in at a quarter to two and Irv had a glass waiting for him by the time he reached the bar.

He was a big man, Steve Prokowski, and sweating like a college crew man right now. "Nothing," he said wearily. "Lots of guys danced with her. Nothing there. Shoe clerks and CPA's and punk kids. There was a guy they called Helgy. That name mean anything to you, Pat?"

Pat lied with a shake of the head. "This Helgy something special?"

"Danced with her a lot. Took her home. Brought her a couple of times. The way it is, I guess, if you really *like* to dance there's only one place to do it where you've got the room and the right music. That's a place like Dreamland.

"I mean you can't catalogue a guy because he goes to a public dancehall any more than you can catalogue people because you saw them in Grand Central Station. All kinds of people like to dance. This Helgy drove a smooth car, a convertible. That's nightclub stuff, right? But he liked to dance, and the story is, he really could."

Steve finished his beer and Irv brought another. Steve said casually, "Now, what do you know, Pat?"

"I'm out of a job. I don't know anything beyond that. The Chief acted on Callender's recommendation, I suppose?"

"I don't know. The lieutenant doesn't always confide in me. What can you do alone, Pat?"

"It wasn't my idea to work alone." Pat climbed off his stool and put a dollar on the bar. "Out of that, Irv, all of them." He put a hand on Steve's shoulder. "Thanks for coming in."

"You're welcome. Thanks for the beer. I still work for the department, remember, Pat."

"I didn't forget it for a minute."

He could feel Steve's eyes on him in the mirror as he walked out.

Once at breakfast, Delia had been reading the paper and she'd said, "Well, imagine that!"

"I'll try," he'd said. "Imagine what?"

"This boy I used to dance with at Dreamland, this Joe Helgeson. He's a composer, it says here. He likes to dance, and always has, and he knows very little about music, but he's composed. And he must be rich. Helgy, we always called him."

"You should have married him," Pat told her, "so you could have your breakfast in bed."

"There's always time," she told him. "But right now I'm happy with you."

After that, Pat had been conscious of the name. He saw it on sheet music, and it disturbed him. He heard Delia talk to friends about the composer she knew, Helgy, as though that was her world.

He swung his coupe away from the curb and headed toward the Drive. He knew the building, Delia had pointed it out to him once.

It was about eleven stories high with terrace apartments overlooking the bay. Helgy had one of the terrace apartments.

There was a clerk in the quiet lobby, too, and his glance said Pat should have used the service entrance.

Pat said, "Would you phone Mr. Helgeson and tell him Delia Kelley's husband would like very much to talk to him?"

The clerk studied him for a moment before picking up the phone. He looked surprised when he said, "Mr. Helgeson will see you, sir."

The elevator went up quickly and quietly, and Pat stepped out onto the lush, sculptured carpeting of the top floor. There was a man waiting for him there, a thin man with blond hair in a crew cut, and alert blue eyes.

"Sergeant Kelley?"

Pat nodded.

"I've — been reading the papers. It's — I really don't know what to say, Sergeant."

"I don't either," Pat said, "except to ask you what you might know about it."

They were walking along the hall, now. They came to the entry hall of the apartment, and Helgeson closed the door behind them. There he faced Pat honestly.

"I've seen her a few times, Sergeant, since she — she left you. There was nothing, well, nothing wrong about it."

"That part doesn't matter," Pat said. "I'm not looking for the men who flirted with her. I'm looking for the man who killed her."

They went into a low, long living room with a beamed ceiling, with floor-length windows facing on the terrace. Helgeson sat in a chair near the huge, bleached mahogany piano.

"I can't help you with that," he said. "I danced with her, at Dreamland. I don't know what attraction the place had for me, except it was the only magic I knew as a kid. I never probed myself for any reasons. She was — a wonderful dancer. I didn't think of her beyond that. That sounds phony, I know, but —" His voice died.

"I'm surprised the Homicide section hasn't sent a man to see you, or have they? You said you'd been reading about it."

"Homicide? No. Why should they?"

"You're pretty well known, and they have your nickname."

"I'm not known down there, not generally. Not as the composer. I'm just another punk, just Helgy, down there. A rather aging punk." He stared at Pat. "But if you know, they know."

Pat shook his head. "I've left the force. I asked to be assigned to this case and was refused."

"Oh," Helgeson rubbed his forehead frowningly. "She told me, when she phoned to break a date yesterday, that she was going back to you. I thought —"

"Yesterday?" Pat interrupted. "She told you *that*, yesterday?"

Helgeson nodded, studying Pat quietly.

Pat could see the pulse in his wrist and he had a passing moment of giddiness. "Where was she living?"

"The Empire Court, over on Hudson."

"Working, was she?"

"I don't think so. She never mentioned it, if she was. She was kind of reticent about all that."

Pat looked at Helgeson levelly. "Was she — living alone?"

Helgeson took a deep breath. "I don't know. I never went in, over there. She was always ready when I called for her." He seemed pale and his voice was unsteady.

Pat felt resentment moving through him, but he couldn't hate them all. Everybody had loved Delia.

He said quietly. "There's nothing you know? She must have mentioned some names, or what she was doing. What the hell did you talk about?"

"We didn't talk much. We danced, that's all. Sergeant, believe me, if I could help I would." His voice was ragged. "If you knew how much I — wanted to help." He shook his head. "There isn't anything I know, not a damned thing."

"All right. I can believe that. If there's anything you hear or happen to remember, *anything at all*, phone me." He gave him the number.

He went from there to the Empire Court, on Hudson. It was a fairly modern, U-shaped building of gray stone, set back on a deep lot. There was a department car among the cars at the curb.

The name in the lobby read: *Delia Revolt.* Pat pressed the button and the door buzzed.

It was on the second floor and he walked up. There were some technical men dusting for prints, and there was Lieutenant Callender, his back to the doorway, standing in the middle of the living room.

He turned and saw Pat. His face showed nothing.

"Anything?" Pat asked him.

"Look, Pat, for the love of —"

"You look," Pat said. "She was my wife. You got a wife, Lieutenant?"

"I'm married to my second, now." He shook his big head and ran a hand through his hair. "The Chief said you'd resigned."

"That's right."

"You've been a cop for fifteen years. You're acting like a rookie."

"I've only been a husband for four years, Lieutenant. I'm not getting in your way."

"We'll probably get a million prints, all but the right ones. We found a dressing robe we're checking, and some pajamas." The lieutenant's eyes looked away. "I'll talk to the Chief, Pat. I'll see that you get your job back."

"I don't want it back — yet. Thanks, anyway, Lieutenant." He kept seeing Delia in the room and somebody else, some formless, faceless somebody, and the giddiness came again and he knew he wouldn't have the stomach to look in any of the other rooms.

He turned his back on the lieutenant and went down the steps to the lobby and out into the hot, bright day. They were right about it, of course. A cop shouldn't be on a family case any more than a surgeon should. Emotion was no asset in this business.

He sat in the car for minutes, trying to get back to reality, trying to forget that cozy apartment and the lieutenant's words. The brightness of the day seemed to put a sharp outline on things, to give them a sense of unreality, like a lighted stage setting.

He heard last night's trumpet again, and started the motor.

The alley was bright, now, but no cleaner. The voices of the freight handlers on the street side of the warehouse were drowned by the racket of the huge trucks bumping past. He walked to the alley's dead end and saw, for the first time, the door that led from the dancehall, a fire exit.

It was open, now, and he could see some men in there, sprinkling the floor with some granulated stuff. There was the sound of a huge rotary brush polisher, but it was outside his line of vision.

He went in through the open door, along a wide hall that flanked the west edge of the bandstand. The men looked at him curiously as he stood there, imagining what it must have been like last night. He could almost hear the music and see the dim lights and the crowded floor.

Along this edge the floor was raised and there were seats up here, for the speculative males, looking over the field, discussing the old favorites and the new finds, wondering what happened to this transient queen and that one. Some had married and not retired.

One of the workers called over, "Looking for the boss, mister?"

"That's right."

"Won't be in this afternoon. The joint's been full of cops and he went out to get some fresh air."

"Okay." Pat turned and went out.

It was nearly five now. He turned the car in a U-turn and headed for Borden. He parked on a lot near Borden and Sixth, and walked the two blocks to Curtes-Husted, Publishers.

Lois was busily typing when he opened the door to the outer office. She looked up at his entrance, and her face seemed to come alive, suddenly.

"Pat!" She got up and came over to the railing.

"I was pretty rough, last night. I thought a drink and dinner might take us back to where we were. Part way, anyway."

"It will, it will. Oh, Pat, if you knew what last night —" She put a hand on his on top of the railing.

The door to Pat's right opened, and a man stood there. He had a masculine, virile face and iron-gray hair. He said, "You can go any time, Lois. I guess Mr. Curtes won't be back."

"Thank you, Mr. Husted," she said. "I'll be going in a minute."

He smiled, and closed the door.

"My boss, the VP," she whispered. "Isn't he handsome?"

"I suppose." Pat could feel her hand trembling.

She said quietly, "You're better, aren't you? You're coming out of it."

"I'm better," he said. "This whole case is one blind alley."

"Delia knew a lot of men — of people. I'll be with you in a minute."

They went to the Lamp Post, an unpretentious restaurant nearby.

They had a martini each, and Lois told him, "Their spare ribs are the best in town."

He ordered the spare ribs.

She seemed animated. She said, "It's going to be all right. It's going to take some time, and then you're going to be really happy, Pat. I'm going to see that you're happy."

He ordered another pair of drinks, and they finished those before the ribs came. They went from the Lamp Post to a spot on the west side, and Pat tried very hard to get drunk. But it didn't work; the alcohol didn't touch him.

They went back to Lois's place. He sat with her in the car in front of her apartment.

"Come on up," she said. "I'll make some coffee."

He shook his head. "I know Husted was paying for that apartment Delia was living in. I've known it for two months, Lois. And you did, too, didn't you?"

Her silence was his answer.

"You probably thought Husted killed her, and yet you've told the police nothing. Delia probably told you yesterday or the day before that she was coming back to me. But you didn't tell me that. Was it yesterday you saw her?"

"The day before. I didn't want her to come back, Pat. And I didn't tell you about my boss because he's got a family, because he's a fundamentally decent man."

"You didn't want her to come back. Because of me?" Pat's voice was hoarse. "You poor damned fool, you don't know me, do you? No matter what she was, Lois, I'll be married to her the rest of my life. But you were the one who could have told me she was coming back. You could have saved her life."

"Pat —"

"Get out, Lois. Get out — quick!"

She scrambled out.

The liquor was getting to him a little now. He finished the note, there on his dinette table, and then went to unlock the front door. Then he called headquarters, gave them the message, and went to pick up the note. He read:

Lieutenant Callender:

I wanted to work with Homicide because I thought it would be safer that way. I could see how close you boys were getting. But it doesn't matter now, because I've no desire to escape you. I killed my wife with a wrecking bar which you'll find in the luggage deck of my car. I couldn't stand the thought of her loving anyone else and I wasn't man enough to rid myself of her. The checking I've done today reveals to me I would probably have escaped detection. I make this confession of my own free will.

Sergeant Patrick Kelley

He waited then, .38 in hand. He waited until he heard the wail of the siren, and a little longer. He waited until he heard the tires screeching outside.

Then he put the muzzle of his .38 to the soft roof of his mouth, and pulled the trigger.

GEORGES SIMENON

AT THE ETOILE DU NORD

In September 1929 a successful Belgian writer named Georges Simenon (b. 1903) was sailing the canals of western Europe. When he had to stop near the Dutch town of Delfzijl for boat repairs, Simenon used the layover time to write The Strange Case of Peter the Lett, *a little book featuring a detective named Jules Maigret. It didn't take him long, and in the next year and a half he wrote eighteen more. Maigret, who moved to Paris in 1923, was well on his way to becoming Europe's most popular policeman. Delfzijl was so delighted with its role in the whole affair that it erected a statue of Maigret.*

Someone must have kept count of the Maigret novels. Although years would go by without a new one, Simenon often turned out a book in eight to eleven days. Besides the Maigret adventures, he also wrote what he called "hard" novels, usually psychological studies that many critics consider his best work.

Maigret's methods of detection are curious. He empathizes with both the victim and the person he tries to imagine as the murderer. He pauses to sip a beer or drops by a café for an apéritif, and somehow it all becomes clear. "But for chance," Maigret muses in the short story "In the Rue Pigalle," "fifty percent of criminals would escape punishment, and . . . but for informers, another fifty percent would remain at liberty."

"L'Etoile du Nord" was published in France in 1944. This translation is by Jean Stewart.

1

A VAGUE MUMBLE over the telephone was the cause of it all, at any rate the cause of Maigret's involvement in this baffling case.

He had almost ceased to belong to the Police Judiciaire. In two more days he would have officially retired. He was expecting to spend these two days, like the previous ones, putting his files in order and sorting out his personal documents and his notes. He had spent thirty years in the office in the Quai des Orfèvres, and he knew every nook and cranny of it better than those of his own house. He had never looked forward impatiently to retirement. But now, forty-eight hours away from freedom, he felt like a boy who has completed his military service, counting the hours, dreaming constantly of the house on the banks of the Loire which was awaiting him and where Madame Maigret was already fixing things up for his arrival.

In order to work in peace he had just spent the night in his office, which was now blue with tobacco smoke. Dawn revealed rain on the embankment, where the street lamps were still burning, and this atmosphere reminded him of the many interrogations which, begun in this very room in the early afternoon, had gone on through the night until the same drab dawn, when a confession was finally wrung from an exhausted offender, while the man who had been questioning him was just as worn out himself.

The telephone rang in a neighboring room. At first Maigret paid no attention, then he raised his head, remembering that the inspector on duty had looked in a few minutes earlier to say he was going out for a drink of hot coffee.

The big house was deserted, its lights burning low in the empty corridors. Maigret went into the inspectors' office, lifted the receiver, and said, "Hello?"

And a man's voice at the end of the line said: "Is that you?"

Why, instead of saying no, or asking for details, did he merely reply with an indistinct mumble?

"This is Pierre . . . We've just been told at Emergencies about a mysterious crime committed at the hotel Etoile du Nord . . . Are you going over there?"

Maigret mumbled again, hung up, and looked around him in some embarrassment. He knew the way these things happen. The inspector on duty had a friend called Pierre at Emergencies Central Office, and this friend was happy to be able to give him a tip.

Only two more days . . .

Maigret filled his pipe and went back to his room, but he lacked the courage to reimmerse himself in the pile of papers; a minute later he put on his bowler hat and his heavy overcoat with the velvet collar, and with a shrug of his shoulders went downstairs.

It was barely six o'clock in the morning. The telephone had worked fast, for when Maigret alighted from his taxi in the Rue de Maubeuge, a stone's throw from the Gare du Nord, there were no onlookers by the door of the hotel, at which a uniformed policeman was standing guard.

"Has the district superintendent come?"

"Not yet. They've gone to fetch him from his home."

"And the doctor?"

"He's just gone up."

The Etoile du Nord was typical of the drab fourth-rate hotels to be found in the neighborhood of all stations. In a small office to the right of the door, Maigret noticed an unmade bed, presumably the night porter's.

The dirty grayness of it all was intensifed by the bleary light of a wet dawn.

"Number 32, on the third floor."

A worn stair-carpet, held down with brass rods. In the passage on the first floor, a few people in their night clothes, some wearing overcoats by way of dressing-gowns over their pajamas, half-awakened faces showing the kind of bewilderment which is a reaction to sudden catastrophe.

Maigret went up and almost collided with a young girl who was coming downstairs, dressed in a dark suit.

"Where are you going?" he asked automatically.

"To catch my train."

"Go back into your room."

"But . . ."

"Nobody is to leave the hotel before I give permission. There's a policeman at the door."

He went on up, forcing her to go backwards up the stairs.

"Will it take long?"

"I don't know. I tell you again, go back to your room."

At the start of an inquiry Maigret was often surly, and this time, into the bargain, he had not slept. A door opened, that of no. 32, and a man emerged who had obviously dressed in a hurry, wearing neither collar nor tie and with slippers on his bare feet.

"The Police Superintendent?"

"No! I'm from the Criminal Investigation Department: Superintendent Maigret."

"Come in, please. I'm the proprietor of the hotel. It's the first time anything like this has happened in the five years I've been in the business . . ."

This was a familiar type: a plaintive bore, a weak character who had invested all his savings in this hotel in the hope of retiring after a few years.

Maigret went into the room. The doctor was putting on his coat, and a man was lying on the bed, stark naked, in a position which concealed his face but revealed a large wound in the middle of the back, roughly on a level with the heart.

"Dead?"

"Almost instantaneously."

"And the blood?"

The doctor pointed to a large pool on the floor, near the door.

"He crawled over there to call for help."

The properitor explained:

"My alarm clock had just rung, for I always get up at half-past five. We cater mainly for travelers and they have to catch early trains. I heard the sound of doors banging . . ."

"One minute. You said doors banging. Do you mean you heard more than one door?"

"I think so . . . I can't be sure — I heard a lot of noise going on . . ."

"And footsteps?"

"Footsteps, certainly!"

"In the passage or on the stairs?"

"That's what I'm wondering . . ."

"Think carefully . . . footsteps on the stairs don't make the same sound as on a floor."

"There may have been both sorts? . . . What did strike me was a cry, a cry that sounded like a man gasping. I was putting on my trousers . . . I opened the door and . . ."

"Excuse me! Where do you sleep?"

"At the end of the passage on the second floor. There's a little closet there which we can't let because it's not got a proper window."

"Go on!"

"That's all! I hurried up. Some guests were opening their doors. This door was standing open and on the threshold a man was kneeling rather than lying, with blood pouring from him . . ."

"Was he naked?"

"I took off his pajamas," the doctor interrupted.

"Stabbed with a knife?"

"Yes, a heavy knife with a broad blade."

The local police superintendent arrived at last and frowned when he saw Maigret already on the scene.

Maigret had a particular loathing for sensational happenings in hotels, and he was already regretting having automatically answered a telephone call which was not meant for him. As usual, travelers were becoming impatient. They came up to him one after the other.

"Excuse me, Superintendent . . . Here are my papers . . . I'm a respectable resident of Béziers . . . I've got to be at Brussels by midday and my train . . ."

The Superintendent could only reply: "Sorry!"

Some of them lost their tempers. Women, after trying blandishments in vain, burst into tears.

"If my husband knew I'd spent the night in this hotel!"

"Be patient, madame!"

Finally, as the crowd was blocking up the passages, he grew angry, and forced them all to return to thir rooms and keep the doors shut.

He had less than a quarter of an hour before him to do a good job. Presently the specialists from the Records Department would be there with their cameras and instruments of every sort.

Then there would be the examining magistrate and his assistant, and the forensic pathologist.

"Is that his luggage? He had nothing else?"

The pallid proprietor shook his head. There was only a small suitcase standing in a corner. Maigret opened it and found nothing but toilet articles and a change of underwear.

On the coatrack hung an iron-gray suit of excellent cut, a half-belted overcoat and a soft felt hat marked with the initials G. B.

In the wallet was a visiting card inscribed: *Georges Bompard, 17 Rue de Miromesnil, Paris.* The wallet contained no money, and there was none to be found anywhere else except some small change in the man's pockets.

Maigret had had the body turned over, and he now beheld a man of about forty-five, well groomed, with particularly finely cut features. Curiously enough his silvery gray hair gave the unknown man a look of remarkable youthfulness as well as a certain distinction.

"Fetch me his registration form!"

The proprietor brought it. The name and address were the same as on the visiting card.

"Was he alone when he arrived?"

"I've just asked the night porter, for he came in at half-past three in the morning. He was alone."

"Where is the night porter?"

"He's waiting downstairs."

"Tell him he's not to leave the hotel until I've finished my inquiry."

As he spoke Maigret bent down and picked up a silk stocking which had been lying half hidden at the foot of the bed.

"Bring me the list of guests, particularly of the women guests."

The silk stocking had been pulled off carelessly and dropped on the floor, as though in the course of hasty undressing. It was flesh-colored, of smallish size and medium quality.

Leaving the local police officer to collect the data for his report and receive the gentlemen from the D.P.P., Maigret went out of the room, still wearing his overcoat, with his hat on his head and his pipe between his lips. But the pipe had gone out, and he was followed by the hotel proprietor rather like a colonel inspecting barracks.

"Who's in here?" he asked in front of one door.

"Madame Geneviève Blanchet, forty-two years of age, widow, from Compiègne."

"Let's go in!"

A first glance showed him that Madame Blanchet was wearing lisle stockings, but he nonetheless obliged her to open her cases, after which, despite her protests, he searched the room.

"You heard nothing?"

She reddened, and he had to insist.

"I got the impression . . . You know! The walls are so thin! . . . I got the impression, as I was saying, that the gentleman was not alone and that he . . . that they . . ."

"Were making love in the next room?" Maigret put it bluntly, for he had a strong dislike of prudish women.

Two old English ladies, further on, gave him some trouble, for they were in possession of several pairs of stockings, new ones, which they were planning to smuggle through the customs for their niece.

A Swiss woman with dubious papers was sent to the Quai des Orfèvres to have her identity checked.

Time was passing, and Maigret had not yet discovered the second stocking. It was on the floor above that he found himself in the presence of the girl in the dark suit whom he had already met on the stairs. He immediately glanced down at her legs.

"Hello, so you don't wear stockings?" he asked with surprise. "At this time of year?"

For the month was March and the weather particularly cold.

"I never wear stockings."

"Have you any luggage?"

"No!"

"Have you filled in a registration form?"

"Yes."

He picked it out of the file. It gave the name of Céline Germain, no occupation, Rue des Saules, Orléans.

"Your name is Céline Germain?"

"Yes."

He observed her more closely, for there was an aggressive decisiveness about her replies.

"Age?"

"Nineteen."

"You're quite sure you never wear stockings?"

He searched the room, pulled the bedclothes about, opened all the drawers of the wardrobe, and suddenly snapped out an order:

"Will you lift up your skirt?"

"What? Are you mad?"

"Please lift up your skirt."

"Look here! Aren't you afraid of my entering a complaint against you, filthy beast?"

"A man has been killed in this hotel!" was all Maigret replied. "Come on! Hurry up!"

She was pale, and her great gold-flecked eyes — a redhead's eyes — expressed contempt and fury.

"Lift it up yourself if you're not afraid to," she declared. "I warn you I shall lodge a complaint!"

He went up to her and touched her hips.

"You're wearing a girdle," he noted.

"So what?"

"You know very well that it's not a foundation garment but a narrow suspender belt . . ."

"What business is that of yours? Can't I dress the way I like?"

"Where's the other stocking?"

"I don't know what you're talking about."

The hotel proprietor was listening with stupefaction to this peculiar dialogue.

"Find me a big monkey wrench!" called out Maigret curtly.

And he used it to dismantle the drainpipe of the washbasin. As he apparently expected, he soon pulled out a small spongy ball which was in fact a silk stocking.

"Come along, my dear," he ordered without displaying the least surprise. "We can discuss things better in my office."

"And suppose I refuse to follow you?"

"Come along!"

He pushed her into the corridor. She tried to put up some resistance. Then he paused for a moment outside no. 32 and glanced into the room.

"I'm off to Headquarters," he told the examining magistrate who had just arrived. "I think I'm on to something interesting."

At that moment his prisoner tried to move away suddenly. But the

Superintendent was just as quick; he grasped her by the arm, and then, with her free hand, she started scratching his face.

"Come now! Quiet!"

"Let me go! . . . I tell you to let me go. You're a swine. You wanted to make me undress. You lifted up my skirt. It was because I refused that you're taking your revenge!"

Doors were being opened, bewildered faces appearing, while Maigret alone remained quite calm, holding the girl firmly by the arm. "Will you shut up?"

"You've no right to take me away! I've done nothing! I want to catch my train . . ."

He led her forcibly down the stairs and, still undiscouraged, she went on shouting shrilly:

"Help! . . . I've done nothing! . . . I'm being ill-treated!"

Perhaps she was hoping for some support from the puzzled crowd, as is the case more often than one thinks. In his early days Maigret had been beaten up because a pickpocket whom he was arresting outside a big department store had started shouting: "Stop thief!"

There were a great many people outside the Etoile du Nord. The Superintendent had taken the precaution of calling a taxi. He nevertheless needed the help of a policeman to control the girl, who went on struggling and trying to fling herself on the ground.

Finally the taxi door closed on them. Maigret straightened his hat and cast a sideways glance at his companion, who was now panting.

"I've seldom seen a more tiresome little bitch," he observed.

"And I've never met a worse brute than you!"

She was a strange girl! The first time he had seen her on the stairs, looking young and slight in her navy blue suit, he had taken her for a respectable young lady. In her room, on the contrary, she had been as ill-tempered and brazen as a tart.

Now her attitude was changing again, as she remarked:

"If you're the famous Maigret, I don't congratulate you, for I thought you'd be cleverer than this!"

He lit his pipe, which had long been out. She sighed.

"I loathe tobacco smoke!"

"Which doesn't prevent you from having cigarettes in your bag!"

"That's my own smoke; I object to yours!"

He went on smoking nonetheless, while watching her from the corner of his eye, since she was quite capable of opening the taxi door and jumping out.

"How long has it been?" he suddenly asked.

"What?"

"That you've been on the game?"

He had the impression that a fleeting smile passed over her thin lips.

"Is that your business?"

"Please yourself! Perhaps you'll be more sensible in my office."

"Shall you still want to look at my girdle?"

"Who knows?"

It was still raining. The streets of Paris were busier now. The taxi slowed down to cross the Halles, and finally reached the embankment.

Maigret was still undecided whether or not he was glad to have taken the telephone call that morning. At all events, he was interested in the singular little creature sitting stiffly by his side.

The battle was on between them, a strange battle in which each side seemed to feel some curiosity about the other.

"I suppose you're going to question me for hours on end without giving me anything to eat or drink? That's your practice, isn't it?"

"Who knows?" he said again.

"I may as well tell you right away that I'm not afraid. I've got nothing on my conscience. You'll be sorry some day for whatever you do to me . . ."

"All right!"

"What have you got against me?"

"I don't know yet."

"Then let me go. That would be much more intelligent of you."

The taxi drew up in the courtyard of Police Headquarters, and Maigret got out. He was about to pull out his wallet and pay when his eyes caught the girl's, and he realized that she was awaiting this opportunity to make a final attempt to escape. He told the driver:

"I'll have the money sent down to you."

Police Headquarters was busy now, and voices could be heard in most of the rooms. Maigret opened the door of his, ushered in Céline Germain, and locked the door from the outside; then he went to see the Director.

They discussed the affair for some ten minutes and reached an agreement about it, after which Maigret went to see the office messenger.

"Send me up coffee and croissants for two."

At last he opened his own door and stood for a moment motionless, seeing all his papers, torn and crumpled, scattered over the floor, the windowpanes cracked and the bust of the Republic, which used to stand on the mantelpiece, lying shattered on the ground.

As for the girl, seated in the Superintendent's own chair, she stared at him defiantly.

"I told you," she said. "And I warn you there's more to come!"

2

This was probably the most disappointing interrogation in all Maigret's career. From beginning to end it took place in exceptional circumstances, in a setting of the utmost chaos, with torn papers on the floor and pieces of plaster which the Superintendent pretended not to see.

Added to which Maigret had not slept, and the girl confronting him was presumably in much the same condition. So that both of them were pale, their eyes shining with that hectic but exhausted brightness that follows long periods of wakefulness.

When he entered his office, Maigret had walked up to his armchair with perfect composure and grasped the girl's arm, saying quietly:

"Do you mind?"

And she had got up, aware that he would have the last word; she had sat down in the place he indicated, facing the window through which the bleak light shone on her as inexorably as a magnesium flare. Did she expect him to start speaking? In that case she must have been seriously disappointed, for the Superintendent began by filling a pipe with meticulous care, then he poked the stove, sharpened a pencil, and finally opened the door for the café waiter who brought in breakfast for two.

"Does it tempt you?" he said gently to his prisoner.

"Isn't there any milk?" she retorted sourly.

"I thought black coffee would keep you awake better."

"I hate coffee without milk."

"In that case don't drink it."

She drank it nonetheless, trying to get accustomed to her companion's ominous placidity. After reviving himself, he lifted the receiver of the telephone.

"Hello! Give me the Orléans Flying Squad."

And when he had his connection:

"Maigret speaking . . . Will you give me some unofficial information . . . If need be I'll send you a rogatory warrant . . . It concerns a certain Céline Germain, residing Rue des Saules in your city . . ."

He thought he saw a brief smile pass over the girl's lips. Meanwhile he frowned. "What? . . . You're sure? . . . Nor in the suburbs of Orléans?"

When he replaced the receiver his gaze dwelt at some length on Céline Germain's face. Finally he asked with a sigh:

"Where do you live?"

"Nowhere!"

"Where did you meet Georges Bompard?"

"In the street."

Now the two of them had joined battle, and each watched the other tensely, while outside the rain still fell and the hooter of some tugboat sounded occasionally as it passed under the bridge.

"In what street?"

"At Montmartre."

"You were soliciting?"

"What about it?"

"What time was it?"

"I don't know."

"Did you go back to the hotel with him?"

She hesitated, realized that he knew her companion had entered the hotel alone, and explained:

"I went in a little before him and took a room. He wanted it that way."

"Where were you born?"

"That's nobody's business."

"You've never been in trouble with the police?"

At the same moment there came a knock at the door. Inspector Janvier seemed reluctant to speak, but Maigret signed to him to go ahead.

"I've come from the Rue de Miromesnil, where I didn't find out much. Georges Bompard really does live there. For the past fifteen years he's occupied a two-room bachelor flat on the fifth floor rear, at a rent of 2,500 francs. The concierge says he's very seldom there, for he's a commercial representative and he travels a good deal."

Maigret felt that the girl was wincing and was about to say something, but the moment passed and she immediately resumed her impassive air.

"Go on."

"That's all! Bompard left his home yesterday morning."

"Had anybody rung him up?"

"He doesn't have a telephone."

"Nothing else?"

"Nothing else. Except for a personal impression. He must have been a gay dog, to judge by the photographs of women that practically covered the walls."

"Did you see a picture of this one?"

"I'm trying to remember . . . I don't think so . . ."

"Go and fetch me all the photographs and the letters, if there are any."

When Janvier had left, Maigret stoked the fire again, patiently, passed a hand over his brow, and yawned.

"So the long and the short of it is that you know nothing. Your name is Céline Germain and you're a streetwalker. Bompard accosted you in the street and took you to the hotel . . ."

"Not right away. We went dancing in nightclubs first."

"And once in the hotel?"

"I went to his room, as we'd agreed. We went to bed."

"I know! A neighbor heard you . . ."

"She must have been a nasty-minded snooper if she got up to listen. Perhaps she looked through the keyhole too?"

"And then? Did anyone come in?"

"I don't know . . . I went back to my room."

"Undressed?"

"I'd got partially dressed. I must have forgotten the stocking I'd dropped under the bed. I was woken up by steps in the corridor and by doors opening and shutting. When I realized what was happening I guessed I should be suspected and I tried to leave. Then you prevented me from leaving. I remembered the stocking and I put the other down the plughole. Now do you know enough?"

Maigret got up, put on his hat but not his coat, opened the door, and simply said: "Come!"

He went along a number of corridors with the girl, keeping a close watch on her; they climbed up narrow stairs and at last reached the Criminal Records Department, where all those arrested during the night are subjected to anthropometric examination.

It was the women's turn. There were still a score of them about, mainly prostitutes of the lowest sort who were used to the ceremony and undressed of their own accord.

At this point, anyone who had not known Maigret would have thought he was just a big fellow automatically doing an uninteresting job.

"Get undressed . . ." he sighed, relighting his pipe.

But he had to turn aside his head so that his prisoner should not see the strange smile that came to his lips.

"Take everything off?"

"Of course!"

He anticipated a conflict. He waited with some anxiety. Finally she literally tore off her jacket and her cream-colored silk blouse, then sat down to remove her shoes.

As he looked down at her, the Superintendent noted that her hands were shaking, and he almost called off the ordeal.

"You still insist that you solicited in the public street?"

She nodded, her eyes in a fixed stare and her teeth clenched; she let her skirt drop. Two small firm breasts were visible under her chemise.

"Now get into line . . . You're going to be examined."

And with an apparently automatic gesture he picked up the clothes and took them into the next room. This was the laboratory where, amid test tubes and projectors, specialists were busy with meticulous research.

"Look, Eloi, what d'you think of this outfit?"

A tall young man picked up the tailor-made suit and felt it knowledgeably. He put his finger on the label first.

"It comes from a shop in Bordeaux. It's excellent quality cloth and it's well made. It must belong to a young woman of good bourgeois family."

"Many thanks."

When he went back to the women's section he heard sounds of loud argument, and shortly afterwards the photographer of the Records Department came over to tell him:

"There's nothing to be done about it! Every time I try to take a picture she shuts her eyes, blows out her cheeks, twists her lips, in a word she manages to make herself quite unrecognizable."

"Let her get dressed again!" Maigret conceded wearily. "No card with her fingerprints, of course?"

"No. She's never been in trouble with the police. Look, here's the doctor looking for you . . ."

The doctor was a young fellow whom Maigret knew well. The two men talked in low voices in a corner for a long time. When they had done the girl reappeared, wearing her suit, her gaze fixed and her face so pale that the Superintendent felt compassion for her.

"Have you decided to speak?"

"I've nothing to say."

They were back in Maigret's office again, and curiously enough a sort of intimacy had grown up between the Superintendent and the girl. Although they did not look on one another as friends but rather the reverse, they were no longer strangers.

"You know what the doctor told me?"

She reddened and was on the verge of bursting into tears.

"I suppose you can guess? It's less than a month since . . ."

"Shut up!"

"You admit, then, that less than a month ago you were still a virgin.

I should like you to admit, too, that you haven't given me your real name."

She retorted, with an attempt at irony: "If you're providing both the questions and the answers!"

"That's right! I shall ask the questions and provide the answers. Or rather I shall try to reconstruct events. You live somewhere in the provinces, I'm not yet sure where, but probably somewhere near Bordeaux . . ."

He noted that the girl betrayed a certain satisfaction: so it was not Bordeaux!

"You were a well-brought-up young girl, probably living with your parents. Georges Bompard came into your life. He made love to you . . . you gave yourself to him and he persuaded you to follow him . . ."

She looked away, realizing that the Superintendent was only talking in order to watch her reactions.

"Are you writing a sentimental novel?" she jeered, trying, not very successfully, to assume a tone of vulgar mockery.

"Almost, since the next chapter is desertion . . ."

"I suppose Georges tells me we must part and I kill him, then I go and hide the knife . . . By the way, where could I have hidden the knife?"

"Excuse me, who told you he was killed with a knife?"

"Why . . . People were saying so . . . in the passages . . ."

"In that case, since you've now become so talkative, go on and tell me where, in fact, you hid the weapon . . ."

"You think you're remarkable, don't you?"

"One thing I'm sure of, you're pretty remarkable yourself! You endured that examination this morning, amongst all those prostitutes, sooner than confess that you'd lied when you spoke of soliciting!"

"You're very naive!"

"Why?"

"Because the fact that I was a virgin a month ago doesn't prove anything. Are you going to keep on questioning me a long time?"

"As long as I need to. By way of warning, I must tell you that three years ago a man spent thirty-seven hours on the chair you're now occupying. He had come in to give evidence. He went off handcuffed, and he is now a convict in Guiana."

She glanced at him with contempt.

"Just as you please!" she said. "I shall wait patiently for your questions. You began by feeling my girdle. Then you managed to see me stripped. I'm wondering whether after all you're just a nasty old man . . ."

Maigret made no reply but, perhaps by way of punishment, kept her for a quarter of an hour waiting for a word, while he studied unimportant papers.

Then he looked up suddenly. "How much did Bompard give you for the night?" he said. "Since he picked you up in the street, it's only to be expected . . ."

"That he should pay me! He gave me a thousand francs . . ."

"Yes, there's a thousand-franc note in your handbag. Were all your customers equally generous?"

"Some of them were."

At such moments Maigret would gladly have slapped her face. The most notorious criminals of the last thirty years had passed through his office. One of them, a former lawyer who had tragically turned to crime, had been so crafty that the Superintendent had more than once had to leave the room to hide his fury.

But on the present occasion he was confronted by a slip of a girl! She said she was nineteen, but he'd not have been surprised to learn that she was only seventeen.

For hours now they had been closeted together, and he had learned nothing, not even her name or where she came from. She was lying brazenly, hardly seeking to conceal the fact. Or rather, she seemed to be saying:

"It's not up to me to tell you the truth, is it? It's up to you to find it out!"

Janvier had returned from the Rue de Miromesnil with a pile of photographs, some of them more than suggestive. Maigret had examined them each in turn, slowly, and had been conscious of his companion's cold fury.

"Jealous?" he asked her.

"Of a casual pick-up!"

At all events, there was no photograph there resembling Céline, while information about Bompard was somewhat meager.

The firm that employed him had been contacted; it was a music publisher in the Boulevard Malesherbes. The publisher, when questioned, had replied:

"Bompard was an odd man; I saw very little of him. He was an excellent representative, but he had certain fads, such as constantly changing his itinerary. He liked to surround himself with mystery, and we in the firm thought he was given to bluffing. Sometimes he implied that he belonged to an illustrious family. He dressed with meticulous care and a certain eccentricity which I thought out of place in his profession . . ."

*

At three in the afternoon, Maigret's office still displayed the same chaos, to which were now added glasses of beer on the table, the remains of sandwiches, ash from Maigret's pipe all over the place and cigarette stubs, since the Superintendent had finally sent for some cigarettes for Céline.

All in all, the situation was almost ridiculous, and this must have become generally known at Headquarters, for Maigret's colleagues kept looking in on obvious pretexts.

At the Etoile du Nord, Sergeant Lucas, Maigret's best collaborator, was carrying out a thorough investigation, to no effect. Not only was the knife nowhere to be found (even though all the toilets had been dismantled!) but no evidence had brought in the slightest clue.

Altogether, the only established facts were these: shortly after 3 A.M. a girl called Céline, about whom nothing was known, had rung at the door of the hotel and asked for a room for the rest of the night.

Less than a quarter of an hour later, Georges Bompard, carrying an overnight case, entered the same hotel and took a room, in which Céline visited him shortly afterwards.

Finally, two hours after that, Bompard opened the door to call for help and collapsed, having been stabbed with a knife in the middle of the back; the girl, meanwhile, endeavored to disappear.

The afternoon papers had just come out. They published a photograph of Céline on the front page, but she was unrecognizable, since she had persisted in making faces at the camera.

"Tell me, my dear, when Bompard accosted you in that street in Montmartre, the name of which you have forgotten, was he carrying his case?"

"No!"

"You went into two night clubs. Was he still without his case? And yet when he came to the hotel he was carrying one . . ."

"We went together to fetch it from a small all-night bistro near the Place Pigalle, where he had deposited it . . ."

"In the bedroom, did he open the case in your presence?"

"No . . . Yes . . . I can't be sure."

"Where did he take the thousand-franc note from?"

"I suppose from his wallet!"

"When we found that wallet it was empty. Presumably Bompard gave you all the money he had with him, keeping only enough change to pay for his room next morning . . ."

"That was no concern of mine!"

Obviously! She had an answer for everything, and the very incoherence of her thesis had its own logic.

What else could he try, to break her composure? Persuasion? Resignedly, Maigret assumed his most good-natured air:

"Don't you think we're both of us becoming rather ridiculous? I'm trying to make you say you killed Bompard, whereas you may not have done so; on the other hand you persist in declaring you know nothing, whereas you really know something . . ."

"I'm in the stronger position, then!" she remarked.

"Well, yes! Only that won't last. Lucas has just called me to say he's got hold of something significant. At any moment now the situation will change and you'll be in an awkward fix . . .

"Let's argue calmly, both of us, and stop me if I'm wrong. To begin with, an undeniable fact: Bompard was stabbed with a knife. Now it's hardly likely, unless we assume premeditation, that you'd have had a knife of that size in your handbag. It can't have been lying about on the table, either. . . . And the overnight case, which might have contained one, was shut . . ."

"I never said that!"

"All right! . . . It doesn't matter whether it was open or shut. The fact remains that a woman of your sort is not likely to use a knife. If you had wanted to do away with a faithless lover or an unscrupulous seducer you'd have bought yourself a revolver.

"Therefore, you did not kill Bompard . . .

"We must assume, then, that someone came in from outside, and I shall prove to you that this person could only have come while you were present . . ."

She had risen and was standing with her face pressed against the windowpane, while dusk fell over rain-drenched Paris.

"For one thing, if you had gone off quietly, after those embraces that don't concern me, you would probably not have left one of your stockings under the bed. You'd have picked up your belongings carefully, like the sensible, self-possessed little person that you are . . ."

He was speaking ironically, for at that moment he saw a sort of shudder run down the back of her neck.

"Are you listening, Céline? For another thing, Bompard was stabbed in the back, which implies either that he was occupied with a third person — yourself — when the murderer appeared, or that he had no reason to mistrust that murderer . . .

"These are the conclusions to which logical argument leads us! Now I've a piece of advice to give you in your own interest: to speak the truth without delay. You want to make me believe that you are a professional streetwalker, not to use a coarser term . . .

"If I were to let myself believe it, I should not fail to point out to you that in that case you've probably also got a steady boyfriend —

there's another name for them too — who, seeing you go into the hotel with an apparently wealthy man, might have thought of robbing him . . .

"You see what I'm driving at? And do you understand at last that it's in your own interest to tell me straight what you saw?"

A long silence followed. The girl went on looking out of the window. Maigret was on the lookout for any reaction from her, but without much hope.

Finally she turned round, as pale as she had been that morning when she left the Records Department. She went back to sit down on her chair wearily, pushing aside with her foot the papers scattered on the floor.

"Is that all?" she sighed.

"Why not confess right away what you'll be forced to confess in an hour or two?"

A bitter smile curled her lips as she remarked dryly:

"Do you think so?"

It looked as though she had given in and was about to speak at last. She sat there, staring at the floor, with her knees crossed and her hands clasped over them. Maigret dared not move for fear of influencing her.

At last she bestirred herself, looked for the cigarettes on the desk, and took one, which she lit offhandedly.

"This is a queer job you're doing!" she remarked. "Doesn't it embarrass you a bit?"

Maigret did not bat an eyelid.

"You think that's a clever story you've made up? And you really imagine you know something about me?"

"I imagine I'm going to find out something," he said with deep earnestness.

"Really?"

It was discouraging. She changed from one minute to the next, reverting to the tone in which, that morning, she had spoken of herself as a streetwalker.

"Is this how you always carry on your inquiries?"

Maigret felt pity rather than anger, for she at last betrayed a latent anguish, a despair which might perhaps overthrow the frail barrier of her will.

"Listen, Céline . . ."

"I'm not called Céline!"

"I know."

"You know nothing at all! You shan't know anything! And if by any misfortune you should get to know anything, you'll bear the weight of it on your conscience. Now send me to prison if you like. Give interviews to journalists who'll write columns about the girl who won't tell her name . . ."

"What were you doing in Bordeaux?"

"When?" she cried with a start.

"Not very long ago. I'll give you the exact date presently. From your accent I'd say you don't come from the south at all, nor from the southwest. And yet . . ."

She sighed, overcome by a weariness which was perfectly genuine: "I've had enough of it! If you sent me to prison I should at least be able to sleep there."

"You can sleep as soon as you've told me . . ."

"Is this blackmail?"

In distress, he blurted: "No, you little fool! Don't you see that what I'm doing is for your own sake? Don't you know that once you've gone out of this door you'll be an accused person and you'll be at the mercy of the D.P.P.? Have you seen me take a single note? Have you seen me write a report of this interrogation?"

She watched him with curiosity.

"You must realize that so long as you're here . . ."

But he did not complete his sentence. He had already said too much. He could have slapped her, like a disobedient child, and yet at other moments . . .

"Shall we begin again from the beginning? Shall I prove to you that your story doesn't hold water?"

She looked up at him and said: "I know!"

"So then?"

"There's nothing else to be done. I'm really at the end of my tether. If you'd let me lie on the floor I'd go to sleep . . ."

The telephone bell rang and Maigret turned his back on the girl, who did, in fact, lie down on the floor and close her eyes.

3

"Hello! . . . Is that you? . . . Are you still working in the office? . . . The electrician has come and is asking whether he should install a light in the toolshed . . ."

Madame Maigret was ringing from far away, from the newly decorated little house at Meung-sur-Loire where he was due in forty-eight hours.

"What sort of weather?" he queried.

"Dry . . . there's a strong wind . . ."

In Paris it was still raining, and Maigret wished the wind from the Loire would come and sweep away the tense, unhealthy atmosphere of his office, where for hours on end an exhausting struggle had been going on.

He held the receiver to his ear, but let his gaze dwell on that enigmatic creature who had been standing up to him with the incredible energy of which only some women are capable, and who had lied as girls know how to lie.

"Yes, I'm listening . . ."

"Can I speak to you a moment longer? The electrician wants to know if he should fix a bell at the front door. I thought the knocker would be enough . . ."

"Sure!"

But his "sure" applied not only to the front door of the Meung house and its electric bell. Maigret had stopped listening. He couldn't wait to hang up and think about something else. He replied noncommittally.

"Yes . . . Good . . . As you prefer . . . That's right . . . Goodbye, darling . . ."

And when he said "darling" the girl's eyes turned to him again with curiosity, since feminine instincts persist in spite of tragic happenings.

Whew! . . . Maigret had a sensation of relief. It seemed to him that after going round in circles for so long without finding a way out, he had at last discovered one. He had recovered his rational powers. His mistake had been to remain too long shut up with this girl in a stifling atmosphere.

"Hello! . . . Is Lucas back? . . . Send him up to my office at once . . . Yes, with all the reports of the Etoile du Nord case . . ."

He lit his pipe, took a drink of beer, and went over to the window, which he opened in spite of the rain.

"Just a minute, to clear the air," he explained.

True, he had not discovered the murderer of Georges Bompard, and there was nothing sensational about the idea that had just occurred to him, but it served to release him from the vicious circle.

His idea was as follows: when the crime was committed the night porter had been on duty on the ground floor, and it was impossible to leave the hotel without his cooperation. Now this night porter declared that he had not opened the door for anybody and had not left his post.

Moreover, on the second floor, the proprietor had been up, putting on his trousers, so he said, and he had hurried upstairs as soon as he heard the cries for help.

Assuming then, as Maigret did, that the girl had not committed the crime . . .

Assuming that she had witnessed it and was keeping silent for some compelling reason . . .

Lucas came in, a bundle of papers in his hand.

"Come in! Sit down! Have you got the night porter's statement?"

And he read it through, muttering the words to himself:

"Joseph Dufieu, born at Moissac . . . Heard the calls for help from the third floor almost at the same time as my boss's footsteps on the stair . . . It was I who rang Emergencies right away, then I called a policeman who was passing and who came to stand sentry in front of the hotel . . ."

Was Maigret deliberately pursuing his inquiry in the girl's presence? She seemed, at all events, to be listening intently, and she betrayed a certain anxiety.

"Have you questioned all the guests in the hotel, Lucas?"

"The statements are here . . . I'm certain that none of them knew the victim and therefore none of them had any motive for attacking him."

"What about the proprietor? Where does he come from?"

"Toulouse."

Maigret's ideas, though still vague, were beginning to take shape, and he walked up and down, his hands behind his back and his pipe between his teeth. He shut the window again, and from time to time took up his stand in front of the girl, who seemed disturbed by his change of attitude.

"Good! Now follow my argument carefully, Lucas! Assume that this young lady did not kill Bompard. It would seem from your inquiries that none of the hotel guests did so. Now two men have asserted that nobody left the hotel. These two are Dufieu the night porter, and the propietor . . . How do we know that one or other isn't a former acquaintance of Bompard's, having an old grudge against him?"

He suddenly broke off, dissatisfied.

"No! It wasn't the night porter, since Bompard saw him on his arrival and handed over his registration form; he'd have had time to recognize the man, and if there had been an argument between them it would have taken place before half-past three in the morning."

Why did the girl relax as though relieved? And why did Maigret go on, still thinking aloud:

"As for the proprietor . . . Let's see! Does he get the night porter to wake him? No, he's got an alarm clock . . . He hadn't gone downstairs when he heard the shouts . . . Dufieu hadn't gone upstairs . . . So the proprietor couldn't know that Bompard was in his hotel . . ."

He sat down heavily. As often happens, he had started out confidently on a trail and now noticed that it led nowhere.

"Get them to bring us up something to drink, Lucas . . . What'll you take, my dear?"

"A coffee!"

"Don't you think you're excitable enough already?"

To think that with a single word she could have cleared up everything and that she remained obstinately silent! He glared at her resentfully. he wanted to solve the problem at all costs. He could not picture himself, at the end of his career, handing the girl over to the examining magistrate and declaring:

"She's either guilty or she isn't. I've been closeted with her for over twelve hours and I've got nothing out of her . . ."

As for Lucas, he knew that on such occasions it was better to remain in the background, and after ordering two beers and a coffee he kept quiet in a corner.

"You follow, Lucas? There's one character I keep coming back to: the night porter. Only he knew that Bompard was in the hotel. Only he could have seen the murderer come out of the room . . . Wait! . . ."

There was a knock on the door. He shouted:

"No! I'm not in! . . . To anyone!"

He was on his feet again, in a state of excitement.

"The list of hotel guests, quickly! You did say the porter came from Moissac? . . . and the proprietor from Toulouse? . . . Let's see about the guests . . . London . . . Amiens . . . Compiègne . . . Marseille . . . Mercy-le-Haut . . . Not one from Moissac! . . . Not one from Toulouse!"

He had scarcely uttered these words when, turning to the girl, he noticed a look of terror in her eyes, while her little teeth were feverishly biting her lower lip.

"Can you guess what I'm getting at, Lucas? Bompard, having made a conquest, as must be usual with him to judge by the photographs that were found in his flat, puts up at a hotel chosen at random near the Gare du Nord . . . Somebody recognizes him, somebody who has a reason to bear him ill will . . . And this obstinate child knows that person, since she refuses to speak, since she invents all sorts of nonsense rather than tell the truth . . . We're getting warm, I'm sure. Damn it, we . . ."

He repeated dreamily:

"Moissac! Toulouse! And the suit comes from a firm in Bordeaux . . ."

He picked up the telephone receiver and passed it to Lucas.

"Get me the music publisher for whom Bompard worked. Ask him where Bompard went on his last round . . ."

At moments like this Maigret seemed to grow larger, to become broader and heavier. He took deep puffs at his pipe and his gaze settled on the girl with crushing power. He seemed to be saying:

"All right! When you saw me you thought I wasn't nearly as clever as some people said. An easy-going duffer, didn't you? Somebody whom a little girl could make randy and who got his fun taking her clothes off; a sentimental duffer into the bargain, soft-hearted and excitable! One minute, my dear . . ."

And to Lucas, at the telephone:

"What does he say?"

"Bompard must have spend the last few months in the southwest."

"That's enough! Ring off!"

He emptied his glass at one gulp, poked the stove for a moment, turned round, suddenly calm, and said to Lucas in so unexpected a tone that the girl could not restrain a smile:

"You might have told me I was making a fool of myself!"

"But, Chief . . ."

"The hotel servants . . . Have you questioned them?"

"Yes, Chief . . . There are only two chambermaids that sleep in the hotel, on the sixth floor. Of course they heard nothing. They were the last to come down, when the hullabaloo woke them up."

"Have you their names?"

"There's Berthe Martineau, nineteen years old . . ."

"Where from?"

"I'm looking . . . Here we are . . . Compiègne!"

"And the other?"

"Lucienne Jouffroy, forty-five, from . . . from Moissac."

And Lucas, who was a short man, looked up at the Superintendent with an expression of mingled astonishment and admiration.

"You've got it, now? Jump into a taxi . . . Go and fetch her . . . Quickly, for heaven's sake!"

And he pushed the sergeant out, then closed the door with weary relief.

He looked at the photographs one after the other, and merely noted that Bompard's mistresses were all young girls, often very young girls.

"Which is she?" he asked his prisoner amicably.

He was almost as sleepy as Céline. She sat hunched up, and instead of replying she shook her head.

"Is Lucienne Jouffroy's picture among these?"

"I can't say anything yet!" she sighed at last, with an effort.

"Why not? Are you waiting till the woman comes? Admit that you're from Moissac yourself!"

"I'll speak later!"

"Why not now?"

"Because!"

"Do you know what I'd do if I had a daughter like you? I'd give her a good smacking from time to time, to teach her a lesson. Now, I bet you began by collecting photographs of film stars, didn't you? No? Then you've read too many novels . . ."

Gently, she corrected him: "I was keen on music . . ."

And she gave a start when Maigret declared emphatically:

"It comes to the same thing! You were romantic! You met Georges Bompard. What surprises me, now, is that you should have fallen for a commercial traveler . . ."

She corrected him again: "He told me he was a composer. He played the piano wonderfully . . ."

Once again an intimacy had grown up between them, that strange intimacy that is formed oftener than one might expect between a policeman and his prisoner. The room was overheated and thick with smoke. The various noises of Police Headquarters could be heard vaguely, phones ringing in neighboring rooms, footsteps down the long corridor, and in the background the hooting of cars on the bridge nearby.

"Did you love him?"

She hung her head without replying.

"You loved him, that's for sure! And I wonder whether it was he who took you away or you that followed him, that hung on to him?"

She answered him straight, raising her eyes:

"It was me, afterwards!"

He understood. He was back in that everyday reality which underlies the most apparently complicated cases.

A commercial traveler with a taste for young girls who gave himself glamour in their eyes by posing as a great composer . . .

A romantic provincial teenager who, after yielding to him, had sought to safeguard her happiness . . .

"Was it he who brought you to Paris?"

"I came on my own."

"Had he given you his address?"

"No . . . He kept everything rather mysterious . . . But he'd told me he used to go to a certain café in the Boulevard Saint-Germain. That was where I found him. I had no luggage and he went to fetch his overnight case. He asked me to stay a few days in the hotel, after which he would be free of certain commitments and would be able to devote himself exclusively to me."

That morning, when she had tried to make herself out a low-class adventuress, Maigret had almost believed her, so well had she played her part. In the course of the day she had shown herself alternately very childish and very much of a woman, now obdurate and now dejected, now aggressive and now disheartened.

"Your inspector's taking a long time," she suddenly said, looking at her wristwatch.

"He's a sergeant . . ."

"I don't know the difference."

"Is it a long time since you left Moissac?"

"I'm not going to say anything yet."

"Do you know Dufieu, the night porter?"

"I shall talk when the sergeant gets back."

"So you believe Lucienne Jouffroy has gone away?"

"I've no idea . . . Can I have some more coffee brought up, please? I'm dying with fatigue."

He rang the messenger. Soon afterwards a call came through for him.

"What? . . . what did you say? Well, can't be helped, my boy. It was only to be expected . . . Yes, we'll have her description sent to all the frontier posts."

He turned to the girl.

"That was Sergeant Lucas. He tells me Lucienne Jouffroy left the hotel late this morning without informing anyone . . ."

And he spoke into the phone again: "Come back at once . . . All right . . ."

He hung up, and saw his companion looking mistrustful.

"I suppose there's nothing to prevent you from talking now?"

"How am I to know you're not lying? Perhaps there wasn't even anyone on the line?"

"Why, what a suspicious person you are! Well, my dear, since that's the way it is, we shall just have to wait till Lucas comes back. Will you believe *him?*"

"Maybe."

They were both on edge by now. A quarter of an hour passed without either of them speaking, and finally Lucas appeared, uneasy and abashed.

"I should have thought of it this morning, Chief . . ."

"How could you have thought of it this morning when I didn't think of it myself? What about the night porter?"

"He's here in the passage."

"What has he got to say?"

"Nothing. He declares he knows nothing . . ."

"Bring him in."

The man came in, stoop-shouldered, and cast a stealthy glance at Maigret.

"What was your connection with Lucienne Jouffroy?"

"She's my sister-in-law."

"Sit down. You needn't be afraid. But answer my questions frankly. Did your sister-in-law have a daughter?"

"Yes, Rosine."

"What has become of her?"

"She died."

"Of what?"

A stubborn silence. Maigret persisted: "Of what?"

And then Céline said in a low voice, turning towards the porter:

"You can tell him, Joseph."

"She died of an operation she had done because she was pregnant. She was sixteen . . ."

"And this happened at Moissac?"

"At Moissac, three years ago."

"And Georges Bompard was traveling there at the time?"

"It was all his fault . . . It was he who took her to the abortionist, when she went to tell him she was pregnant."

"One minute, Dufieu! I assume that it was following these events that your sister-in-law came to Paris, and that it was you who found her a job as chambermaid at the Etoile du Nord?"

The man nodded.

"Last night you must have been astonished when you saw a girl you knew turn up at that hotel at three in the morning, a girl of good family from Moissac . . ."

"Mademoiselle Blanchon," he muttered involuntarily.

"The daughter of Judge Blanchon?"

Dufieu turned to the girl in alarm, and she replied clearly and composedly:

"Yes, I'm Geneviève Blanchon, Superintendent. My father knows nothing about it. It was only yesterday morning that I left Moissac. Bompard had promised to write to me there, and I'd had no news from him . . ."

"One minute, please. So, Dufieu, you were surprised when you saw the young lady, but you were far more surprised when Bompard appeared. As a night porter, you could not have been misled by the fact that he arrived a few minutes later than the girl."

"No, Superintendent."

"So you went up to the sixth floor to tell your sister-in-law."

"Yes, I did."

"Did you suspect that things might take such a dramatic turn?"

"I knew my sister-in-law wanted to be revenged on that man."

Maigret turned to the sergeant.

"Lucas! Take him to your room, will you?"

He wanted to be left alone with the girl, who had now quite dropped her defiant air.

"Did Lucienne Jouffroy come in while you were there?"

"Yes."

"Did you know her daughter had been Bompard's mistress?"

"Yes."

"And that he had taken her to the abortionist?"

"Yes."

"In spite of which you came to Paris to be with him?"

Unmoved, but lowering her voice, she replied:

"I loved him! He told me Rosine had had other lovers . . ."

"If I were your father . . ." growled Maigret.

"What would you do?"

"I don't know, but . . . So you left home without money and without luggage . . . And it was Bompard who gave you a thousand francs to keep you at the Etoile du Nord until . . ."

"I loved him," she repeated.

"And now?"

"Now I don't know . . . I wanted to prevent Lucienne Jouffroy being arrested, and my father finding out . . ."

"You don't think that's going to be easy, do you?"

The telephone bell rang. Maigret answered, crossly:

"Yes . . . All right . . . Can't be helped . . . Of course . . ."

Then, replacing the receiver:

"Lucienne Jouffroy has not even tried to get across the frontier. She wandered about Paris for hours and she's just gone into a police station to give herself up and confess everything . . . She didn't mention you; she just declared that Bompard was in bed with a prostitute whom she didn't know . . ."

"What will happen?"

"If I know the jurymen of the Seine district, she'll certainly be acquitted . . ."

"And what about me?"

"You?"

He stood up and, suddenly yielding to a desire he had restrained too long, he slapped the girl's face. She was so taken aback that she remained speechless.

"Come along!"

"Where?"

"Never you mind."

He took her along the corridors and into the dark courtyard of Police Headquarters.

"Hi! . . . Taxi! . . .

He made her get in, muttering as though to himself:

"There are two doors . . . Suppose, in the midst of the crowd, somebody should get out of one of them . . ."

Then he fell silent. The car drove along the Rue de Rivoli. The girl sat motionless.

"Listen," growled Maigret, "have you lost your wits?"

"I'm sleepy," she sighed.

"Well, you'll be able to sleep later . . . I warn you that if in one minute you don't . . ."

She opened one of the doors and hesitated.

And Maigret shouted furiously: "Get off with you, for heaven's sake, you great goose! . . ."

The driver turned round, saw only one person in his taxi, and was about to stop, but the Superintendent lowered the pane between them and muttered:

"Draw up in front of some good brasserie . . . I've such a mighty thirst!"

JOHN D.
MACDONALD

I ALWAYS GET THE CUTIES

John D. MacDonald (1916–1986) struck it rich with Travis McGee, a part-time thief who works outside the law to retrieve stolen property from thieves who are even farther outside the law than he and don't share his moral scruples. Those cataloguers of crime literature, Jacques Barzun and Wendell Hertig Taylor, called him "more the private avenger than the private eye." There is a studied similarity to his dozens of adventures. Each has a different color in its title: **The Turquoise Lament, The Green Ripper, The Dreadful Lemon Sky,** *and so on. There's always the Fort Lauderdale setting and his live-in boat, the* **Busted Flush** *(in every novel you seem to learn how McGee won it in a card game). And just about always, MacDonald manages to fit in a reference to Utica, New York, his home as a teenager.*

MacDonald's roots, though, are in the old pulp magazines, and in the late 1940s he was producing so many stories that he published under three names besides his own. The following story, which was first published in 1954, has the sly flair of pulp literature at its best.

KEEGAN CAME into my apartment, frosted with winter, topcoat open, hat jammed on the back of his hard skull, bringing a noisy smell of the dark city night. He stood in front of my birch fire, his great legs planted, clapping and rubbing hard palms in the heat.

He grinned at me and winked one narrow gray eye. "I'm off duty, Doc. I wrapped up a package. A pretty package."

"Will bourbon do, Keegan?"

"If you haven't got any of that brandy left. This is a brandy night."

When I came back with the bottle and the glasses, he had stripped off his topcoat and tossed it on the couch. The crumpled hat was on the floor, near the discarded coat. Keegan had yanked a chair closer to the fire. He sprawled on the end of his spine, thick ankles crossed, the soles of his shoes steaming.

I poured his brandy and mine, and moved my chair and the long coffee table so we could share either end of it. His story was bursting in him. I knew that. I've only had the vaguest hints about his home life. A house crowded with teen-age daughters, cluttered with their swains. Obviously no place to talk of his dark victories. And Keegan is not the sort of man to regale his co-workers with talk of his prowess. So I am, among other things, his sounding board. He bounces successes off the politeness of my listening, growing big in the echo of them.

"Ever try to haggle with a car dealer, Doc?" he asked.

"In a mild way."

"You are a mild guy. I tried once. Know what he told me? He said, 'Lieutenant, you try to make a car deal maybe once every two years. Me, I make ten a day. So what chance have you got?'"

This was a more oblique approach than Keegan generally used. I became attentive.

"It's the same with the cuties, Doc — the amateurs who think they can bring off one nice clean safe murder. Give me a cutie every time. I eat 'em alive. The pros are trouble. The cuties leave holes you can drive diesels through. This one was that woman back in October. At that cabin at Bear Paw Lake. What do you remember about it, Doc?"

I am always forced to summarize. It has got me into the habit of reading the crime news. I never used to.

"As I remember, Keegan, they thought she had been killed by a prowler. Her husband returned from a business trip and found the body. She had been dead approximately two weeks. Because it was the off season, the neighboring camps weren't occupied, and the people in the village thought she had gone back to the city. She had been strangled, I believe."

"Okay. So I'll fill you in on it. Then you'll see the problem I had. The name was Grosswalk. Cynthia and Harold. He met her ten years ago when he was in med. school. He was twenty-four and she was thirty. She was loaded. He married her and he never went back to med. school. He didn't do anything for maybe five, six years. Then he gets a job selling medical supplies, surgical instruments, that kind of stuff. Whenever a wife is dead, Doc, the first thing I do is check on how they were getting along. I guess you know that."

"Your standard procedure," I said.

"Sure. So I check. They got a nice house here in the city. Not many friends. But they got neighbors with ears. There are lots of brawls. I get the idea it is about money. The money is hers — was hers, I should say. I put it up to this Grosswalk. He says okay, so they weren't getting along so good, so what? I'm supposed to be finding out who killed her, sort of coordinating with the State Police, not digging into his home life. I tell him he is a nice suspect. He already knows that. He says he didn't kill her. Then he adds one thing too many. He says he couldn't have killed her. That's all he will say. Playing it cute. You understand. I eat those cuties alive."

He waved his empty glass. I went over and refilled it.

"You see what he was doing to me, Doc. He was leaving it up to me to prove how it was he couldn't have killed her. A reverse twist. That isn't too tough. I get in touch with the sales manager of the company. Like I thought, the salesmen have to make reports. He was making a western swing. It would be no big trick to fly back and sneak into the camp and kill her, take some money and junk to make it look good, and then fly back out there and pick up where he left off. She was killed on maybe the tenth of October, the medical examiner says. Then he finds her on the twenty-fourth. But the sales manager tells me something that needs a lot of checking. He says that this Grosswalk took sick out west on the eighth and went into a hospital, and he was in that hospital from the eighth to the fifteenth, a full seven days. He gave me the name of the hospital. Now you see how the cutie made his mistake. He could have told me that easy enough. No, he has to be cute. I figure that if he's innocent he would have told me. But he's so proud of whatever gimmick he rigged for me that he's got to let me find out the hard way."

"I suppose you went out there," I said.

"It took a lot of talk. They don't like spending money for things like that. They kept telling me I should ask the L.A. cops to check because that's a good force out there. Finally I have to go by bus, or pay the difference. So I go by bus. I found the doctor. Plural — doctors. It is a clinic deal, sort of, that this Grosswalk went to. He gives them his symptoms. They say it looks to them like the edge of a nervous breakdown just beginning to show. With maybe some organic complications. So they run him through the course. Seven days of tests and checks and observations. They tell me he was there, that he didn't leave, that he *couldn't* have left. But naturally I check the hospital. They reserve part of one floor for patients from the clinic. I talked to the head nurse on that floor, and to the nurse that had the most to do with Grosswalk. She showed me the schedule and charts. Every day, every night, they were fooling around with the guy, giving him injections of this and that. He couldn't have got out. The people at the clinic told me the results. He was okay. The rest had helped him a lot. They told him to slow down. They gave him a prescription for a mild sedative. Nothing organically wrong, even though the symptoms seemed to point that way."

"So the trip was wasted?"

"Not entirely. Because on a hunch I ask if he had visitors. They keep a register. A girl came to see him as often as the rules permitted. They said she was pretty. Her name was Mary MacCarney. The address is there. So I go and see her. She lives with her folks. A real tasty kid. Nineteen. Her folks think this Grosswalk is too old for her. She is tall, Irish, all black and white and blue. It was warm and we sat on the porch. I soon find out this Grosswalk has been feeding her a line, telling her that his wife is an incurable invalid not long for this world, that he can't stand hurting her by asking for a divorce, that it is better to wait, and anyway, she says, her parents might approve of a widower, but never a guy who has been divorced. She has heard from Grosswalk that his wife has been murdered by a prowler and he will be out to see her as soon as he can. He has known her for a year. But, of course, I have told him not to leave town. I tell her not to get her hopes too high because it begins to look to me like this Grosswalk has knocked off his wife. Things get pretty hysterical, and her old lady gets in on it, and even driving away in the cab I can hear the old lady yelling at her.

"The first thing I do on getting back is check with the doctor who took care of Mrs. Grosswalk, and he says, as I thought he would, that she was as healthy as a horse. So I go back up to that camp and unlock it again. It is a snug place, Doc. Built so you could spend the winter there if you wanted to. Insulated and sealed, with a big fuel-oil furnace and modern kitchen equipment and so on. It was aired out a lot better than the first time I was in it. Grosswalk stated that he hadn't touched a thing. He said it was unlocked. He saw her and backed right out and went to report it. And the only thing touched had been the body.

"I poked around. This time I took my time. She was a tidy woman. There are twin beds. One is turned down. There is a very fancy nightgown laid out. That is a thing which bothered me. I looked at her other stuff. She has pajamas which are the right thing for October at the lake. They are made from that flannel stuff. There is only one other fancy nightgown, way in the back of a drawer. I have found out here in the city that she is not the type to fool around. So how come a woman who is alone wants to sleep so pretty? Because the husband is coming back from a trip. But he couldn't have come back from the trip. I find another thing. I find deep ruts off in the brush beside the camp. The first time I went there, her car was parked in back. Now it is gone. If the car was run off where those ruts were, anybody coming to the door wouldn't see it. If the door was locked, they wouldn't even knock maybe, knowing she wouldn't be home. That puzzles me. She might do it if she didn't want company. I prowl some more. I look in the deep freeze. It is well stocked. No need to buy stuff for a hell of a while. The refrigerator is the same way. And the electric is still on."

He leaned back and looked at me expectantly.

"Is that all you had to go on?" I asked.

"A murder happens here and the murderer is in Los Angeles at the time. I got him because he tried to be a cutie. Want to take a try, Doc?"

I knew I had to make an attempt. "Some sort of device?"

"To strangle a woman? Mechanical hands? You're getting too fancy, Doc."

"Then he hired somebody to do it?"

"There are guys you can hire, but they like guns. Or a piece of pipe in an alley. I don't know where you'd go to hire a strangler. He did it himself, Doc."

"Frankly, Keegan, I don't see how he could have."

"Well, I'll tell you how I went after it. I went to the medical examiner and we had a little talk. Cop logic, Doc. If the geography is wrong, then maybe you got the wrong idea on timing. But the medico checks it out. He says definitely the woman has been dead twelve days to two weeks when he makes the examination. I ask him how he knows. He says because of the extent of decomposition of the body. I ask him if that is a constant. He says no — you use a formula. A sort of rule-of-thumb formula. I ask him the factors. He says cause of death, temperature, humidity, physical characteristics of the body, how it was clothed, whether or not insects could have got to it, and so on.

"By then I had it, Doc. It was cute. I went back to the camp and looked around. It took me some time to find them. You never find a camp without them. Candles. They were in a drawer in the kitchen. Funny-looking candles, Doc. Melted down, sort of. A flat side against the bottom of the drawer, and all hardened again. Then I had another idea. I checked the stove burners. I found some pieces of burned flaked metal down under the heating elements.

"Then it was easy. I had this Grosswalk brought in again. I let him sit in a cell for four hours and get nervous before I took the rookie cop in. I'd coached that rookie for an hour, so he did it right. I had him dressed in a leather jacket and work pants. I make him repeat his story in front of Grosswalk. 'I bought a chain saw last year,' he says, acting sort of confused, 'and I was going around to the camps where there are people and I was trying to get some work cutting up fireplace wood. So I called on Mrs. Grosswalk. She didn't want any wood, but she was nice about it.' I ask the rookie when that was. He scratches his head and says, 'Sometime around the seventeenth, I think it was.' That's where I had to be careful. I couldn't let him be positive about the date. I say she was supposed to be dead a week by then and was he sure it was her. 'She wasn't dead then. I know her. I'd seen her in the village. A kind of heavy-set woman with blonde hair. It was her all right, Lieutenant.' I asked him was he sure of the date and he said yes, around the seventeenth like he said, but he could check his records and find the exact date.

"I told him to take off. I just watched that cutie and saw him come apart. Then he gave it to me. He killed her on the sixteenth, the day he got out of the hospital. He flew into Omaha. By then I've got the stenographer taking it down. Grosswalk talks, staring at the floor, like he was talking to himself. It was going to be a dry run. He wasn't going to do it if she'd been here in the city or into the village in the previous seven days. But, once she got in the camp, she seldom went out, and the odds were all against any callers. On his previous trip to Omaha he had bought a jalopy that would run. It would make the fifty miles to the lake all right. He took the car off the lot where he'd left it and drove to the lake. She was surprised to see him back ahead of schedule. He explained the company car was being fixed. He questioned her. Finally she said she hadn't seen or talked to a living soul in ten days. Then he knew he was set to take the risk.

"He grabbed her neck and hung on until she was dead. He had his shoulders hunched right up around his ears when he said that. It was evening when he killed her, nearly bedtime. First he closed every window. Then he turned on the furnace as high as it would go. There was plenty of oil in the tank. He left the oven door open and the oven turned as high as it would go. He even built a fire in the fireplace, knowing it would be burned out by morning and there wouldn't be any smoke. He filled the biggest pans of water he could find and left them on the top of the stove. He took the money and some of her jewelry, turned out the lights, and locked the doors. He ran her car off in the brush where nobody would be likely to see it. He said by the time he left the house it was like an oven in there.

"He drove the jalopy back to Omaha, parked it back in the lot, and caught an eleven-fifteen flight to Los Angeles. The next morning he was making calls. And keeping his fingers crossed. He worked his way east. He got to the camp on the twenty-fourth — about ten in the morning. He said he went in and turned things off and opened up every window, and then went out and was sick. He waited nearly an hour before going back in. It was nearly down to normal temperature. He checked the house. He noticed she had turned down both beds before he killed her. He remade his. The water had boiled out of the pans and the bottoms had burned through. He scaled the pans out into the lake. He said he tried not to look at her, but he couldn't help it. He had enough medical background to know that it had worked, and also to fake his own illness in L.A. He went out and was sick again, and then he got her car back where it belonged. He closed most of the windows. He made another inspection trip and then drove into the village. He was a cutie, Doc, and I ate him alive."

There was a long silence. I knew what was expected of me. But I had my usual curious reluctance to please him. He held the glass cradled in his hand, gazing with a half smile into the dying fire. His face looked like stone.

"That was very intelligent, Keegan," I said.

"The pros give you real trouble, Doc. The cuties always leave holes. I couldn't bust geography, so I had to bust time." He yawned massively and stood up. "Read all about it in the morning paper, Doc."

"I'll certainly do that."

I held his coat for him. He's a big man. I had to reach up to get it properly onto his shoulders. He mashed the hat onto his head as I walked to the door with him. He put his big hand on the knob, turned, and smiled down at me without mirth.

"I always get the cuties, Doc. Always."

"You certainly seem to," I said.

"They are my favorite meat."

"So I understand."

He balled one big fist and pumped it lightly against my chin, still grinning at me. "And I'm going to get you too, Doc. You know that. You were cute. You're just taking longer than most. But you know how it's going to come out, don't you?"

I don't answer that anymore. There's nothing to say. There hasn't been anything to say for a long time now.

He left, walking hard into the wild night. I sat and looked into my fire. I could hear the wind. I reached for the bottle. The wind raged over the city, as monstrous and inevitable as Keegan. It seemed as though it was looking for food — the way Keegan is always doing.

But I no longer permit myself the luxury of imagination.

JIM THOMPSON **THIS WORLD, THEN THE FIREWORKS**

It would be hard to invent a literary career as bizarre as Jim Thompson's (1906–1977). It is too bad he didn't live to see how his fame has spread. Five years ago no one besides a few diehard fans and collectors would have recognized his name. Now there have been full-page appreciations of him in News-week, *furrowed-brow essays in the* New York Review of Books *("His novels are morally so rotten as to be of nearly clinical interest"), and hardcover reissues bearing Stephen King's imprimatur ("My favorite crime novelist"). The feisty California publisher Black Lizard Books seems to be trying to reprint as many of the twenty-nine Thompson novels as it can get its hands on (most were twenty-five-cent paperback originals), and* The Killer Inside Me *is an authentic cult novel on college campuses.*

As Thompson tells his story, he was a journeyman reporter and editor who kept a job only as long as he could stay sober. He claimed, in "An Alcoholic Looks at Himself," that over a three-year period he was hospitalized twenty-seven times. But he was also director of the Oklahoma branch of the Federal Writers Project. His first two novels were issued by respectable publishers, not pulp houses, and were praised by the likes of Richard Wright and The New Yorker. *In the late 1950s he wrote the film script for Stanley Kubrick's brilliantly upsetting* Paths of Glory.

"This World, Then the Fireworks" was not published during Thompson's lifetime. Now, however it happened, he has found his readers.

1-Minus

I REMEMBER THE NIGHT well. It was our fourth birthday, Carol's and mine. We'd had a small cake and a half-pint of ice cream with our dinner. Mom was putting us to bed when we heard the blast of the shotgun.

She stood staring down at us, her eyes getting wider, and then — I think she must have suspected Dad's highjinks — she tore out of the house and across the street. Carol and I got up and followed her.

We were pretty scared. We paused on our front porch, wondering if we dared proceed further in our nightclothes. Then, we heard a second blast and what sounded like a scream from Mom, and we were too scared to stay where we were.

It was early summer. The air was balmy, sweet with the smell of new-ly budded trees, and the horizon still glowed with the golden pastels of the late-setting sun. We crossed the street, hand in hand, walking in great beauty.

We crossed the lawn of the other house, the grass kissing and ca-ressing our bare feet. We went up the steps and peered through the open door.

Mom had caught part of the second blast as she burst into the house. She wasn't seriously injured, merely branded for life. We didn't know she'd been injured at all, despite the spurting pinpricks on her face. So meager was our knowledge of life, of good and bad; and Mom was laughing so loudly.

She screamed, yelled with laughter, spraying the blood that trickled down into her mouth. Carol and I gripped hands tightly, and slowly stared at one another. We were twins, as I've indicated, and our re-semblance was indeed strong at that age. We not only looked alike, but our thoughts were very nearly identical.

So we stared at each other. And as my eyes misted doubtfully, so did hers. And her lips trembled as mine trembled. And as she — I laughed.

We burst into laughter simultaneously. It was so funny, you see. It was funnier even than Charlie Chaplin in the movies, or Krazy Kat in the funny papers.

The man on the floor didn't have any head, hardly any head at all. And that was funny, wasn't it? And it was funny the way Mom was laughing, spraying out pink stuff and making shiny red bubbles with her mouth. But the funniest thing, what we laughed loudest about, was Dad and the woman. The woman who was the wife of the man without any head. The wife of the man Dad had killed to keep from getting killed.

Dad and the woman. Dad who went to the electric chair, and the woman who committed suicide. Standing there naked.

We laughed and laughed, Carol and I. We were still laughing occasionally — shrieking and screaming — weeks later. It was so funny. It seemed so funny, I remember.

And I remember the night well.

1

Most of the city lay below the railway station.

My taxi took me down through the business section, sparkling and scrubbed-looking at this early hour, and on down a wide palm-bordered hill overlooking the ocean. Carol and Mom's house did not front on the water, as the best homes did, but it was still very nice, considering. After all, Mom had no income, and Carol's alimony was a mere two hundred and fifty a month.

My cab fare came to ninety-five cents. I had a total of two dollars. I would have had much more, but at the last moment I'd literally turned out my pockets to Ellen. It had to be done, I felt, her folks being the type they were. They wouldn't bar their doors to her, of course. But they doubtless would be very difficult — extraordinarily so — if she and the two kids could not pay a good share of their upkeep.

I can't understand people like that, can you? I mean, people who would extend adult conflict into the defenseless world of children. I don't condemn them, mind you; everyone is as he is for sound reasons, because circumstance has so formed him. Still, I cannot understand such people, and they make me a little ill at my stomach.

I gave the cab driver my two dollars. I started up the walk to the house, broke but happier than I had been in years. It did not matter about being broke — Carol, dear child, had usually been very expert at obtaining money, and she was obviously in good form now. Anyway, broke or not, money or not, it didn't and wouldn't matter. We were together again. After three long years, the longest we had ever been separated, Carol and I were at last together. And nothing else seemed to matter.

Mom had heard the cab arrive and was waiting at the door for me. She drew me inside, smiling with strained warmth, murmuring banal words of welcome.

I set down my suitcases and returned the kiss she'd given me. She stepped back and stared up into my face. Gazed at me with a kind of awed wonder, wonder that was at once worried and unwillingly proud.

"I just can't believe it, Marty." She shook her head. "You're even handsomer than you used to be."

"Oh, now," I laughed. "You'll make me blush, Mom."

"You and Carol. You get better-looking all the time. You never seem to grow a day older."

I said that she didn't look a bit older either, but of course she did. I had the impression, in fact, that she had aged about ten years since I stepped through the door of the house. There was a haunted, sickish look in her eyes. The only brightness in the sallow flesh of her face were the bluish pocks of that long-ago shotgun blast.

I remember how she got those pocks. I remember it well. It was our fourth birthday, Carol's and mine, and —

"Where's Carol?" I asked. "Where's that red-headed sis of mine?"

"You eat your breakfast," Mom said. "I have it all ready."

"She's still in bed?" I said. "Which is her room?"

"Come and eat your breakfast, Marty, I know you must be tired and hungry, and —"

"Mom. MOM!" I said.

Her eyes wavered nervously. She sighed and turned away toward the kitchen. "At the head of the stairs, next to the bath. And Marty . . ."

"Yes?" — I was already at the stairs.

"You and Carol — you won't get into any trouble this time?"

"Get into trouble?" I said. "Why, that's pretty unfair, Mom. When were we ever in any trouble?"

"Please, Marty. I j-just — I don't think I can take any more. Get yourself a job right away, son. You can do it. There's three newspapers here in town, and with your talent and experience and looks —"

"Now, Mom," I laughed. "You're making me blush again."

"Bring your family on right away. Set up your own household. I know how hard it must be on you to be around someone like Ellen, but you did marry her —"

"Better stop right there. Right there," I said.

"You'll do it, won't you? You won't stay here a bit longer than you have to?"

"Why, Mom," I said. "I know you don't mean it that way, but you almost sound as though I wasn't welcome."

I looked at her sorrowfully, with genuine sorrow. For it is rather sad, you know, when one's own mother fears and even dislikes him. It was almost unbearable, and I say this as one who has done a great deal of bearing.

"This saddens me, Mom," I said. "I quote you from Section B, Commandment One-minus: If thy son be birthed with teeth in his tail, kick him not thereon. For this is but injury upon injury, and thou may loseth a foot."

A faint flush tinged her sallowness. She turned abruptly and entered the kitchen.

I went up the stairs.

I eased open the door to Carol's room, tiptoed across the floor and sat down on the edge of her bed.

2

We are only fraternal twins, fortunately; fortunately, since it would be a shame if she were as big as I. As it is, she is approximately a foot shorter — five feet to my six — and about eighty pounds lighter; and our physical similarities are largely a matter of coloring, skin texture, bone structure and contour.

I looked at her silently, thinking that I could look forever and never tire.

I am confident that she was awake. But knowing how much I like to see her awaken, she played 'possum for two or three minutes. Then, at last, she slowly opened her eyes — my eyes — revealing their startling blueness to me.

And her lips curled softly, revealing the perfect white teeth.

"Mr. Martin Lakewood," she said.

"Mrs. Carol Lakewood Wharton," I said.

"Sister," we said, "You wonderful, darling redhead!"

"Brother!"

And for the next few minutes we had no time nor breath for talk.

Finally, I got her robe for her and accompanied her into the bathroom. I sat on the edge of the tub while she washed and primped before the mirror.

"Darling — Marty." She touched a lipstick to her mouth. "How did that — uh — matter turn out in Chicago? I know you couldn't write me about it, and I was a little worried."

I didn't answer her immediately; I was only vaguely conscious of hearing the question. I was looking at her, you see, and now, so soon after our reunion, it was difficult to look at her and think of anything else.

"Mmm, darling?" she said. "You know the matter I mean. It was right afterwards that Mom went on her rampage, and dragged me out here."

I blinked and came out of my trance. I said that certainly I remembered. "Well, that worked out pretty well, darling. The cops had a guy on ice for a couple of other mur — matters. He was indubitably guilty of them, understand? So they braced him that one, and he obligingly confessed."

"Oh, how sweet of him! But of course, he had nothing to lose, did he?"

"Well, he was really a very nice guy," I said. "It's hard to repay a favor like that, but I did the little that I could. Always took him cigarettes or some little gift whenever I interviewed him for the paper."

She turned her head for a moment, gave me a fondly tender smile. "That's like you, Marty! You always were so thoughtful."

"It was nothing," I said. "I was only glad that I could make his last days a little happier."

Mom called up the stairway to us. Carol kicked the door shut and picked up her eyebrow pencil.

"Goddamn her, anyway," she murmured. "I'll go down and slap the hell out of her in a minute. Well, I will, Marty! I'll —"

"I'm sorry," I laughed. "I'm not laughing at you, darling. It's just that it always seems so incongruous to me, the things you say and the way you look. Such words from such a tiny sweet-faced doll!"

I had reason to know that her words, her threats, were not idle ones. But still I was amused. She laughed with me, good sport that she was, but it was patently an effort.

"I guess I'm losing my sense of humor," she sighed. "I don't like to complain, but honestly, I never saw such a town! Things have really been very difficult, Marty. I can't remember when I've seen a hundred-dollar bill."

"Oh? I thought it was supposed to be quite a lively place."

"Well, it may be. It may be just my luck."

"It'll change now," I said. "Things will be a lot better from now on."

"I'm sure they will be. I certainly hope so. I think if I go to bed with one more sailor I'll start saluting. Well" — she finished her primping and turned around facing me. "Now, what about you, darling? What was this little, uh, misunderstanding you were involved in?"

I said it was nothing at all, really. More a problem of semantics than ethics. The paper called it blackmail and extortion. I considered it a personally profitable public service.

"Uh-huh. But just what did you do, Marty?"

"Well, I was on the city hall beat, you know, and I had the good fortune to ferret out some smelly figurative bodies and to identify the office-holders responsible for them . . ." I took out my cigarettes and lighted two for us. I dragged the smoke in deeply, exhaled and went on. "Now, the paper's attitude was that I should have reported the story, but I couldn't see it that way. I couldn't and I still can't, Carol."

"Mmm-hmm. Yes, darling?"

"It would have simply meant the ousting of one bunch of crooks and the election of another. They'd either be crooked, the second bunch, or too stupid to be; incompetents, in other words. So . . . so I did the best possible thing, as I saw it. I made a deal with a friend of mine, an insurance salesman, and he had some confidential talks with the malefactors in question. They all bought nice policies. They seemed to feel pretty much as I did — that they were paying a just penalty for their malfeasance, and that I was no more than justly rewarded for a civic duty."

Carol laughed delightedly. "But how did you happen to get caught, Marty? You're always so clever about these things."

How? Why? I wasn't sure of the answer to that question. Or perhaps, rather, I was more sure than I cared to be . . . I'd wanted to be caught? I'd subconsciously brought about my own downfall? I was tired, fed up, sick of the whole mess and life in general?

I wasn't conscious of feeling that way. I didn't want to believe that I did. For if I did, then I and, inevitably, she were lost. Time was already in the process of taking care of us. Of course, if we could accept the truth, see the danger and completely alter our way of life — But how could we? We would have to, but how? Where the compromise between the imperative and the impossible?

On either side, the possible truth showed the same hideous face. It could neither be accepted nor denied, and so I did neither. At any rate, I did my incoherent best to warn Carol, to put her on guard, without alarming her.

"That question," I said. "I'm a little wary of it, baby. I may have simply bungled or had some bad luck. Or it may have been another way. I could give you an explanation, and it would be completely believable. And it might even be true. But whether it actually was or not . . ." I shook my head, tossed my cigarette butt into the toilet. "As I say, I'm a little afraid of this one. It's too basic, the implications are too grave. At some point, you know — at *some* point — you'd better look squarely at the truth or look squarely away from it. You can't risk rationalizations. There is the danger that the rationalization may become the truth to you, and when you have arrived at this certain point —"

I broke off abruptly. It had struck me with startling suddenness that this might be that certain point and this, the words I was speaking, a rationalization.

I sat stunned, unseeing, my eyes turned inward. For a terrifying moment, I raced myself about a swiftly narrowing circle. Faster and faster and — and never fast enough.

And then Carol was down on her knees in front of me. Hugging my knees. Her voice at once hate-filled and loving, her face an angel's and a fiend's.

"Shall I kill her, darling? Would you like sister to kill her?" The words were blurred together, smeared with tenderness and fury. "I don't mind. Brother would always do anything for sister, always, anything, so s-sister will j-just —"

"What?" I said. "What?"

"She was mean to you, wasn't she? She got you upset, and — a-and I'll kill her for you, Marty! She deserves to die, the old scar-faced hag! I ought to have killed her long ago, and now —"

"Don't!" I said. "DON'T, CAROL!"

"B-but, darling she —"

"It's too basic, understand? We can't think of such things. We can't use words like deserve and ought."

"Well . . ." The glaze went out of her eyes, and for a few seconds there was no expression in them at all. They were merely empty blue pools, blue and white pools. Blue emptiness and empty crystalline whiteness.

Then, I smiled, and instantly she smiled. We laughed, uncomfortably . . . and lightly.

"Now, didn't I sound silly!" she said. "I don't know what got into me."

"Forget it," I said. "Just put it out of your mind."

I boosted her to her feet, and she helped me to mine. We went down to breakfast.

3

I was prepared for Mom to be discomfiting, but she was not particularly so. Not nearly to the extent, at least, that she was capable of. I suspect that she was still a little cowed by Carol's outburst. Moreover, so soon after my arrival, she was unwilling — I might say, unable — to toss her weight around. To be annoying, a mild nuisance, was all the prosaic instincts would permit.

She was sure, she said, that Ellen and the kids would love this city. As for herself, an older person, she was beginning to feel that it might not be very healthy. It was too damp, you know, but for Ellen and the kids . . .

Did Ellen's folks still feel as they had? she said. Did they feel they had been unconscionably imposed upon, and were Ellen and the kids made to feel the brunt of their attitude?

She said — Well, that is about all she said. Her most annoying remarks.

I said virtually nothing, being busy with my breakfast.

Carol and I left the house soon after breakfast. We walked toward town a few blocks, then sat down on a bench in a small wayside park. Carol was very much concerned about the children. She was concerned for Ellen, too, of course — she and Ellen have always been fond of each other. But Ellen was an adult. She was able to absorb things that children could not and should not.

"Do you remember that time at Uncle Andrew's house, Marty? Uncle Frank had put us out because everyone in town was talking about us, and . . ."

I remembered. Uncle Andrew's three big boys had dragged Carol behind the barn, and when I took a club to them — I'd gotten the life half-beaten out of me. By Uncle Andrew, with Mom helplessly looking on. I'd lied, you see. It was the boys' word against Carol's and mine, and our word was worthless.

"I remember," I laughed, "but you know how we look on those things, Carol. They were normal, just what they should have been, broadly speaking. We weren't discriminated against, mistreated. What we endured was simply the norm; for us, for those particular times and situations."

"Yes, I know. But — but —"

But there could be no buts about this. You may be wrong, and exist comfortably in a world of righteousness. But you may not be right and live in a world of error, the kind of world we had once *seemed* to live in. It is impossible. Believe me, it is. The growing weight of injustice becomes impossible to bear.

"The norm is constantly changing," I said. "It is different with every person, every time, every situation. One person's advantage may be the disadvantage of another, but the position of both is always normal."

"Uh-huh. Of course, Marty," said Carol. "But, anyway . . ."

She took a roll of bills from her purse and thumbed through them rapidly. She pulled off a few of them for herself, probably a total of forty dollars, and pressed the others into my hand.

"You take this, Marty. I insist, now, darling! Keep what you need —

I imagine you're broke, aren't you — and send the rest to Ellen. Wire it to her so she'll get it right away."

I counted the money. I looked up from it suddenly, with deliberate suddenness, and I saw something in her face I didn't like. I couldn't analyze the expression, say why it troubled me. And that in itself was alarming. We were so much alike, you know, we thought so much alike, that it was as though my brain and body had separated and I had lost contact with my own thoughts.

"You said things had been tough," I said. "But there's more than three hundred dollars here . . ."

"So?" She laughed nervously. "Three hundred dollars is *money?*"

"Your alimony would just about pay your rent," I went on slowly. "And you said Mom's doctor bills ran very high. So with your other living expenses, your clothes, groceries, household bills, personal expense —"

She laughed again, laying one of her beautifully delicate hands on my knee. "Marty! Stop making like an auditor, will you? I've never heard such a fuss over a little bit of money."

"It's not a little bit, under the circumstances. It's around four hundred dollars with what you've kept. What's the answer, Carol?"

"Well . . ." She hesitated. "Well, you see, Marty, I was — I was saving this for something. I've saved it a few dollars at a time, and I knew that if you knew I needed — wanted — it for myself, you wouldn't want to —"

"Oh," I said, and I could feel my face clearing. "What was it you wanted, baby?"

"A — a mink. A cape stole. But I don't have to have it, darling. Anyway, now that you're here, we'll be rolling in money pretty soon."

I shoved the bills into my pocket. I hated to deprive her of anything, but since it was only temporary and not of vital importance . . .

She didn't have the clothes, the accessories, she used to have. I'd noticed that in glancing around her room that morning. She had sufficient to be very smartly turned out, mind you, but it was little by her standards. She had no jewelry at all. Even her wedding ring was gone — pawned, I supposed.

"Well, darling?" She smiled at me, her head cocked on one side. "Are you satisfied, now?"

I nodded. I had no reason to be anything else. Only a vague feeling of disquiet.

"Satisfied," I said.

We walked into town. It was a quiet walk, being largely uphill. But we had had so little time together, and the walking gave us a chance to talk.

As I had imagined was the case, knowing her independent nature, she was carrying on on her own. The local vice syndicate was a laughable outfit. They had no real stand-in with the police, and their hoods were spineless oafs. Once, shortly after she had come here, they had tried to take Carol in tow, but they had left her strictly alone since then.

"Two of them came to the house, Marty. I gave them some money, and then I fixed them both a nice big drink. And can you imagine, darling? — they gulped it down like lambs. I do believe they'd never heard of chloral hydrate! Well, fortunately, I had a car at the time, so . . ."

So when the stupes had awakened, they were out in the middle of the desert, sans clothes and everything else they owned. It was almost a week before the highway patrol found them. One of them died a few months later, and the other had to be committed to an insane asylum.

"That's my sister," I murmured. "That's my sweet little sis . . . Mom didn't know about the deal?"

"We-ell, she didn't *know*. She was out somewhere that evening. But you know her. She always seemed to sort of feel it when — when something's happened, and she was fussing around, nagging at me, for days. It was simply terrible, Marty! I almost went out and got a job just to shut her up."

"A *job*?" I said. "She wanted you to take a *job*?"

"Isn't it incredible?" Carol shook her head. "But what about you, Marty? You won't let her hound you into going to work, will you?"

I said that I wouldn't let anyone force me to do anything: my norm period for being forced had expired. Still, I probably would go to work. For a while, and when the notion struck me. A job could be amusing and often very useful.

"I suppose," Carol nodded. "I guess it wouldn't hurt to work a *little* bit." She gave my hand a squeeze, smiled up at me sunnily. "I'll have to leave you here, darling. Have a nice day, and be sure to wire the money to Ellen."

She started toward the entrance of a swank cocktail lounge, her principal base of operations. Then she paused and turned around again.

"Send a telegram with it too, will you, Marty? To the kids. Tell them Aunt Carol loves them more and more every day, and she wants them to be real good for their mother."

4

I went to work the following day on the first paper I applied to. I had no difficulty about it. Not since I was a child — and a very small child — have I had any difficulty in getting work. It would be very strange if I did. Personably and in intelligence, I am a generous cut above average; I must admit to this, immodest as it seems. Also, and when I choose to, I can be exceedingly ingratiating. Then, there is my experience in job-getting — my childhood training by earnest teachers. One gets work readily when the penalty for failure is a clubbing. Well-clubbed — a minor fracture or so always helps — he learns not to take no for an answer.

Carol did not get this valuable training. Being sorely undernourished and frequently raped, she had little energy and time for other endeavors.

However, as I was saying . . .

It was the best and biggest paper in town, which is not to say, of course, that it was either very good or very big. Most of the staffers were fair, about average, I suppose. They had been getting by nicely until I came along. Then, well, there I was, a *real* newspaper man, a towering beacon of ability. And by comparison, these average people looked like submoronic dolts.

The publisher no longer made his face to shine upon them. He griped at everyone — except me. No one — except me — could do anything to suit him.

Whenever I've cared to, when I've had an amusing objective in mind, I've always advanced in my work. But I set an all-time record on that paper. I was assistant city editor at the end of that week. Two weeks later, I was made city editor. And at the end of the month — correction. It was the beginning of my fifth week . . .

By this time, the city room was in a mess. All the staffers were jumpy — almost to the point of total incompetence. The news editor had resigned. The copy-desk chief had reverted to alcoholism. The Newspaper Guild was raising hell. The — well, as I say, it was a mess. Exactly the situation I had wanted. If it wasn't straightened out fast, the paper would be on the skids.

Now, the managing editor *was* a pretty good man. So much so that given a little time, and even with me around, he could have righted things. But the publisher was in no mood to give his time. The m.e. was a bum, he declared — in so many words. He was at the root of all the trouble, he would have to go. And his replacement should be you-know-who.

I held the job for two days, just long enough to make sure that the previous incumbent had left town. Then, I resigned. Needless to say, the publisher was shocked silly.

I couldn't do it! he sputtered. I simply couldn't do it! And when I pointed out that I had just done it, he virtually went down on his knees to me . . . Why was I doing it? he pleaded. What did I want from him?

I told him I already had what I wanted, and I was doing it because he was a wicked old man. He had violated Commandment One-minus, the commandment that had never been written, since even a god-damned fool could be expected to know it.

"Yea, verily," I said. "It is the pointed moral of all happening from the beginning of creation; to wit: Take not advantage of thy neighbor with his pants down, for to each man there comes this season and in my house there are many mansions, and in the mansions are many bastards longer-donged than thyself."

He didn't argue with me any more. He was afraid to, I imagine, believing me insane and himself in actual physical danger.

I collected my pay from the cashier and walked out.

It was now around three in the afternoon — my normal quitting time, since most of the work on afternoon papers is done in the morning. I had a couple drinks in a nearby bar. Then, feeling rather at loose ends, I wandered on down the street to the public square.

It was in the approximate center of the business district, a departure and arrival point for most of the city's bus lines. I found an unoccupied bench near the pseudo-Moorish fountain and sat down. Letting my mind wander comfortably. Pleased with myself. A little amazed, as I sometimes am, that I could have risen so relatively high.

I had almost no formal education, no more than a few months of grammar school. I had learned to read from the newspapers — from the newspapers I had hustled. And squeezing past this first barricade, leaping over it, rather, I had raced up the casually tortuous trail of the newspapers. Street sales. Wholesale street. Ciruclation slugger. Copy boy. Cub reporter . . . The newspapers were grade school, high school and college. They were broad education, practically applied. And they never asked but one question, they were interested in only one thing. Could you do your job? I always could. I always had to.

Now, rather for some years past, I no longer had to. My norm for having to had expired; I had expired it, if you forgive the verb. And for the future, the present —

I was quite pleased with myself. At the same time, the abrupt cessation of intense activity left me with a hanging-in-the-air feeling —

restless and mildly ill at ease. And while what I had done was entirely logical and fitting, I was afraid I might have acted a trifle selfishly.

Carol wouldn't think so, of course. She would appreciate the joke as much as I. But still, her luck was running very bad — there was still no prize chump in the offing, no one like that character in Chicago. And since she'd insisted on sending most of my salary to Ellen —

Well, what the hell? I thought. We were bound to get a break before long. She'd latch onto some well-heeled boob, set him up where I could safely get at him, and that would be the end of him, and the end of our financial troubles.

I yawned and leaned back against the bench. Then, I sat up again; casually, oh so very casually, but very much alert. I got up, went down the flagstoned pathway and stopped squarely in the middle of the sidewalk.

She smacked right into me. She'd been trying to look at me and not look at me for the past ten minutes, so we piled right together.

I had to catch her by the shoulders to keep her from going over backwards. I continued to hold onto her, smiling down into her face.

It was what you might call a well-organized face, one that would have been pretty except for its primness and the severity of her brushed-back, skinned-back hairdo. Not that I place my emphasis on prettiness, understand. My wife Ellen is the ugliest woman I have ever seen.

She, this one, wore glasses, a white blouse and a blue suit and hat. The blouse was nicely top-heavy, and the suit was curved in a way its maker had never intended.

"Well," I said, "if it isn't Alice Blueclothes! Boo, pretty Alice."

She was trying to look stern, grim, but she just wasn't up to it. Under my hands, I could feel her flesh trembling. I could feel it burn.

"L-let — let go of me!" she gasped. "I'm warning you, Mister, let go of me instantly —"

"Not 'instantly,' " I said. "Marty. You're thinking about my brother, Alice. He has pretty red hair, too."

"You l-let — I'll fix you! I'll —"

"But, Alice," I said. "We haven't had our waltz yet — or would you rather make it a square dance? I'm sure these smiling bystanders would be glad to join in."

She tore herself free. Red-faced, acutely conscious of the aforesaid bystanders, she thrust a hand into her purse, came out with a leather-backed badge.

"P-police officer," she said. "You're under arrest!"

5

I went along willingly, as the saying is. I had been sure from the beginning that she was a cop. She had a firm grip on my arm as we left the square, a grip strong with fury. But it rapidly grew weaker and weaker, and as we turned into a side street she let go entirely. She stopped. I stopped. I glanced at the plain black car at the curb, noted the absence of official insignia.

"All right, Mister," she said, trying to look very stern, to sound very harsh. "I should take you in, but I'm off duty and —"

"Is this your car, Alice?" I said. "It matches your shoes, doesn't it?"

"Shut up! If you don't behave yourself, p-promise to behave, I'll —"

"Yes, it's an exact match," I said. "It matches your hair too. Are you brunette all over, Alice, or just where it shows?"

Her face went white. White, then red again, about three shades redder than it had been. She turned away from me suddenly, jerked open the door of the car and literally stumbled inside. I slid into the seat with her.

"G-go away," she whispered. "Please, go 'way . . ."

"I will," I said. "You say it like you mean it, and I will."

She hesitated. Then, she turned toward me, faced me, her chin thrust out. And her lips formed the words. But she did not speak them. I have played this same scene a hundred times, five hundred times, and never have I heard the words spoken.

Her eyes wavered helplessly. She looked down into her lap, shame-faced, her fingers twisting and untwisting the strap of her purse.

"W-we could . . ." She hesitated, went on in a barely audible whisper. "We c-could . . . go some place for a drink?"

"I wouldn't think of it!" I shook my head firmly. "I know something of your city, you see, and I know that cops in uniform may not drink."

"But —"

"I know something else, too. Local lady cops must be single; marriage is grounds for immediate dismissal. And one would also be dismissed, naturally — promptly — if her conduct were anything less than circumspect. She can't sleep around as other women might. A very small breath of scandal, and she'd be out. So — so what is our lady to do, anyway? What is she to do, say, if her womanly desires are somewhat stronger than normal ones, if she is highly sexed, loaded with equipment which screams for action? What — yes, dear? You'll have to speak a little louder."

She wasn't blushing anymore. *Yet* is the word. I had to bend over to hear what she said.

"Well," I nodded, "that's fine. I'd like to go to your house. I always hate to take a woman to a hotel."

"No! I m-meant we could have dinner. We c-could talk. We — it's on the beach. We could swim, if you like and —"

I told her that of course, we could — and we would, if she still wanted to. We'd get right in bed first, and if she wasn't too tired afterwards . . .

I paused, looking at her inquiringly. I put a hand on the door latch.

"It's entirely up to you, dear. Don't consider me at all. I can walk a city block and pick up a half-dozen women."

"I k-know . . ." she muttered humbly. "I know you could. But —"

"Well?"

"I — *c-can't!* You'd think I was awful! It would be bad enough, if we were acquainted and —"

"Don't apologize." I swung the door open. "It's quite all right."

"Wait — c-could I call you somewhere? If — if I th-thought about it and decided t-to —"

"But suppose I decided not to?" I pointed out. "No, I think we'd better forget it."

"B-but —" She was almost crying. "I c-couldn't respect myself! You wouldn't respect me! You'd t-think I was terrible, and — wait! *Wait!*"

I smiled at her. I got out and slammed the door and started up the street.

I really didn't care, you know. At least, I cared very little. She was a cop, of course, and it was a cop that Dad had killed. But I wasn't sure that I cared to do anything about that or her, to take care of that by taking care of her. I just didn't know. The situation seemed to offer possibilities, but I just didn't know. Whether I wanted to do anything about it and her. Whether there was anything suitable to do if I did want.

She called after me. She called louder, more desperately. I kept going.

I heard the car door open. Slam. She called once more. Then she was silent, she was running after me, a fiercely silent animal racing after an escaping prey.

She caught up with me. Her fingers sank into my arm, half yanked me around. And her face was dead white now, even her lips were white. And her eyes were blazing.

"D-don't you go 'way!" she panted. "Don't you dare go 'way! You come with me! Come right now, you hear? *N-now!* Now now now NOW or I'll —"

"But you won't respect me," I said. "You'll think I'm terrible."

"You better! You j-just better! You don't, I'll — *I'll do it here!*"

. . . It was the latter part of February, but it can be warm there in February and it was this night. Not hot-warm, but cool-warm. Balmy. The kind of night when bedclothes are unnecessary and naked bodies warm each other comfortably.

I raised up on one elbow, reached across her to the ashtray. I held the cigarette over her a moment, letting its glow fall upon her body, moving the glow slowly downward from her breasts. Then, I crushed it out in the tray, and lay back down again.

"Very pretty," I said. "A very lovely bush. Not as extensive as my wife's, but then you don't have her area."

"Crazy!" She snuggled against me. "You and your four-hundred-pound wife!"

"She probably weighs more than that now. She gets bigger all the time, you know. Elephantiasis. It's not fat, but growth. I imagine her head alone weighs as much as you do."

"I'll bet!" she snickered. "I can see you marrying a wife like that!"

"But who else would have married her? And wasn't she entitled to marriage, to everything that could possibly be given her? It would have been better, of course, if she had been put to sleep at birth, as our first three children were —"

"Uh-huh. Oh, sure!"

"It's done. What kinder thing can you do for three hopeless Mongoloids? One you might take care of, but three of them — triplets —"

"Mmmm-hmm?" She yawned drowsily. "And what's wrong with the other two, the two you have now? They don't have all their parts, I suppose?"

"Well," I said, "they're my children. So, no, I don't suppose they do. Something is certain to be missing . . ."

A balmy gust of wind puffed through the partially open window, swirling the curtains, sucking them back against the screen. They rustled there, scratchily, flattening themselves. Trying to push out into the moonlight. Then, they gave up limply, came creeping back over the sill. And slid down into the darkness.

I closed my eyes. I drew her into my arms and pulled her tightly against me.

She shivered. Her lips moved hungrily over my face, burning, pressing harder and harder. Whispering in ecstatic abandon. *"Marty . . .Oh Marty, Marty, Marty! Y-you — you know what I'm going to d-do to you?"*

I had a pretty good idea, but I didn't say. She probably thought it was something original — her own invention — and there was no point in playing the kill-sport.

What I said was that that was beside the point. "It isn't what you're going to do to me, lady. It's what I'm going to do to you."

6

It was very late when I reached home. Mom was asleep — the doctor had come and given her a sedative. Carol let me in the door and we swapped news briefly. Then, since both of us were tired and didn't want Mom waking up on us, we turned in.

I had trouble getting to sleep — I don't think I'd slept more than an hour or so when my alarm sounded off. But I got up anyway, promptly at seven. Mom didn't know I'd quit my job. The longer she could be kept in ignorance the better.

I left the house and had breakfast in a drugstore. Afterwards, I sauntered down to that little park I've mentioned and sat down to wait for Carol. We hadn't had a chance to talk much last night. She'd indicated that she had things to tell me, and I of course had things to tell her.

I yawned, blinking my eyes against the warm morning sunlight. I yawned again and put on my sunglasses. Thinking about last night, about my lady cop. Putting together the bits of personal data I'd been able to get out of her.

Her name was Archer, Lois Archer. She was about twenty-eight years old. (My guess — she hadn't told me.) She'd been with the police department for five years. She'd worked as a secretary for three years, then there'd been an opening on the force so she'd shifted over to that. The pay was considerably higher. The work had promised to be much more interesting. She'd detested the job almost from the beginning — she simply wasn't the cop type. But she'd felt that she had to stick with it. Good jobs, even reasonably good jobs, were hard to get out there. So many people came here for the climate and were willing to work for next-to-nothing to remain.

She had a brother overseas in the army. He and she owned the house jointly. She — well, that was about the size of things. The sum total of what I knew about her, and probably all it was important to know.

I saw Carol approaching. I stood up and waved to her. I'd been so busy that I'd hardly gotten a good look at her for weeks. And I noticed now that she seemed to have put on a little weight. It was hard to spot on anyone as small-boned as she; doubtless no one but I would have spotted it. I thought it made her even more attractive than she had been, and I told her so.

She laughed, making a face at me. "Now, that's a nice thing to say to a girl! You say that to your cop, and she'll probably pinch you."

"Well, turnabout." I shrugged. "Turnabout. I think she'll wish she could, incidentally, when she goes to sit down."

I filled her in on Lois, on the setup as a whole. I said that it looked quite promising.

"The house is on the outer outskirts of town; the nearest neighbor is blocks away. Of course, that's not all to the good. It would be worth a lot more if it was closer in."

"Uh-huh." Carol nodded. "But it's a nice place, you said, and it's on the waterfront."

"Yes. So, well, I'd say about fifteen thousand. That's at a forced sale — a fast sale — which naturally it would have to be. Now, this brother angle presents a bit of a problem. She'll have to get his okay, and I got the impression he might be a pretty tough customer. She seemed rather uncomfortable whenever she mentioned him. But . . ."

I paused, remembering the way she'd acted. After a moment, I went on again . . . She'd been uncomfortable, conscience-stricken, about the whole situation, hadn't she? Afraid I wouldn't respect her, that I'd think she was awful and so on.

"I think it can be worked out," I said. "Say the house is worth fifteen thousand at the outside. She cables him she has an offer for twenty, and he'll leap at it."

"Will it take very long, Marty?"

"I don't think so. She's already got the going-away notion — you know, just the two of us going off somewhere together. Possibly, probably I can swing it in a month."

"Oh," said Carol slowly. "Well, I suppose if" — she saw my expression, gave me a quick smile. "Now, don't you worry about me, darling. We'll get by all right. I'm a little behind on some of the bills, but my alimony is due next week and — well, something will turn up."

"I don't see how I can do it much faster," I said. "Not the main deal. But I might be able to promote a few hundred. Her brother is pretty certain to be half-owner of the car and furniture, but there's quite a bit of pawnable stuff around, hunting and fishing gear that belongs to him, and —"

I broke off. It wasn't a good idea. In reaching for a few hundred, I might blow the main chance.

Carol said I shouldn't do it. She studied my face searchingly, so intently that I wanted to look away.

"Marty . . . You like her, don't you?"

"I like everyone," I said. "Except, possibly, for one William Wharton the Third — your ex-husband, in case you've been able to forget."

"You know how I feel about Ellen, Marty, and it's not out of pity. When a person thinks you're wonderful, knowing just about everything there is to know — well, I just about have to feel as I do. But . . . but I've thought a lot about it, Marty, and I think sometimes you really did it for me. You couldn't do anything about my marriage, but you could make yourself as miserable as I was."

"I didn't do it for you," I said. "I would have done it for you, of course — that, or anything else. But I didn't. Don't you remember, Carol? I did what I said I was going to do, back when we were kids. What we both said we were going to do."

"I know, darling, but —"

"Someone that no one else wanted. Someone scorned and shamed and cast aside. Someone who had never known real love, or even simple kindness, and would never know unless we —"

Her hand closed over mine. She smiled at me mistily, winking back the tears in her sky-blue eyes.

I felt sick all over. I felt like my guts were being ripped out of me, and for a moment I wished they had been.

"Don't," I said. "For God's sake, don't cry, darling! I don't know how I could have been so stupid as to —"

"I-it's all right, Marty." She made the tears go away. "You didn't do it. I just happened to think of something, something that Mom said to me one night, and —"

"What? What was it?"

"Nothing. I mean, she didn't actually say it. She started to, and then she — she just shut up. Let's forget it, hmmm?" She patted my hand, cocking her head on one side. "I'm probably wrong about it. She probably didn't intend to say anything at all like I thought she did."

"Well," I said, "I don't know what she could say that she hasn't said already."

"She didn't. She really didn't say anything, darling. Lend me your handkerchief, will you?"

I gave it to her, and she blew her nose. She opened her purse, took out her compact and studied herself in the mirror.

"About afterwards, Marty. Will you have to dispose of her — Lois?"

"I don't know," I said. "I don't think I'd have to — I imagine she'd be too ashamed to squawk. But that still leaves the question of whether I should. It would seem kind of fitting, you know, something virtually required."

"Yes?" said Carol. "Well, perhaps. It seems that it would be, but on the other hand . . ." She shook her head thoughtfully, returning the compact to her purse. "Whatever you think, Marty, whatever you want. I just don't want you to feel you have to do it on my account."

"I won't," I promised. "For that matter . . . well. Skip it. I have a feeling that it should be done, that it must, but —"

"Yes?"

"I don't know," I said. "I just don't know."

7

We walked into town together, and I left her at the cocktail lounge. I had a light second breakfast and settled down in the public square. Except for a very vague sense of uneasiness, of something left undone, I felt quite happy. I had Carol; we were brought together again. I had Lois — at least, I would have her for a while. Life was back in balance, then, poised perfectly on the two essential kinds of love. And there was little more to be asked of it. There was much to be grateful for, to feel happy about.

I lolled back on my bench, basking in the sunlight. Warm inwardly and outwardly. Deciding that I should be able to send for the family in a few weeks. This would be a beautiful place for Ellen to die, I thought. And, of course, she was dying. I had been temporarily unable to go on watching the process — and I had felt that her folks should be forced to do so. But in a few weeks, as soon as my emotional resources were replenished, and theirs, if they had any, depleted . . .

I would give her a beautiful death. It would make up for many things.

As for the present . . .

I got up quickly and went out to the sidewalk.

The cocktail lounge was about a block away. Carol and a young navy officer had just emerged from it and started up the street. And a man who had been loitering near the entrance had followed them.

I ran across the intersection. I ran partway up the block, then slowed to a walk as they, and subsequently he, rounded the corner. I reached the corner myself and crossed to the other side of the street. I stood there, my back half-turned, ostensibly looking into a shop window.

They turned in at the entrance of one of those small, lobbyless hotels. He glanced up at its neon signs, consulted his watch and took out a notebook. He wrote in it briefly, looking again at his watch. Then he returned it to his pocket and walked on down the street.

I followed him at a discreet distance.

Some four blocks away, he entered a small office building.

It was a shabby place, a diseases-of-men, rubber novelties, massage-parlor kind of building. At the foot of the steps, immediately inside the door, was a white-lettered office directory. It was divided into five sections, one for each story. Since the building was a walk-up, tenants became fewer and fewer after the second floor. And on the fifth there was only one.

He was all alone up there. J. Krutz, Private Investigations, "Divorce Cases a Specialty," was all alone.

I pulled my hat down low, readjusted my sunglasses and started up the steps.

There was a small lavatory, a chipped-enamel sink, in one corner of his office. He was bent over it, his back turned to the door, when I arrived, and I stood back from the threshold for a moment, giving him time to dry his hands and face. Then, I strode in brusquely, curtly introduced myself and sat down without waiting for an invitation.

He was a flabby-looking, owl-faced fellow. Obviously wounded by my manner — servilely hostile, if you know what I mean — he sat down across from me — at a scarred, untidy desk; memos to himself on a paper spike and an ashtray probably appropriated from a hotel overflowed with cigarette butts.

He was cert'n'ly glad, he said, to meet Mr. Wharton's West Coast representative. But wasn't we kind of rushing things? After all, he'd only been on the job four days; yessir, it was just four days since he'd got Mr. Wharton's wire from New York, and he'd already sent in two reports.

He paused, giving me a wounded look.

I ripped out a handsome curse.

"That Wharton" — I shook my head. "Always driving someone. Always trying to put on the squeeze. Why, he gave me the impression you'd been on the case for weeks!"

"Well," he hesitated cautiously. "I'm not criticizing, y'understand. But . . ."

"You should," I said firmly. "You have every right to, Mr. Krutz.

Doubtless he can't help it, I bear him not the slightest ill will, but the man is a bastard. This case itself is proof of the fact."

"Well . . ." He hesitated again. Then he leaned forward eagerly, an oily grin on his owl's face. "Ain't it the truth?" he said. "Yessir, you really got something there, Mr. Allen. I know all about the case, even if there wasn't much of it got on the papers. Why, the guy was just as low-down as they get — washed-up, worn-out punk, pimping for a living. He was nothin', know what I mean, ten times lower than nothing. So somehow this swell little dish decides to marry him — I never will be able to figure that one out — and she starts getting him back on his feet. There's nothing he's any good at, so she supports 'em both. What time she ain't knocking herself out on the job, she's working to build him up. Nursing him, waiting on him hand and foot, actually making somethin' out of nothing, y'know, and she does so good at it that his family decides to take him back. Then . . ."

Then he'd given her a big fat dose of syphilis and divorced her for having it. She was very young, then. She was too dazed to fight. Probably she didn't care to fight.

"I see you know all the facts, Mr. Krutz," I said. "You're thoroughly grounded in the case."

"Sure. That's my business, know what I mean? . . . What's the matter with the guy, Mr. Allen? I'm tickled to have the job, naturally, but why does he want it done? How can he do a thing like this just to save himself a few bucks?"

"I wonder," I said. "How can you do it to make yourself a few bucks?"

"Me? Well, uh" — he laughed uncertainly. "I mean, what the hell, anyway? That's my job. If I didn't do it, someone else would. I — say ain't I seen you somewhere be —"

"Would they do it?" I said. "How can you be sure they would, Mr. Krutz? Have you ever thought about the potentials in a crusade for not doing the things that someone else would do if you didn't?"

"Say n-now," he stammered. "Now, l-looky here, Mister —"

"I'm afraid you have sinned," I said. "You have violated Section A of Commandment One-minus. Yea, verily, Krutz —"

"Now, l-looky. Y-you — you —" He stood shakily. "You c-can't blame me f-for —"

"Yea, verily, sayeth the Lord Lakewood, better the blind man who pisseth through a window than the knowing servant who raises it for him."

I smiled and thrust out my hand. He took it automatically.

I jerked him forward — and down. He came down hard on his

desk, on its sharp steel paper spike. It went through his open mouth and poked out the back of his head.

I left.

It just about had to be done that way, to look like an accident. But still I was not at all pleased with myself. It was too simple, a stingy complement to the complex process of birth, and there is already far too much of such studied and stupid simplicity in life. Catchword simplicity — "wisdom." Idiot ideology. Drop-a-bomb-on-Moscow, the-poor-are-terribly-happy thinking. Men are forced to live with this nonsense, this simplicity, and they should have something better in death.

That is and was my feeling, at least, and Carol shared it.

"The poor man," she said. "I wish I could have had him in bed with me. They're always so happy that way."

She did not, of course, receive her alimony check.

8

I went to work the following week and quit at the end of it. Although I felt uncomfortable in doing so, I sent most of the money to Ellen at Carol's insistence. Mom was very cross that night, the eve of my resignation. She had learned, meanwhile, of my quitting the first job. And this seemed to be a little more than she could take.

"You just don't want to amount to anything!" she said furiously. "Neither of you do — you do your best not to! Well, all I have to say is . . ."

We were eating dinner at the time. Carol had been eating very little, and now she was beginning to look ill. I held up my hand, cutting off all that Mom had to say, which was obviously interminable.

"Before you go any further," I said. "Before you say anything more, perhaps you should establish your qualifications for saying it."

"What — how do you mean?"

"I don't know how to make it any plainer. Not without being much more pointed than I care to."

She didn't understand for a moment; she was too absorbed in her tirade against us. Then she understood, and her face sagged and her eyes went sick. Mouth working, she stared down dully at her plate.

"I . . . I couldn't help it," she mumbled. "I — I did the best I could."

I said I was sure of it. Carol and I didn't blame her at all. "Now, why don't we finish our dinners and forget all about it?"

"I — I don't feel like eating." She pushed back her plate and stood up. "I think I'd better lie —" She staggered.

I jumped up and caught her by the arm, and Carol and I helped her up the stairs to bed. We fixed her some of the sleeping potion. She drank it down, looked up at us from her pillow, eyes dragging shut, face a crumpled, blue-dotted parchment.

"Just don't," she whispered. "Just don't do anything else."

And she fell asleep.

I was seeing Lois that night. Carol was also going out, having had poor luck that day; and she stood at the curb with me for a few minutes, while I waited for Lois to come by.

"Now, don't you worry about me, Marty." She smiled. "I feel fine, and — and, well, after all, it's really the only way we can do anything very profitable."

"I know," I said. "But . . ." But it *was* the only way. If she was to pick up, or rather be picked up by, a prize chump, there could be no witnesses to the act. It must be done unobserved, and night offered the least chance of observation.

"Well. Don't wear yourself out," I said. "It's not necessary. I should be able to swing this other matter very soon."

"Don't you wear *yourself* out," she said. "Don't do anything at all, if you don't want to."

I promised I wouldn't. I added that I still hadn't decided what Lois's final disposition should be.

"It's an odd thing," I said, "but I have a feeling that it isn't necessary for me to decide. The fitting thing will be done, but I will have nothing to do with it."

Carol left as Lois drove up. We rode out to her house, and she was pouting and peevish throughout the trip. She just didn't see *why*, she kept exclaiming. My sister had money. She just had to have, the way she dressed and living in that big house — and everything! So why —

"She'd die if she didn't live that way," I said. "She lived too long another way."

"Oh, stop talking nonsense! Tell me why, Marty. Just tell me why I should be expected to give up everything when you could just as well ask that fine sister of yours to —"

We had stopped in front of her house, in the driveway, rather. I turned suddenly and slapped her across the mouth.

Her eyes flashed. Her hand lashed out in instant, angry reaction — then stopped, just short of my jaw.

"Well?" I said. "Well, Lois, my peevish bluecoat?"

She bit her lip helplessly, trying to smile, to pass it off as a joke.

"Well, how about *this*?" I said, and I swung my hand again — I kept swinging it. "And this and this and —"

"P-please, Marty!" She tried to cover her face. "It'll sh-show — I have to work, and —"

"All right," I said. "All right, my inky-haired incontinent, my sloe-eyed slut, my copulating cop. How about this?"

I caught my hand into the front of her blouse, her brassiere. I yanked, and her naked breasts bloomed out through the torn cloth. And . . . and she flung herself forward, crushing them against me.

"H-harder, dearest! Oh, Marty, I — I —"

"I'm trying to do you a favor," I said. "I love you, Lois, and I'm trying to —"

"D-don't talk, darling. J-just — Marty! Where are you going?"

"Home," I said. "I'm walking up to the highway and catching a cab."

"*No!* D-don't you dare! You just t-try to, and —"

I did try to, after certain preliminaries. But I didn't make it. Got as far as the highway, three blocks; then I gave up and went back. Carrying her in my arms. Carrying her as I'd left her in the car. With every stitch of her clothes ripped off.

9

I stayed there that night. The next morning she phoned in to the department, reported herself sick and was given the day off. So I kept on staying.

It was a pretty wild day, a sweetly wild day. A perfect commingling of sweetness and wildness. We had breakfast. We took a bath together. We had a half-dozen drinks. Then, we stripped every damned picture in the house from the walls, dug up a couple of her brother's rifles and lugged the lot down to the beach.

They were the most hideous kind of crap, those pictures. Cute stuff — dime-store junk. Pictures of kewpie-doll babies with their pants falling off and dogs smoking pipes and cats rolling a ball of yarn. Her brother liked such junk, it seemed; he also liked to have his own way. So we carried it down to the beach, and we blasted it to pieces. Taking turns at it. One of us tossing an item into the air for the other to shoot at.

It was noon by that time. We went back to the house, ate and drank some more and took another bath. We rested, dozed in each other's arms. We got up and went on another romp.

Her brother belonged to some half-assed lodge — one of those dress-up outfits. She got out his uniform hat, pulled the plumes off of it and made herself into a peacock.

She was a very lovely peacock. She crawled around on the floor, wiggling her bottom and making the plumes sway. I crawled around after her, snapping at them, barking and yipping like a dog. I caught up with her. We rolled around on the floor, locked together, working up static electricity from the carpet. We rolled into the living room — laughing, yelling and jerking with jolts of electricity. We knocked over the tables and chairs and lamps, making a mess of the place. And then I grabbed a bottle of whiskey and we rolled back into the bedroom and under the bed.

We came out finally. We took our third bath, washing away the dirt and lint and climbed into bed again. It was night. The balmy, cool-warm breeze of the night was drifting through the window. My back was to it, and she was afraid I might catch cold. She bent over me, shaking out her soft, black, waist-length hair; she tucked it over and under my shoulders, her face pressed tightly to my chest, drawing herself against me with her hair. And we wrapped together.

We had said nothing about money all day; we were afraid of spoiling that sweet wildness. We were afraid of spoiling this now, this gentle sweetness, so we still did not speak of money. We ignored that chasm and placed ourselves in the wonderland beyond, the green pastures of accomplished fact.

"Huh-uh, Marty . . ." she murmured. "I don't want you on any old newspapers. I want us to be all alone, away off somewhere by ourselves."

"Well, let's see, then," I said. "We might run a dairy. None of this mechanized stuff, mind you. I would operate it by hand, and you, my lamb, or I should say —"

"Now, Marty!" she snickered. "That's dirty."

"Well, I could write my book," I said, "my treatise on taxation. 'Cornucopia of Constipation, or the Martin Lakewood Bowel Movement Single Tax.' "

"Crazy! You — *ha, ha* — you crazy sweet thing!"

"I would do away with all taxes on food and other necessities," I said, "and the only levy would be on bowel movements. It's really a very sensible plan, Lois. The most just, most equitable plan ever invented. The less money a man has, the less he eats, the less are his taxes."

"Uh-hmmm, and suppose he didn't have any money at all. What would he do then?"

"What does he do now?" I said.

"Oh, Marty! *Ha, ha, ha* . . ."

"What's so funny about it?" I said. "If it's right to let a man starve, then it's right to let him die of constipation. It's more right, goddammit! At least we give him a choice, a little control over his own destiny. We can deny him food, but we can't keep him from holding in his bowels. If he can hold in long enough — What's so funny! Goddammit, what are you laughing about?"

"Why, Marty!" She laughed nervously. "We're just talking, joking. There's nothing to be angry about."

"But"— I caught myself. "Yeah, sure," I said. "It's all a joke, and a pretty bad one; not even original. Just about the oldest joke there is."

We lay silent for a time. The curtains scratched restlessly against the screen, and far in the distance somewhere there was the faint howling of a dog.

"Marty . . ." She pressed in on me at the hips. "Love me, Marty? Love me very much?"

"Yes," I said. "I'm afraid I do."

"More than anyone else?"

We had been on this line before. I imagine every man has, and has been as frustrated by it as I.

"Do you, Marty? Love me more than you do your sister?"

"I've told you," I said. "It's two different things; entirely different kinds of love. The two aren't comparable."

"But you have to love one of us more than the other. You *have* to, Marty."

I said that, goddammit, I didn't have to, and no one out of his infancy would say that I did. It was a milk-and-highball proposition. Both were satisfying, but each in its own way. "Take your brother, now. As a brother, you love him more than —"

"I do not! I only love you, and I love you more than anyone else in the world!"

"Well," I said helplessly. "Well —"

The phone rang. She murmured to let it go, and I let it go. And after the second ring it stopped.

It was Carol's signal. I waited tensely for her to call back, and Lois waited for something else. She nudged me again, pressed forward with her thighs. The phone rang.

I turned suddenly and grabbed for it. Lois let out with an angry *"Ouch!"* and sat up glaring at me, rubbing her scalp.

"What's the matter with you? You knew my hair was —"

"Please," I said. "Be quiet a minute!"

It was Carol. She spoke rapidly, her voice pitched just above a whisper.

". . . understand, Marty? A hunting lodge . . . take the left turn at the crossroad, and . . ."

"Of course, I understand," I said. "I'll start right away, Carol. As soon as mother gets to feeling better, I can come back."

We hung up. I gave Lois a kiss and apologized for yanking her hair.

"I'll have to leave for a while now, baby. My mother's taken ill — nothing serious, but Carol thinks I ought to be there, and —"

"Oh, she does, huh?" She pushed me away from her. "Well, go on then, and call yourself a cab! You're not going to use my car to rush home to her!"

I started dressing. If I had to — and I was sure I wouldn't have to — I could get along without her car. It would take extra time; I'd have to go into town and rent one there. But I could do it.

"You and your darling Carol! I've seen the way you act around each other. You know what I think about you?"

"Something nasty, I'm sure," I said. "Something very naughty. Otherwise, you wouldn't be wearing that pretty blush."

She told me what she thought. Rather, she yelled it. And I laughed and kissed her again. Because she didn't actually think it, of course. She didn't mean it; it was meaningless. It was mere words, said not out of hate but love.

She was crying, apologizing, as soon as they were spoken.

"I'm s-sorry, darling. I just l-love you so much, and —"

"It's all right," I said. "I have to run now, baby."

I took the car, naturally. She insisted on it.

10

The lodge was about thirty miles up in the mountains, about a mile off the main mountain road. It was heavily wooded country up there. I shut off the car lights as soon as I left the road and weaved my way through the trees by moonlight. I drove very slowly, holding the motor to a quiet purr. After a few minutes of this creeping, I stopped and got out.

I was on the edge of a clearing. The lodge was about fifty yards. It was a low, log-and-frame structure with a lean-to at one end. Inside the lean-to was a black sports coupe.

I glanced up at the sky, watched the moon drift behind a mass of clouds. In the brief darkness, as it vanished from view, I raced stooping across the clearing. I stopped in the sheltering alcove of the door, getting my wind back, reconstructing the interior of the place from the description Carol had given me.

This, immediately beyond the door, was the living room. The kitchen was straight on through. There was a bedroom on the right — of the living room, that is — and another at its left extreme. They were supposed to be in the one to the right.

Pressed gently down on the latch. I pushed against the door, ever so easily, and it moved silently open. I stepped inside.

A small lamp was burning on the fireplace mantel. I looked swiftly around the room, then crossed it and glanced into the kitchen. I couldn't see very well, but I could see enough. A wood stove with a row of implements above it. I lifted down one of them, a heavy meat cleaver, and reentered the living room.

It was an old place, and the floors were not what they had been. Several times, as I went toward the bedroom, there were dangerously loud squeaks. And just as I reached the door there was a *pop* like that of an exploding firecracker.

I stopped dead still in my tracks. Holding my breath. Listening.

There was no sound for a moment. Then, I heard the rattle of bedsprings, the rustle of bedclothes thrown back. The quiet but unmistakable sound of feet touching the floor. And crossing it.

I stepped to one side of the door. I raised the cleaver. I stood on tiptoe as the latch clicked softly, then clicked back into place. From the other side of the panels, there came a nervous whisper:

"M-Marty . . . ?"

"Carol!" I laughed out loud with relief. "Are you all right, darling?"

"Fine" — she didn't sound exactly fine. "He let me fix him a drink, and — well, it's all over, Marty. I'll be out as soon as I dress."

I wiped the cleaver off and returned it to the kitchen. I sat down on a cowhide-covered lounge, and after a few minutes she came out. She sat down next to me, running a comb through her thick red hair, touching up the make-up on her innocent child's face.

There'd be no trouble, she said. There was no danger of future trouble. The guy had picked her up on a dark street and they'd come directly to this place. Being unmarried and on a vacation, it might be days before inquiries were made about him.

"So it's all right — *that* part's all right." Carol smiled tiredly. "But look at this, Marty."

She opened her purse and handed it to me, a thick sheaf of bills with a rubber band around each end. I riffled it and silently handed it back. It was a Kansas City roll, big bills, a couple of fifties on the outside; the inside, little stuff, ones and fives and a few tens.

"Five hundred dollars. Just about five hundred." Carol looked down at it, her blue eyes dull and empty. "And Marty, he apologized for it.

He gave it to me — afterwards, when it was already done and there was nothing I could . . ."

I shook my head silently. It hardly seemed the time for words. I did a little wiping up with my handkerchief and then we left.

She was sick once on the way back to town. I had to stop the car and let her out by the roadside. We drove on again, she huddling against me, shivering with the cold mountain air. I talked to her — to myself. I talked to both of us, and for both of us. And if it was rationalization, so be it. Perhaps the power to rationalize is the power to remain sane. Perhaps the insane are so because they cannot escape the truth.

We were culpable, I said, only to the degree that all life, all society, was culpable. We were no more than the pointed instruments of that life, activated symbols in an allegory whose authors were untold billions. And only they, acting in concert, could alter a line of its text. And the alterations could best be impelled by remaining what we were. Innocence outraged, the sacred defiled, the useful made useless. For in universal horror there could be universal hope, in ultimate bestiality the ultimate in beauty and good. The blind should be made to see — so it was written. *They should be made to see!* And, lo, the Lord World was an agonized god, and he looked not kindly upon the bandaging of his belly whilst his innards writhed with cancer.

"Yea, verily," I said. "If thy neighbor's ass pains him, do thou not divert him with bullshit, but rather kick him soundly thereon. Yea, even though it maketh him thine enemy. For it is better that he should howl for a doctor than to drown in dung."

We had reached the house. Carol sat up, blinking her eyes sleepily.

"Don't worry about the money," she said as she got out of the car. "It'll be a big help, more than I need, really."

I drove on out to Lois's house. I went inside just long enough to give her an ultimatum. She was to cable her brother immediately or at least the first thing in the morning. Otherwise, we were washed up.

She was too startled, too furious to speak for a moment. When she did it was to tell me to go to hell, that she would neither cable him in the morning nor any other time.

I got away fast — pleased, saddened. Glad that I had tried, but knowing that I had changed nothing. She was certain to relent. She had to. For she was a symbol also, one more character in the allegory of unalterable lines.

I don't know why I had been so long in identifying her and seeing the part she had to play. Certainly, I should have seen it long before.

I got home and went quietly to bed. A few minutes later my bedroom door opened, and silently closed again. I sat up. I held out my hands in the darkness, and Carol found them, and I drew her down into the bed. I stroked her hair, whispered to her softly.

"Bad?" I said. "Is it bad, little sister?"

"B-bad . . ." She shuddered violently. "Oh, M-Marty, I keep —"

"Don't," I said. "Don't think, don't remember. It was the way it had to be. It was the best way, and you'll see that it was."

She shuddered again. And again. I drew her closer, whispering, and gradually the shaking subsided.

"It — the Things will go away in the morning, Marty? They'll go far away?"

"Yes. Just like they used to, remember? When day came, the night Things went away, and when night came the day Things went —"

"Y-yes," she said. "Yes! Tell me a story, Marty."

I hesitated. I had told her so many stories, and I was not sure of the kind she wanted.

"Well . . ." I said. "Well, once upon a time there were three billion bastards who lived in a jungle. They ate dirt, these bastards, of which there was more than enough for all. A total of six sextillion, four hundred and fifty quintillion short tons, to be exact. But being bastards, they were not content with —"

"Marty."

"Another one? A different kind?"

"*The* other one, Marty. You know."

I knew. I remembered. How could I help but remember?

"Once upon a time," I said. "Once upon a time, there was a little boy and a little girl, and the little boy was her father and the little girl was his mother. They —"

The door banged open. The light went on.

Mom stood staring at us, her chest rising and falling. Her eyes gleaming with a kind of evil triumph.

I sat up. Carol and I both sat up. One of her breasts had slipped out of her nightgown, and I tucked it back inside.

"Yes, Mom?" I said. "I hope we didn't wake you up."

"I'll bet you do! I'll just bet you do!"

"But" — I frowned, puzzled. "Of course, I hope so. We tried to be as quiet as we could. Carol had a little trouble sleeping, so I was just —"

"I know what you were doing! The same thing you've been doing for years! Scum, filth — no wonder everyone hated you! They saw through you all right, you didn't fool them any. They should have beaten you to death, starved you to death, you r-rotten . . ."

She believed it. She had made herself belief it. It was justification; it excused everything, the moral cowardice, the silence in the face of wrong, the years of all-absorbing, blindly selfish self-pity. She had hoped for this — what she believed this was. Doubtless, she had hoped for it right from the beginning. That abysmal degradation had been her hope for her children. And who knew, who was to say, how much that hope had been expressed in our lives?

I wanted to say something, do something to comfort Carol. I could not.

I lay back down on the pillow and covered my face with my hands. Carol laid one of her hands over mine.

She spoke very quietly, but somehow her voice rose above the tirade.

"You made Marty cry," she said. "You made my brother cry."

"I'll — I'll do worse than that!" Mom panted. "I'll —"

"There is nothing worse than that. Go to your room."

"Now — now, see here," Mom faltered. "Don't you tell me to —"

"Go to your room."

There was silence, complete suspension of movement, for a moment. Then Carol threw back the covers — I felt her throw them back. She climbed out of bed and pointed — I could see her pointing.

"N-no!" It was Mom, but it was not her voice. "NO, Carol! I'm sorry! I d-didn't mean it! I —"

"You meant it. I mean it. Go to your room."

"No! You can't! I'm your mother. Y-you —"

"Are you? Were you?" — she was moving away from the bed, and Mom was moving out of the door. Backing away as Carol advanced. "Go on. Go. You have to go to sleep."

"No!"

"Yes."

Their voices grew fainter and fainter. Then, right at the last, they rose again. Not strident but clear. A little tired but peaceful.

"That's right. Drink it all down. Now, you'll be a lot better."

"Thank you. Thank you, very much, Carol . . ."

11

Figuratively, at least, most people do die of oversedation; fumbling about fearfully, blindly, they grasp the sweet-smelling potions handed them with never a look at the label, and suddenly they are dead. They died "natural" deaths, then. As she died. At any rate, the doctor chose to call it natural — heart failure — and we could not, of course, dispute his word.

He, the doctor, left after a period of condoling with us. The undertaker came to supervise the removal of the body and remained to discuss funeral arrangements. He thought something very nice could be done for about twelve hundred dollars, something that our loved one would have loved. The price fell gradually, his face falling with it, until he was down to the rock bottom of "adequacy" which bore a price tag of four hundred and fifty.

Carol paid him. The funeral was set for the following afternoon. It was a little after he left us, with a barely pleasant good morning, that Lois called.

"I've just got one thing to say to you," she began. "If you think for one minute that you can — Marty! Marty, darling! What's the matter?"

I couldn't answer her. How did I know what the matter was? Carol took the phone out of my hand and talked to her.

They talked for several minutes, and I could hear her weeping as Carol hung up. An hour or so later, as Carol was getting ready to go to town, she called back. I still couldn't talk, so Carol took a message for me.

Would I please, please call her as soon as I could? She didn't want to disturb me, feeling as I must, so — would I, please? It was important. It concerned something that I wanted.

I lay down. I hadn't felt at all sleepy, but I fell asleep instantly, and night had come when I awakened.

I called out to Carol. I got up and ran into her room, and there was a note pinned to her pillow:

Marty darling:
   I storied to you about what I was going to do today. I knew you'd be worried, and there's really no need to because I'm going to be perfectly all right. I'll be with you as soon as I can, but I won't be able to be there for the funeral. Don't you go either, if it bothers you. And tell me a story tonight, darling. I'll be listening for it.

The signature was mixed up, jumbled. The initial letter was both *M* and *C* and the second letter was both *o* and *a*.

I fixed a bite of dinner. I shaved and started out to look for her, and then I remembered that this was tonight, so I came back. I went up to her room. I stretched out on her bed and took her into my arms. And I told her a story, I told it all through the night. She was so frightened. She was trembling and shaking constantly. So I talked on and on, on and on through the night, holding her tightly against me.

Day came, at last.

At last, she slipped quietly out of my arms.

At last, she was asleep.

I lay watching her for a time, selfishly hoping that she would awaken. Because I had always loved to watch that awakening, the coming to life of purity and beauty, reborn by night and as yet untarnished by day. I waited and watched, but she did not awaken. She did not come to life. And finally I fell asleep at her side.

When I awoke, she was gone. I was anxious about her, naturally — I wondered where she had gone. I sat for a long time wondering, about her and the others who went. Then it was almost time for the funeral, and I had to leave.

I went to the funeral, but I did not stay. I strolled away from the graveside and off toward the bus line, meandering casually through the hummocked greensward, the marble- and copper-bordered streets of The City of Wonderful People. It was a crowded city; neighbor elbowed against neighbor. Yet no one felt the need for more room. They dwelt peacefully side by side, content with what they had. No one needing more than what he had, nor wanting more than he needed. Because they were so wonderful, you see. They were all so wonderful.

There was Annie, for example, devoted wife of Samuel. And there was William, faithful husband of Nora. There was Henry, dutiful son, and Mabel, loving daughter, and Father and Mother, who were not only devoted, faithful, dutiful and loving, but God-fearing to boot. One had to look closely to see that they were all these things, their gravestones being only slightly larger than a cigarette package. But one always does have to look closely to see virtue, and as in this case, it is always worth the trouble.

Yes, hell. Yes, oh, God, yes it was a wonderful place, The City of Wonderful People. Everyone in it was everything that everyone should be. Some had a little more on the ball, of course, than others; there was one guy, for instance, who was only humble. But think of that! Think of its possibilities! Think of what you could do with a guy like that on a world tour. Or if war prevented, as it indubitably would, you could put him on television. A nationwide hookup. You could go to the network and say, Look, I've got something different here. Something unique. I've got a guy that's — No, he doesn't do card tricks, he's not a singer or dancer. Well, he does have a sense of humor, but he doesn't tell — No, I'm afraid he doesn't have big tits, and his ass looks just like yours and mine. What's he's got is something different. Something there's a hell of a need for. And if you'll just give him a chance . . .

They'd never go for it.

You'd have to nail him to a cross first.

Only here, only in the City of the Wonderful People, was the wonderful wonderful.

12

The phone was ringing. Ringing again or still.

I let it.

It would only be Lois, weeping and apologizing and commiserating with me. Telling me she'd sent the cable. Begging to see me. Telling me she quit her job, that she was giving up everything for me, so wouldn't I — couldn't I — come out for just a little while?

Yes, it would only be Lois. And, of course, I would go to see her — I had to. But it was not time yet. She had sent the cable to Japan four days ago. Even in a suspicious world, where days were hours and miles were feet, it was not yet time.

So I let the phone ring, even when it rang with that flat finality which phones assume when ringing for the last time. I did not want to talk. Carol would not want to talk. Carol was asleep and must not be disturbed, and —

It wasn't Lois calling. Lois was answering it. The front door was open, and she was speaking into the phone. Frowning, stammering, her face slowly turning gray. She mumbled something that sounded like, "J-just a minute, doctor" — which made no sense at all, naturally. She looked at me concernedly.

"Can you talk, Marty? It's some doctor down in Mexico. Just across the border. He says — it's about Carol, darling — h-he says that . . . Oh, Marty, I'm so s-sorry — he says th-that —"

I took the phone away from her. It couldn't be about Carol, but she was obviously in no condition to talk.

It was a poor connection, and his English was poor. I had to keep asking him to repeat things, and even then he was almost impossible to understand.

"You must be mistaken," I said. "Five months pregnant? What the hell kind of doctor would abort a five-month pregnancy?"

"But I do not know, señor. She tell me is barely three months, and it do not show mooch, you know. She is so small, an' —"

But he'd know, dammit. Any kind of doctor would. If he wasn't completely stupid, willing to run any risk to pick up a few dollars . . .

"I am so sorry señor. I do my ver' best. It is not mooch, perhaps —
but for twenty-five dollars, what would you? Soch as I am, as leetle
as I know, I —"

"Well, it doesn't matter," I said. "It's all a mistake. You've got the
wrong party."

"No! Wait, señor!"

"Well?" I said.

"What should I do? What do you wish done? I am poor man, and
you must know —"

"I tell you what I know," I said. "You're trying to work some kind
of racket, and if you bother me again I'll sic the authorities on
you."

"Señor! Please" — he was almost crying. "I mus' — you mus' do something! Almost four days it has been, an' the weather she is so hot, an' —
What shall I do?"

I laughed. I imagined it must be a hell of a mess.

"What the hell do I care what you do?" I said. "Throw it in the
ocean. Throw it on the garbage dump. Throw it out in the alley for
the dogs to piss on."

"But she is —"

"Don't lie to me! I know where my sister is!"

I slammed up the phone.

Lois wet her lips. She came toward me hesitantly, wanting to protest,
to take charge, to do what her essential primness and ingrained propriety demanded. She wanted to say, You'd better go, Marty. You
must or I'll do it. But she did not say that; she could not say it, I
suppose. Her instincts had not changed during these past few weeks,
but she was no longer sure of them. She no longer relished and took
pride in them. They were something to be scorned, ignored, pushed
out of the path of desire.

"Let's go out to my house, Marty. You need to get away from here."

"I think so, too," I said. "It's about time that I did."

13

I needed to be diverted. I needed to forget. I needed to make merry.
I did. She said I did. And who does not? So there was the sweet
wildness again. Then, wildness without sweetness. Wilder and wilder
wildness. Babel.

There was the lewd peacock, the weird, waggling, wiggling mutation
of woman and bird. There was the breastless woman, the woman with

three faces, with two bedaubed grinning faces for breasts. There was the serpent woman, the frog woman, the woman who was man. There was the man who looked like a dog, the man horse, the man who was woman, the man who was not man. There were the shrieks, the fierce grunts and growls, the howls and snarls, the cluckings, groanings, whinings, barkings, yippings, moanings. There was the rolling and crawling, the laughter and the prayers, the talk in unknown tongues. There was Babel.

And there was peace.

And there was night, and I was wrapped in Circe's hair.

". . . don't think I'm awful, do you, Marty? He's just, well, nothing. And he doesn't want to be anything. Just a big, stupid, hateful boor. He's lucky I didn't do something like this long ago!"

"You should have," I said. "You should have split up with him and gone your own way."

"Sweet"— She brushed her lips against my face. "You do think I'm right, then, don't you, Marty? He deserves to lose every last penny he's got! Every penny he put into this place."

"Why didn't you split with him?" I asked. "Why didn't you get married? Of course, there was your job, the department's single-woman policy. But couldn't you have kept it a secret?"

She hesitated. Her body moved in a small shrug. "I suppose, but you know how it is. I guess I just got in a rut, and, well, I guess there wasn't anyone I cared about marrying."

I reached over and lit a cigarette. We smoked it, taking turns, and I crushed it out in the ashtray. I turned a little on my side, looked out into the quiet night. It was early summer now. The air was sweet with the smell of budding trees, and the horizon still glowed with the golden pastels of the late-setting sun.

Lois laughed venomously; she could just see her brother, she said, when he received her cable. "He's always been so slow and stodgy, but I'll bet he moves fast for once. I told him I'd been offered thirty thousand dollars for the house."

I laughed with her. Thirty thousand dollars for *this* place! Yes, that would make him move all right.

"You don't think I'm awful, do you, Marty? About everything, I mean. You don't think I'm cheap and trashy and — and —"

"I want to tell you something," I said. "I want to tell you about my dad."

"But what's he — No, huh-uh, Marty. Don't tell me any of those crazy stories about —"

"Well, we'll say it's just a story," I said. "It isn't true, we'll say, but just a story."

"Well" — she squirmed uncomfortably. "Oh, all right! I suppose, if you simply *have* to."

"I've often wondered about him, Lois. He wasn't any genius, but he had at least average good sense. He must have known that fooling around with another man's wife — and a cop's wife, at that — was certain to cost him a lot more than it was worth. It was a continuing relationship, you see. Not just a one-night stand. She wasn't that kind of woman, and he wouldn't have been interested in her if she had been that kind. So I kept asking myself, why did he do it? Why did he carry on an affair that could only end in one way? And why did she, a woman of excellent reputation, ostensibly a model of womanly virtue —"

"Marty." She put her fingers over my mouth. "Please don't. Let's just talk about us, mmm?"

"We will." I pushed her hand away. "The woman killed herself that night, the same night Dad killed her husband. She didn't live long enough to explain, and Dad never chose to. It wouldn't have helped him any, and there was no point in looking like a bigger fool than he did already. So . . . so, Lois, I was left with a riddle. One that's nagged me for an answer for almost thirty years. And yet the answer's been before me all the time. In people. In hypocrisy and deception and self-deception. In walling ourselves up in our own little worlds.

"There was the husband, for example, a real cold fish. He minded his own business — was sufficient unto himself. We were his neighbors, but only geographically. So far as social contact went, we might just as well have been on another planet. . . . It was a bad attitude. Inevitably, as it always does, it got him killed."

"*K-killed!* . . . Marty, please don't talk any —"

"It was a factor, certainly. If he'd been a little more sociable, friendly, talkative . . . But let's leave him there, and take up his wife. She was what you call a nice woman, as I say. Very proper. At the same time, she resented her husband. She might have gone to work on him, talked things out with him, reformed him into a reasonable facsimile of the man she'd loved and married. But that would have been a lot of trouble, and she'd convinced herself that it wasn't worthwhile. It was easier to pick up another man — Dad. And there was a way she could do it and still cling to a few shreds of propriety. He was married, of course, and that was bad. But she could believe that it was his badness, rather than hers. If he thought, if he was willing to think that she —" I paused, stroking her hair gently. "Don't cry, Lois. It can't be changed. There are not enough tears for this sorrow."

"M-Marty! Oh, Marty, Marty! H-how you must hate me!"

She wept uncontrollably. The tears were hot against my chest, and her flesh was icy.

"I've never hated anyone," I said. "Never anyone."

The lawn was bright in the moonlight. Soon a little girl would come trudging across the grass, it seemed that I could see her coming now, and she would be frightened because she was alone. And then she would not be alone . . .

"I love you, Lois," I said. "We're going to go away together. We'll all go away together."

A cab stopped in front of the house.

A man in uniform got out.

And, of course, it wasn't her brother.

MICKEY SPILLANE

THE
GOLD
FEVER
TAPES

*Mickey Spillane (b. 1918) is the tough-guy writer everyone has heard of, along
with his private eye Mike Hammer. Spillane appears in television beer com-
mercials. When his name was an answer on the* Wheel of Fortune *TV game
show, it was guessed immediately (category: author, a job description he claims
to loathe; the preferred title is writer, and readers are called customers). In
the 1950s, well-thumbed paperback copies of* I, the Jury *were passed around
high school locker rooms as though they were pornography — which says more
about the 1950s than about the salacious quality of the novel.*

I, the Jury *was published in 1947,* Vengeance Is Mine! *and* My Gun
Is Quick *in 1950,* Kiss Me, Deadly *in 1952. The Mike Hammer novels,
about a dozen in all, arrived with the postwar paperback boom. A later, less
popular (and more political) Spillane hero is Tiger Mann, who spends a good
deal of his time battling Soviet agents.*

*Perhaps his paperback popularity harmed his critical reputation; Spillane
has never won the intellectual following that more down-and-out hard-boiled
writers have attracted.*

*"The Gold Fever Tapes," anachronistic as it may seem, was first published
in the 1973 issue of* Stag Annual.

THEY KILLED SQUEAKY WILLIAMS on the steps of the Criminal
Courts Building with two beautifully placed slugs in the middle of his
back and got away into traffic before anybody really knew what had
happened.

But I knew what had happened, and my guts felt all tight and dry
just standing there looking at his scrawny, frozen face in the drawer

of the morgue locker. One eye was still partly open and was staring at me.

"Identify him?" the attendant asked.

"He doesn't have to," the other voice said, and I turned around.

Charlie Watts had made captain since I had seen him last, but ten years and a few promotions had only screwed tighter the force of hate he had for people like me.

"An old cellmate of yours, Fallon . . . isn't he?" Even his voice had that same grating quality, like a file on a knife blade.

I nodded. "Six months' worth," I said.

"How'd you manage it, Fallon? What'd you have on the wheels to get paroled out like that? What bunch of suckers would let a damned crooked cop like you out after the bust you took?"

"Maybe they needed my room," I told him.

The drawer slammed shut and Squeaky went back into the cold locker and the last I saw of him was that half-open eye.

"And maybe you ought to come over and talk about this little hassle in more familiar surroundings," Watts told me.

"Why?"

"Because there might be something interesting to discuss when ex-cons get shot down on public property and old buddies show up to make sure he's dead."

"I came in to identify the body. As of this morning he wasn't I.D.'d."

"The picture in the paper wasn't all that good, Fallon."

"Not to you, maybe."

"Knock it off and let's go."

"Drop dead," I said and held out my open wallet.

After a few seconds he said, "Son-of-a-bitch. A reporter. An *effing* newspaper reporter. Now who the hell would give you a job as a reporter?"

"Orley News Service, Charlie. They believe that criminals can be rehabilitated. Ergo . . . I have a reason for being here since I can write a great personal piece on the deceased."

"Ergo shit," he said.

"If you want to check my credentials . . ."

"Go screw yourself and get out of here."

"Ease off. The past is behind us."

"Not as far as I'm concerned," he said. "You'll always be just a lousy cop who took a payoff and loused things up for the rest of us. It's too bad that con didn't kill you up at Sing."

"Squeaky took that knife for me," I reminded him.

"So pay your last respects and blow."

"My pleasure, Captain." I put my wallet back and walked across the room. At the door I stopped and looked back. "Your leg ever hurt when it rains?"

"I don't owe you any favors for deflecting a slug for me, Fallon. I've taken three since then."

"Too bad," I grinned. "That hole in my side still bugs me."

Why some women look naked with their clothes on is beyond me, but with Cheryl I finally figured it out. She was what I called posture-naked. She always did those damn things that made a man look at her, like bending stiff-legged over the bottom drawer of the filing cabinet so that her mini-skirt hiked up to her hips, or leaning across my desk in those loose-fitting peasant blouses so that I forgot whatever she was trying to point out to me.

When I walked into the office Orley News Service had provided me with, she was scratching her tail with the utter abandon of a little kid and I said, "Will you stop that!"

"I'm itchy."

"What've you got?"

Cheryl glared at me a second, then laughed. "Nothing. I'm peeling. I got my behind sunburned skinny-dipping in my friend's pool."

"Great guys you go with."

"My friend is a girl I was in the chorus line with. She married a millionaire."

"Why didn't you do the same thing?"

"I have ambition."

"To be a typist?"

"Orley pays me as a secretary and researcher."

"They're wasting their money," I said.

She gave me that silly smirk of hers that irritated the hell out of me. "So I'm a sex object the brass likes to keep around."

"Yeah, but why around me?"

"Maybe you need help."

"Not that kind."

"That kind especially."

"Everybody was safer when you were a social worker."

"Parole officer."

"Same difference."

"Like hell," she said. Then her eyes went into that startling directness and she asked, "What happened this morning?"

"It was Squeaky. He's dead."

"Then write the story and stay out of it."

"Don't play parole officer with me, kiddo."

Her eyes wouldn't let me alone. "You know what your job is."

"Squeaky saved my ass for me," I said.

"And now he's dead." She studied my face for a long stretch of time, then caught her lower lip between her teeth. "You know why?"

I swung around in my chair and looked out the window over the Manhattan skyline. It wasn't very pretty any more. Absolute cubism had taken over architectural design. The city used to be sexy. Now it was passing into its menopause. "No," I said.

"In the pig's ass you don't," Cheryl told me softly. "Don't forget what your job is. You stick your neck out and everybody gets hurt."

When the door shut to the outer office I pulled the little cassette tape from my pocket and shoved it into the recorder. I wanted to hear it again just to be sure.

And Squeaky sure had a hell of a story to tell in a matter of two and a half minutes.

He had come out of the big house after a six-year stretch and opened a radio repair shop just off Seventh Avenue, made enough bread to consider marrying a chubby little streetwalker who lived in the next tenement and got himself killed before he got on the freebie list in exchange for marital security. But that part wasn't on the tape. That part I knew because we had kept in touch.

The tape was a recording of two voices, one wondering how the hell the Old Man was going to get eight hundred pounds of solid gold out of the country into Europe and the other telling him not to sweat it because anybody who could get it together could get it out and with the prices they were paying for the stuff over there it was all worth the risk even if five people had already been killed putting it into one lump. All they had to do was knock off the mechanic who had made it possible and they got their share and to hell with it.

The miserable little bastard, I thought. He had taken a cassette recorder with a built-in microphone into the restaurant to work on it during his lunch hour and picked up the conversation in the next booth. The trouble was he knew one of the guys by his voice and tried to put the bite on him for a lousy grand.

But they didn't call him Squeaky for nothing. His voice went across to the other end and he was staked out for a kill before he knew what was happening. All he could do was send me the tape and try to get into protective custody before they nailed him, and he never did make the top steps of the Criminal Courts Building. Whoever was protecting eight hundred pounds of solid gold for overseas shipment had taken a chip off the lump and paid for a contract kill on my old cellblock buddy.

Peg it at one hundred bucks an ounce minimum and eight hundred pounds came to damn near a million and a quarter bucks. Less the cost of shipping and a few dead bodies. One was Squeaky's.

Little idiot. He was too hysterical trying to run out a few inches of tape to remember to identify the guys on the other segment. All I had was their voices and the single name, *the Old Man.*

I stuck the tape in the envelope with the graphic voice print pattern Eddie Connors had pulled for me and filed it in the back of the drawer with my bills and locked it shut. My stomach had that ugly feeling again and I was remembering how blood smelled when it was all spread out in a pool on hot pavement and that half-open eye of Squeaky Williams was looking at me from under the frozen eyelid. I said something dirty under my breath and pulled the .45 out from the desk and stuck it in my belt.

Everything was going to hell and I couldn't care less. All I could remember was Squeaky stepping in front of that knife Water Head Ardmore had tried to shove into me just because I had been a cop.

A lot of them wouldn't look at me because I had gone sour, but there were those who had done exactly what I had done without making the mistake of getting caught, and the burly lieutenant was one of them and couldn't take the chance of not meeting me without taking the chance of me pulling the string on him. He was as uncomfortable as hell because he had been forced into it, and even though he had cut himself loose, he had done it and damn well knew it.

We sat together in the back of the Chinese restaurant and over the chow mein I said, "Who's collecting gold, Al?"

"Who isn't?"

"I'm talking about a million and a quarter's worth."

"It's illegal," he said, "except for manufacturing purposes."

"Sure, and it's too heavy to ship. But that didn't stop them from forming it into aircraft seat brackets, phoney partitions and faked machine parts."

Al Grossino forked up another mouthful of noodles and glared at me. "Look, I haven't heard of . . ."

"Don't crap me, Al. They've reopened the old mines since the price went up and technology advanced to the point where they can make them productive. Those companies are processing the stuff on the site to cut costs. It's all government supervised and if there has been any rumbles you're in the position to know it."

"Damn it, Fallon . . ."

"You make me push it and I will," I said.

He waited a few seconds, his eyes passing me to survey the rest of the place until he was satisfied. "Hell, you're always going to get the looters. Small-time crap."

"What's the rumble?"

He gave a small shrug of resignation and said, "Two Nevada outfits and one in Arizona are hassling with the unions. They started missing stuff before it got to the ingot stage. So far nothing's showed up on the New York market."

"As far as you know anyway."

"Don't lip me, Fallon."

I grinned and waited.

Al Grossino said, "We got a wire to keep an eye out but so far it doesn't look like anything. Those companies will use any excuse for a tax deduction."

"Horseshit."

"You that dumb that you don't know how the feds cover every grain of gold mined in this country?"

"You that dumb that you don't know the difference between the official price and the black market?" I said.

"Okay, so the speculators . . ."

"Crap on the speculators. Spell it out in hard language. Who are the biggest speculators over here? Who built Las Vegas? Who handles the narcotics traffic? Who . . ."

"The mob isn't moving into gold, Fallon," he snapped. "They're too damned smart to play around with currency."

"Why do they handle counterfeit?" I asked him with a nasty grin.

He threw his napkin down and swallowed the last of his cold tea. "Make your point and let me get out of here."

"Find out how much those companies think they're missing," I said.

"Why?"

"I'm a reporter, remember?"

"It's hard to picture you that way."

"Your time might come, Al. By the way, who's the Old Man?"

"Hell, you're not that stupid, Fallon. You were in the army. You were a cop. Anybody who runs anything is the Old Man." He picked up his hat, stuck me with the check and left me sitting there.

I looked at the cop on the door, showed my press card and took a handful of garbage from him until I spotted Lucas of the *News* inside and read him off with some language from the U.S. Constitution and

walked into Charlie Watts running an interrogation scene on a weepy
Marlene Peters. He was backed up by two detectives and an assistant
D.A. But the chunky little street hustler who had been slated to marry
Squeaky Williams had been busted too often not to know all the tricks,
and now she was turning on her ultimate weapon of salty tears. She
had the guardians of civic virtue all shook up. Lucas was there ready
to put it all down and I was wondering who had the warrant or did
they get themselves invited in.

Apparently I was a welcome relief and my old commander said, "I
was expecting to see you sooner or later."

"Which one is it?"

"Sooner," he said. "No doubt you know the lady."

"No doubt."

"Professionally?"

"I never paid for it yet, Charlie."

The D.A.'s man couldn't have been out of his twenties and made
the mistake of saying, "What the hell are you doing here?"

I said, "I'm about to throw your ass out of here, kid. I mean physically and with blood all over the place unless you ease on out of here
on your own. And take your friends with you."

Charlie Watts made a real grin, hoping something would happen,
but I was right about the warrant. They didn't have one. That's why
they all got up and glanced at the red-faced D.A.'s man, and Lucas
put his notes away with disgust, reading the whole thing right down
to the button. I waited until the door was closed, then tossed my hat
on the table and said, "How're you doing, Marlene?"

There weren't any tears now. She was dry-eyed and scared, but not
because the cops had been there. Her tongue kept flicking over her
lips and she couldn't keep her hands still at all. "Please, Fallon . . ."

"You worried about me?"

"No."

"You love Squeaky?"

"A little bit. He was the only guy who ever wanted to marry me."

"You know why he was killed?"

"Yes."

That crawly feeling went up my spine again. "Why?"

"He didn't tell me. He just knew something, that's all. He said he
could prove it and it would make us the big bundle that could get us
the hell out of this town. He had a tape recording of something."

"Oh?"

She spun around, eyes as big as wristwatches. "But I don't have it!
He sent it to somebody just before he went up to see that judge who

sentenced him and told me to get out quick — and all of a sudden he was dead."

"Why didn't you go?"

"Are you kidding?" She covered her face with her hands and this time the tears were for real. "Why do you think the street's so empty for? They're outside waiting for me, that's why. Shit, I'm dead too. I'm as dead as Squeaky and I don't even know what for."

"You're not dead, Marlene."

"Go look out the window. There's a car on each end of the street. Oh, you won't see anybody. They're just waiting there for the right time and when you all leave I'm nothing more than a dead screwed-up whore who crossed up her pimp and got her throat cut for the trouble."

"So I won't leave." I pulled her hands away from her face. "Squeaky say anything at all? Come on, think about it."

Marlene shook her head and pulled away from me. "Let me alone."

"That didn't answer the question."

"What difference does it make?"

"No sense dying, is there?"

The tone of my voice got her then and she turned around. "I'm not talking to any cops."

"I'm an ex-con," I said, "Squeaky's old roommate, remember?"

"He wanted to marry me. He really did."

"I know."

"I would have, too. He wasn't much, but nobody else ever asked me."

"Somebody will. What did he tell you?"

"Nothing. All he said was he knew who the rat was and this time he'd put him in his hole." She made a pathetic gesture with her hands and her eyes got wet again. "How am I going to get out of here?"

"I'll take you," I said.

So we went downstairs to the back of the landing and felt our way to the basement steps, inching our way past the garbage and the empty baby carriages until we made the crumbling concrete steps that led out to the rear court and the night and stood there long enough before we crossed to the rotted fence that separated her building from the one opposite, ducking under the hanging wash and skirting the crushed cartons and tipped-over garbage cans.

But they had been guarding the night longer than we had and their vision was adjusted to the dark so that when the first cough of a muted gun spit out all I saw was the flash and felt a slug breeze by. All I could do was shove her aside while I clawed at the .45 in my belt.

The white spit came again, then another, but this time I had the big end of the Colt and the roar of the blast tore the night open, whose only echo was a choking, gurgling gasp, until I heard the little whimper from my left and feet slamming away in front of me.

I said, "Marlene . . . ?"

And the little whimper answered, "He really would have married me. You know that, don't you?"

I lit a match and looked into blank, dead eyes. "I know, kid," I said.

Windows were banging open and someplace a woman screamed. Some guy was swearing into the night and another nut had a flashlight trying to probe into the darkness but couldn't tell where it had all come from. I walked over to the fence, found the body and lit another match.

The guy didn't have much of a face left at all. But he did have a wallet in his right hip pocket and I put it in mine and got out just as the guy with the flashlight almost picked me out of the shadows.

Maybe my guts should have been all churned up again. Maybe that crawly feeling should have had my shoulders tight as hell. In an hour Charlie Watts would have an APB out on me and in two hours the papers would be running the old story on the front pages with my pictures in the centerfold or even splashed on page one and there wouldn't be any place at all for me to surface.

But for the first time in a long time I felt nice and easy.

I even wished I had Cheryl handy.

Fallon, you slob, I thought, *you got a real death desire.*

Somebody else did too . . . now. They had a man dead and knew this kind of an ex-con didn't let his old cellmate down. And wherever he was, the Old Man would be sweating because the possibility was there that a real live killer knew about all that gold just waiting to reach the European market.

Ma Christy was one of those old-time New York pros with no eyes, ears or memory who ran a boarding house right close to the docks where the Cunards used to unload and all she did was point with her thumb and say, "The broad's in number two, Fallon."

I told her thanks and went up to where Cheryl was waiting in the dingy room with a hamburger in one fist and a copy of the *News* in the other. At least this time I was well on the inside pages and when she looked at me over the top of the sheet she said, "You sure did it, boss man."

"Pull your skirt down. Ma thinks I rented the room for an assignation."

"It's too short. Besides, assignation sounds like a dirty word."

"There's only one 'ass' in it."

"A pity," she said.

I closed the door and locked it, then crossed the room and pulled the blinds closed. She still hadn't looked up from the paper. "What did you get?"

"You're wanted for murder," Cheryl told me.

"Great," I said.

"His name was Arthur Littleworth, alias Shim Little, alias Little Shim, alias Soho Little, alias . . ."

"I know."

"Contract killer out of Des Moines, Iowa. The .357 Magnum he carried was the same one used in two other hits, one in Los Angeles, one in New York."

"Which one in the city?"

"Your friend's. Squeaky's."

"They have an angle on it, don't they?"

"Sure. He was in the can with Squeaky before you were. They were enemies."

"I don't remember him."

"He got out before you got in. I checked the dates. Your hit was pure retribution." She put the paper down and watched me with those big round eyes of hers. "You're on everybody's kill list now."

"How about that?" I said.

"Why do you have to ask for it?"

"Screw it. What do you care?"

"You don't know much about women, do you?"

"Kitten, I've been there and back."

"Learn anything?"

"Enough to stay away from you sex objects," I told her.

"One phone call and you'd be busted."

"So would you, doll."

"I'm no virgin."

"But there are other ways and the busting hurts worse."

"Sounds interesting."

"Try me," I said.

"Maybe later."

"You're lucky. Right now I'm spooky of little typists with a sex drive."

I got that silly grin again. "You bastard," she said. "Why do I have to be torn between duty and schoolgirl love?"

"What do I look like to you?"

"A big ugly bum with a record. You don't even know how to dress properly. Ex-cop, ex-con, neophyte reporter, currently wanted criminal."

"Thanks," I said. "It's been a stinking two days."

"Can I help you out?"

"Feel like being an accessory?"

She looked at the half-made bed and grinned again. "Sometimes I wonder about myself."

"Ummm?"

"I talk better when I'm being loved," she said.

We lay there a little while afterwards and she said, "You haven't got any chance at all, you know that."

"Who ever did?"

"It was all decided a long time ago."

"No Kismet crap, baby."

"Face reality. Your whole future was based on programmed performance."

"Screw it, parole officer."

"It was an assigned risk." She was looking at the ceiling, deadly serious. "They thought it would be worth it."

"They forgot about the incidental factors," I said.

"He was only a person in the same cell."

"Try living in prison. See what the person in the upper bunk is like."

"Worth dying for?"

"Isn't everybody?"

"Us too?"

"All I'm doing is screwing . . . not saying 'I love you, sweetheart.' "

"Screwing's enough for a parole officer," she told me.

"Not for a typist," I said. "Now tell me what you found out."

"Charlie thinks you'd be better off dead."

"Nice."

"He's not the only one. There's a contract out on you."

"That's what I figured," I said, then turned over and wrapped my arm around all that lovely soft flesh and fell asleep. I still was feeling nice and easy. My last coherent thought was how far a doll would go for a guy.

The thing they call gold fever is a thing you can't hide. Like giving the clap to your wife and the neighbor next door. So your wife won't squeal, but the neighbor will when she gives it to her husband and he's peeing red peppers in the bowl and hanging onto the rafters while he howls and he's ready to blow the whistle on everybody.

And gold sure makes them pee.

Loco Bene was so terrified of seeing a first-rate killer standing in front of his bed that he damned near browned out at the sight of the dirty end of a .45 and said, "No shit, Fallon, I never heard of nuthin' except what gets talked up on the street."

"Bene . . . you roomed with Shim Little." I was remembering what Cheryl had filled me in on.

"Yeah, yeah, I know. We wasn't no pals, though. Just because he had a couple of mob connections we were just crap to him."

"Okay, Loco, you've done your share of the delivery work in the narcotics rackets. How're the new routes set up?"

"Come on, come on! Like you're givin' me a choice between who knocks me off. If them routes get tapped, you think they won't know who was talking? Besides, they're all incoming tracks. I never ship outside."

"Loco, the word's out. There's gold going to be passed and you're a first-class route man. Don't tell me you haven't heard any buzz on it."

"Fallon . . ."

I thumbed the hammer back and the metallic snick sounded like thunder.

He swallowed first, then made a gesture with his shoulders. "Sure, I heard some talk. Like somebody wants to contact Gibbons only they don't know he's pullin' a stretch in a Mexican jail."

"Adrian Gibbons?"

"Sure. He used to handle heavy stuff, mostly expensive machine parts. He was an artist the way he could build them into cheap gizmos to fake out the inspectors. Never had a bust until he tried to rape that Mex chick."

"They won't ship gold like that," I said. "Who else are they looking for?"

"Nobody tells me . . . hell, the Chinaman turned down an offer because he's still hot from that picture deal he made with the museum. And anyway, he uses legit routes. But gold . . ."

"Who's the Mechanic, Loco?"

"Huh?"

"You heard me."

"Like for cars . . . or a card sharp?"

"Who would Shim Little call the Mechanic?"

His hands pulled at each other and he wet his lips down again. "Was a guy in the joint they called the Mechanic, only he used to set up cars to run hash and junk in from across the border."

"Remember his name?"

"Naw, but he had a double eight on the end of his number. He got out before me. Now how about laying off, Fallon? I gave you . . ."

I eased the hammer down on the rod and stuck it back in my belt. "Maybe I'll come around again, Loco," I said. "So keep your ears open."

The television and newspaper coverage I had gotten over that damned back yard shootout had turned me into a night person. Every cop in the department would be alerted and there weren't many of the street people you could afford to take a chance on. Not when you knew they wouldn't mind scoring a few brownie points with the cops by pointing a finger your way. But there were a few no better off than myself and these were the ones with the best antennae in the system because it was their best survival device and they had words to say.

Cheryl's information had been exact, all right. A fat, open contract was out on me, and some new faces with old reputations had shown up in places I generally frequented. O'Malley, the doorman at my apartment building, who was a real, solid buddy, was glad to hear from me and was pretty damn sure somebody had my place staked out. He was going to pack a change of clothes for me and leave them in his locker in the basement, with the private rear entrance key stashed over the doorsill. Long ago I had anticipated a possible tap on the office phone line and had arranged an alternate communication system with Cheryl. She was picking up the same information, going through repeated questioning by the police, the reporters and two of the D.A.'s men.

There was an irritated note in her voice when she said, "You're going to blow this one sure as hell, Fallon."

"It's too late now to cut out."

"You know better than that," she said.

"Sure," I told her. "I can prove self-defense and claim the gun was one of Squeaky's but who gets that contract lifted off me?"

"That's the odd part, isn't it?"

"Damn odd. It's too high a price to pay for an ex-con who knocked off a punk hit man, but when you're protecting somebody who's sitting on a big lump of gold, it's only like paying a nuisance tax."

"Okay, don't lecture me. Just tell me what to do."

What I wanted, I told her, was to find a guy they referred to as the Mechanic. I gave her the approximate dates of his stay in the joint and the last two digits of his number. She was to get those voice print patterns and the tape from my file, that Japanese mini recorder I had, and meet me at Ma Christy's at two A.M. That gave her just four hours.

Then I went back into the night again. Somebody had to know who the Mechanic was, and if the Old Man was scheduling him for a kill too, the quickest way to flush him out was to put the word around. Whatever the Mechanic was doing would get jammed in a hurry if he knew the payoff was to be made with a bullet. All that gold was just too big and too heavy to be moved around without somebody getting wise, so it would have to be shipped in a pretty special way. Small parcels would involve just too many different operations, too many people and accumulated risks, so my bet was that it would go as a single unit directly to a market. All I had to know was where it was, who had it and how it was going. And what I was going to do about it if I ever found out.

Sure, I could lay the story on Charlie Watts and the good captain would dutifully process it, but if this were a possible mob operation there were always those pipelines into the bureaucratic maze of officialdom that would send out the warning signal and all that yellow metal would go right back into hiding until another time.

No, I wanted one shot at it myself first.

By midnight I had the story out in three different quarters and had picked up a little more on Shim Little. He was a loner who shuttled around between cheap midtown motels, never keeping a permanent address, always seemed to have enough money in his pocket and didn't have any regular friends anyone remembered. A few times he was seen with the same guy, a nondescript type who didn't talk much, but Paddy Ables, the night bartender at the Remote Grill, said he knew the guy packed a gun and the couple of times he saw him he had an out-of-state newspaper with him. He couldn't remember the name, but it had a big eagle in the masthead. Paddy was pretty nervous talking to me, so I told him thanks and left.

Outside, a fine mist was blowing in from the river and you could smell the rain in the air.

I walked down Seventh Avenue to the cross street the builders hadn't gotten around to remodeling yet, sniffing at the acrid smells that were worn into the bricks like grease in an old frying pan, and turned west to the last address Shim Little had used. It was a decrepit hotel with rooms by the day or week but used mostly by the hour or minute by the jaded whores hitting the leftover trade from Broadway or the idiot tourists who thought getting clapped up or rolled in New York would make a great story to tell in the locker rooms back home.

The young kid with the dirty fingernails behind the desk made my type but not my face and was satisfied with a quick look at my press card and a five-buck tip to tell me that the cops had scoured Shim Little's room and come up with nothing but a suitcase of personal belongings and a portable radio. As far as he knew Little never had any guests and never said anything, either.

I asked, "How about dames?"

His eyes made a joke of it. "You kidding? What kind of a place you think this is?"

"So he didn't bring any in."

"All he had to do was knock on any door. This is a permanent H.Q. for two dozen three-way ten-buck hookers. A few even got super specialties if you're a weirdo."

I let him see another five and he flicked it out of my fingers. "What was he?"

He waved a thumb toward the tiny lobby. A chunky broad in a short tight dress was coming through the doors, her face grim with fatigue. "Ask Sophia there. She knew the guy." He made a motion with his head and when she spotted me the grim look disappeared like somebody turned a switch and the professional smile flashed across her face. She didn't even bother to be introduced. She simply hooked her arm into mine and took me up two flights to her room, unlocked the door and had her clothes off in half a minute. She turned around, held out her hand and said, "Ten bucks and take your pick."

I gave her a twenty and told her to put her clothes back on. Between the appendectomy slash, the caesarean scar, an ass full of striation marks and a shaved pussy red-flecked with pimples from a dull razor, she didn't exactly radiate my kind of sexuality.

But for the twenty she did what she was told. "You a freak?" she asked curiously. "I got some dresses if you like it with clothes on."

"Just a conversationalist," I told her.

This time her smile was tired and real. "Oh, great, mister." She flopped into a chair and yanked the black wig off her head. Her hair was a short mop of tight curls. "Tonight I'm glad to see you. It's been rough here. Now, you want dirty talk, the story of my sex life, some . . ."

"Information."

Her eyes narrowed down a little bit. "You can't be a cop because you already passed the bread."

"Reporter, Sophia."

"What the hell have I got to say? You doing a piece on whores? Hell, man, who needs to research that? All you have to do is . . ."

"Shim Little."

"Man, he's dead." Her face said that's about all she was going to say.

"I know," I told her. "I killed him."

She recognized me then. She was remembering the photos in the paper and was putting it all together and letting her imagination gouge horrible thoughts in her mind. "Mister . . . ," her voice was hoarse and scared. "I only laid him twice. Just a straight job. He was . . . okay."

"He lived here for two weeks, kid. Don't tell me you don't know about your neighbors."

"So we talked a little bit. He wasn't much of a talker. In this business you're on and off if you want to make a buck."

"How much did he pay you?"

"Fifty . . . both times. He was a good tipper. You don't get many like that."

"With him you'd spend a little extra time the second time around."

"Why not?"

I grinned at her and it scared her again. "Where'd he get his loot?"

"Honest, mister . . . hell, we just . . ."

My grin got bigger and she wiped the back of her mouth with her hand. "He was . . . one of the boys. Not very big. He wanted me to think so but I could tell. He said he had a nice safe job now and laughed when he said it. Yeah, he really laughed at that, but I didn't go asking any nosy damn fool questions. He was the kind who could get mean as hell and he had that crazy gun with him all the time. He even put it on the other pillow while we were screwing."

"No names?"

"Just that it was the safest job he ever had. He kept laughing about it."

"How about friends?"

"Not around here. I saw him on Eighth Avenue once with some guy, that's all."

I got up and she shrank back into her chair. "I don't have to remind you to forget about making any telephone calls, do I?"

"Mister," she said. "You got your conversation, I got my bread, now just let's forget it."

"Good enough." I looked at my watch. It was quarter to two.

Cheryl had beaten me to Ma Christy's by five minutes and had a bag of hamburgers and a container of coffee ready for me when I got there. She had deliberately dressed as sloppily as she could, using no makeup at all with a hairpiece I hated pegged to her head, but even the attempt at disguise couldn't quite hide all that woman if you looked hard enough.

I said, "Hello, gorgeous."

"Two detectives were covering my apartment. They were expecting a ravishing creature."

"No trouble?"

"They're still back watching out for Miss Ravishing. I exited through the building next door just to be sure."

"Bring the stuff?"

"Yeah, but eat first."

I had forgotten how hungry I was and wolfed down the chow. When I finished I pulled the notes from the manila envelope she had brought and spread them out on the bed. The contacts had come through and it was all there.

The guy they called the Mechanic was one Henry Borden, fifty-nine years old, arrested for possession and selling of narcotics, suspected of reworking car bodies for transportation of illegal items. By trade he was a tool and die man, sheetmetal worker, and was currently employed in an aluminum casting foundry in Brooklyn. His current address was down in the Village.

Little things were beginning to tie in now. The connecting link was *metal*.

I took the package, slid it under the rickety dresser without disturbing any of the dust and said, "Let's take a ride."

"Now?"

"Now," I told her.

"You look like you could use some rest," she said impishly.

"No. I have to keep what strength I have."

Downstairs we picked up a cab on the corner and gave an address two blocks from Henry Borden's and walked the rest of the way. The drizzle had started and we had the empty street to ourselves. We found the house number and the basement apartment Borden occupied and didn't have any trouble getting in at all because whoever had been there before us didn't bother to lock up on the way out.

He had just left the Mechanic lying there with his throat cut almost all the way through in a huge glob of blood that was draining toward the back of the room on the warped floor.

The apartment was too small to take long to search, but the frisk had been efficient enough. Everything was turned inside out, including the pockets of everything he owned, with an empty billfold lying in plain sight to give the earmarks of a robbery. Even the lining of Borden's work jacket had been torn loose and the zipper pocket yanked off. Still dangling from the flap were two ball point pens and a small clip-on screwdriver. I tugged them off, tossed the screwdriver on the chair and stuck the pens in my own pocket. Borden wasn't going to use them again.

In back of me, Cheryl was beginning to gag. I got her outside, walked her until she felt better, then grabbed a cab and got her back home. She went in through the other building and I went back to Ma Christy's. Nobody followed me.

For a little while I sat on the edge of the bed and listened to the tape again on the mini recorder. The voices were talking about knocking off the Mechanic, which completed the job, and the stuff would be ready to ship. Well, now it was ready to go and I'd fall with it. I took out my pen and jotted down a few notes for tomorrow. It skipped on the paper so I put it down and used the other one. I finished what I was doing before I saw the printed name on the pen. It read, *Reading Associates, Rare Books, First Editions.* The address was on Madison Avenue in the lower fifties. I looked at the other pen. It was another cheap giveaway with *MacIntosh and Stills, Aluminum Casting* printed on it. I shrugged and flopped back on the bed. I was asleep in a minute.

So the old cop instinct comes out and you check all the possibilities, but the con instinct was there too and you do it as unobtrusively as possible because you know about the eyes that are watching and how fast it could end if you weren't careful.

I checked the papers, but the morning editions didn't have anything at all about the body down in the Village and unless somebody purposely checked in on Henry Borden he might not even be found until the odors of decomposition started to smell up the neighborhood.

At ten-thirty I took the elevator up to the fourth floor of the building that housed Reading Associates. It was a multi-office operation with a staff of a dozen or so and already getting some traffic from some elderly scholarly types. A few collegiate types were browsing through the racks and examining manuscripts in the glass-topped cases.

I wasn't much of an authority on rare books, but apparently the collectors were a breed apart and assumed anyone there had to be an enthusiast. A tiny old guy gave me a friendly nod and immediately wanted to know if I was going to exhibit at the show. I faked my way around the question and let him do the talking. He had already attended the one in Los Angeles, was going to be at the one here in New York next week, but unfortunately had to skip the one in London the end of the month. Of course, the main event would be the Chicago showing in six weeks where it was hoped some new finds would be put on display.

I even shook hands with Mr. Reading himself, an owlish man in his middle thirties with thick glasses and a bright smile who was in the middle of three conversations at once. The main topic seemed to be the surprise he was preparing for the Chicago exhibit.

When I broke loose I roamed around long enough to get a quick look into the offices, but there was nothing more than the crackle of papers coming from any of them. The door to Reading's office stood wide open, a book-lined room with a single antique desk stacked with papers and an archaic safe with the door swung out stuffed full of folders.

I was about to leave when a pair of magazine photographers I recognized came in and I squeezed back behind the shelves, backing into a smudged-faced girl in a smock and knocking the waste basket out of her hands. She let out a startled, "Oh!"

I said, "Sorry, Miss," and bent down to put the junk back in the basket.

She laughed and brushed her hair out of her eyes. "Here, let me do that. You'll get your hands all dirty and you know what Mr. Reading thinks about that." She picked up the used carbons and stencils, wrapped a paper around the mimeograph ink cans and the two paint spray cans, dropped the empty beer bottle on top of the lot and edged around me.

The photographers were clustered around Reading, pointing out something in the cases, and when I had a clear field I went back to the corridor and punched the button for the elevator.

It was a good try, but that's all it was. A real, fat fizzle.

When I reached the street the rain had started again, but it gave me a good excuse for keeping my head tipped down under my hat. I went across town to the big newsstand that carried out-of-state papers and scanned the racks without finding any with the big eagle in the masthead. I tried one more and didn't make it there either. The later local editions were out, but there still wasn't any mention of Henry Borden's death.

Time was always on the side of the killer when these things happened. You can't just let them drop when you trip over them no matter what the score is. I found an empty booth in a Times Square cigar store, looked up MacIntosh and Stills in Brooklyn and got an irritated manager on the other end. When I asked him if Borden had been in he half-shouted. "That bastard hasn't shown all day and we're sitting here with an order ready to go out."

"Maybe something's wrong with him," I suggested.

"Sure. We let him use our tools to do a moonlight job and now he forgets where they belong. He's the only guy here who can handle this damn job, but if he doesn't get his ass in we'll damn well do without him."

"I'll go check on him."

"Somebody oughta," he said and hung up.

I checked by calling 911, the police emergency number, and told them where to look for a mutilated corpse and didn't bother to leave my name. I made one more call to Al Grossino and arranged for a meet at nine o'clock. That was still a long way off and I didn't want to go prowling around the city in the daylight. The answer was in a crummy little bar on Eighth Avenue that didn't believe in overlighting and didn't care how long you sipped at a beer as long as you kept them coming.

By six o'clock I was starting to feel bloated and was ready to cut out, but the TV news came on and the pre-show rundown made a big splash about another gruesome killing in Manhattan, so I called for another brew. It was great coverage, all right. They didn't show any body shots, but the announcer on the street was giving a running commentary on what the police had found after an anonymous tip. Half the residents in the neighborhood were gawking and waving into the camera or pointing at the rubber body bag being loaded into the morgue wagon, but by that time I had stopped listening and was watching the background, because there was one character there standing on his toes to look over the heads in front and folded in his pocket was a newspaper with a big, rangy eagle in the masthead. He walked out of camera range as I was leaving for the phone booth in the back of the room, and this time I didn't have to leave my name because Charlie Watts recognized my voice the second I said hello to him.

"You coming in, Fallon?"

"You want another commendation in your file, Charlie?"

"They don't give out medals for nailing people like you."

"How about that body with its throat cut?"

Charlie let a beat go by, then: "I'm listening."

"Your guy got himself on television tonight without realizing it. A real good shot, front face and profile. He's on the six o'clock news with a newspaper in his pocket . . . one with an eagle across the front."

"How do you know?"

"Check him out, buddy. You'll have his mug shots somewhere. If that's his hometown newspaper you can go through his local department. I got the feeling this guy's still got some of the amateur left in him. No pro is going back to make sure the body is growing cold."

"You ought to know."

"Get with the legwork, Charlie. You don't have to say thanks." I cradled the receiver before he could get a trace through, left a buck on the counter for the bartender and went out to join the rush hour crowd getting home. I had spent too much time in the same clothes and was getting sloppy and soggy looking. Right then I could smell myself and I didn't feel like getting tapped for being a bum, so I hustled up the avenue, turned east where the buildings partially kept the rain off me and headed toward the street that ran behind my building.

It took better than a half-hour and nobody was around to see the underground route I took to my own place. I crossed the yard behind Patsy's, pushed the boards in the fence out so I could squeeze through and went in the rear entrance to the service personnel's locker room.

O'Malley had left everything I needed, including a shaving kit and a towel. When I had showered and gotten the beard off my face I changed into my fresh clothes, packed the old stuff back into the locker and slid the .45 under my belt.

Outside the thunder rumbled and I slung my raincoat on. Something was bugging me and I couldn't quite reach out and touch it. Squeaky had handed it to me on a platter, but killing one lousy punk had thrown the whole thing out of kilter. All I had to do was sit through an interrogation by the cops and everything would have been blown sky high. Routine police work could have jammed the entire operation, but Squeaky had to go and try to take a bite out of it. Damn it, that nice little guy was a born loser and he went down the hard way, scared half out of his mind with no way out. He didn't even have sense enough to let somebody else make that call to Shim Little, and him with a voice you could spot like a snowball in a coalpile.

Now the operation had bought its time and I was the only one who could stop the clock. But I couldn't surface very easily and they'd know that too, so all the options were on their side.

That little bug inside kept nagging at me. It had a big grinning face like it knew all the answers and I did too, only I couldn't put it together like the bug did.

Darkness had finally settled in and I went into it gratefully. I edged around the row of plastic garbage bags and headed for the fence, my hand feeling for the loose boards. I was halfway through when I realized how stupid I had been, because there were other people who thought like I did too.

But this one's stupidity was not putting the boards back the way I had left them and I had the bare second to dive and roll under the knife blade that hacked a huge sliver out of the post above my head and there wasn't a chance in the world of reaching for the gun I had buried under my clothes.

He didn't get a second chance with the blade because this was my kind of fight and my boot caught his elbow and the steel clattered against the concrete walkway. I had a fistful of hair, yanking his face into the dirt beside me, one fist driving into his ribs and he tried to let out a yell but the ground muffled it all.

For ten seconds he turned tiger, then I flipped him over, got my knee against his spine, my forearm locked under his chin and arched him like a bow until there was a sudden crack from inside him and he went death-limp in my hands.

He should have used the gun he kept in the shoulder sling, or maybe he just enjoyed the steel more. Or he never should have gotten into the pro ranks in the big town. There wasn't any wallet on him, or any keys, but he wouldn't be too hard to identify. The newspaper was still in his pocket, a three-day-old weekly from a small town in Florida.

What really was interesting came out of his side pocket. He had sixty bucks in tens and fives and ten one-hundreds. Only the C notes had been torn in half and somebody else was holding the other sections. I had to grin at that old dodge. It was a neat piece of insurance to make sure somebody got a job done and could prove it before he collected the other part of his loot. I took the sixty bucks and two of the torn bills and tucked them in my billfold.

I almost missed something else, but it flashed in the light and I took that too and the little bug inside me grinned bigger.

Al Grossino huddled behind the wheel of the car, filling the interior with foul-smelling cigar smoke. He handed me two sheets of paper, and I said, "Just tell me, Al."

"Those companies keep up a constant weighing system. That gold got lost before it was poured into ingots. The Nevada bunch think they figured it out. It was siphoned off with the same vacuums they use to pick up the residue on the floor."

"Somebody would be checking the containers."

"They found a by-pass."

"Yeah?"

"Three guys walked off the job a month ago. Security ran checks on their job records and they were all phoney."

"So it was engineered," I said.

Al wouldn't commit himself besides a shrug. "Could be. It's a federal case now."

"What was the final count?"

"About a thousand pounds."

"That's one hell of a bundle of loot."

He took another deep pull on the cigar and looked at me. "Who's got it, Fallon?"

"You want to be a hero?"

"Why not?"

"Let's make it some other time."

"You're getting to own me this time, buddy."

"Fine. I'll make you half-hero." I told him where to look to find a dead man and how he could play it if he were smart, then I backed out of the car and watched while he drove off.

When I called Cheryl from the booth on the corner I gave her the code message that meant an immediate meet and in twenty minutes I saw her coming toward me. She passed me in the doorway while I made sure she wasn't being followed, then when she crossed and doubled back I went over to join her.

"Any trouble?"

"That car was still there."

"Charlie's men?"

"Department registration. I checked."

"What about the office?"

"They have a man there too."

"Any squawks from Orley?"

"I didn't want to give you the bad news," she said.

"So?"

"You, my friend, are under the boom. They're about to lower it."

"A hell of a way to end a career." I grinned at her.

"Well, if the worst comes to the worst, I'll support you." She kissed her fingertip and touched my mouth with it.

"I like it better the other way around. Maybe Orley will see it my way." Then I told her what had happened and even in the dim light from the street I could see her go pale.

She shook her head a little sadly. "They won't see anything now. You know how fast Charlie can work when he wants to. He'll pull out every stop just to nail your hide."

"But if I come up with the big package it won't hurt so bad." I gave her hand a squeeze. "Your training with parolees ever teach you anything?"

"Just to keep my skirt down and my blouse buttoned up with the ones fresh out."

"How about breaking and entering?"

"I've read up on the subject."

"Let's give it a try." I took out the two half-bills, scribbled a note across one and told her what to do. She repeated the instructions back to me, her mouth tight with worry, but she knew the score and she knew the alternatives and didn't question what I told her. The thing could go two ways now, but when you consider egos or fear or reprisals you could place your bets with the odds slightly in your favor and hope Lady Luck would give you the edge you needed. At least she seemed to frown on trivial stupidity and minor coincidences when they both locked hands to build a beautiful infield error.

I rang the night bell in the building and the sleepy-looking watchman unlocked the door and said, "Yeah? The place is closed up."

I showed him my press card and he shook his head. "That don't mean nothing."

Fifty of the sixty bucks I had taken from the corpse did mean something though and he agreed to a five-minute talk because his coffee would get cold.

"There been any night work going on here?" I asked him.

"Sure. Maintenance, cleaning . . . all the time."

"How about Reading Associates?"

"Night deliveries sometimes. They had their shelves reworked two months ago."

"I mean lately."

He thought for a moment, then nodded. "Some guy was let up to install new glass cases in the place, only Mr. Reading was with him most of the time."

"Use much equipment?"

This time I got a frown. "Yeah, a big tool box and a small crate. Wooden one with steel bands around it. The day man said they had some welding bottles up there too. Why? They finished all that stuff the other day. Nobody's been here since."

"You like to make a hundred on top of that fifty?"

He started to get pictures in his mind then and his eyes got a flinty look in them. "Like hell, mister. You get your tail out of here like now. Come on, buddy, scram."

I took off my hat and let him see the edges of my teeth. "Take a good look, feller. You might have seen my picture in the paper recently." When I held my coat open he saw the gun in my belt too and it all came through fast and he wore the same expression Loco and Sophia did when their mouths went suddenly dry.

I looked at my watch. "I won't be long. You'll get your hundred on the way out. But if I were you I'd stay right in the doorway where a buddy outside can see you, and if anybody comes in here you just ring that office once. Just once, understand?"

He couldn't talk. My reputation and the big story in the paper had put a knot in his belly and a lump in his throat. He nodded and I walked to the elevator, took it up to the floor I wanted and pushed the down button to get it back to the ground floor before I got out.

Getting into the office wasn't hard at all. It took two minutes with the picks and I was inside with all the musty paper smell and when my eyes were adjusted I went across to Reading's office and sat down behind his desk. If the schedule worked out I was twenty minutes early.

But the little Lady of the Luck was on my side for a change and I was only two minutes early, because the desk phone rang once and quit and I knew he was on the way up. I heard the keys work the lock, saw a single overhead light snap on and heard him come into his office. He had a gun in his hand, but it was dangling while mine was aiming for a spot right between those owlish eyes of his and he just stood there because a face-to-face shootout wasn't that end of his job at all. He had planned on an ambush and could have made it stick with me as a prowler but it hadn't worked out at all.

I said, "Drop it, Reading."

He let the gun clatter to the floor.

"Sit down. Over there."

"Listen, you came for a payoff. All right, I'll . . ."

"It's going to be more than the six hundred you offered your boy to wipe me out."

"Okay, we'll deal. How much?"

"All of it."

At first he didn't get what I meant, then the message went through, but a wily expression clouded his eyes and I knew he was thinking of his insurance policy. Too bad he didn't know about mine. "You're not very smart, Fallon."

"Cutting in on mob money isn't supposed to be, buddy. But neither is killing a guy's old pal very smart either. And I don't think organizing a few extra kills on your own without authority from higher headquarters is very bright thinking."

"You're out of your mind."

"Finding those torn bills under your door has made you pretty skitterish, pal."

"What torn bills?"

"The ones you knew had to come from a dead man. But before that man was dead he talked to me and told me who gave them to him. That's what you thought. So it was just fine to meet with me right here and lay me out when I came in because the story would look good. Hell, man, you had me pegged when I came in today. Oh, you were cool about it, but you knew you had to work fast. There were others that saw me and could identify me as having looked over your collection and a heist of a few of those first editions of yours could net me a bundle in the right places. Yeah, it really would have looked good. And that hood you picked was a little smarter than I thought he was. He had the stakeouts pegged and knew I'd probably make a try to get back home some way. I was beginning to look too seedy to be roaming the streets any more."

"Fallon . . ."

"Your own men blew it on you, kiddo." I was remembering what Shim Little had told the whore in the hotel. "But the big blooper was your own. You had those giveaway pens lying around and it's just natural for people to pick them up."

"Those pens are distributed in every bookstore in town."

"But they don't turn up in the pockets of odd people," I told him.

His smile was hard, going over the technicality, and he knew damn well it wouldn't stand up as evidence at all. He was still banking on his own insurance.

I said, "All of it, Reading. I want it all."

We both heard the door slam open and the pounding of feet on the floor. He let out a little laugh and said, "None of it, Fallon," then called out, "In here, officers."

They came through the doors in a rush and I nodded to Charlie Watts and the other three and laid the .45 on the top of the desk. "You took long enough to get here."

I was staring at all those police .38s and it wasn't a very pretty sight at all. "You're finally down, Fallon. You're finally going to get that great big fall."

When I smiled at him he didn't like it a bit. There was just too damn much confidence in it and he turned to tell Reading to shut up because he was cop enough to get a smell that wasn't supposed to be there at all. It hung in the room like smoke and he was the only one who could smell it.

"Read me my rights, then let's give it fifteen minutes and we'll do it all downtown like the old days. Later they'll give you and Al Grossino that new commendation and everybody will be happy."

I was thinking of what he was going to say when he heard the tapes, when they did voice prints from interrogation tapes on Shim Little and his dead buddy and tied in the dead Mechanic, then got a statement from little squat Sophia and tied it all in with the double-edged hook I was ready to throw.

So he gave me the fifteen minutes which was exactly the right amount of time for Cheryl to get there, escorted in by another patrolman.

Reading was still making noise, insisting I had called him under the pretense of blackmailing him for holding stolen rare books and like a good citizen had immediately called the police to intercept the action. The gun on the floor was his and he had a license to carry it, but I had gotten there first and was threatening his life.

Sure, it was true enough. It was what I had figured he'd do. I said to Charlie, "You get the rest of those torn bills from Al?"

The captain watched me a moment and nodded. "I have some more on me." I glanced over at Reading. "He has the other halves."

Once more I got that crafty look and he stated with indignant sincerity, "That's ridiculous!"

"Cheryl?"

"After I delivered the first two I watched through the window. He got an envelope out of his desk drawer and tossed it in the fireplace. He made one phone call then got out of there in a hurry. I went in through the window and pulled the envelope off the fire. It's under the rug in his den right now."

"Money doesn't burn very easily, Reading," I said.

"You're not planting evidence on me, Fallon. I demand . . ."

"Shut up," I said. "Charlie, come here."

My old commander walked across the room and I took out my wallet. I opened the back compartment and showed him something new. "For your eyes only, captain. Orley News Service is just a staged setup for this outfit. My being busted out of the department and doing that short stretch was all part of the staging."

I almost wanted to laugh because although he'd check it out in detail later he knew every part of it was true and he was hating himself for never having given me any benefit of doubt at all.

Reading was having a fit in front of the other officers, demanding to call a lawyer, and I said nice and loud and clear, "He's holding the gold, Charlie. It was going to be shipped out of the country right along with him and his little prized book collection and when he gets ready to talk you'll get all the names you want because Mr. Reading here doesn't want to get any contract put out for him for gross negligence in handling mob cash, and prison walls are a lot thicker than the ones he has here."

But Reading was thinking he still held the trump card. I reached for the .45 on the desk and asked Charlie, "Mind?"

He didn't say anything, but the other cops were still holding hard on me. "Shim Little said he was on the safest job in the world. Let's see if he was right."

I thumbed the hammer of the .45 back and aimed it at the open door of the archaic safe and touched the trigger. The roar in the room was momentarily deafening and the stink of cordite was sharp.

Everybody had jerked back waiting to hear the whistle of a ricocheting slug bounce off the steel, but there wasn't any at all. There was just a neat hole punched in the door and under the dull black finish was the shiny yellow that only gold can reflect and over in the corner Reading slumped into the chair and began to choke on his own fear.

"Downtown now, Charlie?"

He smiled at me for the first time in years. "Yeah, you bastard."

"Let's keep it that way if we can. It's better for our business."

"The broad too?"

"She's one of us, buddy."

"I'll be damned."

Downstairs I paid the night watchman with a hundred bucks of Cheryl's money and we all went out to the cars together. I never thought it would happen again, but this time I got to ride in the front seat with my old commander. Just this once. Washington wouldn't approve of the fraternization after all the work they went through.

When we were getting in, Cheryl said, "We can't even hire a hotel room tonight, you slob. You took all my cash."

"There's always home," I told her.

She grinned and squeezed my hand. Like a little trap. And I was caught in it. But it felt good anyway.

ROSS MACDONALD

WILD GOOSE CHASE

Ross Macdonald (1915–1983) is the class act, the Cary Grant of American mystery writers. He is smart, he is stylish, and he astonishes without telling you he is astonishing.

He was born Kenneth Millar and grew up in Canada. The first Lew Archer story was signed John Macdonald to avoid confusion with his wife, mystery writer Margaret Millar; later ones were signed John Ross Macdonald (to avoid confusion with John D. MacDonald), and finally he dropped the first name. There were eighteen Lew Archer novels in all, from The Moving Target *in 1949 to* The Blue Hammer *in 1976.*

"I'm not Archer, exactly, but Archer is me," he said more than once, and it is as succinct a statement of the relationship between author and creation as you can find. But, he added, "fictional detectives tend to be idealized versions of their authors, the kind of men we would choose to be if we were men of action instead of the solitary fantasists we are."

"The typical detective hero in contemporary American fiction," he once wrote, "speaks for our common humanity. He has an impatience with special privilege, a sense of interdependence among men, and a certain modesty." As for Archer himself, Macdonald wrote on a different occasion, he "is less a doer than a questioner, a consciousness in which the meanings of other lives emerge."

"Wild Goose Chase" was first published in 1954.

THE PLANE turned in toward the shoreline and began to lose altitude. Mountains detached themselves from the blue distance. Then there was a city between the sea and the mountains, a little city made of sugar cubes. The cubes increased in size. Cars crawled like colored beetles between the buildings, and matchstick figures hustled jerkily along the white morning pavements. A few minutes later I was one of them.

The woman who had telephoned me was waiting at the airport, as she had promised. She climbed out of her Cadillac when I appeared at the entrance to the waiting room, and took a few tentative steps toward me. In spite of her height and her blondeness, the dark harlequin glasses she wore gave her an oddly Oriental look.

"You must be Mr. Archer."

I said I was, and waited for her to complete the exchange of names — she hadn't given me her name on the telephone. All she had given me, in fact, was an urgent request to catch the first plane north, and assurances that I would be paid for my time.

She sensed what I was waiting for. "I'm sorry to be so mysterious. I really can't afford to tell you my name. I'm taking quite a risk in coming here at all."

I looked her over carefully, trying to decide whether this was another wild goose chase. Although she was well-groomed in a sharkskin suit, her hair and face were slightly disarranged, as if a storm had struck a glancing blow. She took off her glasses to wipe them. I could see that the storm was inside of her, roiling the blue-green color of her eyes.

"What's the problem?" I said.

She stood wavering between me and her car, beaten by surges of sound from the airfield where my plane was about to take off again. Behind her, in the Cadillac's front seat, a little girl with the coloring of a Dresden doll was sitting as still as one. The woman glanced at the child and moved farther away from the car:

"I don't want Janie to hear. She's only three and a half but she understands a great deal." She took a deep gasping breath, like a swimmer about to dive. "There's a man on trial for murder here. They claim he murdered his wife."

"Glenway Cave?"

Her whole body moved with surprise. "You know him?"

"No, I've been following the trial in the papers."

"Then you know he's testifying today. He's probably on the witness stand right now." Her voice was somber, as if she could see the courtroom in her mind's eye.

"Is Mr. Cave a friend of yours?"

She bit her lip. "Let's say that I'm an interested observer."

"And you don't believe he's guilty."

"Did I say that?"

"By implication. You said they *claim* he murdered his wife."

"You have an alert ear, haven't you? Anyway, what I believe doesn't matter. It's what the jury believes. Do you think they'll acquit him?"

"It's hard to form an opinion without attending the trial. But the average jury has a prejudice against the idea of blowing off your wife's head with a twelve-gauge shotgun. I'd say he stands a good chance of going to the gas chamber."

"The gas chamber." Her nostrils dilated, and she paled, as if she had caught a whiff of the fatal stuff. "Do you seriously think there's any danger of that?"

"They've built a powerful case against him. Motive. Opportunity. Weapon."

"What motive?"

"His wife was wealthy, wasn't she? I understand Cave isn't. They were alone in the house; the housekeeping couple were away for the weekend. The shotgun belonged to Cave, and according to the chemical test his driving gloves were used to fire it."

"You *have* been following the trial."

"As well as I could from Los Angeles. Of course you get distortions in the newspapers. It makes a better story if he looks guilty."

"He isn't guilty," she said in a quiet voice.

"Do you know that, or merely hope it?"

She pressed one hand across her mouth. The fingernails were bitten down to the quick. "We won't go into that."

"Do you know who murdered Ruth Cave?"

"No. Of course not."

"Am I supposed to try and find out who did?"

"Wouldn't that be very difficult, since it happened so long ago? Anyway, it doesn't really matter to me. I barely knew the woman." Her thoughts veered back to Cave. "Won't a great deal depend on the impression he makes on the witness stand?"

"It usually does in a murder trial."

"You've seen a lot of them, haven't you?"

"Too many. I take it I'm going to see another."

"Yes." She spoke sharply and definitely, leaning forward. "I don't dare go myself. I want you to observe the jurors, see how Glen — how Mr. Cave's testimony affects them. And tell me if you think he's going to get off."

"What if I can't tell?"

"You'll have to give me a yes or no." Her breast nudged my arm. She was too intent on what she was saying to notice. "I've made up my mind to go by your decision."

"Go where?" I said.

"To hell if necessary — if his life is really in danger."

"I'll do my best. Where shall I get in touch with you?"

"I'll get in touch with you. I've made a reservation for you at the Rubio Inn. Right now I'll drop you at the courthouse. Oh, yes — the money." She opened her leather handbag, and I caught the gleam of a blue revolver at the bottom of the bag. "How much?"

"A hundred dollars will do."

A few bills changed hands, and we went to the car. She indicated the right rear door. I went around to the left so that I could read the white slip on the steering column. But the leatherette holder was empty.

The little girl stood up in the front seat and leaned over the back of it to look at me. "Hello. Are you my daddy?" Her eyes were as blue and candid as the sky.

Before I could answer, her mother said: "Now Janie, you know he isn't your daddy. This is Mr. Archer."

"Where is my daddy?"

"In Pasadena, darling. You know that. Sit down, Janie, and be still."

The little girl slid down out of my sight. The engine roared in anger.

It was ten minutes past eleven by the clock on the courthouse tower. Superior Court was on the second floor. I slid into one of the vacant seats in the back row of the spectators' section. Several old ladies turned to glare at me, as though I had interrupted a church service.

The trial was more like an ancient tribal ceremony in a grotto. Red draperies were drawn over the lofty windows. The air was dim with human exhalations. Black iron fixtures suspended from the ceiling shed a wan light on the judge's gray head, and on the man on the witness stand.

I recognized Glenway Cave from his newspaper pictures. He was a big handsome man in his early thirties who had once been bigger and handsomer. Four months in jail waiting for trial had pared him down to the bone. His eyes were pressed deep into hollow sockets. His double-breasted gabardine suit hung loosely on his shoulders. He looked like a suitable victim for the ceremony.

A broad-backed man with a straw-colored crewcut was bent over the stenograph, talking in an inaudible voice to the court reporter. Harvey, chief attorney for the defense. I had met Rod Harvey several times in the course of my work, which was one reason why I had followed the trial so closely.

The judge chopped the air with his hatchet face: "Proceed with your examination, Mr. Harvey."

Harvey raised his clipped blond head and addressed the witness: "Mr. Cave, we were attempting to establish the reason behind your — ah — misunderstanding with your wife. Did you and Mrs. Cave have words on the evening of May nineteenth?"

"We did. I've already told you that." Cave's voice was shallow, with high-pitched overtones.

"What was the nature of the conversation?"

"It was more of an argument than a conversation."

"But a purely verbal argument?" Harvey sounded as if his own witness had taken him by surprise.

A sharp-faced man spoke up from the prosecution end of the attorneys' table. "Objection. The question is leading — not to say *misleading*."

"Sustained. The question will be stricken."

Harvey shrugged his heavy tweed shoulders. "Tell us just what was said then, Mr. Cave. Beginning at the beginning."

Cave moved uncomfortably, passing the palm of one hand over his eyes. "I can't recall it verbatim. It was quite an emotional scene —"

Harvey cut him off. "Tell us in your own words what you and Mrs. Cave were talking about."

"The future," Cave said. "Our future. Ruth was planning to leave me for another man."

An insect-buzzing rose from the spectators. I looked along the row where I was sitting. A couple of seats to my right, a young woman with artificial violets at her waist was leaning forward, her bright dark eyes intent on Cave's face. She seemed out of place among the frowsy old furies who surrounded her. Her head was striking, small and boyishly chic, its fine bony structure emphasized by a short haircut. She turned, and her brown eyes met mine. They were tragic and opaque.

The D.A.'s voice rose above the buzzing. "I object to this testimony. The witness is deliberately blackening the dead woman's reputation, without corroborative evidence of any kind, in a cowardly attempt to save his own neck."

He glanced sideways at the jury. Their faces were stony. Cave's was as white as marble. Harvey's was mottled red. He said, "This is an essential part of the case for the defense. A great deal has been made of Mr. Cave's sudden departure from home on the day of his wife's death. I am establishing the reason for it."

"We know the reason," the D.A. said in a carrying undertone.

Harvey looked up mutely at the judge, whose frown fitted the lines in his face like an old glove.

"Objection overruled. The prosecution will refrain from making unworthy comments. In any case, the jury will disregard them."

But the D.A. looked pleased with himself. He had made his point, and the jury would remember. Their twenty-four eyes, half of them female, and predominantly old, were fixed on Cave in uniform disapproval.

Harvey spoke in a voice thickened by emotion. "Did your wife say who the man was that she planned to leave you for?"

"No. She didn't."

"Do you know who it was?"

"No. The whole thing was a bolt from the blue to me. I don't believe Ruth intended to tell me what she had on her mind. It just slipped out, after we started fighting." He caught himself up short. "Verbally fighting, I mean."

"What started this verbal argument?"

"Nothing important. Money trouble. I wanted to buy a Ferrari, and Ruth couldn't see any sense in it."

"A Ferrari motor car?"

"A racing car, yes. I asked her for the money. She said that she was tired of giving me money. I said that I was equally tired of taking it from her. Then it came out that she was going to leave me for somebody else." One side of Cave's mouth lifted in a sardonic smile. "Somebody who would love her for herself."

"When did she plan to leave you?"

"As soon as she could get ready to go to Nevada. I told her to go ahead, that she was free to go whenever and wherever she wanted to go, with anybody that suited her."

"And what did you do then?"

"I packed a few clothes and drove away in my car."

"What time did you leave the house?"

"I don't know exactly."

"Was it dark when you went?"

"It was getting dark, but I didn't have to use my headlights right away. It couldn't have been later than eight o'clock."

"And Mrs. Cave was alive and well when you left?"

"Certainly she was."

"Was your parting friendly?"

"Friendly enough. She said good-bye and offered me some money. Which I didn't take, incidentally. I didn't take much of anything, except for bare essentials. I even left most of my clothes behind."

"Why did you do that?"

"Because she bought them for me. They belonged to her. I thought perhaps her new man might have a use for them."

"I see."

Harvey's voice was hoarse and unsteady. He turned away from Cave, and I could see that his face was flushed, either with anger or impatience. He said without looking at the prisoner, "Did the things you left behind include a gun?"

"Yes. A twelve-gauge double-barreled shotgun. I used it for shooting rabbits, mostly, in the hills behind the house."

"Was it loaded?"

"I believe so. I usually kept it loaded."

"Where did you leave your shotgun?"

"In the garage. I kept it there. Ruth didn't like to have a gun in the house. She had a phobia —"

Harvey cut in quickly. "Did you also leave a pair of driving gloves, the gloves on the table here marked by the prosecution as Exhibit J?"

"I did. They were in the garage, too."

"And the garage door — was it open or closed?"

"I left it open, I think. In any case, we never kept it locked."

"Mr. Cave," Harvey said in a deep voice, "did you kill your wife with the shotgun before you drove away?"

"I did not." In contrast with Harvey's, Cave's voice was high and thin and unconvincing.

"After you left around eight o'clock, did you return to the house again that night?"

"I did not. I haven't been back since, as a matter of fact. I was arrested in Los Angeles the following day."

"Where did you spend the night — that is, after eight o'clock?"

"With a friend."

The courthouse began to buzz again.

"What friend?" Harvey barked. He suddenly sounded like a prosecutor cross-examining a hostile witness.

Cave moved his mouth to speak, and hesitated. He licked his dry lips. "I prefer not to say."

"Why do you prefer not to say?"

"Because it was a woman. I don't want to involve her in this mess."

Harvey swung away from the witness abruptly and looked up at the judge. The judge admonished the jury not to discuss the case with anyone, and adjourned the trial until two o'clock.

I watched the jurors file out. Not one of them looked at Glenway Cave. They had seen enough of him.

Harvey was the last man to leave the well of the courtroom. I waited for him at the little swinging gate which divided it from the spectators' section. He finished packing his briefcase and came toward me, carrying the case as if it was weighted.

"Mr. Harvey, can you give me a minute?"

He started to brush me off with a weary gesture, then recognized my face. "Lew Archer? What brings you here?"

"It's what I want to talk to you about."

"This case?"

I nodded. "Are you going to get him off?"

"Naturally I am. He's innocent." But his voice echoed hollowly in the empty room and he regarded me doubtfully. "You wouldn't be snooping around for the prosecution?"

"Not this time. The person who hired me believes that Cave is innocent. Just as you do."

"A woman?"

"You're jumping to conclusions, aren't you?"

"When the sex isn't indicated, it's usually a woman. Who is she, Archer?"

"I wish I knew."

"Come on now." His square pink hand rested on my arm. "You don't accept anonymous clients any more than I do."

"This one is an exception. All I know about her is that she's anxious to see Cave get off."

"So are we all." His bland smile tightened. "Look, we can't talk here. Walk over to the office with me. I'll have a couple of sandwiches sent up."

He shifted his hand to my elbow and propelled me toward the door. The dark-eyed woman with the artificial violets at her waist was waiting in the corridor. Her opaque gaze passed over me and rested possessively on Harvey.

"Surprise." Her voice was low and throaty to match her boyish look. "You're taking me to lunch."

"I'm pretty busy, Rhea. And I thought you were going to stay home today."

"I tried to. Honestly. But my mind kept wandering off to the courthouse, so I finally up and followed it." She moved toward him with a queer awkwardness, as if she was embarrassingly conscious of her body, and his. "Aren't you glad to see me, darling?"

"Of course I'm glad to see you," he said, his tone denying the words.

"Then take me to lunch." Her white-gloved hand stroked his lapel. "I made a reservation at the club. It will do you good to get out in the air."

"I told you I'm busy, Rhea. Mr. Archer and I have something to discuss."

"Bring Mr. Archer along. I won't get in the way. I promise." She turned to me with a flashing white smile. "Since my husband seems to have forgotten his manners, I'm Rhea Harvey."

She offered me her hand, and Harvey told her who I was. Shrugging his shoulders resignedly, he led the way outside to his bronze convertible. We turned toward the sea, which glimmered at the foot of the town like a fallen piece of sky.

"How do you think it's going, Rod?" she said.

"I suppose it could have been worse. He could have got up in front of the judge and jury and confessed."

"Did it strike you as that bad?"

"I'm afraid it was pretty bad." Harvey leaned forward over the wheel in order to look around his wife at me. "Were you in on the debacle, Archer?"

"Part of it. He's either very honest or very stupid."

Harvey snorted. "Glen's not stupid. The trouble is, he simply doesn't care. He pays no attention to my advice. I had to stand there and ask the questions, and I didn't know what crazy answers he was going to come up with. He seems to take a masochistic pleasure in wrecking his own chances."

"It could be his conscience working on him," I said.

His steely blue glance raked my face and returned to the road. "It could be, but it isn't. And I'm not speaking simply as his attorney. I've known Glen Cave for a long time. We were roommates in college. Hell, I introduced him to his wife."

"That doesn't make him incapable of murder."

"Sure, any man is capable of murder. That's not my point. My point is that Glen is a sharp customer. If he had decided to kill Ruth for her money, he wouldn't do it that way. He wouldn't use his own gun. In fact, I doubt very much that he'd use a gun at all. Glen isn't that obvious."

"Unless it was a passional crime. Jealousy can make a man lose his sophistication."

"Not Glen. He wasn't in love with Ruth — never has been. He's got about as much sexual passion as a flea." His voice was edged with contempt. "Anyway, this tale of his about another man is probably malarkey."

"Are you sure, Rod?"

He turned on his wife almost savagely. "No, I'm not sure. I'm not sure about anything. Glen isn't confiding in me, and I don't see how I can defend him if he goes on this way. I wish to God he hadn't forced me into this. He knows as well as I do that trial work isn't my forte. I advised him to get an attorney experienced in this sort of thing, and he wouldn't listen. He said if I wouldn't take on his case that he'd defend himself. And he flunked out of law school in his second year. What could I do?"

He stamped the accelerator, cutting in and out of the noon traffic on the ocean boulevard. Palm trees fled by like thin old wild-haired madmen racing along the edge of the quicksilver sea.

The beach club stood at the end of the boulevard, a white U-shaped building whose glass doors opened "For Members and Guests Only." Its inner court contained a swimming pool and an alfresco dining space dotted with umbrella tables. Breeze-swept and sluiced with sunlight, it was the antithesis of the dim courtroom where Cave's fate would be decided. But the shadow of the courtroom fell across our luncheon and leached the color and flavor from the food.

Harvey pushed away his salmon salad, which he had barely disturbed, and gulped down a second martini. He called the waiter to order a third. His wife inhibited him with a barely perceptible shake of her head. The waiter slid away.

"This woman," I said, "the woman he spent the night with. Who is she?"

"Glen told me hardly anything more than he told the court." Harvey paused, half gagged by a lawyer's instinctive reluctance to give away information, then forced himself to go on. "It seems he went straight from home to her house on the night of the shooting. He spent the night with her, from about eight-thirty until the following morning. Or so he claims."

"Haven't you checked his story?"

"How? He refused to say anything that might enable me to find her or identify her. It's just another example of the obstacles he's put in my way, trying to defend him."

"Is this woman so important to his defense?"

"Crucial. Ruth was shot sometime around midnight. The p.m. established that through the stomach contents. And at the time, if he's telling the truth, Glen was with a witness. Yet he won't let me try to locate her, or have her subpoenaed. It took me hours of hammering at him to get him to testify about her at all, and I'm not sure that wasn't a mistake. That miserable jury —" His voice trailed off. He was back in court fighting his uphill battle against the prejudices of a small elderly city.

And I was back on the pavement in front of the airport, listening to a woman's urgent whisper: *You'll have to give me a yes or no. I've made up my mind to go by your decision.*

Harvey was looking away across the captive water, fishnetted under elastic strands of light. Under the clear September sun I could see the spikes of gray in his hair, the deep small scars of strain around his mouth.

"If I could only lay my hands on the woman." He seemed to be speaking to himself, until he looked at me from the corners of his eyes. "Who do *you* suppose she is?"

"How would I know?"

He leaned across the table confidentially. "Why be so cagey, Archer? I've let down my hair."

"This particular hair doesn't belong to me."

I regretted the words before I had finished speaking them.

Harvey said, "When will you see her?"

"You're jumping to conclusions again."

"If I'm wrong, I'm sorry. If I'm right, give her a message for me. Tell her that Glen — I hate to have to say this, but he's in jeopardy. If she likes him well enough to —"

"Please, Rod." Rhea Harvey seemed genuinely offended. "There's no need to be coarse."

I said, "I'd like to talk to Cave before I do anything. I don't know that it's the same woman. Even if it is, he may have reasons of his own for keeping her under wraps."

"You can probably have a few minutes with him in the courtroom." He looked at his wristwatch and pushed his chair back violently. "We better get going. It's twenty to two now."

We went along the side of the pool, back toward the entrance. As we entered the vestibule, a woman was just coming in from the boulevard. She held the heavy plate-glass door for the little flaxen-haired girl who was trailing after her.

Then she glanced up and saw me. Her dark harlequin glasses flashed in the light reflected from the pool. Her face became disorganized behind the glasses. She turned on her heel and started out, but not before the child had smiled at me and said: "Hello. Are you coming for a ride?" Then she trotted after her mother.

Harvey looked quizzically at his wife. "What's the matter with the Kilpatrick woman?"

"She must be drunk. She didn't even recognize us."

"You know her, Mrs. Harvey?"

"As well as I care to." Her eyes took on a set, glazed expression — the look of congealed virtue faced with its opposite. "I haven't seen

Janet Kilpatrick for months. She hasn't been showing herself in public much since her divorce."

Harvey edged closer and gripped my arm. "Would Mrs. Kilpatrick be the woman we were talking about?"

"Hardly."

"They seemed to know you."

I improvised. "I met them on the Daylight one day last month, coming down from Frisco. She got plastered, and I guess she didn't want to recall the occasion."

That seemed to satisfy him. But when I excused myself, on the grounds that I thought I'd stay for a swim in the pool, his blue ironic glance informed me that he wasn't taken in.

The receptionist had inch-long scarlet fingernails and an air of contemptuous formality. Yes, Mrs. Kilpatrick was a member of the club. No, she wasn't allowed to give out members' addresses. She admitted grudgingly that there was a pay telephone in the bar.

The barroom was deserted except for the bartender, a slim white-coated man with emotional Mediterranean eyes. I found Mrs. Janet Kilpatrick in the telephone directory: her address was 1201 Coast Highway. I called a taxi, and ordered a beer from the bartender.

He was more communicative than the receptionist. Sure, he knew Glenway Cave. Every bartender in town knew Glenway Cave. The guy was sitting at this very bar the afternoon of the same day he murdered his wife.

"You think he murdered her?"

"Everybody else thinks so. They don't spend all that money on a trial unless they got the goods on them. Anyway, look at the motive he had."

"You mean the man she was running around with?"

"I mean two million bucks." He had a delayed reaction. "What man is that?"

"Cave said in court this morning that his wife was going to divorce him and marry somebody else."

"He did, eh? You a newspaperman by any chance?"

"A kind of one." I subscribed to several newspapers.

"Well, you can tell the world that that's a lot of baloney. I've seen quite a bit of Mrs. Cave around the club. She had her own little circle, see, and you can take it from me she never even looked at other guys. *He* was always the one with the roving eye. What can you expect, when a young man marries a lady that much older than him?" His faint accent lent flavor to the question. "The very day of the murder he was making a fast play for another dame, right here in front of me."

"Who was she?"

"I wouldn't want to name names. She was pretty far gone that afternoon, hardly knew what she was doing. And the poor lady's got enough trouble as it is. Take it from me."

I didn't press him. A minute later a horn tooted in the street.

A few miles south of the city limits a blacktop lane led down from the highway to Mrs. Kilpatrick's house. It was a big old-fashioned red-wood cottage set among trees and flowers above a bone-white beach. The Cadillac was parked beside the vine-grown veranda, like something in a four-color advertisement. I asked my driver to wait, and knocked on the front door.

A small rectangular window was set into the door. It slid open, and a green eye gleamed like a flawed emerald through the aperture.

"You," she said in a low voice. "You shouldn't have come here."

"I have some questions for you, Mrs. Kilpatrick. And maybe a couple of answers. May I come in?"

She sighed audibly. "If you must." She unlocked the door and stood back to let me enter. "You will be quiet, won't you? I've just put Janie to bed for her afternoon nap."

There was a white silk scarf draped over her right hand, and under the silk a shape which contrasted oddly with her motherly concern — the shape of a small handgun.

"You'd better put that thing away. You don't need it, do you?"

Her hand moved jerkily. The scarf fell from the gun and drifted to the floor. It was a small blue revolver. She looked at it as if it had somehow forced its way into her fist, and put it down on the telephone table.

"I'm sorry. I didn't know who was at the door. I've been so worried and frightened —"

"Who did you think it was?"

"Frank, perhaps, or one of his men. He's been trying to take Janie away from me. He claims I'm not a fit mother. And maybe I'm not," she added in the neutral tones of despair. "But Frank is worse."

"Frank is your husband?"

"My ex-husband. I got a divorce last year and the court gave me custody of Janie. Frank has been fighting the custody order ever since. Janie's grandmother left her a trust fund, you see. That's all Frank cares about. But I'm her mother."

"I think I see what it's all about," I said. "Correct me if I'm wrong. Cave spent the night with you — the night he was supposed to have shot his wife. But you don't want to testify at his trial. It would give your ex-husband legal ammunition to use in the custody fight for Janie."

"You're not wrong." She lowered her eyes, not so much in shame as in submission to the facts. "We got talking in the bar at the club that afternoon. I hardly knew him, but I — well, I was attracted to him. He asked if he could come and see me that night. I was feeling lonely, very low and lonely. I'd had a good deal to drink. I let him come."

"What time did he arrive?"

"Shortly after eight."

"And he stayed all night?"

"Yes. He couldn't have killed Ruth Cave. He was with me. You can understand why I've been quietly going crazy since they arrested him — sitting at home and biting on my nails and wondering what under heaven I should do." Her eyes came up like green searchlights under her fair brow. "What *shall* I do, Mr. Archer?"

"Sit tight for a while yet. The trial will last a few more days. And he may be acquitted."

"But you don't think he will be, do you?"

"It's hard to say. He didn't do too well on the stand this morning. On the other hand, the averages are with him, as he seems to realize. Very few innocent men are convicted of murder."

"He didn't mention me on the stand?"

"He said he was with a woman, no names mentioned. Are you two in love with each other, Mrs. Kilpatrick?"

"No, nothing like that. I was simply feeling sorry for myself that night. I needed some attention from a man. He was a piece of flotsam and I was a piece of jetsam and we were washed together in the dark. He did get rather — emotional at one point, and said that he would like to marry me. I reminded him that he had a wife."

"What did he say to that?"

"He said his wife wouldn't live forever. But I didn't take him seriously. I haven't even seen him since that night. No, I'm not in love with him. If I let him die, though, for something I know he didn't do — I couldn't go on living with myself." She added, with a bitter grimace. "It's hard enough as it is."

"But you do want to go on living."

"Not particularly. I have to because Janie needs me."

"Then stay at home and keep your doors locked. It wasn't smart to go to the club today."

"I know. I needed a drink badly. I'm out of liquor, and it was the nearest place. Then I saw you and I panicked."

"Stay panicked. Remember, if Cave didn't commit that murder, somebody else did — and framed him for it. Somebody who is still at large. What do you drink, by the way?"

"Anything. Scotch, mostly."

"Can you hold out for a couple of hours?"

"If I have to." She smiled, and her smile was charming. "You're very thoughtful."

When I got back to the courtroom, the trial was temporarily stalled. The jury had been sent out, and Harvey and the D.A. were arguing in front of the judge's bench. Cave was sitting by himself at the far end of the long attorneys' table. A sheriff's deputy with a gun on his thigh stood a few feet behind him, between the red-draped windows.

Assuming a self-important legal look, I marched through the swinging gate into the well of the courtroom and took the empty chair beside Cave. He looked up from the typed transcript he was reading. In spite of his prison pallor he was a good-looking man. He had a boyish look about him and the kind of curly brown hair that women are supposed to love to run their fingers through. But his mouth was tight, his eyes dark and piercing.

Before I could introduce myself, he said, "You the detective Rod told me about?"

"Yes. Name is Archer."

"You're wasting your time, Mr. Archer, there's nothing you can do for me." His voice was a dull monotone, as if the cross-examination had rolled over his emotions and left them flat.

"It can't be that bad, Cave."

"I didn't say it was bad. I'm doing perfectly well, and I know what I'm doing."

I held my tongue. It wouldn't do to tell him that his own lawyer had lost confidence in his case. Harvey's voice rose sharp and strained above the courtroom mutter, maintaining that certain questions were irrelevant and immaterial.

Cave leaned toward me and his voice sank lower. "You've been in touch with her?"

"She brought me into the case."

"That was a rash thing for her to do, under the circumstances. Or don't you know the circumstances?"

"I understand that if she testifies she risks losing her child."

"Exactly. Why do you think I haven't had her called? Go back and tell her that I'm grateful for her concern but I don't need her help. They can't convict an innocent man. I didn't shoot my wife, and I don't need an alibi to prove it."

I looked at him, admiring his composure. The armpits of his gabardine suit were dark with sweat. A fine tremor was running through him.

"Do you know who did shoot her, Cave?"

"I have an opinion. We won't go into it."

"Her new man?"

"We won't go into it," he repeated, and buried his aquiline nose in the transcript.

The judge ordered the bailiff to bring in the jury. Harvey sat down beside me, looking disgruntled, and Cave returned to the witness stand.

What followed was moral slaughter. The D.A. forced Cave to admit that he hadn't had gainful employment since his release from the army, that his sole occupations were amateur tennis and amateur acting, and that he had no means of his own. He had been completely dependent on his wife's money since their marriage in 1946, and had used some of it to take extended trips in the company of other women.

The prosecutor turned his back on Cave in histrionic disgust. "And you're the man who dares to impugn the morals of your dead wife, the woman who gave you everything."

Harvey objected. The judge instructed the D.A. to rephrase his "question."

The D.A. nodded, and turned on Cave. "Did you say this morning that there was another man in Mrs. Cave's life?"

"I said it. It was true."

"Do you have anything to confirm that story?"

"No."

"Who is this unknown vague figure of a man?"

"I don't know. All I know is what Ruth told me."

"She isn't here to deny it, is she? Tell us frankly now, Mr. Cave, didn't you invent this man? Didn't you make him up?"

Cave's forehead was shining with sweat. He took a handkerchief out of his breast pocket and wiped his forehead, then his mouth. Above the white fabric masking his lower face, he looked past the D.A. and across the well of the courtroom. There was silence for a long minute.

Then Cave said mildly, "No, I didn't invent him."

"Does this man exist outside your fertile brain?"

"He does."

"Where? In what guise? Who is he?"

"I don't know," Cave said on a rising note. "If you want to know, why don't you try and find out? You have plenty of detectives at your disposal."

"Detectives can't find a man who doesn't exist. Or a woman either, Mr. Cave."

The D.A. caught the angry eye of the judge, who adjourned the trial until the following morning. I bought a fifth of scotch at a downtown liquor store, caught a taxi at the railroad station, and rode south out of town to Mrs. Kilpatrick's house.

When I knocked on the door of the redwood cottage, someone fumbled the inside knob. I pushed the door open. The flaxen-haired child looked up at me, her face streaked with half-dried tears.

"Mummy won't wake up."

I saw the red smudge on her knee, and ran in past her. Janet Kilpatrick was prone on the floor of the hallway, her bright hair dragging in a pool of blood. I lifted her head and saw the hole in her temple. It had stopped bleeding.

Her little blue revolver lay on the floor near her lax hand. One shot had been fired from the cylinder.

The child touched my back. "Is Mummy sick?"

"Yes, Janie. She's sick."

"Get the doctor," she said with pathetic wisdom.

"Wasn't he here?"

"I don't know. I was taking my nap."

"Was anybody here, Janie?"

"Somebody was here. Mummy was talking to somebody. Then there was a big bang and I came downstairs and Mummy wouldn't wake up."

"Was it a man?"

She shook her head.

"A woman, Janie?"

The same mute shake of her head. I took her by the hand and led her outside to the cab. The dazzling postcard scene outside made death seem unreal. I asked the driver to tell the child a story, any story so long as it was cheerful. Then I went back into the grim hallway and used the telephone.

I called the sheriff's office first. My second call was to Frank Kilpatrick in Pasadena. A manservant summoned him to the telephone. I told him who I was and where I was and who was lying dead on the floor behind me.

"How dreadful!" He had an Ivy League accent, somewhat withered by the coastal sun. "Do you suppose that Janet took her own life? She's often threatened to."

"No," I said, "I don't suppose she took her own life. Your wife was murdered."

"What a tragic thing!"

"Why take it so hard, Kilpatrick? You've got the two things you wanted — your daughter, and you're rid of your wife."

It was a cruel thing to say, but I was feeling cruel. I made my third call in person, after the sheriff's men had finished with me.

The sun had fallen into the sea by then. The western side of the sky was scrawled with a childish finger-painting of colored cirrus clouds. Twilight flowed like iron-stained water between the downtown buildings. There were lights on the second floor of the California-Spanish building where Harvey had his offices.

Harvey answered my knock. He was in shirtsleeves and his tie was awry. He had a sheaf of papers in his hand. His breath was sour in my nostrils.

"What is it, Archer?"

"You tell me, lover-boy."

"And what is that supposed to mean?"

"You were the one Ruth Cave wanted to marry. You were going to divorce your respective mates and build a new life together — with her money."

He stepped backward into the office, a big disordered man who looked queerly out of place among the white-leather and black-iron furniture, against the limed-oak paneling. I followed him in. An automatic door closer shushed behind me.

"What in hell is this? Ruth and I were good friends and I handled her business for her — that's all there was to it."

"Don't try to kid me, Harvey. I'm not your wife, and I'm not your judge . . . I went to see Janet Kilpatrick a couple of hours ago."

"Whatever she said, it's a lie."

"She didn't say a word, Harvey. I found her dead."

His eyes grew small and metallic, like nailheads in the putty of his face. "Dead? What happened to her?"

"She was shot with her own gun. By somebody she let into the house, somebody she wasn't afraid of."

"Why? It makes no sense."

"She was Cave's alibi, and she was on the verge of volunteering as a witness. You know that, Harvey — you were the only one who did know, outside of Cave and me."

"I didn't shoot her. I had no reason to. Why would I want my client convicted?"

"No, you didn't shoot her. You were in court at the time that she was shot — the world's best alibi."

"Then why are you harassing me?"

"I want the truth about you and Mrs. Cave."

Harvey looked down at the papers in his hand, as if they might suggest a line to take, an evasion, a way out. Suddenly his hands came together and crushed the papers into a misshapen ball.

"All right, I'll tell you. Ruth was in love with me. I was — fond of her. Neither of us was happily married. We were going to go away together and start over. After we got divorces, of course."

"Uh-huh. All very legal."

"You don't have to take that tone. A man has a right to his own life."

"Not when he's already committed his life."

"We won't discuss it. Haven't I suffered enough? How do you think I felt when Ruth was killed?"

"Pretty bad, I guess. There went two million dollars."

He looked at me between narrowed lids, in a fierce extremity of hatred. But all that came out of his mouth was a weak denial. "At any rate, you can see I didn't kill her. I didn't kill either of them."

"Who did?"

"I have no idea. If I did, I'd have had Glen out of jail long ago."

"Does Glen know?"

"Not to my knowledge."

"But he knew that you and his wife had plans?"

"I suppose he did — I've suspected it all along."

"Didn't it strike you as odd that he asked you to defend him, under the circumstances?"

"Odd, yes. It's been terrible for me, the most terrible ordeal."

Maybe that was Cave's intention, I thought, to punish Harvey for stealing his wife. I said, "Did anybody besides you know that Janet Kilpatrick was the woman? Did you discuss it with anybody?"

He looked at the thick pale carpeting between his feet. I could hear an electric clock somewhere in the silent offices, whirring like the thoughts in Harvey's head. Finally he said, "Of course not," in a voice that was like a crow cawing.

He walked with an old man's gait into his private office. I followed and saw him open a desk drawer. A heavy automatic appeared in his hand. But he didn't point it at me. He pushed it down inside the front of his trousers and put on his suit jacket.

"Give it to me, Harvey. Two dead women are enough."

"You know, then?"

"You just told me. Give me that gun."

He gave it to me. His face was remarkably smooth and blank. He turned his face away from me and covered it with his hands. His entire body hiccuped with dry grief. He was like an overgrown child who had lived on fairy tales for a long time and now couldn't stomach reality.

The telephone on the desk chirred. Harvey pulled himself together and answered it.

"Sorry, I've been busy, preparing for re-direct . . . Yes, I'm finished now . . . Of course I'm all right. I'm coming home right away."

He hung up and said, "That was my wife."

She was waiting for him at the front door of his house. The posture of waiting became her narrow, sexless body, and I wondered how many years she had been waiting.

"You're so thoughtless, Rod," she chided him. "Why didn't you tell me you were bringing a guest for dinner?" She turned to me in awkward graciousness. "Not that you're not welcome, Mr. Archer."

Then our silence bore in on her. It pushed her back into the high white Colonial hallway. She took up another pose and lit a cigarette with a little golden lighter shaped like a lipstick. Her hands were steady, but I could see the sharp edges of fear behind the careful expression on her face.

"You both look so solemn. Is something wrong?"

"Everything is wrong, Rhea."

"Why, didn't the trial go well this afternoon?"

"The trial is going fine. Tomorrow I'm going to ask for a directed acquittal. What's more, I'm going to get it. I have new evidence."

"Isn't that grand?" she said in a bright and interested tone. "Where on earth did you dig up the new evidence?"

"In my own backyard. All these months I've been so preoccupied trying to cover up my own sordid little secret that it never occurred to me that you might have secrets, too."

"What do you mean?"

"You weren't at the trial this afternoon. Where were you? What were you doing?"

"Errands — I had some errands. I'm sorry, I didn't realize you — wanted me to be there."

Harvey moved toward her, a threat of violence in the set of his shoulders. She backed against a closed white door. I stepped between them and said harshly, "We know exactly where you were, Mrs. Harvey. You went to see Janet Kilpatrick. You talked your way into her house, picked up a gun from the table in the hall, and shot her with it. Didn't you?"

The flesh of her face was no more than a stretched membrane.

"I swear, I had no intention — All I intended to do was talk to her. But when I saw that she realized, that she *knew* —"

"Knew what, Mrs. Harvey?"

"That I was the one who killed Ruth. I must have given myself away, by what I said to her. She looked at me, and I saw that she knew. I saw it in her eyes."

"So you shot her?"

"Yes. I'm sorry." She didn't seem to be fearful or ashamed. The face she turned on her husband looked starved, and her mouth moved over her words as if they were giving her bitter nourishment. "But I'm not sorry for the other one, for Ruth. You shouldn't have done it to me, Rod. I warned you, remember? I warned you when I caught you with Anne that if you ever did it to me again — I would kill the woman. You should have taken me seriously."

"Yes," he said drearily. "I guess I should have."

"I warned Ruth, too, when I learned about the two of you."

"How did you find out about it, Mrs. Harvey?"

"The usual way — an anonymous telephone call. Some friend of mine, I suppose."

"Or your worst enemy. Do you know who it was?"

"No. I didn't recognize the voice. I was still in bed, and the telephone call woke me up. He said — it was a man — he said that Rod was going to divorce me, and he told me why. I went to Ruth that very morning — Rod was out of town — and I asked her if it was true. She admitted it was. I told her flatly I'd kill her unless she gave you up, Rod. She laughed at me. She called me a crazy woman."

"She was right."

"Was she? If I'm insane, I know what's driven me to it. I could bear the thought of the other ones. But not her! What made you take up with *her,* Rod — what made you want to marry that gray-haired old woman? She wasn't even attractive, she wasn't nearly as attractive as I am."

"She was well-heeled," I said.

Harvey said nothing.

Rhea Harvey dictated and signed a full confession that night. Her husband wasn't in court the following morning. The D.A. himself moved for a directed acquittal, and Cave was free by noon. He took a taxi directly from the courthouse to the home of his late wife. I followed him in a second taxi. I still wasn't satisfied.

The lawns around the big country house had grown knee-high and had withered in the summer sun. The gardens were overgrown with rank flowers and ranker weeds. Cave stood in the drive for a while after he dismissed his taxi, looking around the estate he had inherited. Finally he mounted the front steps.

I called him from the gate. "Wait a minute, Cave."

He descended the steps reluctantly and waited for me, a black scowl twisting his eyebrows and disfiguring his mouth. But they were smooth and straight before I reached him.

"What do you want?"

"I was just wondering how it feels."

He smiled with boyish charm. "To be a free man? It feels wonderful. I guess I owe you my gratitude, at that. As a matter of fact, I was planning to send you a check."

"Save yourself the trouble. I'd send it back."

"Whatever you say, old man." He spread his hands disarmingly. "Is there something else I can do for you?"

"Yes. You can satisfy my curiosity. All I want from you is a yes or no." The words set up an echo in my head, an echo of Janet Kilpatrick's voice. "Two women have died and a third is on her way to prison or the state hospital. I want to hear you admit your responsibility."

"Responsibility? I don't understand."

"I'll spell it out for you. The quarrel you had with your wife didn't occur on the nineteenth, the night she was murdered. It came earlier, maybe the night before. And she told you who the man was."

"She didn't have to tell me. I've known Rod Harvey for years, and all about him."

"Then you must have known that Rhea Harvey was insanely jealous of her husband. You thought of a way to put her jealousy to work for you. It was you who telephoned her that morning. You disguised your voice, and told her what her husband and your wife were planning to do. She came to this house and threatened your wife. No doubt you overheard the conversation. Seeing that your plan was working, you left your loaded shotgun where Rhea Harvey could easily find it and went down to the beach club to establish an alibi. You had a long wait at the club, and later at Janet Kilpatrick's house, but you finally got what you were waiting for."

"They also serve who only stand and wait."

"Does it seem so funny to you, Cave? You're guilty of conspiracy to commit murder."

"I'm not guilty of anything, old man. Even if I were, there's nothing you could possibly do about it. You heard the court acquit me this morning, and there's a little rule of law involving double jeopardy."

"You were taking quite a risk, weren't you?"

"Not so much of a risk. Rhea's a very unstable woman, and she had to break down eventually, one way or the other."

"Is that why you asked Harvey to defend you, to keep the pressure on Rhea?"

"That was part of it." A sudden fury of hatred went through him, transfiguring his face. "Mostly I wanted to see him suffer."

"What are you going to do now, Cave?"

"Nothing. I plan to take it easy. I've earned a rest. Why?"

"A pretty good woman was killed yesterday on account of you. For all I know you planned that killing the same way you planned the other. In any case, you could have prevented it."

He saw the mayhem in my eyes and backed away. "Take it easy, Archer. Janet was no great loss to the world, after all."

My fist smashed his nervous smile and drove the words down his throat. He crawled away from me, scrambled to his feet and ran, jumping over flowerbeds and disappearing around the corner of the house. I let him go.

A short time later I heard that Cave had been killed in a highway accident near Palm Springs. He was driving a new Ferrari at the time.

STANLEY ELLIN

THE
NINE-TO-
FIVE MAN

Stanley Ellin (1916–1986) wrote some of the most highly praised crime stories of the past fifty years. His "Specialty of the House" is near the top of just about everyone's list of favorite short stories. And Alfred Hitchcock's half-hour version was the high-water mark of his television series. Most of Ellin's stories were published in Ellery Queen's Mystery Magazine, *but none seems to follow any of the traditional formats. And in a business where writers are praised for the number of novels they can produce per year, Ellin's single annual story, which usually took him a year to write and rewrite, was an event.*

As a Brooklyn high school student, Ellin recalled, the two magazines he read with the greatest interest were The New Yorker, *"although it sometimes bothered me that so many of its stories seemed to fix on nothing more than terribly sensitive people bound and determined to give themselves a hard time," and* Black Mask, *because the "clipped, flat, declarative style colored by dialogue with a frequently sardonic edge had the texture of the neighborhood I lived in." Both publications left their mark on the Ellin style.*

"The Nine-to-Five Man" was published in Ellery Queen's Mystery Magazine *in 1963.*

THE ALARM CLOCK sounded, as it did every weekday morning, at exactly 7:20, and without opening his eyes Mr. Keesler reached out a hand and turned it off. His wife was already preparing breakfast — it was her modest boast that she had a built-in alarm to get her up in the morning — and a smell of frying bacon permeated the bedroom. Mr. Keesler savored it for a moment, lying there on his back with his eyes closed, and then wearily sat up and swung his feet out of bed.

His eyeglasses were on the night table next to the alarm clock. He put them on and blinked in the morning light, yawned, scratched his head with pleasure, and fumbled for his slippers.

The pleasure turned to mild irritation. One slipper was not there. He kneeled down, swept his hand back and forth under the bed, and finally found it. He stood up, puffing a little, and went into the bathroom. After lathering his face he discovered that his razor was dull, and discovered immediately afterward that he had forgotten to buy new blades the day before. By taking a few minutes more than usual he managed to get a presentable, though painful, shave out of the old blade. Then he washed, brushed his teeth carefully, and combed his hair. He liked to say that he was in pretty good shape since he still had teeth and hair enough to need brushing.

In the bedroom again, he heard Mrs. Keesler's voice rising from the foot of the stairway. "Breakfast, dear," she called. "It's on the table now."

It was not really on the table, Mr. Keesler knew; his wife would first be setting the table when he walked into the kitchen. She was like that, always using little tricks to make the house run smoothly. But no matter how you looked at it, she was a sweetheart all right. He nodded soberly at his reflection in the dresser mirror while he knotted his tie. He was a lucky man to have a wife like that. A fine wife, a fine mother — maybe a little bit too much of an easy mark for her relatives — but a real sweetheart.

The small annoyance of the relatives came up at the breakfast table.

"Joe and Betty are expecting us over tonight, dear," said Mrs. Keesler. "Betty called me about it yesterday. Is that all right with you?"

"All right," said Mr. Keesler amiably. He knew there was nothing good on television that evening anyhow.

"Then will you remember to pick up your other suit at the tailor's on the way home?"

"For Betty and Joe?" said Mr. Keesler. "What for? They're only in-laws."

"Still and all, I like you to look nice when you go over there, so please don't forget." Mrs. Keesler hesitated. "Albert's going to be there, too."

"Naturally. He lives there."

"I know, but you hardly ever get a chance to see him, and, after all, he's our nephew. He happens to be a very nice boy."

"All right, he's a very nice boy," said Mr. Keesler. "What does he want from me?"

Mrs. Keesler blushed. "Well, it so happens he's having a hard time getting a job where —"

"No," said Mr. Keesler. "Absolutely not." He put down his knife and fork and regarded his wife sternly. "You know yourself that there's hardly enough money in the novelties line to make us a living. So for me to take in a lazy —"

"I'm sorry," said Mrs. Keesler. "I didn't mean to get you upset about it." She put a consoling hand on his. "And what kind of thing is that to say, about not making a living? Maybe we don't have as much as some others, but we do all right. A nice house and two fine sons in college — what more could we ask for? So don't talk like that. And go to work, or you'll be late."

Mr. Keesler shook his head. "What a softie," he said. "If you only wouldn't let Betty talk you into these things —"

"Now don't start with that. Just go to work."

She helped him on with his coat in the hallway. "Are you going to take the car today?" she asked.

"No."

"All right, then I can use it for the shopping. But don't forget about the suit. It's the tailor right near the subway station." Mrs. Keesler plucked a piece of lint from his coat collar. "And you make a very nice living, so stop talking like that. We do all right."

Mr. Keesler left the house by the side door. It was an unpretentious frame house in the Flatbush section of Brooklyn, and like most of the others on the block it had a small garage behind it. Mr. Keesler unlocked the door of the garage and stepped inside. The car occupied nearly all the space there, but room had also been found for a clutter of tools, metal cans, paint brushes, and a couple of old kitchen chairs which had been partly painted.

The car itself was a four-year-old Chevrolet, a little the worse for wear, and it took an effort to open the lid of its trunk. Mr. Keesler finally got it open and lifted out his big leather sample case, groaning at its weight. He did not lock the garage door when he left, since he had the only key to it, and he knew Mrs. Keesler wanted to use the car.

It was a two-block walk to the Beverly Road station of the I.R.T. subway. At a newsstand near the station Mr. Keesler bought a *New York Times,* and when the train came in he arranged himself against the door at the end of the car. There was no chance of getting a seat during the rush hour, but from long experience Mr. Keesler knew how to travel with the least inconvenience. By standing with his back braced against the door and his legs astride the sample case he was able to read his newspaper until, by the time the train reached 14th Street, the press of bodies against him made it impossible to turn the pages.

At 42nd Street he managed to push his way out of the car using the sample case as a battering ram. He crossed the platform and took a local two stations farther to Columbus Circle. When he walked up the stairs of the station he saw by his wristwatch that it was exactly five minutes to nine.

Mr. Keesler's office was in the smallest and shabbiest building on Columbus Circle. It was made to look even smaller and shabbier by the new Coliseum which loomed over it on one side and by the apartment hotels which towered over it on the other. It had one creaky elevator to service its occupants, and an old man named Eddie to operate the elevator.

When Mr. Keesler came into the building Eddie had his mail all ready for him. The mail consisted of a large bundle of letters tied with a string, and a half dozen small cardboard boxes. Mr. Keesler managed to get all this under one arm with difficulty, and Eddie said, "Well, that's a nice big load the same as ever. I hope you get some business out of it."

"I hope so," said Mr. Keesler.

Another tenant picked up his mail and stepped into the elevator behind Mr. Keesler. "Well," he said, looking at the load under Mr. Keesler's arm, "it's nice to see that somebody's making money around here."

"Sure," said Mr. Keesler. "They send you the orders all right, but when it comes to paying for them where are they?"

"That's how it goes," said Eddie.

He took the elevator up to the third floor and Mr. Keesler got out there. His office was in Room 301 at the end of the corridor, and on its door were painted the words KEESLER NOVELTIES. Underneath in quotation marks was the phrase *"Everything for the trade."*

The office was a room with a window that looked out over Central Park. Against one wall was a battered rolltop desk that Mr. Keesler's father had bought when he himself had started in the novelties business long ago, and before it was a large, comfortable swivel chair with a foam-rubber cushion on its seat. Against the opposite wall was a table, and on it was an old L. C. Smith typewriter, a telephone, some telephone books, and a stack of magazines. There was another stack of magazines on top of a large filing cabinet in a corner of the room. Under the window was a chaise-longue which Mr. Keesler had bought second-hand from Eddie for five dollars, and next to the rolltop desk were a wastepaper basket and a wooden coat-rack he had bought from Eddie for fifty cents. Tenants who moved from the building sometimes found it cheaper to abandon their shopworn furnishings than to pay cartage for them, and Eddie did a small business in selling these articles for whatever he was offered.

Mr. Keesler closed the office door behind him. He gratefully set the heavy sample case down in a corner, pushed open the desk, and dropped his mail and the *New York Times* on it. Then he hung his hat and coat on the rack, checking the pockets of the coat to make sure he had forgotten nothing in them.

He sat down at the desk, opened the string around the mail, and looked at the return address on each letter. Two of the letters were from banks. He unlocked a drawer of the desk, drew out a notebook, and entered the figures into it. Then he tore the receipts into small shreds and dropped them into the wastepaper basket.

The rest of the mail was easily disposed of. Mr. Keesler took each of the smaller envelopes and, without opening it, tore it in half and tossed it into the basket on top of the shredded deposit slips. He then opened the envelopes which were thick and unwieldy, extracted their contents — brochures and catalogues — and placed them on the desk. When he was finished he had a neat pile of catalogues and brochures before him. These he dumped into a drawer of the filing cabinet.

He now turned his attention to the cardboard boxes. He opened them and pulled out various odds and ends — good-luck charms, a souvenir coin, a plastic keyring, several packets of cancelled foreign stamps, and a small cellophane bag containing one chocolate cracker. Mr. Keesler tossed the empty boxes into the wastepaper basket, ate the cracker, and pushed the rest of the stuff to the back of the desk. The cracker was a little bit too sweet for his taste, but not bad.

In the top drawer of the desk were a pair of scissors, a box of stationery, and a box of stamps. Mr. Keesler removed these to the table and placed them next to the typewriter. He wheeled the swivel chair to the table, sat down, and opened the classified telephone directory to its listing of dentists. He ran his finger down a column of names. Then he picked up the phone and dialed a number.

"Dr. Glover's office," said a woman's voice.

"Look," said Mr. Keesler, "this is an emergency. I'm in the neighborhood here, so can I come in during the afternoon? It hurts pretty bad."

"Are you a regular patient of Dr. Glover's?"

"No, but I thought —"

"I'm sorry, but the doctor's schedule is full. If you want to call again tomorrow —"

"No, never mind," said Mr. Keesler. "I'll try someone else."

He ran his finger down the column in the directory and dialed again.

"This is Dr. Gordon's office," said a woman's voice, but much more youthful and pleasant than the one Mr. Keesler had just encountered. "Who is it, please?"

"Look," said Mr. Keesler. "I'm suffering a lot of pain, and I was wondering if the doctor couldn't give me a couple of minutes this afternoon. I'm right in the neighborhood here. I can be there any time that's convenient. Say around two o'clock?"

"Well, two o'clock is already filled, but I have a cancellation here for three. Would that be all right?"

"That would be fine. And the name is Keesler." Mr. Keesler spelled it out carefully. "Thanks a lot, miss, and I'll be there right on the dot."

He pressed the bar of the phone down, released it, and dialed again. "Is Mr. Hummel there?" he said. "Good. Tell him it's about the big delivery he was expecting this afternoon."

In a moment he heard Mr. Hummel's voice. "Yeah?"

"You know who this is?" asked Mr. Keesler.

"Sure I know who it is."

"All right," said Keesler, "then meet me at four o'clock instead of three. You understand?"

"I get it," said Mr. Hummel.

Mr. Keesler did not continue the conversation. He put down the phone, pushed aside the directory, and took a magazine from the pile on the table. The back pages of the magazine were full of advertisements for free gifts, free samples, and free catalogues. *Mail us this coupon,* most of them said, *and we will send you absolutely free* —

Mr. Keesler studied these offers, finally selected ten of them, cut out the coupons with his scissors, and addressed them on the typewriter. He typed slowly but accurately, using only two fingers. Then he addressed ten envelopes, sealed the coupons into them, and stamped them. He snapped a rubber band around the envelopes for easier mailing and put everything else in the office back into its proper place. It was now 10:25, and the only thing left to attend to was the *New York Times.*

By twelve o'clock, Mr. Keesler, stretched comfortably out on the chaise-longue, had finished reading the *Times.* He had, however, by-passed the stock market quotations as was his custom. In 1929 his father's entire capital had been wiped out overnight in the market crash, and since that day Mr. Keesler had a cold and cynical antipathy to stocks and bonds and anything connected with them. When talking to people about it he would make it a little joke. "I like to know that my money is all tied up in cash," he would say. But inwardly he had been deeply scarred by what his father had gone through after the debacle. He had been very fond of his father, a gentle and hard-working man, well liked by all who knew him, and had never forgiven the stock market for what it had done to him.

Twelve o'clock was lunchtime for Mr. Keesler, as it was for almost everyone else in the building. Carrying his mail, he walked downstairs along with many others who knew that it would take Eddie quite a while to pick them up in his overworked elevator at this hour. He dropped the letters into a mailbox on the corner, and banged the lid of the mailbox a couple of times for safety's sake.

Near 58th Street on Eighth Avenue was a cafeteria which served good food at reasonable prices, and Mr. Keesler had a cheese sandwich, baked apple, and coffee there. Before he left he had a counterman wrap a cinnamon bun in waxed paper and place it in a brown paper bag for him to take along with him.

Swinging the bag in his hand as he walked, Mr. Keesler went into a drugstore a block away and bought a roll of two-inch-wide surgical bandage. On his way out of the store he surreptitiously removed the bandage from its box and wrapper and dropped the box and wrapper into a little basket on the street. The roll of bandage itself he put into the bag containing the cinnamon bun.

He repeated this process in a drugstore on the next block, and then six more times in various stores on his way down Eighth Avenue. Each time he would pay the exact amount in change, drop the box and wrappings into a little basket, put the roll of bandage into his paper bag. When he had eight rolls of bandage in the bag on top of the cinnamon bun he turned around and walked back to the office building. It was exactly one o'clock when he got there.

Eddie was waiting in the elevator, and when he saw the paper bag he smiled toothlessly and said as he always did, "What is it this time!"

"Cinnamon buns," said Mr. Keesler. "Here, have one." He pulled out the cinnamon bun wrapped in its waxed paper, and Eddie took it.

"Thanks," he said.

"That's all right," said Mr. Keesler. "There's plenty here for both of us. I shouldn't be eating so much of this stuff anyhow."

At the third floor he asked Eddie to hold the elevator, he'd be out in a minute. "I just have to pick up the sample case," he said. "Got to get to work on the customers."

In the office he lifted the sample case to the desk, put the eight rolls of bandage in it, and threw away the now empty paper bag into the wastepaper basket. With the sample case weighing him down he made his way back to the elevator.

"This thing weighs more every time I pick it up," he said to Eddie as the elevator went down, and Eddie said, "Well, that's the way it goes. We're none of us as young as we used to be."

A block away from Columbus Circle, Mr. Keesler took an Independent Line subway train to East Broadway, not far from Manhattan Bridge. He ascended into the light of Straus Square, walked down to Water Street, and turned left there. His destination was near Montgomery Street, but he stopped before he came to it and looked around.

The neighborhood was an area of old warehouses, decaying tenements, and raw, new housing projects. The street Mr. Keesler was interested in, however, contained only warehouses. Blackened with age, they stood in a row looking like ancient fortresses. There was a mixed smell of refuse and salt water around them that invited coveys of pigeons and seagulls to fly overhead.

Mr. Keesler paid no attention to the birds, nor to the few waifs and strays on the street. Hefting his sample case, he turned into an alley which led between two warehouses and made his way to the vast and empty lot behind them. He walked along until he came to a metal door in the third warehouse down the row. Using a large, old-fashioned key he opened the door, stepped into the blackness beyond it, and closed it behind him, locking it from the inside and testing it to make sure it was locked.

There was a light switch on the wall near the door. Mr. Keesler put down his sample case and wrapped a handkerchief loosely around his hand. He fumbled along the wall with that hand until he found the switch, and when he pressed it a dim light suffused the building. Since the windows of the building were sealed by metal shutters, the light could not be seen outside. Mr. Keesler then put away the handkerchief and carried the sample case across the vast expanse of the warehouse to the huge door of the delivery entrance that faced on the street.

Near the door was a long plank table on which was a time-stamper, a few old receipt books, and some pencil stubs. Mr. Keesler put down the sample case, took off his coat, neatly folded it and laid it on the table, and placed his hat on top of it. He bent over the sample case and opened it. From it he took the eight rolls of bandage, a large tube of fixative called Quick-Dry, a four-inch length of plumber's candle, two metal cans each containing two gallons of high octane gasoline, six paper drinking cups, a two-yard length of fishline, a handful of soiled linen rags, and a pair of rubber gloves much spattered with drops of dried paint. All this he arranged on the table.

Now donning the rubber gloves, he picked up the length of fishline and made a series of loops in it. He fitted a roll of bandage into each loop and drew the string tight. When he held it up at arm's length it looked like a string of white fishing bobbers.

Each gasoline tin had a small spout and looked as if it were tightly sealed. But the lid of one could be removed entirely and Mr. Keesler pried at it until it came off. He lowered the line of rolled bandages into the can, leaving the end of the string dangling over the edge for ready handling. A few bubbles broke at the surface of the can as the gauze bandages started to soak up gasoline. Mr. Keesler observed this with satisfaction, and then, taking the tube of Quick-Dry with him, he made a thoughtful tour of inspection of the warehouse.

What he saw was a broad and high steel framework running through the center of the building from end to end and supporting a great number of cardboard boxes, wooden cases, and paper-covered rolls of cloth. More boxes and cases were stacked nearly ceiling-high against two walls of the room.

He surveyed everything carefully, wrinkling his nose against the sour odor of mold that rose around him. He tested a few of the cardboard boxes by pulling away loose pieces, and found them all as dry as dust.

Then having studied everything to his satisfaction he kneeled down at a point midway between the steel framework and the angle of the two walls where the cases were stacked highest and squeezed some fixative on the wooden floor. He watched it spread and settle, and then went back to the table.

From the pocket of his jacket he drew out a finely whetted penknife and an octagon-shaped metal pencil which was also marked off as a ruler. He looked at his wristwatch, making some brief calculations, and measured off a length of the plumber's candle with the ruler. With the penknife he then sliced through the candle and trimmed away some wax to give the wick clearance. Before putting the knife back into his pocket he cleaned the blade with one of the pieces of cloth on the table.

When he looked into the can which contained the bandages soaking in gasoline he saw no more bubbles. He picked up the can and carried it to the place on the floor where the fixative was spread. Slowly reeling up the string so that none of the gasoline would spatter him, he detached each roll of wet bandage from it. He loosened a few inches of gauze from six of the bandages and pressed the exposed gauze firmly into the fixative, which was now gummy.

Unspooling the bandage as he walked he then drew each of the six lengths of gauze in turn to a designated point. Three went among the boxes of the framework and three went into the cases along the walls. They were nicely spaced so that they radiated like the main strands of a spiderweb to points high among the packed cases. To reach the farthest points in the warehouse Mr. Keesler knotted the extra rolls of bandage to two of those which he had pulled out short of the mark. There was a sharp reek of gasoline in the warehouse now, added to its smell of mold.

Where the ends of the bandages were thrust between the boxes, Mr. Keesler made sure that the upper box was set back a little to provide a narrow platform. He took the paper drinking cups from the table, filled each with gasoline, and set it on top of the end of the bandage, resting on this platform.

The fixative was now put to work again. Mr. Keesler squeezed some of it over the juncture of the six bandages on the floor, which were sealed there by the previous application. While it hardened he went to the table, took a handful of rags, and brought them to the open gasoline can. He lowered each rag in turn into the can, squeezed some of the excess gasoline back into the can after he pulled it out, and arranged all the rags around the fixative.

Then he took the stump of plumber's candle which he had prepared and pressed it down into the drying fixative. He tested it to make sure it was tightly set into place, looped the gasoline-saturated fishline around and around its base, and pushed the rags close up against it. He made sure that a proper length of candle was exposed, and then stood up to view his handiwork. Everything, as far as he could see, was in order.

Humming a little tune under his breath, Mr. Keesler took the two cans of gasoline and disposed of their contents among the boxes. He handled the cans expertly, splashing gasoline against the boxes where the bandages were attached, pouring it between the boxes wherever he detected a draft stirring in the dank air around him. When the cans were empty he wiped them thoroughly with a rag he had reserved for the purpose and added the rag to the pile around the candle.

Everything that needed to be done had now been done.

Mr. Keesler went back to the table, tightly sealed the gasoline cans, and placed them in the sample case. He pulled off the rubber gloves and put them and the remnants of plumber's candle into the case, too. Then he locked the case and put on his hat and coat.

He carried the case to a point a few feet away from the candle on the floor, set it down, and took out a book of matches from his pocket. Cupping a hand around the matchbook he lit one, and walking with great care while shielding the flame, he approached the candle, bent over it, and lit it. The flame guttered and then took hold.

Mr. Keesler stood up and put out the match, not by shaking it or blowing it, but by wetting his thumb and forefinger in his mouth and squeezing out the light between them. He dropped the used match into his pocket, went to the back door, switched off the electric light there with his handkerchiefed hand, and drew open the door a few inches.

After peering outside to make sure no one was observing him, Mr. Keesler stepped through the door, locked it behind him, and departed.

He returned to his office by the same route he had come. In the elevator he said to Eddie, "All of a sudden my tooth is killing me. I guess I'll have to run over to the dentist," and Eddie said, "Your teeth sure give you a lot of trouble, don't they?"

"They sure do," said Mr. Keesler.

He left the sample case in his room, washed his hands and face in the lavatory at the opposite end of the hallway, and took the elevator down. The dentist's office was on 56th Street near Seventh Avenue, a few minutes' walk away, and when Mr. Keesler entered the reception room the clock on the wall there showed him that it was two minutes before three. He was pleased to see that the dentist's receptionist was young and pretty and that she had his name neatly entered in her appointment book.

"You're right on time," she said as she filled out a record card for him. She handed him the card. "Just give this to Dr. Gordon when you go into the office."

In the office Mr. Keesler took off his glasses, put them in his pocket, and sat back in the dentist's chair. His feet hurt, and it felt good to be sitting down.

"Where does it hurt?" said Dr. Gordon, and Mr. Keesler indicated the back of his lower right jaw. "Right there," he said.

He closed his eyes and crossed his hands restfully on his belly while the doctor peered into his open mouth and poked at his teeth with a sharp instrument.

"Nothing wrong on the surface," Dr. Gordon said. "Matter of fact, your teeth seem to be in excellent shape. How old are you?"

"Fifty," said Mr. Keesler with pride. "Fifty-one next week."

"Wish my teeth were as good," said the dentist. "Well, it might possibly be that wisdom tooth under the gum that's giving the trouble. But all I can do now is put something soothing on it and take X-rays. Then we'll know."

"Fine," said Mr. Keesler.

He came out of the office at 3:30 with a sweet, minty taste in his mouth and with his feet well rested. Walking briskly he headed for the B.M.T. subway station at 57th Street and took a train down to Herald Square. He climbed to the street there and took a position among the crowd moving slowly past the windows of R. H. Macy's Department Store, keeping his eyes fixed on the windows as he moved.

At four o'clock he looked at his watch.

At five minutes after four he looked at it with concern.

Then in the window of the store he saw a car coming up to the curb. He walked across the street and entered it, and the car immediately drew away from the curb and fell in with the rest of the traffic on the street.

"You're late, Hummel," said Mr. Keesler to the driver. "Nothing went wrong, did it?"

"Nothing," said Mr. Hummel tensely. "It must have started just about 3:30. The cops called me ten minutes ago to tell me about it. The whole building's going, they said. They wanted me to rush over right away."

"Well, all right," said Keesler. "So what are you so upset about? Everything is fine. In no time at all you'll have sixty thousand dollars of insurance money in your pocket, you'll be rid of that whole load of stuff you were stuck with — you ought to be a happy man."

Mr. Hummel awkwardly manipulated the car into a turn that led downtown. "But if they find out," he said. "How can you be so sure they won't? At my age to go to jail —!"

Mr. Keesler had dealt with overwrought clients many times before. "Look, Hummel," he said patiently, "the first job I ever did was thirty years ago for my own father, God rest his soul, when the market cleaned him out. To his dying day he thought it was an accident, he never knew it was me. My wife don't know what I do. Nobody knows. Why? Because I'm an expert. I'm the best in the business. When I do a job I'm covered up every possible way — right down to the least little thing. So quit worrying. Nobody will ever find out."

"But in the daytime," said Mr. Hummel. "With people around. I still say it would have been better at night."

Mr. Keesler shook his head. "If it happened at night, the Fire Marshal and the insurance people would be twice as suspicious. And what do I look like, anyhow, Hummel, some kind of bum who goes sneaking around at night? I'm a nine-to-five man. I go to the office and I come home from the office like anybody else. Believe me, that's the best protection there is."

"It could be," said Mr. Hummel, nodding thoughtfully. "It could be."

A dozen blocks away from the warehouse, thick black smoke could be seen billowing into the air above it. On Water Street, three blocks away, Mr. Keesler put a hand on Mr. Hummel's arm.

"Stop here," he said. "There's always marshals and insurance people around the building looking at people, so this is close enough. You can see all you have to from here."

Mr. Hummel looked at the smoke pouring from the building, at the tongues of flame now and then shooting up from it, at the fire engines and tangles of hose in the street, and at the firemen playing water against the walls of the building. He shook his head in awe. "Look at that," he said, marveling. "Look at that."

"I did," said Mr. Keesler. "So how about the money?"

Mr. Hummel stirred himself from his daze, reached into his trouser pocket, and handed Mr. Keesler a tightly folded roll of bills. "It's all there," he said. "I had it made up the way you said."

There were fourteen hundred-dollar bills and five twenties in the roll. Bending low and keeping the money out of sight Mr. Keesler counted it twice. He had two bank deposit envelopes all filled out and ready in his pocket. Into one which credited the money to the account of K. E. Esler he put thirteen of the hundred-dollar bills. Into the other which was made out in the name of Keesler Novelties he put a single hundred-dollar bill. The five twenties he slipped into his wallet, and from the wallet took out the key to the warehouse.

"Don't forget this," he said, handing it to Mr. Hummel. "Now I have to run along."

"Wait a second," said Mr. Hummel. "I wanted to ask you about something, and since I don't know where to get in touch with you —"

"Yes?"

"Well, I got a friend who's in a very bad spot. He's stuck with a big inventory of fur pieces that he can't get rid of, and he needs cash bad. Do you understand?"

"Sure," said Mr. Keesler. "Give me his name and phone number, and I'll call him up in a couple of weeks."

"Couldn't you make it any sooner?"

"I'm a busy man," said Mr. Keesler. "I'll call him in two weeks." He took out the book of matches and inside it wrote the name and number Mr. Hummel gave him. He put away the matches and opened the door to the car. "So long, Hummel."

"So long, Esler," said Mr. Hummel.

For the second time that day Mr. Keesler traveled in the subway from East Broadway to Columbus Circle. But instead of going directly to his office this time, he turned down Eighth Avenue and dropped the sealed envelope which contained the $1300 into the night-deposit box of the Merchant's National Bank. Across the street was the Columbus National Bank, and into its night-deposit box he placed the envelope containing the hundred dollars. When he arrived at his office it was ten minutes before five.

Mr. Keesler opened his sample case, threw in the odds and ends that had come in the mail that morning, shut the sample case, and closed the rolltop desk, after throwing the *New York Times* into the wastebasket. He took a magazine from the pile on the filing cabinet and sat down in the swivel chair while he looked at it.

At exactly five o'clock he left the office, carrying the sample case.

The elevator was crowded, but Mr. Keesler managed to wedge himself into it. "Well," said Eddie on the way down, "another day, another dollar."

In the subway station Mr. Keesler bought a *World-Telegram,* but was unable to read it in the crowded train. He held it under his arm, standing astride the sample case, half dozing as he stood there. When he got out of the station at Beverly Road he stopped at the stationery store on the corner to buy a package of razor blades. Then he walked home slowly, turned into the driveway, and entered the garage.

Mrs. Keesler always had trouble getting the car into the garage. It stood there now at a slight angle to the wall so that Mr. Keesler had to squeeze past it to get to the back of the garage. He opened the sample case, took out the piece of plumber's candle and the tube of Quick-Dry, and put them into a drawer of the workbench there. The drawer was already full of other bits of hardware and small household supplies.

Then he took the two gasoline cans from the sample case and a piece of rubber tubing from the wall and siphoned gasoline from the tank of the car into the cans until they were full. He put them on the floor among other cans which were full of paint and solvent.

Finally he took out the rubber gloves and tossed them on the floor under one of the partly painted chairs. The spatters of paint on the gloves were the exact color of the paint on the chairs.

Mr. Keesler went into the house by the side door, and Mrs. Keesler, who had been setting the kitchen table, heard him. She came into the living room and watched as Mr. Keesler turned the sample case upside down over the table. Trinkets rolled all over the table, and Mrs. Keesler caught the souvenir charm before it could fall to the floor.

"More junk," she said good-naturedly.

"Same as always," said Mr. Keesler, "just stuff from the office. I'll give them to Sally's kids." His niece Sally had two pretty little daughters of whom he was very fond.

Mrs. Keesler put her hand over her mouth and looked around. "And what about the suit?" she said. "Don't tell me you forgot about the suit at the tailor's!"

Mr. Keesler already had one arm out of his coat. He stood there helplessly.

"Oh, no," he said.

His wife sighed resignedly.

"Oh, yes," she said. "And you'll go right down there now before he closes."

Mr. Keesler thrust an arm out behind him, groping for the sleeve of his coat, and located it with his wife's help. She brushed away a speck on the shoulder of the coat, and then patted her husband's cheek affectionately.

"If you could only learn to be a little methodical, dear," said Mrs. Keesler.

ED McBAIN

SMALL
HOMICIDE

In the traditional detective novel the police are a blundering lot who need considerable outside help solving their cases. In the dozens of 87th Precinct novels that Ed McBain has written since 1956, the police often blunder, but they are persistent, they know their jobs, and they make their arrests. Real private detectives, McBain has said, don't solve crimes, and no policeman ever solves a crime alone. That is why his books have no one particular hero or detective but an entire precinctful of cops, and the precinct house itself is often a major presence in the story.

Back in the 1950s, when Evan Hunter (b. 1926) had just published The Blackboard Jungle *and wanted to branch into crime writing, he was warned that the move would ruin his reputation as a serious novelist. So he adopted the McBain pseudonym. (Chris Steinbrunner and Otto Penzler in their* Encyclopedia of Mystery and Detection *say that Evan Hunter itself is a pseudonym for Salvatore Lombino, who attended Evander Childs High School and Hunter College. They also say Hunter denies that where he went to school has anything to do with his name.)*

The chronicles of the 87th Precinct are short novels propelled by peppery dialogue. They are probably the best police procedural yarns in the business and have made Ed McBain one of the most imitated — and influential — crime writers of his generation.

"Small Homicide" was first published in 1953.

HER FACE WAS SMALL and chubby, the eyes blue and innocently rounded, but seeing nothing. Her body rested on the seat of the wooden bench, one arm twisted awkwardly beneath her.

The candles near the altar flickered and cast their dancing shadows on her face. There was a faded pink blanket wrapped around her, and against the whiteness of her throat were the purple bruises that told us she'd been strangled.

Her mouth was open, exposing two small teeth and the beginnings of a third.

She was no more than eight months old.

The church was quiet and immense, with early-morning sunlight lighting the stained-glass windows. Dust motes filtered down the long, slanting columns of sunlight, and Father Barron stood tall and darkly somber at the end of the pew, the sun touching his hair like an angel's kiss.

"This is the way you found her, Father?" I asked.

"Yes. Just that way." The priest's eyes were a deep brown against the chalky whiteness of his face. "I didn't touch her."

Pat Travers scratched his jaw and stood up, reaching for the pad in his back pocket. His mouth was set in a tight, angry line. Pat had three children of his own. "What time was this, Father?"

"At about five-thirty. We have a six o'clock mass, and I came out to see that the altar was prepared. Our altar boys go to school, you understand, and they usually arrive at the last moment. I generally attend to the altar myself."

"No sexton?" Pat asked.

"Yes, we have a sexton, but he doesn't arrive until about eight every morning. He comes earlier on Sundays."

I nodded while Pat jotted the information in his pad. "How did you happen to see her, Father?"

"I was walking to the back of the church to open the doors. I saw something in the pew, and I . . . well, at first I thought it was just a package someone had forgotten. When I came closer, I saw it was . . . was a baby." He sighed deeply and shook his head.

"The doors were locked, Father?"

"No. No, they're never locked. This is God's house, you know. They were simply closed. I was walking back to open them. I usually open them before the first mass in the morning."

"They were unlocked all night?"

"Yes, of course."

"I see." I looked down at the baby again. "You . . . you wouldn't know who she is, would you, Father?"

Father Barron shook his head again. "I'm afraid not. She may have been baptized here, but infants all look alike, you know. It would be different if I saw her every Sunday. But . . . ." He spread his hands wide in a helpless gesture.

Pat nodded, and kept looking at the dead child. "We'll have to send some of the boys to take pictures and prints, Father. I hope you don't mind. And we'll have to chalk up the pew. It shouldn't take too long, and we'll have the body out as soon as possible."

Father Barron looked down at the dead baby. He crossed himself then and said, "God have mercy on her soul."

I was sipping my hot coffee when the buzzer on my desk sounded. I pushed down the toggle and said, "Levine here."

"Dave, want to come into my office a minute? This is the lieutenant."

"Sure thing," I told him. I put down the cup and said, "Be right back," to Pat, and headed for the Skipper's office.

He was sitting behind his desk with our report in his hands. He glanced up when I came in and said, "Sit down, Dave. Hell of a thing, isn't it?"

"Yes," I said.

"I'm holding it back from the papers, Dave. If this breaks, we'll have every mother in the city telephoning us. You know what that means?"

"You want it fast."

"I want it damned fast. I'm pulling six men from other jobs to help you and Pat. I don't want to go to another precinct for help because the bigger this gets, the better its chances of breaking print are. I want it quiet and small, and I want it fast." He stopped and shook his head, and then muttered, "Goddamn thing."

"We're waiting for the autopsy report now," I said. "As soon as we get it, we may be able to —"

"What did it look like to you?"

"Strangulation. It's there in our report."

The lieutenant glanced at the typewritten sheet in his hands, mumbled, "Uhm," and then said, "While you're waiting, you'd better start checking the Missing Persons calls."

"Pat's doing that now, sir."

"Good, good. You know what to do, Dave. Just get me an answer to it fast."

"We'll do our best, sir."

He leaned back in his leather chair, "A little girl, huh?" He shook his head. "Damn shame. Damn shame." He kept shaking his head and looking at the report, and then he dropped the report on his desk and said, "Here're the boys you've got to work with." He handed me a typewritten list of names. "All good, Dave. Get me results."

"I'll try, sir."

Pat had a list of calls on his desk when I went outside again. I picked it up and glanced through it rapidly. A few older kids were lost, and there had been the usual frantic pleas from frantic mothers who should have watched their kids more carefully in the first place.

"What's this?" I asked. I put my forefinger alongside a call clocked in at eight-fifteen. A Mrs. Wilkes had phoned to say she'd left her baby outside in the carriage, and the carriage was gone.

"They found the kid," Pat said. "Her older daughter had simply taken the kid for a walk. There's nothing there, Dave."

"The Skipper wants action, Pat. The photos come in yet?"

"Over there." He indicated a pile of glossy photographs on his desk. I picked up the stack and thumbed through it. They'd shot the baby from every conceivable angle, and there were two good close-ups of her face. I fanned the pictures out on my desk top and phoned the lab. I recognized Caputo's voice at once.

"Any luck, Cappy?"

"That you, Dave?"

"Yep."

"You mean on the baby?"

"Yeah."

"The boys brought in a whole slew of stuff. A pew collects a lot of prints, Dave."

"Anything we can use?"

"I'm running them through now. If we get anything, I'll let you know."

"Fine. I want the baby's footprints taken and a stat sent to every hospital in the state."

"Okay. It's going to be tough if the baby was born outside, though."

"Maybe we'll be lucky. Put the stat on the machine, will you? And tell them we want immediate replies."

"I'll have it taken care of, Dave."

"Good. Cappy, we're going to need all the help we can get on this one. So . . ."

"I'll do all I can."

"Thanks. Let me know if you get anything."

"I will. So long, Dave. I've got work."

He clicked off, and I leaned back and lighted a cigarette. Pat picked up one of the baby's photos and glumly studied it.

"When they get him, they should cut off his . . ."

"He'll get the chair," I said. "That's for sure."

"I'll pull the switch. Personally. Just ask me. Just ask me and I'll do it."

The baby was stretched out on the long white table when I went down to see Doc Edwards. A sheet covered the corpse, and Doc was busy typing up a report. I looked over his shoulder:

POLICE DEPARTMENT

City of New York

Date: June 12, 1953

From: Commanding Officer, Charles R. Brandon, 77th Pct.

To: Chief Medical Examiner

SUBJECT: DEATH OF Baby girl (unidentified)

Please furnish information on items checked below in connection with the death of the above named. Body was found on June 12, 1953 at Church of the Holy Mother, 1220 Benson Avenue, Bronx, New York

Autopsy performed or examination made? Yes

By Dr. James L. Edwards, Fordham Hospital Mortuary

Date: June 12, 1953 Where? Bronx County

Cause of death: Broken neck

Doc Edwards looked up from the typewriter.
"Not nice, Dave."
"No, not nice at all." I saw that he was ready to type in the RESULT OF CHEMICAL ANALYSIS space. "Anything else on her?"
"Not much. Dried tears on her face. Urine on her abdomen, but-

tocks, and genitals. Traces of Desitin and petroleum jelly there, too. That's about it."

"Time of death?"

"I'd put it at about three A.M. last night."

"Uh-huh."

"You want a guess?"

"Sure."

"Somebody doesn't like his sleep to be disturbed by a crying kid. That's my guess."

"Nobody likes his sleep disturbed," I said. "What's the Desitin and petroleum jelly for? That normal?"

"Yeah, sure. Lots of mothers use it. Mostly for minor irritations. Urine burn, diaper rash, that sort of thing."

"I see."

"This shouldn't be too tough, Dave. You know who the kid is yet?"

"We're working on that now."

"Well, good luck."

"Thanks."

I turned to go, and Doc Edwards began pecking at the typewriter again, completing the autopsy report on a dead girl.

There was good news waiting for me back at the office. Pat rushed over with a smile on his face and a thick sheet of paper in his hands.

"Here's the ticket," he said.

I took the paper and looked at it. It was the photostat of a birth certificate.

U.S. NAVAL HOSPITAL   St. Albans, N.Y.   Birth Certificate

This certifies that ____Louise Ann Dreiser_____was born to

____Alice Dreiser____ in this hospital at ____4:15 P.M.____ on

the ____tenth____ day of____November, 1952____

Weight ____7____ lbs. ____6____ ozs.

In witness whereof, the said hospital has caused this certificate to be issued, properly

signed and the seal of the hospital hereunto affixed.

Gregory Freeman, Lt(jg) MC USN

Gregory Freeman, LTJG MC USN

Attending Physician

Frederick L. Mann

Frederick L. Mann, CAPTAIN MC

Commanding Officer USN

"Here's how they got it," Pat said, handing me another stat. I looked at it quickly. It was obviously the reverse side of the birth certificate.

Baby's Footprint   (Permanent Evidence of Identity)

Left foot   Right foot

Sex of child _____Female_____

Weight at birth _____7_____ lbs.

_____6_____ ozs.

Certificate of birth should be carefully preserved as record of value for future use:

1. To identify relationship

2. To establish age to enter school

There were several more good reasons why a birth certificate should be kept in the sugar bowl, and then below that:

Official registration at _____ 148-15 Archer Avenue,

Jamaica, L.I., N.Y.

Mother's left thumb   Mother's right thumb

"Alice Dreiser," I said.

"That's the mother. Prints and all. I've already sent a copy down to Cappy to check against the ones they lifted from the pew."

"Fine. Pick one of the boys from the list the Skipper gave us, Pat. Tell him to get whatever he can on Alice Dreiser and her husband. They have to be sailors or relations to get admitted to a naval hospital, don't they?"

"Yeah. You've got to prove dependency."

"Fine. Get the guy's last address, and we'll try to run down the woman, or him, or both. Get whoever you pick to call right away, will you?"

"Right. Why pick anyone? I'll make the call myself."

"No, I want you to check the phone book for any Alice Dreisers. In the meantime, I'll be looking over the baby's garments."

"You'll be down at the lab?"

"Yeah. Phone me, Pat."

"Right."

Caputo had the garments separated and tagged when I got there.

"You're not going to get much out of these," he told me.

"No luck, huh?"

He held out the pink blanket. "Black River Mills. A big trade name. You can probably buy it in any retail shop in the city." He picked up the small pink sweater with the pearl buttons. "Toddlers, Inc., ditto. The socks have no markings at all. The undershirt came from Gilman's here in the city. It's the largest department store in the world, so you can imagine how many of these they sell every day. The cotton pajamas were bought there, too."

"No shoes?"

"No shoes."

"What about the diaper?"

"What about it? It's a plain diaper. No label. You got any kids, Dave?"

"One."

"You ever see a diaper with a label?"

"I don't recall."

"If you did, it wasn't in it long. Diapers take a hell of a beating."

"Maybe this one came from a diaper service."

"Maybe. You can check that."

"Safety pins?"

"Two. No identifying marks. Look like five-and-dime stuff."

"Any prints?"

"Yeah. There are smudged prints on the pins, but there's a good partial thumbprint on one of the pajama snaps."

"Whose?"

"It matches the right thumbprint on the stat you sent down. Mrs. Dreiser's."

"Uh-huh. Did you check her prints against the ones from the pew?"

"Nothing, Dave. None of her, anyway."

"Okay, Cappy. Thanks a lot."

Cappy shrugged. "I get paid," he said. He grinned and waved as I walked out and headed upstairs again. I met Pat in the hallway, coming down to the lab after me.

"What's up?" I asked.

"I called the Naval Hospital. They gave me the last address they had for the guy. His name is Carl Dreiser, lived at 831 East 217th Street, Bronx, when the baby was born."

"How come?"

"He was a yeoman, working downtown on Church Street. Lived with his wife uptown, got an allotment. You know the story."

"Yeah. So?"

"I sent Artie to check at that address. He should be calling in soon now."

"What about the sailor?"

"I called the Church Street office, spoke to the commanding officer, Captain"— he consulted a slip of paper —"Captain Thibot. This Dreiser was working there back in November. He got orders in January, reported aboard the U.S.S. Hanfield, DD 981, at the Brooklyn Navy Yard on January fifth of this year."

"Where is he now?"

"That's the problem, Dave."

"What kind of problem?"

"The Hanfield was sunk off Pyongyang in March."

"Oh."

"Dreiser is listed as missing in action."

I didn't say anything. I nodded, and waited.

"A telegram was sent to Mrs. Dreiser at the Bronx address. The Navy says the telegram was delivered and signed for by Alice Dreiser."

"Let's wait for Artie to call in," I said.

We ordered more coffee and waited. Pat had checked the phone book, and there'd been no listing for either Carl or Alice Dreiser. He'd had a list typed of every Dreiser in the city, and it ran longer than my arm.

"Why didn't you ask the Navy what his parents' names are?" I said.

"I did. Both parents are dead."

"Who does he list as next of kin?"

"His wife. Alice Dreiser."

"Great."

In a half hour, Artie called in. There was no Alice Dreiser living at the Bronx address. The landlady said she'd lived there until April and had left without giving a forwarding address. Yes, she'd had a baby daughter. I told Artie to keep the place staked out, and then buzzed George Tabin and told him to check the Post Office Department for any forwarding address.

When he buzzed back in twenty minutes, he said, "Nothing, Dave. Nothing at all."

We split the available force of men, and I managed to wangle four more men from the lieutenant. Half of us began checking on the Dreisers listed in the phone directory, and the rest of us began checking the diaper services.

The first diaper place I called on had a manager who needed only a beard to look like Santa Claus. He greeted me affably and offered all his assistance. Unfortunately, they'd never had a customer named Alice Dreiser.

At my fourth stop, I got what looked like a lead.

I spoke directly to the vice-president, and he listened intently.

"Perhaps," he said, "perhaps." He was a big man, with a wide waist, a gold watch chain straddling it. He leaned over and pushed down on his intercom buzzer.

"Yes, sir?"

"Bring in a list of our customers. Starting with November of 1952."

"Sir?"

"Starting with November of 1952."

"Yes, sir."

We chatted about the diaper business in general until the list came, and then he handed it to me and I began checking off the names. There were a hell of a lot of names on it. For the month of December, I found a listing for Alice Dreiser. The address given was the one we'd checked in the Bronx.

"Here she is," I said. "Can you get her records?"

The vice-president looked at the name. "Certainly, just a moment." He buzzed his secretary again, told her what he wanted, and she brought the yellow file cards in a few minutes later. The cards told me that Alice Dreiser had continued the diaper service through February. She'd been late on her February payment, and had cancelled service in March. She'd had the diapers delivered for the first week in March but had not paid for them. She did not notify the company that she was moving. She had not returned the diapers they'd sent her that first week in March. The company did not know where she was.

"If you find her," the vice-president told me, "I'd like to know. She owes us money."

"I'll keep that in mind," I said.

The reports on the Dreisers were waiting for me back at the precinct. George had found a couple who claimed to be Carl's aunt and uncle. They knew he was married. They gave Alice's maiden name as Grant. They said she lived somewhere on Walton Avenue in the Bronx, or at least *had* lived there when Carl first met her; they hadn't seen either her or Carl for months. Yes, they knew the Dreisers had had a daughter. They'd received an announcement card. They had never seen the baby.

Pat and I looked up the Grants on Walton Avenue, found a listing for Peter Grant, and went there together.

A bald man in his undershirt, his suspenders hanging over his trousers, opened the door.

"What is it?" he asked.

"Police officers," I said. "We'd like to ask a few questions."

"What about? Let me see your badges."

Pat and I flashed our buzzers and the bald man studied them.

"What kind of questions do you want to ask?"

"Are you Peter Grant?"

"Yeah, that's right. What's this all about?"

"May we come in?"

"Sure, come on in." We followed him into the apartment, and he motioned us to chairs in the small living room. "Now, what is it?" he asked.

"Your daughter is Alice Dreiser?"

"Yes," he said.

"Do you know where she lives?"

"No."

"Come on, mister," Pat said. "You know where your daughter lives."

"I don't," Grant snapped, "and I don't give a damn, either."

"Why? What's wrong, mister?"

"Nothing. Nothing's wrong. It's none of your business, anyway."

"Her daughter had her neck broken," I said. "It is our business."

"I don't give a . . ." he started to say. He stopped then and looked straight ahead of him, his brows pulled together into a tight frown. "I'm sorry. I still don't know where she lives."

"Did you know she was married?"

"To that sailor. Yes, I knew."

"And you know she had a daughter?"

"Don't make me laugh," Grant said.

"What's funny, mister?" Pat said.

"Did I know she had a daughter? Why the hell do you think she married the sailor? Don't make me laugh!"

"When was your daughter married, Mr. Grant?"

"Last September." He saw the look on my face, and added, "Go ahead, you count it. The kid was born in November."

"Have you seen her since the marriage?"

"No."

"Have you ever seen the baby?"

"No."

"Do you have a picture of your daughter?"

"I think so. Is she in trouble? Do you think she did it?"

"We don't know who did it yet."

"Maybe she did," Grant said softly. "She just maybe did. I'll get you the picture."

He came back in a few minutes with a picture of a plain girl wearing a cap and gown. She had light eyes and straight hair, and her face was intently serious.

"She favors her mother," Grant said, "God rest her soul."

"Your wife is dead?"

"Yes. That picture was taken when Alice graduated high schcool. She graduated in June and married the sailor in September. She's . . . she's only just nineteen now, you know."

"May we have this?" He hesitated and said, "It's the only one I've got. She . . . she didn't take many pictures. She wasn't a very . . . pretty kid."

"We'll return it."

"All right," he said. His eyes began to blink. "She . . . If she's in trouble, you'll . . . you'll let me know, won't you?"

"We'll let you know."

"Kids . . . kids make mistakes sometimes." He stood up abruptly. "Let me know."

We had copies of the photo made, and then we staked out every church in the neighborhood in which the baby was found. Pat and I covered the Church of the Holy Mother, because we figured the suspect was most likely to come back there.

We didn't talk much. There is something about a church of any denomination that makes a man think rather than talk. Pat and I knocked off at about seven every night, and the night boys took over then. We were back on the job at seven in the morning, every morning.

It was a week before she came in.

She was a thin girl, with the body of a child and a pinched, tired face. She stopped at the font in the rear of the church, dipped her hand in the holy water, and crossed herself. Then she walked to the altar, stopped before an idol of the Virgin Mary, lighted a candle, and knelt before it.

"That's her," I said.

"Let's go," Pat answered.

"Not here. Outside."

Pat's eyes locked with mine for an instant. "Sure," he said.

She knelt before the idol for a long time, and then got to her feet slowly, drying her eyes. She walked up the aisle, stopped at the font, crossed herself, and then walked outside.

We followed her out, catching up with her at the corner. I pulled up on one side of her and Pat on the other.

"Mrs. Dreiser?" I asked.

She stopped walking. "Yes?"

I showed my buzzer. "Police officers," I said. "We'd like to ask some questions."

She stared at my face for a long time. She drew a trembling breath then, and said, "I killed her. I . . . Carl was dead, you see. I . . . I guess that was it. It wasn't right — his getting killed, I mean. And she was crying." She nodded blankly. "Yes, that was it. She just cried all the time, not knowing that I was crying inside. You don't know how I cried inside. Carl . . . he was all I had. I . . . I couldn't stand it anymore. I told her to shut up and when she didn't I . . . I . . ."

"Come on now, ma'am," I said.

"I brought her to the church." She nodded, remembering it all now. "She was innocent, you know. So I brought her to the church. Did you find her there?"

"Yes, ma'am," I said. "That's where we found her."

She seemed pleased. A small smile covered her mouth and she said, "I'm glad you found her."

She told the story again to the lieutenant. Pat and I checked out and on the way to the subway, I asked him, "Do you still want to pull the switch, Pat?"

He didn't answer.

CHESTER HIMES

BLIND MAN WITH A PISTOL

With his black policemen Grave Digger Jones and Coffin Ed Johnson, Chester Himes (1909–1984) brought the detective novel to Harlem, and he brought it with a bang. His crime novels, which include Cotton Comes to Harlem, All Shot Up, *and* The Real Cool Killers, *all proved to be more popular in Europe, where Himes spent the last thirty-five years of his life, than in America. His noncrime novels include* Pinktoes *and* If He Hollers Let Him Go, *his first novel, published in 1948.*

When Blind Man with a Pistol *was published in 1969, Himes wrote: "A friend of mine . . . told me this story about a blind man with a pistol shooting at a man who stopped him on a subway train and killing an innocent by-stander reading his newspaper across the aisle and I thought, damn right, sounds like today's news, riots in the ghettos, war in Vietnam, masochistic goings-on in the Mideast . . . and thought further that all unorganized violence is like a blind man with a pistol."*

Himes was born in Missouri, spent several years at both Ohio State University and Ohio State Penitentiary, beginning his career as a writer in the latter institution, where he was serving time for armed robbery.

The following excerpt from Blind Man with a Pistol *is the novel's conclusion; it can stand as an independent short story.*

IT WAS JUST the blind man didn't want anyone to know he was blind. He refused to use a cane or a Seeing Eye dog and if anyone tried to help him across the street more than likely they'd be rewarded with insults. Luckily, he remembered certain things from the time when he could see, and these remembrances were guides to his behavior.

For the most part he tried to act like anyone else and that caused all the trouble.

He remembered how to shoot dice from the time that he could see well enough to lose his pay every Saturday night. He still went to crap games and still lost his bread. That hadn't changed.

Since he had become blind he had become a very stern looking, silent man. He had skin the color and texture of brown wrapping paper; reddish, unkempt, kinky hair that looked burnt; and staring, milky, unblinking eyes with red rims that looked cooked. His eyes had the menacing stare of a heat-blind snake, which, along with his stern demeanor, could be very disconcerting.

However, he wasn't impressive physically. If he could have seen, anyone would have taken him on. He was tall and flabby and didn't look strong enough to squash a chinch. He wore a stained seersucker coat with a torn right sleeve over a soiled nylon sport shirt, along with baggy brown pants and scuffed and runover army shoes which had never been cleaned. He always looked hard up but he always managed to get hold of enough money to shoot dice. Old-timers said when he was winning he'd bet harder than lightning bumps a stump. But he was seldom winning.

He was up to the dice game at Fo-Fo's "Sporting Gentlemen's Club" on the third floor of a walkup at the corner of 135th Street and Lenox Avenue. The dice game was in the room that had formerly been the kitchen of the cold-water flat Fo-Fo had converted into a private club for "sporting gentlemen," and the original sink was still there for losers to wash their hands, although the gas stove had been removed to make room for the billiard table where the dice did their dance. It was hot enough in the room to fry brains and the unsmiling soul brothers stood packed about the table, grease running from their heads down into the sweat oozing from their black skin, watching the running of the dice from muddy, bloodshot, but alert eyes. There was nothing to smile about, it was a serious business. They were gambling their bread.

The blind man stood at the head of the table where Abie the Jew used to run his field, winning all the money in the game by betting the dice out, until a Black Muslim brother cut his throat because he wouldn't take a nickel bet. He tossed his last bread into the ring and said defiantly, "I'll take four to one that I come out on 'leven." Maybe Abie the Jew might have given it, but soul brothers are superstitious about their gambling and they figure a blind man might throw anything anytime.

But the back man covered the sawbuck and let the game go on.

The stick man tossed the dice into the blind man's big soft trembling right hand, which closed about them like a shell about an egg.

The blind man shook them, saying, "Dice, I beg you," and turned them loose in the big corral. He heard them jump the chain and bounce off the billiard table's lower lip and the stick man cry, "Five-four — *nine!* Nine's the point. Take 'em, Mister Shooter, and see what you can do."

The blind man caught the dice again when they were tossed to him and looked around at the black sweaty faces he knew were there, pausing to stare a moment at each in turn and then said aggressively, "Bet one to four I jump it like I made it."

Abie the Jew might have taken that too, but the blind man knew there wasn't a chance of getting that bet from his soul brothers, he just felt like being contrary. Mother-rapers just waiting to get the jump on him, he thought, but if they fucked with him he'd cost them.

"Turn 'em loose, shooter," the stick man barked. "You done felt 'em long enough, they ain't titties."

Scornfully, the blind man turned them loose. They rolled down the table and came up seven.

"Seven!" the stick man cried. "Four-trey — the country way. Seven! The loser!"

"The dice don't know me," the blind man said, then on second thought asked to see them. "Here, lemme see them dice."

With a "what-can-you-do?" expression, the stick man tossed him the dice. The blind man caught them and felt them. "Got too hot," he pronounced.

"I tole you they weren't titties," the stick man said and cried, "Shooter for the game."

The next shooter threw down and the stick man looked at the blind man. "Sawbuck in the center," he said. "You want him, back man?"

The blind man was the back man but he was a broke man too. "I leave him," he said.

"One gone," the stick man chanted. "Saddest words on land or sea, Mister Shooter, pass by me. Next sport with money to lose."

The blind man stopped at the sink to wash his hands and went out. On his way down the stairs he bumped into a couple of church sisters coming up the stairs and didn't even move to one side. He just went on without apologizing or uttering one word.

"Ain't got no manners at all!" the duck-bottom sister exclaimed indignantly.

"Why is our folks like that?" her lean black sister complained. "Ain't a Christian bone in 'em."

"He's lost his money in that crap game upstairs," sister duck-bottom said. "I knows."

"Somebody oughta tell the police," sister lean-and-black ventured spitefully. "It's a crying shame."

"Ain't it the truth? But they might send 'round some of them white mother-rapers — 'scuse me, Lawd, you's white too."

The blind man heard that and muttered to himself as he groped down the stairs, "Damn right, He white; that's why you black bitches mind him."

He was feeling so good with the thought he got careless and when he stepped out onto the sidewalk he ran head-on into another soul brother hurrying to a funeral.

"Watch where you going, mother-raper!" the brother snarled. "You want all the sidewalk?"

The blind man stopped and turned his face. "You want to make something of it, mother-raper?"

The brother took one look at the blind man's menacing eyes and hurried on. No need of him being no stand-in, he was only a guest, he thought.

When the blind man started walking again, a little burr-headed rebel clad in fewer rags than a bushman's child ran up to him and said breathlessly, "Can I help you, suh?" He had bet his little buddies a Pepsi-Cola top he wasn't scared to speak to the blind man, and they were watching from the back door of the Liberian First Baptist Church, a safe distance away.

The blind man puffed up like a puff adder. "Help me what?"

"Help you across the street, suh?" the little rebel piped bravely, standing his ground.

"You better get lost, you little black bastard, 'fore I whale the day-lights out of you!" the blind man shouted. "I can get across the street as good as anybody."

To substantiate his contention the blind man cut across Lenox Avenue against the light, blind eyes staring straight ahead, his tall flabby frame moving nonchalantly like a turned-on zombie. Rubber burnt asphalt as brakes squealed. Metal crashed as cars telescoped. Drivers cursed. Soul people watching him could have bitten off nail-heads with their ass-holes. But hearing the commotion the blind man just thought the street was full of bad drivers.

He followed the railing about the kiosk down into the subway station and located the ticket booth by the sound of coins clinking. Pushing in that direction, he stepped on the pet corn of a dignified, elegant, gray-haired, light-complexioned soul sister and she let out a bellow.

"Oh! Oh! Oh! Mother-raping cocksucking turdeating bastard, are you blind?" Tears of rage and pain flooded from her eyes. The blind man moved on unconcernedly; he knew she wasn't talking to him, he hadn't done anything.

He shoved his quarter into the ticket window, took his token and nickel change and went through the turnstile out onto the platform following the sound of footsteps. But instead of getting someone to help him at that point he kept on walking straight ahead until he was teetering on the edge of the tracks. A matronly white woman, standing nearby, gasped and clutched him by the arm to pull him back to safety.

But he shook off her hand and flew into a rage. "Take your hands off me, you mother-raping dip!" he shouted. "I'm on to that pickpocket shit!"

Blood flooded the woman's face. She snatched back her hand and instinctively turned to flee. But after taking a few steps outrage overcame her and she stopped and spat, "Nigger! Nigger! Nigger!"

Some mother-raping white whore got herself straightened, he interpreted, listening to the train arrive. He went in with the others and groped about surreptitiously until he found an empty seat and quickly sat next to the aisle, holding his back ramrod straight and assuming a forbidding expression to keep anyone from sitting beside him. Exploring with his feet he ascertained that two people sat on the wall seat between him and the door, but they hadn't made a sound.

The first sound above the general movement of passengers which he was able to distinguish came from a soul brother sitting somewhere in front of him talking to himself in a loud, uninhibited tone of voice: "Mop the floor, Sam. Cut the grass, Sam. Kiss my ass, Sam. Manure the roses, Sam. Do all the dirty work, Sam. *Shit!*"

The voice came from beyond the door and the blind man figured that the loudmouthed soul brother was sitting in the first cross seat facing toward the rear. He could hear the angry resentment in the soul brother's voice but he couldn't see the vindictiveness in his little red eyes or see the white passengers wince.

As though he'd made his eyes red on purpose, the soul brother said jubilantly, "That nigger's dangerous, he's got red eyes. Hey-hey! Red-eyed nigger!" He searched the white faces to see if any were looking at him. None were.

"What was that you said, Sam?" he asked himself in a sticky falsetto, mimicking someone, probably his white mistress.

"Mam?"

"You said a naughty word, Sam."

"*Nigger?* Y'all says it all the time."

"I don't mean that."

"Weren't none other."

"Don't you sass me, Sam. I heard you."

"*Shit?* All I said was mo' shit mo' roses."

"I *knew* I heard you say a naughty word."

"Yass mam, if ya'll weren't lissenin' y'all wouldn't a' heerd."

"We have to listen to know what you people are thinking."

"Haw-haw-haw! Now ain't that some sure enough shit?" Sam asked himself in his natural voice. "Lissenin', spyin', sniffin' around. Say they caint stand niggers and lean on yo' back to watch you work. Rubbin' up against you. Gettin in yo' face. Jes so long as you workin' like a nigger. Ain't that somep'n?"

He stared furiously at two middle-aged white passengers on the wall seat on his side of the door, trying to catch them peeking. But they were looking steadily down into their laps. His red eyes contracted then expanded, theatrically.

This red-eyed soul brother was fat and black and had red lips, too, that looked freshly skinned, against a background of blue gums and a round puffy face dripping with sweat. His bulging-bellied torso was squeezed into a red print sport shirt, open at the collar and wet in the armpits, exposing huge muscular biceps wrapped in glistening black skin. But his legs were so skinny they made him look deformed. They were encased in black pants, as tight as sausage skins, which cut into his crotch, chafing him mercilessly and smothering what looked like a pig in a sack between his legs. To add to his discomfort, the jolting of the coach gave him an excruciating nutache.

He looked as uncomfortable as a man can be who can't decide whether to be mad at the mother-raping heat, his mother-raping pants, his cheating old lady, or his mother-raping picky white folks.

A huge, lumpy-faced white man across the aisle, who looked as though he might have driven a twenty-ton truck since he was born, turned and looked at the fat brother with a sneer of disgust. Fat Sam caught the look and drew back as if the man had slapped him. Looking quickly about for another brother to appease the white man's rage, he noticed the blind man in the first seat facing him beyond the door. The blind man was sitting there tending to his own business, staring at Fat Sam without seeing him, and frowning as hard as going up a hill at his bad luck. But Fat Sam bitterly resented being stared at, like all soul brothers, and this mother-raper was staring at him in a way that made his blood boil.

"What you staring at, mother-raper?" he shouted belligerently.

The blind man had no way of knowing Fat Sam was talking to him, all he knew was the loudmouthed mother-raper who'd come in talking to his mother-raping self was now trying to pick a fight with some other mother-raper who was just looking at him. But he could understand why the mother-raper was so mad, he'd caught some mother-raping whitey with his old lady. The mother-raper ought to be more careful, he thought unsympathetically, if she were that kind of whore he ought to watch her more; leastways he ought to keep his business to himself. Involuntarily, he made a downward motion, like a cat buzzing to the object Jeff, "Don't rank it, man, don't rank it!"

The gesture hit Fat Sam like a bolt of white lightning and a ray of white heat, and he jumped on it with his two black feet, as they say in that part of the world. Mother-raper wavin' him down like he was a mother-rapin' dog, he thought. Here in front of all these sneakin' white mother-rapers. He was more incensed by the white passengers' furtive smiles than by the blind man's gesture, although he hadn't discovered yet the old man was blind. White mother-rapers kickin' him in the ass from every which-a-side anyhow, he thought furiously, and here his own mother-rapin' soul brother just as much to say, keep yo' ass still, boy, so these white folks can kick it better.

"You doan like how I talk, you ol' mother-raper, you can kiss my black ass!" he shouted at the blind man. "I know you shit-colored Uncle Tom mother-rapers like you! You think I'm a disgrace to the race."

The first the blind man knew the soul brother was talking to him was when he heard some soul sister say protestingly, "That ain't no way to talk to that old man. You oughta be 'shamed of yo'self, he weren't bothering you."

He didn't resent what the soul brother had said as much as the meddling-ass sister calling him an "old man," otherwise he wouldn't have replied.

"I don't give a mother-rape whether you're a disgrace to the race or not!" he shouted, and because he couldn't think of anything else to say, added, "All I want is my bread."

The big white man looked at Fat Sam accusingly, like he'd been caught stealing from a blind man.

Fat Sam caught the look, and it made him madder at the blind man. "Bread!" he shouted. "What mother-raping bread?"

The white passengers looked around guiltily to see what had happened to the old man's bread.

But the blind man's next words relieved them. "What you and those other mother-rapers cheated me out of," he accused.

"Me?" Fat Sam exclaimed innocently. Me cheated you outer yo' bread? I ain't even seen you before, mother-raper!"

"If you ain't seen me, mother-raper, how come you talking to me?"

"Talkin' to you? I ain't talkin' to you, mother-raper. I just ast who you starin' at, and you go tryna make these white folks think I's cheated you."

"White folks?" the blind man cried. He couldn't have sounded more alarmed if Fat Sam had said the coach was full of snakes. "Where? Where?"

"Here, mother-raper!" Fat Sam crowed triumphantly. "All 'round you. Everywhere!"

The other soul people on the coach looked away before someone thought they knew those brothers, but the white passengers stole furtive peeks.

The big white man thought they were talking about him in a secret language known only to soul people. He reddened with rage.

It was then the sleek, fat, yellow preacher in the black mohair suit and immaculate dog collar, sitting beside the big white man, sensed the rising racial tension. Cautiously he lowered the open pages of the *New York Times*, behind which he had been hiding, and peered over the top at his argumentative brothers.

"Brothers! Brothers!" he admonished. "You can settle your differences without resorting to violence."

"Violence, hell!" the big white man exclaimed. "What these niggers need is discipline."

"Beware, mother-raper! Beware!" the blind man warned. Whether he was warning the fat black man or the big white man, no one ever knew. But his voice sounded so dangerous the fat yellow preacher ducked back out of sight behind his newspaper.

But Fat Sam thought it was himself the old man threatened. He jumped to his feet. "You talkin' to me, mother-raper?"

The big white man jumped up an instant later and pushed him back down.

Hearing all the movement, the blind man stood up too; he wasn't going to get caught sitting down.

The big white man saw him and shouted, "And you sit down, too!"

The blind man didn't pay him any attention, not knowing the white man meant him.

The white man charged down the aisle and pushed him down. The blind man looked startled. But all might have ended peacefully if the big white man hadn't slapped him.

The blind man knew it was the white man who had pushed him down, but he thought it was the soul brother who had slapped him, taking advantage of the white man's rage.

It figured. He said protestingly, "What you hit me for, mother-raper?"

"If you don't shut up and behave yourself, I'll hit you again," the white man threatened.

The blind man knew then it was the white man who had slapped him. He stood up again, slowly and dangerously, groping for the back of the seat to brace himself. "If'n you hit me again, white folks, I'll blow you away," he said.

The big white man was taken aback, because he had known all along the old man was blind. "You threatening me, boy?" he said in astonishment.

Fat Sam stood up in front of the door as though whatever happened he was going to be the first one out.

Still playing peacemaker, the fat yellow preacher said from behind his newspaper, "Peace, men, God don't know no color."

"Yeah?" the blind man questioned and pulled out a big .45 caliber revolver from underneath his old seersucker coat and shot at the big white man point-blank.

The blast shattered windows, eardrums, reason and reflexes. The big white man shrunk instantly to the size of a dwarf and his breath swooshed from his collapsed lungs.

Fat Sam's wet black skin dried instantly and turned white.

But the .45 caliber bullet, as sightless as its shooter, had gone the way the pistol had been aimed, through the pages of the *New York Times* and into the heart of the fat yellow preacher. "Uh!" his reverence grunted and turned in his Bible.

The moment of silence was appropriate but unintentional. It was just that all the passengers had died for a moment following the impact of the blast.

Reflexes returned with the stink of burnt cordite which peppered nostrils, watered eyes.

A soul sister leaped to her feet and screamed, "BLIND MAN WITH A PISTOL!" as only a soul sister, with four hundred years of experience, can. Her mouth formed an ellipsoid big enough to swallow the blind man's pistol, exposing the brown tartar stains on her molars and a white-coated tongue flattened between her bottom teeth and humped in the back against the tip of her palate which vibrated like a blood-red tuning fork.

"BLIND MAN WITH A PISTOL! BLIND MAN WITH A PISTOL!"

It was her screaming which broke everyone's control. Panic went off like Chinese firecrackers.

The big white man leaped ahead from reflex action and collided violently with the blind man, damn near knocking the pistol from his hand. He did a double take and jumped back, bumping his spine against a tubular iron upright. Thinking he was being attacked from behind by the other soul brother, he leaped ahead again. If die he must, he'd rather it came from the front than behind.

Assaulted the second time by a huge smelly body, the blind man thought he was surrounded by a lynch mob. But he'd take some of the mother-rapers with him, he resolved, and shot twice indiscriminately.

The second blasts were too much. Everyone reacted immediately. Some thought the world was coming to an end; others that the Venusians were coming. A number of the white passengers thought the niggers were taking over; the majority of the soul people thought their time was up.

But Fat Sam was a realist. He ran straight through the glass door. Luckily the train had pulled into the 125th Street station and was grinding to a stop. Because one moment he was inside the coach and the next he was outside on the platform, on his hands and knees, covered with blood, his clothes ripped to ribbons, shards of glass sticking from the sweaty blood covering his wet black skin like the surrealistic top of a Frenchman's wall.

Others trying to follow him got caught in the jagged edges of glass and were slashed unmercifully when the doors were opened. Suddenly the pandemonium had moved to the platform. Bodies crashed in headlong collision, went sprawling on the concrete. Legs kicked futilely in the air. Everyone tried to escape to the street. Screams fanned the panic. The stairs became strewn with the bodies of the fallen. Others fell too as they tried senselessly to run over them.

The soul sister continued to scream, "BLIND MAN WITH A PISTOL!"

The blind man groped about in the dark, panic-stricken, stumbling over the fallen bodies, waving his pistol as though it had eyes. "Where?" he cried piteously. "Where?"

The people of Harlem were as mad as only the people of Harlem can be. The New York City government had ordered the demolition of condemned slum buildings in the block on the north side of 125th Street between Lenox and Seventh avenues, and the residents didn't have any place to go. Residents from other sections of Harlem were mad because these displaced people would be dumped on them, and their neighborhoods would become slums. It was a commercial block too, and the proprietors of small businesses on the ground floors of the condemned buildings were mad because rent in the new buildings would be prohibitive.

The same applied to the residents, but most hadn't thought that far as yet. Now they were absorbed by the urgency of having to find immediate housing, and they bitterly resented being evicted from the homes where some had been born, and their children had been born, and some had married, and friends and relatives had died, no matter if these homes were slum flats that had been condemned as unfit for human dwelling. They had been forced to live there, in all the filth and degradation, until their lives had been warped to fit, and now they were being thrown out. It was enough to make a body riot.

One angry sister, who stood watching from the opposite sidewalk, protested loudly, "They calls this *urban renewal*, I calls it poor folks removal."

"Why don't she shut up, she cain't do nuthin'?" a young black teeny-bopper said scornfully.

Her black teeny-bopper companion giggled. "She look like a rolled-up mattress."

"You shut up, too. You'll look like that yo'self w'en you get her age."

Two young sports who'd just come from the YMCA gym glanced at the display of books in the window of the National African Memorial Bookstore next to the credit jewelers on the corner.

"They gonna tear down the black bookstore, too," one remarked. "They don't want us to have nothing."

"What I care?" the other replied. "I don't read."

Shocked and incredulous, his friend stopped to look at him. "Man, I wouldn't admit it. You ought to learn how to read."

"You don't dig me, man. I didn't say I can't read, I said I don't read. What I want to read all this mother-raping shit whitey is putting down for?"

"Umh!" his friend conceded and continued walking.

However, most of the soul people stood about apathetically, watching the wrecking balls swing against the old crumbling walls. It was a hot day and they sweated copiously as they breathed the poisonous air clogged with gasoline fumes and white plaster dust.

Farther eastward, at the other end of the condemned block, where Lenox Avenue crosses 125th Street, Grave Digger and Coffin Ed stood in the street, shooting the big gray rats that ran from the condemned buildings with their big long-barrelled, nickel-plated .38 caliber pistols on .44 caliber frames. Every time the steel demolition ball crashed against a rotten wall, one or more rats ran into the street indignantly, looking more resentful than the evicted people.

Not only rats but startled droves of bedbugs stampeded over the ruins and fat black cockroaches committed suicide by jumping from high windows.

They had an audience of rough-looking jokers from the corner bar who delighted in hearing the big pistols go off.

One rugged stud warned jokingly, "Don't shoot no cats by mistake."

"Cats are too small," Coffin Ed replied. "These rats look more like wolves."

"I mean two-legged cats."

At that moment a big rat came out from underneath a falling wall, and pawed the sidewalk, snorting.

"Hey! Hey! Rat!" Coffin Ed called like a toreador trying to get the attention of his bull.

The soul brothers watched in silence.

Suddenly the rat looked up through murderous red eyes and Coffin Ed shot it through the center of its forehead. The big brass-jacketed .38 bullet knocked the rat's body out of its fur.

"Olé!" the soul brothers cried.

The four uniformed white cops on the other corner eastward stopped talking and looked around anxiously. They had left their police cars parked on each side of 125th Street, beyond the demolition area, as though to keep any of the dispossessed from crossing the Triborough Bridge into the restricted neighborhoods of Long Island.

"He just shot another rat," one said.

"Too bad it weren't a nigger rat," the second cop said.

"We'll leave that for you," the first cop replied.

"Damn right," the second cop declared. "I ain't scared."

"As big as those rats are those niggers could cook 'em and eat 'em," the third cop remarked cynically.

"And get off relief," the second cop put in.

Three of them laughed.

"Maybe those rats been cooking and eating those niggers is why they're so big," the third cop continued.

"You men are not funny," the fourth cop protested.

"Then why'd you sneak that laugh?" the second cop observed.

"I was retching is all."

"That's all you hypocrites do — retch," the second cop came back.

The third cop caught a movement out of the corner of his eye and jerked his head about. He saw a fat black man shoot up from the subway, leaking blood, sweat and tears, bringing pandemonium with him. The other bleeding people who erupted behind him looked crazed with terror, as though they had escaped from the bad man.

But it was the sight of the bleeding, running, black man which galvanized the white cops into action. A bleeding, running black man spelled trouble, and they had the whole white race to protect. They went off running in four directions with drawn revolvers and squinting eyes.

Grave Digger and Coffin Ed watched them in amazement.

"What happened?" Coffin Ed asked.

"Just that fat blacky showing all that blood," Grave Digger said.

"Hell, if it was serious he'd have never got this far," Coffin Ed passed it off.

"You don't get it, Ed," Grave Digger explained. "Those white officers have got to protect white womanhood."

Seeing a white uniformed cop skid to a stop and turn to head him off, the fat black man broke in the direction of the Negro detectives. He didn't know them but they had pistols and that was enough.

"He's getting away!" the first cop called from behind.

"I'll cool the nigger!" the front cop said. He was the third cop who thought niggers ate rats.

At that moment the big white man who had started all the fracas came up the stairs, heaving and gasping as though he'd just made it. "That ain't the nigger!" he yelled.

The third cop skidded to a halt, looking suddenly bewildered.

Then the blind man stumbled up the stairs, tapping the railing with his pistol.

The big white man leaped aside in blind terror. "There's the nigger with the pistol," he screamed, pointing at the blind man coming up the subway stairs like "shadow" coming out of the East River.

At the sound of his voice the blind man froze. "You still alive, mother-raper?" He sounded shocked.

"Shoot him quick!" the big white man warned the alert white cops.

As though the warning had been for him, the blind man upped with his pistol and shot at the big white man the second time. The big white man leaped straight up in the air as though a firecracker had exploded in his ass-hole.

But the bullet had hit the white cop in the middle of the forehead, as he was taking aim, and he fell down dead.

The soul brothers who had been watching the antics of the white cops, petrified with awe, picked up their feet and split.

When the three other uniformed white cops converged on the blind man he was still pulling the trigger of the empty double-action pistol. Quickly they cut him down.

The soul brothers, who had got as far as doorways and corners, paused for a moment to see the results.

"Great Godamighty!" one of them exclaimed. "The mother-raping white cops has shot down that innocent brother!"

He had a loud, carrying voice, as soul brothers are apt to have, and a number of other soul people who hadn't seen it heard him. They believed him.

Like wildfire the rumor spread.

"DEAD MAN! DEAD MAN! . . ."

"WHITEY HAS MURDERED A SOUL BROTHER!"

"THE MOTHER-RAPING WHITE COPS, THAT'S WHO!"

"GET THEM MOTHER-RAPERS, MAN!"

"JUST LEAVE ME GET MY MOTHER-RAPING GUN!"

An hour later Lieutenant Anderson had Grave Digger on the radio-phone. "Can't you men stop that riot?" he demanded.

"It's out of hand, boss," Grave Digger said.

"All right, I'll call for reinforcements. What started it?"

"A blind man with a pistol."

"What's that?"

"You heard me, boss."

"That don't make any sense."

"Sure don't."

PAUL CAIN

PIGEON
BLOOD

George Sims (1902–1966), who called himself Paul Cain, seems almost a
prototype of the unknown pulp magazine writer. The son of a Des Moines,
Iowa, policeman, he went to California with his mother after that marriage
broke up. He hung around the fringes of the motion picture business, where
his most lasting contribution, perhaps, was convincing Myrna Williams to
change her last name to Loy. Cain wrote a series of pulp stories featuring a
hard-living gunman from the East Coast, and after one was turned into a
Cary Grant vehicle, Gambling Ship, he reworked the stories into a novel
called Fast One. As Peter Ruric he was credited with a few screenplays,
including The Black Cat with Boris Karloff and Bela Lugosi and Grand
Central Murder with Van Heflin. In 1950 a few Paul Cain pulp stories,
including "Pigeon Blood," were published as a collection, Seven Slayers.
Sixteen years later he drank himself to death.
    Joseph Shaw, editor of Black Mask, has been quoted as saying, "In the
matter of grim hardness, while . . . Dashiell paused on the threshold, Paul
went all the way."

THE WOMAN was bent far forward over the steering wheel of the
open roadster. Her eyes, narrowed to long black-fringed slits, moved
regularly down and up, from the glistening road ahead, to the small
rear-view mirror above the windshield. The two circles of white light
in the mirror grew steadily larger. She pressed the throttle slowly,
steadily downward; there was no sound but the roar of the wind and
the deep purr of the powerful engine.
    There was a sudden sharp crack; a little frosted circle appeared on

the windshield. The woman pressed the throttle to the floor. She was pale; her eyes were suddenly large and dark and afraid, her lips were pressed tightly together. The tires screeched on the wet pavement as the car roared around a long, shallow curve. The headlights of the pursuing car grew larger.

The second and third shots were wild, or buried themselves harmlessly in the body of the car; the fourth struck the left rear tire and the car swerved crazily, skidded halfway across the road. Very suddenly there was bright yellow light right ahead, at the side of the road. The woman jammed on the brakes, jerked the wheel hard over; the tires slid, screamed raggedly over the gravel in front of the gas station, the car stopped. The other car went by at seventy-five miles an hour. One last shot thudded into the back of the seat beside the woman and then the other car had disappeared into the darkness.

Two men ran out of the gas station. Another man stood in the doorway. The woman was leaning back straight in the seat and her eyes were very wide; she was breathing hard, unevenly.

One of the men put his hand on her shoulder, asked: "Are you all right, lady?"

She nodded.

The other man asked: "Hold-ups?" He was a short, middle-aged man and his eyes were bright, interested.

The woman opened her bag and took out a cigarette. She said shakily: "I guess so." She pulled out the dashboard lighter, waited until it glowed red and held it to her cigarette.

The younger man was inspecting the back of the car. He said: "They punctured the tank. It's a good thing you stopped — you couldn't have gone much farther."

"Yes — I guess it's a very good thing I stopped," she said, mechanically. She took a deep drag of her cigarette.

The other man said: "That's the third hold-up out here this week."

The woman spoke to the younger man. "Can you get me a cab?"

He said: "Sure." Then he knelt beside the blown-out tire, said: "Look, Ed — they almost cut it in two."

The man in the doorway called to her: "You want a cab, lady?"

She smiled, nodded, and the man disappeared into the gas station; he came back to the doorway in a minute, over to the car. "There'll be a cab here in a little while, lady," he said.

She thanked him.

"This is one of the worst stretches of road on Long Island — for highwaymen." He leaned on the door of the car. "Did they try to nudge you off the road — or did they just start shooting?"

"They just started shooting."

He said: "We got a repair service here — do you want us to fix up your car?"

She nodded. "How long will it take?"

"Couple days. We'll have to get a new windshield from the branch factory in Queens — an' take off that tank . . ."

She took a card out of her bag and gave it to him, said: "Call me up when it's finished."

After a little while, a cab came out of the darkness of a side street, turned into the station. The woman got out of the car and went over to the cab, spoke to the driver: "Do you know any shortcuts into Manhattan? Somebody tried to hold me up on the main road a little while ago, and maybe they're still laying for me. I don't want any more of it — I want to go home." She was very emphatic.

The driver was a big red-faced Irishman. He grinned, said: "Lady — I know a million of 'em. You'll be as safe with me as you'd be in your own home."

She raised her hand in a gesture of farewell to the three men around her car and got into the cab. After the cab had disappeared, the man to whom she had given the card took it out of his pocket and squinted at it, read aloud: "Mrs. Dale Hanan — Five-eighty Park Avenue."

The short, middle-aged man bobbed his head knowingly. "Sure," he said —"I knew she was class. She's Hanan's wife — the millionaire. Made his dough in oil — Oklahoma. His chauffeur told me how he got his start — didn't have a shoestring or a place to put it, so he shot off his big toe and collected ten grand on an accident policy — grub-stake on his first well. Bright boy. He's got a big estate down at Roslyn."

The man with the card nodded. He said: "That's swell. We can soak him plenty." He put the card back into his pocket.

When the cab stopped near the corner of Sixty-third and Park Avenue the woman got out, paid the driver and hurried into the apartment house. In her apartment, she put in a long-distance call to Roslyn, Long Island; when the connection had been made, she said: "Dale — it's in the open now. I was followed, driving back to town — shot at — the car was nearly wrecked. . . . I don't know what to do. Even if I call Crandall now, and tell him I won't go through with it — won't go to the police — he'll probably have me killed, just to make sure. . . . Yes, I'm going to stay in — I'm scared. . . . All right, dear. 'Bye."

She hung up, went to a wide center table and poured whiskey into a tall glass, sat down and stared vacantly at the glass — her hand was shaking a little. She smiled suddenly, crookedly, lifted the glass to her mouth and drained it. Then she put the glass on the floor and leaned back and glanced at the tiny watch at her wrist. It was ten minutes after nine.

At a few minutes after ten a black Packard town-car stopped in front of a narrow building of gray stone on East Fifty-fourth Street; a tall man got out, crossed the sidewalk and rang the bell. The car went on. When the door swung open, the tall man went into a long, brightly lighted hallway, gave his hat and stick to the checkroom attendant, went swiftly up two flights of narrow stairs to the third floor. He glanced around the big, crowded room, then crossed to one corner near a window on the Fifty-fourth Street side and sat down at a small table, smiled wanly at the man across from him, said: "Mister Druse, I believe."

The other man was about fifty, well set up, well groomed in the way of good living. His thick gray hair was combed sharply, evenly back. He lowered his folded newspaper to the table, stared thoughtfully at the tall man.

He said: "Mister Hanan," and his voice was very deep, metallic.

The tall man nodded shortly, leaned back and folded his arms across his narrow chest. He was ageless, perhaps thirty-five, forty-five; his thin, colorless hair was close-clipped, his long, bony face deeply tanned, a sharp and angular setting for large seal-brown eyes. His mouth was curved, mobile.

He asked: "Do you know Jeffrey Crandall?"

Druse regarded him evenly, expressionlessly for a moment, raised his head and beckoned a waiter. Hanan ordered a whiskey sour.

Druse said: "I know Mister Crandall casually. Why?"

"A little more than an hour ago, Crandall, or Crandall's men, tried to murder Mrs. Hanan, as she was driving back from my place at Roslyn." Hanan leaned forward: his eyes were wide, worried.

The waiter served Hanan's whiskey sour, set a small bottle of Perrier and a small glass on the table in front of Druse.

Druse poured the water into the glass slowly. "So what?"

Hanan tasted his drink. He said: "This is not a matter for the police, Mister Druse. I understand that you interest yourself in things of this nature, so I took the liberty of calling you and making this appointment. Is that right?" He was nervous, obviously ill at ease.

Druse shrugged. "*What* nature? I don't know what you're talking about."

"I'm sorry — I guess I'm a little upset." Hanan smiled. "What I mean is that I can rely on your discretion?"

Druse frowned. "I think so," he said slowly. He drank half of the Perrier, squinted down at the glass as if it tasted very badly.

Hanan smiled vacantly. "You do not know Mrs. Hanan?"

Druse shook his head slowly, turned his glass around and around on the table.

"We have been living apart for several years," Hanan went on. "We are still very fond of one another, we are very good friends, but we do not get along — together. Do you understand?"

Druse nodded.

Hanan sipped his drink, went on swiftly: "Catherine has — has always had — a decided weakness for gambling. She went through most of her own inheritance — a considerable inheritance — before we married. Since our separation she has lost somewhere in the neighborhood of a hundred and fifteen thousand dollars. I have, of course, taken care of her debts." Hanan coughed slightly. "Early this evening she called me at Roslyn, said she had to see me immediately — that it was very important. I offered to come into town but she said she'd rather come out. She came out about seven."

Hanan paused, closed his eyes and rubbed two fingers of one hand slowly up and down his forehead. "She's in a very bad jam with Crandall." He opened his eyes and put his hand down on the table.

Druse finished his Perrier, put down the glass and regarded Hanan attentively.

"About three weeks ago," Hanan went on, "Catherine's debt to Crandall amounted to sixty-eight thousand dollars — she had been playing very heavily under the usual gambler's delusion of getting even. She was afraid to come to me — she knew I'd taken several bad beatings on the market — she kept putting it off and trying to make good her losses, until Crandall demanded the money. She told him she couldn't pay — together, they hatched out a scheme to get it. Catherine had a set of rubies — pigeon blood — been in her family five or six generations. They're worth, perhaps, a hundred and seventy-five thousand — her father insured them for a hundred and thirty-five, forty years ago and the insurance premiums have always been paid. . . ." Hanan finished his whiskey sour, leaned back in his chair.

Druse said: "I assume the idea was that the rubies disappear; that Mrs. Hanan claim the insurance, pay off Crandall, have sixty-seven thousand left and live happily forever after."

Hanan coughed; his face was faintly flushed. "Exactly."

"I assume further," Druse went on, "that the insurance company did not question the integrity of the claim; that they paid, and that Mrs. Hanan, in turn, paid Crandall."

Hanan nodded. He took a tortoise-shell case out of his pocket, offered Druse a cigarette.

Druse shook his head, asked: "Are the insurance company detectives warm — are they making Crandall or whoever he had do the actual job, uncomfortable?"

"No. The theft was well engineered. I don't think Crandall is worrying about that." Hanan lighted a cigarette. "But Catherine wanted her rubies back — as had, of course, been agreed upon." He leaned forward, put his elbows on the table. "Crandall returned paste imitations to her — she only discovered they weren't genuine a few days ago."

Druse smiled, said slowly: "In that case, I should think it was Crandall who was in a jam with Mrs. Hanan, instead of Mrs. Hanan who was in a jam with Crandall."

Hanan wagged his long chin back and forth. "This is New York. Men like Crandall do as they please. Catherine went to him and he laughed at her; said the rubies he had returned were the rubies that had been stolen. She had no recourse, other than to admit her complicity in defrauding the insurance company. That's the trouble — she threatened to do exactly that."

Druse widened his eyes, stared at Hanan.

"Catherine is a very impulsive woman," Hanan went on. "She was so angry at losing the rubies and being made so completely a fool that she threatened Crandall. She told him that if the rubies were not returned within three days she would tell what he had done; that he had stolen the rubies — take her chances on her part in it coming out. Of course she wouldn't do it, but she was desperate and she thought that was her only chance of scaring Crandall into returning the rubies — and she made him believe it. Since she talked to him, Wednesday, she has been followed. Tomorrow is Saturday, the third day. Tonight, driving back to town, she was followed, shot at — almost killed."

"Has she tried to get in touch with Crandall again?"

Hanan shook his head. "She's been stubbornly waiting for him to give the rubies back — until this business tonight. Now she's frightened — says it wouldn't do any good for her to talk to Crandall now because he wouldn't believe her — and it's too easy for him to put her out of the way."

Druse beckoned the waiter, asked him to bring the check. "Where is she now?"

"At her apartment — Sixth-third and Park."

"What do you intend doing about it?"

Hanan shrugged. "That's what I came to you for. I don't know what to do. I've heard of you and your work from friends. . . ."

Druse hesitated, said slowly: "I must make my position clear."

Hanan nodded, lighted a fresh cigarette.

"I am one of the few people left," Druse went on, "who actually believes that honesty is the best policy. Honesty is my business — I am primarily a business man — I've made it pay."

Hanan smiled broadly.

Druse leaned forward. "I am not a fixer," he said. "My acquaintance is wide and varied — I am fortunate in being able to wield certain influences. But above all I seek to further justice — I mean real justice as opposed to *book* justice — I was on the bench for many years and I realize the distinction keenly." His big face wrinkled to an expansive grin. "And I get paid for it — *well* paid."

Hanan said: "Does my case interest you?"

"It does."

"Will five thousand be satisfactory — as a retaining fee?"

Druse moved his broad shoulders in something like a shrug. "You value the rubies at a hundred and seventy-five thousand," he said. "I am undertaking to get the rubies back, and protect Mrs. Hanan's life." He stared at Hanan intently. "What value do you put on Mrs. Hanan's life?"

Hanan frowned self-consciously, twisted his mouth down at the corners. "That is, of course, impossible to —"

"Say another hundred and seventy-five." Druse smiled easily. "That makes three hundred and fifty thousand. I work on a ten per cent basis — thirty-five thousand — one-third in advance." He leaned back, still smiling easily. "Ten thousand will be sufficient as a retainer."

Hanan was still frowning self-consciously. He said: "Done," took a checkbook and fountain pen out of his pocket.

Druse went on: "If I fail in either purpose, I shall, of course, return your check."

Hanan bobbed his head, made out the check in a minute, illegible scrawl and handed it across the table. Druse paid for the drinks, jotted down Hanan's telephone number and the address of Mrs. Hanan's apartment. They got up and went downstairs and out of the place; Druse told Hanan he would call him within an hour, got into a cab. Hanan watched the cab disappear in east-bound traffic, lighted a cigarette nervously and walked towards Madison Avenue.

Druse said: "Tell her I've come from Mister Hanan."

The telephone operator spoke into the transmitter, turned to Druse. "You may go up — Apartment Three D."

When, in answer to a drawled, "Come in," he pushed open the door and went into the apartment, Catherine Hanan was standing near the center table, with one hand on the table to steady herself, the other in the pocket of her long blue robe. She was beautiful in the mature way that women who have lived too hard, too swiftly, are sometimes beautiful. She was very dark; her eyes were large, liquid, black and dominated her rather small, sharply sculptured face. Her mouth was large, deeply red, not particularly strong.

Druse bowed slightly, said: "How do you do."

She smiled, and her eyes were heavy, nearly closed. "Swell — and you?"

He came slowly into the room, put his hat on the table, asked: "May we sit down?"

"Sure." She jerked her head towards a chair, stayed where she was.

Druse said: "You're drunk."

"Right."

He smiled, sighed gently. "A commendable condition. I regret exceedingly that my stomach does not permit it." He glanced casually about the room. In the comparative darkness of a corner, near a heavily draped window, there was a man lying on his back on the floor. His arms were stretched out and back, and his legs were bent under him in a curious broken way, and there was blood on his face.

Druse raised his thick white eyebrows, spoke without looking at Mrs. Hanan: "Is *he* drunk, too?"

She laughed shortly. "Uh-huh — in a different way." She nodded towards a golf-stick on the floor near the man. "He had a little too much niblick."

"Friend of yours?"

She said: "I rather doubt it. He came in from the fire-escape with a gun in his hand. I happened to see him before he saw me."

"Where's the gun?"

"I've got it." She drew a small black automatic half out of the pocket of her robe.

Druse went over and knelt beside the man, picked up one of his hands. He said slowly: "This man is decidedly dead."

Mrs. Hanan stood, staring silently at the man on the floor for perhaps thirty seconds. Her face was white, blank. Then she walked unsteadily to a desk against one wall and picked up a whiskey bottle, poured a stiff drink. She said: "I know it." Her voice was choked, almost a whisper. She drank the whiskey, turned and leaned against the desk, stared at Druse with wide unseeing eyes. "So what?"

"So pull yourself together, and forget about it — we've got more important things to think about for a little while." Druse stood up. "How long ago? . . ."

She shuddered. "About a half-hour — I didn't know what to do. . . ."

"Have you tried to reach Crandall? I mean before this happened — right after you came in tonight?"

"Yes — I couldn't get him."

Druse went to a chair and sat down. He said: "Mister Hanan has turned this case over to me. Won't you sit down, and answer a few questions . . . ?"

She sank into a low chair near the desk. "Are you a detective?" Her voice was still very low, strained.

Druse smiled. "I'm an attorney — a sort of extra-legal attorney." He regarded her thoughtfully. "If we can get your rubies back, and assure your safety, and" — he coughed slightly — "induce Mister Hanan to reimburse the insurance company, you will be entirely satisfied, will you not?"

She nodded, started to speak.

Druse interrupted her: "Are the rubies themselves — I mean intrinsically, as stones — awfully important to you? Or was this grandstand play of yours — this business of threatening Crandall — motivated by rather less tangible factors — such as self-respect, things like that?"

She smiled faintly, nodded. "God knows how I happen to have any self-respect left — I've been an awful ass — but I have. It was the idea of being made such a fool — after I've lost over a hundred thousand dollars to Crandall — that made me do it."

Druse smiled. "The rubies themselves," he said — "I mean the rubies as stones — entirely apart from any extraneous consideration such as self-respect — would more seriously concern Mister Hanan, would they not?"

She said: "Sure. He's always been crazy about stones."

Druse scratched his tip of his long nose pensively. His eyes were wide and vacant, his thick lips compressed to a long downward curved line. "You are sure you were followed when you left Crandall's Wednesday?"

"As sure as one can be without actually knowing — it was more of a followed feeling than anything else. After the idea was planted I could have sworn I saw a dozen men, of course."

He said: "Have you ever had that feeling before — I mean before you threatened Crandall?"

"No."

"It may have been simply imagination, because you expected to be followed — there was reason for you to be followed?"

She nodded. "But it's a cinch it wasn't imagination this evening."

Druse was leaning forward, his elbows on his knees. He looked intently at her, said very seriously: "I'm going to get your rubies back, and I can assure you of your safety — and I think I can promise that the matter of reimbursement to the insurance company will be taken care of. I didn't speak to Mister Hanan about that, but I'm sure he'll see the justice of it."

She smiled faintly.

Druse went on: "I promise you these things — and in return I want you to do exactly as I tell you until tomorrow morning."

Her smile melted to a quick, rather drunken laugh. "Do I have to poison any babies?" She stood up, poured a drink.

Druse said: "*That's* one of the things I *don't* want you to do."

She picked up the glass, frowned at him with mock seriousness. "You're a moralist," she said. "That's one of the things I *will* do."

He shrugged slightly. "I shall have some very important, very delicate work for you a little later in the evening. I thought it might be best."

She looked at him, half smiling, a little while, and then she laughed and put down the glass and went into the bathroom. He leaned back comfortably in the chair and stared at the ceiling; his hands were on the arms of the chair and he ran imaginary scales with his big blunt fingers.

She came back into the room in a little while, dressed, drawing on gloves. She gestured with her head towards the man on the floor, and for a moment her more or less alcoholic poise forsook her — she shuddered again — her face was white, twisted.

Druse stood up, said: "He'll have to stay where he is for a little while." He went to the heavily draped window, to the fire-escape, moved the drape aside and locked the window. "How many doors are there to the apartment?"

"Two." She was standing near the table. She took the black automatic from a pocket of her suit, took up a gray suede bag from the table and put the automatic into it.

He watched her without expression. "How many keys?"

"Two." She smiled, took two keys out of the bag and held them up. "The only other key is the pass-key — the manager's."

He said: "That's fine," went to the table and picked up his hat and put it on. They went out into the hall and closed and locked the door. "Is there a side entrance to the building?"

She nodded.

"Let's go out that way."

She led the way down the corridor, down three flights of stairs to a door leading to Sixty-third Street. They went out and walked over Sixty-third to Lexington and got into a cab; he told the driver to take them to the corner of Fortieth and Madison, leaned back and looked out the window. "How long have you and Mister Hanan been divorced?"

She was quick to answer: "Did he say we were divorced?"

"No." Druse turned to her slowly, smiled slowly.

"Then what makes you think we are?"

"I don't. I just wanted to be sure."

"We are *not*." She was very emphatic.

He waited, without speaking.

She glanced at him sidewise and saw that he expected her to go on. She laughed softly. "He wants a divorce. He asked me to divorce him several months ago." She sighed, moved her hands nervously on her lap. "That's another of the things I'm not very proud of — I wouldn't do it. I don't quite know why — we were never in love — we haven't been married, really, for a long time — but I've waited, hoping we might be able to make something out of it. . . ."

Druse said quietly: "I think I understand — I'm sorry I had to ask you about that."

She did not answer.

In a little while the cab stopped; they got out and Druse paid the driver and they cut diagonally across the street, entered an office building halfway down the block. Druse spoke familiarly to the Negro elevator boy; they got off at the forty-fifth floor and went up two flights of narrow stairs, through a heavy steel fire-door to a narrow bridge and across it to a rambling two-story penthouse that covered all one side of the roof. Druse rang the bell and a thin-faced Filipino boy let them in.

Druse led the way into a very big, high-ceilinged room that ran the length and almost the width of the house. It was beautifully and brightly furnished, opened on one side onto a wide terrace. They went through to the terrace; there were steamer-chairs there and canvas swings and low round tables, a great many potted plants and small trees. The tiled floor was partially covered with strips of coco-matting. There was a very wide, vividly striped awning stretched across all one side. At the far side, where the light from the living room faded into darkness, the floor came to an abrupt end — there was no railing or parapet — the nearest building of the same height was several blocks away.

Mrs. Hanan sat down and stared at the twinkling distant lights of

Upper Manhattan. The roar of the city came up to them faintly, like surf very far away. She said: "It is very beautiful."

"I am glad you find it so." Druse went to the edge, glanced down. "I have never put a railing here," he said, "because I am interested in Death. Whenever I'm depressed I look at my jumping-off place, only a few feet away, and am reminded that life is very sweet." He stared at the edge, stroked the side of his jaw with his fingers. "Nothing to climb over, no windows to raise — just walk."

She smiled wryly. "A moralist — and morbid. Did you bring me here to suggest a suicide pact?"

"I brought you here to sit still and be decorative."

"And you?"

"I'm going hunting." Druse went over and stood frowning down at her. "I'll try not to be long. The boy will bring you anything you want — even *good* whiskey, if you can't get along without it. The view will grow on you — you'll find one of the finest collections of books on satanism, demonology, witchcraft, in the world inside." He gestured with his head and eyes. "Don't telephone anyone — and, above all, *stay* here, even if I'm late."

She nodded vaguely.

He went to the wide doors that led into the living room, turned, said: "One thing more — who are Mister Hanan's attorneys?"

She looked at him curiously. "Mahlon and Stiles."

He raised one hand in salute. "So long."

She smiled, said: "So long — good hunting."

He went into the living room and talked to the Filipino boy a minute, went out.

In the drugstore across the street from the entrance to the building, he went into a telephone booth, called the number Hanan had given him. When Hanan answered, he said: "I have very bad news. We were too late. When I reached Mrs. Hanan's apartment, she did not answer the phone — I bribed my way in and found her — found her dead. . . . I'm terribly sorry, old man — you've got to take it standing up. . . . Yes — strangled."

Druse smiled grimly to himself. "No, I haven't informed the police — I want things left as they are for the present — I'm going to see Crandall and I have a way of working it so he won't have a single out. I'm going to pin it on him so that it will stay pinned — and I'm going to get the rubies back, too. . . . I know they don't mean much to you now, but the least I can do is get them back — and see that Crandall is stuck so he can't wriggle out of it." He said the last very emphatically, was silent for a little while, except for an occasionally interjected "Yes" or "No."

Finally he asked: "Can you be in around three-thirty or four? . . . I'll want to get in touch with you then. . . . Right, I know how you must feel — I'm terribly sorry. . . . Right. Good-bye." He hung up and went out into Fortieth Street.

Jeffrey Crandall was a medium-sized man with a close-cropped mustache, wide-set greenish-gray eyes. He was conservatively dressed, looked very much like a prosperous real estate man, or broker.

He said: "Long time no see."

Druse nodded abstractedly. He was sitting in a deep red leather chair in Crandall's very modern office, adjoining the large room in a midtown apartment building that was Crandall's "Place" for the moment. He raised his head and looked attentively at the pictures on the walls, one after the other.

"Anything special?" Crandall lighted a short stub of green cigar.

Druse said: "Very special," over his shoulder. He came to the last picture, a very ordinary Degas pastel, shook his head slightly, disapprovingly, and turned back to Crandall. He took a short-barreled derringer out of his inside coat-pocket, held it on the arm of his chair, the muzzle focused steadily on Crandall's chest.

Crandall's eyes widened slowly; his mouth hung a little open. He put one hand up very slowly and took the stub of a cigar out of his mouth.

Druse repeated: "Very special." His full lips were curved to a thin, cold smile.

Crandall stared at the gun. He spoke as if making a tremendous effort to frame his words casually, calmly: "What's it all about?"

"It's all about Mrs. Hanan." Druse tipped his hat to the back of his head. "It's all about you gypping her out of her rubies — and her threatening to take it to the police — and you having her murdered at about a quarter after ten tonight, because you were afraid she'd go through with it."

Crandall's tense face relaxed slowly; he tried very hard to smile. He said: "You're crazy," and there was fear in his eyes, fear in the harsh, hollow sound of his voice.

Druse did not speak. He waited, his cold eyes boring into Crandall's.

Crandall cleared his throat, moved a little forward in his chair and put his elbows on the wide desk.

"Don't ring." Druse glanced at the little row of ivory push buttons on the desk, shook his head.

Crandall laughed soundlessly as if the thought of ringing had never entered his mind. "In the first place," he said, "I gave her back the stones that were stolen. In the second place, I never believed her gag about telling about it." He leaned back slowly, spoke very slowly and distinctly as confidence came back to him. "In the third place, I couldn't be chump enough to bump her off with that kind of a case against me."

Druse said: "Your third place is the one that interests me. The switched rubies, her threat to tell the story — it all makes a pip of a case against you, doesn't it?"

Crandall nodded slowly.

"That's the reason," Druse went on, "that if I shoot you through the heart right now, I'll get a vote of thanks for avenging the lady you made a sucker of, and finally murdered because you thought she was going to squawk."

All the fear came back into Crandall's face suddenly. He started to speak.

Druse interrupted him, went on: "I'm going to let you have it when you reach for your gun, of course — that'll take care of any technicalities about taking the law into my own hands — anything like that."

Crandall's face was white, drained. He said: "How come I'm elected? What the hell have you got against me?"

Druse shrugged. "You shouldn't jockey ladies into trying to nick insurance companies. . . ."

"It was her idea."

"Then you should have been on the level about the rubies."

Crandall said: "So help me God! I gave her back the stuff I took!" He said it very vehemently, very earnestly.

"How do you know? How do you know the man you had do the actual job didn't make the switch?"

Crandall leaned forward. "Because *I* took them. She gave me her key and I went in the side way, while she was out, and took them myself. They were never out of my hands." He took up a lighter from the desk and relighted the stump of cigar with shaking hands. "That's the reason I didn't take her threat seriously. I thought it was some kind of extortion gag she'd doped out to get some of her dough back. She got back the stones I took — and if they weren't genuine they were switched before I took them, or after I gave them back."

Druse stared at him silently for perhaps a minute, finally smiled, said: "Before."

Crandall sucked noisily at his cigar. "Then, if you believe me" — he glanced at the derringer — "what's the point?"

"The point is that if I didn't believe you, you'd be in an awfully bad spot."

Crandall nodded, grinned weakly.

"The point," Druse went on, "is that you're still in an awfully bad spot because no one else will believe you."

Crandall nodded again. He leaned back and took a handkerchief out of his breast pocket and dabbed at his face.

"I know a way out of it." Druse moved his hand, let the derringer hang by the trigger-guard from his forefinger. "Not because I like you particularly, nor because I think you particularly deserve it — but because it's right. I can turn up the man who really murdered her — if we can get back the rubies — the real rubies. And I think I know where they are."

Crandall was leaning far forward, his face very alive and interested.

"I want you to locate the best peterman we can get." Druse spoke in a very low voice, watched Crandall intently. "We've got to open a safe — I think it'll be a safe — out on Long Island. Nothing very difficult — there'll probably be servants to handle but nothing more serious than that."

Crandall said: "Why can't I do it?" He smiled a little. "I used to be in the box business, you know — before I straightened up and got myself a joint. That's the reason I took the fake rubies myself — not to let anyone else in on it."

Druse said: "That'll be fine."

"When?" Crandall stood up.

Druse put the derringer back in his pocket. "Right now — where's your car?"

Crandall jerked his head towards the street. They went out through the crowded gambling room, downstairs, got into Crandall's car. Crossing Queensborough Bridge, Druse glanced at his watch. It was twenty minutes past twelve.

At three thirty-five Druse pushed the bell of the penthouse, after searching, vainly as usual, for his key. The Filipino boy opened the door, said: "It's a very hot night, sir."

Druse threw his hat on a chair, smiled sadly at Mrs. Hanan, who had come into the little entrance-hall. "I've been trying to teach him English for three months," he said, "and all he can say is 'Yes sir,' and 'No, sir,' and tell me about the heat." He turned to the broadly grinning boy. "Yes, Tony, it is a very hot night."

They went through the living room, out onto the terrace. It was cool there, and dim; a little light came out through the wide doors, from the living room.

Mrs. Hanan said: "I'd about given you up."

Druse sat down, sighed wearily. "I've had a very strenuous evening — sorry I'm so late." He looked up at her. "Hungry?"

"Starved."

"Why didn't you have Tony fix you something?"

"I wanted to wait." She had taken off her suit-coat, hat; in her smartly cut tweed skirt, white mannish shirt, she looked very beautiful.

Druse said: "Supper, or breakfast, or something will be ready in a few minutes — I ordered it for four." He stood up. "Which reminds me — we're having a guest. I must telephone."

He went through the living room, up four broad, shallow steps to the little corner room that he used as an office. He sat down at the broad desk, drew the telephone towards him, dialed a number.

Hanan answered the phone. Druse said: "I want you to come to my place, on top of the Pell Building, at once. It is very important. Ring the bell downstairs — I've told the elevator boy I'm expecting you. . . . I can't tell you over the phone — please come alone, and right away." He hung up and sat staring vacantly at his hands a little while, and then got up and went back to the terrace, sat down.

"What did you do with yourself?"

Mrs. Hanan was lying in one of the low chairs. She laughed nervously. "The radio — tried to improve my Spanish and Tony's English — chewed my fingernails — almost frightened myself to death with one of your damned demon books." She lighted a cigarette. "And you?"

He smiled in the darkness. "I earned thirty-five thousand dollars."

She sat up, said eagerly: "Did you get the rubies?"

He nodded.

"Did Crandall raise much hell?"

"Enough."

She laughed exultantly. "Where are they?"

Druse tapped his pocket, watched her face in the pale orange glow of her cigarette.

She got up, held out her hand. "May I see them?"

Druse said: "Certainly." He took a long flat jewel-case of black velvet out of his inside coat-pocket and handed it to her.

She opened the case and went to the door to the living room, looked at its contents by the light there, said: "They are awfully beautiful, aren't they?"

"They are."

She snapped the case closed, came back and sat down.

Druse said: "I think I'd better take care of them a little while longer."

She leaned forward and put the case on his lap; he took it up and put it back in his pocket. They sat silently, watching the lights in buildings over towards the East River. After a while the Filipino boy came out and said that they were served.

"Our guest is late." Druse stood up. "I make a rule of never waiting breakfast — anything but breakfast."

They went together through the living room, into the simply furnished dining room. There were three places set at the glittering white and silver table. They sat down and the Filipino boy brought in tall and spindly cocktail glasses of iced fruit; they were just beginning when the doorbell rang. The Filipino boy glanced at Druse, Druse nodded, said: "Ask the gentleman to come in here." The Filipino boy went out and there were voices in the entrance-hall, and then Hanan came into the doorway.

Druse stood up. He said: "You must forgive us for beginning — you are a little late." He raised his hand and gestured towards the empty chair.

Hanan was standing in the doorway with his feet wide apart, his arms stiff at his sides, as if he had been suddenly frozen in that position. He stared at Mrs. Hanan and his eyes were wide, blank — his thin mouth was compressed to a hard, straight line. Very suddenly his right hand went towards his left armpit.

Druse said sharply: "Please sit down." Though he seemed scarcely to have moved, the blunt derringer glittered in his hand.

Mrs. Hanan half rose. She was very pale; her hands were clenched convulsively on the white tablecloth.

Hanan dropped his hand very slowly. He stared at the derringer and twisted his mouth into a terribly forced smile, came slowly forward to the empty chair and sat down.

Druse raised his eyes to the Filipino boy who had followed Hanan into the doorway, said: "Take the gentleman's gun, Tony — and serve his cocktail." He sat down, held the derringer rigidly on the table in front of him.

The Filipino boy went to Hanan, felt gingerly under his coat, drew out a small black automatic and took it to Druse. Then he went out through the swinging door to the kitchen. Druse put the automatic in his pocket. He turned his eyes to Mrs. Hanan, said: "I'm going to tell you a story. After I've finished, you can both talk all you like — but please don't interrupt."

He smiled with his mouth — the rest of his face remained stonily impassive. His eyes were fixed and expressionless, on Hanan. He said: "Your husband has wanted a divorce for some time. His principal reason is a lady — her name doesn't matter — who wants to marry him — and whom he wants to marry. He hasn't told you about her because he has felt, perhaps justifiably, that your knowing about her would retard, rather than hasten, an agreement. . . ."

The Filipino boy came in from the kitchen with a cocktail, set it before Hanan. Hanan did not move, or look up. He stared intently at the flowers in the center of the table. The Filipino boy smiled self-consciously at Druse and Mrs. Hanan, disappeared into the kitchen.

Druse relaxed a little, leaned back; the derringer was still focused unwaveringly on Hanan.

"In the hope of uncovering some adequate grounds for bringing suit," Druse went on, "he has had you followed for a month or more — unsuccessfully, need I add? After you threatened Crandall, you discovered suddenly that you were being followed and, of course, ascribed it to Crandall."

He paused. It was entirely silent for a moment, except for the faint, faraway buzz of the city and the sharp, measured sound of Hanan's breathing.

Druse turned his head towards Mrs. Hanan. "After you left Mister Hanan at Roslyn, last night, it suddenly occurred to him that this was his golden opportunity to dispose of you, without any danger to himself. You wouldn't give him a divorce — and it didn't look as if he'd be able to force it by discovering some dereliction on your part. And now, you had threatened Crandall — Crandall would be logically suspected if anything happened to you. Mister Hanan sent his men — the men who had been following you — after you when you left the place at Roslyn. They weren't very lucky."

Druse was smiling, slightly. Mrs. Hanan had put her elbows on the table, her chin in her hands; she regarded Hanan steadily.

"He couldn't go to the police," Druse went on —"they would arrest Crandall, or watch him, and that would ruin the whole plan. And the business about the rubies would come out. That was the last thing he wanted"— Druse widened his smile —"because he switched the rubies himself — some time ago."

Mrs. Hanan turned to look at Druse; very slowly she matched his smile.

"You never discovered that your rubies were fake," he said, "because that possibility didn't occur to you. It was only after they'd been given back by Crandall that you became suspicious and found out they weren't genuine." He glanced at Hanan and the smile went from his face, leaving it hard and expressionless again. "Mister Hanan is *indeed* 'crazy about stones.' "

Hanan's thin mouth twitched slightly; he stared steadily at the flowers.

Druse sighed. "And so — we find Mister Hanan, last night, with several reasons for wishing your — shall we say, disappearance? We find him with the circumstances of being able to direct suspicion at Crandall, ready to his hand. His only serious problem lay in finding a third, responsible, party before whom to lay the whole thing — or enough of it to serve his purpose."

Mrs. Hanan had turned to face Hanan. Her eyes were half closed and her smile was very hard, very strange.

Druse stood up slowly, went on: "He had the happy thought of calling me — or perhaps the suggestion. I was an ideal instrument, functioning as I do, midway between the law and the underworld. He made an appointment, and arranged for one of his men to call on you by way of the fire-escape, while we were discussing the matter. The logical implication was that I would come to you when I left him, find you murdered, and act immediately on the information he had given me about Crandall. My influence and testimony would have speedily convicted Crandall. Mister Hanan would have better than a divorce. He'd have the rubies, without any danger of his having switched them ever being discovered — and he'd have"— Druse grinned sourly —"the check he had given me as an advance. Failing in the two things I had contracted to do, I would of course return it to him."

Hanan laughed suddenly; a terribly forced, high-pitched laugh.

"It is very funny," Druse said. "It would all have worked very beautifully if you" — he moved his eyes to Mrs. Hanan — "hadn't happened to see the man who came up the fire-escape to call on you, before he saw you. The man whose return Mister Hanan has been impatiently waiting. The man" — he dropped one eyelid in a swift wink — "who confessed to the whole thing a little less than an hour ago."

Druse put his hand into his inside pocket and took out the black velvet jewel-case, snapped it open and put it on the table. "I found them in the safe at your place in Roslyn," he said. "Your servants there objected very strenuously — so strenuously that I was forced to tie them up and lock them in the wine cellar. They must be awfully uncomfortable by now — I shall have to attend to that."

He lowered his voice to a discreet tone. "And your lady was there, too. She, too, objected very strenuously, until I had had a long talk with her and convinced her of the error of her — shall we say, affection, for a gentleman of your instincts. She seemed very frightened at the idea of becoming involved in this case — I'm afraid she will be rather hard to find."

Druse sighed, lowered his eyes slowly to the rubies, touched the largest of them delicately with one finger. "And so," he said, "to end this vicious and regrettable business — I give you your rubies" — he lifted his hand and made a sweeping gesture towards Mrs. Hanan — "and your wife — and now I would like your check for twenty-five thousand dollars."

Hanan moved very swiftly. He tipped the edge of the table upward, lunged up and forward in the same movement; there was a sharp, shattering crash of chinaware and silver. The derringer roared, but the bullet thudded into the table. Hanan bent over suddenly — his eyes were dull, and his upper lip was drawn back over his teeth — then he straightened and whirled and ran out through the door to the living room.

Mrs. Hanan was standing against the big buffet; her hands were at her mouth, and her eyes were very wide. She made no sound.

Druse went after Hanan, stopped suddenly at the door. Hanan was crouched in the middle of the living room. The Filipino boy stood beyond him, framed against the darkness of the entrance-hall; a curved knife glittered in his hand and his thin yellow face was hard, menacing. Hanan ran out on the terrace and Druse went swiftly after him. By the dim light from the living room he saw Hanan dart to the left, encounter the wall there, zigzag crazily towards the darkness of the outer terrace, the edge.

Druse yelled: "Look out!" ran forward, Hanan was silhouetted a moment against the mauve glow of the sky; then with a hoarse, cracked scream he fell outward, down.

Druse stood a moment, staring blindly down. He took out a handkerchief and mopped his forehead, then turned and went into the living room and tossed the derringer down on the big center table. The Filipino boy was still standing in the doorway. Druse nodded at him and he turned and went through the dark entrance-hall into the kitchen. Druse went to the door to the dining room; Mrs. Hanan was still standing with her back to the buffet, her hands still at her mouth, her eyes wide, unseeing. He turned and went swiftly up the broad steps to the office, took up the telephone and dialed a number. When the connection had been made, he asked for MacCrae.

In a minute or so MacCrae answered; Druse said: "You'll find a stiff in Mrs. Dale Hanan's apartment on the corner of Sixty-third and Park, Mac. She killed him — self-defense. You might find his partner downstairs at my place — waiting for his boss to come out. . . . Yeah, his boss was Hanan — he just went down — the other way. . . . I'll file charges of attempted murder against Hanan, and straighten it all out when you get over here. . . . Yeah — hurry."

He hung up and went down to the dining room. He tipped the

table back on its legs and picked up the rubies, put them back into the case. He said: "I called up a friend of mine who works for Mahlon and Stiles. As you probably know, Mister Hanan has never made a will." He smiled. "He so hated the thought of death that the idea of a will was extremely repugnant to him."

He picked up her chair and she came slowly across and sank into it.

"As soon as the estate is settled," he went on. "I shall expect your check for a hundred and thirty-five thousand dollars, made out to the insurance company."

She nodded abstractedly.

"I think these" — he indicated the jewel-case — "will be safer with me, until then."

She nodded again.

He smiled. "I shall also look forward with a great deal of pleasure to receiving your check for twenty-five thousand — the balance on the figure I quoted for my services."

She turned her head slowly, looked up at him. "A moralist," she said — "morbid — and mercenary."

"Mercenary as hell!" He bobbed his big head up and down violently.

She looked at the tiny watch at her wrist, said: "It isn't morning yet, strictly speaking — but I'd rather have a drink than anything I can think of."

Druse laughed. He went to the buffet and took out a squat bottle, glasses, poured two big drinks. He took one to her, raised the other and squinted through it at the light. "Here's to crime."

They drank.

DONALD E. WESTLAKE

JUST ONE OF THOSE DAYS

As Richard Stark, Donald Westlake (b. 1933) has written some of the toughest hard-boiled crime novels around, featuring a grim professional thief named Parker, no first name, just Parker. As Tucker Coe, he has written about a broken ex-police officer who solves crimes as part of his psychological rehabilitation. Who knows how many other pseudonyms he has employed over the years?

But under his own name Westlake writes comedies, and he is that rarity, a writer who produces "comic" mysteries that are also successful comic novels. The typical comic mystery is all too often simply a standard crime novel into which the author has thrown a few supposedly funny characters who come in, do their vaudeville turns, and then get out of the way so the serious crime solving can take place. (The experienced reader knows that these visiting comedians can never be taken seriously as suspects.) Westlake novels such as The Hot Rock, God Save the Mark, *and* Trust Me on This *actually use humor to solve the mystery or advance the story. More often than not, the result is good mystery as well as good comedy.*

"Just One of Those Days" was first published in 1966.

HARRY CAME into the motel room as I was putting my shoulder holster on. "Forget it, Ralph," he said.

I looked at him. "Forget it? What do you mean, forget it?"

He took off his coat and tossed it on the bed. "The bank's closed," he said.

"It can't be closed," I said. "This is Tuesday."

"Wrong," he said. He flipped his automatic out of his holster and tossed it on the bed. "It can be closed," he said. "Everything can be closed. This is Griffin's Day."

"This is *what's* Day?"

"Griffin's," he said. He shrugged out of his shoulder holster and tossed it on the bed. "Kenny Griffin's Day," he said.

"I give up," I said. "What's a Kenny Griffin?"

"Astronaut," he said. He opened his shirt collar and tossed himself onto the bed. "Comes from this burg," he said. "It's his Homecoming Day. They're having a big parade for him."

"By the bank?" I asked.

"What difference?" He moved his automatic out from under his hip, adjusted his pillow, and shut his eyes. "The bank's closed anyway," he said.

I cocked my head, and from far away I heard band music. "Well, if that isn't nice," I said.

"They're gonna give him the key to the city," Harry said.

"That is real nice," I said.

"Speeches, and little kids giving him flowers."

"That's so nice I can't stand it," I said.

"He was in orbit," Harry said.

"He should of stayed in orbit," I said.

"So we'll do it tomorrow," said Harry.

"I know," I said. "But it's just irritating."

It was more irritating to me than to Harry, because, after all, I was the planner. I hated it when a plan went wrong or had to be changed around, no matter how minor the change. Like planning a caper on Tuesday and having to do it on Wednesday instead. A small alteration, an unimportant shift, but we'd have to stay in this town one day longer than expected, which increased the chances of identification at some later date. We'd have to change our airline reservations, which maybe some smart clerk would think about afterward. We'd show up at the Miami hotel a day late, which would tend to make us conspicuous there, too. Nothing vital, sure, nothing desperate, but it only takes a tiny leak to sink a mighty battleship. I remember reading that on a poster once when I was a kid, and it made a big impression on me.

I am the natural planner type. I had cased this bank and this town for three weeks *before* making my plan, and then for another five days *after* it was set. I worked out just the right method, the right time, the right getaway, the right everything.

The one thing I didn't work out was one of those astronauts hailing from this town and deciding on *my* day he'll come on back again. As I later said to Harry, why couldn't he of just phoned?

So we did it on Wednesday. We went to the bank at precisely two fifty-four, flipped the masks up over our faces, and announced, "This is a stick-up. Everybody freeze."

Everybody froze. While I watched the people and the door, Harry went behind the counter and started filling the bag.

Actually, Wednesday worked just as well as Tuesday so far as the mechanics of the plan were concerned. On all three midweek days, Tuesday and Wednesday and Thursday, all but three of the bank employees were at lunch at two fifty-four P.M., having to take a later-than-normal lunch because the bank was at its busiest during usual lunch hours. On the days I had checked it, there had never been any more than three customers here at this time, and the average had been only slightly over one. Today, for instance, there was just one, a small and elderly lady who carried an umbrella despite the bright sun outside.

The rest of the plan would work as well on Wednesday as on Tuesday, too. The traffic lights I'd timed worked the same every day of the week, the plane schedule out at the airport was the same as yesterday, and the traffic we could expect on the Belt Highway was no different, either. Still, I did hate to have things changed on me.

Harry was done filling the bag at one minute to three, which was a full minute ahead of time. We both stood by the door and waited, and when the second hand was done with its sweep once more, Harry put his gun away, flipped his mask off, picked up the bag and went out to where we'd parked the stolen Ford in front of the fire hydrant.

I now had forty seconds. I was looking everywhere at once, at my watch, at the three employees and the little old lady customer and at Harry out front in the Ford. If he didn't manage to get it started in time, we'd have to wait another minute and ten seconds.

But he did. After thirty-one seconds he gave me the sign. I nodded, let nine more seconds go by and dashed out of the bank. Eighteen running paces while I stuffed the gun away and stripped off the mask, and then I was in the car and it was rolling.

There was a traffic light at the corner. "Twenty-two miles an hour," I said, looking at that light, seeing it red down there in front of us.

"I know," said Harry. "Don't worry, I know."

The light turned green just as we reached the intersection. We sailed on through. I looked back, and saw people just erupting from the bank.

Midway down this block there was an alley on the right that led through to the next block. Harry made the turn, smooth and sweet, into a space hardly any wider than our car, and ahead of us was the MG. Harry hit the brakes, I grabbed the bag, and we jumped out of the Ford. Harry opened the Ford's hood and grabbed a handful of wires and yanked. Then he shut the hood and ran to the MG.

I was already in it, putting on the beard and the sunglasses and the cap and the yellow turtleneck sweater. Harry put on his beard and sunglasses and beret and green sports jacket. He started the engine, I stared at the second hand of my watch.

"Five," I said. "Four. Three. Two. One. Go!"

We shot out of the alley, turned left, made the light just before it went to red, turned right, made the lights perfectly for three blocks, then hit the Schuyler Avenue ramp to the Belt Highway.

"You watch the signs," Harry said. "I'll watch the traffic."

"Naturally," I said.

Almost every city has one of these by-pass highways now, a belt that makes a complete circuit of the city. Not only can travelers passing through use it to avoid getting involved in city traffic, but local citizens can use it for high-speed routing from one part of the city to the other. This one, called the Belt Highway, was an elevated road all the way around, giving a fine view of the town and the countryside.

But it was neither the town nor the surrounding countryside I was interested in at the moment. Right now my primary concern was the Airport Road exit. As Harry steered us through the light midweek afternoon traffic, I watched the signs.

One thing I have to admit, they did put up plenty of signs. Like for the first exit we came to, which was called Callisto Street Exit. First there was there a sign that said, "Callisto Street Exit, ¼ Mile." A little after that, there was a sign that said, "Callisto Street Exit, Keep Right." And then finally, at the exit itself, a sign with an arrow pointing to the down-ramp and the words, "Callisto Street Exit."

Of course, all of this was mostly geared for local citizens, so there wasn't any sign telling you where Callisto Street itself might take you, but if you knew it was Callisto Street you wanted, there wasn't a chance in the world that you'd miss it.

Harry buzzed us along in the white MG, just exactly at the fifty-mile-an-hour speed limit, and I watched the exits go by, with the standard three signs for each one: Woodford Road, Eagle Avenue, Griffin Road, Crowell Street, Five Mile Road, Esquire Avenue . . .

I looked at my watch. I said, "Harry, are you going too slow? You're supposed to go fifty."

Harry was insulted; he prides himself on being one of the best drivers in the business. "I *am* going fifty," he said, and gestured for me to take a look at the speedometer myself.

But I was too intent on watching for signs. Airport Road I wanted; Airport Road. I said, "It shouldn't be taking anywhere near *this* long, I know."

"I'm doing fifty — and I *been* doing fifty."

I looked at my watch, then back out at the highway. "Maybe the speedometer's busted. Maybe you're only doing forty."

"I'm doing fifty," Harry said. "I can *tell*. I know what fifty feels like, and I'm doing fifty."

"If we miss that plane," I said, "we're in trouble."

"We won't miss it," said Harry grimly, and hunched over the wheel.

"The cops will be asking questions all around the neighborhood back there now," I said. Sooner or later they'll find somebody that saw this car come out of the alley. Sooner or later they'll be looking for us in *this* car and with *these* descriptions."

"You just watch the signs," said Harry.

So I watched the signs. Remsen Avenue, De Witt Boulevard, Green Meadow Park, Seventeenth Street, Glenwood Road, Powers Street . . .

Harry said, "You must of missed it."

I said, "Impossible. I've read every sign. Every sign. Your speedometer's off."

"It isn't."

Earhart Street, Willoughby Lane, Firewall Avenue, Broad Street, Marigold Hill Road . . .

I looked at my watch. "Our plane just took off," I said.

"You keep looking at your watch," Harry said. "That's how come you missed it."

"I did not miss it," I said.

"Here comes Schuyler Avenue again," he said. "Isn't that where we got on?"

"How did I miss it?" I cried. "Hurry, Harry! We'll get it this time! They'll have a plane going *somewhere!*"

Harry crouched over the steering wheel.

They stopped us halfway around the circuit again. Some smart cop had seen us — the description was out by now, of course — and radioed in, and they set up a nice little road block across their elevated highway, and we drove right around to it and stopped, and they put the arm on us.

As I was riding in the back of a police car, going in the opposite direction on the Belt now, I asked the detective I was handcuffed to, "Do you mind telling me what you did with Airport Road?"

He grinned at me and pointed out the window, saying, "There it is."

The sign he pointed at said, "Griffin Road, ¼ Mile."

I said, "Griffin Road? I wanted *Airport* Road."

"That's it," he said. "We changed the name yesterday, in honor of Kenny Griffin. You know, the astronaut. We're all real proud of Kenny around here."

"I better not say anything against him then," I said.

JOSEPH HANSEN

ELECTION DAY

With Dave Brandstetter, Joseph Hansen (b. 1923) did not create the first gay detective. George Baxt's outrageous Pharaoh Love — for one — was introduced in 1966 (A Queer Kind of Death), four years before Brandstetter's debut in Fadeout. But Brandstetter caught the public's attention, perhaps because he was more like the typical southern California insurance investigator next door than Love, a larger-than-life black policeman who seems to call everyone cat.

Hansen has said that his desire to refute myths about homosexual stereotypes preceded his desire to write mysteries and that making Brandstetter an insurance company employee was an inside joke because insurance companies "won't knowingly employ homosexuals." He says, "I wanted to tell a rattling good mystery yarn, but I also wanted to turn a few more common beliefs about homosexuals inside out and upside down." There have been nine Brandstetter novels so far, with more in sight. Hansen's other series detective is Hank Bohannon, owner of a California boarding stable, who, apparently, has no stereotypes that need straightening out.

"Election Day" was first published in a 1984 issue of Ellery Queen's Mystery Magazine.

SHABBY BRICK STORE-FRONTS slept against a background of brown hills in October sunlight that hadn't yet warmed up. It was early, but a place that served breakfast ought to be awake. Dave looked for it. This drab east end of Hollywood rarely saw much traffic. Now it consisted of a single faded peewee pickup truck, inching its way along at the curb, a mohawk-haired college-age boy in sweat pants and tank top trotting beside it. When the truck paused, he reached into it for a poster, red with white lettering. He slapped the poster against the naked trunk of a soaring palm tree and, with a shiny gun, stapled the poster in place. CATTON FOR CONGRESS. He and the truck moved on.

FAMOUS FARMHOUSE BREAKFASTS had a snappy new sign, and an artfully antiqued plank front covering the original brick. A width of inky new blacktop beside it was painted with white bias lines. Dave left his Jaguar there and tried the knob of a door under a little outcrop of shingled roof. The knob turned but the door didn't give. He blinkered his eyes with cupped hands and peered through the glass. No one sat on counter stools nor at the small tables surfaced with gingham-patterned Formica. Behind the counter, glass coffee pots gleamed empty. Through a wide service window sheltered by another shingled roof edge, Dave saw no one moving in the kitchen. Things looked a little dusty.

He frowned at his watch. Seven thirty-two. *Open daily, 6:00 A.M. till 2:00 P.M.* was crisply lettered on the door glass. But CLOSED, a cardboard sign said, *Sorry We Missed You.* Dave glanced up and down the street. No one headed on foot for Famous Farmhouse Breakfasts. Only one car was in sight, parked up the block on the other side. Had Harvey and Carolyn Sweetzer given up? If so, where were they? They weren't at home. He'd been to their boxy stucco tract house before the dew had evaporated from the composition roof. No one had answered his ring at the front door nor his knock at the back. No car had stood in the driveway, none in the garage. He had misjudged the time they left for work. But they plainly weren't at work. So where were they? Carolyn Sweetzer's sister Elizabeth was dead, but they wouldn't be at a mortuary — not this early.

He sighed. His practice of not telephoning ahead sometimes wasted time in this way. He liked face-to-face encounters. People's expressions, the look in their eyes, the way they fidgeted if they did, or stiffened if they did, often told him what words wouldn't on the phone. The element of surprise sometimes made people blurt things out before they'd had a chance to think. He turned away. He'd gauged locating the Sweetzers to be a sure bet. Little businesses like this held people close. He'd been wrong, hadn't he? There were no sure bets. He was dropping into the leather seat of the Jaguar when a car caromed into the parking lot and squealed to a sharp stop. A thin, balding man jumped out of it. He wore a beige polyester suit.

"Harvey Sweetzer?" he said.

"Sorry," Dave said. He had seen the man before, at the marshal's, at the court house. He was a process server. Carmichael? Some name like that. "What's wrong?"

Carmichael had reached into the inside pocket of his jacket and half drawn out a paper. His face fell, and he pushed the paper back out of sight. "I know you," he said. "Damn, I thought I was getting a break." He frowned, chewed a thin, pale lower lip, then brightened. "Insurance, right? Death claims? Wait, I got a name to go with it. Brandstetter." Dave nodded, and shook the cool, lifeless hand the man offered. The man's smile faded. "Oh, no. You don't mean to tell me he's dead. Oh, boy — is that going to leave a lot of people hung out to dry."

"Creditors?" Dave said.

"All that remodeling." The man waved a thin arm. "Outside, inside. Stoves, refrigerators, ventilation — you know what restaurant equipment costs? Contractors, painters, electricians, plumbers. He was crazy. Everybody who gave him credit was crazy." He waved at the street. "Look at this neighborhood. Who do you see? Nobody. Three months ago, six, maybe, yeah. There was a plant where they assembled ballpoint pens, all right? Fifty, sixty workers. There was a lens-grinding lab, you know? Eyeglasses? Say another couple dozen people. But they folded. I mean, the country is in the worst shape since the Depression, so Harvey Sweetzer goes in hock twenty thousand bucks to fix up a broken-down beanery. What did it do — dawn on him? Did he kill himself? Is that why you're here?"

"It's about Bess Jessup," Dave said.

"The one that used to be a singer?" Carmichael nodded, sunlight glaring off his scalp. "Murdered. I saw it on the TV news. What's she got to do with Sweetzer?"

"She was his sister-in-law," Dave said.

Carmichael drew breath for another question, then didn't ask it. He turned his head a little, regarded Dave from the corners of his eyes, frowning. He gave a soft whistle. "Oh, hey. I get it. She had a life insurance policy, right? And it just so happens Harvey Sweetzer is the beneficiary?"

Dave pulled his legs into the Jaguar, closed the door, ran the window down. "Could be," he said, and started the engine. He smiled. "You could get your money, yet. Can I ask you to move your car?"

"Yeah, sure. I got a lot of other suckers to hunt for." Carmichael got into his no-color, no-model car. "Two things there's no shortage of." He slammed the door. "Optimism and bad debts." He backed the car into the empty street.

The fair-haired, blue-eyed boy in orange jail coveralls said, "He knocked, and it was a code knock she knew from before. She whispered to be quiet and he'd go away. But he knew she was there. And in a minute, he was tramping through the place, yelling her name. The bedroom door slaps open, and he calls her bitch, drags her out of the bed, and starts punching her out."

Rader was the boy's name, and he sat looking glum, on a gray-green steel chair, forearms resting on a gray-green steel table. Dave had seen his record. Rader had worn jail coveralls before. He still looked as if he should be rehearsing the role of an angel in a Christmas pageant. The man who looked as if he belonged in jail coveralls stood behind Rader, leaning against a gray-green wall, hands pocketed. Squat, swarthy, low-browed, Bren Larkin was a public defender. His tough appearance always amused Dave. The man was a model of decency.

Dave sat opposite Rader. He reached behind him and probed the pockets of the blue denim jacket he'd hung on the back of the chair. He brought out cigarettes, and pushed the pack across the table. Rader took a cigarette. Dave lit it for him. Rader said, "What kind of watch is that?"

Dave put away the lighter. "Matthiesen," he said. "So you jumped him with your knife."

"Which you were not supposed to have," Larkin said, "under the conditions of your parole."

"The conditions are stupid," Rader said. "This is Los Angeles, not Sweetwater. In Los Angeles, big, black pimps come charging in on you when you're doing it with your girl." He looked through cigarette smoke at Dave. "The knife was in my jeans. On the floor. I yelled at him to cool it. Hell, he didn't even look my way. So I dove and got the knife and ran at him. He got the knife away from me and I got cut, didn't I?" He rubbed his ribs, wincing. "Bess was passing out, I was spouting blood, okay? Nothing happened to him. But he was the one who ran."

"No one saw him," Larkin said, "come or go. You ran, though. Stancliff saw you. The landlord."

"Hats Jimmerson was there." Rader looked sullen and stubborn. I can't help it if the landlord didn't see him. Damn right I ran. It was my knife, wasn't it, and I wasn't supposed to have it, and I wasn't supposed to be consorting with ex-convicts and criminals, and I wasn't supposed to get in fights. The landlord was coming. 'What's happening? What's the matter?' I grabbed my clothes and went out the bedroom window and down the alley."

"Forgetting the five thousand dollars?" Larkin said.

"I never heard of a Matthiesen watch," Rader said. "It looks expensive."

"It isn't," Dave said. "Not very."

"There wasn't any five thousand dollars," Rader said.

Larkin said, "In a brown supermarket sack."

"Give up." Rader looked disgust over his shoulder. "The detectives said it was wrapped in white plastic." He looked at Dave with a thin, pitying smile. "They're all alike. Think everybody's as stupid as they are. He wants me to say, 'No, it was wrapped in newspapers,' right?"

"He's on your side," Dave said.

"Nobody's on my side." Rader reached for a Pepsi can on the table. The bright chains on his wrists rattled. He tapped ash off his cigarette into the small opening in the top of the can. "I didn't see any five thousand dollars in any sack or plastic or newspapers or anything."

"It was there when they found her dead that night."

"She was alive when I left her," Rader said.

"It was your knife that killed her," Larkin said.

"Last I saw it, Hats had it," Rader said, "staring at it like it scared him shitless. My blood all over it. He must have dropped it before he ran out." Rader dragged on the cigarette and coughed. "Look, even the cops admit my fingerprints aren't on the knife."

"Only Bess Jessup's," Larkin said. "But it was your knife, you had a loud argument with your girl, you beat her up — the bruises are there to show it. The landlord heard the fight and saw you run. You have a record of robbery with violence. You used to beat up your wife when you had one."

Rader nodded. He looked thoughtfully at the manacles on his wrists. He slowly moved his wrists apart, stretching the chain, as if measuring it for something. "If she'd had five thousand dollars," he said, "she would have told me about it. She'd have been wild with excitement. She'd been trying every which way to raise money for that record deal. She didn't say anything."

"Maybe she knew you the way the police know you," Larkin said. "Maybe she was afraid you'd steal it."

Rader smiled wryly at Dave. "And he's on my side?"

"He's thinking the way the D.A. would think," Dave said.

"Bullshit," Rader said. "I didn't take the money. It was there. You call that thinking?" He twisted his head to look at Larkin again. "Make sense, will you? Was it hidden — the five thou? Wasn't it out in plain sight? Didn't somebody say it was laying on the coffee table with her guitar?"

"That's where it was," Dave said.

"That doesn't mean she didn't have it in a closet," Larkin said, "and you found it, and she came in from the store or something and caught you taking it, and that was when the fight started, and you killed her."

"And then went off without the money?"

"You panicked. The landlord was banging on the door."

"I panicked, but I remembered to wipe my prints off the knife? Shit." Rader poked his cigarette into the Pepsi can, and stood up. "I want to go back to my cell. And I want another lawyer. Why didn't I take the knife with me?"

"Why didn't Jimmerson bring her the five thousand?"

"She was scared of him, she was hiding from him, for Christ sake. Ask him for money? He'd have her peddling her ass in bars again. He'd have her back on heroin. She was through with that life. She was going back to her singing career. She was good, you know? Beautiful. Listen to her tapes. She hadn't touched a twelve-string in years, but she was getting it all back. She was really working at it."

"Maybe Jimmerson killed her," Larkin said. "Finding her in bed with you. Before she went to prison for dealing, she was his lady. Maybe you're covering for him because if you don't, he'll kill you too. He cut you to warn you."

Rader shook his head. "She was alive when I left."

"Yup." Larkin sighed, pushed away from the wall, rapped thick knuckles on the interrogation room door. "I wish to hell she'd called the police."

"She didn't want me going back to Q," Rader said.

A uniformed officer opened the door from the hall.

Stancliff walked from his door down a long white room with skylights to a big broad drafting table, where he picked up a white mug with "S" on it. He slurped coffee from the mug and raised inquiring brows at Dave. "Coffee?"

"No thanks." Dave looked at the drafting table. Cut-up sheets of printed matter on high-gloss paper lay there. Photographs. Miscellaneous letters of the alphabet in various type sizes and faces. Steel rulers, triangles, T-squares, French curves in thick amber plastic. X-acto knives and blue pencils. "Her place isn't sealed any longer. What have you done with her possessions?"

"Nothing. I only straightened up the worst of the mess." Stancliff set down the mug and perched on a stool at the table. "Stuff was thrown every which way. Drawers, clothes, couch cushions. Otherwise, it's the way I found it." He was an attenuated man, with a trimmed gray beard, gray hair over his ears, horn-rim glasses. Cheap white cotton gloves covered his bony hands. "Fall is my busy season. Usually it's only Christmas — advertising fliers, all that. But this year it's elections, too. All I do is work and sleep." His laugh was wry. "And not really all that much of the latter." He pushed papers around, looking for something. "It will be January before I get down there." He found a brush with long, soft bristles, and gently ran these over a pristine sheet of tagboard. He began to rule the tagboard with blue lines and corners, frowning, careful but quick.

Dave walked into a kitchenette at the far end of the room. Breakfast dishes were in the sink. There were vague smells of bacon and toast. A window was over the sink. He looked out and down. Below were garages, a small patio with floppy green plants in corners, a redwood gate to an alley. "I'd like a look at the place," he said.

"Here's the key." Stancliff rummaged among push-pins, ruling pens, erasers, in a gray metal fishing-tackle box. "She didn't have much. She'd just come out of a drug rehab program, you know. Clothes, guitar, tape recorder, and a carton of old clippings — that was about it. Everything else came with the apartment." He laid a key in Dave's hand.

"Thank you." Dave went down the long room again. Books were stacked everywhere. Art magazines. On a roughly built plank loft in a corner lay a mattress with tumbled blankets. On the ladder to the loft cast-off clothes hung — none of them women's clothes. Dave stopped at the door. "She was right down below you. A musician. Trying to write new songs, take up a career again. Wasn't it noisy?"

"Nothing distracts me when I'm working. Concentration. That's the secret of success. Look around you. Conspicuous, isn't it — my tremendous success in life?" He drew another blue line. "Only the fights. They bothered me."

"You mean with Mike Rader? Had he beaten her before?"

"Not that. Just arguments. She was high-strung, lost her temper easily. He didn't know how to handle it. Sometimes I wondered if I'd been wise, renting to her. I didn't like that kid. What did she want with him, anyway? He was young enough to be her son. A convict, a thief. She needed someone mature, steady, decent."

"So when you saw him running away after the fight, it seemed logical to you that he was the one who'd killed her."

"Not then, no. I didn't know anyone had killed anyone. I'd run downstairs, shouting to them to stop, but I don't think they heard me. I ran back up here to phone the police, but then it went quiet. I was giving myself a belt of nerve-steadier in the kitchen, when I saw him run across the patio. Hop. He was trying to put on his pants. He was stark naked. I remember laughing."

"He was bleeding," Dave said.

"I didn't see that. Later, the police showed me the blood-smears on the windowsill, and the drops across the patio, but I didn't notice it when he ran off."

"You didn't phone the police?"

"What for?" Stancliff shrugged. "It was over."

"Completely," Dave said. "You didn't go downstairs to check whether she was all right?"

Stancliff looked away. "I should have, shouldn't I? The truth is, I'd been working around the clock to meet a deadline — not eating, keeping myself going on coffee and uppers. And that double Scotch hit me like a two-by-four. I passed out. When I came to, it was dark. That didn't bother me so much as the silence. I was used to hearing her music all the time. The silence was eerie. It worried me. So then I did go down to see if she was all right."

"And she was dead," Dave said.

"And she was dead." Pain muffled Stancliff's words. Tears wet his eyes. "She was a wonderful, beautiful person. She'd had a rotten run of luck, but that was over. Marvelous talent." He gave a soundless, sorry laugh. "I thought I wanted that once — talent. Not for music, for art. But from what I've seen, it involves too much suffering. Read their lives. Talented people have a miserable time of it."

Dave opened the door. "I'll bring the key back," he said, and went out and closed the door.

The curtains were drawn, so the light was dim. He found pull ropes and rattled the curtains open. The twelve-string guitar lay on a coffee table. It was blotched with fingerprint powder. So were the room's other surfaces. The guitar was all that showed anyone special had lived here. That and the big reel-to-reel tape recorder. Its brightwork caught the light. He put on reading glasses, switched on the amplifier and tape deck, and set the reels turning. Bargain loudspeakers sat on a dusty hardwood floor. From the speakers came a sweet, steady voice singing lyrics that rhymed "protects" with "MX" as in missile. Rader exaggeraged. Nervously was how she managed the twelve-string. Dave switched off the system and tucked away his glasses.

Nothing had been tidied in the kitchen. Tins that had held TV dinners lay in the sink, a faucet dripping into them. There were soiled forks. Empty diet soft-drink cans stood on the counter beside the sink. Cupboard doors hung slightly open. Inside waited a few clean plates, drinking glasses, mugs. The empty shelves were just that — empty. So was the refrigerator freezer compartment, whose ice cube tray held only ice cubes. The main part of the refrigerator contained a carton of skim milk, a six-pack of diet cola, a jar of grapefruit juice. The wastebasket under the sink was stuffed with stained hamburger wrappers, pizza tins, fried chicken buckets, more soft-drink cans. The stove top wore a film of dust.

The bedroom held bed, chest, mirror, lamp, clock. The bed had been stripped. The police lab would have wanted a look at Rader's bloodstains. The closet contained mostly jeans and blouses, a couple of skirts, no dresses. Bright colors, though — brave, humorous. A pair of shiny fake leather boots, worn Adidas, no carton of clippings. In the chest of drawers, sweaters, gaudy T-shirts, pantyhose, a couple of bras in boxes yet to be opened. Penney's, Woolworth's. Nothing uncommon in the bathroom medicine cabinet — aspirin, cold capsules, antacid tablets, tampons. Only one prescription drug — a folder of contraceptive pills. No forbidden drugs. No syringes, needles, rubber tubing. He closed the mirrored door, and stretched to run his hand along the top of the cabinet. A dusty key, the flat kind, stamped out. Nothing to identify it except a number, twenty-three. He dropped it into his pocket.

Under the lid of the toilet tank he found no plastic envelopes of cocaine, heroin, marijuana, PCP, Quaaludes. No drugs lay anchored in balloons in the bottom of the tank. In the clothes hamper, a tall basket woven of split bamboo, was nothing but dirty laundry. He crouched and opened the vanity doors under the wash basin. Toilet bowl cleaner, air freshener, a flat, dry, blue cellulose sponge, a pink-bristled toilet bowl brush, two bars of bath soap. He unwrapped these to be sure. The perfume of the soap was strong. He felt around carefully in the dark corners behind pipes under the basin. Nothing. He closed the doors, rose, switched off the light, left the bathroom.

When he stepped into the livingroom again, he thought he saw for an instant a face at the window. He went to the window. Nothing stirred outside. The landscaping was desert plants set in coarse white gravel. No one hurried off up the sunny street on foot. Not a car moved. He turned back, frowning. If not to buy drugs, why had someone brought Bess Jessup five thousand dollars in small bills? He sat on a smudged couch and lifted the guitar from the coffee table. When he laid it on the floor, its strings hummed.

The table was strewn with music manuscript and blue-lined notebook pages. On these, in ballpoint pen, were written the words of songs. Dave put on his reading glasses again. Her subjects were Three Mile Island, Times Beach, and how war kills children. He laid music and words aside, pushed away glossy campaign mailers, *Catton for Congress*. Beneath lay letters with the logos of recording companies.

What the letters indicated was that Bess Jessup had sent reminders of her long-lapsed career, along with new audition tapes, to a number of places that didn't care.

And to one that did. A little bit. Jawal Singh was cautiously friendly. He was president of Seesaw Records. His letter Dave folded and pushed into a pocket. He put away his glasses, closed the curtains, locked the apartment, and returned the door key to Stancliff. The found key he showed the gaunt man who took it in white-gloved fingers, frowning. "Belong to anything of yours?" Dave asked.

"Never saw it before," Stancliff said. "You want it?"

"For a little while," Dave said.

He was a few steps down the concrete strip between the white-graveled plantings when he heard a hiss behind him. He turned. At a corner of the building, a worried-looking man made a beckoning gesture. He wore a Levi's outfit he was too fat for, and a billed cap with *Dr Pepper* stitched on its front. Behind the man, a VW van's windshield reflected the sun. It was noon, and the sun was hot by now. Dave crunched across the gravel to the man, who whispered:

"Brandstetter? The insurance man?"

"That's me," Dave handed him a card.

"Harvey Sweetzer," the man said. "They told me at the insurance company office that you'd be coming here. Something wrong? Aren't we going to get the money?" He kept looking past Dave up and down the street, and he hurried his words. "I really need that money. For my business."

"I know," Dave said. A fat woman was staring at him through the windshield of the van. She wore sunglasses, but neither these nor the fleshiness of her cheeks hid her likeness to her dead sister, of whom the police had photographs Dave had seen. "Why did someone toss her apartment?"

"What?" Sweetzer said. "What?"

"The landlord said that when he found your sister-in-law's body, the apartment was a wreck, everything thrown every which way. Why?"

"How the hell would I know?" Sweetzer said. "We didn't associate with her. We're not that kind of people."

"She kept a box of clippings. It's not in the police report, and it's not in the apartment."

"Probably old stuff from when she was a singer. She had a start, you know." The door of the van opened. Sweetzer turned. "Carolyn, never mind." He said to Dave, "Then the Vietnam war ended, and all that radical stuff dried up. And first it was drugs, then prostitution. A hooker." He wagged his head glumly. "My own wife's sister."

"You didn't take the clippings? You didn't tear the apartment up, looking for this key? She had it hidden."

"Me?" Sweetzer's eyes opened as wide as the pouches of fat around them allowed. "We've never even been here. Look — when do we get the check? I've got a lot of people I owe money to, breathing down my neck."

Carolyn called from the van, "We can't even show our faces, can't open the cafe, can't even go home." She sounded on the verge of tears. "You have to help us."

"The check won't be sent until I clear it," Dave said, "and I have a lot of questions about your sister's death."

"That no-good convict kid stabbed her," Sweetzer said. "The one she was living with, sleeping with. Ex-druggie, like herself. That's how that kind of people live. That's how she'd been living for fifteen years. What are you talking about? What questions?"

"If she was so contemptible," Dave said, "why did you keep up the payments on her life insurance? You didn't want anything to do with her. You never came to see her. She was trying to start a new life, no more drugs, no more prostitution. She'd been through rehabilitation. She was writing songs, trying for a record deal. You didn't care."

Sweetzer's laugh was sour and pitying. "You don't know much about those kind of people, I guess. You know how many times she'd told Carolyn and me she was through with all that sordid stuff, she was going to start over with her music and all that? So many times I lost count."

Now Carolyn did clamber down from the van. A scarf was tied over her head. Her fat hips were packed into jeans. She came at a ding-toed walk to stand beside her husband. "We helped her. Helped her again and again. We never knew in the middle of the night when the phone would ring, and she'd be in jail again, or at some hospital, and crying for us to come and bail her out, or whatever."

"That's why I took out the life insurance," Sweetzer said. "Because the way she was living — hell, she was living with a black man, did you know that? — anybody with a grain of sense knew she was going to end up dead one of these times. Murdered. It was in the cards."

"We tried to save her." Tears leaked from under Carolyn's dark glasses. "We brought her from jail that time, to live with us, her own room and all. Gave her a job waitressing at the cafe."

Sweetzer snorted. "How long do you think that lasted?"

Carolyn blew her nose loudly on a Kleenex.

"We're her only family," Sweetzer said. "We'd have to bury her when the day came. That's why I kept up the policy."

"Fifty thousand dollars will buy a lot of funeral," Dave said.

"Listen," Sweetzer said, "I don't add up what I do out of the goodness of my heart. But we're not rich people, and over the years we emptied our pockets for her, paid her back rent, utilities, got her guitar out of hock, paid her bailbondsmen, paid her fines. When it's your own wife's sister, you do what you have to do. You think I'm some kind of mean, grasping guy, wanting this insurance money. Well, I never asked her for a dime back, when she was alive."

"You have to help us," Carolyn said. "We're being hounded like we were animals. We have to sleep in the van. People can only keep that up so long."

Dave said, "Where do you park it to sleep in it?"

Sweetzer shrugged. "Beach. Out-of-the-way places."

"The night she was killed?" Dave said.

"Oh, my goodness." Carolyn took a step backward.

Sweetzer tried to sound truculent but he only squeaked. "What the hell do you mean by that?" Sweat broke out on his upper lip. "Are you accusing us?"

"No, but I don't think Mike Rader killed her," Dave said. "He didn't have a reason."

"And we do?" Carolyn cried. "My own sister?"

"Drug addicts don't need reasons," Sweetzer said.

"The tests show he's clean of drugs," Dave said.

"We were in Griffith Park. We weren't in anybody's way. Couldn't even be seen from the road. But the patrol found us and rousted us out," Sweetzer said in disgust.

"What time was that?" Dave said.

"Let's go, Carolyn." Sweetzer took her fat arm and steered her ahead of him back to the van. "We don't have to answer his questions."

"It will be on the park patrol records," Dave said. "You may as well tell me. Or won't it be on the records?"

"Yeah." Sweetzer pushed Carolyn up into the van. "It's on the damn records. They issued us a citation. We haven't got enough troubles. A little after seven." He slammed the passenger door, and walked around to the driver's side. He opened the door there. "Who do I go to at that insurance company to get some action?"

"I never heard of anyone like that at an insurance company," Dave said.

Dave entered Max Romano's restaurant through the kitchen as usual. The air was hot and steamy, heady with smells of garlic, parmesan, basil. He gave a lift of the hand to the somber, gaunt head chef Alex, spoke the names of the other kitchen help, and pushed into the restaurant that hummed and clinked with conversation, eating, drinking. Max drew a good lunch-time crowd. Dave glanced toward the corner table Max always reserved for him. He expected to see Cecil Harris waiting there. A television news field reporter, Cecil was young, black, gangly as a basketball player. He lived with Dave. But he wasn't sitting at the corner table. Hats Jimmerson was, a huge hulk of a man in a shiny black mohair suit, green shirt, wide flame-colored necktie. Max Romano appeared at Dave's elbow, clutching menus, worried.

"I'm sorry," he said. "He insisted."

"You did the right thing," Dave said. Heart pounding, he edged his way between tables. Jimmerson glowered at him. Dave said, "What the hell does this mean?"

"It mean," Jimmerson rumbled, "never send a boy on a man's errand. How can anybody so smart act so stupid? Sit down. You attracting attention. I don't need that."

"Where is Cecil?" Dave said.

"I said, sit down. If you do like I say in every way, Cecil going to be okay." Jimmerson looked at a wristwatch studded with diamonds. Diamonds glittered in rings on his thick fingers. "I expect he is enjoying lunch at this moment with some of my people. Barbecued ribs? Barbecued chicken? I forget today's menu."

Dave sat down because his legs felt weak. Cecil's assignment had been only to locate Jimmerson. Dave had warned him not to go near the man, not to take any risks. Jimmerson was right. Dave had been stupid. Max came now and set down a stocky glass of Glenlivet on the rocks. He and Dave had been friends for almost forty years. They always exchanged small talk. Not today. Max hovered for a nervous moment, then went doubtfully away.

"What did he do?" Dave tasted the Scotch. "Come ring your door-bell?"

Jimmerson shook his head. "He was just asking too many people too many questions. I have a great many friends. One of them was bound to phone me up. Just because a man is black don't mean he'll go unnoticed in the black community. I assume you were thinking along those lines?"

"Something like that," Dave said. "And he's a good investigator. He told you why I wanted to locate you?"

Jimmerson's drink was green. He took a sip of it and nodded. "Yes. You want to clear a young prevaricator of a murder charge against a lady I once knew."

"Were you there?" Dave said. "For my information only. I won't make any trouble for you. I don't want Cecil hurt."

Jimmerson said slowly and distinctly, "I have not laid eyes on Bess Jessup since we split up two years ago, when they busted her for dealing cocaine. I didn't even know she was out of prison, let alone where she was living. And don't jive me, Mr. Brandstetter, please. Wherever you go, trouble ain't but two, three steps behind."

"You know where everybody's living," Dave said.

"Including you." Jimmerson picked up a hat from the carpet. It was shiny black straw with a wide brim and a cerise plume wrapped around the band. "It so happen"— got to his feet; he was a good six foot five, a good three hundred pounds —"that on that afternoon, with twenty other distinguished guests, I was having cocktails with the President at the Annenberg estate in Palm Springs."

"The district attorney wants Mike Rader dead," Dave said. "He's no boy scout, but he doesn't deserve that."

"He be all right." Jimmerson put on the hat and smiled. A diamond glittered in each of his incisors. "He got a friend. That what we all of us need in this life. Friends. That why the po-lice have such a lot of bad luck when it come to me. See, the po-lice, they just naturally ain't got no friends." He chuckled, picked up his glass, finished off the green drink, set the glass down, licked his lips. "But me — I got nothing but friends. That way the po-lice didn't look very hard for me when this felonious child told them his story. That why you shouldn't have put your skinny young associate to the trouble. The day Bess Jessup lost her life, I was with my friends. It don't matter which of my friends gets asked was I with them — I was with them. All right?"

"Someone brought her five thousand dollars in small bills that day," Dave said. "Any idea who that would be?"

"Not me." The diamonds in Jimmerson's teeth flashed again. "I don't deliver. I collect."

"She owned a box of clippings," Dave said. "It's gone."

"She always had that. It didn't mean nothing. Just old, no-good memories. Trash. Nobody would steal that."

"This mean anything to you?" Dave laid the key down.

Jimmerson frowned at it, turned it over with sparkling fingers. "It's a key. Where to? Don't look like much."

Dave put the key away. "When do I see Cecil?"

"Relax. Enjoy your lunch. And I think I can promise you" — Jimmerson consulted the jeweled watch again — "that he will be joining you for dessert."

"Captain Barker will like hearing that," Dave said.

"Give the Captain my regards," Jimmerson said, "and tell him that

I am going to be traveling abroad, indefinitely. I think it is time for me to go check on my Swiss bank accounts." He tilted his hat and strolled out. A good many people stopped eating to watch him.

Dave got up to follow and sat down again. But he did not relax, did not enjoy his lunch. He nibbled at the spinach salad, choked down a bite or two of bread, left untouched the best Alfredo in town. He was on his third Scotch, staring into it, disgusted with himself, when Cecil dropped into his customary chair and grinned at him.

"Thank God," Dave said. "They didn't hurt you."

"I don't like barbecue that spicy," Cecil said, "but you better believe I ate it without complaining." He sobered. "Look, I'm sorry I messed up. I thought I was being discreet. Then, all of a sudden, I'm riding off between two gorillas in a long, black limousine, just like on TV. 'Mr. Jimmerson would like a few words with you.' Whoo-ee!"

"Don't apologize," Dave said. "It was my mistake. I'm thankful you came out unscathed. He was there, all right."

"He admitted it?" Cecil looked surprised.

"No, but those cuts on Bess Jessup's face came from his rings — I'd bet on it. If we could search his place, we'd find clothes of his with her blood on them. And Rader's."

"You search his place," Cecil said. "I'll stay home."

"There's no point," Dave said, and watched Max set down a green Heineken bottle and a tall, frosty glass for Cecil. Dave said, "Max? You all right?"

"That man looked like some kind of criminal," Max said. "I was ready to call the police."

"You're a shrewd judge of character," Dave said.

"In this business, you get to know." With a sage nod into his double chins, Max waddled away.

Cecil measured beer into his glass, tasted it, wiped foam from his upper lip. "No point?" he said.

"Hats didn't kill her. Her bruises had time to develop, darken, swell. She was killed later. The body temperature test allows a two-hour leeway. The examiner wrote down five-thirty because Stancliff said that was the time of the fight."

"Hats could have come back," Cecil said. "So could Rader."

"And left without the five thousand dollars?" Dave said.

"You're a shrewd judge of character," Cecil said.

Seesaw Records' offices and studios were on the second floor of a weary brick building in a district where no one swept the sidewalks. Big cardboard cartons of records narrowed a dim hallway at the top of the stairs up from the street. Microphone booms, coiled black rubber cables, leaning guitar cases. Dave stepped around the tarnished carcass of an old Scully tape deck to knock on a door whose cracked opaque glass was lettered with Jawal Singh's name. A high, musical voice told him to come in. The office needed fresh paint. The ceiling showed that, not the walls — they were covered with posters, album jackets, yellowing photographs of singers and instrumentalists, and eight or ten gold records mounted behind dusty plexiglass. A tiny brown man with long, smoky black hair sat at a desk stacked with reels of tape, albums, cassettes, strewn with papers, and little white cartons that had once held Chinese take-out food. The tiny man had big, glistening brown eyes, and dazzling teeth.

"How can I help you?" He rose, held out a tiny hand. TAXIDERMY was lettered across his T-shirt. The elaborate calligraphy had faded. Dave shook the hand. Jawal Singh said, "You don't look like someone in the music business." Dave gave him a card. He read the card, frowned, smiled once more. "I have heard of you. Yes, I think I have even seen you on the television. What an honor. Please sit down."

"Thank you." Dave looked for a chair that wasn't stacked with records, tapes, copies of *Rolling Stone*, and didn't see one. He set the stack from the chair nearest the desk on the floor and sat down. "I've come about Bess Jessup. For the company that insured her life."

"Ah. What a tragedy. A talented girl. I think she was just beginning to get it together." Singh's speech was elegant and precise, a touch of London in it, a memory of Delhi. "She had been through many difficult years. Now she wanted to resume the career that drugs destroyed."

"Also changing times," Dave said.

"The world is always surprising us," Singh said. "Who could have guessed that all our marches of protest, our speeches and songs and petitions could have brought about the ending of that war? And by Mr. Nixon! I was totally taken by surprise." He glanced around the woebegone office. "I sometimes wonder if I will ever recover. I was deeply committed to peace. But I was not prepared for it. This operation of mine was not like other record companies. It was a crusade on my part. I chose my artists for the message they had to bring the world. Peace, brotherhood."

"And the world lost interest," Dave said. He nodded at Singh's T-shirt. "Taxidermy?"

"Ah." Singh touched the letters with a sheepish smile. "Yes. They were my one successful bid to break with the crusading past, to enter the world of — what did they call it?— 'the me generation'?"

"That's what they called it."

"Taxidermy were very gifted young people. Rock artists. For a little while, they enjoyed great fame and fortune. Regularly they topped the charts." He waved at the gold records. "Those were theirs. It was a time of unwonted prosperity for me." He smiled wistfully for a moment, remembering, then grew mournful. "But they were too young to cope with the success, the money, the adulation. One by one, they destroyed themselves with drugs."

"Are you satisfied that Bess Jessup had really gone off drugs for good? On the night she was killed, someone brought her five thousand dollars. She couldn't have been dealing again?"

"One cannot, of course, predict human behavior," Singh said. "I should be deeply disturbed to think it. But she was having a difficult time raising the required ten thousand dollars for me to produce her new album."

"Is that the custom?" Dave said. "For the artist to put up part of the money?"

"It is the custom when a company is as near extinction as this one." Singh smiled faintly. "And when one knows that human behavior cannot be predicted, particularly that of addictive personalities, however good their intentions."

"In other words," Dave said, "you thought that if she had to raise a bundle to put into the album, it might keep her straight."

Singh nodded. "But not principally. The truth is, I have the recording facilities here, and I have still a fair distribution system, but almost no capital, and certainly no capital to waste." He frowned. "I do hope that she did not resort to drug dealing to raise that money. Guilt for that would be upon me for the rest of my days, doubly so, since it apparently resulted in her death."

"You were going to handle the advertising and publicity too, I suppose," Dave said. "Did she happen to bring you a box of clippings about her career in the sixties?"

"How did you know?" Singh's brows rose.

"It should have been in her apartment and it wasn't."

Singh popped out of his chair. "It is right here." He shifted tapes, albums, and papers off another chair and laid in Dave's hands a department-store suit box. Dave sat down and took off its sunken lid. He found loose clippings, photographs, scrapbooks. The box was too roomy for them. "Please feel free to examine it all. It will show you why she might indeed have come back. She was hoping, once the album was released, to fly to West Germany and join in the protests against the U.S. deployment of missiles there. There it is as it used to be here. Excuse me." He went to the office door. "I have some editing to do. I will be in studio A, if you need me."

"Thank you," Dave said.

When Singh came back, Dave was fitting the lid onto the box. He lifted it once more and took out to show to Singh a newspaper feature, grown yellow around its edges, cracked at its folds. There was a photograph three columns wide. It showed a platform filled with war protest celebrities. Peace posters waved in the picture's foreground. Banners hung over the platform and along its edge. Bess Jessup stood at a microphone with her guitar, her hair blowing in the wind. A young man, tall, slender, fair, stood beside her, clutching a sheaf of papers. Dave pointed him out to Singh. "You think that's the same Jack Catton who's now running for Congress?"

Singh nodded. "I asked her that very question. She said yes, but so bitterly that I regretted having spoken. She and Jack Catton were lovers, then. They lived together. Both were very active in the antiwar movement. He earned his living as a journalist for the *Free Press, Open City*, the other counter-culture papers — all vanished now." Singh's laugh was sad. "How long ago that was."

"Maybe not," Dave said.

Catton came at a long-legged stride up the brightly lighted airport tunnel from the Sacramento four o'clock shuttle flight. He was in a crowd of other passengers, but he stood out. For one thing, he was taller. For another, his hair shone brassy as a new trumpet. He was handsome, and his pace, the way he swung his attaché case, spelled energy. Here was a man not just leaving an aircraft and heading for office or home. Here was a man going someplace important. He'd put on weight since the sixties, but he was still trim. A plump young woman hurried along beside him on short legs. He talked to her. Rapidly. Dave stepped into his way, handed him a card.

"Mr. Catton? Dave Brandstetter. Can I talk to you?"

Catton blinked at him, at the card. "Insurance? I'm sorry. I have all I need." He started to step around Dave.

"I'm a death claims investigator," Dave said. "It's about Elizabeth Jessup. Bess. You used to know her."

Catton's skin had a childlike transparency. He blushed. He looked sharply at the plump girl. "Lucy — go phone and say the flight was late. I'm running behind. I'll be there as soon as I can. Wait for me at the car, okay?"

"I'll bring it around," she said. "Don't be long, Jack. It's the mayor, remember." She looked harried, sweaty, rumpled, but she summoned a smile for Dave. "Try not to keep him long," she pleaded.

"Let's go to the coffee shop," Catton said.

"The bar will be less crowded," Dave said.

Catton drank Perrier water. "All I know about it is that she was murdered. Her lover stabbed her. I really don't have time to read a newspaper these days. When I see television it's because it's going in a room I'm running through. I'm sorry she's dead. She meant a lot to me once. Everything. But that was in megalithic times."

Dave drank Scotch — not very good Scotch but it was all there was. "Why did the two of you break up?"

Catton read his watch. "Dear God, that was nineteen seventy, man. Fourteen years ago. I haven't seen her since. I was in New York for five years —"

"In journalism," Dave said. "Starting with the *Village Voice,* and branching out to the national liberal weeklies — the *Nation,* the *New Republic.* It got you name recognition." Dave had spent an hour researching Catton at the library after leaving Jawal Singh. "Then, when you decided to go into politics, you came back to Los Angeles."

"It was home," Catton said. "My roots are here."

"First the Gene McCarthy presidential campaign, then the school board, then the state assembly, now congress. And you never looked up Bess Jessup? Why not?"

"I heard what had happened to her." Catton looked somber. "Drugs, prostitution, prison." He gazed at the far glass wall, beyond which glossy white jet liners taxied white runways. "Anyway, we were through. She was a dreamer. I was" — his smile was thin, one-cornered — "into action, right? And we'd both been very young. I thought we believed in the same ideals. But for her, it was all just a big emotional high."

"You were into all of it," Dave said, "from draft-card burning to women's lib, even the black activists." Dave smiled slightly, eyeing Catton's blondness. "Ideals? Not just politics — building for your future?"

"This isn't getting us anyplace. What do you want?"

Dave told Catton Bess Jessup's story. "She wasn't having much luck raising the money. Some of your campaign literature was on her coffee table. I wondered if she'd come to you for a loan."

Catton stared. "Are you serious? She hated me. Two people never broke up with less chance of ever getting together again. Come to me for money? Bess? No way."

"You didn't feel sorry for her and take her five thousand dollars out of your campaign fund? Cash? Small bills? In a supermarket sack? You didn't deliver it?"

"I'm not listening to any more." Catton snatched up his briefcase from an empty chair and stood. "You go tell whoever sent you that trying to link my name to Bess Jessup's now isn't going to do a damn bit of good. I haven't seen her. If she did come to me, I'd refuse to see her. I'm sorry she's had a rough life, but it's also been a well-publicized life, and every story was more squalid than the last. And I'm not having my name connected to a woman like that. No politician would." He started off again.

"No one sent me." Dave fell in beside him. "I'm investigating her murder, that's all. If there's no need to bring your name into it, I won't bring it in."

"Believe me," Catton snarled, "there's no need."

"Whoever brought her that money," Dave said, "also ransacked her apartment. Can you suggest why?"

"Obviously looking for drugs," Catton said. He pushed out through glass doors to a broad sidewalk busy with luggage carts, with men, women, children arriving, departing. Cars inched along, bumper to bumper, or paused at curbside, unloading passengers and baggage. "There's my ride," Catton said.

"One last thing." Dave held out the key. "I found this hidden in her apartment. She kept souvenirs from the past. Is this one? Does it recall anything to you?"

Catton snatched it, scowling, turned it over in his hand, gave it back. "Nothing. Now, will you excuse me, please? I have a very important appointment." He ran toward a shiny black Seville at the curb. The plump young woman, who leaned across to open the passenger door for him, looked ready to weep with impatience.

Dave dropped the key back into his pocket.

One look at the airport terminal lockers showed him the key wouldn't work in their doors. He took the long way home from the airport and stopped at the Greyhound bus station in Santa Monica. The key went grudgingly into the lock of number twenty-three, but it wouldn't turn. It almost refused to come loose again. Dusk had reached the canyon before him. High overhead the sky held transparent blue-green light, but down here between the shaggy, shadowy hills, cars had to climb the crooked road with their headlights on. It was night for sure by the time Dave jounced down into his yard off Horseshoe Canyon Road. His headlights flared back at him from the long row of French doors that fronted his odd house. He parked the Jaguar, switched off the lights, climbed wearily out. He rounded the front building, and crossed the uneven bricks of the courtyard under a dark, spreading oak whose dry leaves crackled beneath his shoes. He switched on lights in the cookshack and built himself a double martini. He would carry it across to the back building where, this morning, he had readied kindling and logs in the big fireplace. With the setting of the sun, October had asserted itself. A chill was in the air. He turned off the cookshack lights, stepped out, carrying the icy drink, and pulled the door shut behind him. He took two steps in the familiar dark. At his back, someone else took a step. He made a sharp half turn. Something hard struck his skull. He went down. The splintering of glass was the last thing he heard for a long time.

"All that blood." Cecil stood at the foot of the bed where Dave sat propped on pillows feeling wan in the morning sunshine that poured down from a skylight not far above him in the raftered plank roof of the sleeping loft. "When I got here at midnight, and saw all that blood, I thought you were dead for sure." He set a bentwood breakfast tray on Dave's knees. "But where were you? I phoned everybody, before I had the sense to look up here. And here you were, sleeping like a little child, head all wrapped in white."

"Nothing bleeds like a scalp wound," Dave said. "I didn't notice the mess I was making. I had to telephone. The paramedics got here in no time. After I was stitched up, the hospital wanted to keep me overnight, but I took a taxi back here. I didn't phone you at work because I didn't want to upset you. Instead, the blood did that."

"Drink the orange juice," Cecil said. "Drink the coffee. You need liquids to replace the blood."

Dave frowned around him. "What went with my clothes?"

"I stuffed them in a plastic bag. They're ruined."

"Look in the left pocket of the jacket," Dave said.

Cecil went down the raw pine plank steps from the loft. He was gone for a few minutes. Dave drank the orange juice. His stomach almost turned over, but not quite. He tried the coffee. Cautiously. That was better. Cecil climbed back up the stairs. "Nothing in the left pocket. Nothing in any of the pockets. Stole your watch, your wallet, your checkbook — even your reading glasses. Why would they leave anything in your pockets?"

"They only wanted the key," Dave said.

The light had changed when Dave woke again. He was sweating. The noon sun beating down on the roof made the loft hot. The smell of pine lumber was strong, and underlying it was a faint memory of hay and horse: these buildings he called home had once been stables. He had tried earlier to get out of bed. His head had reacted badly. He tried again now, tentatively, a few inches at a time. If he took it slow, it felt as if it would be all right. He got to the stairs. They appeared to swim. He gripped the rail until the dizziness stopped. Then he made his way carefully down to the bathroom. When he came out of the bathroom, Cecil had returned and was standing, studying him, worried.

"You look sick." He took Dave's arm. "Back to bed."

"What did you find?" Dave said.

"You were right. She chose the place nearest to where she lived — the Trailways depot. But they'd been and gone. Key was in the lock. Inside looked empty." Cecil's support was welcome. Dave seemed to want to fall over. "And I started to leave it, when I saw a piece of paper. It was stuck in the weld at the back. Half a piece of paper."

"Let me see it," Dave said.

"When we've got you up these stairs," Cecil said.

It was an old photocopy, discolored and sooty. Part of a letter. Happily, the part that bore the letterhead. STUDENTS AGAINST WAR. And the date, 15 August 1970. Dave missed his reading glasses, but by squinting he made out some of the typing. The sense of it was lost in the past, however. It was a fragment from the middle of some ongoing plan of action — a rally, a demonstration, a march? Dave studied the letterhead again. The address was on Vermont Avenue, near City College. But Students Against War wouldn't be there now. Students Against War wouldn't be anywhere now. A list of officers ran partway down the left edge of the page in tiny type. Dave handed the paper to Cecil.

"Can you read those names?"

Cecil read them to him. Dave smiled.

Andy Levitan had freckles and kinky red hair. Dave knew him because he was a junior partner of Abe Greenglass, Dave's attorney. He didn't know him well, merely to speak to. But Dave had asked Abe Greenglass to send Andy Levitan to his house. Now he sat on the edge of Dave's bed and frowned through horn-rim glasses with very large, round lenses, at the torn scrap of letterhead, and smiled with irony, and slowly shook his head. He handed the paper back.

"Where the hell did you get that?"

"Bess Jessup had it," Dave said.

"I saw where she was murdered. You looking into that?"

"Was she part of Students Against War?" Dave said.

"She sang at all our rallies, but she wasn't a member. Boy, I never expected to see that letterhead again. That was a thousand years ago. 'Andy Levitan, Executive Secretary.' How seriously we took ourselves." He tilted his head at Dave, forehead creased. "You think this had something to do with her death? How could that be? Anyway, what was she doing with it?"

"I was hoping you could tell me," Dave said.

"I thought we destroyed every piece of paper in that office," Levitan said. "In one very large, very hasty bonfire. You see, we'd planned a major assault on the system — a raid on a draft board, to burn their records."

Cecil whistled. "What happened?"

"It was a close secret, all right? But somebody told the police, and they were there, waiting for us in the dark. Surprise! They let us splash the kerosene around, almost let us light the match, before they switched on the lights. We got out on bail, but we figured we were done for, that we'd spend the rest of our lives in prison. They'd sealed our offices, put a guard on, but we broke in the back and stole our own files and destroyed them."

"You had a spy in your midst," Dave said.

Levitan nodded. "Bob Broughton. It had to be him. He didn't get prosecuted — 'insufficient evidence.' After which he joined the Marines. Jack Catton wanted to kill him." Levitan's laugh was short and bleak. "As it turned out, Vietnam killed him."

Behind a sprawling Tudor-style house, very black beams, mullioned windows, very white plaster, a long lawn sloped down to a lake with swans and rushes. Trees threw lacy shade on the grass, and on colorful flowerbeds. The women were colorful too, in picture hats against the blazing sun. The men wore summer whites. Left-liberal campaign contributors, they held drinks and little bowls of strawberries in clotted cream. Untidy rows of folding chairs had been abandoned — the politicking was over. Dave spotted Catton and moved through the chatting, laughing crowd to stand waiting for him to quit scattering charm for a moment. When he did, Dave stepped in.

"What happened to you?" Catton frowned. "Accident?"

"Impatience," Dave said. "Not mine. Someone else's. They wanted that key I showed you, and they must have assumed I wouldn't give it to them if they simply asked."

"What did they want with it?" Catton led Dave aside. "I had the idea you didn't know what it was for."

"I do now. It fit a locker in a bus station. Not far from where Bess Jessup lived."

"That was where she had the drugs hidden?"

"Not drugs." Dave's head pounded. The heat was punishing. "A bunch of photocopies of documents from the nineteen sixties — when you two lived together."

Catton looked blank. "Documents?"

"Letters from outfits like Students Against War."

Catton expelled a short, bewildered laugh. "Why would Bess have hung onto junk like that?"

"You tell me. You were in Students Against War."

"So were hundreds of decent kids." Catton looked worriedly across the lawn, as if afraid of missing a chance to shake a hand. "What could it have to do with her death?"

"The five thousand wasn't for drugs," Dave said. "So what does that leave?"

"What? Sorry. Excuse me." Catton started away, up the grassy slope. "There's Councilman Greevey."

"Wait," Dave said. "It leaves blackmail, right?"

"You've lost me," Catton said. Then his expression changed. "Hell, we destroyed the SAW papers. You see —"

"Andy Levitan told me," Dave said. "But obviously some escaped. He figures the police spy made copies, and somehow Bess got hold of them. But he says the spy was Bob Broughton, and Broughton is dead. You can't blackmail a dead man."

"So it wasn't blackmail," Catton started off again.

"Unless the spy was someone else," Dave said. "Maybe all of you were mistaken about Broughton. It would be nice to know, wouldn't it?"

Catton halted, turned back. "There's no way. The police department is being sued right now. For undercover activities against political organizations." His smile was wry. "They never stop, do they? But it means the records will be sealed."

"Not to everyone," Dave said. "I'll have Captain Ken Barker check them for me. He's an old friend. And he owes me. He's out of town today, but he'll be back tomorrow. I'll phone you, shall I? When he gives me the name?"

Catton was staring at Dave, but without seeing him. "What? Oh, yes. I mean, no." He made a despairing gesture with his hand. "Don't bother. I'll be honest with you. I took her the five thousand. Yes, she came to me and begged. You were right — I felt sorry for her. I felt even sorrier for her when I saw her at that miserable, torn-up apartment. Her face was a mass of cuts and bruises. But there was no blackmail. You can forget that part. And she was alive when I left her, soaking her face with cold towels."

"What time?" Dave said.

"A little after seven." Catton laid a trembling hand on Dave's arm. "You won't let it come out, will you? What I said at the airport was true — a candidate connected with a woman like that: voters wouldn't understand. At the scene of a murder, the night it happened? It would finish me. And what good would it do Bess?"

"I'll telephone you with that name," Dave said.

It was colder tonight, and damp. Rain was due. At sundown, clouds had blown in from the sea. They hung low and thick over the canyon now and made the darkness beneath the old oak complete. A bench circled the stout trunk of the oak. Ordinarily plants in pots occupied the bench, but Dave had set some of them on the ground. He sat on the bench, back against the oak, and waited. He wore two sweaters and a coat with a sheepskin lining, but the cold got through. He shivered, his head hurt, and he kept falling asleep.

He jerked awake and pushed up the thick sleeve at his wrist to read his new watch. Ten past ten. Had he been wrong? It wouldn't be the first time, but it would surprise hell out of him. He pushed his cold hands into the slash pockets of the coat and dozed off again. He couldn't make out what woke him the next time. He looked at the front building, where he had left lamps on and a classical music station playing through the stereo. He wished he was in there with the fire blazing with a big globe of brandy.

He read his watch again. Five of eleven. The hell with it. He got up stiffly from the bench, yawned, started to raise his arms to stretch, when headlight beams crossed the dark, shaggy heads of the trees out front. The underside of the car scraped paving. Dave smiled thinly. He was always meaning to get the humpy drop from the road into his yard graded. The glow of the headlights beyond the front building winked out. A car door closed. Dave stepped behind the trunk of the oak.

There was no scuffing of shoes on the bricks. The soles must be soft. But they still crackled dry leaves. Dave listened to them. A man appeared in silhouette against the door to the front building, a heavy old door with thick squares of glass. Something was odd-looking about the man's head. It took a second to understand — he was wearing a ski mask. He lifted a hand to press the button in the frame of the door. But he didn't use a finger or a thumb. He used the barrel of a gun. It glinted in the light that came out through the door. Dave launched himself at the man, caught his arm. He meant to twist the arm behind the man's back, make him drop the gun.

The man was stronger than he was. He used the leverage of Dave's grip on his arm to slam Dave hard against the shingle wall of the building. Dave's head met the wall with a crack. The pain was blinding. He went down. "You have to understand," the man said. Dave couldn't understand anything. He was only very dimly aware of being hauled to his feet, of the door opening, of himself a stagger of unaccountable legs into the room where the softly glowing lamps reeled around him, slowly, sickeningly. He sprawled on a couch. "You have to understand," the man said again, and pulled off the ski mask.

"Ah," Dave said hollowly, trying to push himself into a sitting posture. "It is you."

"You're going to die," Catton said, "but you have to understand how it was." He sat on a couch that faced the one where Dave was. A coffee table was between them, Mexican pottery on it, painted terracotta, a wide-eyed cat with its paws tucked up, three jars of different sizes. "They had me on a dope charge. Marijuana. I was selling it on campus at LACC. They were going to lock me up forever. Unless I told them what was going on inside the movement."

"I'm in too much pain to cry," Dave said. "Let me tell you. Bess found out you were spying on your friends, selling out the peaceniks. That's why you left so suddenly for New York. She told you if you didn't go, she'd expose you. She loved you, or she'd have done it regardless."

"She hated me," Catton said. "I never saw such hate."

"Did you know she had a stack of material you'd stolen from Students Against War and the rest?"

"Not until she came to me last week. Asking for ten thousand dollars to pay that racketeering record producer. When I gave it to her, she'd give me the papers." Catton's laugh was bitter. "Everybody sells out. It just takes some of us a little longer."

"You only took her five thousand," Dave said.

Catton shrugged sourly. "What the hell. She was on her beam ends, a drug addict, a whore. Five thousand would look like a fortune to her."

"Why did you kill her?" Dave said.

"It was an accident. It was her fault. That rotten temper of hers. I asked her for the documents, and she wouldn't give them up. She said she had them hidden in a safe place, and until I brought her the rest of the money, they'd stay there. I started tearing the place apart to find them, and she picked up this switchblade and went for me."

"And you tried to take it away from her?"

"We struggled. Some pimp had beat hell out of her but she was strong. The blade slid into her. I don't know how." Catton stared away numbly. "Christ, I didn't mean to kill her."

"But you went wearing gloves," Dave said. "Your prints aren't on that money. They're not on the sack."

"Just so she couldn't prove I gave it to her and wreck my campaign. I tell you, I never meant to hurt her."

"Only to save yourself," Dave said. "I understand."

"So do I," Ken Barker said. He came from behind the shadowy bar at the upper end of the long room. "Perfectly."

Catton scrambled to his feet and fired his gun. But wildly. Barker's gun went off at almost the same moment, and the impact of the bullet spun Catton around. He fell across the coffee table, knocking the Mexican pottery off, shattering it. He slumped from table to floor and lay still. Dave saw blood. Barker, a big-shouldered man with a broken nose and steel-gray hair, knelt over Catton, laid fingers on the candidate's neck below the jaw hinge. He looked up at Dave. "He's alive. Can you use a phone?"

"I can try." Dave pushed dizzily to his feet, tottered a few steps, picked up a receiver, punched buttons. While the phone rang at the other end of the line, Cecil came through the door at a run. That would make it midnight, the hour he always arrived home from work. Raindrops sparkled in his hair, and his eyes were round with alarm.

"Fourth of July in here?" he said.

"Election day," Dave said.

SUE GRAFTON

THE PARKER SHOTGUN

Sue Grafton (b. 1940) was a novelist (The Lolly Madonna War), *a screen-writer, and a television writer (movies-of-the-week, a few episodes of* Rhoda) *before she discovered crime. Her twice-divorced detective Kinsey Millhone lives in a place that sounds a lot like Santa Barbara and acts like a tried-and-true goddaughter of Marlowe and Spade. The first Kinsey Millhone novel was* A Is for Alibi, *then came* B Is for Burglar, C Is for Corpse, D Is for Deadbeat, E Is for Evidence, *and* F Is for Fugitive. *She swears she will keep going until she hits Z (no saying, as yet, for what).*

Just as Flaubert proclaimed "I am Emma," Grafton confided to a News-week reporter: "I am Kinsey Millhone." Whether it applies to the author or not, Kinsey once described herself this way: "My standard outfit consists of boots or tennis shoes, form-fitting jeans, and a tank top or turtleneck, depending on the season. Sometimes I wear a windbreaker or a denim vest, and I've always got a large leather shoulder bag, which sometimes (but not often) contains my little .32."

"The Parker Shotgun" was first published in 1986.

THE CHRISTMAS HOLIDAYS had come and gone, and the new year was under way. January, in California, is as good as it gets — cool, clear, and green, with a sky the color of wisteria and a surf that thunders like a volley of gunfire in a distant field. My name is Kinsey Millhone. I'm a private investigator, licensed, bonded, insured; white, female, age thirty-two, unmarried, and physically fit. That Monday morning, I was sitting in my office with my feet up, wondering what life would bring, when a woman walked in and tossed a photograph on my desk. My introduction to the Parker shotgun began with a graphic view of its apparent effect when fired at a formerly nice-looking man at close range. His face was still largely intact, but he had no use now for a pocket comb. With effort, I kept my expression neutral as I glanced up at her.

"Somebody killed my husband."

"I can see that," I said.

She snatched the picture back and stared at it as though she might have missed some telling detail. Her face suffused with pink, and she blinked back tears. "Jesus. Rudd was killed five months ago, and the cops have done shit. I'm so sick of getting the runaround I could scream."

She sat down abruptly and pressed a hand to her mouth, trying to compose herself. She was in her late twenties, with a gaudy prettiness. Her hair was an odd shade of brown, like cherry Coke, worn shoulder length and straight. Her eyes were large, a lush mink brown; her mouth was full. Her complexion was all warm tones, tanned, and clear. She didn't seem to be wearing makeup, but she was still as vivid as a magazine illustration, a good four-color run on slick paper. She was seven months pregnant by the look of her; not voluminous yet, but rotund. When she was calmer, she identified herself as Lisa Osterling.

"That's a crime lab photo. How'd you come by it?" I said when the preliminaries were disposed of.

She fumbled in her handbag for a tissue and blew her nose. "I have my little ways," she said morosely. "Actually I know the photographer and I stole a print. I'm going to have it blown up and hung on the wall just so I won't forget. The police are hoping I'll drop the whole thing, but I got news for *them*." Her mouth was starting to tremble again, and a tear splashed onto her skirt as though my ceiling had a leak.

"What's the story?" I said. "The cops in this town are usually pretty good." I got up and filled a paper cup with water from my Sparklett's dispenser, passing it over to her. She murmured a thank you and drank it down, staring into the bottom of the cup as she spoke. "Rudd was a cocaine dealer until a month or so before he died. They haven't said as much, but I know they've written him off as some kind of small-time punk. What do they care? They'd like to think he was killed in a drug deal — a double cross or something like that. He wasn't, though. He'd given it all up because of this."

She glanced down at the swell of her belly. She was wearing a kelly green T-shirt with an arrow down the front. The word "Oops!" was written across her breasts in machine embroidery.

"What's your theory?" I asked. Already I was leaning toward the official police version of events. Drug dealing isn't synonymous with longevity. There's too much money involved and too many amateurs getting into the act. This was Santa Teresa — ninety-five miles north of the big time in L.A., but there are still standards to maintain. A shotgun blast is the underworld equivalent of a bad annual review.

"I don't have a theory. I just don't like theirs. I want you to look into it so I can clear Rudd's name before the baby comes."

I shrugged. "I'll do what I can, but I can't guarantee the results. How are you going to feel if the cops are right?"

She stood up, giving me a flat look. "I don't know why Rudd died, but it had nothing to do with drugs," she said. She opened her handbag and extracted a roll of bills the size of a wad of socks. "What do you charge?"

"Thirty bucks an hour plus expenses."

She peeled off several hundred-dollar bills and laid them on the desk.

I got out a contract.

My second encounter with the Parker shotgun came in the form of a dealer's appraisal slip that I discovered when I was nosing through Rudd Osterling's private possessions an hour later at the house. The address she'd given me was on the Bluffs, a residential area on the west side of town, overlooking the Pacific. It should have been an elegant neighborhood, but the ocean generated too much fog and too much corrosive salt air. The houses were small and had a temporary feel to them, as though the occupants intended to move on when the month was up. No one seemed to get around to painting the trim, and the yards looked like they were kept by people who spent all day at the beach. I followed her in my car, reviewing the information she'd given me as I urged my ancient VW up Capilla Hill and took a right on Presipio.

The late Rudd Osterling had been in Santa Teresa since the sixties, when he migrated to the West Coast in search of sunshine, good surf, good dope, and casual sex. Lisa told me he'd lived in vans and communes, working variously as a roofer, tree trimmer, bean picker, fry cook, and forklift operator — never with any noticeable ambition or success. He'd started dealing cocaine two years earlier, apparently netting more money than he was accustomed to. Then he'd met and married Lisa, and she'd been determined to see him clean up his act. According to her, he'd retired from the drug trade and was just in the process of setting himself up in a landscape maintenance business when someone blew the top of his head off.

I pulled into the driveway behind her, glancing at the frame and stucco bungalow with its patchy grass and dilapidated fence. It looked like one of those households where there's always something under construction, probably without permits and not up to code. In this case, a foundation had been laid for an addition to the garage, but the weeds were already growing up through cracks in the concrete. A wooden outbuilding had been dismantled, the old lumber tossed in an unsightly pile. Closer to the house, there were stacks of cheap pecan wood paneling, sun-bleached in places and warped along one edge. It was all hapless and depressing, but she scarcely looked at it.

I followed her into the house.

"We were just getting the house fixed up when he died," she remarked.

"When did you buy the place?" I was manufacturing small talk, trying to cover my distaste at the sight of the old linoleum counter, where a line of ants stretched from a crust of toast and jelly all the way out the back door.

"We didn't really. This was my mother's. She and my stepdad moved back to the Midwest last year."

"What about Rudd? Did he have any family out here?"

"They're all in Connecticut, I think, real la-di-dah. His parents are dead, and his sisters wouldn't even come out to the funeral."

"Did he have a lot of friends?"

"All cocaine dealers have friends."

"Enemies?"

"Not that I ever heard about."

"Who was his supplier?"

"I don't know that."

"No disputes? Suits pending? Quarrels with the neighbors? Family arguments about the inheritance?"

She gave me a "no" on all four counts.

I had told her I wanted to go through his personal belongings, so she showed me into the tiny back bedroom, where he'd set up a card table and some cardboard file boxes. A real entrepreneur. I began to search while she leaned against the door frame, watching.

I said, "Tell me about what was going on the week he died." I was sorting through canceled checks in a Nike shoe box. Most were written to the neighborhood supermarket, utilities, telephone company.

She moved to the desk chair and sat down. "I can't tell you much because I was at work. I do alterations and repairs at a dry cleaner's up at Presipio Mall. Rudd would stop in now and then when he was out running around. He'd picked up a few jobs already, but he really wasn't doing the gardening full time. He was trying to get all his old business squared away. Some kid owed him money. I remember that."

"He sold cocaine on *credit*?"

She shrugged. "Maybe it was grass or pills. Somehow the kid owed him a bundle. That's all I know."

"I don't suppose he kept any records."

"Nuh-uh. It was all in his head. He was too paranoid to put anything down in black and white."

The file boxes were jammed with old letters, tax returns, receipts. It all looked like junk to me.

"What about the day he was killed? Were you at work then?"

She shook her head. "It was a Saturday. I was off work, but I'd gone to the market. I was out maybe an hour and a half, and when I got home, police cars were parked in front, and the paramedics were here. Neighbors were standing out on the street." She stopped talking, and I was left to imagine the rest.

"Had he been expecting anyone?"

"If he was, he never said anything to me. He was in the garage, doing I don't know what. Chauncy, next door, heard the shotgun go off, but by the time he got here to investigate, whoever did it was gone."

I got up and moved toward the hallway. "Is this the bedroom down here?"

"Right. I haven't gotten rid of his stuff yet. I guess I'll have to eventually. I'm going to use his office for the nursery."

. I moved into the master bedroom and went through his hanging clothes. "Did the police find anything?"

"They didn't look. Well, one guy came through and poked around some. About five minutes' worth."

I began to check through the drawers she indicated were his. Nothing remarkable came to light. On top of the chest was one of those brass and walnut caddies, where Rudd apparently kept his watch, keys, loose change. Almost idly, I picked it up. Under it there was a folded slip of paper. It was a partially completed appraisal form from a gun shop out in Colgate, a township to the north of us. "What's a Parker?" I said, when I'd glanced at it. She peered over the slip.

"Oh. That's probably the appraisal on the shotgun he got."

"The one he was killed with?"

"Well, I don't know. They never found the weapon, but the homicide detective said they couldn't run it through ballistics, anyway — or whatever it is they do."

"Why'd he have it appraised in the first place?"

"He was taking it in trade for a big drug debt, and he needed to know if it was worth it."

"Was this the kid you mentioned before or someone else?"

"The same one, I think. At first, Rudd intended to turn around and sell the gun, but then he found out it was a collector's item so he decided to keep it. The gun dealer called a couple of times after Rudd died, but it was gone by then."

"And you told the cops all this stuff?"

"Sure. They couldn't have cared less."

I doubted that, but I tucked the slip in my pocket anyway. I'd check it out and then talk to Dolan in homicide.

The gun shop was located on a narrow side street in Colgate, just off the main thoroughfare. Colgate looks like it's made up of hardware stores, U-haul rentals, and plant nurseries; places that seem to have half their merchandise outside, surrounded by chain link fence. The gun shop had been set up in someone's front parlor in a dinky white frame house. There were some glass counters filled with gun paraphernalia, but no guns in sight.

The man who came out of the back room was in his fifties, with a narrow face and graying hair, gray eyes made luminous by rimless glasses. He wore a dress shirt with the sleeves rolled up and a long gray apron tied around his waist. He had perfect teeth, but when he talked I could see the rim of pink where his upper plate was fit, and it spoiled the effect. Still, I had to give him credit for a certain level of good looks, maybe a seven on a scale of ten. Not bad for a man his age. "Yes ma'am," he said. He had a trace of an accent, Virginia, I thought.

"Are you Avery Lamb?"

"That's right. What can I help you with?"

"I'm not sure. I'm wondering what you can tell me about this appraisal you did." I handed him the slip.

He glanced down and then looked up at me. "Where did you get this?"

"Rudd Osterling's widow," I said.

"She told me she didn't have the gun."

"That's right."

His manner was a combination of confusion and wariness. "What's your connection to the matter?"

I took out a business card and gave it to him. "She hired me to look into Rudd's death. I thought the shotgun might be relevant since he was killed with one."

He shook his head. "I don't know what's going on. This is the second time it's disappeared."

"Meaning what?"

"Some woman brought it in to have it appraised back in June. I made an offer on it then, but before we could work out a deal, she claimed the gun was stolen."

"I take it you had some doubts about that."

"Sure I did. I don't think she ever filed a police report, and I suspect she knew damn well who took it but didn't intend to pursue it. Next thing I knew, this Osterling fellow brought the same gun in. It had a beavertail fore-end and an English grip. There was no mistaking it."

"Wasn't that a bit of a coincidence? His bringing the gun in to you?"

"Not really. I'm one of the few master gunsmiths in this area. All he had to do was ask around the same way she did."

"Did you tell her the gun had showed up?"

He shrugged with his mouth and a lift of his brows. "Before I could talk to her, he was dead and the Parker was gone again."

I checked the date on the slip. "That was in August?"

"That's right, and I haven't seen the gun since."

"Did he tell you how he acquired it?"

"Said he took it in trade. I told him this other woman showed up with it first, but he didn't seem to care about that."

"How much was the Parker worth?"

He hesitated, weighing his words. "I offered him six thousand."

"But what's its value out in the marketplace?"

"Depends on what people are willing to pay."

I tried to control the little surge of impatience he had sparked. I could tell he'd jumped into his crafty negotiator's mode, unwilling to tip his hand in case the gun showed up and he could nick it off cheap. "Look," I said, "I'm asking you in confidence. This won't go any further unless it becomes a police matter, and then neither of us will have a choice. Right now, the gun's missing anyway, so what difference does it make?"

He didn't seem entirely convinced, but he got my point. He cleared his throat with obvious embarrassment. "Ninety-six."

I stared at him. "Thousand dollars?"

He nodded.

"Jesus. That's a lot for a gun, isn't it?"

His voice dropped. "Ms. Millhone, that gun is priceless. It's an A-1 Special 28-gauge with a two-barrel set. There were only two of them made."

"But why so much?"

"For one thing, the Parker's a beautifully crafted shotgun. There are different grades, of course, but this one was exceptional. Fine wood. Some of the most incredible scrollwork you'll ever see. Parker had an Italian working for him back then who'd spend sometimes five thousand hours on the engraving alone. The company went out of business around 1942, so there aren't any more to be had."

"You said there were two. Where's the other one, or would you know?"

"Only what I've heard. A dealer in Ohio bought the one at auction a couple years back for ninety-six. I understand some fella down in Texas has it now, part of a collection of Parkers. The gun Rudd Osterling brought in has been missing for years. I don't think he knew what he had on his hands."

"And you didn't tell him."

Lamb shifted his gaze. "I told him enough," he said carefully. "I can't help it if the man didn't do his homework."

"How'd you know it was the missing Parker?"

"The serial number matched, and so did everything else. It wasn't a fake, either. I examined the gun under heavy magnification, checking for fill-in welds and traces of markings that might have been overstamped. After I checked it out, I showed it to a buddy of mine, a big gun buff, and he recognized it, too."

"Who else knew about it besides you and this friend?"

"Whoever Rudd Osterling got it from, I guess."

"I'll want the woman's name and address if you've still got it. Maybe she knows how the gun fell into Rudd's hands."

Again he hesitated for a moment, and then he shrugged. "I don't see why not." He made a note on a piece of scratch paper and pushed it across the counter to me. "I'd like to know if the gun shows up," he said.

"Sure, as long as Mrs. Osterling doesn't object."

I didn't have any other questions for the moment. I moved toward the door, then glanced back at him. "How could Rudd have sold the gun if it was stolen property? Wouldn't he have needed a bill of sale for it? Some proof of ownership?"

Avery Lamb's face was devoid of expression. "Not necessarily. If an avid collector got hold of that gun, it would sink out of sight, and that's the last you'd ever see of it. He'd keep it in his basement and never show it to a soul. It'd be enough if he knew he had it. You don't need a bill of sale for that."

*

I sat out in my car and made some notes while the information was fresh. Then I checked the address Lamb had given me, and I could feel the adrenaline stir. It was right back in Rudd's neighborhood.

The woman's name was Jackie Barnett. The address was two streets over from the Osterling house and just about parallel; a big corner lot planted with avocado trees and bracketed with palms. The house itself was yellow stucco with flaking brown shutters and a yard that needed mowing. The mailbox read "Squires," but the house number seemed to match. There was a basketball hoop nailed up above the two-car garage and a dismantled motorcycle in the driveway.

I parked my car and got out. As I approached the house, I saw an old man in a wheelchair planted in the side yard like a lawn ornament. He was parchment pale, with baby-fine white hair and rheumy eyes. The left half of his face had been disconnected by a stroke, and his left arm and hand rested uselessly in his lap. I caught sight of a woman peering through the window, apparently drawn by the sound of my car door slamming shut. I crossed the yard, moving toward the front porch. She opened the door before I had a chance to knock.

"You must be Kinsey Millhone. I just got off the phone with Avery. He said you'd be stopping by."

"That was quick. I didn't realize he'd be calling ahead. Saves me an explanation. I take it you're Jackie Barnett."

"That's right. Come in if you like. I just have to check on him," she said, indicating the man in the yard.

"Your father?"

She shot me a look. "Husband," she said. I watched her cross the grass toward the old man, grateful for a chance to recover from my gaffe. I could see now that she was older than she'd first appeared. She must have been in her fifties — at that stage where women wear too much makeup and dye their hair too bold a shade of blonde. She was buxom, clearly overweight, but lush. In a seventeenth-century painting, she'd have been depicted supine, her plump naked body draped in sheer white. Standing over her, something with a goat's rear end would be poised for assault. Both would look coy but excited at the prospects. The old man was beyond the pleasures of the flesh, yet the noises he made — garbled and indistinguishable because of the stroke — had the same intimate quality as sounds uttered in the throes of passion, a disquieting effect.

I looked away from him, thinking of Avery Lamb instead. He hadn't actually told me the woman was a stranger to him, but he'd certainly implied as much. I wondered now what their relationship consisted of.

Jackie spoke to the old man briefly, adjusting his lap robe. Then she came back and we went inside.

"Is your name Barnett or Squires?" I asked.

"Technically it's Squires, but I still use Barnett for the most part," she said. She seemed angry, and I thought at first the rage was directed at me. She caught my look. "I'm sorry," she said, "but I've about had it with him. Have you ever dealt with a stroke victim?"

"I understand it's difficult."

"It's impossible! I know I sound hard-hearted, but he was always short-tempered and now he's frustrated on top of that. Self-centered, demanding. Nothing suits him. Nothing. I put him out in the yard sometimes just so I won't have to fool with him. Have a seat, hon."

I sat. "How long has he been sick?"

"He had the first stroke in June. He's been in and out of the hospital ever since."

"What's the story on the gun you took out to Avery's shop?"

"Oh, that's right. He said you were looking into some fellow's death. He lived right here on the Bluffs, too, didn't he?"

"Over on Whitmore . . ."

"That was terrible. I read about it in the papers, but I never did hear the end of it. What went on?"

"I wasn't given the details," I said briefly. "Actually, I'm trying to track down a shotgun that belonged to him. Avery Lamb says it was the same gun you brought in."

She had automatically proceeded to get out two cups and saucers, so her answer was delayed until she'd poured coffee for us both. She passed a cup over to me, and then she sat down, stirring milk into hers. She glanced at me, self-consciously. "I just took that gun to spite *him*," she said with a nod toward the yard. "I've been married to Bill for six years and miserable for every one of them. It was my own damn fault. I'd been divorced for ages and I was doing fine, but somehow when I hit fifty, I got in a panic. Afraid of growing old alone, I guess. I ran into Bill, and he looked like a catch. He was retired, but he had loads of money, or so he said. He promised me the moon. Said we'd travel. Said he'd buy me clothes and a car and I don't know what all. Turns out he's a penny-pinching miser with a mean mouth and a quick fist. At least he can't do that anymore." She paused to shake her head, staring down at her coffee cup.

"The gun was his?"

"Well, yes, it was. He has a collection of shotguns. I swear he took better care of them than he did of me. I just despise guns. I was always after him to get rid of them. Makes me nervous to have them in the house. Anyway, when he got sick, it turned out he had insurance, but it only paid eighty percent. I was afraid his whole life savings would go up in smoke. I figured he'd go on for years, using up all the money, and then I'd be stuck with his debts when he died. So I just picked up one of the guns and took it out to that gun place to sell. I was going to buy me some clothes."

"What made you change your mind?"

"Well, I didn't think it'd be worth but eight or nine hundred dollars. Then Avery said he'd give me six thousand for it, so I had to guess it was worth at least twice that. I got nervous and thought I better put it back."

"How soon after that did the gun disappear?"

"Oh, gee, I don't know. I didn't pay much attention until Bill got out of the hospital the second time. He's the one who noticed it was gone," she said. "Of course, he raised pluperfect hell. You should have seen him. He had a conniption fit for two days, and then he had another stroke and had to be hospitalized all over again. Served him right if you ask me. At least I had Labor Day weekend to myself. I needed it."

"Do you have any idea who might have taken the gun?"

She gave me a long, candid look. Her eyes were very blue and couldn't have appeared more guileless. "Not the faintest."

I let her practice her wide-eyed stare for a moment, and then I laid out a little bait just to see what'd she'd do. "God, that's too bad," I said. "I'm assuming you reported it to the police."

I could see her debate briefly before she replied. Yes or no. Check one. "Well, of course," she said.

She was one of those liars who blush from lack of practice.

I kept my tone of voice mild. "What about the insurance? Did you put in a claim?"

She looked at me blankly, and I had the feeling I'd taken her by surprise on that one. She said, "You know, it never even occurred to me. But of course he probably would have it insured, wouldn't he?"

"Sure, if the gun's worth that much. What company is he with?"

"I don't remember offhand. I'd have to look it up."

"I'd do that if I were you," I said. "You can file a claim, and then all you have to do is give the agent the case number."

"Case number?"

"The police will give you that from their report."

She stirred restlessly, glancing at her watch. "Oh, lordy, I'm going to have to give him his medicine. Was there anything else you wanted to ask while you were here?" Now that she'd told me a fib or two, she was anxious to get rid of me so she could assess the situation. Avery Lamb had told me she'd never reported it to the cops. I wondered if she'd call him up now to compare notes.

"Could I take a quick look at his collection?" I said, getting up.

"I suppose that'd be all right. It's in here," she said. She moved toward a small paneled den, and I followed, stepping around a suitcase near the door.

A rack of six guns was enclosed in a glass-fronted cabinet. All of them were beautifully engraved, with fine wood stocks, and I wondered how a priceless Parker could really be distinguished. Both the cabinet and the rack were locked, and there were no empty slots. "Did he keep the Parker in here?"

She shook her head. "The Parker had its own case." She hauled out a handsome wood case from behind the couch and opened it for me, demonstrating its emptiness as though she might be setting up a magic trick. Actually, there was a set of barrels in the box, but nothing else.

I glanced around. There was a shotgun propped in one corner, and I picked it up, checking the manufacturer's imprint on the frame. L. C. Smith. Too bad. For a moment I'd thought it might be the missing Parker. I'm always hoping for the obvious. I set the Smith back in the corner with regret.

"Well, I guess that'll do," I said. "Thanks for the coffee."

"No trouble. I wish I could be more help." She started easing me toward the door.

I held out my hand. "Nice meeting you," I said. "Thanks again for your time."

She gave my hand a perfunctory shake. "That's all right. Sorry I'm in such a rush, but you know how it is when you have someone sick."

Next thing I knew, the door was closing at my back and I was heading toward my car, wondering what she was up to.

I'd just reached the driveway when a white Corvette came roaring down the street and rumbled into the drive. The kid at the wheel flipped the ignition key and cantilevered himself up onto the seat top. "Hi. You know if my mom's here?"

"Who, Jackie? Sure," I said, taking a flyer. "You must be Doug."

He looked puzzled. "No, Eric. Do I know you?"

I shook my head. "I'm just a friend passing through."

He hopped out of the Corvette. I moved on toward my car, keeping an eye on him as he headed toward the house. He looked about seventeen, blond, blue-eyed, with good cheekbones, a moody, sensual mouth, lean surfer's body. I pictured him in a few years, hanging out in resort hotels, picking up women three times his age. He'd do well. So would they.

Jackie had apparently heard him pull in, and she came out onto the porch, intercepting him with a quick look at me. She put her arm through his, and the two moved into the house. I looked over at the old man. He was making noises again, plucking aimlessly at his bad hand with his good one. I felt a mental jolt, like an interior tremor shifting the ground under me. I was beginning to get it.

I drove the two blocks to Lisa Osterling's. She was in the backyard, stretched out on a chaise in a sunsuit that made her belly look like a watermelon in a laundry bag. Her face and arms were rosy, and her tanned legs glistened with tanning oil. As I crossed the grass, she raised a hand to her eyes, shading her face from the winter sunlight so she could look at me. "I didn't expect to see you back so soon."

"I have a question," I said, "and then I need to use your phone. Did Rudd know a kid named Eric Barnett?"

"I'm not sure. What's he look like?"

I gave her a quick rundown, including a description of the white Corvette. I could see the recognition in her face as she sat up.

"Oh, him. Sure. He was over here two or three times a week. I just never knew his name. Rudd said he lived around here somewhere and stopped by to borrow tools so he could work on his motorcycle. Is he the one who owed Rudd the money?"

"Well, I don't know how we're going to prove it, but I suspect he was."

"You think he killed him?"

"I can't answer that yet, but I'm working on it. Is the phone in here?" I was moving toward the kitchen. She struggled to her feet and followed me into the house. There was a wall phone near the back door. I tucked the receiver against my shoulder, pulling the appraisal slip out of my pocket. I dialed Avery Lamb's gun shop. The phone rang twice.

Somebody picked up on the other hand. "Gun shop."

"Mr. Lamb?"

"This is Orville Lamb. Did you want me or my brother, Avery?"

"Avery, actually. I have a quick question for him."

"Well, he left a short while ago, and I'm not sure when he'll be back. Is it something I can help you with?"

"Maybe so," I said. "If you had a priceless shotgun — say, an Ithaca or a Parker, one of the classics — would you shoot a gun like that?"

"You could," he said dubiously, "but it wouldn't be a good idea, especially if it was in mint condition to begin with. You wouldn't want to take a chance on lowering the value. Now if it'd been in use previously, I don't guess it would matter much, but still I wouldn't advise it — just speaking for myself. Is this a gun of yours?"

But I'd hung up. Lisa was right behind me, her expression anxious. "I've got to go in a minute," I said, "but here's what I think went on. Eric Barnett's stepfather has a collection of fine shotguns, one of which turns out to be very, very valuable. The old man was hospitalized, and Eric's mother decided to hock one of the guns in order to do a little something for herself before he'd blown every asset he had on his medical bills. She had no idea the gun she chose was worth so much, but the gun dealer recognized it as the find of a lifetime. I don't know whether he told her that or not, but when she realized it was more valuable than she thought, she lost her nerve and put it back."

"Was that the same gun Rudd took in trade?"

"Exactly. My guess is that she mentioned it to her son, who saw a chance to square his drug debt. He offered Rudd the shotgun in trade, and Rudd decided he'd better get the gun appraised, so he took it out to the same place. The gun dealer recognized it when he brought it in."

She stared at me. "Rudd was killed over the gun itself, wasn't he?" she said.

"I think so, yes. It might have been an accident. Maybe there was a struggle and the gun went off."

She closed her eyes and nodded. "Okay. Oh, wow. That feels better. I can live with that." Her eyes came open, and she smiled painfully. "Now what?"

"I have one more hunch to check out, and then I think we'll know what's what."

She reached over and squeezed my arm. "Thanks."

"Yeah, well, it's not over yet, but we're getting there."

When I got back to Jackie Barnett's, the white Corvette was still in the driveway, but the old man in the wheelchair had apparently been moved into the house. I knocked, and after an interval, Eric opened the door, his expression altering only slightly when he saw me.

I said, "Hello again. Can I talk to your mom?"

"Well, not really. She's gone right now."

"Did she and Avery go off together?"

"Who?"

I smiled briefly. "You can drop the bullshit, Eric. I saw the suitcase in the hall when I was here the first time. Are they gone for good or just for a quick jaunt?"

"They said they'd be back by the end of the week," he mumbled. It was clear he looked a lot slicker than he really was. I almost felt bad that he was so far outclassed.

"Do you mind if I talk to your stepfather?"

He flushed. "She doesn't want him upset."

"I won't upset him."

He shifted uneasily, trying to decide what to do with me.

I thought I'd help him out. "Could I just make a suggestion here? According to the California penal code, grand theft is committed when the real or personal property taken is of a value exceeding two hundred dollars. Now that includes domestic fowl, avocados, olives, citrus, nuts, and artichokes. Also shotguns, and it's punishable by imprisonment in the county jail or state prison for not more than one year. I don't think you'd care for that."

He stepped away from the door and let me in.

The old man was huddled in his wheelchair in the den. The rheumy eyes came up to meet mine, but there was no recognition in them. Or maybe there was recognition but no interest. I hunkered beside his wheelchair. "Is your hearing okay?"

He began to pluck aimlessly at his pant leg with his good hand, looking away from me. I've seen dogs with the same expression when they've done pottie on the rug and know you've got a roll of newspaper tucked behind your back.

"Want me to tell you what I think happened?" I didn't really need to wait. He couldn't answer in any mode that I could interpret. "I think when you came home from the hospital the first time and found out the gun was gone, the shit hit the fan. You must have figured out that Eric took it. He'd probably taken other things if he'd been doing cocaine for long. You probably hounded him until you found out what he'd done with it, and then you went over to Rudd's to get it. Maybe you took the L. C. Smith with you the first time, or maybe you came back for it when he refused to return the Parker. In either case, you blew his head off and then came back across the yards. And then you had another stroke."

I became aware of Eric in the doorway behind me. I glanced back at him. "You want to talk about this stuff?" I asked.

"Did he kill Rudd?"

"I think so," I said. I stared at the old man.

His face had taken on a canny stubbornness, and what was I going to do? I'd have to talk to Lieutenant Dolan about the situation, but the cops would probably never find any real proof, and even if they did, what could they do to him? He'd be lucky if he lived out the year.

"Rudd was a nice guy," Eric said.

"God, Eric. You *all* must have guessed what happened," I said snappishly.

He had the good grace to color up at that, and then he left the room. I stood up. To save myself, I couldn't work up any righteous anger at the pitiful remainder of a human being hunched in front of me. I crossed to the gun cabinet.

The Parker shotgun was in the rack, three slots down, looking like the other classic shotguns in the case. The old man would die, and Jackie would inherit it from his estate. Then she'd marry Avery and they'd all have what they wanted. I stood there for a moment, and then I started looking through the desk drawers until I found the keys. I unlocked the cabinet and then unlocked the rack. I substituted the L. C. Smith for the Parker and then locked the whole business up again. The old man was whimpering, but he never looked at me, and Eric was nowhere in sight when I left.

The last I saw of the Parker shotgun, Lisa Osterling was holding it somewhat awkwardly across her bulky midriff. I'd talk to Lieutenant Dolan all right, but I wasn't going to tell him everything. Sometimes justice is served in other ways.

PAUL THEROUX

THE JOHORE MURDERS

*Although he was born and raised in the Boston suburbs and spent his university years in New England and New York, Paul Theroux (b. 1941) has made a literary career out of acting like an Englishman. Or, at least, writing as though he were an English writer. His fiction (seventeen novels and short story collections) is more often than not set in Britain or some backwater of the old empire. Critics tend to drop names such as Graham Greene, Evelyn Waugh, or Somerset Maugham when they write about Theroux. His tartly dyspeptic nonfiction books (*The Great Railway Bazaar *and* The Old Patagonian Express, *for example) are ideal antidotes to the usual travel writer's gush.*

The following story, set in a small Malaysian city, is written in Theroux's more avuncular, Maugham-ish mode. It appeared in his 1977 collection The Consul's File.

THE FIRST VICTIM was a British planter, and everyone at the Club said what a shame it was that after fifteen years in the country he was killed just four days before he planned to leave. He had no family, he lived alone; until he was murdered no one knew very much about him. Murder is the grimmest, briefest fame. If the second victim, a month later, had not been an American I probably would not have given the Johore murders a second thought, and I certainly would not have been involved in the business. But who would have guessed that Ismail Garcia was an American?

The least dignified thing that can happen to a man is to be murdered. If he dies in his sleep he gets a respectful obituary and perhaps a smiling portrait; it is how we all want to be remembered. But murder is the great exposer: here is the victim in his torn underwear, face down on the floor, unpaid bills on his dresser, a meager shopping list, some loose change, and worst of all the fact that he is alone. Investigation reveals what he did that day — it all matters — his habits are examined, his behavior scrutinized, his trunks rifled, and a balance sheet is drawn up at the hospital giving the contents of his stomach. Dying, the last private act we perform, is made public: the murder victim has no secrets.

So, somewhere in Garcia's house, a passport was found, an American one, and that was when the Malaysian police contacted the Embassy in Kuala Lumpur. I was asked to go down for the death certificate, personal effects, and anything that might be necessary for the report to his next of kin. I intended it to be a stopover, a day in Johore, a night in Singapore, and then back to Ayer Hitam. Peeraswami had a brother in Johore; Abubaker, my driver, said he wanted to pray at the Johore mosque; we pushed off early one morning, Abubaker at the wheel, Peeraswami playing with the car radio. I was in the back seat going over newspaper clippings of the two murders.

In most ways they were the same. Each victim was a foreigner, unmarried, lived alone in a house outside town, and had been a resident for some years. In neither case was there any sign of a forced entry or a robbery. Both men were poor, both men had been mutilated. They looked to me like acts of Chinese revenge. But on planters? In Malaysia it was the Chinese *towkay* who was robbed, kidnapped, or murdered, not the expatriate planters who lived from month to month on provisioners' credit and chit-signing in bars. There were two differences: Tibbets was British and Ismail Garcia was American. And one other known fact: Tibbets, at the time of his death, was planning to go back to England.

A two-hour drive through rubber estates took us into Johore, and then we were speeding along the shore of the Straits, past the lovely casuarina trees and the high houses on the leafy bluff that overlooks the swampland and the marshes on the north coast of Singapore. I dropped Peeraswami at his brother's house, which was in one of the wilder suburbs of Johore and with a high chain-link fence around it to assure even greater seclusion. Abubaker scrambled out at the mosque after giving me directions to the police headquarters.

Garcia's effects were in a paper bag from a Chinese shop. I signed for them and took them to a table to examine: a cheap watch, a cheap ring, a copy of the Koran, a birth certificate, the passport.

"We left the clothes behind," said Detective-Sergeant Yusof. "We just took the valuables."

Valuables: there wasn't five dollars' worth of stuff in the bag.

"Was there any money?"

"He had no money. We're not treating it as robbery."

"What *are* you treating it as?"

"Homicide, probably by a friend."

"Some friend."

"He knew the murderer, so did Tibbets. You will believe me when you see the houses."

I almost did. Garcia's house was completely surrounded by a high fence, and Yusof said that Tibbets's fence was even higher. It was not unusual; every large house in Malaysian cities had an unclimbable fence or a wall with spikes of glass cemented on to the top.

"The lock wasn't broken, the house wasn't tampered with," said Yusof. "So we are calling it a sex crime."

"I thought you were calling it a homicide."

Yusof smirked at me. "We have a theory. The Englishmen who live here get funny ideas. Especially the ones who live alone. Some of them take Malay mistresses, the other ones go around with Chinese boys."

"Not Malay boys?"

Yusof said, "We do not do such things."

"You say Englishmen do, but Garcia was an American."

"He was single," said Yusof.

"I'm single," I said.

"We couldn't find any sign of a mistress."

"I thought you were looking for a murderer."

"That's what I'm trying to say," said Yusof. "These queers are very secretive. They get jealous. They fight with their boyfriends. The body was mutilated — that tells me a Chinese boy is involved."

"So you don't think it had anything to do with money?"

"Do you know what the rubber price is?"

"As a matter of fact, I do."

"And that's not all," said Yusof. "This man Garcia — do you know what he owed his provisioner? Eight hundred-over dollars! Tibbets was owing five hundred."

I said, "Maybe the provisioner did it."

"Interesting," said Yusof. "We can work on that."

Tibbets was English, so over lunch I concentrated on Garcia. There was a little dossier on him from the Alien Registration Office. Born 1922 in the Philippines; fought in World War II; took out American citizenship in Guam, came to Malaysia in 1954, converted to Islam and changed his name. From place to place, complicating his identity, picking up a nationality here, a name there, a religion somewhere else. And why would he convert? A woman, of course. No man changed his religion to live with another man. I didn't believe he was a homosexual, and though there was no evidence to support it I didn't rule out the possibility of robbery. In all this there were two items that interested me — the birth certificate and the passport. The birth certificate was brown with age, the passport new and unused.

Why would a man who had changed his religion and lived in a country for nearly twenty years have a new passport?

After lunch I rang police headquarters and asked for Yusof.

"We've got the provisioner," he said. "I think you might be right. He was also Tibbets's provisioner — both men owed him money. He is helping us with our inquiries."

"What a pompous phrase for torture," I said, but before Yusof could reply I added, "About Garcia — I figure he was planning to leave the country."

Yusof cackled into the phone. "Not at all! We talked to his employer — Garcia had a permanent and pensionable contract."

"Then why did he apply for a passport two weeks ago?"

"It is the law. He must be in possession of a valid passport if he is an expatriate."

I said, "I'd like to talk to his employer."

Yusof gave me the name of the man, Tan See Leng, owner of the Tai-Hwa Rubber Estate. I went over that afternoon. At first Tan refused to see me, but when I sent him my card with the consulate address and the American eagle on it, he rushed out of his office and apologized. He was a thin evasive man with spiky hair, and though he pretended not to be surprised when I said Garcia was an American national I could tell this was news to him. He said he knew nothing about Garcia, apart from the fact that he'd been a good foreman. He'd never seen him socially. He confirmed that Garcia lived behind an impenetrable fence.

"Who owned the house?"

"He did."

"That's something," I said. "I suppose you knew he was leaving the country."

"He was not leaving. He was wucking."

"It would help if you told me the truth," I said.

Tan's bony face tightened with anger. He said, "Perhaps he intended to leave. I do not know."

"I take it business isn't so good."

"The rubber price is low, some planters are switching to oil palm. But the price will rise if we are patient."

"What did you pay Garcia?"

"Two thousand a month. He was on permanent terms — he signed one of the old contracts. We were very generous in those days with expatriates."

"But he could have broken the contract."

"Some men break."

"Up in Ayer Hitam they have something called a 'golden handshake.' If they want to get rid of a foreigner they offer him a chunk of money as compensation for loss of career."

"That is Ayer Hitam," said Tan. "This is Johore."

"And they always pay cash, because it's against the law to take that much money out of the country. No banks. Just a suitcase full of Straits dollars."

Tan said nothing.

I said, "I don't think Garcia or Tibbets were queer. I think this was robbery, pure and simple."

"The houses were not broken into."

"So the papers say," I said. "It's the only thing I don't understand. Both men were killed at home during the day."

"Mister," said Tan. "You should leave this to the police."

"You swear you didn't give Garcia a golden handshake?"

"That is against the law, as you say."

"It's not as serious as murder, is it?"

In the course of the conversation, Tan had turned to wood. I was sure he was lying, but he stuck to his story. I decided to have nothing more to do with the police or Yusof and instead to go back to the house of Peeraswami's brother, to test a theory of my own.

The house bore many similarities to Garcia's and to what I knew of Tibbets's. It was secluded, out of town, rather characterless, and the high fence was topped with barbed wire. Sathya, Peeraswami's brother, asked me how I liked Johore. I told him that I liked it so much I wanted to spend a few days there, but that I didn't want the Embassy to know where I was. I asked him if he would put me up.

"Oh, yes," he said. "You are welcome. But you would be more comfortable in a hotel."

"It's much quieter here."

"It is the country life. We have no car."

"It's just what I'm looking for."

After I was shown to my bedroom I excused myself and went to the offices of the *Johore Mail*, read the classified ads for the previous few weeks and placed an ad myself. For the next two days I explored Johore, looked over the Botanical Gardens and the Sultan's mosque, and ingratiated myself with Sathya and his family. I had arrived on a Friday. On Monday I said to Sathya, "I'm expecting a phone call today."

Sathya said, "This is your house."

"I feel I ought to do something in return," I said. "I have a driver and a car — I don't need them today. Why don't you use them? Take your wife and children over to Singapore and enjoy yourself."

He hesitated, but finally I persuaded him. Abubaker, on the other hand, showed an obvious distaste for taking an Indian family out for the day.

"Peeraswami," I said, "I'd like you to stay here with me."

"*Tuan*," he said, agreeing. Sathya and the others left. I locked the gate behind them and sat by the telephone to wait.

There were four phone calls. Three of the callers I discouraged by describing the location, the size of the house, the tiny garden, the work I said had to be done on the roof. And I gave the same story to the last caller, but he was insistent and eager to see it. He said he'd be right over.

Rawlins was the name he gave me. He came in a new car, gave me a hearty greeting, and was not at all put off by the slightly ramshackle appearance of the house. He smoked a cheroot which had stained his teeth and the center swatch of his mustache a sticky yellow, and he walked around with one hand cupped, tapping ashes into his palm.

"You're smart not to use an agent," he said, looking over the house. "These estate agents are bloody thieves."

I showed him the garden, the lounge, the kitchen.

He sniffed and said, "You like curry."

"My cook's an Indian." He went silent, glanced around suspiciously, and I added, "I gave him the day off."

"You lived here long?"

"Ten years. I'm chucking it. I've been worried about selling this place ever since I broke my contract."

"Rubber?" he said, and spat a fragment of the cheroot into his hand.

"Yes," I said. "I was manager of an estate up in Kluang."

He asked me the price and when I told him he said, "I can manage that." He took out a checkbook. "I'll give you a deposit now and the balance when contracts are exchanged. We'll put our lawyers in touch and Bob's your uncle. Got a pen?"

I went to the desk and opened a drawer, but as I rummaged he said, "Okay, turn around slow and put your hands up."

I did as I was told and heard the cheroot hitting the floor. Above the kris Rawlins held his face was fierce and twisted. In such an act a man reverts; his face was pure monkey, threatening teeth and eyes. He said, "Now hand it over."

"What is this?" I said. "What do you want?"

"Your money, all of it, your handshake."

"I don't have any money."

"They always lie," he said. "They always fight, and then I have to do them. Just make it easy this time. The money —"

But he said no more, for Peeraswami in his bare feet crept behind him from the broom cupboard where he had been hiding and brought a cast-iron frying pan down so hard on his skull that I thought for a moment I saw a crack show in the man's forehead. We tied Rawlins up with Sathya's neckties and then I rang Yusof.

On the way to police headquarters, where Yusof insisted the corpse be delivered, I said, "This probably would not have happened if you didn't have such strict exchange control regulations."

"So it was robbery," said Yusof, "but how did he know Tibbets and Garcia had had golden handshakes?"

"He guessed. There was no risk involved. He knew they were leaving the country because they'd put their houses up for sale. Expatriates who own houses here have been in the country a long time, which means they're taking a lot of money out in a suitcase. You should read the paper."

"I read the paper," said Yusof. "Malay and English press."

"I mean the classified ads, where it says, 'Expatriate-owned house for immediate sale. Leaving the country. No agents.' Tibbets and Garcia placed that ad, and so did I."

Yusof said, "I should have done that. I could have broken this case."

"I doubt it — he wouldn't have done business with a Malay," I said. "But remember, if a person says he wants to buy your house you let him in. It's the easiest way for a burglar to enter — through the front door. If he's a white man in this country no one suspects him. We're supposed to trust each other. As soon as I realized it had something to do with the sale of a house I knew the murderer would be white."

"He didn't know they were alone."

"The wife and kids always fly out first, especially if daddy's breaking currency regulations."

"You foreigners know all the tricks."

"True," I said. "If he was a Malay or a Chinese I probably wouldn't have been able to catch him." I tapped my head. "I understand the mind of the West."

JANWILLEM VAN
DE WETERING

SURE, BLUE, AND DEAD, TOO

When Janwillem van de Wetering (b. 1931) reached military age, he took the option Holland offered its young men and went into the police force rather than the army. "I was really a draft dodger," he recalled several years ago, "and thought working as a reserve policeman would be a great joke. I was in for a great surprise." That was nearly thirty years ago. Since then he has become a Zen Buddhist, spent time in a Buddhist monastery in Japan (his first book, The Empty Mirror, *was about that experience), moved to Maine, and written a dozen books — novels and short story collections — inspired by his experience as a part-time policeman.*

The Amsterdam police, he says, are not brilliant, but they are dogged: "Since there are only about five murders a year, they have to solve them." Although van de Wetering has often expressed his admiration for Robert van Gulik, the Dutch diplomat who wrote the Judge Dee stories ("I never met him, but I went to his funeral"), his own detectives — Adjutant Grijpstra, Sergeant de Gier, and their co-workers — seem to owe less to the good judge than to Ed McBain and the boys at the 87th Precinct.

Van de Wetering originally wrote his books in Dutch and then translated them into English. Now he writes in English and translates them — sometimes adding additional characters — for the folks back home.

"Sure, Blue, and Dead, Too" was first published in Ellery Queen's Mystery Magazine *in 1983.*

THE EVENING had passed and night was due, but it wasn't quite dark yet. Sergeant de Gier had noticed the mysterious moment of change and passed the information on to Adjutant Grijpstra. "Evening gone, night not quite come." He went further and drew the adjutant's attention to the faint coloring of the sky that curved like a tight metallic-blue sheet above the city of Amsterdam, iridescent in its entirety, intensified by the first pulsating stars.

"Quite," Grijpstra answered.

"Blue," Sergeant de Gier said, "but not your everyday blue. A most noteworthy shade of blue, don't you think?"

"So what are we doing here again?" Grijpstra asked.

"We're police detectives," de Gier explained, caressing his full mustache and delicately curved nose. "We're waiting for the heroin dealers about to meet and exchange merchandise for money."

"And when are they due?"

"We don't know."

"And what do they look like?"

"We don't know that either."

Adjutant and sergeant, members of the Amsterdam Murder Brigade, were assisting — because no murders had been reported recently — the Dangerous Drug Department. They were doing so quietly, dressed like innocent civilians, comfortably reclining in their unmarked blue Volkswagen, parked on Brewers' Square, opposite the Concert Building, pointed at Museum Square. They had been reclining for a while now.

"And how do we know that the dealers will meet?"

"Because," the sergeant answered, "Detection passed on the message. Our very own Detection, with the whispering voice of a handsome man like me, who in turn had heard another whispering voice — in the restroom of a better brothel, perhaps. A large quantity of the evil drug will pass hands tonight. For us to see. For us to apprehend, together with the hands that pass it."

Grijpstra spilled cigar-ash on his neat pin-striped waistcoat. He also arranged his bristly gray hair. "Bah."

"Bah how?"

"Both in general," the adjutant explained, "and in particular. What can we see? The sky. Numberless passersby. Do you honestly think that we would be able to spot a suspect popping up, parcel in hand, to greet and do business with another?"

"The sky is lovely," said de Gier. "Do look before the blue becomes black. Now is the time to be impressed."

Grijpstra looked up, grunted, and looked down. He grunted again, more emotionally.

"Nice woman," de Gier agreed. "Same color as the sky. Blue summer coat, blue scarf, blue high heels. I can't see her face, but from her general bearing I would deduct she is crying. Why is she crying?"

The woman's hands dropped away from her face. "She's only crying a little," Grijpstra said. "We could investigate the mystery, but we don't want to push our duty. A crying woman hardly disturbs the peace of our city."

De Gier sat up. "I feel like working. We were sent on a fool's errand. We aren't fools. I suspect the subject of being a prostitute and want to question her. Are you coming, Adjutant?"

"Prostitution isn't illegal."

"It is, too," de Gier said. "*Here* it is. We are within two hundred feet of the Concert Building, which contains a bar. Prostitution within two hundred feet of a public place where alcoholic beverages are sold is illegal."

"Leave the woman in peace," Grijpstra said gently. "We're after heroin."

"Very well, Adjutant. But now look at that. What do you see? A handcart loaded with rags. Parked under a no-parking sign. And a subject climbing into it. A most suspicious agglomeration of events." He put his hand on the handle of his door. "May I?"

"You may not. Leave Blue Pete alone."

"You know the subject?"

"An old acquaintance."

"Tell me about him," the sergeant said. "I feel a trifle restless. Your tale will calm me down."

"Anything to keep your youthful enthusiasm within suitable bounds.

"Some years ago," Adjutant Grijpstra intoned pleasantly, "when the local station here hadn't been computerized away, I happened to be behind the counter and Blue Pete came in, accompanied by his dear wife, a fat woman, just like mine. Maybe even fatter, if that could be possible. She pushed Blue Pete aside and lodged a complaint. He was part of the complaint, so she had brought him along."

"Yes?" de Gier prodded.

"If you interrupt me, I won't tell the tale."

"Right. But over there goes a gentleman carrying a parcel. Does it contain heroin? No, it's a present for a loved one, adorned with a ribbon. Perhaps his wife has her birthday. Go on, Adjutant."

"Her name was Anne, Blue Pete's wife's was, and probably still is, and she was suffering from a venereal disease at the time."

"That was the complaint?"

"Part of it. She had contracted it from her neighbor and passed it on to Blue Pete."

"Shall I inquire about the nature of the contents of the parcel the gent is carrying? Now look at that, will you? A well-dressed, well-educated gentleman, probably holding an important position in our society, on his way home where his wife awaits him, is bothering our blue lady. Just because she is crying. Let me arrest the scoundrel."

"He has stopped bothering her," Grijpstra said. "He's still carrying the parcel. Has he perhaps exchanged it for a similar parcel the lady was hiding under her coat?"

"No, I had a full view from here. Nothing passed hands."

"I never have a full view of anything," Grijpstra complained mildly. "Very well, Anne's charge was that her neighbor presented her with a venereal disease. She carried proof."

"She showed you her microbes?"

"Her pills. And a prescription for more, signed by her physician. Proof of her affliction."

"The complaint is not clear to me."

"Because you're too young," Grijpstra explained. "You're not familiar with yesteryear's laws. Whippersnappers like your good self gambol about while totally unaware of the great happenings. The present connects with the past. You have no past yet."

"Since when is the spreading of venereal disease prohibited?"

"It was during the war. A German Occupation law, to protect the Nazi soldiery."

"And Blue Pete?"

"A detached personality. Blue Pete drinks methyl alcohol, a well-known killer of microbes, and he only came along to support his wife in her struggle with the paramour next door."

The sergeant looked at the ragman, now settled comfortably on his cart. "You have a marvelous memory, Adjutant."

"Blue Pete showed up again that very same night, the night of the complaint. I was driving a patrol car through an alley and nearly ran into the blighter's cart. No lights. I was going to fine him, but he did have a light, he said. He showed me a candle that he hadn't lit. There was a bit of a breeze, you see, and the light might have been blown out."

"Did you fine him?"

"Nah," Grijpstra said. "Mustn't bother the poor too much."

The sergeant looked out of the window again. "Not even when they keep breaking the law? Parking under no-parking signs? How sad it all is. And the blue lady is still crying. What could be the matter with her?"

"The fourteen-six?" the radio under the blue Volkswagen's dashboard asked.

Grijpstra grabbed the microphone. "Go ahead. This is the fourteen-six."

"Not correct," the radio said. "Even the Murder Brigade has to adhere to the rules. First you have to confirm your number and then you should ask me for orders."

"Yes, ducks. Sorry, ducks."

"Ducks?"

De Gier took over the microphone. "The fourteen-six here, Marie. Sergeant de Gier. What can we do for you?"

"Darling," the radio purred. "Do go to Headquarters. The constables guarding the building are being bothered by a man."

"We're on our way."

The Volkswagen veered away from the curb.

"And our heroin?" Grijpstra asked.

"Will wait for us," de Gier said. "The radio room is in Headquarters, too, and who knows what will happen if that terrible man penetrates to Marie's whereabouts. She's a constable, of course, but rather vulnerable because of her beauty. Onward at once."

Grijpstra clutched the dashboard. "Please, Sergeant, this is an unmarked car. Nobody knows we're the police. Oh, Sweet Savior —"

"That pedestrian got away, didn't he?" de Gier asked, glancing at his rearview mirror. "Sporty type, climbing a tree now."

"Whoa!"

"I can't slow down for joyriding cyclists. Assistance to endangered colleagues is our most prized emergency."

"Red light ahead."

"Not anymore."

"The streetcar!"

"Police always have the right of way and streetcars have powerful brakes. Ha-ha, look at all those people sliding off their seats. Right, here we are. Headquarters."

"What's happening here?" Grijpstra asked.

"Well," the constable coming from the doorman's lobby said, "we're supposed to guard this building, right? This is no police station, this is Headquarters itself, but this subject walks straight in, drunk and all, and bothers us. What can we do? We can't guard the building and arrest him at the same time."

"But aren't there two of you?" de Gier asked. "You could arrest the subject while your colleague guards the building."

"The subject wants to be violated," the constable whispered.

"Violence," de Gier whispered, "is lawfully permitted under special circumstances. Didn't they teach you that at police school?"

"The subject is somewhat big," the constable whispered.

The subject was in the lobby, well over six feet, barrel-chested, and waving large fists. He was dressed neatly and swayed slowly. He smiled. "You're a cop, too?" he asked the sergeant.

"Sergeant de Gier, at your service entirely."

"Serve me," the subject said. "If you don't, I'll kill you. I already killed tonight — an innocent bystander. I deserve to suffer suitable punishment. I wish to wither away in a dank cell."

Grijpstra moved forward and addressed the other constable.

"Tell your side of it," Grijpstra said.

The constable backed out of the drunk's earshot. "He didn't kill anyone, Adjutant, he just happens to have been indulging. He says he knocked someone down with his car on Brewers' Square, but we have our radio here and no accident has been reported in that area."

"When would the mishap have occurred?"

"An hour ago, and he has been here ever since, yelling at us. How can we guard the building with the subject distracting us?"

Grijpstra breathed deeply. He reshaped his smile. "Constable, we're of the Criminal Investigation Department. We are highly trained. We learned how to count, for instance. Am I mistaken if I count two of you?"

"I'm not familiar with the ways of the supercops, Adjutant," the constable said pleasantly, "but we regular officers work in couples. My mate and I form just one couple — and couples, we were taught at police school, may never be split. The subject is big. It will need a complete couple to arrest him. If we arrest him, we cannot guard the building."

Grijpstra faced the drunk. "Sir."

The subject continued to sway and to smile.

"You're under arrest. Follow me."

The subjects balled his hands to fists.

"Let's go," Grijpstra bellowed.

The subject hit Grijpstra. Grijpstra fell down. De Gier jumped forward. The subject's arm flew up and turned behind his back, yanked expertly by de Gier's arms. Handcuffs clicked.

"The subject is now a suspect," de Gier told the constables. "I suspect him of harassing the police. Watch him." He squatted next to Grijpstra. "How are you doing?"

Grijpstra groaned.

"Ambulance," de Gier said. A constable picked up a phone.

The suspect kicked. De Gier, still squatting, bent sideways and clutched the suspect's leg. The suspect fell over backward and hit the floor with the full impact of his own strength and weight.

"Take him to a cell," de Gier said. The constables dragged the suspect away.

A siren howled in the street. De Gier opened the door.

"Evening," the ambulance driver said. "You guys damaged a subject again?"

"A colleague is hurt," de Gier said. "Be careful with him; he's my friend."

"We're always careful." The driver turned to his assistant. "Ready? Let's pick him up."

Grijpstra opened his eyes.

"Don't relax too much," the driver said. "Otherwise we can't get you on the stretcher. You're a bit heavy, you know."

"I'm not heavy," Grijpstra said, "and I have no intention of cooperating. I was out for a moment, but I'm back again. Where's the suspect, Sergeant?"

"He's in his cell and you're on your way to the doctor."

"No," Grijpstra started to his feet.

"Grab him," de Gier said to the driver.

The driver shook his head. "Not if the patient refuses."

De Gier held his fist under the driver's nose. "Take him along."

He held his fist under Grijpstra's nose. "Be taken along. Your skull hit the stone floor, and I want to know whether it's cracked or not. You can come back if the doctor releases you."

"Who outranks who?" the driver asked.

"I'm outranked," de Gier said, "but I happen to be more aggressive than he is and I'm good at judo."

"Let's pick him up and get out of here," the driver's assistant said.

"I'll be on my way, too," de Gier said to the constables. "Have a good night now, the two of you."

The blue Volkswagen was parked on Brewers' Square again, opposite the Concert Building, pointed at Museum Square. De Gier was at the wheel. He picked up the microphone. "The fourteen-six."

"Darling."

"I'm back doing what I was doing," de Gier said, "and I have a request."

"Yes?"

"Please ask one of the constables guarding your building to speak to me on the radio."

"Sergeant?" one of the constables asked a few moments later.

"Listen," de Gier said. "The situation was somewhat bewildering just now. What exactly was bothering your suspect when he first approached you?"

"An excess of alcohol," the constable said.

"Anything else?"

"He said he had run someone down on Brewers' Square."

"Details?"

The constable grinned noisily. "He ran down a blue one."

"What does that mean?"

"I wouldn't know, Sergeant."

"Thanks." De Gier pushed the microphone back into its clip.

Over there, de Gier observed, the blue lady is still crying. Patiently. Into her handkerchief. Seeing that no one is restraining me now, I'll go and find out what causes her lengthy grief. He got out and walked over.

"Good evening."

"Please leave me alone."

"I only wanted to ask you something," de Gier said. "I am a —"

A patrol car stopped next to the conversing couple. Two constables got out. They had left their caps in the car. "What's going on here?" one of them asked.

"This man is annoying me," the lady said.

The constables turned to de Gier. "We've been watching you for a while, sir. You were ogling the lady and now you're actually waylaying her. Move along — and be glad that we don't intend, for the moment, to pursue the misdemeanor."

De Gier showed his police card.

The constables edged him along the sidewalk. "Look here," the older of the two said, "even we aren't allowed to bother crying females. It's tempting, I will admit, for when they're in tears, they're easy to push over, but we shouldn't, don't you agree?"

De Gier showed his watch. "You see the seconds change numbers?"

"Yes?"

"Five more numbers and the two of you are back in your car and driving away. I have to talk to the lady. Make yourselves scarce. All right?"

"I don't know whether you recognize the sergeant," the younger constable advised his partner, "but Rinus de Gier has just been declared judo and karate champion of Amsterdam. Let's go. Good evening, Sergeant champion."

The patrol car drove off. De Gier walked back to the lady. He showed her his police card. "Miss," he said in a low and pleasant voice, "you seem to be unhappy. Did a car run into you a while ago?"

The lady sobbed.

"Let's have nothing but the truth," de Gier said. "Crying only makes your eyes bulge. You have been run into by a car and you had a bad fright. Share your misery."

"No," the lady said. . . . "Do my eyes really bulge?"

"Not really. Would you like a cigarette?"

"I never smoke in the street."

"Smoke in my car."

The lady adjusted her skirt and drew on her cigarette.

"Well?" de Gier asked.

"I'll tell you. I'm having an affair with a certain Mr. Dams and he promised to marry me."

"He did?" de Gier said.

"So he would have to divorce his wife."

"He would."

"But he didn't. And I had enough of waiting. Tonight I decided to go to his house."

De Gier waited.

"His wife opened the door. I said, 'I'm your husband's girlfriend and I want to know about the divorce.' She let me in and he switched off the TV and looked at both of us. His wife said, 'What's this about a divorce?' He got up and went to the kitchen and came back with a bottle of gin and drank it all."

De Gier waited.

"And then he left the house, and his wife said it was all my fault. I ran out of the house and followed his car, in my own."

De Gier waited.

"He could hardly drive, but he managed to get as far as here and to park it. He walked off before I could park."

"Mr. Dams is a big man?"

"Oh, yes." She blew her nose.

"Three-piece suit? Wide-shouldered?"

"Yes."

"Where's his car?"

"The big Chevrolet over there."

"You saw him park. Did he hit anyone?"

"He drove over the island, where the pedestrians wait for the street-car."

"Your friend, Mr. Dams," de Gier said, "has been arrested. He hit an officer. He won't be released until tomorrow morning. I would advise you to go home and sleep well."

De Gier unclipped the microphone. "Headquarters? The fourteen-six."

"Darling?"

"Could I speak to that constable again?"

"Sergeant?" the constable asked.

"Go to the suspect's cell and ask him about his accident. Then come back and tell me exactly what he answers."

Heroin, de Gier thought, brought me here, and I haven't seen any trace of it yet and never will, I'm sure, for soon the Concert Building will empty and there will be thousands of people on the square and they can give each other parcels forever without me seeing any of it. Let's solve puzzles that can be solved. Like what's with the blue lady and her Mr. Dams?

"The fourteen-six?" the radio asked.

"Right here."

"Sergeant," the constable said. "Sure, blue, and dead, too."

"What?"

"That's what the suspect said just now."

"That's all?"

"All."

If there's anything, de Gier thought, that really annoys me, it's a simple situation I can't comprehend. Blue. What blue? Blue what? The lady was blue, but the suspect didn't hit the lady. The sergeant looked out of the car. The cart loaded with rags was still parked under the no-parking sign. The rags were moving. De Gier got out.

"Is this where you sleep?" de Gier asked.

"I have a bed at home," Blue Pete said, "but my wife is in it and she's watching TV. I'd rather be here. Resting. Drinking a little." He held up a bottle. "Care for a sip?"

"Methylated spirits?" de Gier asked.

"The best Dutch gin," Blue Pete said. "What with welfare on the up again, methyl alcohol has become too cheap for me. Pity in a way. I really prefer methylated spirits — the taste is a bit sharper."

"But you're still blue," de Gier said.

"That'll never wear off. Sure you don't want a nip?"

De Gier pushed the bottle away. "Tell me, Pete, did anyone happen to run into you tonight with his car?"

"No."

"Are you sure?"

"Yes!" shouted Blue Pete. "Do you think I need to lie to anyone? With my welfare going up and up and up?"

"Pete," de Gier said. "Relax, it's a beautiful night. But someone drove into 'a blue one' tonight, and you are blue."

"If I'd been involved in an accident," Blue Pete said, "I would have made a fuss. Maybe I'm just a simple textile dealer, but nobody drives over *me*, not even if the millionaire drives a brand-new Chevrolet!"

"Aha," said de Gier. "A Chevrolet, eh? The one over there, perhaps?"

"But it never drove into me," Blue Pete said. "It drove across the traffic island over there. It was stopped by the little pillar with the blue light in it." He laughed raucously. "And it had just been fixed. I watched a uniformed chap fussing with it with a screwdriver and pliers. Fixed it finally and bang, there comes the millionaire with the Chevrolet and bends it all out of shape again. Ho-ho."

De Gier walked back to his car. He thought as he walked. He changed his direction and investigated the pillar. It was bending over a few degrees and scratched, but the light still burned. He walked over to the Chevrolet. Its bumper was dented a little and some of the paint from the pillar was stuck in the dent. The Sergeant slid back into the Volkswagen, sighing contently. Facts fitted once again. Here was Mr. Dams, an upright citizen trapped by another woman. Temporarily insane, Mr. Dams got himself drunk and hit a pillar. How easy everything was once seen from the correct angle.

He released the microphone. "The fourteen-six."

"Darling?"

"Hello, Marie," de Gier said. "Please don't call me darling. The channel is open — any police car can listen in."

"Yes, my beloved."

"Any news about the adjutant's condition?"

"A sore chin. He's on his way to you."

Grijpstra tapped on the window. De Gier opened the door for him.

"Nothing the matter with me," the adjutant said. "You forced me to make a spectacle of myself."

"I'm sorry," de Gier said. "I'll never do it again. Next time you're out cold on the floor, I will stand on your head."

"Thanks," Grijpstra said. "How's our heroin deal?"

"What heroin?"

"Our original assignment."

"Ah, that." De Gier cursed. "I thought I had it all figured out — and now this." He pointed.

"Are you pointing at the man in the blue uniform opening the little door in the pillar with the blue light in it?"

"I am."

"What could be wrong with that? The man is employed by the electric company and he's checking the pillar."

"I just found out," the sergeant said, "that the light was checked a little while ago. Besides, it's burning. What's he fiddling with the insides of the pillar for?"

"Replacing a fuse?" Grijpstra asked lazily. "Dusting connections? Scraping the socket? Should we care?"

"I think so," de Gier said. "Because he's doing none of that. He's removing some small cellophane packages. You go right; I'll take the left. Pull your gun."

The man in the uniform also pulled a gun. There were two shots. De Gier dropped when the shots went off and kicked the suspect's legs from under him. Grijpstra caught the falling suspect. Handcuffs clicked.

"He didn't hit you, did he?" de Gier asked.

"No," Grijpstra said. "But I hit him. He's bleeding from the chest. I don't think the cuffs were necessary."

"Come right in," the superintendent said. "The chief is waiting for you. Good work — but it's a pity the suspect didn't survive his arrest."

The chief got up from behind his desk and smiled down at his visitors. "Adjutant. Sergeant. My congratulations. The suspect has been identified and important clues have been found in his home that will lead to further arrests. What brilliant reasoning led you to believe that the man masquerading as an electric company worker was your man?"

Grijpstra didn't say anything. De Gier was quiet.

"Well?"

"No brilliant reasoning, sir," de Gier said. "A melody perhaps — one blue note leading to another."

The chief smiled patiently. "Tell me about it."

Grijpstra reported.

"I see," the chief said. "Who put the heroin *into* the pillar?"

Grijpstra shrugged. "We didn't see that. The big dealer presumably."

"And the small dealer took it out?"

"So it seems."

"The pillar merely served as a third party? The dealers didn't want to meet?"

Grijpstra nodded. "The less they know, the less they can tell."

"And the lady in blue?"

"No connection, sir. Neither was Blue Pete."

"Yet the *events* connected," the chief said. "A typical example of proper police work. What do you think, Superintendent? These men are from your department. Don't you agree that they did well?"

The superintendent was standing near the door. He came forward and studied his assistants. His eyes rested on de Gier's brow. "You're pale, Sergeant."

"Blue," de Gier mumbled. "It's such a beautiful shade. It's pursued us all night, leading to death."

The commissaris led the sergeant to the door. Grijpstra followed.

"What was that?" the chief asked when the superintendent returned.

"An erratic statement," the superintendent said. "It's a while since you and I were assigned to street duty. After a violent death a colleague may tend toward erratic behavior." He looked out the window. The sky curved like a tight metallic-blue sheet above the city of Amsterdam, iridescent in its entirety, intensified by the first pulsating stars. "It's the blue hour again," he said to the chief. "Let's go across the street. You may allow me to buy you a drink."

SARA PARETSKY

Sara Paretsky (b. 1947) grew up in Kansas, then moved to Chicago and became an insurance company executive and the creator of V. I. Warshawski. V.I., sometimes called Vicky, is a former Chicago public defender turned private eye. She is the daughter of a Polish cop and a half-Jewish, half-Italian mother, and she seems to have a knack for getting involved in cases that touch on social issues. In such novels as Deadlock, Indemnity Only, Bitter Medicine, *and* Blood Shot *the issues include patients' rights in for-profit hospitals, abortion and the right-to-life movement, insurance malpractice, corrupt unions, and — perhaps more traditionally — hanky-panky in a Dominican priory.*

Vicky, like Sue Grafton's Kinsey Millhone, is a dedicated jogger, but she is hardly a methodical sleuth; in one adventure she wistfully — or waspishly — praises Kinsey for her "immaculate record keeping." Vicky describes her own methods this way: "I solve my problems better by acting than thinking. That's what makes me a good detective."

"Skin Deep" was first published in 1987.

1

THE WARNING BELL clangs angrily and the submarine dives sharply. Everyone to battle stations. The Nazis pursuing closely, the bell keeps up its insistent clamor, loud, urgent, filling my head. My hands are wet: I can't remember what my job is in this cramped, tiny boat. If only someone would turn off the alarm bell. I fumble with some switches, pick up an intercom. The noise mercifully stops.

"Vic! Vic, is that you?"

"What?"

"I know it's late. I'm sorry to call so late, but I just got home from work. It's Sal, Sal Barthele."

"Oh, Sal. Sure." I looked at the orange clock readout. It was four-thirty. Sal owns the Golden Glow, a bar in the south Loop I patronize.

"It's my sister, Vic. They've arrested her. She didn't do it. I know she didn't do it."

"Of course not, Sal — Didn't do what?"

"They're trying to frame her. Maybe the manager . . . I don't know."

I swung my legs over the side of the bed. "Where are you?"

She was at her mother's house, 95th and Vincennes. Her sister had been arrested three hours earlier. They needed a lawyer, a good lawyer. And they needed a detective, a good detective. Whatever my fee was, she wanted me to know they could pay my fee.

"I'm sure you can pay the fee, but I don't know what you want me to do," I said as patiently as I could.

"She — they think she murdered that man. She didn't even know him. She was just giving him a facial. And he dies on her."

"Sal, give me your mother's address. I'll be there in forty minutes."

The little house on Vincennes was filled with neighbors and relatives murmuring encouragement to Mrs. Barthele. Sal is very black, and statuesque. Close to six feet tall, with a majestic carriage, she can break up a crowd in her bar with a look and a gesture. Mrs. Barthele was slight, frail, and light-skinned. It was hard to picture her as Sal's mother.

Sal dispersed the gathering with characteristic firmness, telling the group that I was here to save Evangeline and that I needed to see her mother alone.

Mrs. Barthele sniffed over every sentence. "Why did they do that to my baby?" she demanded of me. "You know the police, you know their ways. Why did they come and take my baby, who never did a wrong thing in her life?"

As a white woman, I could be expected to understand the machinations of the white man's law. And to share responsibility for it. After more of this meandering, Sal took the narrative firmly in hand.

Evangeline worked at La Cygnette, a high-prestige beauty salon on North Michigan. In addition to providing facials and their own brand-name cosmetics at an exorbitant cost, they massaged the bodies and feet of their wealthy clients, stuffed them into steam cabinets, ran them through a Bataan-inspired exercise routine, and fed them herbal teas. Signor Giuseppe would style their hair for an additional charge.

Evangeline gave facials. The previous day she had one client booked after lunch, a Mr. Darnell.

"Men go there a lot?" I interrupted.

Sal made a face. "That's what I asked Evangeline. I guess it's part of being a Yuppie — go spend a lot of money getting cream rubbed into your face."

Anyway, Darnell was to have had his hair styled before his facial, but the hairdresser fell behind schedule and asked Evangeline to do the guy's face first.

Sal struggled to describe how a La Cygnette facial worked — neither of us had ever checked out her sister's job. You sit in something like a dentist's chair, lean back, relax — you're naked from the waist up, lying under a big down comforter. The facial expert — cosmetician was Evangeline's official title — puts cream on your hands and sticks them into little electrically heated mitts, so your hands are out of commission if you need to protect yourself. Then she puts stuff on your face, covers your eyes with heavy pads, and goes away for twenty minutes while the face goo sinks into your hidden pores.

Apparently while this Darnell lay back deeply relaxed, someone had rubbed some kind of poison into his skin. "When Evangeline came back in to clean his face, he was sick — heaving, throwing up, it was awful. She screamed for help and started trying to clean his face — it was terrible, he kept vomiting on her. They took him to the hospital, but he died around ten tonight.

"They came to get Baby at midnight — you've got to help her, V.I. — even if the guy tried something on her, she never did a thing like that — she'd haul off and slug him, maybe, but rubbing poison into his face? You go help her."

2

Evangeline Barthele was a younger, darker edition of her mother. At most times, she probably had Sal's energy — sparks of it flared now and then during our talk — but a night in the holding cells had worn her down.

I brought a clean suit and makeup for her: justice may be blind but her administrators aren't. We talked while she changed.

"This Darnell — you sure of the name? — had he ever been to the salon before?"

She shook her head. "I never saw him. And I don't think the other girls knew him either. You know, if a client's a good tipper or a bad one they'll comment on it, be glad or whatever that he's come in. Nobody said anything about this man."

"Where did he live?"

She shook her head. "I never talked to the guy, V.I."

"What about the PestFree?" I'd read the arrest report and talked briefly to an old friend in the M.E.'s office. To keep roaches and other vermin out of their posh Michigan Avenue offices, La Cygnette used a potent product containing a wonder chemical called chorpyrifos. My informant had been awe-struck —"Only an operation that didn't know shit about chemicals would leave chorpyrifos lying around. It's got a toxicity rating of five — it gets you through the skin — you only need a couple of tablespoons to kill a big man if you know where to put it."

Whoever killed Darnell had either known a lot of chemistry or been lucky — into his nostrils and mouth, with some rubbed into the face for good measure, the pesticide had made him convulsive so quickly that even if he knew who killed him he'd have been unable to talk, or even reason.

Evangeline said she knew where the poison was kept — everyone who worked there knew, knew it was lethal and not to touch it, but it was easy to get at. Just in a little supply room that wasn't kept locked.

"So why you? They have to have more of a reason than just that you were there."

She shrugged bitterly. "I'm the only black professional at La Cygnette — the other blacks working there sweep rooms and haul trash. I'm trying hard not to be paranoid, but I gotta wonder."

She insisted Darnell hadn't made a pass at her, or done anything to provoke an attack — she hadn't hurt the guy. As for anyone else who might have had opportunity, salon employees were always passing through the halls, going in and out of the little cubicles where they treated clients — she'd seen any number of people, all with legitimate business, in the halls, but she hadn't seen anyone emerging from the room where Darnell was sitting.

When she finally got to bond court later that morning, I tried to argue circumstantial evidence — any of La Cygnette's fifty or so employees could have committed the crime, since all had access and no one had motive. The prosecutor hit me with a very unpleasant surprise: the police had uncovered evidence linking my client to the dead man. He was a furniture buyer from Kansas City who came to Chicago six times a year, and the doorman and the maids at his hotel had identified Evangeline without any trouble as the woman who accompanied him on his visits.

Bail was denied. I had a furious talk with Evangeline in one of the interrogation rooms before she went back to the holding cells.

"Why the hell didn't you tell me? I walked into the courtroom and got blindsided."

"They're lying," she insisted.

"Three people identified you. If you don't start with the truth right now, you're going to have to find a new lawyer and a new detective. Your mother may not understand, but for sure Sal will."

"You can't tell my mother. You can't tell Sal!"

"I'm going to have to give them some reason for dropping your case, and knowing Sal it's going to have to be the truth."

For the first time she looked really upset. "You're my lawyer. You should believe my story before you believe a bunch of strangers you never saw before."

"I'm telling you, Evangeline, I'm going to drop your case. I can't represent you when I know you're lying. If you killed Darnell we can work out a defense. Or if you didn't kill him and knew him we can work something out, and I can try to find the real killer. But when I know you've been seen with the guy any number of times, I can't go into court telling people you never met him before."

Tears appeared on the ends of her lashes. "The whole reason I didn't say anything was so Mama wouldn't know. If I tell you the truth, you've got to promise me you aren't running back to Vincennes Avenue talking to her."

I agreed. Whatever the story was, I couldn't believe Mrs. Barthele hadn't heard hundreds like it before. But we each make our own separate peace with our mothers.

Evangeline met Darnell at a party two years earlier. She liked him, he liked her — not the romance of the century, but they enjoyed spending time together. She'd gone on a two-week trip to Europe with him last year, telling her mother she was going with a girlfriend.

"First of all, she has very strict morals. No sex outside marriage. I'm thirty, mind you, but that doesn't count with her. Second, he's white, and she'd murder me. She really would. I think that's why I never fell in love with him — if we wanted to get married I'd never be able to explain it to Mama."

This latest trip to Chicago, Darnell thought it would be fun to see what Evangeline did for a living, so he booked an appointment at La Cygnette. She hadn't told anyone there she knew him. And when she found him sick and dying she'd panicked and lied.

"And if you tell my mother of this, V.I. — I'll put a curse on you. My father was from Haiti and he knew a lot of good ones."

"I won't tell your mother. But unless they nuked Lebanon this morning or murdered the mayor, you're going to get a lot of lines in the paper. It's bound to be in print."

She wept at that, wringing her hands. So after watching her go off with the sheriff's deputies, I called Murray Ryerson at the *Herald-Star* to plead with him not to put Evangeline's liaison in the paper. "If you do she'll wither your testicles. Honest."

"I don't know, Vic. You know the *Sun-Times* is bound to have some kind of screamer headline like DEAD MAN FOUND IN FACE-LICKING SEX ORGY. I can't sit on a story like this when all the other papers are running it."

I knew he was right, so I didn't push my case very hard.

He surprised me by saying, "Tell you what: you find the real killer before my deadline for tomorrow's morning edition and I'll keep your client's personal life out of it. The sex scoop came in too late for today's paper. The *Trib* prints on our schedule and they don't have it, and the *Sun-Times* runs older, slower presses, so they have to print earlier."

I reckoned I had about eighteen hours. Sherlock Holmes had solved tougher problems in less time.

3

Roland Darnell had been the chief buyer of living-room furnishings for Alexander Dumas, a high-class Kansas City department store. He used to own his own furniture store in the nearby town of Lawrence, but lost both it and his wife when he was arrested for drug smuggling ten years earlier. Because of some confusion about his guilt — he claimed his partner, who disappeared the night he was arrested, was really responsible — he'd only served two years. When he got out, he moved to Kansas City to start a new life.

I learned this much from my friends at the Chicago police. At least, my acquaintances. I wondered how much of the story Evangeline had known. Or her mother. If her mother didn't want her child having a white lover, how about a white ex-con, ex- (presumably) drug-smuggling lover?

I sat biting my knuckles for a minute. It was eleven now. Say they started printing the morning edition at two the next morning, I'd have to have my story by one at the latest. I could follow one line, and one line only — I couldn't afford to speculate about Mrs. Barthele — and anyway, doing so would only get me killed. By Sal. So I looked up the area code for Lawrence, Kansas, and found their daily newspaper.

The *Lawrence Daily Journal-World* had set up a special number for handling press inquiries. A friendly woman with a strong drawl told me Darnell's age (forty-four); place of birth (Eudora, Kansas); ex-wife's name (Ronna Perkins); and ex-partner's name (John Crenshaw). Ronna Perkins was living elsewhere in the country and the *Journal-World* was protecting her privacy. John Crenshaw had disappeared when the police arrested Darnell.

Crenshaw had done an army stint in Southeast Asia in the late sixties. Since much of the bamboo furniture the store specialized in came from the Far East, some people speculated that Crenshaw had set up the smuggling route when he was out there in the service. Especially since Kansas City immigration officials discovered heroin in the hollow tubes making up chair backs. If Darnell knew anything about the smuggling, he had never revealed it.

"That's all we know here, honey. Of course, you could come on down and try to talk to some people. And we can wire you photos if you want."

I thanked her politely — my paper didn't run too many photographs. Or even have wire equipment to accept them. A pity — I could have used a look at Crenshaw and Ronna Perkins.

La Cygnette was on an upper floor of one of the new marble skyscrapers at the top end of the Magnificent Mile. Tall, white doors opened onto a hushed waiting room reminiscent of a high-class funeral parlor. The undertaker, a middle-aged highly made-up woman seated at a table that was supposed to be French provincial, smiled at me condescendingly.

"What can we do for you?"

"I'd like to see Angela Carlson. I'm a detective."

She looked nervously at two clients seated in a far corner. I lowered my voice. "I've come about the murder."

"But — but they made an arrest."

I smiled enigmatically. At least I hoped it looked enigmatic. "The police never close the door on all options until after the trial." If she knew anything about the police she'd know that was a lie — once they've made an arrest you have to get a presidential order to get them to look at new evidence.

The undertaker nodded nervously and called Angela Carlson in a whisper on the house phone. Evangeline had given me the names of the key players at La Cygnette; Carlson was the manager.

She met me in the doorway leading from the reception area into the main body of the salon. We walked on thick, silver pile through a white maze with little doors opening onto it. Every now and then we'd pass a white-coated attendant who gave the manager a subdued hello. When we went by a door with a police order slapped to it, Carlson winced nervously.

"When can we take that off? Everybody's on edge and that sealed door doesn't help. Our bookings are down as it is."

"I'm not on the evidence team, Ms. Carlson. You'll have to ask the lieutenant in charge when they've got what they need."

I poked into a neighboring cubicle. It contained a large white dentist's chair and a tray covered with crimson pots and bottles, all with the cutaway swans which were the salon's trademark. While the manager fidgeted angrily I looked into a tiny closet where clients changed — it held a tiny sink and a few coat hangers.

Finally she burst out, "Didn't your people get enough of this yesterday? Don't you read your own reports?"

"I like to form my own impressions, Ms. Carlson. Sorry to have to take your time, but the sooner we get everything cleared up, the faster your customers will forget this ugly episode."

She sighed audibly and led me on angry heels to her office, although the thick carpeting took the intended ferocity out of her stride. The office was another of the small treatment rooms with a desk and a menacing phone console. Photographs of a youthful Mme. de Leon, founder of La Cygnette, covered the walls.

Ms. Carlson looked through a stack of pink phone messages. "I have an incredibly busy schedule, Officer. So if you could get to the point . . ."

"I want to talk to everyone with whom Darnell had an appointment yesterday. Also the receptionist on duty. And before I do that I want to see their personnel files."

"Really! All these people were interviewed yesterday." Her eyes narrowed suddenly. "Are you really with the police? You're not, are you? You're a reporter. I want you out of here now. Or I'll call the real police."

I took my license photostat from my wallet. "I'm a detective. That's what I told your receptionist. I've been retained by the Barthele family. Ms. Barthele is not the murderer and I want to find out who the real culprit is as fast as possible."

She didn't bother to look at the license. "I can barely tolerate answering police questions. I'm certainly not letting some snoop for hire take up my time. The police have made an arrest on extremely good evidence. I suppose you think you can drum up a fee by getting

Evangeline's family excited about her innocence, but you'll have to look elsewhere for your money."

I tried an appeal to her compassionate side, using half-forgotten arguments from my court appearances as a public defender. (Outstanding employee, widowed mother, sole support, intense family pride, no prior arrests, no motive.) No sale.

"Ms. Carlson, you the owner or the manager here?"

"Why do you want to know?"

"Just curious about your stake in the success of the place and your responsibility for decisions. It's like this: you've got a lot of foreigners working here. The immigration people will want to come by and check out their papers.

"You've got lots and lots of tiny little rooms. Are they sprinklered? Do you have emergency exits? The fire department can make a decision on that.

"And how come your only black professional employee was just arrested and you're not moving an inch to help her out? There are lots of lawyers around who'd be glad to look at a discrimination suit against La Cygnette.

"Now if we could clear up Evangeline's involvement fast, we could avoid having all these regulatory people trampling around upsetting your staff and your customers. How about it?"

She sat in indecisive rage for several minutes: how much authority did I have, really? Could I offset the munificent fees for the salon and the building owners paid to various public officials just to avoid such investigations? Should she call headquarters for instruction? Or her lawyer? She finally decided that even if I didn't have a lot of power I could be enough of a nuisance to affect business. Her expression compounded of rage and defeat, she gave me the files I wanted.

Darnell had been scheduled with a masseuse, the hair expert Signor Giuseppe, and with Evangeline. I read their personnel files, along with that of the receptionist who had welcomed him to La Cygnette, to see if any of them might have hailed from Kansas City or had any unusual traits, such as an arrest record for heroin smuggling. The files were very sparse. Signor Giuseppe Fruttero hailed from Milan. He had no next-of-kin to be notified in the event of an accident. Not even a good friend. Bruna, the masseuse, was Lithuanian, unmarried, living with her mother. Other than the fact that the receptionist had been born as Jean Evans in Hammond but referred to herself as Monique from New Orleans, I saw no evidence of any kind of cover-up.

Angela Carlson denied knowing either Ronna Perkins or John Crenshaw or having any employees by either of those names. She had never been near Lawrence herself. She grew up in Evansville, Indiana, came to Chicago to be a model in 1978, couldn't cut it, and got into the beauty business. Angrily she gave me the names of her parents in Evansville and summoned the receptionist.

Monique was clearly close to sixty, much too old to be Roland Darnell's ex-wife. Nor had she heard of Ronna or Crenshaw.

"How many people knew that Darnell was going to be in the salon yesterday?"

"Nobody knew." She laughed nervously. "I mean, of course *I* knew — I made the apointment with him. And Signor Giuseppe knew when I gave him his schedule yesterday. And Bruna, the masseuse, of course, and Evangeline."

"Well, who else could have seen their schedules?"

She thought frantically, her heavily mascaraed eyes rolling in agitation. With another nervous giggle she finally said, "I suppose anyone could have known. I mean, the other cosmeticians and the makeup artists all come out for their appointments at the same time. I mean, if anyone was curious they could have looked at the other people's lists."

Carlson was frowning. So was I. "I'm trying to find a woman who'd be forty now, who doesn't talk much about her past. She's been divorced and she won't have been in the business long. Any candidates?"

Carlson did another mental search, then went to the file cabinets. Her mood was shifting from anger to curiosity and she flipped through the files quickly, pulling five in the end.

"How long has Signor Giuseppe been here?"

"When we opened our Chicago branch in 1980 he came to us from Miranda's — I guess he'd been there for two years. He says he came to the States from Milan in 1970."

"He a citizen? Has he got a green card?"

"Oh, yes. His papers are in good shape. We are very careful about that at La Cygnette." My earlier remark about the immigration department had clearly stung. "And now I really need to get back to my own business. You can look at those files in one of the consulting rooms — Monique, find one that won't be used today."

It didn't take me long to scan the five files, all uninformative. Before returning them to Monique I wandered on through the back of the salon. In the rear a small staircase led to an upper story. At the top was another narrow hall lined with small offices and storerooms. A large mirrored room at the back filled with hanging plants and bright lights housed Signor Giuseppe. A dark-haired man with a pointed beard and a bright smile, he was ministering gaily to a thin, middle-aged woman, talking and laughing while he deftly teased her hair into loose curls.

He looked at me in the mirror when I entered. "You are here for the hair, Signora? You have the appointment?"

"No, Signor Giuseppe. Sono qui perchè la sua fama se è sparsa di fronte a lei. Milano è una bella città, non è vero?"

He stopped his work for a moment and held up a deprecating hand. "Signora, it is my policy to speak only English in my adopted country."

"Una vera stupida e ignorante usanza io direi." I beamed sympathetically and sat down on a high stool next to an empty customer chair. There were seats for two clients. Since Signor Giuseppe reigned alone, I pictured him spinning at high speed between customers, snipping here, pinning there.

"Signora, if you do not have the appointment, will you please leave? Signora Dotson here, she does not prefer the audience."

"Sorry, Mrs. Dotson," I said to the lady's chin. "I'm a detective. I need to talk to Signor Giuseppe, but I'll wait."

I strolled back down the hall and entertained myself by going into one of the storerooms and opening little pots of La Cygnette creams and rubbing them into my skin. I looked in a mirror and could already see an improvement. If I got Evangeline sprung maybe she'd treat me to a facial.

Signor Giuseppe appeared with a plastically groomed Mrs. Dotson. He had shed his barber's costume and was dressed for the street. I followed them down the stairs. When we got to the bottom I said, "In case you're thinking of going back to Milan — or even to Kansas — I have a few questions."

Mrs. Dotson clung to the hairdresser, ready to protect him.

"I need to speak to him alone, Mrs. Dotson. I have to talk to him about bamboo."

"I'll get Miss Carlson, Signor Giuseppe," his guardian offered.

"No, no, Signora. I will deal with this crazed woman myself. A million thanks. *Grazie, grazie.*"

"Remember, no Italian in your adopted America," I reminded him nastily.

Mrs. Dotson looked at us uncertainly.

"I think you should get Ms. Carlson," I said. "Also a police escort. Fast."

She made up her mind to do something, whether to get help or flee I wasn't sure, but she scurried down the corridor. As soon as she had disappeared, he took me by the arm and led me into one of the consulting rooms.

"Now, who are you and what is this?" His accent had improved substantially.

"I'm V. I. Warshawski. Roland Darnell told me you were quite an expert on fitting drugs into bamboo furniture."

I wasn't quite prepared for the speed of his attack. His hands were around my throat. He was squeezing and spots began dancing in front of me. I didn't try to fight his arms, just kicked sharply at his shin, following with my knee to his stomach. The pressure at my neck eased. I turned in a half circle and jammed my left elbow into his rib cage. He let go.

I backed to the door, keeping my arms up in front of my face and backed into Angela Carlson.

"What on earth are you doing with Signor Giuseppe?" she asked.

"Talking to him about furniture." I was out of breath. "Get the police and don't let him leave the salon."

A small crowd of white-coated cosmeticians had come to the door of the tiny treatment room. I said to them, "This isn't Giuseppe Fruttero. It's John Crenshaw. If you don't believe me, try speaking Italian to him — he doesn't understand it. He's probably never been to Milan. But he's certainly been to Thailand, and he knows an awful lot about heroin."

4

Sal handed me the bottle of Black Label. "It's yours, Vic. Kill it tonight or save it for some other time. How did you know he was Roland Darnell's ex-partner?"

"I didn't. At least not when I went to La Cygnette. I just knew it had to be someone in the salon who killed him, and it was most likely someone who knew him in Kansas. And that meant either Darnell's ex-wife or his partner. And Giuseppe was the only man on the professional staff. And then I saw he didn't know Italian — after praising Milan and telling him he was stupid in the same tone of voice and getting no response it made me wonder."

"We owe you a lot, Vic. The police would never have dug down to find that. You gotta thank the lady, Mama."

Mrs. Barthele grudgingly gave me her thin hand. "But how come those police said Evangeline knew that Darnell man? My baby wouldn't know some convict, some drug smuggler."

"He wasn't a drug smuggler, Mama. It was his partner. The police have proved all that now. Roland Darnell never did anything wrong." Evangeline, chic in red with long earrings that bounced as she spoke, made the point hotly.

Sal gave her sister a measuring look. "All I can say, Evangeline, is it's a good thing you never had to put your hand on a Bible in court about Mr. Darnell."

I hastily poured a drink and changed the subject.

WILLIAM MARSHALL

DEATH BY WATER

Australian-born William Marshall (b. 1944) is a former journalist (his official biography lists his other occupations as playwright, teacher, and morgue attendant) who has written, to date, thirteen novels set in a down-at-the-heels multiracial Hong Kong police precinct he calls Yellowthread Street.

Marshall has taken the format perfected by Ed McBain and turned it on its ear; words such as "bizarre," "surrealistic," and "black comedy" tend to pop up in reviews of his novels. His perversely deadpan sense of humor and love of the grotesque set him apart from other police procedural writers. And his feeling for the ethnic subtleties of Hong Kong, where he lived for years and where his wife grew up, seems unparalleled. He has also written a crime series set in Manila.

Now living in New York City, Marshall has most recently written a historical novel set in 1883, The New York Detective.

"Death by Water" is the curtain-raiser to his 1976 novel Gelignite.

HOP PEI COVE, on the western side of the Hong Kong police district of Hong Bay, smelled of fish. Not fresh, live fish, nor even dead fish, but fish long, long dead, not fresh, not yesterday's or the day before yesterday's fish, but extinct fish, obsolete fish, fish long gone to their fishy after-life, fish of a monumental and ancient age, antique fish, phantom fish, the ghosts of fish, fish drawn, quartered, gulleted, filleted, forked, fed into, finished and fishy. Fish of high, bygone and long dead odour. Stinking fish. Detective Inspector Phil Auden said, "Blecht — fish!"

It was 5:30 in the morning on Fisherman's Beach at Hop Pei Cove and the driver of one of the police cars parked on the hard-packed sand rubbed his hands together and opened a tin of rich-smelling body wax to polish the decal on the door of the driver's side of his vehicle. The decal said HONG KONG POLICE on a banner below a picture of a nineteenth-century quayside scene surrounded by laurel leaves. He leaned forward into his task and saturated his fish-filled nostrils with the smell of the wax. A fisherman mending his nets and watching four detectives and two uniformed constables in thighwaders wading thigh-high in the water off the beach shook his head. He looked at the driver again and repaired a break in his net.

On the water, the wind changed and took the smell of fish back to the beach. Auden said, "The wind's changed." He drew a breath of relatively pure air. Something floated past him on the surface of the water and he reached for it with his rubber-gloved hands. It was a twig. He let it pass on the current.

Detective Senior Inspector Christopher Kwan O'Yee looked at him. O'Yee was a Eurasian, a little more used from his boyhood in San Francisco (another great stop on the International Fish Sniffer's World Route of Fish Sniffy Beaches) to odours of all ilks, but he still did not like sniffing fish. He glanced down at something near his section of the water. It was Auden's twig doing a quick circuit. He flipped it back to Auden. Auden looked at it and flipped it behind him towards the beach. The wind changed again.

Detective Chief Inspector Harry Feiffer asked, "What was that?"

"A twig."

"You're sure?"

Detective Inspector Spencer said, "It was a twig."

Doctor Macarthur's voice called out from somewhere near the resuscitation equipment in the ambulance near the waxed police car on the beach, "What was that?" Resuscitation equipment meant nice deep whiffs of unfishy oxygen anytime you liked.

Macarthur called again, "What was that?"

Feiffer called back, "A twig!"

"A what?"

(Ambulances meant you didn't have to wade about waist high in dirty South China Sea effluvia and smell the smell of fish.)

"A bloody twig!"

"— Thank you!"

A little farther out in the effluvia Constable Sun called out, "Here!" He touched at something an inch below the surface with his rubber glove. He called out again, "Here!" and took a long plastic bag from a packet inside his shirt. He called out, "It's a leg —" and opened the bag underwater to scoop it up.

Doctor Macarthur's head went zipp! — phew! out of the ambulance doors as he stuck his oxygen-filled Roman nose into the world to see what had happened. He called out, "What's been found?"

"A leg!"

"Good! Good!"

Sun sealed the bag with a length of wire attached to it and went sloshing in towards shore dragging the leg and water-filled plastic bag a little behind him.

Spencer watched him go. Something else floated by and he leaned towards the surface of the water to see what it was. It was a fish. The fish swam off. "What's the tally?"

O'Yee said, "Part of a shoulder, two legs and a hand."

Auden said, "And part of a hip and pelvis."

"Yeah." O'Yee looked at the surface of the water for any further bits of the anatomical jigsaw. O'Yee said, "The hip and pelvis were the bits found by the swimmer."

Auden said, "Anyone who swims in this muck at half past four in the morning *deserves* to find a hip and pelvis." He asked O'Yee, "Did you take the call?"

"Constable Lee took it."

Auden turned to Lee, a hundred feet away in the ragged line of waders, "What was he doing at half past four in the morning?"

"Who?"

"The person who reported finding the first part."

Constable Lee said, "He was swimming." He looked across to where Constable Sun was dragging the plastic bag across the sand towards the ambulance and Doctor Macarthur was waiting like an anxious birthday-boy to receive it. "He was out for a swim."

"At half past four in the morning?"

Lee watched as Sun handed the object to Macarthur and caught a heavy whiff of fish. Lee said, "I don't think he'll be doing it again for a while."

Feiffer ordered, "Stop that talking. Keep spread out." He was thinking of the work piling up at the station and the faces of the North Point detectives who had agreed, grudgingly, to cover it. He said to Auden, "I don't want anything missed." He glanced at the beach and saw Sun wading back through the light swell as Macarthur carried his trophy into the ambulance. "We need the complete body." The wind changed again and he wished he had been born without his olfactory lobes. He said irritably to Spencer who was concentrating very hard on his particular part of the job, "Just try and concentrate on your particular part of the job, will you?" and turned down windward.

A crowd had gathered along the beach seawall and stood like Roman spectators in an amphitheatre watching the disposal men dispose of the Christians after the lions had disposed of the Christians. Their muttering made a heavy humming sound and the wax-in-the-nose police driver thought briefly that he might go up and move them on, noted that the way to the wall was mined with the lethality of anti-personnel fishstinks, and decided against it. He glanced towards the open doors of the ambulance where the Government Medical Examiner was happily assembling parts of a body on a steel tray and took another blob of wax for the decal. He looked at the decal before blobbing it. The decal shone.

O'Yee shivered. Later, when the sun got higher, it would be a warm spring day, but now, up to his waist in night-cold water, it was cold. He looked at the humming crowd and then back to the water. Something white was floating there, a few inches below the surface. He watched it come. It moved with the current and then turned in a little eddy below the surface. It was another hand. O'Yee closed his eyes and took out a plastic bag.

Spencer said, "I've got something!" He said, "Oh — Jesus —" He looked away.

O'Yee directed the mouth of the plastic bag over the hand and sealed the top.

Spencer said, "It's a stomach —" His own turned. He took out a plastic bag with an effort of will and snared it.

Constable Lee said, "I've got something!" It was a section of chest, still wearing a shirt. The shirt was waterlogged and torn. It seemed to be brown in colour. He took out his bag.

Auden looked at O'Yee and Spencer going towards the shore with their bags. Something touched him on the leg. He looked down expecting to see a fish. It was a head.

Feiffer said, "What is it?"

Auden looked at him.

"Is it the head?"

Auden nodded.

Auden said, "I can't guide it into the plastic bag —"

"Has it got any hair?"

Auden nodded. The head had strands of black hair floating out around it like seaweed.

Feiffer said, "Pick it up by the hair." He saw something next to his own leg and looked down to make out what it was. It was a section of shoulder. He took out a bag to get it.

The crowd on the wall went "Oooo . . ." Feiffer glanced across. Auden had the head by the hair and was trying to get it into the mouth of the bag. His hand slipped from the wet hair and the head fell back into the water with a splash. The crowd made a heavy moaning sound.

The section of shoulder floated neatly into the open plastic bag. Feiffer sealed the bag and held it below the water. He heard Auden say, "Got it —!" and then the sound of him sloshing quickly in towards shore. Feiffer heard a heavy sigh from the crowd. He waited until O'Yee and Lee were back on station in the water and went in with the shoulder as Auden came sloshing back towards Spencer.

Spencer asked Auden, "The head?"

Auden nodded.

Spencer asked, "Young man or old?"

"Young."

Spencer nodded. He said self-encouragingly, "There isn't much more now." He saw Feiffer reach the ambulance and hand his bag in to Macarthur through the open rear doors. Spencer looked at the crowd. They seemed very still. One of them seemed to ask the driver something, but the driver waved his hands to say he couldn't answer. The crowd seemed to make a heavy droning sound.

O'Yee said softly to someone, "They're worried."

He spoke very quietly and no one heard him.

O'Yee said, "They're worried that we mightn't find all of him. Before we found the head it was just a pile of legs and arms and bits, but now we've found the head it's someone who's died in water." He said, "The Chinese have two great fears: drowning at sea and of being put into their graves with bits missing from them." He said to Spencer, "In the old days, the families of condemned men used to pay the axeman to sew the head back on the people he executed." He said, "It's a Chinese belief that the soul won't rest if the body's been lost at sea or dismembered." He said to Spencer, "I don't believe that." He said in an odd voice, "The European part of me says that it's a load of crap." He looked down into the water and blinked at something.

Feiffer came back through the slight swell and took up his position. He asked Auden, "Any more?"

"No. How much more to go?"

Feiffer looked back at the ambulance and the unseeable thing that was being assembled inside it on a steel tray. "Not much." He said hopefully, "We'll be finished soon. It's a younger man in his twenties, slightly undernourished, been in the water for six hours or so." He said, "Macarthur says that the lungs suggest he was dead when he went in." He said quickly, "So let's get it over with." He shook his head to clear the picture of the inside of the ambulance.

A long way out in the cove a water-police launch went by at top speed in the direction of Stanley Bay, its twin props slicing a foaming white cleavage of water away from its bow. There were two figures on the flying bridge and another in the stern. The launch changed course briefly for something, and then went around the point out of sight. Its trailing wake went from white to green and came to the shore as rolling eddies and waves. Spencer felt one of the little wavelets push against him and then travel past. He said to Feiffer, "They'll never find anything —!"

"They're not looking. The current's bringing all the stuff in here. They're searching for wreckage." He said defensively, "They've been out since the first report this morning." He looked at the wake coming towards him in progressively smaller undulations, "Maybe they've found something already."

O'Yee looked back at the crowd. They were still and silent. He thought, "I'm not Chinese, I'm Eurasian, and the European side of me tells me it doesn't matter whether you drown, get shot, die of old age, or simply rust to pieces." He thought, "And it makes no difference whether you're found in one bit or thousands, you're just as dead." He thought, "The Chinese don't know what they're talking about." He thought, "Western science has just discovered after thousands of years that the Chinese knew what they were talking about with acupuncture." He thought, "And I read somewhere that the traditional Chinese cure-all, ginseng, has just been found to really work." He thought, "The Chinese knew that all along." He thought, "But drowning, and souls, and being in bits, is just a load of crap." The crowd on the seawall were totally silent. He thought, "The European part of me knows it's a load of crap." He thought, "On balance, I prefer the Western side of my background." Something floated past him, but it was only another twig. He thought, "That's right." He thought about the crowd. He said to himself, "It's all nonsense." He went to reach for the twig again and remembered it was the second time it had floated past. He flipped it firmly away with his hand and said to anyone or to no one, "Twig."

Feiffer rolled his rubber glove forward onto his knuckles to see his watch. It read 6 A.M. Water had seeped in through the glove, and the watch and leather watchband were both wet. He wondered if it was waterproof. His wife had given it to him as a present. He thought, "It must be. It says *Waterproof* on the back where she had my name engraved on it and she certainly wouldn't buy something that wasn't all it was supposed to be." He thought, "I wish I was at home." He thought, "I hope she hasn't heard about this on the radio." He thought, "Not now while she's pregnant." He thought, "I'd feel a bit funny about it if she knew I'd been touching dead things all morning." He looked at the murky water, remembered the workload at the station, and for no reason apparent to any of the others said, "*Shit —!*"

Spencer looked across at the beach. Doctor Macarthur had emerged from the ambulance and was motioning to them. He was shouting something, but Spencer couldn't make out the words. He looked quickly down at the water to check if it was clear and then moved in closer to shore to hear what Macarthur was saying. A little way in towards the beach he saw something half submerged and went over to see what it was. It was a hand.

"Do you hear me?" Macarthur called out.

Spencer took out another plastic bag and moved it over the hand.

"The shoulders —" Macarthur called out, and then *something — something — something —* understand? It means —" and then, "*something — something — something —*"

Spencer closed the top of the plastic bag. He thought, "A hand?" He thought, "But we've —"

Macarthur called out, " — don't match — do you understand?"

"Oh my God!" Spencer said. They had already found two hands. He said, "There are two of them!"

There was a hum from the crowd. Then talking and then someone — the crowd had grown and was a dark, solid mass along the stone wall of the beach front — shouted to someone close by, "Gay-daw gaw yan?"

Feiffer nodded back to Macarthur and waved his hand. Macarthur acknowledged him and went hurriedly back inside the ambulance.

The voices in the crowd asked the driver on the beach insistently, "Gay-daw?"

The driver shook his head.

Someone else in the crowd demanded, "Leong gaw?" He was asking if it was true that there were two of them.

The driver nodded. He watched the six policemen in the water. There was a deep humming sound from the crowd, and then it fell silent.

O'Yee glanced at the crowd. They were like a dark cloth spread along the seawall with, here and there, specks and flashes of colour from shirts and dresses, coats and bags. O'Yee thought, "They're waiting to see if we find the other man." He thought, "The rest of the other man." He thought, "They're waiting to see if we understand about things and we're prepared to pay the executioner to sew the head back on." He thought, "They look like the drawings in old picture books of Chinamen standing on the rim of China looking out at the rest of the world." He said to Feiffer, "We are going to wait until we get it all, Harry, aren't we?"

"Yes." Feiffer said, "It's a murder job now. We have to get it all for identification."

"Identification. Yes."

O'Yee looked back to the crowd. He thought, "My mother was Irish. She believed in all sorts of things." He thought, "My Chinese father doesn't believe in much at all." He thought, "He'd believe in this." He glanced back at the crowd and felt their presence on him. He thought, "They look like the drawings in old books." He fixed his eyes onto the surface of the sea and looked for artifacts from antiquity.

Spencer straightened up. Then he leaned over and did something in the water.

Auden said, "Well?"

"Nothing."

Auden said, "Don't get the idea you can go in the water if you want a piss. It pollutes the evidence."

Spencer looked shocked. "I was adjusting my waders!"

Feiffer said, "Shut up and get on with it." He felt in his shirt pocket with his wet gloves for his cigarettes, remembered he had left them in the car with his coat, and extracted his wet glove from his now equally wet pocket with distaste. Farther out, Constable Sun said, "Sir — !" and bent down into the water to retrieve something. Feiffer went over. The water was colder and deeper and came up to his already saturated pocket and thoroughly flooded it. Sun had hold of something a little below the surface. He pulled it up and over like a waterlogged surfboard and pushed it in Feiffer's direction for his inspection. It was a complete body.

Constable Sun said quietly, "Now there are three of them."

Feiffer turned the body over. The face was pale and blotched, but at one time it had been a young male Chinese. There was a long ragged gash that ran from the left shoulder diagonally across the chest to the hip, and specks of white bone under the shirt showed where the flesh had been opened up to the ribs. It was a dull chopping wound made by a single sweep, but not deep enough to cause death unless by loss of blood. Feiffer said, "You know what did it, don't you?" and Sun nodded. Feiffer said, "I'll take the scruff of the neck and you guide the feet."

They took the body in to the beach.

Spencer called, "I've got another one! It's complete!" He called Auden over to help him take it in.

"Four." O'Yee thought, "There are four of them. We've got two complete ones and one Macarthur can put together, but we've only found a piece of the other one." He heard someone in the crowd ask something and then someone else — probably the driver — shout an answer back and then there were the sounds of Feiffer and Sun and Auden and Spencer sloshing back into the sea from the beach.

Auden called out, "Something else!" and O'Yee wondered how long it would be before the current changed and whatever else was out there in the sea floating into shore would be taken away forever. He looked at the crowd, but it was silent and immobile.

Auden called out, "An arm and part of a torso!" He called out to someone, "It's the same! It's a ship's propeller wound! It isn't murder at all!" but O'Yee thought, "That doesn't make any difference." He looked at the crowd. They were beginning to edge forwards onto the beach and he thought, "They *know*. They're keeping count and they *know*." Macarthur's voice called, "What was that?" and Spencer's voice called back, "An arm! I've got an arm!"

O'Yee closed his eyes. He thought, "My father was very particular about how and where his body was to be buried." He thought, "He showed me. He made it very clear to me what elder sons were supposed to do with their father's remains." He looked at the crowd. The humming was there again. They were on the beach and the police driver was trying to get them to move back to the seawall. He thought, "They won't move." Something floated up against him and he looked down. It was a hand and an arm. He took out a plastic bag and guided them into the bag very carefully.

Feiffer looked over at him, but O'Yee took the bag and its contents to shore without speaking. He passed the bag into Macarthur's charnel house in the back of the ambulance and went back into the sea.

The crowd watched him. The other three detectives were Europeans. There were two Chinese constables (three, if you counted the driver), but the four detectives were inspectors and they were in charge. The crowd looked at him. They saw he was half-Chinese. He heard the humming.

The driver on the beach went quickly to the police car to answer the buzzing of the radio telephone. He motioned to O'Yee to wait, but O'Yee ignored him. The driver saw Feiffer watching him.

The driver nodded at something someone said on the radio — at a distance nodding into a telephone struck Feiffer as ludicrous (he wondered if he did it himself) — and then the driver came to the edge of the sand.

O'Yee said, "It was an arm," and Feiffer nodded.

Auden said, "A leg and chest!" He bent down with his bag.

Feiffer asked O'Yee quietly, "Are you all right, Christopher?"

"Yes."

"They're propeller wounds. It looks like the four of them were caught up in a ship's propeller somewhere out at sea." He said, "Macarthur says they were already dead, so they must have drowned." He looked down at the water, but there was nothing there.

Sun called, "More!" He called to Feiffer, "An arm!" He reached inside his shirt for his packet of plastic bags.

"Sir —!" the driver's voice called out.

Feiffer shouted back, "Yes?"

"The Water Police report they've stopped a junk full of illegal immigrants!" He called out again, "Illegal immigrants! The Captain says four of them died and he threw the bodies overboard!"

At the water's edge Spencer said, "Good old Water Police."

Feiffer shouted back, "How did they die?"

"What?"

"How did they *die?*"

"They suffocated! The Captain says it was an accident! The Water Police say you can leave it — they'll pick up whatever's left later! They say it isn't that important now!"

"OK!"

"They say leave it now —!"

"Right!"

"No!" O'Yee said.

Feiffer said, "What was that?"

O'Yee said, "There's still some missing."

"What? Bodies?"

O'Yee looked down at the water. He heard the crowd humming. He thought, "My father would have —" He said, *"Bits!"*

Spencer said suddenly, "I've found the head!" His tone changed. He said, "Oh . . . God!" He leaned forward in the water to pick it up the way Auden had done.

Feiffer said, "That's four."

O'Yee said, "There's still some missing."

"What?"

"I don't know! I haven't been keeping bloody score!" He glanced back at the crowd. They *had* been keeping score and they knew there was still some missing. He said, "Something! There's still some missing!" He shouted out to Macarthur at his ambulance, "What's missing?"

"What?" Macarthur shouted back.

"Missing! What's still missing?"

Macarthur glanced back into his ambulance. "A leg!" He shrugged. He shouted back, "It's just a leg! Don't worry about it!" He shouted to them all as one. "You can come in now!"

O'Yee said to Feiffer, "There's a leg missing!"

"Does that matter?"

"Doesn't it?"

Feiffer looked across the cove. The current was changing with the beginning of the morning tide. He said, "The tide's starting to turn. It'll be too late anyway in fifteen minutes." He said, "We've done pretty well, considering, and if the Water Police are certain it isn't a murder investigation —"

"It's because they're bloody Chinese, isn't it!"

"What the hell are you talking about?"

"If they were bloody Europeans you'd think it mattered!"

Feiffer said, "I'm not even going to answer that one." He said with concern in his voice, "I don't know what's gotten into you, Christopher. I know this has been a bloody awful job, but you've seen worse —"

Macarthur called out, "You can leave it now! I'm taking the ambulance in!" He went to the cab of the ambulance and roused the driver to shut the back doors.

O'Yee said, "I just think we should find all of it, that's all."

"There isn't the time. We could be here for the rest of the week." He called to Auden and Spencer, "OK, you can go in now —!" Feiffer looked over to Sun and Lee. "You can go now. Off you go."

Sun and Lee hesitated. They looked at O'Yee.

"Go on," Feiffer said.

Sun and Lee looked at the crowd.

Feiffer said, "That's an order!"

Sun said, "Yes, sir." He glanced at Lee and made a motion of resignation with his head. He and Lee waded past with Auden and Spencer.

Feiffer said to O'Yee, "And you too."

On the beach the ambulance passed through the crowd and out of sight.

O'Yee said, "I think we should stay and find the leg."

"No."

"I think we should."

"Why?"

"I — I just think we should, that's all."

"The Water Police'll find it, or it'll be washed up on the evening tide, or tomorrow. Maybe never. It's just a leg. If it was a head it'd be different, but after all, it's only a bloody leg —"

"I think we should stay."

Feiffer looked at him. He said, "Unless you can give me some sort of strong reason, you can forget it. For all I know you just have a fascination about putting all the little wooden pieces together in bloody puzzles and jigsaws. For all I know, you —"

"You shut your goddamned mouth!"

"What the *hell* is the matter with you?"

"Nothing's the matter with —"

Feiffer said evenly, "I'm ordering you go to to shore and that's all there is to it. We'll probably hear the leg's been found tomorrow or the next day and that'll all be fine and neat, but we do have other cases current in this district and I'm not about to waste all my detectives for the rest of the bloody day just to find a bit of dead meat that's probably been eaten by the bloody fishes anyway! *Now bloodywell get back to shore!*"

O'Yee looked at the beach. The crowd was moving forward past Auden and Spencer to where Sun and Lee took off their waders by the second police car. Sun said something to Lee and they both got quickly into the vehicle and drove off. The crowd turned to the shoreline and looked out at O'Yee.

Feiffer said, "Go on. In."

"I'd like to stay, Harry."

"No."

"I mean it."

"So do I. We've got other work and it's just as important — more so."

"If you could just spare me for —"

"No."

O'Yee said, "You can't have any objection if I —" He said, "This isn't the scene of a possible crime anymore. I mean, now anyone can come here and —"

"Anyone who's off duty. But you're not."

O'Yee looked at the crowd. He said, "I meant, *them!*"

"They can do what they like."

O'Yee said, "I've never had very much time for religion or — for that sort of thing . . ."

Feiffer began wading in towards the shore.

O'Yee thought, "If I call out to them — to the crowd — they'll come in and look for the leg because they all believe it." He thought, "They ought to. Maybe they don't." He thought, "Maybe it's just me. Maybe it's the European side of me trying to be so goddamned Chinese there isn't a Chinese on earth who'd know what the hell I was talking about." He thought, "Maybe I'm imagining it all. Maybe they're just curious ghouls counting the grisly remains." He thought, "If I don't call them, I'll imagine they'll all be looking at me and feeling disgusted." He thought, "And if I do call them and they don't know what I mean, I'll look foolish." He thought, "It'll be a loss of face, Chinese or no." He thought, "They're all from this district: I have to make them take me seriously as a policeman or I'll be finished." Something in the water bumped against his knee. He thought, "If I don't say anything I'll never know."

Feiffer said irritably, thinking of the caseload, "Are you coming?"

The object bumped his knee again. O'Yee thought, "I'll never know." He knew what the object was without looking at it. He took out a plastic bag and bent down to recover it.

He took the leg in to shore with a puzzled expression on his face.

CAROLYN WHEAT

FLAKE PIECE

Carolyn Wheat's (b. 1946) two novels, Dead Man's Thoughts *and* Where Nobody Dies, *both feature Cassandra (Cass) Jameson, a Legal Aid defender turned detective/lawyer who lives in a renovated Brooklyn brownstone and gets involved more deeply in the problems of her clients than is probably professionally wise. Cass graduated from Kent State, Wheat from the University of Toledo, but their careers are otherwise similar. Wheat, too, was a public defender. Now she works with the New York City Police Department as an associate attorney on cases involving minors. She, too, lives among the Brooklyn brownstones.*

Because she has so often worked closely with the police, Wheat feels that she is probably more sympathetic than most private eye writers to the everyday problems faced by policemen. In a new series of short stories she has put aside Cass to deal directly with the men in uniform. The following story is one of these.

HE CAME OUTTA NOWHERE. I swear to God. One minute I'm walkin' with my partner, tryin' to say somethin' he won't rag me about later. Which isn't easy, on account of the Hairbag hasn't got much respect for rookies. Night's as calm as a warm bath. Next thing I know, this kid comes flyin' out of the alley. Nearly knocks my partner over. The Hairbag looks at me. I look at him. He's got thirty years and fifty pounds on me, so guess who chases the kid.

I start running. Behind me I hear yelling, Spanish and English. Sounds like some lady in the tenement got broken into.

Kid runs down Avenue A, then takes a sharp right on East Seventh, right below the park. His sneakers skid on the cobbles. I puff along behind, my heavy cop shoes pounding the pavement. It feels like we'll run that way throughout eternity, him just ahead, me just behind, forever and ever, amen.

"Stop!" I shout at the top of my lungs, but all that comes out is a winded croak. I yell it again. "Stop, goddamn it. I'm a cop." Voice is louder this time, kid's gotta hear me. He's gotta. I just can't run no more. Stitch in my side and I'm breathing like an eighty-year-old with asthma.

Kid disappears. *Where the hell —*

My head swivels. *I can't lose him. I was so close.* A vacant lot on the corner. Has to be. Kid has to be there.

I run toward the emptiness. It's dark as hell. Real hell, the kind Father Fahey used to scare us shitless with at ten o'clock Mass. Slippery, too. God knows what kind of filth people throw in here.

My breath sounds like a steam radiator on a below-zero night. I hear his breath, too, but hearing's all I can do. There's no light at all.

Ice-cold sweat pours down the inside of my tunic. Gun hand's wet and shaky. I point at God knows what.

A movement. I feel it. I don't see it until the kid steps into the streetlight glare. His heel slides and he catches himself. He's into a half-crouch and suddenly I see the glint of shiny metal in his hand.

A gun. Oh Jesus, a gun. Freakin' kid's carryin'. I'm gonna die, I'm gonna die. Oh Mama, I'm gonna die.

My finger jumps on the trigger, pulls back like my whole body energy was pumped into that one place. I hear noise. Could be one shot, could be more. Could be mine, could be his.

Kid crumples. Like a freakin' housa cards the kid crumples to the ground. He writhes a minute, then lays still. Too goddamn still.

I feel weird. Breath gasping like a landed fish. I'm shaking like I'm having a fit. My crotch is wet, just like that time in second grade. Oh Mama, look at the hero, shoots a kid and pisses on himself.

I walk toward the kid. Big red hole in his stomach. *Big* freakin' red hole. Oh God, I don't wanna look — I hafta look. Kid is not alive. No way he's alive with a hole like that in his —

You stupid little turkey, why did you make me kill you?

My eyes move toward the kid's hand. The hand with the gun. It takes me a minute but finally I see what's in front of me. No gun.

No gun. Christ, let my legs hold me up, don't let me fall. No gun. There's gotta be a gun, for God's sake, please, there's *gotta* be a gun.

There's no gun. No metal in the kid's hand at all. Freakin' kid's unarmed. Sweet Jesus, don't let it be true. I *saw* metal gleam in his hand. I wouldn't shoot an unarmed kid. I'm not that kind of a cop.

I drop to my knees. There's shit all over the lot — garbage, dog crap, discarded rubbers, used needles. I don't care. I paw through all of it. I need that gun. There has to be a gun, goddamn it, there *has* to be a gun, there has to be a gun, *there has to be a gun.*

My breath's coming in sobs. I'm on my knees in the crud of the city. My hand touches a furry dead thing and I jump back with the willies. Christ, what the hell was that; it's only a dead puppy. Coulda been a rat. *God what am I doing here?* Freakin' kid shouldn't of turned on me, metal gleaming in his hand.

What could I think? What could I do? I saw my death coming. I had no choice. I had *no* choice.

I see the headline:

COP SHOOTS UNARMED BOY

His mother cryin' on the six o'clock news. My mother cryin' on the eleven. I'm in the grand jury beggin' for time to talk to my lawyer before I answer the next question. Me, a cop, jerking the system around just like the lowlifes I'm always bustin'. And when it's all over, the best that can happen — the *best,* goddamn it! — is that I get a rubber gun and ride a desk. No more street cop. No more me.

I seen it happen before. Guy named Garrigan, in the Five-Four. Dropped a kid in a shoot-out in an abandoned building. Got to where he spent more time in hearing rooms than he did on the job. Worst part was even guys that knew him, guys that shoulda stood by him, walked the other way when he came by. Like he had AIDS or something. Like he wasn't in the family no more.

COP SHOOTS UNARMED BOY. No, sweet Jesus, *no!*

There has to be a gun. Freakin' kid coulda threw it. I reach deeper into the garbage. A whole potful of burned rice. A bloody tampon. A rotten banana. The pizza I had at Sal's rises in my throat. I swallow it back and sit on my heels. I look down at myself and realize I've been wiping my hand on my pants leg for I don't know how long. Little pieces of rotten banana cling to the blue serge.

No gun. No freakin' gun. I shot an unarmed kid. I might as well put the gun in my mouth and pull the trigger.

COP SHOOTS UNARMED BOY, KILLS SELF

I'm rockin' back and forth in the garbage, thinkin' about how bad it's gonna be and pretty soon the blood's pounding in my head and it hurts like hell, only behind the pounding I'm starting to hear words.

Slap, slap, jack him up. Slap, slap, jack him up. Slap, slap, *jack him up, jack him up, jack him up.*

My first week in cop school. Too freakin' green to even be a rookie. Guy givin' the lecture asks what wouldja do if a loudmouth drunk comes along and starts cursing you out, calling you names. He's not breaking the law or anything, just acting like an asshole. What would you do, Cadet Petrizzo?

Vic thinks about it. In the back of the room Holmesey, whose brother's in the Four-Six, starts the whisper. He slaps his hand into his palm like he's got a blackjack and he says, real soft, jack him up. Pretty soon there's three or four guys doin' it. Slap, slap, jack him up. Slap, slap, jack him up. Slap, slap, *jack* him up, *jack him up.* By the end, everybody's doin' it. Even the lieutenant teaching the class grins as he gives us the standard bullshit about jacks being illegal and drunks having rights like everyone else. His grin says, I gotta say it but nobody says you gotta listen.

The only guy not slapping his palm and saying *jack him up* is me. When Holmesey asks me about it after class, I shrug and say I'm not that kind of a cop. He laughs, but not like he means it, and says that's fine in the classroom, shithead, but whatcha gonna do on the street? *You're a cop, not a freakin' social worker.* When he walks away, he shakes his head in disgust.

On the street, it's the same. My partner's this old hairbag with more time on the job than God. His first advice to me: check out the places where it's okay to eat on the arm. His second: get a flake piece.

I'm not that kind of a cop, is what I said. He said, oh yes you are. You're either that kind of a cop or you ain't a cop at all and you goddamn well better decide which it's gonna be, kid, 'cause nobody's gonna want you for a partner if you ain't a stand-up guy.

What's bein' a stand-up guy got to do with carryin' an extra gun around just so you can plant it on some dude and say he tried to shoot you? I asked.

The Hairbag shook his head like Holmesey and said I'd learn sooner or later and personally he was hoping it wouldn't be on his tour of duty.

I'm not that kind of a cop, I said as he walked away. I didn't say it real loud, but I said it. And I meant it.

The thing is, I've got the piece.

I didn't mean to keep it. I took it off a smart-mouth kid who found it in the subway. I saw that story on *60 Minutes* about the five-year-old who shot his sister, so I decided I couldn't let that kid keep the gun no matter what. I was gonna take it to Property but I worked overtime Tuesday, and then Thursday was the funeral for the sergeant from the Seven-Six who never got outta the coma, God rest his soul, so I hadda get my dress uniform from the cleaners and I never did get the freakin' piece to Property like I said I would, so it's in my back pocket and nobody knows I've got it. Not even the Hairbag, since I was off duty at the time. The kid won't say anything, and the punk who dropped it in the subway won't be showing up to put in his claim neither.

It's a perfect flake piece. Put it in the hand of the kid with the big red hole and I'm golden. Well, maybe not golden. There'll still be a helluva stink, lots of questions, but at least I'll have a chance of some-body believing me when I say I had to shoot to save my life. Just wipe my prints off and put the gun in the kid's hand.

I'm not that kind of a cop.

Slap, slap, jack him up.

Slap, slap, *jack* him up.

Slap, slap, *jack him up, jack him up,* JACK HIM UP, JACK HIM UP.

Voices are so freakin' loud. Pounding in my head. Head hurts so bad. I'm not that kind of a cop, *just shut up,* the voices are getting louder, *shut up, you bastards,* I'm not that kind of a cop. I'M NOT THAT KIND OF A COP!

It's quiet now. I look up like I'm seeing everything for the first time. The garbage, the ghost-light from the street lamp behind me, the dirty brick wall behind the kid. Wind whips through me, hitting the cold spots. My underarms, my crotch. I shiver, then stand up. I holster my gun, then watch my hand go toward my pocket, pulling out the other one. I go over to the kid with the big red hole. I wipe off the piece with my handkerchief and bend over.

I look down at the kid with the big red hole and the black gun in his hand. I don't have any memory of putting the gun there, but there it is. Just as if he'd really pulled it on me.

The sound of cop shoes running is heard in the distance. The Hairbag puffs his way along the street. He runs like an old lady tryin' to catch a bus, little shuffling steps and no wind.

"What . . . happened?" he asks between gasps, bending over like he's just broken the marathon record.

I can't believe how steady my voice is. "I followed the perp into the alley. He pulled a piece on me. I hadda shoot. I think he's dead."

The Hairbag stumbles toward the body. His breath is still coming in ragged gulps. He looks down at the kid, then turns back to me. There's a funny look on his face. A cold trickle runs down my back. Something's wrong.

"Not . . . the perp," the Hairbag says, panting between words. "Russo and . . . Johnson picked . . . him up at the . . . corner."

I look into the mud-gray eyes of the partner I've despised for eight months, the partner I would have given anything not to be like. *I'm not that kind of a cop,* I said to myself a hundred times, listening to his stories of the old days, the good days, the freewheeling days before Serpico and the Knapp Commission and college degrees. Those eyes are like a mirror now, a tarnished mirror with the silver all but washed away by time.

I *am* that kind of a cop.

LOREN D.
ESTLEMAN

Perhaps it is a local tradition, but just as General Motors, Ford, and Chrysler produce cars in all sorts of makes and models, Michigan writer Loren D. Estleman (b. 1952) turns out Westerns, new adventures of Sherlock Holmes (Sara Paretsky says his Dr. Jekyll & Mr. Holmes *is the best of the recent rash of Holmes updates), private eye novels in the Hammett tradition (with Detroit detective Amos Walker), and a line of hard-boiled adventures featuring a mob hit man named Peter Macklin. Robert J. Randisi, founder of the Private Eye Writers of America, has called Macklin "the toughest character — hero or anti-hero — to arrive in crime fiction since Richard Stark's Parker."*

A former police reporter, Estleman claims that he "started thinking more like a cop than a reporter, and decided it was time to get out of newspapering." Amos Walker, who appears in the following story, is one of the few modern detectives who remains true to one of the least fashionable private eye traditions of the 1930s: he wears a hat.

"Dead Soldier" was first published in 1982.

1

NHA NELSON'S ORIENTAL FACE was shaped like an inverted raindrop, oval with a chin that came to a point. She just crested five feet and ninety pounds in a tight pink sweater and a black skirt that caught her legs just below the knees. Her eyes slanted down from a straight nose and her complexion was more beige than ivory. She was as Vietnamese as a punji stick.

I said, "My name's Amos Walker. I think we spoke on the telephone about a package I have for Mr. Nelson." I held up the bottle in the paper sack.

"Come in." She gave every consonant its full measure.

Carrying my wine like a partygoer, I followed her into a neat living room where two men sat watching television. One rose to grasp my hand. Reed Nelson was my height and age — just six feet and on the wrong side of thirty — but he had football shoulders under his checked shirt and wore his brass-colored hair cut very close. His brittle smile died short of his eyes. "My neighbor, Steve Minor."

I nodded to the other man, fortyish and balding, who grunted back but kept his seat. He was watching the Lions lose to Pittsburgh.

"Nha said a private detective called." Nelson's eyes went to the bottle. "It's about the tontine, isn't it?"

I said it was. He asked Steve Minor to excuse him, got a grunt in reply, and we adjourned to a paneled basement. Hunting prints covered the walls. Rifles and handguns occupied two glassed-in display cases, and a Browning automatic lay in pieces on a workbench stained with gun oil and crowded with cartridge-loading paraphernalia. My host cleared a stack of paper targets off one of a pair of crushed-leather armchairs and we sat down.

"Expecting someone?" I asked.

He smiled the halfway smile. "Friend of mine owns a range outside Dearborn. I was a sharpshooter in the army and I'd rather not lose the edge. If I were you I wouldn't smoke; you're sitting on a case of black powder."

I looked down at the edge of a carton stenciled EXPLOSIVE sticking out between the legs of my chair and put away my pack of Winstons.

"David Kurch hired me to find you and deliver the bottle," I said. "He's the lawyer you and the others left it with when you formed the tontine."

"I remember. He was an ARVN then, stationed in Que Noc." Nelson's expression turned in on itself. "That was only twelve years ago. It's hard to believe they're all dead."

"They are, though. Chuck Dundas stepped on a mine two feet shy of the DMZ in 'seventy. Albert Rule was MIA for seven years and has been declared dead. Fred Burlingame shot himself in New York last year, and Jerry Lynch died of cancer in August. Congratulations." I handed him the bottle.

He slid it out of the sack, fondled it. "It was bottled in some Frenchman's private vineyard in 'thirty-seven. Al found it in a ruined cellar near Hue, probably left behind when the French bugged out. The tontine was Fred's idea. The last man left was supposed to get the bottle. Were you over there?"

"Two years."

"Then you know how preoccupied we were with death. But, hell, I forgot all about this till you showed up. When I saw the package I remembered."

I passed him my receipt pad with a pen clipped to it. "If you'll sign this I'll shove off."

He read it swiftly and scribbled his name. "How'd you find me? I just moved to Detroit from Southfield, and my number's unlisted." He gave back the pad and pen.

"Kurch said you were an engineer at General Motors. I got it from Personnel."

"They have a hell of a nerve, after I just got fired."

"They cutting back again?"

He moved his head from side to side, but his eyes stayed on me. "They said I was a poor risk from a psychiatric standpoint."

"Are you?"

"You were in Nam. What do you think?"

I let that ride and got up. Crowd noise filtered down from the TV set upstairs. Someone had just made a touchdown. Nelson said, "You drink?"

I sat back down. "Do they make cars in Tokyo?"

This time his smile made it all the way. He turned his head and called, "Nha? Two glasses, please."

"What about your neighbor?" I asked.

"He'll understand. Steve and I aren't all that close. I only invite him over because I knew him slightly in Nam and he put me on to this house, not that that was such a favor with this mortgage staring at my throat. He introduced me to my wife."

On cue, Nha appeared, set a pair of stemmed glasses down on the workbench, and withdrew. She seemed flushed. Nelson scooped a Swiss Army knife out of a drawer in the bench and used the corkscrew to unstop the bottle. When the glasses were full of dark red liquid, he handed one over and raised his. "Chuck, Al, Fred, and Jerry. Four among the fifty thousand."

We sipped. It was good, but nothing beats twelve-year-old Scotch. "Were you married over there?"

He nodded. "She was working in a Saigon orphanage. Grew up there, after her parents got napalmed in 'sixty-five. You like being a private eye?"

We drank wine and told each other our biographies. There wasn't much to tell beyond the gaping hole of Vietnam. After an hour or so, the noise upstairs ceased abruptly. Steve Minor had switched off the set. Nelson replaced the cork in the bottle, which was now half empty. "There's another afternoon's drinking in here," he said, rising.

I was already on my feet. "Share it with your wife, or with someone else close."

"She's a teetotaler. And if there were anyone else close, do you think I'd be wasting it on a shamus I don't even know?" His eyes pleaded.

I said I'd call him. Upstairs, Nha saw me out without speaking. Minor had left.

2

It was three weeks before I made it back. I had spent much of that time following a city councilman's wife from male friend to male friend while her husband was on a junket to Palm Springs. Nelson greeted me at the door, explaining that Nha was out shopping. We killed the bottle in near-silence. He hadn't found a job and he wasn't talking much. It looked as if the novelty had worn off our relationship. We parted.

The rest of the month died painlessly. The Lions blew a late-season rally just before the playoffs. Snow was on the ground most other places. Detroit's streets were clogged with brown slush. Reed Nelson called me at the office on a Saturday and asked me to meet him somewhere for lunch.

"I've got a job interview in Houston next week," he said, when we were sharing a table in my favorite restaurant, one where the chef wore a shirt and didn't swat flies with his spatula. "Only the bank ate my last unemployment check and the savings account is down to double figures. When I applied for a loan, the manager of my friendly dependable finance company snickered and called in his assistant because he said he needed cheering up."

I blew on a spoonful of steaming chili. "What about old Steve? Army buddies are usually good for a few bucks."

"The hell with him."

I glanced up at Nelson's face. He'd lost weight. His cheeks were shadowed and there were purple thumbprints under his eyes. "How's Nha?" I asked.

"She's fine." The words cracked out like shots from a .22.

We ate. I said, "I'll give you two hundred for the Browning."

He hesitated. "It's not worth that. The trigger mechanism's sloppy and the barrel needs bluing."

"I always was a rotten businessman. We'll stop at my bank on the way back to the office. I'll come by later and pick up the automatic."

"Thanks, Amos. You ever need anything, just name it."

"Pass the salt."

3

I returned from a tail job early Monday afternoon. Whoever said travel is broadening never followed a possibly larcenous salesman clear to Toledo and sat up all night in a freezing car. I hadn't eaten since Sunday. Nursing the crick in my neck, I turned on the TV in my living room and lurched into the kitchen to find something to defrost. The volume was too high. When the sound came on, the name "Steven Minor" pasted me to the ceiling.

The picture was just blossoming on when I got back in. Floodlights illuminated two paramedics sliding a stretcher into the back of an ambulance. Then the camera cut to a male model in an overcoat standing in front of a house I recognized with a microphone in one hand. Police flashers throbbed sullenly in the street nearby.

"Police aren't saying yet what may have caused Nelson to shoot his neighbor and barricade himself in his house. But evidence suggests that the tragedy of Vietnam has just claimed another victim." The model identified himself and his grim face disappeared, to be replaced by a smiling one back at the Eyewitness News Desk. I left the set running and got out of there.

4

John Alderdyce was the lieutenant in charge of the investigation. He spoke to a big sergeant from the Tactical Mobile Unit, who reluctantly let me through the cordon. John's black and has been a friend since childhood, or as much of one as a plastic badge can hope to find among the blue brotherhood. "What's your billing in this?" he demanded when we were inside Nelson's house.

"Friend of the family." I scuffed a sole on a red stain on the carpet. It was still fresh, and it wasn't wine. The room was a shambles of overturned furniture and broken crockery. "When did Minor die?"

"He was DOA at Detroit Receiving." Alderdyce's face fluttered. "Damn it, who told you he's dead?"

"I'm a detective. Rumor has it you're with Homicide." I fed my face a butt. "What did I miss?"

"Right now it looks like this guy Nelson popped his cap, plugged his neighbor with a thirty-two auto, then locked himself in, holding his wife hostage. Hostage Negotiations people talked him into surrendering. He's wearing handcuffs in the basement. Vietnam vet, certified psycho, unemployed. They ought to print up a form report for this kind of thing with blanks where we can fill in the names, save on overtime."

"Any witnesses?"

"Don't need 'em. Nelson confessed. We're just waiting for the press to clear out so we can take him downtown and get it on tape. He and Minor were talking downstairs when he flipped. You ought to see that gun room. I guess you have." He nailed me. "Since when are you anybody's friend?"

"Even the garbageman rates a cup of coffee now and then. What's Nha say? That's his wife."

"I met her. Pretty. Did I ever tell you I had a crush on Nancy Kwan before I was married? She was hysterical when I got here. Nelson's wife, not Nancy. We called her doctor. He just left. She's in the bedroom, under sedation."

"I wonder how she got along without it when they burned her parents to death." I blew smoke. "Can I see Nelson?"

Alderdyce's eyes glittered in narrow slits. "As what? Friend or representative?"

I said friend. He considered, then nodded as if agreeing with himself and started for the stairs. I dogged his heels. Drops of blood mottled the steps. I halted.

"Where'd Minor get it?" I asked.

"In the right lung." The lieutenant looked back up at me from the bottom step. "He staggered up the stairs, bounced off some furniture on his way through the living room, and collapsed by the front door. Hospital says he drowned in his own blood. Anything wrong with that?"

"Are you asking as a friend or a policeman?"

He made a rude noise and resumed moving.

A cop in uniform and a plainclothesman I didn't know were guarding the prisoner, who was sitting in the chair I had occupied on my two visits, manacled wrists dangling between his knees. His shirt was soaked through with sweat. When I entered, he looked up and a tired smile tugged at the corners of his mouth. His features were cadaverous.

"I used your gun," he said. "Sorry."

"What's he mean, your gun?" snapped Alderdyce.

"Private joke," I said. "What happened, Reed?"

"They're saying I killed Steve. I was shooting at Charlie."

"Charlie?" Alderdyce's brow puckered.

"Viet Cong." I ditched my cigarette in an ashtray on the workbench. "Shrinks call it Vietnam Flashback. Years after a vet leaves the jungle, something triggers his subconscious and he suddenly thinks he's back there surrounded by the enemy. He reacts accordingly."

"Oh yeah, that. As if murderers didn't have enough loopholes to squirm through as it was."

The telephone rang upstairs. Alderdyce jerked his head at the uniform, who went up to answer it.

"It's a legitimate dodge," I said. "Only not in this case, right, Reed? Steve Minor was the target all along."

The uniform's feet on the stairs were very loud in the silence that followed. "It's for you, Lieutenant," he said. "The lab."

His superior pointed at me. "Hold that thought." He left us.

Five minutes later he returned. His eyes were very bright. "Blow your diminished capacity plea a kiss quick, Nelson. We're going Murder One."

5

"The D.A. won't buy it," said the plainclothesman, after a moment.

"Bet me. The lab found powder burns on Minor's shirt, but guess what? There weren't any around the wound. I called the hospital and checked."

"Proving?" I asked.

"Proving he wasn't wearing it when he was shot. Someone held it up and fired a bullet through it, then put it on him while he was dying upstairs to make us think otherwise. We know you were at Metro Airport an hour before the shooting, Nelson, and that the airline lost your reservation on a flight to Houston. Was Minor in bed with your wife when you came home, or did he just have time to take off his shirt?"

The prisoner leaped to his feet, but was shoved back into it by the other two officers. He opened his mouth, then closed it. Slouched.

"Neighbors reported only one shot, Lieutenant," the plainclothesman pointed out. "And there was just one cartridge gone from the gun."

"They didn't hear the first because it was fired in the basement. And don't you think a man smart enough to know we'd question a chest wound without a corresponding hole in the shirt and then make up that psycho story to cover himself is smart enough to replace one of the spent shells? I want a crew here to search every inch of this house until they find where that second bullet went." He nailed me. "You knew Minor was the target. How? Did you know about him and Nelson's wife?"

"No, and I still don't," I said. "You're zero for two. Nelson never shot anyone. Not in this hemisphere, anyway."

Nelson glanced at me, then away. I continued before Alderdyce could ask any more questions.

"Reed was a sharpshooter over there. Still is; he told me he keeps in practice. There's no way, if he thought Minor was a Viet Cong, that he'd miss the heart at this range and give Charlie a chance to retaliate. And if it was Minor he wanted to kill, he would've made sure his victim didn't hang around long enough to talk. It's my guess he was shot before Reed got here."

"No! I killed him!" This time the cops held the prisoner in his chair.

"His car was parked in the driveway when the neighbors heard the gun go off," protested Alderdyce. The skin on his face was drawn so tight it shone blue, as it often did when I was speaking.

"You said yourself it was the second shot they heard," I reminded him. "That one was his, to keep anyone from wondering why Minor didn't have his shirt on in his neighbor's house, and he did it upstairs because he knew it wasn't safe to pull a trigger in the basement with so much black powder lying around. Just one other person could have fired the fatal bullet. Just one other person was in the house at the time." I breathed some air. "What were Nha and Steve Minor to each other back in Vietnam, Reed?"

"Prostitute and pimp."

Alderdyce and I turned. Nha Nelson, barefoot in a Chinese house dress, her hair down and disheveled, was leaning against the wall at the bottom of the stairwell. Her face was streaked and puffy.

"Don't, Nha," pleaded her husband.

"I should not have let it come this far." She spoke slowly, like a record winding down. The doctor's sedative had furred the fine edge. "Minor made money on the side running prostitutes in Saigon. I was one of six. When his tour ended, he introduced us all to GIs he knew, hoping some of us would marry and he could blackmail the husbands later by threatening to tell all their friends and business associates what their wives used to do for a living.

"Reed was an engineer for a large corporation, the perfect victim. But he lost his job before Minor could begin squeezing him. Then he blackmailed me, but not for money. He was a depraved man. He said if I did not have sex with him he would tell Reed I lied about my past. I agreed."

Her eyes filled and ran over. Nelson said her name. She acted as if she hadn't heard. "I love my husband. I was afraid he would leave me if he knew the truth. Minor waited until Reed left for the airport and then he came over to collect. But I could not do it. I had done it many times, with many men, but that was in Vietnam, before I had Reed. I excused myself while Minor was undressing and came down here for a gun. I wanted only to scare him, to make him leave. He suspected something and followed me. When I heard him on the stairs I panicked. I turned and —" Bitter tears strangled her.

I gave her my handkerchief. She wiped her eyes and nose. Nelson was weeping too, his face buried in his hands, the chain dangling between the wrists. Quiet rolled in and sat down. Alderdyce booted it out. "Do you have the names of the other five women?"

"Three of them," she said. "The other two didn't marry the men Minor wanted them to. I even know the husbands' names and what cities they lived in. He bragged to me about how he had traveled around the country all this time, setting up shop wherever a victim was. That's what he called it, 'setting up shop.' "

The uniform took her elbow gently and steered her around as if she were a sleepy child. Nelson stood.

"Thanks for nothing, Walker."

I said, "I'll be surprised if the D.A. presses charges. If he does he'll lose."

"So what? I'm going to end up in the nut ward sooner or later. My way it counted for something. Why'd you have to take that away from me? We were friends for a while.

I had nothing to throw at that. The plainclothesman prodded him forward and up the steps.

Alderdyce hung back. He had spotted the empty wine bottle, standing in a back corner of the workbench behind a can of gun stock refinisher. "That looks out of place here. Maybe I should have it dusted."

"Forget it." I picked it up and chucked it into the wastebasket. "Dead soldier."

RAYMOND
CHANDLER AND
BILLY WILDER

DOUBLE INDEMNITY

The 1944 film version of James M. Cain's Double Indemnity was Chandler's first movie job. The collaboration with director Billy Wilder (b. 1906) was not a particularly happy one. Chandler thought Wilder vulgar, Wilder thought Chandler pretentious (and Chandler thought Cain "a writer of the faux naïf type, which I particularly dislike"), but the result is a memorable film script and that rarity, a script that reads well.

Writing to Cain just after the movie opened, Chandler said: "For once an emotionally integrated story has got on the screen in the mood in which it was written." And then he went on to explain to Cain that although his dialogue looked good on the page of a novel it didn't sound realistic when read aloud. The film's dialogue is Chandler's, not Cain's.

Years later Chandler described the role of the screenwriter to a British publisher in terms that sound suspiciously like a parody of that old "Simple Art of Murder" description of a private eye: "The wise screen writer is he who wears his second-best suit, artistically speaking, and doesn't take things too much to heart. He should have a touch of cynicism, but only a touch. . . . He should do the best he can without straining at it. He should be scrupulously honest about his work, but he should not expect scrupulous honesty in return."

This version of the Chandler-Wilder screenplay first appeared in Best Film Plays — 1945, edited by John Gassner and Dudley Nichols.

PART ONE

A DOWNTOWN INTERSECTION in Los Angeles fades in: It is night, about two o'clock, very light traffic. At the left and in the immediate foreground a semaphore traffic signal stands at GO. Approaching it at about thirty miles per hour is a Dodge 1938 coupe. It is driven erratically and weaving a little, but not out of control. When the car is about forty feet away, the signal changes to STOP. The car makes no attempt to stop but comes on through as a light newspaper truck is seen crossing the intersection at right angles. It swerves and skids to avoid the Dodge, which goes on as though nothing had happened. The truck stops with a panicky screech of tires. There is a large sign on the truck: READ THE LOS ANGELES TIMES. The truck driver's infuriated face stares after the coupe.

The coupe continues along the street, still weaving, then slows down and pulls over toward the curb in front of a tall office building. The coupe stops. The headlights are turned off. For a second nothing happens, then the car door opens slowly. A man eases himself out onto the sidewalk and stands a moment, leaning on the open door to support himself. He's a tall man, about thirty-five years old. From the way he moves there seems to be something wrong with his left shoulder. He straightens up and painfully lowers his left hand into his jacket pocket. He leans into the car. He brings out a light-weight overcoat and drapes it across his shoulders. He shuts the car door and walks toward the building.

The entrance of the building comes into view. Above the closed, double plate glass doors is lettered: PACIFIC BUILDING. To the left of the entrance there is a drugstore, closed, dark except for a faint light in the back. The man comes stiffly up to the doors. He tries the doors. They are locked. He knocks on the glass. Inside, over his shoulder, the lobby of the building is visible: a side entrance to the drugstore on the left, in the rear a barber shop and cigar and magazine stand closed up for the night, and to the right two elevators. One elevator is open and its dome light falls across the dark lobby.

The man knocks again. The night watchman sticks his head out of the elevator and looks toward the entrance. He comes out with a newspaper in one hand and a half-eaten sandwich in the other. He finishes the sandwich on the way to the doors, looks out and recognizes the man outside, unlocks the door and pulls it open.

NIGHT WATCHMAN. Why, hello there, Mr. Neff.

Neff walks in past him without answering. Then he crosses the lobby, heading for the elevator. The night watchman looks after him, relocks the door, and follows him to the elevator. Neff enters it.

In the elevator Neff stands leaning against the wall. He is pale and haggard with pain, but "deadpans" as the night watchman joins him.

NIGHT WATCHMAN. Working pretty late aren't you, Mr. Neff?
NEFF (*tight-lipped*). Late enough.
NIGHT WATCHMAN. You look kind of all in at that.
NEFF. I'm fine. Let's ride.
The night watchman pulls the lever; the doors close and the elevator rises.
NIGHT WATCHMAN. How's the insurance business, Mr. Neff?
NEFF. Okay.
NIGHT WATCHMAN. They wouldn't ever sell me any. They say I've got something loose in my heart. I say it's rheumatism.
NEFF (*scarcely listening*). Uh-huh.

The night watchman looks around at him, turns away again, and the elevator stops.

NIGHT WATCHMAN (*surly*). Twelve.

The door opens. Across a small dark reception room a pair of frosted glass doors is lettered: PACIFIC ALL-RISK INSURANCE COMPANY — FOUNDED 1906 — MAIN OFFICE. There is a little light beyond the glass doors. Neff straightens up and walks heavily out of the elevator, across the reception room to the doors. He pushes them open. The night watchman stares after him morosely, works the lever, and the elevator doors start to close.

The twelfth-floor insurance office: (The insurance company occupies the entire eleventh and twelfth floors of the building. On the twelfth floor are the executive offices and claims and sales departments. These all open off a balcony which runs all the way around. From the balcony one can see the eleventh floor below: one enormous room filled with desks, typewriters, filing cabinets, business machines, etc.) Neff comes through the double entrance doors from the reception room. The twelfth floor is dark. Some light shines up from the eleventh floor. Neff takes a few steps then holds on to the balcony railing and looks down and we see:

The eleventh floor, from Neff's point of view. Two colored women are cleaning the offices. One is dry-mopping the floor, the other is moving chairs back into position. A colored man is emptying waste baskets into a big square box. He shuffles a little dance step as he moves, and hums a little tune.

Neff moves away from the railing with a faint smile on his face, and walks past two or three offices toward a glass door with number twenty-seven on it and three names: HENRY B. ANDERSON, WALTER NEFF, LOUIS L. SCHWARTZ. Neff opens the door.

Neff's office: Three desks, filing cabinets, one typewriter on a stand, one dictaphone on a fixed stand are against the wall with a rack of records underneath. There are telephones on all three desks. We see a water cooler with an inverted bottle and paper cup holder beside it. There are two windows facing toward the front of the building — venetian blinds, no curtains. The waste basket is full — ash trays unemptied. The office has not been cleaned.

Neff enters, switches on the desk lamp. He looks across at the dictaphone, goes heavily to it and lifts off the fabric cover. He leans down hard on the dictaphone stand as if feeling faint. Then he turns away, takes a few uncertain steps and falls heavily into a swivel chair. His head goes far back, his eyes close, cold sweat shows on his face. For a moment he stays like this, exhausted, then his eyes open slowly and look down at his left shoulder. His good hand flips the overcoat back; he unbuttons his jacket, loosens his tie and shirt. This was quite an effort. He rests for a second, breathing hard. With the help of his good hand he edges his left elbow up on the arm-rest of the chair, supports it there and then pulls his jacket wide. A heavy patch of dark blood shows on his shirt. He pushes his chair along the floor toward the water cooler, using his feet and his right hand against the desk, takes out a handkerchief, presses with his hand against the spring faucet of the cooler, soaks the handkerchief in water and tucks it, dripping wet, against the wound inside his shirt. Next, he gets a handful of water and splashes it on his face. The water runs down his chin and drips. He breathes heavily, with closed eyes. He fingers a pack of cigarettes in his shirt pocket, pulls it out, looks at it. There is blood on it. He wheels himself back to the desk and dumps the loose cigarettes out of the packet. Some are bloodstained, a few are clean. He takes one, puts it between his lips, gropes around for a match, then lights the cigarette. He takes a deep drag and lets smoke out through his nose.

He pulls himself toward the dictaphone again, still in the swivel chair, reaches it, lifts the horn off the bracket and the dictaphone makes a low buzzing sound. He presses the button switch on the horn. The sound stops, the record revolves on the cylinder. He begins to speak:

NEFF. Office memorandum, Walter Neff to Barton Keyes, Claims Manager. Los Angeles, July 16th, 1938. Dear Keyes: I suppose you'll call this a confession when you hear it. I don't like the word confession.

I just want to set you right about one thing you couldn't see, because it was smack up against your nose. You think you're such a hot potato as a claims manager, such a wolf on a phony claim. Well, maybe you are, Keyes, but let's take a look at this Dietrichson claim, Accident and Double Indemnity. You were pretty good in there for a while, all right. You said it wasn't an accident. Check. You said it wasn't suicide. Check. You said it was murder. Check and double check. You thought you had it cold, all wrapped up in tissue paper, with pink ribbons around it. It was perfect, except that it wasn't, because you made a mistake, just one tiny little mistake. When it came to picking the killer, you picked the wrong guy, if you know what I mean. Want to know who killed Dietrichson? Hold tight to that cheap cigar of yours, Keyes. I killed Dietrichson. Me, Walter Neff, insurance agent, thirty-five years old, unmarried, no visible scars — (*He glances down at his wounded shoulder.*) — until a little while ago, that is. Yes, I killed him. I killed him for money — and a woman — and I didn't get the money and I didn't get the woman. Pretty, isn't it?

He interrupts the dictation, lays down the horn on the desk. He takes his lighted cigarette from the ash tray, puffs it two or three times, and kills it. He picks up the horn again.

NEFF (*his voice now quiet and contained*). It all began last May. Around the end of May, it was. I'd been out to Glendale to deliver a policy on some dairy trucks. On the way back I remembered this auto renewal on Los Feliz Boulevard. So I drove over there.

As he goes on speaking, the scene slowly dissolves to the Dietrichson home in the Los Feliz district: Palm trees line the street of middle-class houses mostly in Spanish style. Some kids are throwing a baseball back and forth across a couple of front lawns. An ice cream wagon dawdles along the block. Neff's coupe meets and passes the ice cream wagon and stops before one of the Spanish houses. Neff gets out.

He carries a briefcase, his hat is a little on the back of his head. His movements are easy and full of ginger. He inspects the house, checks the number, goes up on the front porch and rings the bell.

NEFF'S VOICE (*synchronized with the scene*). It was one of those California Spanish houses everyone was nuts about ten or fifteen years ago. This one must have cost somebody about 30,000 bucks — that is, if he ever finished paying for it.

The Dietrichson home: We see the entrance door as Neff rings the bell again and waits. The door opens. A maid, about forty-five, rather slatternly, opens the door.

NEFF. Mr. Dietrichson in?
MAID. Who wants to see him?
NEFF. The name is Neff. Walter Neff.
MAID. If you're selling something —
NEFF. Look, it's Mr. Dietrichson I'd like to talk to, and it's not magazine subscriptions.

He pushes her into the house, and enters the hallway. It is "Spanish" in style, as is the house throughout. A wrought-iron staircase curves down from the second floor. A fringed Mexican shawl hangs down over the landing. A large tapestry hangs on the wall. Downstairs, the dining room to one side, living room on the other side are visible through a wide archway. All of this — architecture, furniture, decorations, etc. — is genuine early Leo Carrillo period. . . . Neff has edged his way in past the maid who still holds the door open.

MAID. Listen, Mr. Dietrichson's not in.
NEFF. How soon do you expect him?
MAID. He'll be home when he gets here, if that's any help to you.

At this point a woman's voice comes from the top of the stairs.

VOICE. What is it, Nettie? Who is it?

As Neff looks up, the scene cuts to the upper landing of the staircase, as seen from below. Phyllis Dietrichson, a blonde woman in her early thirties, stands there looking down. She holds a large bath-towel around her very appetizing torso, down to about two inches above her knees. Her legs are bare. She wears a pair of high-heeled bedroom slippers with pompons, on her left ankle a gold anklet.

MAID'S VOICE. It's for Mr. Dietrichson.
PHYLLIS (*looking down at Neff*). I'm Mrs. Dietrichson. What is it?

Neff looks up, and takes his hat off.

NEFF. How do you do, Mrs. Dietrichson. I'm Walter Neff, Pacific All-Risk.

Following this we see Phyllis and Neff alternately, each of them in the previous setting.

PHYLLIS. Pacific all-what?

NEFF. Pacific All-Risk Insurance Company. It's about some renewals on the automobiles, Mrs. Dietrichson. I've been trying to contact your husband for the past two weeks. He's never at his office.

PHYLLIS. Is there anything I can do?

NEFF. The insurance ran out on the fifteenth. I'd hate to think of your getting a smashed fender or something while you're not — uh — fully covered.

PHYLLIS (*glancing over her towel costume; with a little provocative smile*). Perhaps I know what you mean, Mr. Neff. I've just been taking a sun bath.

NEFF. No pigeons around, I hope. . . . About those policies, Mrs. Dietrichson — I hate to take up your time —

PHYLLIS. That's all right. If you can wait till I put something on, I'll be right down. Nettie, show Mr. Neff into the living room.

She turns away as gracefully as one can with a towel for a wrapper, following which the scene cuts to the entrance hall as Neff watches Phyllis out of sight. He speaks to the maid while still looking up.

NEFF. Where would the living room be?

MAID. In there, but they keep the liquor locked up.

NEFF. That's okay. I always carry my own keys.

He goes through the archway, while the maid goes off the other way, and the scene cuts to the living room, as the narrator's voice (that is, Neff's talking into the dictaphone) starts again:

NEFF'S VOICE (*synchronized with the scene*). The living room was still stuffy from last night's cigars. The windows were closed and the sunshine coming in through the venetian blinds showed up the dust in the air. The furniture was kind of corny and old-fashioned, but it had a comfortable look, as if people really sat in it. On the piano, in a couple of fancy frames, were Mr. Dietrichson and Lola, his daughter by his first wife. They had a bowl of those little red goldfish on the table behind the davenport, but, to tell you the truth, Keyes, I wasn't a whole lot interested in goldfish right then, nor in auto renewals, nor in Mr. Dietrichson and his daughter Lola. I was thinking about

that dame upstairs, and the way she had looked at me, and I wanted
to see her again, close, without that silly staircase between us.

Neff comes into the room and throws his briefcase on the plush
davenport and tosses his hat on top of it. He looks around the room,
then moves over to a baby grand piano with a sleazy Spanish shawl
dangling down one side and two cabinet photographs standing in a
staggered position on top. Neff glances them over: Mr. Dietrichson,
age about fifty-one, a big, blocky man with glasses and a Rotarian look
about him; Lola Dietrichson, age nineteen, wearing a filmy party dress
and a yearning look in her pretty eyes. Neff walks away from the
piano and takes a few steps back and forth across the rug. His eyes
fall on a wrinkled corner. He carefully straightens it out with his foot.
His back is to the archway as he hears high heels clicking on the
staircase. He turns and looks through the arch.

The scene cuts to the staircase, from Neff's point of view, as Phyllis
Dietrichson is coming downstairs. First we see her feet, with pompon
slippers and the gold anklet on her left ankle. Then the view pulls
back slowly as she descends, until we see all of her. She is wearing a
pale blue summer dress.

PHYLLIS' VOICE. I wasn't long, was I?

NEFF'S VOICE. Not at all, Mrs. Dietrichson.

PHYLLIS (*as the scene pulls back with her into the living room*). I hope
I've got my face on straight.

NEFF. It's perfect for my money.

PHYLLIS (*crossing to the mirror over the fireplace*). Won't you sit down,
Mr. — Neff is the name, isn't it?

NEFF. With two f's, like in Philadelphia, if you know the story.

PHYLLIS. What story?

NEFF. The Philadelphia story. What are we talking about?

PHYLLIS (*working with her lipstick*). About the insurance. My husband
never tells me anything.

NEFF. It's on your two cars, the LaSalle and the Plymouth.

He crosses to the davenport to get the policies from his briefcase.
She turns away from the mirror and sits in a big chair with her legs
drawn up sideways, the anklet now clearly visible.

NEFF. We've been handling this insurance for three years for Mr.
Dietrichson . . . (*His eyes have caught the anklet.*) That's a honey of an
anklet you're wearing, Mrs. Dietrichson. (*Phyllis smiles faintly and covers*

the anklet with her dress.) We'd hate to see the policies lapse. Of course, we give him thirty days. That's all we're allowed to give.

PHYLLIS. I guess he's been too busy down at Long Beach in the oil fields.

NEFF. Could I catch him home some evening for a few minutes?

PHYLLIS. I suppose so. But he's never home much before eight.

NEFF. That would be fine with me.

PHYLLIS. You're not connected with the Automobile Club, are you?

NEFF. No, the All-Risk, Mrs. Dietrichson. Why?

PHYLLIS. Somebody from the Automobile Club has been trying to get him. Do they have a better rate?

NEFF. If your husband's a member.

PHYLLIS. No, he isn't.

NEFF (*as Phyllis rises and walks up and down, paying less and less attention*). Well, he'd have to join the club and pay a membership fee to start with. The Automobile Club is fine. I never knock the other fellow's merchandise, Mrs. Dietrichson, but I can do just as well for you. I have a very attractive policy here. It wouldn't take me two minutes to put it in front of your husband. (*He consults the policies he is holding.*) For instance, we're writing a new kind of fifty percent retention feature in the collision coverage.

PHYLLIS (*stopping in her walk*). You're a smart insurance man, aren't you, Mr. Neff?

NEFF. I've had eleven years of it.

PHYLLIS. Doing pretty well?

NEFF. It's a living.

PHYLLIS. You handle just automobile insurance, or all kinds? (*She sits down again, in the same position as before.*)

NEFF. All kinds. Fire, earthquake, theft, public liability, group insurance, industrial stuff and so on right down the line.

PHYLLIS. Accident insurance?

NEFF. Accident insurance? Sure, Mrs. Dietrichson. (*His eyes fall on the anklet again.*) I wish you'd tell me what's engraved on that anklet.

PHYLLIS. Just my name.

NEFF. As for instance?

PHYLLIS. Phyllis.

NEFF. Phyllis. I think I like that.

PHYLLIS. But you're not sure?

NEFF. I'd have to drive it around the block a couple of times.

PHYLLIS (*standing up again*). Mr. Neff, why don't you drop by tomorrow evening about eight-thirty. He'll be in then.

NEFF. Who?

PHYLLIS. My husband. You were anxious to talk to him, weren't you?

NEFF. Sure, only I'm getting over it a little. If you know what I mean.

PHYLLIS. There's a speed limit in this state, Mr. Neff. Forty-five miles an hour.

NEFF. How fast was I going, officer?

PHYLLIS. I'd say about ninety.

NEFF. Suppose you get down off your motorcycle and give me a ticket.

PHYLLIS. Suppose I let you off with a warning this time.

NEFF. Suppose it doesn't take.

PHYLLIS. Suppose I have to whack you over the knuckles.

NEFF. Suppose I bust out crying and put my head on your shoulder.

PHYLLIS. Suppose you try putting it on my husband's shoulder.

NEFF. That tears it. (*Neff takes his hat and briefcase.*) Eight-thirty tomorrow evening then, Mrs. Dietrichson.

PHYLLIS. That's what I suggested.

As they both move toward the archway, the scene cuts to the hallway, and Phyllis and Neff are seen going toward the entrance door.

NEFF. Will you be here, too?

PHYLLIS. I guess so. I usually am.

NEFF. Same chair, same perfume, same anklet?

PHYLLIS (*opening the door*). I wonder if I know what you mean.

NEFF (*walking out*). I wonder if you wonder.

Outside the Dietrichson home, looking past Neff's parked car toward the entrance door, which is just closing: Neff comes toward the car, swinging his briefcase. He opens the car door and looks back with a confident smile. Next we see the entrance door, as the peep window in the upper panel opens and Phyllis looks out after him. Neff sits in his car and presses the starter button, looking back toward the little window in the entrance door, as the peep window is quickly closed from the inside. And then we see the street as Neff makes a U-turn and drives back down the block.

NEFF'S VOICE (*over the scene*). She liked me. I could feel that. The way you feel when the cards are falling right for you, with a nice little pile of blue and yellow chips in the middle of the table. Only what I didn't know then was that I wasn't playing her. She was playing me — with a deck of marked cards — and the stakes weren't any blue and yellow chips. They were dynamite. It was a hot afternoon and I can still remember the smell of honeysuckle all along that street. How could I have known that murder can sometimes smell like honeysuckle. Maybe you would have known, Keyes, the minute she mentioned accident insurance, but I didn't. I felt like a millionaire.

The scene dissolves to the insurance office on the twelfth floor. There is activity on the eleventh floor below: typewriters working, adding machines, filing clerks, secretaries, and so forth. Neff, wearing his hat and carrying his briefcase, enters from the vestibule. He walks toward his office. He passes a few salesmen. There is an exchange of greetings.

NEFF'S VOICE: I went back to the office to see if I had any mail. It was the day you had that truck driver from Inglewood on the carpet. Remember, Keyes?

Just as Neff reaches his office a secretary comes out. She stops.

SECRETARY. Oh, Mr. Neff, Mr. Keyes wants to see you. He's been yelling for you all afternoon.

NEFF. Is he sore, or just frothing at the mouth a little? Here, park these for me, sweetheart.

He hands her his hat and briefcase and the scene moves with him as he continues to a door lettered: BARTON KEYES — CLAIMS MANAGER. Keyes' voice is heard inside, quite loud. Neff grins as he opens the door and goes in. Then the scene cuts to Keyes' office: It is a minor executive office, not too tidy: a large desk across one corner, good carpet, several chairs, filing cabinet against one wall, a dictaphone on the corner of the desk. Keyes is sitting behind the desk with his coat off but his hat on. A cigar is clamped in his mouth, ashes falling like snow down his vest, a gold chain and elk's tooth across it. On the other side of the desk sits Sam Gorlopis. He is a big, dumb bruiser, six feet three inches tall — rough, untidy hair, broad face, small piggish eyes — wearing a dirty work shirt and corduroy pants. He holds a sweat-soaked hat on his knee with a hairy hand. He is chewing gum rapidly. As Neff opens the door, Keyes is giving it to Gorlopis, the truck driver.

KEYES. Come on, come on, Gorlopis. You're not kidding anybody with that line of bull. You're in a jam and you know it.

GORLOPIS. Sez you. All I want is my money.

KEYES. Sez you. All you're gonna get is the cops.

He sees Neff standing inside the door.

KEYES. Come in, Walter. This is Sam Gorlopis from Inglewood.

NEFF. Sure, I know Mr. Gorlopis. Wrote a policy on his truck. How are you, Mr. Gorlopis?

GORLOPIS. I ain't so good. My truck burned down. (*He looks sideways cautiously at Keyes.*)

KEYES. Yeah, he just planted his big foot on the starter and the whole thing blazed up in his face.

GORLOPIS. Yes, sir.

KEYES. And didn't even singe his eyebrows.

GORLOPIS. No sir. Look, mister. I got twenty-six hundred bucks tied up in that truck. I'm insured with this company and I want my money.

KEYES. You got a wife, Gorlopis?

GORLOPIS. Sure I got a wife.

KEYES. You got kids?

GORLOPIS. Two kids.

KEYES. What you got for dinner tonight?

GORLOPIS. We got meat loaf.

KEYES. How do you make your meat loaf, Gorlopis?

GORLOPIS. Veal and pork and bread and garlic. Greek style.

KEYES. How much garlic?

GORLOPIS. Lotsa garlic, Mr. Keyes.

KEYES. Okay, Gorlopis. Now listen here. Let's say you just came up here to tell me how to make meat loaf. That's all, understand? Because if you came up here to claim on that truck, I'd have to turn you over to the law, Gorlopis, and they'd put you in jail. No wife. No kids —

GORLOPIS. What for?

KEYES (*yelling*). — And no meat loaf, Gorlopis!

GORLOPIS. I didn't do nothin'.

KEYES. Yeah? Now, look, Gorlopis. Every month hundreds of claims come to this desk. Some of them are phonies, and I know which ones. How do I know, Gorlopis? (*He speaks as if to a child.*) Because my little man tells me.

GORLOPIS. What little man?

KEYES. The little man in here. (*He pounds the pit of his stomach.*) Every time one of those phonies comes along he ties knots in my stomach. And yours was one of them, Gorlopis. That's how I knew your claim was crooked. So what did I do? I sent a tow car out to your garage this afternoon and they jacked up that burned-out truck of yours. And what did they find, Gorlopis? They found what was left of a neat pile of shavings.

GORLOPIS. What shavings?

KEYES. The ones you soaked with kerosene and dropped a match on.

GORLOPIS (*cringing under the impact*). Look, Mr. Keyes, I'm just a poor man. Maybe I made a mistake.

KEYES. Well, that's one way of putting it.

GORLOPIS (*starting to leave*). I ain't feelin' so good, Mr. Keyes.

KEYES. Here, just a minute. Sign this and you'll feel fine. (*He puts a blank form in front of him and points.*) Right there. It's a waiver on your claim. (*Gorlopis hesitates, then signs laboriously.*) Now you're an honest man again.

GORLOPIS. But I ain't got no more truck.

KEYES. Goodbye, Gorlopis.

GORLOPIS (*still bewildered*). Goodbye, Mr. Keyes. (*He stands up and goes slowly to the door and turns there.*) Twenty-six hundred bucks. That's a lot of dough where I live.

KEYES. What's the matter, Gorlopis? Don't you know how to open the door? Just put your hand on the knob, turn it to the right, now pull it toward you —

GORLOPIS (*doing just as Keyes says*). Like this, Mr. Keyes?

KEYES. That's the boy. Now the same thing from the outside.

GORLOPIS (*stupefied*). Thank you, Mr. Keyes.

He goes out, closing the door after him. Keyes takes his cigar stub from his mouth and turns it slowly in the flame of a lighted match. He turns to Neff.

KEYES. What kind of an outfit is this anyway? Are we an insurance company, or a bunch of dimwitted amateurs, writing a policy on a mugg like that?

NEFF. Wait a minute, Keyes. I don't rate this beef. I clipped a note to that Gorlopis application to have him thoroughly investigated before we accepted the risk.

KEYES. I know you did, Walter. I'm not beefing at you. It's the company. The way they do things. The way they don't do things. The way they'll write anything just to get it down on the sales sheet. And I'm the guy that has to sit here up to my neck in phony claims so they won't throw more money out of the window than they take in at the door.

NEFF (*grinning*). Okay, turn the record over and let's hear the other side.

KEYES. I get darn sick of picking up after a gang of fast-talking salesmen dumb enough to sell life insurance to a guy that sleeps in the same bed with four rattlesnakes. I've had twenty-six years of that, Walter, and I —

NEFF. And you loved every minute of it, Keyes. You love it, only you worry about it too much, you and your little man. You're so darn conscientious you're driving yourself crazy. You wouldn't even say today is Tuesday without you looked at the calendar, and then you would check if it was this year's or last year's calendar, and then you would find out what company printed the calendar, then find out if their calendar checks with the World Almanac's calendar.

KEYES. That's enough from you, Walter. Get out of here before I throw my desk at you.

NEFF. I love you, too.

He walks out, still grinning, and we next see the exterior of the offices. Neff comes out of Keyes' office and walks back along the balcony, where there is great activity of secretaries going in and out of doors. Neff enters his own office. Anderson, a salesman, is sitting at one of the desks, filling out a report. Neff goes to his own desk. He looks down at some mail. On top there is a typewritten note. He reads it, sits down, and leafs through his desk calendar.

We get a closeup of a calendar page showing the date:

THURSDAY

23
May

and five or six appointments pencilled in tightly on the page.

NEFF'S VOICE (*over the scene*). I really did, too, you old crab, always yelling your fat head off, always sore at everyone. But behind the cigar ashes on your vest I kind of knew you had a heart as big as a house . . . Back in my office there was a phone message from Mrs. Dietrichson about the renewals. She didn't want me to come tomorrow evening. She wanted me to come Thursday afternoon at three-thirty instead. I had a lot of stuff lined up for that Thursday afternoon, including a trip down to Santa Monica to see a couple of live prospects about some group insurance. But I kept thinking about Phyllis Dietrichson and the way that anklet of hers cut into her leg.

The entrance hall of the Dietrichson home fades in. There is a moving view of Phyllis Dietrichson's feet and ankles as she comes down the stairs, her high heels clicking on the tiles. The anklet glistens on her leg as she moves. Phyllis reaches the entrance hall, and as she walks toward the front door her whole body becomes visible. She wears a gay print dress with a wide sash over her hips. She opens the door. Outside is Neff, wearing a sport coat and flannel slacks. He takes his hat off.

PHYLLIS. Hello, Mr. Neff. (*As he stands there with a little smile*) Aren't you coming in?

NEFF (*starting to go inside*). I'm considering it.

PHYLLIS. I hope you didn't mind my changing the appointment. Last night wasn't so convenient.

NEFF. That's okay. I was working on my stamp collection.

Phyllis leads Neff toward the living room, and they go in through the archway. She then heads toward the davenport, in front of which is a low tea table holding tall glasses, ice cubes, lemon, and a pot of tea.

PHYLLIS. I was just fixing some iced tea. Would you like a glass?

NEFF. Unless you have a bottle of beer that's not working.

PHYLLIS. There might be some. I never know what's in the ice box. (*Calling*) Nettie! . . . (*She pours herself a glass of tea.*) About those renewals, Mr. Neff. I talked to my husband about it.

NEFF. You did?

PHYLLIS. Yes. He'll renew with you, he told me. In fact, I thought he'd be here this afternoon.

NEFF. But he's not?

PHYLLIS. No.

NEFF. That's terrible.

PHYLLIS (*calling again, impatiently*). Nettie! . . . *Nettie!* . . . Oh, I forgot, it's the maid's day off.

NEFF. Don't bother, Mrs. Dietrichson. I'd like some iced tea very much.

PHYLLIS. Lemon? Sugar?

NEFF. Fix it your way.

She fixes him a glass of tea while he looks around. He sits down slowly. (We see them together and separately in close shots throughout the conversation.)

NEFF. Seeing it's the maid's day off maybe there's something I can do for you. (*As she hands him the tea*) Like running the vacuum cleaner.

PHYLLIS. Fresh.

NEFF. I used to peddle vacuum cleaners. Not much money but you learn a lot about life.

PHYLLIS. I didn't think you'd learned it from a correspondence course.

NEFF. Where did you pick up this tea drinking? You're not English, are you?

PHYLLIS. No. Californian. Born right here in Los Angeles.

NEFF. They say native Californians all come from Iowa.

PHYLLIS. I wanted to ask you something, Mr. Neff.

NEFF. Make it Walter.

PHYLLIS. Walter?

NEFF. That's right.

PHYLLIS. Tell me, Walter, on this insurance — how much commission do you make?

NEFF. Twenty percent. Why?

PHYLLIS. I thought maybe I could throw a little more business your way.

NEFF. I can always use it.

PHYLLIS. I was thinking about my husband. I worry a lot about him, down in those oil fields. It's very dangerous.

NEFF. Not for an executive, is it?

PHYLLIS. He doesn't just sit behind a desk. He's right down there with the drilling crews. It's got me worried sick.

NEFF. You mean a crown block might fall on him some rainy night?

PHYLLIS. Please don't talk like that.

NEFF. But that's the idea.

PHYLLIS. The other day a casing line snapped and caught the foreman. He's in the hospital with a broken back.

NEFF. Bad.

PHYLLIS. It's got me jittery just thinking about it. Suppose something like that happened to my husband?

NEFF. It could.

PHYLLIS. Don't you think he ought to have accident insurance?

NEFF. Uh-huh.

PHYLLIS. What kind of insurance could he have?

NEFF. Enough to cover doctors' and hospital bills. Say a hundred and twenty-five a week cash benefit. And he'd rate around fifty thousand capital sum.

PHYLLIS. Capital sum? What's that?

NEFF. In case he gets killed. Maybe I shouldn't have said that.

PHYLLIS. I suppose you have to think of everything in your business.

NEFF. Well, your husband would understand. I'm sure I could sell him on the idea of some accident protection. Why don't I talk to him about it?

PHYLLIS. You could try. But he's pretty tough going.

NEFF. They're all tough at first.

PHYLLIS. He has a lot on his mind. He doesn't want to listen to anything except maybe a baseball game on the radio. Sometimes we sit all evening without saying a word to each other.

NEFF. Sounds pretty dull.

PHYLLIS (*shrugging*). So I just sit and knit.

NEFF. Is that what you married him for?

PHYLLIS. Maybe I like the way his thumbs hold up the wool.

NEFF. Any time his thumbs get tired — only with me around you wouldn't have to knit.

PHYLLIS. Wouldn't I?

NEFF. You bet your life you wouldn't. (*After taking a sip of the iced tea*) I wonder if a little rum would get this up on its feet!

PHYLLIS. I want to ask you something, Walter. Could I get an accident policy for him — without bothering him at all?

NEFF. How's that again?

PHYLLIS. That would make it easier for you, too. You wouldn't even have to talk to him. I have a little allowance of my own. I could pay for it and he needn't know anything about it.

NEFF. Why shouldn't he know?

PHYLLIS. Because he doesn't want accident insurance. He's superstitious about it.

NEFF. A lot of people are. Funny, isn't it?

PHYLLIS. If there was a way to get it like that, all the worry would be over. You see what I mean, Walter?

NEFF. Sure. I've got good eyesight. You want him to have the policy without him knowing it. And that means without the insurance company knowing that he doesn't know. That's the set-up, isn't it?

PHYLLIS. Is there anything wrong with it?

NEFF. No, I think it's lovely. And then, some dark wet night, if that crown block did fall on him —

PHYLLIS. What crown block?

NEFF. Only sometimes they have to have a little help. They can't quite make it on their own.

PHYLLIS. I don't know what you're talking about.

NEFF. Of course, it doesn't have to be a crown block. It can be a car backing over him, or he can fall out of an upstairs window. Any little thing like that, as long as it's a morgue job.

PHYLLIS. Are you crazy?

NEFF. Not that crazy. Goodbye, Mrs. Dietrichson. (*He picks up his hat.*)

PHYLLIS (*jumping up*). What's the matter?

NEFF (*starting to leave*). Look, baby, you can't get away with it.

PHYLLIS. Get away with what?

NEFF. You want to knock him off, don't you, baby.

PHYLLIS. That's a horrible thing to say!

NEFF. What'd you think I was, anyway? A guy that walks into a good-looking dame's front parlor and says "Good afternoon, I sell accident insurance on husbands. You got one that's been around too long? Somebody you'd like to turn into a little hard cash? Just give me a smile and I'll help you collect." Boy, what a dope you must think I am.

PHYLLIS. I think you're rotten.

NEFF. I think you're swell. So long as I'm not your husband.

PHYLLIS. Get out of here.

NEFF. You bet I will. You bet I'll get out of here, baby. But quick. (*He goes out.*)

She looks after him and we then see the outside of the Dietrichson house, Neff's voice coming over this, as he talks into the dictaphone.

NEFF'S VOICE (*over the scene*). So I let her have it, straight between the eyes. She didn't fool me for a minute, not this time. I knew I had hold of a red-hot poker and the time to drop it was before it burned my hand off. I stopped at a drive-in for a bottle of beer, the one I had wanted all along, only I wanted it worse now, to get rid of the sour taste of her iced tea, and everything that went with it. I didn't want to go back to the office, so I dropped by a bowling alley at Third and Western and rolled a few lines to get my mind thinking about something else for a while.

As Neff bangs the front door shut, walks quickly to his car and drives away, the scene dissolves to the drive-in of a restaurant, "shooting" past Neff sitting behind the wheel of his car. The car hop hangs a tray on the door and serves him a bottle of beer. This dissolves to the interior of a bowling alley where Neff is bowling. He rolls the ball with an effort at concentration, but his mind is not really on the game. This dissolves to the exterior of an apartment house. It is late afternoon. The apartment house is called the Los Olivos Apartments. It is a six-story building in the Normandie-Wilshire district, with a basement garage. The view moves up the front of the building to the top floor windows, as a little rain starts to fall.

NEFF'S VOICE (*continuing*). I didn't feel like eating dinner when I left, and I didn't feel like a show, so I drove home, put the car away and went up to my apartment.

We now see the living room of Neff's apartment at dusk. It is a double apartment of conventional design, with kitchen, dinette, and bathroom, square-cut overstuffed borax furniture. Gas logs are lit in the imitation fireplace. Neff stands by the window with his coat off and his tie loose. Raindrops strike against the glass. He turns away impatiently, paces up and down past a caddy bag with golf clubs in it, pulls one out at random, makes a couple of short swings, throws the club on the couch, and paces again.

NEFF'S VOICE (*continuing*). It had begun to rain outside and I watched it get dark and didn't even turn on the light. That didn't help me either. I was all twisted up inside, and I was still holding on to that red-hot poker. And right then it came over me that I hadn't walked out on anything at all, that the hook was too strong, that this wasn't the end between her and me. It was only the beginning. So at eight o'clock the bell would ring and I would know who it was without even having to think, as if it was the most natural thing in the world.

The doorbell rings. Neff goes to the door and opens it, revealing Phyllis standing there.

PHYLLIS. Hello. (*As Neff just looks at her in amazement*) You forgot your hat this afternoon. (*She has nothing in her hands but her bag.*)

NEFF. Did I? (*He looks down at her hands.*)

PHYLLIS. Don't you want me to bring it in?

NEFF. Sure. Put it on the chair. (*She comes in. He closes the door.*) How did you know where I live?

PHYLLIS. It's in the phone book. (*Neff switches on the standing lamp.*) It's raining.

NEFF. So it is. Peel off your coat and sit down. (*She starts to take off her coat.*) Your husband out?

PHYLLIS. Long Beach. They're spudding in a new well. He phoned he'd be late. About nine-thirty. (*He takes her coat and lays it across the back of a chair.*) It's about time you said you're glad to see me.

NEFF. I knew you wouldn't leave it like that.

PHYLLIS. Like what?

NEFF. Like it was this afternoon.

PHYLLIS. I must have said something that gave you a terribly wrong impression. You must surely see that. You must never think anything like that about me, Walter.

NEFF. Okay.

PHYLLIS. It's not okay. Not if you don't believe me.

NEFF. What do you want me to do?

PHYLLIS. I want you to be nice to me. Like the first time you came to the house.

NEFF. It can't be like the first time. Something has happened.

PHYLLIS. I know it has. It's happened to us.

NEFF. That's what I mean.

Phyllis has moved over to the window. She stares out through the wet windowpane.

NEFF. What's the matter now?

PHYLLIS. I feel as if he was watching me. Not that he cares about me. Not any more. But he keeps me on a leash. So tight I can't breathe. I'm scared.

NEFF. What of? He's in Long Beach, isn't he?

PHYLLIS. I oughtn't to have come.

NEFF. Maybe you oughtn't.

PHYLLIS. You want me to go?

NEFF. If you want to.

PHYLLIS. Right now?

NEFF. Sure. Right now.

By this time, he has hold of her wrists. He draws her to him slowly and kisses her. Her arms tighten around him. After a moment he pulls his head back, still holding her close. Then they break away from each other, and she puts her head on his shoulder.

NEFF. I'm crazy about you, baby.

PHYLLIS. I'm crazy about you, Walter.

NEFF. That perfume on your hair. What's the name of it?

PHYLLIS. I don't know. I bought it down at Ensenada.

NEFF. We ought to have some of that pink wine to go with it. The kind that bubbles. But all I have is bourbon.
PHYLLIS. Bourbon is fine, Walter.

He lets her go and moves toward the dinette. We then see the dinette and kitchen, which contains a small table and some chairs. A low glass-and-china cabinet is built betweeen the dinette and kitchen, leaving a space like a doorway. The kitchen is the usual apartment house kitchen, with stove, ice-box, sink, etc. It is quite small. Neff goes to the ice-box and Phyllis drifts in after him.

NEFF. Soda?
PHYLLIS. Plain water, please.
NEFF. Get a couple of glasses, will you.

He points at the china closet. He has taken a tray of ice cubes from the refrigerator and is holding it under the hot-water faucet.

NEFF. You know, about six months ago a guy slipped on the soap in his bathtub and knocked himself out cold and drowned. Only he had accident insurance. So they had an autopsy and she didn't get away with it.

Phyllis has the glasses now. She hands them to him. He dumps some ice cubes into the glasses.

PHYLLIS. Who didn't?
NEFF. His wife. (*He reaches for the whiskey bottle on top of the china closet.*) And there was a case of a guy found shot and his wife said he was cleaning a gun and his stomach got in the way. All she collected was a three-to-ten stretch in Tehachapi.
PHYLLIS. Perhaps it was worth it to her.

Neff hands her a glass.

NEFF. See if you can carry this as far as the living room. (*They move back toward the living room.*)

The living room as Phyllis and Neff go toward the davenport: she is sipping her drink and looking around.

PHYLLIS. It's nice here, Walter. Who takes care of it for you?

NEFF. A colored woman comes in twice a week.

PHYLLIS. You get your own breakfast?

NEFF. Once in a while I squeeze a grapefruit. The rest I get at the corner drugstore. (They sit on the davenport, fairly close together.)

PHYLLIS. It sounds wonderful. Just strangers beside you. You don't know them. You don't hate them. You don't have to sit across the table and smile at him and that daughter of his every morning of your life.

NEFF. What daughter? Oh, that little girl on the piano.

PHYLLIS. Yes. Lola. She lives with us. He thinks a lot more of her than he does of me.

NEFF. Ever think of a divorce?

PHYLLIS. He wouldn't give me a divorce.

NEFF. I suppose because it would cost him money.

PHYLLIS. He hasn't got any money. Not since he went into the oil business.

NEFF. But he had when you married him?

PHYLLIS. Yes, he had. And I wanted a home. Why not? But that wasn't the only reason. I was his wife's nurse. She was sick for a long time. When she died, he was all broken up. I pitied him so.

NEFF. And now you hate him.

PHYLLIS. Yes, Walter. He's so mean to me. Every time I buy a dress or a pair of shoes he yells his head off. He won't let me go anywhere. He keeps me shut up. He's always been mean to me. Even his life insurance all goes to that daughter of his. That Lola.

NEFF. Nothing for you at all, huh?

PHYLLIS. No. And nothing is just what I'm worth to him.

NEFF. So you lie awake in the dark and listen to him snore and get ideas.

PHYLLIS. Walter, I don't want to kill him. I never did. Not even when he gets drunk and slaps my face.

NEFF. Only sometimes you wish he was dead.

PHYLLIS. Perhaps I do.

NEFF. And you wish it was an accident, and you had that policy. For fifty thousand dollars. Is that it?

PHYLLIS. Perhaps that too. (*She takes a long drink.*) The other night we drove home from a party. He was drunk again. When we got into the garage he just sat there with his head on the steering wheel and the motor still running. And I thought what it would be like if I didn't switch it off, just closed the garage door and left him there.

NEFF. I'll tell you what it would be like, if you had that accident policy, and tried to pull a monoxide job. We have a guy in our office named Keyes. For him a set-up like that would be just like a slice of rare roast beef. In three minutes he'd know it wasn't an accident. In ten minutes you'd be sitting under the hot lights. In half an hour you'd be signing your name to a confession.

PHYLLIS. But, Walter, I didn't do it. I'm not going to do it.

NEFF. Not if there's an insurance company in the picture, baby. So long as you're honest they'll pay you with a smile, but you just try to pull something like that and you'll find out. They know more tricks than a carload of monkeys. And if there's a death mixed up in it, you haven't got a prayer. They'll hang you as sure as ten dimes will buy a dollar, baby. (*She begins to cry, and he puts his arms around her and kisses her.*) Just stop thinking about it, will you.

He holds her tight. Their heads touch, side by side, as the scene slowly starts to recede and then dissolves to Neff's office at night. Neff is sitting in the swivel chair, talking into the dictaphone. He has hooked the wastebasket under his feet to sit more comfortably. As he talks, a little cough shakes him now and then.

NEFF. So we just sat there, and she kept on crying softly, like the rain on the window, and we didn't say anything. Maybe she had stopped thinking about it, but I hadn't. I couldn't. Because it all tied up with something I had been thinking about for years, since long before I ever ran into Phyllis Dietrichson. Because, in this business you can't sleep for trying to figure out the tricks they could pull on you. You're like the guy behind the roulette wheel, watching the customers to make sure they don't crook the house. And then one night, you get to thinking how you could crook the house yourself. And do it smart. Because you've got that wheel right under your hands. And you know every notch in it by heart. And you figure all you need is a plant out in front, a shill to put down the bet. And suddenly the doorbell rings and the whole set-up is right there in the room with you . . . Look, Keyes, I'm not trying to whitewash myself. I fought it, only maybe I didn't fight it hard enough. The stakes were fifty thousand dollars, but they were the life of a man, too, a man who'd never done me any dirt. Except he was married to a woman he didn't care anything about, and I did . . .

The scene dissolves back to Neff's living room and the view moves slowly toward the davenport again. Neff sits in one corner with his feet on the low table. He is smoking his cigarette and staring at the ceiling. Phyllis has been sitting fairly close to him. She gets up slowly and crosses to her raincoat, lying over the chair.

PHYLLIS. I've got to go now, Walter. (*Neff does not answer. He keeps on staring at the ceiling. She starts to put the raincoat on.*) Will you phone me, Walter? (*As Neff still does not answer*) Walter! (*He looks at her slowly, almost absently.*) I hate him. I loathe going back to him. You believe me, don't you, Walter?

NEFF. Sure I believe you.

PHYLLIS. I can't stand it anymore. What if they did hang me?

NEFF. You're not going to hang, baby —

PHYLLIS. It's better than going on this way.

NEFF. — you're not going to hang, baby. Not ever. Because you're going to do it the smart way. Because I'm going to help you.

PHYLLIS. You!

NEFF. Me.

PHYLLIS. Do you know what you're saying?

NEFF. Sure I know what I'm saying.

He gets up and grips her arm.

NEFF. We're going to do it together. We're going to do it right. And I'm the guy that knows how.

There is fierce determination in his voice. His fingers dig into her arm.

PHYLLIS. Walter, you're hurting me.

NEFF. There isn't going to be any slip-up. Nothing sloppy. Nothing weak. It's got to be perfect. (*He kisses her.*) You go now. (*He leads her toward the door.*) Call me tomorrow. But not from your house. From a booth. And watch your step. Every single minute. It's got to be perfect, understand. Straight down the line.

They have now reached the door. Neff opens it. Phyllis stands in the doorway, her lips white.

PHYLLIS. Straight down the line.

She goes quietly. He watches her down the corridor. Slowly he closes the door and goes back into the room. He moves across to the window and opens it wide. He stands there, looking down into the dark street. From below comes the sound of a car starting and driving off. The rain drifts in against his face. He just stands there motionless. His mind is going a hundred miles a minute, and the scene fades out.

NEFF'S VOICE (*synchronized with the scene*). That was it, Keyes. The machinery had started to move and nothing could stop it.

PART TWO

NEFF'S OFFICE fades in at night. Neff sits slumped in his chair before the dictaphone. On the desk next to him stands a used record. The cylinder on the dictaphone is not turning. He is smoking a cigarette. He puts it down, then lifts the needle and slides off the record which is on the machine and stands it on end on the desk beside the other used record. He reaches down painfully to take another record from the rack beneath the dictaphone, looks at it against the light to make sure it has not been used, then slides it into place on the machine and resets the needle. He lifts the horn and resumes his dictation.

NEFF. The first thing we had to do was to fix him up with that accident policy. I knew he wouldn't buy, but all I wanted was his signature on an application. So I had to make him sign without his knowing what he was signing. And I wanted a witness other than Phyllis to hear me give him the sales talk. I was trying to think with your brains, Keyes. I wanted all the answers ready for all the questions you were going to spring as soon as Dietrichson was dead.

Neff takes a last drag on his cigarette and kills it by running it under the ledge of the dictaphone stand. He drops the stub on the floor and resumes.

NEFF. A couple of nights later I went to the house. Everything looked fine, except I didn't like the witness Phyllis had brought in. It was Dietrichson's daughter Lola, and it made me feel a little queer in the belly to have her right there in the room, playing Chinese checkers, as if nothing was going to happen.

This dissolves to a board of Chinese checkers. The view then moves back and gradually reveals the Dietrichson living room at night. The checkerboard is on the davenport between Phyllis and Lola. Mr. Dietrichson sits in a big easy chair. His coat and tie are over the back of the chair, and the evening paper is lying tumbled on the floor beside him. He is smoking a cigar with the band on it. He has a drink in front of him and several more inside him. In another chair sits Neff, his briefcase on the floor, leaning against his chair. He holds his rate book partly open, with a finger in it for a marker. He is going full swing.

NEFF. I suppose you realize, Mr. Dietrichson, that, not being an employee, you are not covered by the State Compensation Insurance Act. The only way you can protect yourself is by having a personal policy of your own.

DIETRICHSON. I know all about that. The next thing you'll tell me I need earthquake insurance and lightning insurance and hail insurance.

Phyllis looks up from the checkerboard and cuts in on the dialogue. Lola listens without much interest.

PHYLLIS (*to Dietrichson*). If we bought all the insurance they can think up, we'd stay broke paying for it, wouldn't we, honey?

DIETRICHSON. What keeps us broke is you going out and buying five hats at a crack. Who needs a hat in California?

NEFF. I always say insurance is a lot like a hot water bottle. It looks kind of useless and silly hanging on a hook, but when you get that stomachache in the middle of the night, it comes in mighty handy.

DIETRICHSON. Now you want to sell me a hot water bottle.

NEFF. Dollar for dollar, accident insurance is the cheapest coverage you can buy, Mr. Dietrichson.

DIETRICHSON. Maybe some other time, Mr. Neff. I had a tough day.

NEFF. Just as you say, Mr. Dietrichson.

DIETRICHSON. Suppose we just settle that automobile insurance tonight.

NEFF. Sure. All we need on that is for you to sign an application for renewal.

Phyllis throws a quick glance at Neff. As she looks back she sees that Lola is staring down at her wristwatch.

LOLA. Phyllis, do you mind if we don't finish this game? It bores me stiff.

PHYLLIS. Got something better to do?

LOLA (*getting up*). Yes, I have. (*To Dietrichson*) Father, is it all right if I run along now?

DIETRICHSON. Run along where? Who with?

LOLA. Just Anne. We're going roller skating.

DIETRICHSON. Anne who?

LOLA. Anne Matthews.

PHYLLIS. It's not that Nino Zachette again?

DIETRICHSON. It better not be that Zachette guy. If I ever catch you with him —

LOLA. It's Anne Matthews, I told you. I also told you we're going roller skating. I'm meeting her at the corner of Vermont and Franklin — the northwest corner, in case you're interested. And I'm late already. I hope that is all clear. Good night, father. Good night, Phyllis. (*She starts to go.*)

NEFF. Good night, Miss Dietrichson.

LOLA. Oh, I'm sorry. Good night, Mr. —

NEFF. Neff.

LOLA. Good night, Mr. Neff.

PHYLLIS. Now you're not going to take my car again.

LOLA. No thanks. I'd rather be dead. (*She goes out through the archway.*)

DIETRICHSON. A great little fighter for her weight.

Dietrichson sucks down a big swallow of his drink. Neff has taken two blank forms from his briefcase. He puts the briefcase on Mr. Dietrichson's lap and lays the forms on top. Phyllis is watching closely.

NEFF. This is where you sign, Mr. Dietrichson.

DIETRICHSON. Sign what?

NEFF. The applications for your auto renewals. So you'll be protected until the new policies are issued.

DIETRICHSON. When will that be?

NEFF. In about a week.

DIETRICHSON. Just so I'm covered when I drive up North.

Neff takes out his fountain pen.

NEFF. San Francisco, Mr. Dietrichson?

DIETRICHSON. Palo Alto.

PHYLLIS. He was a Stanford man, Mr. Neff. And he still goes to his class reunion every year.

DIETRICHSON. What's wrong with that? Can't I have a little fun even once a year?

NEFF. Great football school, Stanford. Did you play football, Mr. Dietrichson?

DIETRICHSON. Left guard. Almost made the varsity, too.

Neff has unscrewed his fountain pen. He hands it to Mr. Dietrichson. Dietrichson puts on his glasses.

NEFF. On that bottom line, Mr. Dietrichson. (*Dietrichson signs. Neff's and Phyllis' eyes meet for a split second.*) Both copies, please.

He withdraws the top copy barely enough to expose the signature line on the supposed duplicate.

DIETRICHSON. Sign twice, huh?

NEFF. One is the agent's copy. I need it for my files.

DIETRICHSON (*in a mutter*). Files. Duplicates. Triplicates.

Dietrichson grunts and signs again. Again Neff and Phyllis exchange a quick glance.

NEFF. No hurry about the check, Mr. Dietrichson. I can pick it up at your office some morning. (*Casually Neff lifts the briefcase and signed applications off Dietrichson's lap.*)

DIETRICHSON. How much you taking me for?

NEFF. One forty-seven fifty, Mr. Dietrichson.

Dietrichson stands up. He is about Neff's height but a little heavier.

PHYLLIS. I guess that's enough insurance for one evening, Mr. Neff.

DIETRICHSON. Plenty.

Dietrichson has poured some more whiskey into his glass. He tries the siphon but it is empty. He gathers up his coat and tie and picks up his glass.

DIETRICHSON. Good night, Mr. Neff.

NEFF (*zipping up his briefcase*). Good night, Mr. Dietrichson. Good night, Mrs. Dietrichson.

DIETRICHSON. Bring me some soda when you come up, Phyllis. (*Dietrichson trundles off toward the archway.*)

PHYLLIS (*to Neff*). I think you left your hat in the hall.

Phyllis leads the way and Neff goes after her, his briefcase under his arm. The scene then cuts to the hallway of the Dietrichson residence as Phyllis enters through the living room archway with Neff behind her. She leads him toward the door. On the way he picks up his hat. In the background Dietrichson begins to ascend the stairs, carrying his coat and glass. Phyllis and Neff move close to the door. They speak in very low voices.

PHYLLIS. All right, Walter?
NEFF. Fine.
PHYLLIS. He signed it, didn't he?
NEFF. Sure he signed it. You saw him.

Phyllis opens the door a crack. Both look at the stairs, where Dietrichson is going up. Phyllis takes her hand off the doorknob and holds on to Neff's arm.

NEFF (*looking up*). Watch it, will you.

Phyllis slowly drops her hand from his arm. Both look up as Dietrichson goes across the balcony and out of sight.

NEFF. Listen. That trip to Palo Alto. When does he go?
PHYLLIS. End of the month.
NEFF. He drives, huh?
PHYLLIS. He always drives.
NEFF. Not this time. You're going to make him take the train.
PHYLLIS. Why?
NEFF. Because it's all worked out for a train.

For a second they stand listening and looking up as if they had heard a sound.

PHYLLIS. It's all right. Go on, Walter.
NEFF. Look, baby. There's a clause in every accident policy, a little something called double indemnity. The insurance companies put it in as a sort of come-on for the customers. It means they pay double on certain accidents. The kind that almost never happen. Like for instance if a guy got killed on a train, they'd pay a hundred thousand instead of fifty.
PHYLLIS. I see. (*Her eyes widen with excitement.*)

NEFF. We're hitting it for the limit, baby. That's why it's got to be a train.

PHYLLIS. It's going to be a train, Walter. Just the way you say. Straight down the line.

They look at each other. The look is like a long kiss. Neff goes out. Slowly Phyllis closes the door and leans her head against it as she looks up the empty stairway.

Outside the Dietrichson residence: Neff, briefcase under his arm, comes down the steps to the street, where his Dodge coupe is parked at the curb. He opens the door and stops, looking in. Sitting there in the dark corner of the car, away from the steering wheel, is Lola. She wears a coat but no hat.

LOLA. Hello, Mr. Neff. It's me. (*She gives him a sly smile.*)

NEFF (*a little annoyed*). Something the matter?

LOLA. I've been waiting for you.

NEFF. For me? What for?

LOLA. I thought you could let me ride with you, if you're going my way.

NEFF (*who doesn't like the idea very much*). Which way would that be?

LOLA. Down the hill. Down Vermont.

NEFF (*remembering*). Oh, sure. Vermont and Franklin. Northwest corner, wasn't it? Be glad to, Miss Dietrichson.

As Neff gets into the car, the scene cuts to the interior of the coupe; Neff puts the briefcase on the ledge behind the driver's seat. He closes the door and starts the car. They drift down the hill.

NEFF. Roller skating, eh? You like roller skating?

LOLA. I can take it or leave it. (*Neff looks at her curiously, and Lola meets his glance.*)

NEFF. Only tonight you're leaving it?

(*This is an embarrassing moment for Lola.*)

LOLA. Yes, I am. You see, Mr. Neff, I'm having a very tough time at home. My father doesn't understand me and Phyllis hates me.

NEFF. That does sound tough, all right.

LOLA. That's why I have to lie sometimes.

NEFF. You mean it's not Vermont and Franklin.

LOLA. It's Vermont and Franklin all right. Only it's not Anne Matthews. It's Nino Zachette. You won't tell on me, will you?

NEFF. I'd have to think it over.

LOLA. Nino's not what father says at all. He just had bad luck. He was doing pre-med at U.S.C. and working nights as an usher in a theatre downtown. He got behind in his credits and flunked out. Then he lost his job for talking back. He's so hot-headed.

NEFF. That comes expensive, doesn't it?

LOLA. I guess my father thinks nobody's good enough for his daughter except maybe the guy that owns Standard Oil. Would you like a stick of gum?

NEFF. Never use it, thanks.

LOLA (*putting a stick of gum in her mouth*). I can't give Nino up. I wish father could see it my way.

NEFF. It'll straighten out all right, Miss Dietrichson.

LOLA. I suppose it will sometime. (*Looking out*) This is the corner right here, Mr. Neff. (*As Neff brings the car to a stop by the curb*) There he is. By the bus stop.

As Neff looks out, the scene cuts to the corner of Vermont and Franklin where Zachette stands waiting, hands in trousers pockets. He is about twenty-five, Italian-looking, open shirt, not well dressed.

Back in the coupe we see Lola and Neff.

LOLA. He needs a haircut, doesn't he. Look at him. No job, no car, no money, no prospects, no nothing — I love him. (*She leans over and honks on the horn.*) Nino!

We get a close view of Zachette as he turns and looks toward the car.

LOLA'S VOICE. Over here, Nino.

Zachette walks toward the car, and the scene cuts to the coupe: Lola has opened the door. Zachette comes up.

LOLA. This is Mr. Neff, Nino.

NEFF. Hello, Nino.

ZACHETTE (*belligerent from the first word*). The name is Zachette.

LOLA. Nino, please. Mr. Neff gave me a ride from the house. I told him all about us.

ZACHETTE. Why does he have to get told about us?

LOLA. We don't have to worry about Mr. Neff, Nino.

ZACHETTE. I'm not doing any worrying. Just don't you broadcast so much.

LOLA. What's the matter with you, Nino? He's a friend.

ZACHETTE. I don't have any friends. And if I did, I like to pick them myself.

NEFF. Look, sonny, she needed the ride and I brought her along. Is that anything to get tough about?

ZACHETTE. All right, Lola, make up your mind. Are you coming or aren't you?

LOLA. Of course I'm coming. Don't mind him, Mr. Neff. (*Lola steps out of the car.*) Thanks a lot. You've been very sweet.

Lola catches up with Zachette, and as they walk away together the scene cuts to the coupe while Neff's dictation is heard. Neff looks after them. Slowly he puts the car in gear and drives on. His face is tight. Behind his head, light catches the metal of the zipper on the briefcase.

NEFF'S VOICE. She was a nice kid, and maybe he was a little better than he sounded. I kind of hoped so for her sake, but right then it gave me a nasty feeling to be thinking about them at all, with that briefcase right behind my head and her father's signature on it — and what that signature meant. It meant that he was a dead pigeon, and it was only a question of time, and not very much time at that. You know that big market in Los Feliz, Keyes? That's the place Phyllis and I had picked for a meeting place.

This dissolves to the super-market. There is a fair amount of activity but the place is not crowded. Neff comes along the sidewalk into the scene. He passes in front of the fruit and vegetable display and goes between the stalls into the market.

NEFF'S VOICE (*continuing*). I already had most of the plan in my head, but a lot of details had to be worked out, and she had to know them all by heart when the time came.

Inside the market: Neff stops by the cashier's desk and buys a pack of cigarettes. As he is opening the pack he looks back casually beyond the turnstile into the rear part of the market.

NEFF'S VOICE. We had to be very careful from now on. We couldn't let anybody see us together — we couldn't even talk to each other on the telephone — not from her house or at my office, anyway. So she was to be in the market every morning about eleven o'clock, buying stuff, and I could sort of run into her there any day I wanted to, sort of accidentally on purpose.

We see rows of high shelves in the market: The shelves are loaded with canned goods and other merchandise. Customers move around selecting articles and putting them in their baskets. Phyllis is seen among them, standing by the soap section. Her basket is partly filled. She wears a simple house dress, no hat, and has a large envelope pocketbook under her arm. And now Neff spots Phyllis. Without haste he passes through the turnstile toward the back. Back at the shelves, Phyllis is putting a can of cleaning powder into her basket. Neff enters the scene and moves along the shelves toward her, very slowly, pretending to inspect the goods. A customer passes and goes on out of the scene. Phyllis and Neff are now very close. During the ensuing low-spoken dialogue, they continue to face the shelves, not looking at each other.

PHYLLIS. Walter —
NEFF. Not so loud.
PHYLLIS. I wanted to talk to you, Walter. Ever since yesterday.
NEFF. Let me talk first. It's all set. The accident policy came through. I've got it in my pocket. I got his check too. I saw him down in the oil fields. He thought he was paying for the auto insurance. The check's just made out to the company. It could be for anything. But you have to send a check for the auto insurance, see. It's all right that way, because one of the cars is yours.
PHYLLIS. But listen, Walter!
NEFF. Quick, open your bag.

She hesitates, then opens it. Neff looks around quickly, slips the policy out of his pocket and drops it into her bag. She snaps the bag shut.

NEFF. Can you get into his safe deposit box?
PHYLLIS. Yes. We both have keys.
NEFF. Fine. But don't put the policy in there yet. I'll tell you when. And listen, you never touched it or even saw it, understand?
PHYLLIS. I'm not a fool.
NEFF. Okay. When is he taking the train?
PHYLLIS. Walter, that's just it. He isn't going.
NEFF. What?
PHYLLIS. That's what I've been trying to tell you. The trip is off.

NEFF. What's happened?

He breaks off as a short, squatty woman, pushing a child in a walker, comes into sight and approaches. She stops beside Neff, who is pretending to read a label on a can. Phyllis puts a few cakes of soap into her basket.

WOMAN (*to Neff*). Mister, could you reach me that can of coffee? (*She points.*) That one up there.
NEFF (*reaching up*). This one?

She nods. Neff reaches a can down from the high shelf, and hands it to her.

WOMAN. I don't see why they always have to put what I want on the top shelf.

She moves away with her coffee and her child. Out of the corner of his eye Neff watches her go. He moves closer to Phyllis again.

NEFF. Go ahead. I'm listening.
PHYLLIS. He had a fall down at the well. He broke his leg. It's in a cast.
NEFF. That knocks it on the head all right.
PHYLLIS. What do we do, Walter?
NEFF. Nothing. Just wait.
PHYLLIS. Wait for what?
NEFF. Until he can take a train. I told you it's got to be a train.
PHYLLIS. We can't wait. I can't go on like this.
NEFF. We're not going to grab a hammer and do it quick, just to get it over with.
PHYLLIS. There are other ways.
NEFF. Only we're not going to do it other ways.
PHYLLIS. But we can't leave it like this. What do you think would happen if he found out about this accident policy?
NEFF. Plenty. But not as bad as sitting in that death-house.
PHYLLIS. Don't ever talk like that, Walter.
NEFF. Just don't let's start losing our heads.
PHYLLIS. It's not our heads. It's our nerve we're losing.
NEFF. We're going to do it right. That's all I said.
PHYLLIS. Walter, maybe it's *my* nerves. It's the waiting that gets me.
NEFF. It's getting me just as bad, baby. But we've got to wait.

PHYLLIS. Maybe we have, Walter. Only it's so tough without you. It's like a wall between us.

Neff looks at his watch.

NEFF. Good-bye, baby. I'm thinking of you every minute.

He goes off. She stares after him, as the scene dissolves to Neff's office. He is wearing a light gray suit and has his hat on. He is standing behind his desk opening some mail, taking a few papers out of his briefcase, checking something in his rate book, making a quick telephone call. But nothing of this is heard.

NEFF'S VOICE. After that a full week went by and I didn't see her once. I tried to keep my mind off her and off the whole idea. I kept telling myself that maybe those fates they say watch over you had gotten together and broken his leg to give me a way out. Then it was the fifteenth of June. You may remember that date, Keyes. I do too, only for a very different reason. You came into my office around three in the afternoon.

NEFF (*as Keyes enters with some papers in his hand*). Hello, Keyes.

KEYES. I just came from Norton's office. The semi-annual sales records are out. You're high man, Walter. That's twice in a row. Congratulations.

NEFF. Thanks. How would you like a cheap drink?

KEYES. How would you like a fifty-dollar cut in salary?

NEFF. How would I — Do I laugh now, or wait until it gets funny?

KEYES. No, I'm serious. I've been talking to Norton. There's too much stuff piling up on my desk. Too much pressure on my nerves. I spend half the night walking up and down in my bed. I've got to have an assistant. I thought that you —

NEFF. Me? Why pick on me?

KEYES. Because I've got a crazy idea you might be good at the job.

NEFF. That's crazy all right. I'm a salesman.

KEYES. Yeah. A peddler, a glad-hander, a back-slapper. You're too good to be a salesman.

NEFF. Nobody's too good to be a salesman.

KEYES. Phooey. All you guys do is ring doorbells and dish out a smooth line of monkey talk. What's bothering you is that fifty-buck cut, isn't it?

NEFF. Well, it'd trouble anybody.

KEYES. Now, look, Walter. The job I'm talking about takes brains and integrity. It takes more guts than there is in fifty salesmen. It's the hottest job in the business.

NEFF. It's still a desk job. I don't want a desk job.

KEYES. A desk job. Is that all you can see in it? Just a hard chair to park your pants on from nine to five. Just a pile of papers to shuffle around, and five sharp pencils and a scratch pad to make figures on, with maybe a little doodling on the side. That's not the way I see it, Walter. To me a claims man is a surgeon, and that desk is an operating table, and those pencils are scalpels and bone chisels. And those papers are not just forms and statistics and claims for compensation. They're alive, they're packed with drama, with twisted hopes and crooked dreams. A claims man, Walter, is a doctor and a blood-hound and a cop and a judge and a jury and a father confessor, all in one.

The telephone rings on Neff's desk. Automatically Keyes grabs the phone and answers.

KEYES. Who? Okay, hold the line. (*He puts the phone down on the desk and continues to Neff:*) And you want to tell me you're not interested. You don't want to work with your brains. All you want to work with is your finger on a doorbell. For a few bucks more a week. There's a dame on your phone.

NEFF (*picking the phone up and answering*). Walter Neff speaking.

The scene cuts to a phone booth in the market: Phyllis is on the phone.

PHYLLIS. I had to call you, Walter. It's terribly urgent. Are you with somebody?

Back in Neff's office: Neff is at the phone. His eye catches Keyes', who is walking up and down.

NEFF. Of course I am. Can't I call you back . . . Margie?

Phyllis at the phone:

PHYLLIS. Walter, I've only got a minute. It can't wait. Listen. He's going tonight. On the train. Are you listening, Walter? Walter!

Neff at the phone: His eyes are on Keyes. He speaks into the phone as calmly as possible.

NEFF. I'm listening. Only make it short . . . Margie.

Phyllis at the phone:

PHYLLIS. He's on crutches. The doctor says he can go if he's careful. The change will do him good. It's wonderful, Walter. Just the way you wanted it. Only with the crutches it's ever so much better, isn't it?

Neff's office, Neff on the phone:

NEFF. One hundred percent better. Hold the line a minute. (*He covers the receiver with his hand and turns to Keyes, who is now standing at the window.*) Suppose I join you in your office, Keyes —

He makes a gesture as if expecting Keyes to leave. Keyes stays right where he is.

KEYES. I'll wait. Only tell Margie not to take all day.

Neff looks at Keyes' back with a strained expression, then lifts the phone again.

NEFF. Go ahead.

Phyllis at the phone:

PHYLLIS. It's the ten-fifteen from Glendale. I'm driving him. Is it still that same dark street?

Back in the office, Neff is still watching Keyes cautiously.

NEFF. Yeah — sure.

A closeup of Phyllis at the phone:

PHYLLIS. The signal is three honks on the horn. Is there anything else?

A closeup of Neff at the phone:

NEFF. What color did you pick out?

PHYLLIS (*seen again*). Color? (*She catches on.*) Oh, sure. The blue suit, Walter. Navy blue. And the cast on his left leg.

NEFF (*seen again*). Navy blue. I like that fine.

PHYLLIS (*seen again*). This is it, Walter. I'm shaking like a leaf. But it's straight down the line now for both of us. I love you, Walter. Goodbye.

Neff's office: Neff is still on the phone.

NEFF. So long, Margie.

He hangs up. His mouth is grim, but he forces a smile as Keyes turns.

NEFF. I'm sorry, Keyes.

KEYES. What's the matter? The dames chasing you again? Or still? Or is it none of my business?

NEFF (*with a sour smile*). If I told you it was a customer —

KEYES. Margie! I bet she drinks from the bottle. Why don't you settle down and get married, Walter?

NEFF. Why don't you, for instance?

KEYES. I almost did, once. A long time ago.

NEFF (*getting up from his desk*). Look, Keyes, I've got a prospect to call on. (*But Keyes drives right ahead:*)

KEYES. We even had the church all picked out, the dame and I. She had a white satin dress with flounces on it. And I was on my way to the jewelry store to buy the ring. Then suddenly that little man in here started working on me. (*He punches his stomach with his fist.*)

NEFF. So you went back and started investigating her. That it?

KEYES (*nodding slowly, a little sad and a little ashamed*). And the stuff that came out. She'd been dyeing her hair ever since she was sixteen. And there was a manic-depressive in her family, on her mother's side. And she already had one husband, a professional pool player in Baltimore. And as for her brother —

NEFF. I get the general idea. She was a tramp from a long line of tramps. (*He picks up some papers impatiently.*)

KEYES. All right, I'm going. What am I to say to Norton? How about that job I want you for?

NEFF. I don't think I want it. Thanks, Keyes, just the same.

KEYES. Fair enough. Just get this: I picked you for the job, not because I think you're so darn smart, but because I thought maybe you were a shade less dumb than the rest of the outfit. I guess I was all wet. You're not smarter, Walter. You're just a little taller.

He goes out, and now Neff is alone. He watches the door close, then turns and goes slowly to the water cooler. He fills a paper cup and stands holding it. His thoughts are somewhere else. After a moment he absently throws the cupful of water into the receptacle under the cooler. He goes back to the desk . . . He takes his rate book out of his briefcase and puts it on the desk. He buttons the top button of his shirt, and pulls his tie right. He leaves the office, with his briefcase under his arm.

NEFF'S VOICE (*synchronized with the above scene*). That was it, Keyes, and there was no use kidding myself any more. Those fates I was talking about had only been stalling me off. Now they had thrown the switch. The gears had meshed. The machinery had started to move and nothing could stop it. The time for thinking had all run out. From here on it was a question of following the time table, move by move, just as we had it rehearsed. I wanted my time all accounted for for the rest of the afternoon and up to the last possible moment in the evening. So I arranged to call on a prospect in Pasadena about a public liability bond. When I left the office I put my rate book on the desk as if I had forgotten it. That was part of the alibi.

The scene dissolves to Neff's apartment house as Neff's coupe comes down the street, swings into the garage and goes down the ramp into the basement.

NEFF'S VOICE (*continuing*). I got home about seven and drove right into the garage. This was another item to establish my alibi.

This cuts to the garage. There are about eight cars parked. A colored attendant in coveralls and rubber boots is washing a car with a hose and sponge. Neff's car comes in and stops near the attendant. Neff gets out with his briefcase under his arm.

ATTENDANT. Hiya there, Mr. Neff.
NEFF. How about a wash job on my heap, Charlie?
ATTENDANT. How soon you want it, Mr. Neff? I got two cars ahead of you.
NEFF. Anytime you get to it, Charlie. I'm staying in tonight.

ATTENDANT. Okay, Mr. Neff. Be all shined up for you in the morning.

NEFF (*crossing to the elevator and speaking back over his shoulder*). That left front tire looks a little soft. Check it, will you?

ATTENDANT. You bet. Check 'em all 'round. Always do.

Neff enters the elevator and the scene dissolves to Neff's apartment as Neff comes in. He walks straight to the phone, dials, and starts speaking into the mouthpiece, but only his dictation is heard.

NEFF'S VOICE. Up in my apartment I called Lou Schwartz, one of the salesmen that shared my office. He lived in Westwood. That made it a toll call and there'd be a record of it. I told him I had forgotten my rate book and needed some dope on the public liability bond I was figuring. I asked him to call me back. This was another item in my alibi, so that later on I could prove that I had been home.

The scene dissolves to Neff's living room. Neff comes into the living room from the bedroom, putting on the jacket of his blue suit. The phone rings. He picks up the receiver and starts talking, unheard, as before. He makes notes on a pad.

NEFF'S VOICE. I changed into a navy blue suit like Dietrichson was going to wear. Lou Schwartz called me back and gave me a lot of figures. . . .

Now he is seen folding a hand towel and stuffing it into his jacket pocket. He then takes a large roll of adhesive tape and puts that into his pants pocket. This scene dissolving, we see a telephone bell box (on the baseboard) and a doorbell above the entrance door as Neff's hand places a small card against the bell clapper in each of these; and this dissolves to the fire stairs of the apartment house at night as the view moves with Neff going down the stairs in his blue suit, with a hat pulled down over his eyes. And this scene dissolving, we next get a distant view of the Dietrichson home at night. There is no traffic. Some windows are lit. Neff comes into view and approaches cautiously. He looks around and then slides open the garage door.

NEFF'S VOICE. I stuffed a hand towel and a big roll of adhesive tape into my pockets, so I could fake something that looked like a cast on a broken leg. . . . Next I fixed the telephone and the doorbell, so that the cards would fall down if the bells rang. That way I would know there had been a phone call or visitor while I was away. I left the apartment house by the fire stairs and side door. Nobody saw me. It was already getting dark. I took the Vermont Avenue bus to Los Feliz and walked from there up to the Dietrichson house. There was that smell of honeysuckle again, only stronger, now that it was evening.

We see the interior of the garage as Neff closes the door. A very faint light comes in at a side window. He opens the rear door of the sedan, gets in and closes the door after him. The dark interior of the car has swallowed him up.

NEFF'S VOICE. Then I was in the garage. His car was backed in, just the way I told Phyllis to have it. It was so still I could hear the ticking of the clock on the dashboard. I kept thinking of the place we had picked out to do it, that dark street on the way to the station, and the three honks on the horn that were to be the signal. . . . About ten minutes later they came down.

Outside the Dietrichson house: The front door has opened and Dietrichson is halfway down the steps. He is walking with crutches, wearing the dark blue suit and a hat. The cast is on his left leg. There is no shoe on his left foot. Only the white plaster shows. Phyllis comes after him, carrying his suitcase and his overcoat. She wears a camel's-hair coat and no hat. She catches up with him.

PHYLLIS. You all right, honey? I'll have the car out in a second.

Dietrichson just grunts. She passes him moving toward the garage, and slides the door open. Then we again see the garage, as we get a low view from the sedan.
(The camera is very low inside the sedan, shooting slightly upward from Neff's hiding place.) The garage door has just been opened. Phyllis comes to the car, and opens the rear door. She looks down (seen very close), and a tight, cool smile flashes across her face. Then, very calmly, she puts the suitcase and overcoat in back on the seat. She closes the door again.
Outside the garage, Dietrichson stands watching Phyllis as she gets into the car and drives out to pick him up. She stops beside him and opens the right-hand door. Dietrichson climbs in with difficulty. She helps him, watching him closely.

PHYLLIS. Take it easy, honey. We've got lots of time.
DIETRICHSON. Just let me do it my own way. Grab that crutch.

She takes one of the crutches from him.

DIETRICHSON. They ought to make these things so they fold up.

For a moment, as he leans his hand on the back of the seat, there is danger that he may see Neff. He doesn't. He slides awkwardly into the seat and pulls the second crutch in after him. He closes the door. The car moves off, and this dissolves to the interior of the car as Phyllis is driving and Dietrichson is beside her. Dietrichson has a partly smoked cigar between his teeth. They are in the middle of a conversation.

DIETRICHSON. Aw, stop squawkin' can't you, Phyllis? No man takes his wife along to a class reunion. That's what class reunions are for.
PHYLLIS. Mrs. Tucker went along with her husband last year, didn't she?
DIETRICHSON. Yeah, and what happened to her? She sat in the hotel lobby for four days straight. Never even saw the guy until we poured him back on the train.

We get a close view of Neff's face, low down in the corner behind Dietrichson. His face is partly covered by the edge of a traveling rug which he has pulled up over him. He looks up at Dietrichson and Phyllis in the front seat.

PHYLLIS' VOICE. All right, honey. Just so long as you have a good time.
DIETRICHSON'S VOICE. I won't do much dancing, I can tell you that.
PHYLLIS (*as we now see their heads and shoulders as observed by Neff*). Remember what the doctor said. If you get careless you might end up with a shorter leg.
DIETRICHSON. So what? I could break the other one and match them up again.
PHYLLIS. It makes you feel pretty good to get away from me, doesn't it?
DIETRICHSON. It's only for four days. I'll be back Monday at the latest.
PHYLLIS. Don't forget we're having the Hobeys for dinner on Monday.
DIETRICHSON. The Hobeys? We had them last. They owe us a dinner, don't they?
PHYLLIS. Maybe they do but I've already asked them for Monday.
DIETRICHSON. Well, I don't want to feed the Hobeys.

We get a closeup of Phyllis' face only: there is a look of tension in her eyes now. She glances around quickly. The car has reached the dark street Neff and she picked out.

DIETRICHSON'S VOICE. And I don't want to eat at their house either. The food you get there, and that rope he hands out for cigars. Call it off, can't you? — This is not the right street! Why did you turn here?

Phyllis does not answer. She doesn't even breathe. Her hand goes down on the horn button. She honks three times. A closeup shows Dietrichson reacting with surprise.

DIETRICHSON. What are you doing that for? What're you honking the horn for?

This is as far as his voice will ever get, as Neff starts to pull himself up. It breaks off and dies down in a muffled groan. There are struggling noises and a dull sound of something breaking. Phyllis drives on and never turns her head. She stares straight in front of her. Her teeth are clenched.

This dissolves to a parking space adjoining Glendale Station, at night. The station is visible about sixty yards away. There is no parking attendant. Ten or twelve cars are parked diagonally, not crowded. The train is not in yet, but there is activity around the station from passengers and their friends, redcaps and baggage men and news vendors.

The Dietrichson sedan comes into view and parks in the foreground at the outer end of the line, several spaces from the next car, facing away from the camera. Both front doors are open. Phyllis gets out and from the other side crutches emerge, and a man (seen entirely from behind, and apparently Dietrichson) climbs out awkwardly. While he is steadying himself on the ground with the crutches, Phyllis has taken out Dietrichson's suitcase and overcoat. She walks around the car and rolls up the right front window. She closes and locks the car door. She tries the right rear door and takes a last look into the dim interior of the car. Then she and the man walk slowly away from the car to the end of the station platform and along it toward the station building. Phyllis walks several steps ahead of the man.

Phyllis and the man are then seen walking a little to one side, so that Phyllis is clearly seen but the man's face is not.

MAN (*in a subdued voice*). You handle the redcap and the conductor.
PHYLLIS. Don't worry.

MAN. Keep them away from me as much as you can. I don't want to be helped.

PHYLLIS. I said don't worry, Walter.

Phyllis and the man are now walking down the platform (facing front), and at this point it is quite clear that the man is Neff.

NEFF. You start just as soon as the train leaves. At the dairy sign you turn off the highway onto the dirt road. From there it's exactly eight-tenths of a mile to the dump beside the tracks. Remember?

PHYLLIS. I remember everything.

NEFF. You'll be there a little ahead of the train. No speeding. You don't want any cops stopping you — with him in the back.

PHYLLIS. Walter, we've been through all that so many times.

NEFF. When you turn off the highway, cut all your lights. I'm going to be back on the observation platform. I'll drop off as close to the spot as I can. Wait for the train to pass, then blink your lights twice.

Phyllis nods. They go on. Over them is heard the noise of the train coming into the station and its lights are seen.

At the Glendale Station platform: the train is just coming to a stop. The passengers move forward to the tracks. Phyllis, carrying the suitcase and overcoat, and Neff, still a little behind her, come toward us. A redcap sees them and runs up. He takes the suitcase out of Phyllis' hand.

REDCAP. San Francisco train, lady?

Phyllis takes an envelope containing Dietrichson's ticket from the pocket of the overcoat. She reads from the envelope.

PHYLLIS. Car nine, section eleven. Just my husband going.

REDCAP. Car nine, section eleven. Yessum, this way please.

Phyllis hands the overcoat to the redcap, who leads her and Neff toward car number nine. Neff still hangs back and keeps his head down, the way a man using crutches might naturally do.

Outside car number nine: the pullman conductor and porter stand at the steps. The conductor is checking the tickets of passengers getting on. The redcap leads Phyllis and Neff into view. The conductor and porter see Neff on his crutches and move to help him.

PHYLLIS. It's all right, thanks. My husband doesn't like to be helped.

The redcap goes up the steps into the car. Neff laboriously swings himself up onto the box and from there up on the steps, keeping his head down. Meantime, Phyllis is holding the attention of the conductor and porter by showing them the ticket.

CONDUCTOR. Car nine, section eleven. The gentleman only. Thank you.

Phyllis nods and takes the ticket back. Neff has reached the top of the steps. She goes up after him and gives him the ticket. They are now close together.

PHYLLIS. Goodbye, honey. Take awful good care of yourself with that leg.
NEFF. Sure, I will. Just you take it easy going home.
PHYLLIS. I'll miss you, honey.

She kisses him. There are shouts of "All Aboard." The redcap comes from inside the car.

REDCAP. Section eleven, suh.

Phyllis takes a quarter from her bag and gives it to the redcap.

PORTER (*shouting*). All aboard!

The redcap descends. Phyllis kisses Neff again quickly.

PHYLLIS. Good luck, honey.

She runs down the steps. The porter picks up the box. He and the conductor get on board the train. Phyllis stands there waving goodbye as the train starts moving, and the porter begins to close the car door. Phyllis turns and walks out of sight in the direction of the parked car.

The scene then cuts to the platform as the train moves on. The light is dim. The conductor is going on into the car. Neff is half turned away from the porter.

NEFF. Can you make up my berth right away?

PORTER. Yes, sir.

NEFF. I'm going back to the observation car for a smoke.

PORTER. This way, sir. Three cars back. (*He holds the vestibule door open, and Neff hobbles through.*)

This dissolves to the Pullman car, which is dimly lit. Most of the berths are made up. As Neff hobbles along, another porter and some passengers make way for the crippled man solicitously. This dissolves to the platform between two cars as the train conductor meets Neff, opens the door for him, and Neff hobbles on through. This in turn dissolves to the parlor car, where four or five passengers are reading or writing. As Neff comes through on his crutches they pull in their feet to make room for him. One old lady, seeing that he is headed for the observation platform, opens the door for him. He thanks her with a nod and hobbles through.

And now the scene cuts to the observation platform. It is dark except for a little light coming from inside the parlor car. The train is going about fifteen miles an hour between Glendale and Burbank. Neff has come out and hobbled to the railing. He stands looking back along the rails. Suddenly a man's voice speaks from behind him.

MAN'S VOICE. Can I pull a chair out for you?

Neff looks around. He sees a man sitting in the corner smoking a hand-rolled cigarette. He is about fifty-five years old, with white hair, and a broad-brimmed Stetson hat. He looks like a small-town lawyer or maybe a mining man. Neff does not like the man's presence there very much. He turns to him just enough to answer.

NEFF. No thanks, I'd rather stand.

MAN. You going far?

NEFF. Palo Alto.

MAN. My name's Jackson. I'm going all the way to Medford. Medford, Oregon. Had a broken arm myself once.

NEFF. Uh-huh.

JACKSON. That darn cast sure itches something fierce, don't it? I thought I'd go crazy with mine. (*Neff stands silent. His mind is feverishly thinking of how to get rid of Jackson.*) Palo Alto's a nice little town. You a Stanford man?

NEFF. Used to be. (*He starts patting his pockets as if looking for something.*)

JACKSON. I bet you left something behind. I always do.

NEFF. My cigar case. Must have left it in my overcoat back in the section.

JACKSON (*taking out a small bag of tobacco and a packet of cigarette papers*). Care to roll yourself a cigarette, Mr. —?

NEFF. Dietrichson. Thanks. I really prefer cigars. (*Looking around*) Maybe the porter —

JACKSON. I could get your cigars for you. Be glad to, Mr. Dietrichson.

NEFF. That's darn nice of you. It's car nine, section eleven. If you're sure it's not too much trouble.

JACKSON. Car nine, section eleven. A pleasure.

He rises and walks into the parlor car. Neff turns slowly and watches Jackson go back through the car. Then he moves to one side of the platform and looks ahead along the track to orientate himself. He gives one last glance back into the parlor car to make sure no one is watching him. He slips the crutches from under his arms and stands on both feet. He drops the crutches off the train onto the tracks, then quickly swings his body over the rail.

We then see the observation car, with Neff hanging onto the railing. He looks down, then lets go and drops to the right-of-way. The train recedes slowly into the night. Neff has fallen on the tracks. He picks himself up, rubs one knee and looks back along the line of the tracks and off to one side.

A dark landscape comes into view, and we see the railroad tracks. Close beyond the edge of the right-of-way, the silhouette of a dump shows up. Beside it looms the dark bulk of the Dietrichson sedan. The headlights blink twice and go out. Neff, seen close, starts running toward the car. He runs a little awkwardly because of the improvised cast on his left foot. Then we see the car in the dark as the front door opens and Phyllis steps out. She closes the door and looks in the direction of the tracks. The uneven steps of Neff running toward her are heard. She opens the back door of the car and leans in. She pulls the rug off the corpse (which is not visible) and stands looking into the car, unable to take her eyes off what she sees, while at the same time her hands mechanically begin to fold the rug. The running steps grow louder and Neff comes into view, breathing hard. He reaches her.

NEFF. Okay. This has to go fast. Take his hat and pick up the crutches.

Neff points back toward the tracks. He reaches into the car and begins to drag out the body by the armpits. Phyllis coolly reaches past him and takes the hat off the dead man's head. She turns to go.

NEFF. Hang on to that rug. I'll need it.

Phyllis moves out of sight carrying the hat and rug, while Neff gets a stronger hold on the dead Dietrichson and drags him free of the car and toward the tracks. The corpse is not seen.

Phyllis reaches the point where one of the crutches lies. She picks it up and goes for the other crutch a short distance away. She carries both crutches, the hat and the rug toward Neff.

Neff has reached the railroad tracks. The corpse is lying beside the tracks, face down. Phyllis comes up to Neff. He takes the crutches and the hat from her. He throws the crutches beside the corpse. He takes the hat from Phyllis and tosses it carelessly along the track.

NEFF. Let's go. Stay behind me.

He takes the rug from her and they move back toward the car, Phyllis first, then Neff walking almost backwards, sweeping the ground over which the body was dragged with the rug as they go. Then we see the car as they reach it together.

NEFF. Get in. You drive.

She gets in. Neff sweeps the ground after him as he goes around the car to get in beside her. He throws the rug into the back of the car.

Inside the car: Phyllis is behind the wheel. Neff beside her is just closing the door. He props his wrapped foot against the dashboard and begins to tear off the adhesive tape while at the same time Phyllis presses the starter button. The starter grinds, but the motor doesn't catch. She tries again. It still doesn't catch. Neff looks at her. She tries a third time. The starter barely turns over. The battery is very low.

Phyllis leans back. They stare at each other desperately. After a moment Neff bends forward slowly and turns the ignition key to the off position. He holds his left thumb poised over the starter button. There is a breathless moment. Then he presses the starter button with swift decision. The starter grinds with nerve-wracking sluggishness. Neff twists the ignition key to on and instantly pulls the hand-throttle wide open. With a last feeble kick of the starter, the motor catches and races. He eases the throttle down and slides back into his place. They look at each other again. The tenseness of the moment still shows in their faces.

NEFF. Let's go, baby.

Phyllis releases the hand brake and puts the car in reverse. Neff is again busy unwrapping the tape from his leg. Then the car, with the headlights out, backs up, swings around and moves off along the dirt road the way it came.

We see the sedan driving along a highway in traffic, and again Neff's voice is heard over the scene. Phyllis and Neff are facing forward. Neff is bent over, peeling the towel and plaster off his foot, which is out of sight. Phyllis is calm, almost relaxed. Neff straightens up. They are talking to each other. Their lips are seen moving but what they say is not heard. They stop talking. Phyllis stares straight ahead. Neff is pulling adhesive tape off the wrapped towel that was on his foot. He folds the adhesive into a tight ball, rolls the towel up, puts both into his pockets.

NEFF'S VOICE (*synchronized with the scene*). On the way back we went over once more what she was to do at the inquest, if they had one, and about the insurance, when that came up. I was afraid she might go to pieces a little, now that we had done it, but she was perfect. No nerves. Not a tear, not even a blink of the eyes. . . .

This dissolves to a dark street near Neff's house as the sedan comes into view and stops without pulling over to the curb.

NEFF'S VOICE. She dropped me a block from my apartment house.

The car door opens. Neff starts to get out.

PHYLLIS. Walter — (*Neff turns back to her.*) What's the matter, Walter. Aren't you going to kiss me?
NEFF. Sure, I'm going to kiss you.
PHYLLIS (*bending toward him and putting her arms around him*). It's straight down the line, isn't it? (*She kisses him. He is passive in the kiss.*) I love you, Walter.
NEFF. I love you, baby.

This dissolves to the fire stairs. Neff is seen going up.

NEFF'S VOICE. It was two minutes past eleven as I went up the fire stairs again. Nobody saw me this time either.

This dissolves to a closeup of Neff's hand opening the telephone bell box and the door bell. The cards are still in position. Neff's hand takes them out.

NEFF'S VOICE. In the apartment I checked the bells. The cards hadn't moved. No calls. No visitors.

This dissolves to the living room, in which the lights are still on. Neff comes from the bedroom, wearing the light gray suit he wore before the murder, only without a tie. He buttons his jacket, looks around the room, and opens the corridor door.

NEFF'S VOICE. I changed the blue suit. There was one last thing to do. I wanted the garage man to see me again.

This dissolves to the basement garage, where fifteen or twenty cars are now parked. Charlie, the attendant, has washed Neff's car and is now polishing the glass and metal-work. Neff comes from the elevator. Charlie sees him. He straightens up.

CHARLIE. You going to need it after all, Mr. Neff? I'm not quite through.
NEFF. It's okay, Charlie. Just walking down to the drug store for something to eat. Been working upstairs all evening. My stomach's getting sore at me.
CHARLIE. Yes, sir, Mr. Neff.

He walks up the ramp toward the garage entrance, and the scene dissolves to the street outside the apartment house. Neff comes out at the top of the ramp and starts to walk down the street, not too fast. He walks about ten or fifteen yards. At first his steps sound hard and distinct on the sidewalk and echo in the deserted street. But slowly, as he goes on, they fade into utter silence. He walks a few feet without sound, then becomes aware of the silence. He stops rigidly and looks back. He stands like that for a moment, then turns forward again. There is a look of horror on his face now. He walks on again, and still his steps make no sound, as the scene fades out.

NEFF'S VOICE (*synchronized with the scene*). That was all there was to it. Nothing had slipped, nothing had been overlooked, there was nothing to give us away. And yet, Keyes, as I was walking down the street to the drug store, suddenly it came over me that everything would go wrong. It sounds crazy, Keyes, but it's true, so help me: I couldn't hear my own footsteps. It was the walk of a dead man.

PART THREE

NEFF'S OFFICE fades in at night. Neff still sits before the dictaphone. There are four cylinders on end on the desk next to him. He gets up from the swivel chair with great effort and stands a moment unsteadily. The wound in his shoulder is paining him. He is very weak as he slowly crosses to the water cooler. He takes the blood-stained handkerchief from inside his shirt and soaks it with fresh water. The office door opens behind him. He turns, hiding the handkerchief behind his back. In the doorway stands the colored man who has been cleaning up downstairs. He is carrying his big trash box by a rope handle.

COLORED MAN. Didn't know anybody was here, Mr. Neff. We ain't cleaned your office yet.
NEFF. Let it go tonight. I'm busy.
COLORED MAN. Whatever you say, Mr. Neff.

He closes the door slowly, staring at Neff with an uneasy expression. Neff puts the soaked handkerchief back on his wounded shoulder, then walks heavily over to his swivel chair and lowers himself into it. He takes the dictaphone horn and speaks into it again.

NEFF. That was the longest night I ever lived through, Keyes, and the next day was worse, when the story broke in the papers, and they were talking about it at the office, and the day after that when you started digging into it. I kept my hands in my pockets because I thought they were shaking, and I put on dark glasses so people couldn't see my eyes, and then I took them off again so people wouldn't get to wondering why I wore them. I was trying to hold myself together, but I could feel my nerves pulling me to pieces . . .

This dissolves to the insurance office on the twelfth floor. Neff comes through the reception room doors on the balcony with his hat on and his briefcase under his arm. He walks toward his office, but halfway there he runs into Keyes. Keyes is wearing his vest and hat, no coat. He is carrying a file of papers and smoking a cigar.

KEYES. Come on, Walter. The big boss wants to see us.
NEFF. Okay. (*He turns and walks beside Keyes.*) That Dietrichson case?
KEYES. Must be.
NEFF. Anything wrong?
KEYES. The guy's dead, we had him insured and it's going to cost us money. That's always wrong.

He stops by a majolica jar full of sand and takes a pencil from his vest. He stands over the jar extinguishing his cigar carefully so as not to damage it.

NEFF. What have you got so far?
KEYES. Autopsy report. No heart failure, no apoplexy, no predisposing medical cause of any kind. He died of a broken neck.
NEFF. When is the inquest?
KEYES. They had it this morning. His wife and daughter made the identification. The train people and some passengers told how he went through to the observation car . . . It was all over in forty-five minutes. Verdict, accidental death.

Keyes puts the half-smoked cigar into his vest pocket with the pencil. They move on.

NEFF. What do the police figure?
KEYES. That he got tangled up in his crutches and fell off the train. They're satisfied. It's not their dough.

They stop at a door lettered in embossed chromium letters: EDWARD S. NORTON, JR. PRESIDENT. Keyes opens the door, and they go in. We then see the reception room of Mr. Norton's office. A secretary is sitting behind a desk. As Keyes and Neff enter, the door to Norton's private office is opened. From inside, Mr. Norton is letting out three legal-looking gentlemen. Norton is about forty-five, very well groomed, rather pompous in manner.

NORTON (*to the men who are leaving*). I believe the legal position is now clear, gentlemen. Please stand by. I may need you later. (*He sees Keyes and Neff.*) Come in, Mr. Keyes. You too, Mr. Neff.

Neff has put down his hat and briefcase. He and Keyes pass the legal-looking men and follow Norton into his office.

In Norton's office: Naturally it is the best office in the building; modern but not modernistic, spacious, very well furnished; flowers, smoking stands, easy chairs, etc. Norton has gone behind his desk. Keyes has come in, and Neff after him closes the door quietly. Norton looks disapprovingly at Keyes' shirt sleeves.

NORTON. You find this an uncomfortably warm day, Mr. Keyes? (*At this Keyes takes his hat off but holds it in his hands.*)

KEYES. Sorry, Mr. Norton. I didn't know this was formal.

NORTON (*smiling frostily*). Sit down, gentlemen. (*To Keyes*) Any new developments? (*Keyes and Neff sit down, Norton remains standing.*)

KEYES. I just talked to this Jackson long distance. Up in Medford, Oregon.

NORTON. Who's Jackson?

KEYES. The last guy that saw Dietrichson alive. They were out on the observation platform together talking. Dietrichson wanted a cigar and Jackson went to get Dietrichson's cigar case for him. When he came back to the observation platform, no Dietrichson. Jackson didn't think anything was wrong until a wire caught up with the train at Santa Barbara. They had found Dietrichson's body on the tracks near Burbank.

NORTON. Very interesting, about the cigar case. (*He walks up and down behind his desk thinking hard.*) Anything else?

KEYES. Not much. Dietrichson's secretary says she didn't know anything about the policy. There is a daughter, but all she remembers is Neff talking to her father about accident insurance at their house one night.

NEFF. I couldn't sell him at first. Mrs. Dietrichson opposed it. He told me he'd think it over. Later on I went down to the oil fields and closed him. He signed the application and gave me his check.

NORTON (*dripping with sarcasm*). A fine piece of salesmanship that was, Mr. Neff.

KEYES. There's no sense in pushing Neff around. He's got the best sales record in the office. Are your salesmen supposed to know that the customer is going to fall off a train?

NORTON. Fall off a train? Are we sure Dietrichson fell off a train? (*There is a charged pause.*)

KEYES. I don't get it.

NORTON. You don't, Mr. Keyes? Then what *do* you think of this case? This policy might cost us a great deal of money. As you know, it contains a double indemnity clause. Just what is your opinion?

KEYES. No opinion at all.

NORTON. Not even a hunch? One of those interesting little hunches of yours?

KEYES. Nope. Not even a hunch.

NORTON. I'm surprised, Mr. Keyes. I've formed a very definite opinion. I think I know — in fact I know I know what happened to Dietrichson.

KEYES. You know you know what?

NORTON. I know it was not an accident. (*He looks from Keyes to Neff and back to Keyes.*) What do you say to that?

KEYES. Me? You've got the ball. Let's see you run with it.

NORTON. There's a widespread feeling that just because a man has a large office —

The dictograph on his desk buzzes. He reaches over and depresses a key and puts the earpiece to his ear.

NORTON (*into the dictograph*). Yes? . . . Have her come in, please. — (*He replaces the earpiece. He turns back to Keyes and Neff.*) — that just because a man has a large office he must be an idiot. I'm having a visitor, if you don't mind. (*Keyes and Neff start to get up.*) No, no. I want you to stay and watch me handle this.

SECRETARY (*opening the door and ushering someone in*). Mrs. Dietrichson.

Neff stands staring at the door. He relaxes with an obvious effort of will. Phyllis comes in. She wears a gray tailored suit, small black hat with a veil, black gloves, and carries a black bag. The secretary closes the door behind her. Mr. Norton goes to meet her.

NORTON. Thank you very much for coming, Mrs. Dietrichson. I assure you I appreciate it. (*He turns a little toward Keyes.*) This is Mr. Keyes.

KEYES. How do you do.

PHYLLIS. How do you do.

NORTON. And Mr. Neff.

PHYLLIS. I've met Mr. Neff. How do you do.

Norton has placed a chair near her. Phyllis sits down. Norton goes behind his desk.

NORTON. Mrs. Dietrichson, I assure you of our sympathy in your bereavement. I hesitated before asking you to come here so soon after your loss. (*Phyllis nods silently.*) But now that you're here I hope you won't mind if I plunge straight into business. You know why we asked you to come, don't you?

PHYLLIS. No. All I know is that your secretary made it sound very urgent.

Keyes sits quietly in his chair with his legs crossed. He has hung his hat on his foot and thrust his thumbs in the armholes of his vest. He looks a little bored. Neff, behind him, stands leaning against the false mantel, completely dead-pan.

NORTON. Your husband had an accident policy with this company. Evidently you don't know that, Mrs. Dietrichson.

PHYLLIS. No. I remember some talk at the house — (*looking toward Neff*) — but he didn't seem to want it.

NEFF. He took it out a few days later, Mrs. Dietrichson.

PHYLLIS. I see.

NORTON. You'll probably find the policy among his personal effects.

PHYLLIS. His safe deposit box hasn't been opened yet. It seems a tax examiner has to be present.

NORTON. Please, Mrs. Dietrichson, I don't want you to think you are being subjected to any questioning. But there are a few things we should like to know.

PHYLLIS. What sort of things?

NORTON. We have the report of the coroner's inquest. Accidental death. We are not entirely satisfied. In fact, we are not satisfied at all. (*Phyllis looks at him coolly; Keyes looks vaguely interested; Neff is staring straight at Phyllis.*) Frankly Mrs. Dietrichson, we suspect suicide. (*Phyllis doesn't bat an eyelash.*) I'm sorry. Would you like a glass of water?

PHYLLIS. Please.

NORTON. Mr. Neff.

He indicates a thermos on a stand near Neff. Neff pours a glass of water and carries it over to Phyllis. She has lifted her veil a little. She takes the glass from his hand.

PHYLLIS. Thank you. (*Their eyes meet for a fraction of a second.*)

NORTON. Had your husband been moody or depressed lately, Mrs. Dietrichson? Did he seem to have financial worries, for instance?

PHYLLIS. He was perfectly all right and I don't know of any financial worries.

NORTON. There must have been something, Mrs. Dietrichson. Let us examine this so-called accident. First, your husband takes out this policy in absolute secrecy. Why? Because he doesn't want his family to suspect what he intends to do.

PHYLLIS. Do what?

NORTON. Commit suicide. Next, he goes on this trip entirely alone. He has to be alone. He hobbles all the way out to the observation platform, very unlikely with his leg in a cast, unless he has a very strong reason. Once there, he finds he is not alone. There is a man there. What was his name, Keyes? (*Norton flips his fingers impatiently at Keyes who doesn't even bother to look up.*)

KEYES. His name was Jackson. Probably still is.

NORTON. Jackson. So your husband gets rid of this Jackson with some flimsy excuse about cigars. And then he is alone. And then he does it. He jumps. Suicide. In which case the company is not liable. — You know that, of course. We could go to court —

PHYLLIS. I don't know anything. In fact I don't know why I came here. (*She makes as if to rise indignantly.*)

NORTON. Just a moment, please. I said we *could* go to court. I didn't say we want to. Not only is it against our practice, but it would involve a great deal of expense, a lot of lawyers, a lot of time, perhaps years. (*As Phyllis rises coldly*) So what I want to suggest is a compromise on both sides. A settlement for a certain sum, a part of the policy value —

PHYLLIS. Don't bother, Mr. Norton. When I came in here I had no idea you owed me any money. You told me you did. Then you told me you didn't. Now you tell me you want to pay me a part of it, whatever it is. You want to bargain with me, at a time like this. I don't like your insinuations about my husband, Mr. Norton, and I don't like your methods. In fact I don't like you, Mr. Norton. Goodbye, gentlemen.

She turns and walks out. The door closes after her. There is a pregnant pause. Keyes straightens up in his chair.

KEYES. Nice going, Mr. Norton. You sure carried that ball. (*As Norton pours himself a glass of water and stands holding it*) Only you fumbled on the goal line. Then you heaved an illegal forward pass and got thrown for a forty-yard loss. Now you can't pick yourself up because you haven't got a leg to stand on.

NORTON. I haven't eh? Let her claim. Let her sue. We can prove it was suicide.

KEYES (*standing up*). Can we? Mr. Norton, the first thing that hit me was that suicide angle. Only I dropped it in the wastepaper basket just three seconds later. You ought to look at the statistics on suicide sometime. You might learn a little something about the insurance business.

NORTON. I was raised in the insurance business, Mr. Keyes.

KEYES. Yeah. In the front office. Come on, you never read an actuarial table in your life. I've got ten volumes on suicide alone. Suicide by race, by color, by occupation, by sex, by seasons of the year, by time of day. Suicide, how committed: by poisons, by fire-arms, by drowning, by leaps. Suicide by poison, subdivided by types of poison, such as corrosive, irritant, systemic, gaseous, narcotic, alkaloid, protein, and so forth. Suicide by leaps, subdivided by leaps from high places, under wheels of trains, under wheels of trucks, under the feet of horses, from steamboats. But, Mr. Norton, of all the cases on record there's not one single case of suicide by leap from the rear end of a moving train. And do you know how fast that train was going at the point where the body was found? Fifteen miles an hour. Now how could anybody jump off a slow-moving train like that with any kind of expectation that he would kill himself? No soap, Mr. Norton. We're sunk, and we're going to pay through the nose, and you know it. May I have this?

Keyes' throat is dry after the long speech. He grabs the glass of water out of Norton's hand and drains it in one big gulp. Norton is watching him almost stupefied. Neff stands with the shadow of a smile on his face. Keyes puts the glass down noisily on Norton's desk.

KEYES. Come on, Walter.

Norton doesn't move or speak. Keyes puts his hat on and crosses toward the door, Neff after him. With the doorknob in his hands Keyes turns back to Norton with a glance down at his own shirt sleeves.

KEYES. Next time I'll rent a tuxedo.

They go out and the scene dissolves to Neff at the dictaphone at night. There is a tired grin on his face as he talks into the horn.

NEFF. I could have hugged you right then and there, Keyes, you and your statistics. You were the only one we were really scared of, and instead you were almost playing on our team . . .

This dissolves to Neff's apartment. It is almost dark in the room. The corridor door opens, letting the light in. Neff enters with his hat on and his briefcase under his arm. He switches the lights on, closes the door, puts the key in his pocket. At this moment the telephone rings. He picks up the phone.

NEFF'S VOICE (*his dictation synchronized with the scene*). That evening when I got home my nerves had eased off. I could feel the ground under my feet again, and it looked like easy going from there on in.
NEFF (*at the telephone*). Hello . . . hello, baby. . . . Sure, everything is fine . . . You were wonderful in Norton's office.

A telephone booth in a drug store: Phyllis is on the phone. She is not dressed as in Norton's office.

PHYLLIS. I felt so funny. I wanted to look at you all the time.
NEFF (*at the telephone in his apartment*). How do you think I felt? Where are you, baby?
PHYLLIS (*at the phone*). At the drug store. Just a block away. Can I come up?

Neff's apartment, with Neff at the phone:

NEFF. Okay. But be careful. Don't let anybody see you.

He hangs up, takes off his hat and drops hat and briefcase on the davenport. He looks around the room and crosses to lower the venetian blinds and draw the curtains. He gathers up the morning paper which is lying untidily on the floor and puts it in the wastepaper basket. The door bell rings. Neff stops in sudden alarm. It can't be Phyllis. The time is too short. For a second he stands there motionless, then crosses to the door and opens it. In the door stands Keyes.

NEFF. Hello, Keyes.

Keyes walks past him into the room. His hands are clasped behind his back. There is a strange, absent-minded look in his eyes. Neff closes the door without taking his eyes off Keyes.

NEFF. What's on your mind?

KEYES (*stopping in the middle of the room and turning*). That broken leg. The guy broke his leg.

NEFF. What are you talking about?

KEYES. Talking about Dietrichson. He had accident insurance, didn't he? Then he broke his leg, didn't he?

NEFF. So what?

KEYES. And he didn't put in a claim. Why didn't he put in a claim? Why?

NEFF. What the dickens are you driving at?

KEYES. Walter, there's something wrong. I ate dinner two hours ago. It stuck half way. (*He prods his stomach with his thumb.*) The little man is acting up again. Because there's something wrong with that Dietrichson case.

NEFF. Because he didn't put in a claim? Maybe he just didn't have time.

KEYES. Or maybe he just didn't know he was insured.

He has stopped in front of Neff. They look at each other for a tense moment. Neff hardly breathes. Then Keyes shakes his head suddenly.

KEYES. No. That couldn't be it. You delivered the policy to him personally, didn't you, Walter? And you got his check.

NEFF (*stiff-lipped, but his voice is as well under control as he can manage*). Sure, I did.

KEYES (*prodding his stomach again*). Got any bicarbonate of soda?

NEFF. No, I haven't.

KEYES (*resuming his pacing*). Listen, Walter. I've been living with this little man for twenty-six years. He's never failed me yet. There's got to be something wrong.

NEFF. Maybe Norton was right. Maybe it was suicide, Keyes.

KEYES. No. Not suicide — But not accident either.

NEFF. What else?

There is another longer pause, agonizing for Neff. Finally Keyes continues:

KEYES. Look. A man takes out an accident policy that is worth a hundred thousand dollars, if he is killed on a train. Then, two weeks later, he *is* killed on a train. And not in a train accident, mind you, but falling off some silly observation car. Do you know what the mathematical probability of that is, Walter? One out of I don't know how many billions. And add to that the broken leg. It just can't be the way it looks, Walter. Something has been worked on us.

NEFF. Such as what?

Keyes doesn't answer. He goes on pacing up and down. Finally Neff can't stand the silence any longer.

NEFF. Murder?

KEYES (*prodding his stomach again*). Don't you have any peppermint or anything?

NEFF. I'm sorry. (*After a pause*) Who do you suspect?

KEYES. Maybe I like to make things easy for myself. But I always tend to suspect the beneficiary.

NEFF. The wife?

KEYES. Yeah. That wide-eyed dame that didn't know anything about anything.

NEFF. You're crazy, Keyes. She wasn't even on the train.

KEYES. I know she wasn't, Walter. I don't claim to know how it was worked, or who worked it, but I know that it *was* worked. (*He crosses to the corridor door.*) I've got to get to a drug store. It feels like a hunk of concrete inside me.

As he puts his hand on the knob to open the door, the scene cuts to the corridor. The lighted hallway is empty except for Phyllis, who has been standing close to the door of Neff's apartment, listening. The door has just started to open. Phyllis moves away quickly and flattens herself against the wall behind the opening door. Keyes is coming out.

KEYES. Good night, Walter.

Neff, behind him, looks anxiously down the hallway for Phyllis. Suddenly his eye catches a glimpse of her through the crack of the partly opened door. He pushes the door wide so as to hide her from Keyes.

NEFF. Good night, Keyes.

KEYES. See you at the office in the morning. (*He has reached the elevator. He pushes the call button and turns.*) But I'd like to move in on her right now, tonight, if it wasn't for Norton and his stripe-pants ideas about company policy. I'd have the cops after her so quick her head would spin. They'd put her through the wringer, and, brother, what they would squeeze out.

NEFF. Only you haven't got a single thing to go on, Keyes.

KEYES (*as the elevator comes up and stops*). Not too much. Twenty-six years experience, all the percentage there is, and this lump of concrete in my stomach.

He pulls back the elevator door and turns to Neff with one last glance of annoyance.

KEYES (*almost angrily*). No bicarbonate of soda.

Keyes gets into the elevator. The door closes. The elevator goes down. Neff stands numb, looking at the spot where Keyes was last visible. Without moving his eyes he pulls the door around toward him with his left hand. Phyllis slowly comes out. Neff motions quickly to her to go into the apartment. She crosses in front of him and enters. He steps in backwards after her.

Neff's apartment: Phyllis has come a few steps into the room. Neff, backing in after her, closes the door from inside and turns slowly. They look at each other for a long moment in complete silence.

PHYLLIS. How much does he know?

NEFF. It's not what he knows. It's those stinking hunches of his.

PHYLLIS. But he can't prove anything, can he?

NEFF. Not if we're careful. Not if we don't see each other for a while.

PHYLLIS. For how long a while? (*She moves toward him but he does not respond.*)

NEFF. Until all this dies down. You don't know Keyes the way I do. Once he gets his teeth into something he won't let go. He'll investigate you. He'll have you shadowed. He'll watch you every minute from now on. Are you afraid, baby?

PHYLLIS. Yes, I'm afraid. But not of Keyes. I'm afraid of us. We're not the same any more. We did it so we could be together, but instead of that it's pulling us apart. Isn't it, Walter?

NEFF. What are you talking about?

PHYLLIS. And you don't really care whether we see each other or not.

NEFF. Shut up, baby.

He pulls her close and kisses her as the scene fades out.

PART FOUR

THE ANTEROOM of the insurance office fades in. Two telephone operators and a receptionist are at work. Several visitors are waiting in chairs. Lola Dietrichson is one of them. She's wearing a simple black suit and hat, indicating mourning. Her fingers nervously pick at a handkerchief and her eyes are watching the elevator doors anxiously. (Now and then the telephone operators in the background are heard saying, "Pacific All-Risk. Good Afternoon.") The elevator comes up and the doors open. Several people come out, among them Neff, carrying his briefcase. Lola sees him and stands up, and, as he is about to pass through the anteroom without recognizing her, she stops him.

LOLA. Hello, Mr. Neff.
NEFF (*looking at her, a little startled*). Hello — (*His voice hangs in the air.*)
LOLA. Lola Dietrichson. Don't you remember me?
NEFF (*on his guard*). Yes. Of course.
LOLA. Could I talk to you, just for a few minutes? Somewhere where we can be alone?
NEFF. Sure. Come on into my office.

He pushes the swing door open and holds it for her. As she passes in front of him his eyes narrow in uneasy speculation. — This cuts to the twelfth floor balcony as Neff comes up level with Lola and leads her toward his office.

NEFF. Is it something to do with — what happened?
LOLA. Yes, Mr. Neff. It's about my father's death.
NEFF. I'm terribly sorry, Miss Dietrichson.

He opens the door of his office and holds it for her. She enters and the scene cuts to the interior of Neff's office where Lou Schwartz, one of the other salesmen, is working at his desk.

NEFF (*to Schwartz*). Lou, do you mind if I use the office alone for a few minutes?
SCHWARTZ. It's all yours, Walter.

He gets up and goes out. Lola has walked over to the window and is looking out so Schwartz won't stare at her. Neff places a chair beside his desk.

NEFF. Won't you sit down?

At the sound of the closing door she turns and speaks with a catch in her voice.

LOLA. Mr. Neff, I can't help it, but I have such a strange feeling that there is something queer about my father's death.

NEFF. Queer? Queer in what way?

LOLA. I don't know why I should be bothering you with my troubles, except that you knew my father and knew about the insurance he took out. And you were so nice to me that evening in your car.

NEFF. Sure. We got along fine, didn't we.

He sits down. His face is grim and watchful.

LOLA. Look at me, Mr. Neff. I'm not crazy. I'm not hysterical. I'm not even crying. But I have the awful feeling that something is wrong, and I had the same feeling once before — when my mother died.

NEFF. When your mother died?

LOLA. We were up at Lake Arrowhead. That was six years ago. We had a cabin there. It was winter and very cold and my mother was very sick with pneumonia. She had a nurse with her. There were just the three of us in the cabin. One night I got up and went into my mother's room. She was delirious with fever. All the bed covers were on the floor and the windows were wide open. The nurse wasn't in the room. I ran and covered my mother up as quickly as I could. Just then I heard a door open behind me. The nurse stood there. She didn't say a word, but there was a look in her eyes I'll never forget. Two days later my mother was dead. (*After a pause*) Do you know who that nurse was?

Neff stares at her tensely. He knows only too well who the nurse was.

NEFF. No. Who?

LOLA. Phyllis. I tried to tell my father, but I was just a kid then, and he wouldn't listen to me. Six months later she married him and I kind of talked myself out of the idea that she could have done anything like that. But now it's all back again, now that something has happened to my father, too.

NEFF. You're not making sense, Miss Dietrichson. Your father fell off a train.

LOLA. Yes, and two days before he fell off that train what was Phyllis doing? She was in her room in front of a mirror, with a black hat on, and she was pinning a black veil to it, as if she couldn't wait to see how she would look in mourning.

NEFF. Look. You've had a pretty bad shock. Aren't you just imagining all this?

LOLA. I caught her eyes in the mirror, and they had that look in them they had before my mother died. That same look.

NEFF. You don't like your step-mother, do you? Isn't it just because she *is* your step-mother?

LOLA. I loathe her. Because she did it. She did it for the money. Only you're not going to pay her, are you, Mr. Neff? She's not going to get away with it this time. I'm going to speak up. I'm going to tell everything I know.

NEFF. You'd better be careful, saying things like that.

LOLA. I'm not afraid. You'll see.

She turns again to the window so he won't see that she is crying. Neff gets up and goes to her.

LOLA. I'm sorry. I didn't mean to act like this.

NEFF. All this that you've been telling me — who else have you told?

LOLA. No one.

NEFF. How about your step-mother?

LOLA. Of course not. I'm not living in the house any more. I moved out.

NEFF. And you didn't tell that boyfriend of yours? Zachette.

LOLA. I'm not seeing him any more. We had a fight.

NEFF. Where are you living then?

LOLA. I got myself a little apartment in Hollywood.

NEFF. Four walls, and you just sit and look at them, huh?

LOLA (*turning from the window with a pathetic little nod; through her tears*). Yes, Mr. Neff.

The scene dissolves to La Golondrina at night. In the foreground, Neff and Lola are having dinner. In the background the usual activity of Olvera Street — sidewalk peddlers, guitar players, etc. This dissolves to Neff's coupe. Neff and Lola are driving along the beach near

Santa Monica. Neff is wearing a light summer suit, very much in contrast to Lola's mourning. Apparently she is telling him a story and now and then she laughs, but there is no sound. (The view moves past her to a closeup of Neff behind the steering wheel.) He is only half listening to Lola. His mind is full of other thoughts.

NEFF'S VOICE (*synchronized with the above scene*). So I took her to dinner that evening at a Mexican joint down on Olvera Street where nobody would see us. I wanted to cheer her up. . . . Next day was Sunday and we went for a ride down to the beach. She had loosened up a bit and she was even laughing. . . . I had to make sure she wouldn't tell that stuff about Phyllis to anybody else. It was dynamite, whether it was true or not. And I had no chance to talk to Phyllis. You were watching her like a hawk, Keyes. I couldn't even phone her for fear you had the wires tapped.

This dissolves to the insurance office as Neff, with his hat on and no briefcase, is walking toward Keyes' office. As he comes up close to the door, he stops with a startled expression on his face. On a chair beside the door sits a familiar figure. He is Jackson, the man from the observation platform of the train. He is wearing his Stetson hat and smoking a cigar. He is studying something in the file folder. Neff recognizes him immediately but Jackson does not look up. Neff controls his expression and goes on to open the door to Keyes' office.

NEFF'S VOICE (*over the above scene*). Monday morning there was a note on my desk that you wanted to see me, Keyes. For a minute I wondered if it could be about Lola. It was worse. Outside your door was the last guy in the world I wanted to see.

Inside Keyes' office: Neff is just closing the door from the inside. Keyes, his coat off, is lying on his office couch, chewing on a cigar, as usual.

KEYES. Come in. Come in, Walter. I want to ask you something. After all the years we've known each other, do you mind if I make a rather blunt statement?
NEFF. About what?
KEYES. About me. Walter, I'm a very great man. This Dietrichson business. It's murder, and murders don't come any neater. As fancy a piece of homicide as anybody ever ran into. Smart and tricky and almost perfect, *but* — (*bouncing off the couch like a rubber ball*) — but, I

think Papa has it all figured out, figured out and wrapped up in tissue paper with pink ribbons on it.

NEFF. I'm listening.

KEYES (*levelling a finger at him*). You know what? That guy Dietrichson was never on the train.

NEFF. He wasn't?

KEYES. No, he wasn't, Walter. Look, you can't be sure of killing a man by throwing him off a train that's going fifteen miles an hour. The only way you can be sure is to kill him first and then throw his body on the tracks. That would mean either killing him on the train, or — and this is where it really gets fancy — you kill him somewhere else and put him on the tracks. Two possibilities, and I personally buy the second.

NEFF. You're way ahead of me, Keyes.

KEYES. Look, it was like this. They killed the guy — the wife and somebody else — and then the somebody else took the crutches and went on the train as Dietrichson, and then the somebody else jumped off, and then they put the body on the tracks where the train had passed. An impersonation, see. And a cinch to work. Because it was night, very few people were about, they had the crutches to stare at, and they never really looked at the man at all.

NEFF. It's fancy all right, Keyes. Maybe it's a little too fancy.

KEYES. Is it? I tell you it fits together like a watch. And now let's see what we have in the way of proof. The only guy that really got a good look at this supposed Dietrichson is sitting right outside my office. I took the trouble to bring him down here from Oregon. Let's see what he has to say. (*Keyes goes to the door and opens it.*) Come in, Mr. Jackson.

JACKSON (*entering with the file folder*). Yes sir, Mr. Keyes. These are fine cigars you smoke. (*He indicates the cigar he himself is smoking.*)

KEYES. Two for a quarter.

JACKSON. That's what I said.

KEYES. Never mind the cigar, Jackson. Did you study those photographs? What do you say?

JACKSON. Yes, indeed, I studied them thoroughly. Very thoroughly.

KEYES. Well? Did you make up your mind?

JACKSON. Mr. Keyes, I'm a Medford man. Medford, Oregon. Up in Medford we take our time making up our minds —

KEYES. Well you're not in Medford now. I'm in a hurry. Let's have it.

JACKSON (*indicating the file folder he is holding*). Are these photographs of the late Mr. Dietrichson?

KEYES. Yes.

JACKSON. Then my answer is no.

KEYES. What do you mean no?

JACKSON. I mean this is not the man that was on the train.

KEYES. Will you swear to that?

JACKSON. I'm a Medford man. Medford, Oregon. And if I say it, I mean it, and if I mean it, of course I'll swear it.

KEYES. Thank you. (*Turning to Neff*) There you are, Walter. There's your proof. (*Keyes remembers he forgot to introduce Jackson.*) Oh, Mr. Jackson, this is Mr. Neff, one of our salesmen.

JACKSON. Pleased to meet you, Mr. Neff. Pleased indeed.

NEFF. How do you do?

JACKSON. Very fine, thank you. Never was better.

KEYES. Mr. Jackson, how would you describe the man you saw on that observation platform?

JACKSON. Well, I'm pretty sure he was a younger man, about ten or fifteen years younger than the man in these photographs.

KEYES. Dietrichson was about fifty, wasn't he, Walter?

NEFF. Fifty-one, according to the policy.

JACKSON. The man I saw was nothing like fifty-one years old. Of course, it was pretty dark on that platform and, come to think of it, he tried to keep his back toward me. But I'm positive just the same.

KEYES. That's fine, Jackson. Now you understand this matter is strictly confidential. We may need you again down here in Los Angeles, if the case comes to court.

JACKSON. Any time you need me, I'm at your entire disposal, gentlemen. Expenses paid, of course.

KEYES (*picking up the telephone on his desk and speaking into it*). Get me Lubin, in the cashier's office.

Meanwhile, Jackson crosses over to Neff and, during the ensuing dialogue between him and Neff, we hear Keyes' low voice on the phone in the background. We do not hear what he says.

JACKSON (*to Neff*). Ever been in Medford, Mr. Neff?

NEFF. Never.

JACKSON. Wait a minute. Do you go trout fishing? Maybe I saw you up Klamath Falls way.

NEFF. Nope. Never fish.

JACKSON. Neff. Neff. I've got it! It's the name. There's a family of Neffs in Corvallis.

NEFF. No relation.

JACKSON. Let me see. This man's an automobile dealer in Corvallis. Very reputable man, too, I'm told.

KEYES (*rejoining them at this point*). All right, Mr. Jackson. Suppose you go down to the cashier's office — room twenty-seven on the eleventh floor. They'll take care of your expense account and your ticket for the train tonight.

JACKSON. Tonight? Tomorrow morning would suit me better. There's a very good osteopath down here I want to see before I leave.

KEYES (*having opened the door for Jackson*). Okay, Mr. Jackson. Just don't put her on the expense account.

JACKSON (*doesn't get it*). Goodbye, gentlemen. A pleasure. (*He goes out.*)

KEYES. There it is, Walter. It's beginning to come apart at the seams already. A murder's never perfect. It always comes apart sooner or later. And when two people are involved it's usually sooner. We know the Dietrichson dame is in it, and somebody else. Pretty soon we're going to know who that somebody else is. He'll show. He's got to show. Sometime, somewhere, they've got to meet. Their emotions are all kicked up. Whether it's love or hate doesn't matter. They can't keep away from each other. They think it's twice as safe because there are two of them. But it's not twice as safe. It's ten times twice as dangerous. They've committed a murder and that's not like taking a trolley ride together where each one can get off at a different stop. They're stuck with each other. They've got to ride all the way to the end of the line. And it's a one-way trip, and the last stop is the cemetery. (*He puts a cigar in his mouth and starts tapping his pockets for matches.*) She put in her claim and I'm going to throw it right back at her. (*Patting his pockets again*) Have you got one of those?

Neff strikes a match for him. Keyes takes the match out of his hand and lights his cigar.

KEYES. Let her sue us if she dares. I'll be ready for her — and that somebody else. They'll be digging their own graves.

The scene dissolves to a telephone booth in Jerry's Market. Neff is in the booth dialing a number, and as he waits he looks around to make sure he is not watched.

NEFF (*into the phone*). Mrs. Dietrichson? . . . This is Jerry's Market. We just got in a shipment of that English soap you were asking about.

Will you be coming by this morning? . . . Thank you, Mrs. Dietrichson. (*Neff hangs up.*)

This dissolves to the exterior of Jerry's Market. The LaSalle stops in front of the market. Phyllis steps out and goes into the market, looking around. Then we see the shelves in the rear of the market.

Neff is moving slowly along them, outwardly calm but with his nerves on edge. From beyond him Phyllis approaches. She stops beside him, facing the same way, with a couple of feet separating them.

PHYLLIS. Hello, Walter.

NEFF (*in a harsh whisper*). Come closer.

PHYLLIS (*moving closer to him*). What's the matter?

NEFF. Everything's the matter. Keyes is rejecting your claim. He's sitting back with his mouth watering, waiting for you to sue. He wants you to sue. But you're not going to.

PHYLLIS. What's he got to stop me?

NEFF. He's got the goods. He's figured out how it was worked. He knows it was somebody else on the train. He's dug up a witness he thinks will prove it.

PHYLLIS. Prove it how? Listen, if he rejects that claim, I *have* to sue.

NEFF. Yeah? And then you're in court and a lot of other things are going to come up. Like, for instance, about you and the first Mrs. Dietrichson.

PHYLLIS (*looking at him sharply*). What about me and the first Mrs. Dietrichson?

NEFF. The way she died. And about that black hat you were trying on — before you needed a black hat.

A customer comes along the aisle toward them. They move apart. The customer passes. Phyllis draws close again.

PHYLLIS. Walter, Lola's been telling you some of her cockeyed stories. She's been seeing you.

NEFF. I've been seeing her, if you want to know. So she won't yell her head off about what *she* knows.

PHYLLIS. Yes, she's been putting on an act for you, crying all over your shoulder, that lying little —

NEFF. Keep her out of it. All I'm telling you is we're not going to sue.

PHYLLIS. Because you don't want the money any more, even if you could get it? Because she's made you feel like a heel all of a sudden.

(*She begins to cry again.*) Maybe I'm just crazy. Maybe it's all just in my mind.

NEFF. Sure, it's all in your mind.

LOLA. I only wish it was, Walter, because I still love him.

Over Neff's face, as he listens to the music comes the dictation:

NEFF'S VOICE. Zachette. That's funny. Phyllis and Zachette. What was he doing up at her house? I couldn't figure that one out. I tried to make sense out of it and got nowhere. But the real brain-twister came the next day. You sprang it on me, Keyes, after office hours, when you caught me down in the lobby of the building.

This dissolves to the lobby of the Pacific Building, about 5:00 P.M. or a little later. A stream of office employees is coming out of an elevator; a second elevator reaches the lobby and some more office employees come out, among them Neff, wearing his hat and carrying his briefcase. The view precedes him as he walks toward the entrance door. He is stopped by Keyes' voice, off to one side.

KEYES' VOICE. Oh, Walter, just a minute.

Neff stops and looks toward the cigar counter, as he moves toward him. Keyes is standing there buying cigars. He is stuffing them into his pockets.

NEFF. Hello, Keyes.

KEYES. Hang onto your hat, Walter.

NEFF. What for?

KEYES. Nothing much. The Dietrichson case just busted wide open.

NEFF. How do you mean?

KEYES. The guy showed. That's how.

NEFF. The somebody else?

KEYES. Yeah. The guy that did it with her.

NEFF. No kidding?

KEYES. She's filed suit against us, and it's okay by me. When we get into that courtroom I'll tear them apart, both of them. Come on — I'll buy you a martini.

NEFF. No thanks, Keyes.

KEYES. With two olives.

NEFF. I've got to get a shave and a shoeshine. I've got a date.

KEYES. Margie. I still bet she drinks from the bottle.

He bites off the end of the cigar and puts the cigar into his mouth. He starts tapping his pockets for a match, as usual. Neff strikes a match for him.

NEFF. They give you matches when they sell you cigars, Keyes. All you have to do is ask for them.

KEYES. I don't like them. They always explode in my pockets. So long, Walter.

Keyes goes toward the street and out of the scene. Neff moves back into the lobby. As he reaches the elevator, he looks back over his shoulder, to make sure Keyes is gone, then steps into the empty elevator.

NEFF (*entering the elevator*). Twelve.

This dissolves to the entrance of the office on the twelfth floor as Neff comes out of the elevator. The receptionist is just tidying up her desk. She has her hat on and is preparing to leave. Neff passes on through the swinging doors to the twelfth-floor balcony. This cuts to the twelfth-floor balcony as Neff enters from the reception room. A couple of belated employees are leaving for the day. Neff goes toward Keyes' office, looks around to make sure he is unobserved, and enters. Keyes' office: Neff has just come in. He goes over to Keyes' desk and searches the papers on it. He tries the desk drawers and finds them locked. His eye falls on the dictaphone on the stand beside the desk. A record is on it, the needle is about two thirds of the way toward the end. He lifts the needle and sets it back to the beginning of the record, sets the switch to play-back position. He lifts the arm off the bracket and starts the machine. Keyes' voice is heard coming from the horn:

KEYES' VOICE. Memo to Mr. Norton. Confidential. Dietrichson File. With regard to your proposal to put Walter Neff under surveillance, I disagree absolutely. I have investigated his movements on the night of the crime, and he is definitely placed in his apartment from 7:15 P.M. on. In addition to this, I have known Neff intimately for eleven years, and I personally vouch for him, without reservation. . . .

Neff stops the machine. He sits down slowly, still holding the horn. He is deeply moved. After a moment, he presses the switch again.

KEYES' VOICE (*from the dictaphone*). . . . Furthermore, no connection whatsoever has been established between Walter Neff and Mrs. Phyllis Dietrichson, whereas I am now able to report that such a connection has been established between her and another man. This man has been observed to visit the Dietrichson home on the night of July 9th, 10th, 11th, 12th and 13th. We have succeeded in identifying him as one Nino Zachette, former medical student, aged twenty-eight, residing at Lilac Court Apartments, 1228½ N. La Brea Avenue. We have checked Zachette's movements on the night of the crime and have found that they cannot be accounted for. I am preparing a more detailed report for your consideration, and it is my belief that we already have sufficient evidence against Zachette and Mrs. Dietrichson to justify police action. I strongly urge that this whole matter be turned over to the office of the District Attorney. Respectfully, Barton Keyes.

Neff sits, staring blankly at the wall. The cylinder goes on revolving, but no more voice comes — only the whir of the needle on the empty record. At last he remembers to replace the horn. He hangs it back on its hook. The machine stops. Neff gets up from the chair, walks slowly to the door and goes out.

We see the twelfth-floor balcony as Neff comes out of Keyes' office. He walks slowly back toward the reception room entrance, then stands there looking out through the glass doors. All the employees have now left. Neff is entirely alone. He moves as if to go out, then stops rigidly as his face lights up with excitement at a sudden idea. He turns quickly and walks on to his own office and enters. Then Neff's office comes into view as Neff walks across to his desk, lifts the telephone and dials a number. (During the ensuing telephone conversation, only what he says is heard. The pauses indicate speeches at the other end of the line.)

NEFF. Phyllis? Walter. I've got to see you . . . Tonight . . . Yes, it has to be tonight . . . How's eleven o'clock? Don't worry about Keyes. He's satisfied . . . Leave the door on the latch and put the lights out. No, nobody's watching the house . . . I told you Keyes is satisfied. It's just for the neighbors . . . That's what I said. Yeah. Eleven o'clock. Goodbye, baby.

Neff hangs up and stands beside the desk with a grim expression on his face, takes a handkerchief out and wipes perspiration from his forehead and the palms of his hands. The gesture has a symbolic quality, as if he were trying to wipe away the murder.

NEFF'S VOICE. I guess I don't have to tell you what I was going to do at eleven o'clock, Keyes. For the first time I saw a way to get clear of the whole mess I was in, and of Phyllis, too, all at the same time. Yeah, that's what I thought. But what I didn't know was that she was all set for me. That she had outsmarted me again, just like she always had . . .

This dissolves to the hall stairway of the Dietrichson home at night. The lights are turned on. Phyllis is coming down the stairs. She wears white lounging pajamas, and she is carrying something small and heavy concealed in a scarf in her right hand. She reaches the front door, opens it slightly, fixes the catch so that the door can be opened from the outside. She switches off the porch light and the hall light. She moves toward the living room, where there is still a light on.

NEFF'S VOICE. She was all set and waiting for me. It could have been something in my voice when I called her up that tipped her off. And it could have been that she had the idea already. And an idea wasn't the only thing she had waiting for me.

The scene cuts to the living room. On the long table behind the davenport, one of the lamps is lit. The only other light in the room is a standing lamp beside the desk. A window toward the back is open, and through it comes the sound of music, probably a neighboring radio. Phyllis enters and crosses to the table. She puts out the lamp, then moves over to the desk and puts out the lamp there. The room is filled with bright moonlight coming in at the windows. Phyllis crosses to the chair by the fireplace (the one she sat in the first time Neff came to the house). She lifts the loose cushion and puts what was in the scarf behind it. As she withdraws the scarf, there is a brief glint of something metallic before she covers the hidden object with the cushion again. She turns to the low table in front of the davenport and takes a cigarette from the box. She takes a match and is about to strike it when, just then, she hears a car coming up the hill. She listens, motionless. The car stops. A car door is slammed. Calmly, Phyllis strikes the match and lights her cigarette. She drops the match casually into a tray, goes back to the chair, sits down and waits, quietly smoking. There are footsteps outside the house. Over the chair in which Phyllis is sitting the hallway is visible through the arch. The front door opens. Neff comes in. He is silhouetted against the moonlight as he stands there. He closes the door again.

PHYLLIS (*in the foreground*). In here, Walter.

Neff comes through the arch and walks slowly toward her.

NEFF. Hello, baby. Anybody in the house?

PHYLLIS. Nobody. Why?

NEFF. What's that music?

PHYLLIS. A radio up the street.

NEFF (*sitting down on the arm of the davenport, close to her*). Just like the first time I was here. We were talking about automobile insurance. Only you were thinking about murder. And I was thinking about that anklet.

PHYLLIS. And what are you thinking about now?

NEFF. I'm all through thinking. This is goodbye.

PHYLLIS. Goodbye? Where are you going?

NEFF. It's you that's going, baby. Not me. I'm getting off the trolley car right at this corner.

PHYLLIS. Suppose you stop being fancy. Let's have it, whatever it is.

NEFF. I have a friend who's got a funny theory. He says when two people commit a murder they're kind of on a trolley car, and one can't get off without the other. They're stuck with each other. They have to go on riding clear to the end of the line. And the last stop is the cemetery.

PHYLLIS. Maybe he's got something there.

NEFF. You bet he has. Two people are going to ride to the end of the line, all right. Only I'm not going to be one of them. I've got another guy to finish my ride for me.

PHYLLIS. So you've got it all arranged, Walter.

NEFF. You arranged it for me. I didn't have to do a thing.

PHYLLIS. Just who are you talking about?

NEFF. An acquaintance of yours. A Mr. Zachette. Come on, baby, I just got into this because I knew a little something about insurance, didn't I? I was just a sucker. I'd have been brushed off as soon as you got your hands on the money.

PHYLLIS. What are you talking about?

NEFF. Save it. I'm telling this. It's been you and that Zachette guy all along, hasn't it?

PHYLLIS. That's not true.

NEFF. It doesn't make any difference whether it's true or not. The point is Keyes believes Zachette is the guy he's been looking for. He'll have him in the gas chamber before he knows what happened to him.

PHYLLIS. And what's happening to me all this time?

NEFF. Don't be silly. What do you expect to happen to you? You helped him do the murder, didn't you? That's what Keyes thinks. And what's good enough for Keyes is good enough for me.

PHYLLIS. Maybe it's not good enough for me, Walter. Maybe I don't go for the idea. Maybe I'd rather talk.

NEFF. Sometimes people are where they can't talk. Under six feet of dirt, for instance. And if it was you, they'd just charge it up to Zachette, wouldn't they. One more item on his account. Sure they would. That's just what they're going to do. Especially since he's coming here tonight . . . Oh, in about fifteen minutes from now, baby. With the cops right behind him. It's all taken care of.

PHYLLIS. And that'd make everything lovely for you, wouldn't it?

NEFF. Right. And it's got to be done before that suit of yours comes to trial, and Lola gets a chance to sound off, and they trip you up on the stand, and you start to fold up and drag me down with you.

PHYLLIS. Listen, Walter. Maybe I had Zachette here so they won't get a chance to trip me up. So we can get that money and be together.

NEFF. That's cute. Say it again.

PHYLLIS. He came here the first time just to ask where Lola was. I made him come back. I was working on him. He's a crazy sort of guy, quick-tempered. I kept hammering into him that she was with another man, so he'd get into one of his jealous rages, and then I'd tell him where she was. And you know what he'd have done to her, don't you, Walter.

NEFF. Yeah, and for once I believe you. Because it's just rotten enough.

PHYLLIS. We're both rotten, Walter.

NEFF. Only you're just a little more rotten. You're rotten clear through. You got me to take care of your husband, and then you got Zachette to take care of Lola, and maybe take care of me too, and then somebody else would have come along to take care of Zachette for you. That's the way you operate isn't it, baby.

PHYLLIS. Suppose it is, Walter. Is what you've cooked up for tonight any better?

NEFF (*getting up from the davenport, listening to the music for a moment*). I don't like this music anymore. It's too close. Do you mind if I shut the window?

Phyllis just stares at him. He goes quietly over to the window and shuts it and draws the curtain. Phyllis speaks to his back:

PHYLLIS (*her voice low and urgent*). Walter!

Neff turns; something changes in his face. There is the report of a gun. He stands motionless for a moment, then very slowly starts toward her. Phyllis stands with the gun in her hand. Neff stops after he has taken a few steps.

NEFF. What's the matter? Why don't you shoot again? Maybe if I came a little closer? (*Taking a few more steps toward her and stopping again*) How's that. Do you think you can do it now?

Phyllis is silent. She doesn't shoot. Her expression is tortured. Neff goes on until he is close to her. Quietly he takes the gun out of her unresisting hand.

NEFF. Why didn't you shoot, baby? (*In reply Phyllis puts her arms around him in complete surrender.*) Don't tell me it's because you've been in love with me all this time.
PHYLLIS. No. I never loved you, Walter. Not you, or anybody else. I'm rotten to the heart. I used you, just as you said. That's all you ever meant to me — until a minute ago. I didn't think anything like that could ever happen to me.
NEFF. I'm sorry, baby. I'm not buying.
PHYLLIS. I'm not asking you to buy. Just hold me close.

Neff draws her close to him. She reaches up to his face and kisses him on the lips. As she comes out of the kiss there is realization in her eyes that this is the final moment.

NEFF. Goodbye, baby.

Out of sight the gun explodes once, twice. Phyllis quivers in his arms. Her eyes fill with tears. Her head falls limp against his shoulder. Slowly he lifts her and carries her to the davenport. He lays her down on it carefully, almost tenderly. The moonlight coming in at the French doors shines on the anklet. He looks at it for the last time and slowly turns away. As he does so, he puts his hand inside his coat and it comes out with blood on it. Only then is it apparent that Phyllis' shot actually did hit him. He looks at the blood on his fingers with a dazed expression and quickly goes out of the room, the way he came.
And now Neff comes out of the Dietrichson home. He closes the front door with his right hand. His left arm hangs limp. He takes a few steps down the walk, then suddenly hears somebody approaching. He moves behind the palm tree near the walk.

A man comes up the steps toward the front door — Zachette. Just as he reaches the door, Neff calls to him.

NEFF. Hey you. Come here a minute. I said come here, Zachette. (*Zachette turns and approaches him slowly.*) The name is Neff.
ZACHETTE. Yeah? And I still don't like it. What do you want?
NEFF. Look, kid, I want to give you a present. (*He takes some loose change out of his pocket and holds out a coin.*) Here's a nice new nickel.
ZACHETTE. What's the gag?
NEFF. Suppose you go back down the hill to a drug store and make a phone call.

Neff starts to drop the nickel into Zachette's handkerchief pocket. Zachette knocks his hand away.

ZACHETTE. Keep your nickel and buy yourself an ice cream cone.
NEFF. The number is Granite 0386. Ask for Miss Dietrichson. The first name is Lola.
ZACHETTE. Lola? She isn't worth a nickel. And if I ever talk to her, it's not going to be over any telephone.
NEFF. Tough, aren't you? Take the nickel. Take it and call her. She wants you to.
ZACHETTE. Yeah? She doesn't want any part of me.
NEFF. I know who told you that, and it's not true. She's in love with you. Always has been. Don't ask me why. I couldn't even guess.

Zachette just stares at him. Neff moves again to put the nickel into Zachette's pocket. This time Zachette allows him to do it.

NEFF. Now beat it. Granite 0386, I told you. (*He motions toward the street below.*) That way.

Zachette goes slowly past him. Neff grabs him and pushes him almost violently down the walk. Zachette goes out of view. The sound of his steps dies away as Neff looks after him, and, far off in the distance, the siren of a police car is heard. Then Neff moves off through the shrubbery toward the side of the house where he parked his car.

This dissolves to Neff's office at night. The desk lamp is still lighted; outside the windows, the dawn is slowly breaking. Neff is still clutching the horn of the dictaphone. There are eight or nine used cylinders on the desk beside him. A widening stain of blood shows on the left shoulder of his gray jacket. He is very weak by now, and his voice holds a note of utter exhaustion.

NEFF. It's almost four-thirty now, Keyes. It's cold. I wonder if she's still lying there alone in that house, or whether they've found her by now. I wonder a lot of things, but they don't matter any more, except I want to ask you to do me a favor. I want you to be the one to tell Lola, kind of gently, before it breaks wide open . . . Yes, and I'd like you to look after her and that guy Zachette, so he doesn't get pushed around too much. Because . . .

Suddenly he stops his dictation with an instinctive feeling that he is not alone in the room.

As he turns in his chair the view draws back slowly. The office is wide open. Keyes is standing a few steps inside it. Behind him, on the balcony outside, stands the night watchman and the colored janitor, peering curiously into the room over Keyes' shoulder. Slowly, and without taking his eyes off Neff's face, Keyes reaches back and pushes the door shut. Neff hangs up the dictaphone horn. He looks at Keyes with a faint, tired grin and speaks very slowly.

NEFF. Hello, Keyes. (*Keyes moves toward him a few steps and stands without answering.*) Up pretty early, aren't you? I always wondered what time you got down to work. (*Keyes, staring at him, still does not answer.*) Or did your little man pull you out of bed.

KEYES. The janitor did. Seems you leaked a little blood on the way in here.

NEFF. Wouldn't be surprised. (*Neff makes a motion indicating the used cylinders standing on the desk.*) I wanted to straighten out that Dietrichson story for you.

KEYES. So I gather.

NEFF. How long have you been standing there?

KEYES. Long enough.

NEFF. Kind of a crazy story with a crazy twist to it. One you didn't quite figure out.

KEYES. You can't figure them all, Walter.

NEFF. That's right. You can't, can you? And now I suppose I get the big speech, the one with all the two-dollar words in it. Let's have it, Keyes.

KEYES. You're all washed up, Walter.

NEFF. Thanks, Keyes. That was short anyway.

They stare at each other for a long moment, then, with an intense effort Neff gets up on his feet and stands there swaying a little. His face is covered with sweat. His shoulder is bleeding. He is on the verge of collapse.

KEYES. Walter, I'm going to call a doctor.

NEFF (*bitterly*). What for? So they can patch me up? So they can nurse me along till I'm back on my feet? So I can walk under my own power into that gas chamber up in San Quentin? Is that it, Keyes?

KEYES. Something like that, Walter.

NEFF. Well, I've got a different idea. Look here. Suppose you went back to bed and didn't find these cylinders till tomorrow morning, when the office opens. From then on you can play it any way you like. Would you do that much for me, Keyes?

KEYES. Give me one good reason.

NEFF. I need four hours to get where I'm going.

KEYES. You're not going anywhere, Walter.

NEFF. You bet I am. I'm going across the border.

KEYES. You haven't got a chance.

NEFF. Good enough to try for.

KEYES. You'll never make the border.

NEFF. That's what you think. Watch me.

Neff starts to move toward the door, staggering a little, holding himself upright with great effort.

KEYES (*in a voice of stony calm*). You'll never even make the elevator.

Neff has reached the door. He twists the knob and drags the door open. He turns in it to look back at Keyes' implacable face.

NEFF. So long, Keyes.

Neff goes out, leaving the door wide open. The view follows his staggering walk along the balcony toward the elevator lobby. The sound of his breathing is so harsh and loud that for a moment it dominates the scene. Finally he reaches the swing doors leading into the lobby and starts to push them open. At this moment he collapses. He clutches the edge of the door and as it swings around with him he falls to the floor. He tries to struggle up but cannot rise. In the background comes the sound of a telephone being dialed.

KEYES' VOICE. Hello . . . Send an ambulance to the Pacific Building on Olive Street . . . Yeah . . . It's a police job.

There is the sound of the phone being replaced in its cradle. Then there are footsteps growing louder along the balcony and Keyes walks slowly into view. He kneels down beside Neff.

KEYES. How you doing, Walter?

Neff manages a faint smile.

NEFF. I'm fine. Only somebody moved the elevator a couple of miles away.

KEYES. They're on their way.

NEFF (*slowly and with great difficulty*). You know why you didn't figure this one, Keyes? Let me tell you. The guy you were looking for was too close. He was right across the desk from you.

KEYES. Closer than that, Walter. (*The eyes of the two men meet in a moment of silence.*)

NEFF. I love you too.

Neff fumbles for the handkerchief in Keyes' pocket, pulls it out and clumsily wipes his face with it. The handkerchief drops from his hand. He gets a loose cigarette out of his pocket and puts it between his lips. Then with great difficulty he gets out a match, tries to strike it, but is too weak. Keyes takes the match out of his hand, strikes it for him and lights his cigarette. The scene fades out.

SOURCES

The following books and essays proved useful in preparing the introductions to the selections in this book.

Auden, W. H. "The Guilty Vicarage," in *The Dyer's Hand*. New York, 1962.
Bruccoli, Matthew J. *Ross Macdonald*. San Diego, 1984.
Haycroft, Howard, ed. *The Art of the Mystery Story*. New York, 1983.
Hoffman, Daniel. *Poe Poe Poe Poe Poe Poe Poe*. New York, 1972.
Macdonald, Ross. "Introduction," in *Lew Archer, Private Detective*. New York, 1977.
MacShane, Frank, ed. *Selected Letters of Raymond Chandler*. New York, 1981.
Most, Glenn W., and William W. Stowe, eds. *The Poetics of Murder*. New York, 1983.
O'Brien, Geoffrey. "Jim Thompson, Dimestore Dostoevsky," in *The Alcoholics*. Berkeley, 1985.
Pronzini, Bill, and Marcia Muller. *1001 Midnights*. New York, 1986.
Steinbrunner, Chris, and Otto Penzler. *Encyclopedia of Mystery and Detection*. New York, 1969.
Symons, Julian. *Bloody Murder*. New York, 1985.
Walsh, John. *Poe the Detective*. New Brunswick, N.J., 1968.
Winks, Robin, ed., *Colloquium on Crime*. New York, 1986.
—— *Modus Operandi*. Boston, 1982.

ACKNOWLEDGMENTS

Paul Cain, "Pigeon Blood," from *Seven Slayers*. Copyright 1950 by Peter Ruric. Used with permission, Black Lizard Books, 833 Bancroft Way, Berkeley, Calif. 94710.

Raymond Chandler, "The Simple Art of Murder," from *The Simple Art of Murder*. Copyright © 1950 by Raymond Chandler. Copyright © renewed 1978 by Helga Greene. Reprinted by permission of Houghton Mifflin Company.

Raymond Chandler and Billy Wilder, "Double Indemnity." Screenplay of the Paramount photoplay *Double Indemnity*, copyright 1944 by Paramount Pictures, Inc. Reprinted by permission of MCA Publishing Rights.

Stanley Ellin, "The Nine-to-Five Man." Copyright © 1965 by Stanley Ellin. Reprinted by permission of Curtis Brown, Ltd.

Loren D. Estleman, "Dead Soldier," from *General Murders*. Copyright © 1988 by Loren D. Estleman. Reprinted by permission of Houghton Mifflin Company.

William Campbell Gault, "Dead-End for Delia." Copyright © 1950 by Popular Publications; renewed 1978 by William Campbell Gault. Reprinted by permission of Don Congdon Associates, Inc.

Sue Grafton, "The Parker Shotgun." Copyright © 1986 by Sue Grafton. Contained in *Mean Streets*, edited by Robert J. Randisi, copyright © 1986 by The Private Eye Writers of America. Reprinted by permission of the Mysterious Press and Warner Books, New York.

Dashiell Hammett, "The Tenth Clew," from *The Continental Op*. Copyright © 1974 by Lillian Hellman, Executrix of the estate of Dashiell Hammett. Reprinted by permission of Random House, Inc.

Joseph Hansen, "Election Day," from *Brandstetter & Others*. Copyright © 1984 by Joseph Hansen. First published in *Ellery Queen's Mystery Magazine*, November 1984. Reprinted by permission of the author.

Chester Himes, chapters 20 and 21 from *Blind Man with a Pistol*. Copyright © 1969 by Chester Himes. Reprinted by permission of Roslyn Targ Literary Agency, Inc., New York.

John D. MacDonald, "I Always Get the Cuties." Copyright 1954 by Mercury

Publications, Inc., copyright © renewed 1982 by John D. MacDonald Publishing, Inc. Reprinted by permission of Diskant and Associates.

Ross Macdonald, "Wild Goose Chase." Copyright 1954 by Kenneth Millar. Copyright renewed 1982 by The Margaret Millar Survivor's Trust u/a. Reprinted by permission of Harold Ober Associates Incorporated.

William Marshall, "Death by Water," from *Gelignite*. Copyright © 1976 by William Marshall. Reprinted by permission of John Farquharson Ltd.

Ed McBain, "Small Homicide." Copyright © 1953 by Evan Hunter, renewed 1981 by Hui Corporation. Reprinted by permission of John Farquharson Ltd.

Sara Paretsky, "Skin Deep." Copyright © 1987 by Sara Paretsky. Reprinted by permission of Dominick Abel Literary Agency, Inc.

Georges Simenon, "At the Etoile du Nord," from *Maigret's Pipe*, copyright and English translation © 1977 by Georges Simenon. Reprinted by permission of Harcourt Brace Jovanovich, Inc.

Mickey Spillane, "The Gold Fever Tapes," from *Tomorrow, I Die*. Copyright © 1983 by Mickey Spillane. Reprinted by permission of the author.

Paul Theroux, "The Johore Murders," from *The Consul's File*. Copyright © 1972, 1974, 1975, 1976, 1977 by Paul Theroux. Reprinted by permission of Houghton Mifflin Company.

Jim Thompson, "This World, Then the Fireworks," from *Fireworks* by Jim Thompson, published by Donald I. Fine, Inc. Copyright © 1987 by the Estate of Jim Thompson. Reprinted with permission.

Janwillem van de Wetering, "Sure, Blue, and Dead, Too," from *The Sergeant's Cat*. Copyright © 1987 by Janwillem van de Wetering. Reprinted by permission of Pantheon Books, a division of Random House, Inc.

Donald Westlake, "Just One of Those Days," from *The Curious Facts Preceding My Execution and Other Fictions*. Copyright © 1966 by Donald Westlake. Reprinted by permission of Random House, Inc.

Carolyn Wheat, "Flake Piece." Copyright © 1988 by Carolyn Wheat. Reprinted by permission of the author.

Yoh Sano, "No Proof." Copyright © 1978 by Yoh Sano. Reprinted from *Ellery Queen's Japanese Golden Dozen*, with special permission of Charles E. Tuttle Co., Inc., Rutland, Vermont.